P9-CME-900

STRANGE DREAMS

Other Books
by Stephen R. Donaldson

Unforgettable

Fantasy

Stories

Selected by

Stephen R.

Donaldson

BANTAM BOOKS

New York   Toronto   London
Sydney   Auckland

STRANGE DREAMS

To Bob and Kathy Johnson:
good friends for a long time

STRANGE DREAMS

See page 530–31 for acknowledgments.

All rights reserved.
Copyright © 1993 by Stephen R. Donaldson.
Cover art copyright © 1993 by Gervasio Gallardo

BOOK DESIGN BY CHRIS WELCH
ISBN 0-553-37103-7
No part of this book may be reproduced or transmitted
in any form or by any means, electronic or mechanical,
including photocopying, recording, or by any information
storage and retrieval system, without permission in
writing from the publisher.
For information address: Bantam Books.

PRINTED IN THE UNITED STATES OF AMERICA

CONTENTS

viii CONTENTS

INTRODUCTION

I love to rationalize.

In fact, rationalization is a healthy exercise, good for one's mental agility—as well as for one's cardiovascular system. However, during this exercise it's important to keep in mind the distinction between the rationalization itself (which happens after the fact) and the decision or process that is being rationalized. When we blur that distinction, we begin to lose our grasp on reality. Then we stop being the kind of people who read fantasy stories, and become the kind of people about whom fantasy stories are written.

With that in mind, let me state categorically that *I* know the difference between the genesis or inspiration of this collection and the rationalization I'm going to provide for it.

The genesis-slash-inspiration occurred in a conversation with that master anthologist, Martin H. Greenberg (without whose involvement none of this would have been possible—or even desirable). We were discussing the basis on which I might be willing—or indeed able—to pull together a collection, and I quickly dismissed the traditional anthological fundaments: Historical Development (where fantasy came from, and how it grew); Defense of Genre (why fantasy is written); Technical Display (how fantasy can be written); and Thematic Modulation (what fantasy has to say about X or Y). Frankly, I don't want to work hard enough to explain where fantasy came from and how it grew. I've already spent too much time trying to tell people why fantasy is written. Most people have a consuming lack of interest in matters of technique. And thematic anthologies have a distressing tendency to show the writers selected at less than their best.

Which is all very well; but once all these bases have been dismissed, why bother to do a collection at all?

Because, I told Martin, I love these stories. Some of them made my viscera twang; some impressed themselves on my memory or on my heart. In fact, there are certain stories included here that I've been quite unable to forget. They aren't just memorable: they're indelible. What's wrong, I asked Martin, with an anthology built on the simple principle that the stories in it are ones I haven't been able to shake from my mind?

In other words—cutting a little closer to the bone—what's wrong with an anthology founded purely and plainly on my own taste? It may be egocentric, but at least it's sincere.

Martin, bless him, was kind enough to say that there's nothing wrong with an anthology like that. And so here we are.

The rationalization, naturally, is another matter entirely.

The fact is, I have an uneasy relationship with my own egocentricity. I'm forever trying to take it apart, see what makes it tick; rationalize it. So once I began pulling together a list of short stories I haven't been able to forget, I inevitably started asking myself: why? Why have these stories stayed with me? What makes them so indelible?

Well, truth comes in curious disguises; and nowhere more than in fantasy. I have argued elsewhere—at some length—that fantasy is the fundamental form of story-telling. The essence of good fiction is its particularity—the specific is the doorway to the universal—but in fantasy this presents unusual requirements and difficulties. In fantasy, more than in any other form of fiction, the outer landscape must serve as a metaphor for the inner. Precisely because a fantasy deals with magical places and supernatural beings, the sheer scale or effectiveness of the particularity it contains must be greater than in the more tangible, demonstrably "real" genres. As a result, the writer of fantasy is compelled, not simply to describe strangeness, but to revel in it; to immerse in it until it becomes a kind of amniotic fluid of the imagination; to birth stories from it with all the mess and vitality of real parturition.

Which is how lunatics are made, right? Doesn't all that magic unhinge the mind? Don't all those supernatural beings and transcendences falsify our grasp on reality? Aren't we abandoning our intellects, our reason, aren't we abandoning *ourselves* when we read (never mind write) fantasy?

Actually, no. After all, dreaming (which always involves strangeness, distortions of tangible fact, imaginative extrapolation—and what are those things if not metaphors of magic?) is the core human experience: babies do little else, and it becomes the cornerstone of identity for the rest of life. Our grasp on reality is confused only when we blur the distinction between what we do and how we perceive what we do. And when we dismiss fantasy, we blur that distinction. One way to understand fantasy fiction is as a rationalization of our dreams, a commentary on the core of who we are; and the better the fiction (or the writer) is, the more useful the rationalization becomes.

This is a rather baroque way of saying that fantasy stories have the capacity to give us knowledge about ourselves that we might not gain from any other source, precisely because their particularity is woven from the stuff of dreams. William Butler Yeats has written, "In dreams begins responsibility." Ralph Waldo Emerson and C. S. Lewis and Carl Sagan have argued that the way to reach out to our fellow human beings in understanding and empathy is to reach into ourselves.

This, I hope, makes my own rationalization clear. The stories here positively refused to be dislodged from my mind because they told me something necessary and true about myself. The disguise may involve Viriconium or Ealdwood or India, but the truth shows clear. In strange dreams we see ourselves most vividly.

I'm egocentric enough to think that stories that shed this much light for me may do the same for other people as well.

THE ALEPH

TO ESTELA CANTO

O God! I could be bounded in a nutshell, and count myself a King
of infinite space. . . .
HAMLET, II, 2

But they will teach us that Eternity is the Standing still of the
Present Time, a *Nunc-stans* (as the Schools call it); which neither
they, nor any else understand, no more than they would a *Hic-stans*
for an Infinite greatness of Place.
LEVIATHAN, IV, 46

On the burning February morning Beatriz Viterbo died, after braving an agony that never for a single moment gave way to self-pity or fear, I noticed that the sidewalk billboards around Constitution Plaza were advertising some new brand or other of American cigarettes. The fact pained me, for I realized that the wide and ceaseless universe was already slipping away from her and that this slight change was the first of an endless series. The universe may change but not me, I thought with a certain sad vanity. I knew that at times my fruitless devotion had annoyed her; now that she was dead, I could devote myself to her memory, without hope but also without humiliation. I recalled that the thirtieth of April was her birthday; on that day to visit her house on Garay Street and pay my respects to her father and to Carlos Argentino Daneri, her first cousin, would be an irreproachable and perhaps unavoidable act of politeness. Once again I would wait in the twilight of the small, cluttered drawing room, once again I would study the details of her many photographs: Beatriz Viterbo in profile and in full color; Beatriz wearing a mask, during the Carnival of 1921; Beatriz at her First Communion; Beatriz on the day of her wedding to Roberto Alessandri; Beatriz soon after her divorce, at a luncheon at the Turf Club; Beatriz at a seaside resort in Quilmes with Delia San Marco Porcel and Carlos Argentino;

Beatriz with the Pekingese lapdog given her by Villegas Haedo; Beatriz, front and three-quarter views, smiling, hand on her chin. . . . I would not be forced, as in the past, to justify my presence with modest offerings of books—books whose pages I finally learned to cut beforehand, so as not to find out, months later, that they lay around unopened.

Beatriz Viterbo died in 1929. From that time on, I never let a thirtieth of April go by without a visit to her house. I used to make my appearance at seven-fifteen sharp and stay on for some twenty-five minutes. Each year, I arrived a little later and stayed a little longer. In 1933, a torrential downpour coming to my aid, they were obliged to ask me to dinner. Naturally, I took advantage of that lucky precedent. In 1934, I arrived, just after eight, with one of those large Santa Fe sugared cakes, and quite matter-of-factly I stayed to dinner. It was in this way, on these melancholy and vainly erotic anniversaries, that I came into the gradual confidences of Carlos Argentino Daneri.

Beatriz had been tall, frail, slightly stooped; in her walk there was (if the oxymoron may be allowed) a kind of uncertain grace, a hint of expectancy. Carlos Argentino was pink-faced, overweight, gray-haired, fine-featured. He held a minor position in an unreadable library out on the edge of the Southside of Buenos Aires. He was authoritarian but also unimpressive. Until only recently, he took advantage of his nights and holidays to stay at home. At a remove of two generations, the Italian "S" and demonstrative Italian gestures still survived in him. His mental activity was continuous, deeply felt, far-reaching, and—all in all—meaningless. He dealt in pointless analogies and in trivial scruples. He had (as did Beatriz) large, beautiful, finely shaped hands. For several months he seemed to be obsessed with Paul Fort—less with his ballads than with the idea of a towering reputation. "He is the Prince of poets," Daneri would repeat fatuously. "You will belittle him in vain—but no, not even the most venomous of your shafts will graze him."

On the thirtieth of April, 1941, along with the sugared cake I allowed myself to add a bottle of Argentine cognac. Carlos Argentino tasted it, pronounced it "interesting," and, after a few drinks, launched into a glorification of modern man.

"I view him," he said with a certain unaccountable excitement, "in his inner sanctum, as though in his castle tower, supplied with telephones, telegraphs, phonographs, wireless sets, motion-picture screens, slide projectors, glossaries, timetables, handbooks, bulletins. . . . "

He remarked that for a man so equipped, actual travel was superfluous.

Our twentieth century had inverted the story of Mohammed and the mountain; nowadays, the mountain came to the modern Mohammed. So foolish did his ideas seem to me, so pompous and so drawn out his exposition, that I linked them at once to literature and asked him why he didn't write them down. As might be foreseen, he answered that he had already done so—that these ideas, and others no less striking, had found their place in the Proem, or Augural Canto, or, more simply, the Prologue Canto of the poem on which he had been working for many years now, alone, without publicity, without fanfare, supported only by those twin staffs universally known as work and solitude. First, he said, he opened the floodgates of his fancy; then, taking up hand tools, he resorted to the file. The poem was entitled *The Earth*; it consisted of a description of the planet, and, of course, lacked no amount of picturesque digressions and bold apostrophes.

I asked him to read me a passage, if only a short one. He opened a drawer of his writing table, drew out a thick stack of papers—sheets of a large pad imprinted with the letterhead of the Juan Crisóstomo Lafinur Library—and, with ringing satisfaction, declaimed:

Mine eyes, as did the Greek's, have known men's towns and fame,
The works, the days in light that fades to amber;
I do not change a fact or falsify a name—
The voyage I set down is . . . autour de ma chambre.

"From any angle, a greatly interesting stanza," he said, giving his verdict. "The opening line wins the applause of the professor, the academician, and the Hellenist—to say nothing of the would-be scholar, a considerable sector of the public. The second flows from Homer to Hesiod (generous homage, at the very outset, to the father of didactic poetry), not without rejuvenating a process whose roots go back to Scripture— enumeration, congeries, conglomeration. The third—baroque? decadent? example of the cult of pure form?—consists of two equal hemistichs. The fourth, frankly bilingual, assures me the unstinted backing of all minds sensitive to the pleasures of sheer fun. I should, in all fairness, speak of the novel rhyme in lines two and four, and of the erudition that allows me—without a hint of pedantry!—to cram into four lines three learned allusions covering thirty centuries packed with literature—first to the *Odyssey*, second to *Works and Days*, and third to the immortal bagatelle bequeathed us by the frolicking pen of the Savoyard, Xavier de

Maistre. Once more I've come to realize that modern art demands the balm of laughter, the scherzo. Decidedly, Goldoni holds the stage!"

He read me many other stanzas, each of which also won his own approval and elicited his lengthy explications. There was nothing remarkable about them. I did not even find them any worse than the first one. Application, resignation, and chance had gone into the writing; I saw, however, that Daneri's real work lay not in the poetry but in his invention of reasons why the poetry should be admired. Of course, this second phase of his effort modified the writing in his eyes, though not in the eyes of others. Daneri's style of delivery was extravagant, but the deadly drone of his metric regularity tended to tone down and to dull that extravagance.*

Only once in my life have I had occasion to look into the fifteen thousand alexandrines of the *Polyolbion*, that topographical epic in which Michael Drayton recorded the flora, fauna, hydrography, orography, military and monastic history of England. I am sure, however, that this limited but bulky production is less boring than Carlos Argentino's similar vast undertaking. Daneri had in mind to set to verse the entire face of the planet, and, by 1941, had already displaced a number of acres of the State of Queensland, nearly a mile of the course run by the River Ob, a gasworks to the north of Veracruz, the leading shops in the Buenos Aires parish of Concepción, the villa of Mariana Cambaceres de Alvear in the Belgrano section of the Argentine capital, and a Turkish baths establishment not far from the well-known Brighton Aquarium. He read me certain long-winded passages from his Australian section, and at one point praised a word of his own coining, the color "celestewhite," which he felt "actually *suggests* the sky, an element of utmost importance in the landscape of the continent Down Under." But these sprawling, lifeless hexameters lacked even the relative excitement of the so-called Augural Canto. Along about midnight, I left.

Two Sundays later, Daneri rang me up—perhaps for the first time in his life. He suggested we get together at four o'clock "for cocktails in the salon-bar next door, which the forward-looking Zunino and Zungri—

---

*Among my memories are also some lines of a satire in which he lashed out unsparingly at bad poets. After accusing them of dressing their poems in the warlike armor of erudition, and of flapping in vain their unavailing wings, he concluded with this verse:

But they forget, alas, one foremost fact—BEAUTY!

Only the fear of creating an army of implacable and powerful enemies dissuaded him (he told me) from fearlessly publishing this poem.

my landlords, as you doubtless recall—are throwing open to the public. It's a place you'll really want to get to know."

More in resignation than in pleasure, I accepted. Once there, it was hard to find a table. The "salon-bar," ruthlessly modern, was only barely less ugly than what I had expected; at the nearby tables, the excited customers spoke breathlessly of the sums Zunino and Zungri had invested in furnishings without a second thought to cost. Carlos Argentino pretended to be astonished by some feature or other of the lighting arrangement (with which, I felt, he was already familiar), and he said to me with a certain severity, "Grudgingly, you'll have to admit to the fact that these premises hold their own with many others far more in the public eye."

He then reread me four or five different fragments of the poem. He had revised them following his pet principle of verbal ostentation: where at first "blue" had been good enough, he now wallowed in "azures," "ceruleans," and "ultramarines." The word "milky" was too easy for him; in the course of an impassioned description of a shed where wool was washed, he chose such words as "lacteal," "lactescent," and even made one up—"lactinacious." After that, straight out, he condemned our modern mania for having books prefaced, "a practice already held up to scorn by the Prince of Wits in his own graceful preface to the *Quixote*." He admitted, however, that for the opening of his new work an attention-getting foreword might prove valuable—"an accolade signed by a literary hand of renown." He next went on to say that he considered publishing the initial cantos of his poem. I then began to understand the unexpected telephone call; Daneri was going to ask me to contribute a foreword to his pedantic hodgepodge. My fear turned out unfounded; Carlos Argentino remarked, with admiration and envy, that surely he could not be far wrong in qualifying with the epithet "solid" the prestige enjoyed in every circle by Álvaro Melián Lafinur, a man of letters, who would, if I insisted on it, be only too glad to dash off some charming opening words to the poem. In order to avoid ignominy and failure, he suggested I make myself spokesman for two of the book's undeniable virtues— formal perfection and scientific rigor—"inasmuch as this wide garden of metaphors, of figures of speech, of elegances, is inhospitable to the least detail not strictly upholding of truth." He added that Beatriz had always been taken with Álvaro.

I agreed—agreed profusely—and explained for the sake of credibility that I would not speak to Álvaro the next day, Monday, but would wait until Thursday, when we got together for the informal dinner that follows every meeting of the Writers' Club. (No such dinners are ever held, but it is an established fact that the meetings do take place on Thursdays, a point which Carlos Argentino Daneri could verify in the daily papers, and which lent a certain reality to my promise.) Half in prophecy, half in cunning, I said that before taking up the question of a preface I would outline the unusual plan of the work. We then said goodbye.

Turning the corner of Bernardo de Irigoyen, I reviewed as impartially as possible the alternatives before me. They were: *a*) to speak to Álvaro, telling him this first cousin of Beatriz' (the explanatory euphemism would allow me to mention her name) had concocted a poem that seemed to draw out into infinity the possibilities of cacophony and chaos; *b*) not to say a word to Álvaro. I clearly foresaw that my indolence would opt for *b*.

But first thing Friday morning, I began worrying about the telephone. It offended me that that device, which had once produced the irrecoverable voice of Beatriz, could now sink so low as to become a mere receptacle for the futile and perhaps angry remonstrances of that deluded Carlos Argentino Daneri. Luckily, nothing happened—except the inevitable spite touched off in me by this man, who had asked me to fulfill a delicate mission for him and then had let me drop.

Gradually, the phone came to lose its terrors, but one day toward the end of October it rang, and Carlos Argentino was on the line. He was deeply disturbed, so much so that at the outset I did not recognize his voice. Sadly but angrily he stammered that the now unrestrainable Zunino and Zungri, under the pretext of enlarging their already outsized "salon-bar," were about to take over and tear down his house.

"My home, my ancestral home, my old and inveterate Garay Street home!" he kept repeating, seeming to forget his woe in the music of his words.

It was not hard for me to share his distress. After the age of fifty, all change becomes a hateful symbol of the passing of time. Besides, the scheme concerned a house that for me would always stand for Beatriz. I tried explaining this delicate scruple of regret, but Daneri seemed not to hear me. He said that if Zunino and Zungri persisted in this outrage, Doctor Zunni, his lawyer, would sue *ipso facto* and make them pay some fifty thousand dollars in damages.

Zunni's name impressed me; his firm, although at the unlikely address of Caseros and Tacuarí, was nonetheless known as an old and reliable one. I asked him whether Zunni had already been hired for the case. Daneri said he would phone him that very afternoon. He hesitated, then with that level, impersonal voice we reserve for confiding something intimate, he said that to finish the poem he could not get along without the house because down in the cellar there was an Aleph. He explained that an Aleph is one of the points in space that contains all other points.

"It's in the cellar under the dining room," he went on, so overcome by his worries now that he forgot to be pompous. "It's mine—mine. I discovered it when I was a child, all by myself. The cellar stairway is so steep that my aunt and uncle forbade my using it, but I'd heard someone say there was a world down there. I found out later they meant an old-fashioned globe of the world, but at the time I thought they were referring to the world itself. One day when no one was home I started down in secret, but I stumbled and fell. When I opened my eyes, I saw the Aleph."

"The Aleph?" I repeated.

"Yes, the only place on earth where all places are—seen from every angle, each standing clear, without any confusion or blending. I kept the discovery to myself and went back every chance I got. As a child, I did not foresee that this privilege was granted me so that later I could write the poem. Zunino and Zungri will not strip me of what's mine—no, and a thousand times no! Legal code in hand, Doctor Zunni will prove that my Aleph is inalienable."

I tried to reason with him. "But isn't the cellar very dark?" I said.

"Truth cannot penetrate a closed mind. If all places in the universe are in the Aleph, then all stars, all lamps, all sources of light are in it, too."

"You wait there. I'll be right over to see it."

I hung up before he could say no. The full knowledge of a fact sometimes enables you to see all at once many supporting but previously unsuspected things. It amazed me not to have suspected until that moment that Carlos Argentino was a madman. As were all the Viterbos, when you came down to it. Beatriz (I myself often say it) was a woman, a child, with almost uncanny powers of clairvoyance, but forgetfulness, distractions, contempt, and a streak of cruelty were also in her, and perhaps these called for a pathological explanation. Carlos Argentino's madness filled me with spiteful elation. Deep down, we had always detested each other.

On Garay Street, the maid asked me kindly to wait. The master was, as usual, in the cellar developing pictures. On the unplayed piano, beside a large vase that held no flowers, smiled (more timeless than belonging to the past) the large photograph of Beatriz, in gaudy colors. Nobody could see us; in a seizure of tenderness, I drew close to the portrait and said to it, "Beatriz, Beatriz Elena, Beatriz Elena Viterbo, darling Beatriz, Beatriz now gone forever, it's me, it's Borges."

Moments later, Carlos came in. He spoke drily. I could see he was thinking of nothing else but the loss of the Aleph.

"First a glass of pseudo-cognac," he ordered, "and then down you dive into the cellar. Let me warn you, you'll have to lie flat on your back. Total darkness, total immobility, and a certain ocular adjustment will also be necessary. From the floor, you must focus your eyes on the nineteenth step. Once I leave you, I'll lower the trapdoor and you'll be quite alone. You needn't fear the rodents very much—though I know you will. In a minute or two, you'll see the Aleph—the microcosm of the alchemists and Kabbalists, our true proverbial friend, the *multum in parvo!*"

Once we were in the dining room, he added, "Of course, if you don't see it, your incapacity will not invalidate what I have experienced. Now, down you go. In a short while you can babble with *all* of Beatriz' images."

Tired of his inane words, I quickly made my way. The cellar, barely wider than the stairway itself, was something of a pit. My eyes searched the dark, looking in vain for the globe Carlos Argentino had spoken of. Some cases of empty bottles and some canvas sacks cluttered one corner. Carlos picked up a sack, folded it in two, and at a fixed spot spread it out.

"As a pillow," he said, "this is quite threadbare, but if it's padded even a half-inch higher, you won't see a thing, and there you'll lie, feeling ashamed and ridiculous. All right now, sprawl that hulk of yours there on the floor and count off nineteen steps."

I went through with his absurd requirements, and at last he went away. The trapdoor was carefully shut. The blackness, in spite of a chink that I later made out, seemed to me absolute. For the first time, I realized the danger I was in: I'd let myself be locked in a cellar by a lunatic, after gulping down a glassful of poison! I knew that back of Carlos' transparent boasting lay a deep fear that I might not see the promised wonder. To keep his madness undetected, to keep from admitting that he was mad, *Carlos had to kill me.* I felt a shock of panic, which I tried to pin to my uncomfortable position and not to the effect of a drug. I shut my eyes— I opened them. Then I saw the Aleph.

I arrive now at the ineffable core of my story. And here begins my despair as a writer. All language is a set of symbols whose use among its speakers assumes a shared past. How, then, can I translate into words the limitless Aleph, which my floundering mind can scarcely encompass?

Mystics, faced with the same problem, fall back on symbols: to signify the godhead, one Persian speaks of a bird that somehow is all birds; Alanus de Insulis, of a sphere whose center is everywhere and circumference is nowhere; Ezekiel, of a four-faced angel who at one and the same time moves east and west, north and south. (Not in vain do I recall these inconceivable analogies; they bear some relation to the Aleph.) Perhaps the gods might grant me a similar metaphor, but then this account would become contaminated by literature, by fiction. Really, what I want to do is impossible, for any listing of an endless series is doomed to be infinitesimal. In that single gigantic instant I saw millions of acts both delightful and awful; not one of them amazed me more than the fact that all of them occupied the same point in space, without overlapping or transparency. What my eyes beheld was simultaneous, but what I shall now write down will be successive, because language is successive. Nonetheless, I'll try to recollect what I can.

On the back part of the step, toward the right, I saw a small iridescent sphere of almost unbearable brilliance. At first I thought it was revolving; then I realized that this movement was an illusion created by the dizzying world it bounded. The Aleph's diameter was probably little more than an inch, but all space was there, actual and undiminished. Each thing (a mirror's face, let us say) was infinite things, since I distinctly saw it from every angle of the universe. I saw the teeming sea; I saw daybreak and nightfall; I saw the multitudes of America; I saw a silvery cobweb in the center of a black pyramid; I saw a splintered labyrinth (it was London); I saw, close up, unending eyes watching themselves in me as in a mirror; I saw all the mirrors on earth and none of them reflected me; I saw in a backyard of Soler Street the same tiles that thirty years before I'd seen in the entrance of a house in Fray Bentos; I saw bunches of grapes, snow, tobacco, lodes of metal, steam; I saw convex equatorial deserts and each one of their grains of sand; I saw a woman in Inverness whom I shall never forget; I saw her tangled hair, her tall figure, I saw the cancer in her breast; I saw a ring of baked mud in a sidewalk, where before there had been a tree; I saw a summer house in Adrogué and a copy of the first English translation of Pliny—Philemon Holland's—and all at the same time saw each letter on each page (as a boy, I used to marvel that the letters in a closed book did not get scrambled and lost overnight); I saw a sunset in Querétaro that seemed to reflect the color of a rose in Bengal; I saw my empty bedroom; I saw in a closet in Alkmaar a terrestrial globe between two mirrors that multiplied it endlessly; I saw horses with flowing manes on a shore of the Caspian Sea at dawn; I saw the delicate bone structure of a hand; I saw the survivors of a battle sending out picture postcards; I saw in a showcase in Mirzapur a pack of Spanish playing cards; I saw the slanting shadows of ferns on a greenhouse floor; I saw tigers, pistons, bison, tides, and armies; I saw all the ants on the planet; I saw a Persian astrolabe; I saw in the drawer of a writing table (and the handwriting made me tremble) unbelievable, obscene, detailed letters, which Beatriz had written to Carlos Argentino; I saw a monument I worshiped in the Chacarita cemetery; I saw the rotted dust and bones that had once deliciously been Beatriz Viterbo; I saw the circulation of my own dark blood; I saw the coupling of love and the modification of death; I saw the Aleph from every point and angle, and in the Aleph I saw the earth and in the earth the Aleph and in the Aleph the earth; I saw my own face and my own bowels; I saw your face; and I felt dizzy and wept, for my eyes had seen that secret and conjectured object whose name is common to all men but which no man has looked upon—the unimaginable universe.

I felt infinite wonder, infinite pity.

"Feeling pretty cockeyed, are you, after so much spying into places where you have no business?" said a hated and jovial voice. "Even if you were to rack your brains, you couldn't pay me back in a hundred years for this revelation. One hell of an observatory, eh, Borges?"

Carlos Argentino's feet were planted on the topmost step. In the sudden dim light, I managed to pick myself up and utter, "One hell of a—yes, one hell of a."

The matter-of-factness of my voice surprised me. Anxiously, Carlos Argentino went on.

"Did you see everything—really clear, in colors?"

At that very moment I found my revenge. Kindly, openly pitying him, distraught, evasive, I thanked Carlos Argentino Daneri for the hospitality of his cellar and urged him to make the most of the demolition to get away from the pernicious metropolis, which spares no one—believe me, I told him, no one! Quietly and forcefully, I refused to discuss the Aleph. On saying goodbye, I embraced him and repeated that the country, that fresh air and quiet were the great physicians.

Out on the street, going down the stairways inside Constitution Station, riding the subway, every one of the faces seemed familiar to me. I was afraid that not a single thing on earth would ever again surprise me; I was afraid I would never again be free of all I had seen. Happily, after a few sleepless nights, I was visited once more by oblivion.

———

Postscript of March first, 1943—Some six months after the pulling down of a certain building on Garay Street, Procrustes & Co., the publishers, not put off by the considerable length of Daneri's poem, brought out a selection of its "Argentine sections." It is redundant now to repeat what happened. Carlos Argentino Daneri won the Second National Prize for Literature.* First Prize went to Dr. Aita; Third Prize, to Dr. Mario Bonfanti. Unbelievably, my own book *The Sharper's Cards* did not get a single vote. Once again dullness and envy had their triumph! It's been some time now that I've been trying to see Daneri; the gossip is that a second selection of the poem is about to be published. His felicitous pen (no longer cluttered by the Aleph) has now set itself the task of writing an epic on our national hero, General San Martín.

I want to add two final observations: one, on the nature of the Aleph; the other, on its name. As is well known, the Aleph is the first letter of the Hebrew alphabet. Its use for the strange sphere in my story may not be accidental. For the Kabbalah, that letter stands for the *En Soph,* the pure and boundless godhead; it is also said that it takes the shape of a man pointing to both heaven and earth, in order to show that the lower world is the map and mirror of the higher; for Cantor's *Mengenlehre,* it is the symbol of transfinite numbers, of which any part is as great as the whole. I would like to know whether Carlos Argentino chose that name or whether he read it—applied to another point where all points converge—in one of the numberless texts that the Aleph in his cellar revealed to him. Incredible as it may seem, I believe that the Aleph of Garay Street was a false Aleph.

Here are my reasons. Around 1867, Captain Burton held the post of British Consul in Brazil. In July, 1942, Pedro Henríquez Ureña came across a manuscript of Burton's, in a library at Santos, dealing with the mirror which the Oriental world attributes to Iskander Zu al-Karnayn, or Alexander Bicornis of Macedonia. In its crystal the whole world was reflected. Burton mentions other similar devices—the sevenfold cup of Kai Kosru; the mirror that Tariq ibn-Ziyad found in a tower (*Thousand and One Nights,* 272); the mirror that Lucian of Samosata examined on the moon (*True History,* I, 26); the mirrorlike spear that the first book of Capella's *Satyricon* attributes to Jupiter; Merlin's universal mirror, which was "round and hollow . . . and seem'd a world of glas" (*The Faerie*

---

*"I received your pained congratulations," he wrote me. "You rage, my poor friend, with envy, but you must confess—even if it chokes you!—that this time I have crowned my cap with the reddest of feathers; my turban with the most *caliph* of rubies."

Queene, III, 2, 19)—and adds this curious statement: "But the aforesaid objects (besides the disadvantage of not existing) are mere optical instruments. The Faithful who gather at the mosque of Amr, in Cairo, are acquainted with the fact that the entire universe lies inside one of the stone pillars that ring its central court. . . . No one, of course, can actually see it, but those who lay an ear against the surface tell that after some short while they perceive its busy hum. . . . The mosque dates from the seventh century; the pillars come from other temples of pre-Islamic religions, since, as ibn-Khaldun has written: 'In nations founded by nomads, the aid of foreigners is essential in all concerning masonry.' "

Does this Aleph exist in the heart of a stone? Did I see it there in the cellar when I saw all things, and have I now forgotten it? Our minds are porous and forgetfulness seeps in; I myself am distorting and losing, under the wearing away of the years, the face of Beatriz.

LADY OF THE SKULLS

The Lady saw them ride across the plain: a company of six. Putting down her watering can, which was the bronze helm of some unfortunate knight, she leaned over the parapet, chin on her hand. They were all armed, their war-horses caparisoned; they glittered under the noon sun with silver-edged shields, jeweled bridles and sword hilts. What, she wondered as always in simple astonishment, did they imagine they had come to fight? She picked up the helm, poured water into a skull containing a miniature rose bush. The water came from within the tower, the only source on the entire barren, sun-cracked plain. The knights would ride around the tower under the hot sun for hours, looking for entry. At sunset, she would greet them, carrying water.

She sighed noiselessly, troweling around the little rose bush with a dragon's claw. If they were too blind to find the tower door, why did they think they could see clearly within it? They, she thought in sudden impatience. They, they, they . . . they fed the plain with their bleached bones; they never learned. . . .

A carrion-bird circled above her, counting heads. She scowled at it; it cried back at her, mocking. *You*, its black eye said, *never die. But you bring the dead to me.*

"They never listen to me," she said, looking over the plain again, her eyes prickling dryly. In the distance, lightning cracked apart the sky; purple clouds rumbled. But there was no rain in them, never any rain; the sky was as tearless as she. She moved from skull to skull along the parapet wall, watering things she had grown stubbornly from seeds that blew from distant, placid gardens in peaceful kingdoms. Some were grasses, weeds, or wildflowers. She did not care; she watered anything that grew.

The men below began their circling. Their mounts kicked up dust, snorting; she heard cursing, bewildered questions, then silence as they paused to rest. Sometimes they called her, pleading. But she could do nothing for them. They churned around the tower, bright, powerful, richly armed. She read the devices on their shields: three of Grenelief, one of Stoney Head, one of Dulcis Isle, one of Carnelaine. After a time, one man dropped out of the circle, stood back. His shield was simple: a red rose on white. Carnelaine, she thought, looking down at him, and then realized he was looking up at her.

He would see a puff of airy sleeve, a red geranium in an upside-down skull. Lady of the Skulls, they called her, clamoring to enter. Sometimes they were more courteous, sometimes less. She watered, waiting for this one to call her. He did not; he guided his horse into the tower's shadow and dismounted. He took his helm off, sat down to wait, burrowing idly in the ground and flicking stones as he watched her sleeve sometimes, and sometimes the distant storm.

Drawn to his calm, the others joined him finally, flinging off pieces of armor. They cursed the hard ground and sat, their voices drifting up to her in the windless air as she continued her watering.

Like others before them, they spoke of what the most precious thing of the legendary treasure might be, besides elusive. They had made a pact, she gathered: If one obtained the treasure, he would divide it among those left living. She raised a brow. The one of Dulcis Isle, a dark-haired man wearing red jewels in his ears, said,

"Anything of the dragon for me. They say it was a dragon's hoard, once. They say that dragon bones are worm-holed with magic, and if you move one bone the rest will follow. The bones will bring the treasure with them."

"I heard," said the man from Stoney Head, "there is a well and a fountain rising from it, and when the drops of the fountain touch ground they turn to diamonds."

"Don't talk of water," one of the three thick-necked, nut-haired men of Grenelief pleaded. "I drank all mine."

"All we must do is find the door. There's water within."

"What are you going to do?" the man of Carnelaine asked. "Hoist the water on your shoulder and carry it out?"

The straw-haired man from Stoney Head tugged at his long moustaches. He had a plain, blunt, energetic voice devoid of any humor. "I'll carry it out in my mouth. When I come back alive for the rest of it, there'll be plenty to carry it in. Skulls, if nothing else. I heard there's a sorceress' cauldron, looks like a rusty old pot—"

"May be that," another of Grenelief said.

"May be, but I'm going for the water. What else could be most precious in this heat-blasted place?"

"That's a point," the man of Dulcis Isle said. Then: "But no, it's dragon-bone for me."

"More to the point," the third of Grenelief said, aggrieved, "how do we get in the cursed place?"

"There's a lady up there watering plants," the man of Carnelaine said, and there were all their faces staring upward; she could have tossed jewels into their open mouths. "She knows we're here."

"It's the Lady," they murmured, hushed.

"Lady of the Skulls."

"Does she have hair, I wonder."

"She's old as the tower. She must be a skull."

"She's beautiful," the man of Stoney Head said shortly. "They always are, the ones who lure, the ones who guard, the ones who give death."

"Is it her tower?" the one of Carnelaine asked. "Or is she trapped?"

"What's the difference? When the spell is gone, so will she be. She's nothing real, just a piece of the tower's magic."

They shifted themselves as the tower shadow shifted. The Lady took a sip of water out of the helm, then dipped her hand in it and ran it over her face. She wanted to lean over the edge and shout at them all: Go home, you silly, brainless fools. If you know so much, what are you doing here sitting on bare ground in front of a tower without a door waiting for a woman to kill you? They moved to one side of the tower, she to the other, as the sun climbed down the sky. She watched the sun set. Still the men refused to leave, though they had not a stick of wood to burn against the dark. She sighed her noiseless sigh and went down to greet them.

The fountain sparkled in the midst of a treasure she had long ceased to notice. She stepped around gold armor, black, gold-rimmed dragon bones, the white bones of princes. She took the plain silver goblet beside the rim of the well, and dipped it into the water, feeling the cooling mist from the little fountain. The man of Dulcis Isle was right about the dragon bones. The doorway was the dragon's open yawning maw, and it was invisible by day.

The last ray of sunlight touched the bone, limned a black, toothed opening that welcomed the men. Mute, they entered, and she spoke.

"You may drink the water, you may wander throughout the tower. If you make no choice, you may leave freely. Having left, you may never return. If you choose, you must make your choice by sunset tomorrow. If you choose the most precious thing in the tower, you may keep all that you see. If you choose wrongly, you will die before you leave the plain."

Their mouths were open again, their eyes stunned at what hung like vines from the old dragon's bones, what lay heaped upon the floor. Flicking, flicking, their eyes came across her finally, as she stood patiently holding the cup. Their eyes stopped at her: a tall, broad-shouldered, barefoot woman in a coarse white linen smock, her red hair bundled untidily on top of her head, her long skirt still splashed with the wine she had spilled in the tavern so long ago. In the torchlight it looked like blood.

They chose to sleep, as they always did, tired by the long journey, dazed by too much rich, vague color in the shadows. She sat on the steps and watched them for a little. One cried in his sleep. She went to the top of the tower after a while, where she could watch the stars. Under the moon, the flowers turned odd, secret colors, as if their true colors blossomed in another land's daylight, and they had left their pale shadows behind by night. She fell asleep naming the moon's colors.

In the morning, she went down to see who had had sense enough to leave.

They were all still there, searching, picking, discarding among the treasures on the floor, scattered along the spiraling stairs. Shafts of light from the narrow windows sparked fiery colors that constantly caught their eyes, made them drop what they had, reach out again. Seeing her, the one from Dulcis Isle said, trembling, his eyes stuffed with riches, "May we ask questions? What is this?"

"Don't ask her, Marlebane," the one from Stoney Head said brusquely. "She'll lie. They all do."

She stared at him. "I will only lie to you," she promised. She took the small treasure from the hand of the man from Dulcis Isle. "This is an acorn made of gold. If you swallow it, you will speak all the languages of humans and animals."

"And this?" one of Grenelief said eagerly, pushing next to her, holding something of silver and smoke.

"That is a bracelet made of a dragon's nostril bone. The jewel in it is its petrified eye. It watches for danger when you wear it."

The man of Carnelaine was playing a flute made from a wizard's thigh bone. His eyes, the odd gray-green of the dragon's eye, looked dream-drugged with the music. The man of Stoney Head shook him roughly.

"Is that your choice, Ran?"

"No." He lowered the flute, smiling. "No, Corbeil."

"Then drop it before it seizes hold of you and you choose it. Have you seen yet what you might take?"

"No. Have you changed your mind?"

"No." He looked at the fountain, but, prudent, did not speak.

"Bram, look at this," said one brother of Grenelief to another. "Look!"

"I am looking, Yew."

"Look at it! Look at it, Ustor! Have you ever seen such a thing? Feel it! And watch: It vanishes, in light."

He held a sword; its hilt was solid emerald, its blade like water falling in clear light over stone. The Lady left them, went back up the stairs, her bare feet sending gold coins and jewels spinning down through the cross-hatched shafts of light. She stared at the place on the horizon where the flat dusty gold of the plain met the parched dusty sky. Go, she thought dully. Leave all this and go back to the places where things grow. Go, she willed them, go, go, go, with the beat of her heart's blood. But no one came out the door beneath her. Someone, instead, came up the stairs.

"I have a question," said Ran of Carnelaine.

"Ask."

"What is your name?"

She had all but forgotten; it came to her again, after a beat of surprise. "Amaranth." He was holding a black rose in one hand, a silver lily in the other. If he chose one, the thorns would kill him; the other, flashing its pure light, would sear through his eyes into his brain.

"Amaranth. Another flower."

"So it is," she said indifferently. He laid the magic flowers on the parapet, picked a dying geranium leaf, smelled the miniature rose. "It has no smell," she said. He picked another dead leaf. He seemed always on the verge of smiling; it made him look sometimes wise and sometimes foolish. He drank out of the bronze watering helm; it was the color of his hair.

"This water is too cool and sweet to come out of such a barren plain," he commented. He seated himself on the wall, watching her. "Corbeil says you are not real. You look real enough to me." She was silent, picking dead clover out of the clover pot. "Tell me where you came from."

She shrugged. "A tavern."

"And how did you come here?"

She gazed at him. "How did you come here, Ran of Carnelaine?"

He did smile then, wryly. "Carnelaine is poor; I came to replenish its coffers."

"There must be less chancy ways."

"Maybe I wanted to see the most precious thing there is to be found. Will the plain bloom again, if it is found? Will you have a garden instead of skull-pots?"

"Maybe," she said levelly. "Or maybe I will disappear. Die when the magic dies. If you choose wisely, you'll have answers to your questions."

He shrugged. "Maybe I will not choose. There are too many precious things."

She glanced at him. He was trifling, wanting hints from her, answers couched in riddles. Shall I take rose or lily? Or wizard's thigh bone? Tell me. Sword or water or dragon's eye? Some had questioned her so before.

She said simply, "I cannot tell you what to take. I do not know myself. As far as I have seen, everything kills." It was as close as she could come, as plain as she could make it: Leave. But he said only, his smile gone, "Is that why you never left?" She stared at him again. "Walked out the door, crossed the plain on some dead king's horse and left?"

She said, "I cannot." She moved away from him, tending some wild-flower she called wind-bells, for she imagined their music as the night air tumbled down from the mountains to race across the plain. After awhile, she heard his steps again, going down.

A voice summoned her: "Lady of the Skulls!" It was the man of Stoney Head. She went down, blinking in the thick, dusty light. He stood stiffly, his face hard. They all stood still, watching.

"I will leave now," he said. "I may take anything?"

"Anything," she said, making her heart stone against him, a ghost's heart, so that she would not pity him. He went to the fountain, took a mouthful of water. He looked at her, and she moved to show him the hidden lines of the dragon's mouth. He vanished through the stones.

They heard him scream a moment later. The three of Grenelief stared toward the sound. They each wore pieces of a suit of armor that made the wearer invisible: one lacked an arm, another a thigh, the other his hands. Subtly their expressions changed, from shock and terror into something more complex. Five, she saw them thinking. Only five ways to divide it now.

"Anyone else?" she asked coldly. The man of Dulcis Isle slumped down onto the stairs, swallowing. He stared at her, his face gold-green in the light. He swallowed again. Then he shouted at her.

She had heard every name they could think of to shout before she had ever come to the tower. She walked up the stairs past him; he did not have the courage to touch her. She went to stand among her plants. Corbeil of Stoney Head lay where he had fallen, a little brown patch of wet earth beside his open mouth. As she looked, the sun dried it, and the first of the carrion-birds landed.

She threw bones at the bird, cursing, though it looked unlikely that anyone would be left to take his body back. She hit the bird a couple of times, then another came. Then someone took the bone out of her hand, drew her back from the wall.

"He's dead," Ran said simply. "It doesn't matter to him whether you throw bones at the birds or at him."

"I have to watch," she said shortly. She added, her eyes on the jagged line the parapet made against the sky, like blunt worn dragon's teeth, "You keep coming, and dying. Why do you all keep coming? Is treasure worth being breakfast for the carrion crows?"

"It's worth many different things. To the brothers of Grenelief it means adventure, challenge, adulation if they succeed. To Corbeil it was something to be won, something he would have that no one else could get. He would have sat on top of the pile, and let men look up to him, hating and envying."

"He was a cold man. Cold men feed on a cold fire. Still," she added, sighing, "I would have preferred to see him leave on his feet. What does the treasure mean to you?"

"Money." He smiled his vague smile. "It's not in me to lose my life over money. I'd sooner walk empty-handed out the door. But there's something else."

"What?"

"The riddle itself. That draws us all, at heart. What is the most precious thing? To see it, to hold it, above all to recognize it and choose it— that's what keeps us coming and traps you here." She stared at him, saw, in his eyes, the wonder that he felt might be worth his life.

She turned away; her back to him, she watered bleeding heart and columbine, stonily ignoring what the crows were doing below. "If you find the thing itself," she asked dryly, "what will you have left to wonder about?"

"There's always life."

"Not if you are killed by wonder."

He laughed softly, an unexpected sound, she thought, in that place. "Wouldn't you ride across the plain, if you heard tales of this tower, to try to find the most precious thing in it?"

"Nothing's precious to me," she said, heaving a cauldron of dandelions into shadow. "Not down there, anyway. If I took one thing away with me, it would not be sword or gold or dragon bone. It would be whatever is alive."

He touched the tiny rose. "You mean, like this? Corbeil would never have died for this."

"He died for a mouthful of water."

"He thought it was a mouthful of jewels." He sat beside the rose, his back to the air, watching her pull pots into shade against the noon light. "Which makes him twice a fool, I suppose. Three times a fool: for being wrong, for being deluded, and for dying. What a terrible place this is. It strips you of all delusions and then it strips your bones."

"It is terrible," she said somberly. "Yet those who leave without choosing never seem to get the story straight. They must always talk of the treasure they didn't take, not of the bones they didn't leave."

"It's true. Always, they take wonder with them out of this tower and they pass it on to every passing fool." He was silent a little, still watching her. "Amaranth," he said slowly. "That's the flower in poetry that never dies. It's apt."

"Yes."

"And there is another kind of Amaranth, that's fiery and beautiful and it dies. . . ." Her hands stilled, her eyes widened, but she did not speak. He leaned against the hot, crumbling stones, his dragon's eyes following her like a sunflower following the sun. "What were you," he asked, "when you were the Amaranth that could die?"

"I was one of those faceless women who brought you wine in a tavern. Those you shout at, and jest about, and maybe give a coin to and maybe not, depending how we smile."

He was silent, so silent she thought he had gone, but when she turned, he was still there; only his smile had gone. "Then I've seen you," he said softly, "many times, in many places. But never in a place like this."

"The man from Stoney Head expected someone else, too."

"He expected a dream."

"He saw what he expected: Lady of the Skulls." She pulled wild mint into a shady spot under some worn tapestry. "And so he found her. That's all I am now. You were better off when all I served was wine."

"You didn't build this tower."

"How do you know? Maybe I got tired of the laughter and the coins and I made a place for myself where I could offer coins and give nothing."

"Who built this tower?"

She was silent, crumbling a mint leaf between her fingers. "I did," she said at last. "The Amaranth who never dies."

"Did you?" He was oddly pale; his eyes glittered in the light as if at the shadow of danger. "You grow roses out of thin air in this blistered plain; you try to beat back death for us with our own bones. You curse our stupidity and our fate, not us. Who built this tower for you?" She turned her face away, mute. He said softly, "The other Amaranth, the one that dies, is also called Love-lies-bleeding."

"It was the last man," she said abruptly, her voice husky, shaken with sudden pain, "who offered me a coin for love. I was so tired of being touched and then forgotten, of hearing my name spoken and then not, as if I were only real when I was looked at, and just something to forget after that, like you never remember the flowers you toss away. So I said to him: no, and no, and no. And then I saw his eyes. They were like amber with thorns of dark in them: sorcerer's eyes. He said, 'Tell me your name.' And I said, 'Amaranth,' and he laughed and laughed and I could only stand there, with the wine I had brought him overturned on my tray, spilling down my skirt. He said, 'Then you shall make a tower of your name, for the tower is already built in your heart.' "

"Love-lies-bleeding," he whispered.

"He recognized that Amaranth."

"Of course he did. It was what died in his own heart."

She turned then, wordless, to look at him. He was smiling again, though his face was still blanched under the hard, pounding light, and the sweat shone in his hair. She said, "How do you know him?"

"Because I have seen this tower before and I have seen in it the woman we all expected, the only woman some men ever know. . . . And every time we come expecting her, the woman who lures us with what's most precious to us and kills us with it, we build the tower around her again and again and again. . . . "

She gazed at him. A tear slid down her cheek, and then another. "I thought it was my tower," she whispered. "The Amaranth that never dies but only lives forever to watch men die."

"It's all of us," he sighed. In the distance, thunder rumbled. "We all build towers, then dare each other to enter. . . . " He picked up the little rose in its skull pot and stood abruptly; she followed him to the stairs.

"Where are you going with my rose?"

"Out."

She followed him down, protesting. "But it's mine!"

"You said we could choose anything."

"It's just a worthless thing I grew, it's nothing of the tower's treasure. If you must take after all, choose something worth your life!"

He glanced back at her, as they rounded the tower stairs to the bottom. His face was bone-white, but he could still smile. "I will give you back your rose," he said, "if you will let me take the Amaranth."

"But I am the only Amaranth."

He strode past his startled companions, whose hands were heaped with *this, no this,* and *maybe this.* As if the dragon's magical eye had opened in his own eye, he led her himself into the dragon's mouth.

AS ABOVE,
SO BELOW

Owen III Count XXI Hanowald watched his sea-captain stump and jingle away, and drummed fingers on the chart upon his dark oak desk. He looked over the inked outline of the Gold Coast. A wondrous profitable voyage, he thought, if the ships return . . . but then they'll not sail if they're not to return, will they, Sherez?

He rolled the map tight and put it in the white sash of his green silk robe. Did it matter to Sherez, that now he wore fine clean silks to visit the dragonium? The Count doubted that it did. He did not doubt that, should it make a difference to Sherez, Owen would put on salty burlap again. And chains, yes.

He walked the corridors of the Serpent Wing: Two turns left, one right, sharp left, up and down a ramp, ignoring the dozens of false passages. A rumble and whine coming from the Artificers' Tower, where they prepared some marvelous and expensive experiment, distracted his thoughts, but his feet knew the way. Owen could walk these halls blindfolded, literally. His father had seen to that.

As he opened the door to the dragonium, Count Hanowald heard Sherez greet him. Smiling faintly, the Count went down the black iron steps, his boots making hollow sounds of doom, the jangle of the grip-chain echoing in his memory.

"Watch your sstep, Owen," Sherez' voice came from the pit, and a moment later the Count stumbled, grabbing the chain with both hands, scraping a heel-tendon on the leading edge of a step, on the iron rasp put there to gash the dragon's belly should he try to ascend . . . escape . . . from the dragonium.

Owen laughed at that, and at the pain in his ankle. Four Counts Hanowald had died mangled on these stairs, Owen's father one of them, all the same way—descending in haste to see Sherez. None had ever fallen while climbing. Who indeed could, with a dragon's counsel upon him as he departed the pit?

I keep the dragonium as have twenty Hanowalds before me, Owen thought, the maze and the stair and the catacomb, and yet if Sherez sprawled on my chair and held my wand in his teeth, would he rule any more than now?

The Count reached the foot of the stair. A shaft of yellow light from Sherez' left eye picked out the lantern on the wall. Before Owen struck the flint, he noticed a small glimmer near the bright beam.

"Your right eye is healing," he said.

"Ssslowly," said Sherez. "I can tell light from dark, now. The blow was well sstruck, Owen. Your grandfather's arm was sstrong."

The lantern blazed up, and the dragonlight was lost. Owen saw a yellow sphere the size of his head, bloodshot and diffuse. The old split in the closed lid beside it was a mere green groove now, the flake-gold luster of dried dragon blood that Owen's brush could never erase nearly gone. Sherez' ropy arms, thinner than Owen's own, were stretched out before the dragon's head, holding a piece of chain. Rust was scoured from some of the links.

"What, Sherez, must you polish your own teeth now? I've given Emael orders that you're not to go three days without a filing."

"Your sson fears me," said the dragon. "He thinkss I sshall ssnap him up."

"So did I, when I was no bigger than your fang. Emael wears a sword now. He can wield a rasp."

"But you will not chain your sson to the stair, as your father did you, will you, Owen? He iss no coward, your sson. Only young, and uncertain."

"He will be Count one day, Sherez, and he must know you."

"No."

Owen stared. "What do you mean by that? What is going to happen to my son?"

"I do not know, Owen."

"Not . . . know?" The Count looked at the dragon's head, twice Owen's own height, and behind it the hunched scaly back and thick hind legs. The vestigial wings were folded flat, fanning open and shut slightly as Sherez breathed. *What a creature is dragon*, the poets sang, *though for his wisdom he resigned the air to crawl*. . . . Years ago, a traveling artificer had displayed a whole dragon brain, preserved in smelly liquid. The arms of three men could not span it round. How could that brain—

As the mazes of the dragonium wound above and below, that brain coiled through time; time past, time future. All moments were one to a dragon, tomorrow as real as yesterday, this very instant the same to it as last year or next generation. Sherez could tell Owen the hour of the Count's death, had he only the courage to ask.

How could that brain *not know?*

"Emael is no less healthy than you were at his age—nor less brave," said Sherez. "But I do not know what will happen to him."

"You mean that you are going to die."

"We do not die, as you know."

"Then tell me who will kill you. I'll put the tongs to him. I'll roast him in an iron box!"

"Even if it were your son?"

Owen lost his voice. After three hard breaths he said, "Yes, even so," and thought oh gods old, oh God new, what have I said?

Sherez closed his eye. "It is not," he said. "It is no such blow at all. But I wondered. . . ."

"Do you know what your artificers do, even now?"

Again Owen could not speak. The dragon *wondered.* Owen had knelt down here with a file and a brush and pans of salt and fresh water—and his own weight of iron on his feet—and cared for Sherez' teeth and blind eye, and the small wounds done by the stones and the deep creatures. After not too much time Owen remained in the dragonium of his own will. Yet though Owen loved Sherez, and knew he loved Sherez, still there were times when he could have raised his hand and put out that other eye.

The wind in his soul subsided. Voice came back. "The artificers are raising some new assemblage. It's consumed pounds of silver, and good steel, but I don't know what it's meant to do."

"They mean to examine causality," said the dragon. "The silver goes for mirrors. The springs hurl pellets, and divide off time, and smash vials of prussic acid so that cats die horribly."

"Cats?"

"It is all in a good cause, the furtherance of knowledge."

"What is 'causality'?"

"They wish to know if the cause of an action must happen before the action, or if perhaps the action may precede the cause."

"For this they use steel and silver? To find if, perhaps, a man may cut down a tree after it falls?"

"It is subtler than that. Ancient philosophies are involved, concerning the nature of light."

"Light or falling trees, who cares? A thing is done; its consequences follow."

"Yet if a dragon said your son was to slay him, you would have put hot iron to the boy to prevent the act. How may I be killed tomorrow by a man who dies today?"

"Then . . . there is no . . . causality."

"Oh, but there is. And the artificers will prove so. It is dragons who are wrong."

Owen pulled the map from his sash. "I would all my advisers were wrong so perfectly."

Sherez clapped his weak hands. Dragons could not laugh. "Count Owen, how exceptional you are. Any of your artificers would be confounded for days by such a paradox, but you deny that paradox can exist in a rational world."

"Can it?"

"Only as long," said Sherez, "as no one notices there *is* a paradox. I think one day the artificers will prove two objects cannot occupy the same place simultaneously; but until then, who knows? Perhaps they can."

"You are saying that, as a result of these mirrors and levers, all dragons are about to die."

"No. No. Dragons cannot die . . . because it is inherent in the concept of dragons that we shall live forever."

"You can be slain by men."

"Because *your* concept of dragons so strongly demands that we can be slain. We were here before your evolution, O man; would you believe me if I said, before that time, no hand could kill us?"

"Then what is to happen to you, if not death? What else is there but death at the end?"

"Many things," said the dragon, "an infinity—but for us, oblivion. It shall, I think, be as if we never were at all."

"I'll remember."

"Perhaps not."

"What of this pit? I'll put up a plaque in gold on silver, that here were dragons."

Sherez applauded, patter-patter-pat. "A worthy gesture, Owen Hanowald, but perhaps not. You will probably recall this place as having been built for human pain and the confinement of those who frighten you or have information of value. Which—pardon me, Owen—is true."

The Count moved near Sherez' right second fang, the one with the bit of ivory-cementum in it, and crouched, not caring a damn for his robes or his dignity. "I will remember," he said. "Is it not in our concept that we remember our friends?"

Sherez rolled his eye. The split lid creaked a little open. "Exsseptional," the dragon said softly. "Yesss, Owen . . . there may be . . . legendsss."

"What should I do without you, dragon?"

"Substitute reason for prophecy."

Owen stood. "Like an artificer? Then it is the end of life." He looked at the map, crumpled in his white-knuckled hand. "How can I send out ships, men, not knowing if they will return?"

Sherez growled, though Owen did not think it was with anger. "It endss nothing. You will send shipss, and ssometimes they will return, and ssometimes they will not, and ssometimes they will be blown off course and disscover new worldsss. . . . Owen, I think this is a good thing, for men."

"To live like artificers? Without faith, except in what hands can touch and measure and take apart?" Owen looked up the stairwell, put his hand on the chain. "I'll smash every one of their mirrors. I'll drive them out with iron and fire!"

"No. There is not even time left. I have thought of a good joke, Owen. . . . Ssuppose this experiment itsself contains a paradox? Ssuppose that, succeeding, their success vanishesss too, matter and memory?" Sherez clapped. "Owen, Owen, be sstill. I tell you, there iss no time to make a differensse."

"Will may do what time might not," the Count shouted. He shuttered the lantern with a blow, and ran up the steps, his boots making them ring like a cathedral full of bells.

"*Salt-Owen!*" roared the dragon, and Count Hanowald . . . *had to . . .* stop.

Eyelight spotted him. "Owen, Sssalt-Owen . . . be careful, on the stairsss."

As he neared the top, climbing as fast as care would permit, Count Hanowald heard sounds from the Artificers' Tower: the grate of a steel mainspring, a crash of glass, the yowl of a cat.

As he stepped from iron onto stone, there was a sucking wind behind him, like the breeze that follows a departing army.

The Count turned round and looked down at the black cold dungeon, and wondered why the Devil the door was open.

EUMENIDES IN THE FOURTH-FLOOR LAVATORY

L iving in a fourth-floor walk-up was part of his revenge, as if to say to Alice, Throw me out of the house, will you? Then I'll live in squalor in a Bronx tenement, where the toilet is shared by four apartments! My shirts will go unironed, my tie will be perpetually awry. *See what you've done to me?*

But when he told Alice about the apartment, she only laughed bitterly and said, "Not anymore, Howard. I won't play those games with you. You win every damn time."

She pretended not to care about him anymore, but Howard knew better. He knew people, knew what they wanted, and Alice wanted *him.* It was his strongest card in their relationship—that she wanted him more than he wanted her. He thought of this often: at work in the offices of Humboldt and Breinhardt, Designers; at lunch in a cheap lunchroom (part of the punishment); on the subway home to his tenement (Alice had kept the Lincoln Continental). He thought and thought about how much she wanted him. But he kept remembering what she had said the day she threw him out: "If you ever come near Rhiannon again I'll kill you."

He could not remember why she had said that. Could not remember and did not try to remember because that line of thinking made him uncomfortable, and one thing Howard insisted on being was comfortable with himself. Other people could spend hours and days of their lives chasing after some accommodation with themselves, but Howard was accommodated. Well adjusted. At ease. I'm okay, I'm okay, I'm okay. Hell with you. "If you let them make you feel uncomfortable," Howard would often say, "you give them a handle on you and they can run your life." Howard could find other people's handles, but they could never find Howard's.

It was not yet winter but cold as hell at three A.M. when Howard got home from Stu's party. A "must attend" party, if you wished to get ahead at Humboldt and Breinhardt. Stu's ugly wife had tried to be tempting, but Howard had played innocent and made her feel so uncomfortable that she dropped the matter. Howard paid careful attention to office gossip and knew that several earlier departures from the company had got caught with, so to speak, their pants down. Not that Howard's pants were an impenetrable barrier. He got Dolores from the front office into the bedroom and accused her of making life miserable for him. "In little ways," he insisted. "I know you don't mean to, but you've got to stop."

"What ways?" Dolores asked, incredulous yet (because she honestly tried to make other people happy) uncomfortable.

"Surely you knew how attracted I am to you."

"No. That hasn't—that hasn't even crossed my mind."

Howard looked tongue-tied, embarrassed. He actually was neither. "Then—well, then, I was—I was wrong. I'm sorry, I thought you were doing it deliberately."

"Doing what?"

"Snub—snubbing me—never mind, it sounds adolescent, just little things, hell, Dolores, I had a stupid schoolboy crush—"

"Howard, I didn't even know I was hurting you."

"God, how insensitive," Howard said, sounding even more hurt.

"Oh, Howard, do I mean that much to you?"

Howard made a little whimpering noise that meant everything she wanted it to mean. She looked uncomfortable. She'd do anything to get back to feeling right with herself again. She was so uncomfortable that they spent a rather nice half-hour making each other feel comfortable again. No one else in the office had been able to get to Dolores. But Howard could get to anybody.

He walked up the stairs to his apartment feeling very, very satisfied. Don't need you, Alice, he said to himself. Don't need nobody, and nobody's who I've got. He was still mumbling the little ditty to himself as he went into the communal bathroom and turned on the light.

He heard a gurgling sound from the toilet stall, a hissing sound. Had someone been in there with the light off? Howard went into the stall and saw nobody. Then looked closer and saw a baby, probably about two months old, lying in the toilet bowl. Its nose and eyes were barely above water; it looked terrified; its legs and hips and stomach were down the drain. Someone had obviously hoped to kill it by drowning—it was inconceivable to Howard that anyone could be so moronic as to think it would fit down the drain.

For a moment he thought of leaving it there, with the big city temptation to mind one's own business even when to do so would be an atrocity. Saving this baby would mean inconvenience: calling the police, taking care of the child in his apartment, perhaps even headlines, certainly a night of filling out reports. Howard was tired. Howard wanted to go to bed.

But he remembered Alice saying, "You aren't even human, Howard. You're a goddamn selfish monster." I am not a monster, he answered silently, and reached down into the toilet bowl to pull the child out.

The baby was firmly jammed in—whoever had tried to kill it had meant to catch it tight. Howard felt a brief surge of genuine indignation that anyone could think to solve his problems by killing an innocent child. But thinking of crimes committed on children was something Howard was determined not to do, and besides, at that moment he suddenly acquired other things to think about.

As the child clutched at Howard's arms, he noticed the baby's fingers were fused together into flipper-like flaps of bone and skin at the end of the arm. Yet the flippers gripped his arms with an unusual strength as, with two hands deep in the toilet bowl, Howard tried to pull the baby free.

At last, with a gush, the child came up and the water finished its flushing action. The legs, too, were fused into a single limb that was hideously twisted at the end. The child was male; the genitals, larger than normal, were skewed off to one side. And Howard noticed that where the feet should be were two more flippers, and near the tips were red spots that looked like putrefying sores. The child cried, a savage mewling that reminded Howard of a dog he had seen in its death throes. (Howard refused to be reminded that it had been he who'd killed the dog by throwing it out in the street in front of a passing car just to watch the driver swerve; the driver hadn't swerved.)

Even the hideously deformed have a right to live, Howard thought, but now, holding the child in his arms, he felt a revulsion that translated into sympathy for whoever, probably the parents, had tried to kill the creature. The child shifted its grip on him, and where the flippers had been Howard felt a sharp, stinging pain that quickly turned to agony as it was exposed to the air. Several huge, gaping sores on his arms were already running with blood and pus.

It took a moment for Howard to connect the sores with the child, and by then the leg flippers were already pressed against his stomach, and the arm flippers already gripped his chest. The sores on the child's flippers were not sores; they were powerful suction devices that gripped Howard's skin so tightly that they ripped it away when the contact was broken. He tried to pry the child off, but no sooner was one flipper free than it found a new place to hold even as Howard struggled to break the grip of another.

What had begun as an act of charity had now become an intense struggle. This was not a child, Howard realized. Children could not hang on so tightly, and the creature had teeth that snapped at his hands and arms whenever they came near enough. A human face, certainly, but not a human being. Howard threw himself against the wall, hoping to stun the creature so it would drop away. It only clung tighter, and the sores where it hung on him hurt more. But at last Howard pried and scraped it off by levering it against the edge of the toilet stall. It dropped to the ground, and Howard backed quickly away, on fire with the pain of a dozen or more stinging wounds.

It had to be a nightmare. In the middle of the night, in a bathroom lighted by a single bulb, with a travesty of humanity writhing on the floor, Howard could not believe that it had any reality.

Could it be a mutation that had somehow lived? Yet the thing had far more purpose, far more control of its body than any human infant. The baby slithered across the floor as Howard, in pain from the wounds on his body, watched in a panic of indecision. The baby reached the wall and cast a flipper onto it. The suction held and the baby began to inch its way straight up the wall. As it climbed, it defecated, a thin drool of green tracing down the wall behind it. Howard looked at the slime following the infant up the wall, looked at the pus-covered sores on his arms.

What if the animal, whatever it was, did not die soon of its terrible deformity? What if it lived? What if it were found, taken to a hospital, cared for? What if it became an adult?

It reached the ceiling and made the turn, clinging tightly to the plaster, not falling off as it hung upside down and inched across toward the light bulb.

The thing was trying to get directly over Howard, and the defecation was still dripping. Loathing overcame fear, and Howard reached up, took hold of the baby from the back, and, using his full weight, was finally able to pry it off the ceiling. It writhed and twisted in his hands, trying to get the suction cups on him, but Howard resisted with all his strength and was able to get the baby, this time headfirst, into the toilet bowl. He held it there until the bubbles stopped and it was blue. Then he went back to his apartment for a knife. Whatever the creature was, it had to disappear from the face of the earth. It had to die, and there had to be no sign left that could hint that Howard had killed it.

He found the knife quickly, but paused for a few moments to put something on his wounds. They stung bitterly, but in a while they felt better. Howard took off his shirt; thought a moment, and took off all his clothes, then put on his bathrobe and took a towel with him as he returned to the bathroom. He didn't want to get any blood on his clothes.

But when he got to the bathroom, the child was not in the toilet. Howard was alarmed. Had someone found it, drowning? Had they, perhaps, seen him leaving the bathroom—or worse, returning with his knife? He looked around the bathroom. There was nothing. He stepped back into the hall. No one. He stood a moment in the doorway, wondering what could have happened.

Then a weight dropped onto his head and shoulders from above, and he felt the suction flippers tugging at his face, at his head. He almost screamed. But he didn't want to arouse anyone. Somehow the child had not drowned after all, had crawled out of the toilet, and had waited over the door for Howard to return.

Once again the struggle resumed, and once again Howard pried the flippers away with the help of the toilet stall, though this time he was hampered by the fact that the child was behind and above him. It was exhausting work. He had to set down the knife so he could use both hands, and another dozen wounds stung bitterly by the time he had the child on the floor. As long as the child lay on its stomach, Howard could seize it from behind. He took it by the neck with one hand and picked up the knife with the other. He carried both to the toilet.

He had to flush twice to handle the flow of blood and pus. Howard wondered if the child was infected with some disease—the white fluid was thick and at least as great in volume as the blood. Then he flushed seven more times to take the pieces of the creature down the drain. Even after death, the suction pads clung tightly to the porcelain; Howard pried them off with the tip of the knife.

Eventually, the child was completely gone. Howard was panting with the exertion, nauseated at the stench and horror of what he had done. He remembered the smell of his dog's guts after the car hit it, and he threw up everything he had eaten at the party. Got the party out of his system, felt cleaner; took a shower, felt cleaner still. When he was through, he made sure the bathroom showed no sign of his ordeal.

Then he went to bed.

It wasn't easy to sleep. He was too keyed up. He couldn't get out of his mind the thought that he had committed murder (not murder, not murder, simply the elimination of something too foul to be alive). He tried thinking of a dozen, a hundred other things. Projects at work . . . but the designs kept showing flippers. His children . . . but their faces turned to the intense face of the struggling monster he had killed. Alice . . . ah, but Alice was harder to think of than the creature.

At last he slept, and dreamed, and in his dream remembered his father, who had died when he was ten. Howard did not remember any of his standard reminiscences. No long walks with his father, no basketball in the driveway, no fishing trips. Those things had happened, but tonight, because of the struggle with the monster, Howard remembered darker things that he had long been able to keep hidden from himself.

"We can't afford to get you a ten-speed bike, Howie. Not until the strike is over."

"I know, Dad. You can't help it." Swallow bravely. "And I don't mind. When all the guys go riding around after school, I'll just stay home and get ahead on my homework."

"Lots of boys don't have ten-speed bikes, Howie."

Howie shrugged, and turned away to hide the tears in his eyes. "Sure, lots of them. Hey, Dad, don't you worry about me. Howie can take care of himself."

Such courage. Such strength. He had gotten a ten-speed within a week. In his dream, Howard finally made a connection he had never been able to admit to himself before. His father had a rather elaborate ham radio setup in the garage. But about that time he had become tired of it, he said, and he sold it off and did a lot more work in the yard and looked bored as hell until the strike was over and he went back to work and got killed in an accident in the rolling mill.

Howard's dream ended madly, with him riding piggy-back on his father's shoulders as the monster had ridden on *him*, tonight—and in his hand was a knife, and he was stabbing his father again and again in the throat.

He awoke in early morning light, before his alarm rang, sobbing weakly and whimpering, "I killed him, I killed him, I killed him."

And then he drifted upward out of sleep and saw the time. Six-thirty. "A dream," he said. And the dream had awakened him early, too early, with a headache and sore eyes from crying. The pillow was soaked. "A hell of a lousy way to start the day," he mumbled. And, as was his habit, he got up and went to the window and opened the curtain.

On the glass, suction cups clinging tightly, was the child.

It was pressed close, as if by sucking very tightly it would be able to slither through the glass without breaking it. Far below were the honks of early morning traffic, the roar of passing trucks, but the child seemed oblivious of its height far above the street, with no ledge to break its fall. Indeed, there seemed little chance it would fall. The eyes looked closely, piercingly, at Howard.

Howard had been prepared to pretend that the night before had been another terribly realistic nightmare.

He stepped back from the glass, watched the child in fascination. It lifted a flipper, planted it higher, pulled itself up to a new position where it could stare at Howard eye to eye. And then, slowly and methodically, it began beating on the glass with its head.

The landlord was not generous with upkeep on the building. The glass was thin, and Howard knew that the child would not give up until it had broken through the glass so it could get to Howard.

He began to shake. His throat tightened. He was terribly afraid. Last night had been no dream. The fact that the child was here today was proof of that. Yet he had cut the child into small pieces. It could not possibly be alive. The glass shook and rattled with every blow the child's head struck.

The glass slivered in a starburst from where the child had hit it. The creature was coming in. And Howard picked up the room's one chair and threw it at the child, threw it at the window. Glass shattered, and the sun dazzled on the fragments as they exploded outward like a glistening halo around the child and the chair.

Howard ran to the window, looked out, and watched as the child landed brutally on the top of a large truck. The body seemed to smear as it hit, and fragments of the chair and shreds of glass danced around the child and bounced down into the street and the sidewalk.

The truck didn't stop moving; it carried the broken body and the shards

of glass and the pool of blood on up the street, and Howard ran to the
bed, knelt beside it, buried his face in the blanket, and tried to regain
control of himself. He had been seen. The people in the street had looked
up and seen him in the window. Last night he had gone to great lengths
to avoid discovery, but today discovery was impossible to avoid. He was
ruined. And yet he could not, could never have, let the child come into
the room.

Footsteps on the stairs. Stamping up the corridor. Pounding on the
door. "Open up! Hey in there!"

If I'm quiet long enough, they'll go away, he said to himself, knowing
it was a lie. He must get up, must answer the door. But he could not
bring himself to admit that he ever had to leave the safety of his bed.

"Hey, you son-of-a-bitch—" The imprecations went on but Howard
could not move until, suddenly, it occurred to him that the child could
be under the bed, and as he thought of it he could feel the tip of the
flipper touching his thigh, stroking and getting ready to fasten itself—

Howard leaped to his feet and rushed for the door. He flung it wide,
for even if it was the police come to arrest him, they could protect him
from the monster that was haunting him.

It was not a policeman at the door. It was the man on the first floor
who collected rent. "You son-of-a-bitch irresponsible pig-kisser!" the man
shouted, his toupee only approximately in place. "That chair could have
hit somebody! That window's expensive! Out! Get out of here, right now,
I want you out of this place, I don't care how the hell drunk you are."

"There was—there was this thing on the window, this creature. . . ."

The man looked at him coldly, but his eyes danced with anger. No,
not anger. Fear. Howard realized the man was afraid of him.

"This is a decent place," the man said softly. "You can take your
creatures and your booze and your pink stinking elephants and that's a
hundred bucks for the window, a hundred bucks right now, and you can
get out of here in an hour, an hour, you hear? Or I'm calling the police,
you hear?"

"I hear." He heard. The man left when Howard counted out five
twenties. The man seemed careful to avoid touching Howard's hands,
as if Howard had become, somehow, repulsive. Well, he had. To himself,
if to no one else. He closed the door as soon as the man was gone. He
packed the few belongings he had brought to the apartment in two suit-
cases and went downstairs and called a cab and rode to work. The cabby
looked at him sourly, and wouldn't talk. It was fine with Howard, if only

the driver hadn't kept looking at him through the mirror—nervously, as if he was afraid of what Howard might do or try. I won't try anything, Howard said to himself, I'm a decent man. Howard tipped the cabby well and then gave him twenty to take his bags to his house in Queens, where Alice could damn well keep them for a while. Howard was through with the tenement—that one or any other.

Obviously it had been a nightmare, last night and this morning. The monster was only visible to him, Howard decided. Only the chair and the glass had fallen from the fourth floor, or the manager would have noticed.

Except that the baby had landed on the truck, and might have been real, and might be discovered in New Jersey or Pennsylvania later today.

Couldn't be real. He had killed it last night and it was whole again this morning. A nightmare. I didn't really kill anybody, he insisted. (Except the dog. Except Father, said a new, ugly voice in the back of his mind.)

Work. Draw lines on paper, answer phone calls, dictate letters, keep your mind off your nightmares, off your family, off the mess your life is turning into. "Hell of a good party last night." Yeah, it was, wasn't it? "How are you today, Howard?" Feel fine, Dolores, fine—thanks to you. "Got the roughs on the IBM thing?" Nearly, nearly. Give me another twenty minutes. "Howard, you don't look well." Had a rough night. The party, you know.

He kept drawing on the blotter on his desk instead of going to the drawing table and producing real work. He doodled out faces. Alice's face, looking stern and terrible. The face of Stu's ugly wife. Dolores's face, looking sweet and yielding and stupid. And Rhiannon's face.

But with his daughter Rhiannon, he couldn't stop with the face.

His hand started to tremble when he saw what he had drawn. He ripped the sheet off the blotter, crumpled it, and reached under the desk to drop it in the wastebasket. The basket lurched, and flippers snaked out to seize his hand in an iron grip.

Howard screamed, tried to pull his hand away. The child came with it, the leg flippers grabbing Howard's right leg. The suction pad stung, bringing back the memory of all the pain last night. He scraped the child off against a filing cabinet, then ran for the door, which was already opening as several of his coworkers tumbled into his office demanding, "What is it? What's wrong? Why did you scream like that?"

Howard led them gingerly over to where the child should be. Nothing.

Just an overturned wastebasket, Howard's chair capsized on the floor. But Howard's window was open, and he could not remember opening it. "Howard, what is it? Are you tired, Howard? What's wrong?"

I don't feel well. I don't feel well at all.

Dolores put her arm around him, led him out of the room. "Howard, I'm worried about you."

I'm worried, too.

"Can I take you home? I have my car in the garage downstairs. Can I take you home?"

Where's home? Don't have a home, Dolores.

"My home, then. I have an apartment, you need to lie down and rest. Let me take you home."

Dolores's apartment was decorated in early Holly Hobby, and when she put records on the stereo it was old Carpenters and recent Captain and Tennille. Dolores led him to the bed, gently undressed him, and then, because he reached out to her, undressed herself and made love to him before she went back to work. She was naïvely eager. She whispered in his ear that he was only the second man she had ever loved, the first in five years. Her inept lovemaking was so sincere it made him want to cry.

When she was gone he did cry, because she thought she meant something to him and she did not.

Why am I crying? he asked himself. Why should I care? It's not my fault she let me get a handle on her. . . .

Sitting on the dresser in a curiously adult posture was the child, carelessly playing with itself as it watched Howard intently. "No," Howard said, pulling himself up to the head of the bed. "You don't exist," he said. "No one's ever seen you but me." The child gave no sign of understanding. It just rolled over and began to slither down the front of the dresser.

Howard reached for his clothes, took them out of the bedroom. He put them on in the living room as he watched the door. Sure enough, the child crept along the carpet to the living room; but Howard was dressed by then, and he left.

He walked the streets for three hours. He was coldly rational at first. Logical. The creature does not exist. There is no reason to believe in it.

But bit by bit his rationality was worn away by constant flickers of the creature at the edges of his vision. On a bench, peering over the back at him; in a shop window; staring from the cab of a milk truck. Howard walked faster and faster, not caring where he went, trying to keep some intelligent process going on in his mind, and failing utterly as he saw the child, saw it clearly, dangling from a traffic signal.

What made it even worse was that occasionally a passerby, violating the unwritten law that New Yorkers are forbidden to look at each other, would gaze at him, shudder, and look away. A short European-looking woman crossed herself. A group of teenagers looking for trouble weren't looking for him—they grew silent, let him pass in silence, and in silence watched him out of sight.

They may not be able to see the child, Howard realized, but they see something.

And as he grew less and less coherent in the ramblings of his mind, memories began flashing on and off, his life passing before his eyes like a drowning man is supposed to see, only, he realized, if a drowning man saw this he would gulp at the water, breathe it deeply just to end the visions. They were memories he had been unable to find for years, memories he would never have wanted to find.

His poor, confused mother, who was so eager to be a good parent that she read everything, tried everything. Her precocious son Howard read it all, too, and understood it better. Nothing she tried ever worked. And he accused her several times of being too demanding, or not demanding enough; of not giving him enough love, or of drowning him in phony affection; of trying to take over with his friends, of not liking his friends enough. Until he had badgered and tortured the woman so that she was timid every time she spoke to him, careful and long-winded and phrasing everything in such a way that it wouldn't offend, and while now and then he made her feel wonderful by giving her a hug and saying "Have I got a wonderful mom," there were far more times when he put a patient look on his face and said, "That again, Mom? I thought we went over that years ago." A failure as a parent, that's what you are, he reminded her again and again, though not in so many words, and she nodded and believed and died inside with every contact they had. He got everything he wanted from her.

And Vaughn Robles, who was just a little bit smarter than Howard and Howard wanted very badly to be valedictorian and so Vaughn and Howard became best friends and Vaughn would do anything for Howard and whenever Vaughn got a better grade than Howard he could not help but notice that Howard was hurt, wondered if he was really worth anything at all. "Am I really worth anything at all, Vaughn? No matter how well I do, there's always someone ahead of me, and I guess it's just that before my father died he told me and told me, 'Howie, be better than your dad.

Be the top.' And I promised him I'd be the top but hell, Vaughn, I'm just not cut out for it. . . . " And once he even cried. Vaughn was proud of himself as he sat there and listened to Howard give the valedictory address at high school graduation. What were a few grades, compared to a true friendship? Howard got a scholarship and went away to college and he and Vaughn almost never saw each other again.

And the teacher he provoked into hitting him and losing his job; and the football player who snubbed him and Howard quietly spread the rumor that the fellow was gay and he was ostracized from the team and finally quit; and the beautiful girls he stole from their boyfriends just to prove that he could do it and the friendships he destroyed just because he didn't like being excluded and the marriages he wrecked and the coworkers he undercut and he walked along the street with tears streaming down his face wondering where all these memories had come from and why, after such a long time in hiding, they had come out now. Yet he knew the answer. The answer was slipping behind doorways, climbing lightpoles as he passed, waving obscene flippers at him from the sidewalk almost under his feet.

And slowly, inexorably, the memories wound their way from the distant past through a hundred tawdry exploitations because he could find people's weak spots without even trying until finally, memory came to the one place where he knew it could not, could not ever go.

He remembered Rhiannon.

Born fourteen years ago. Smiled early, walked early, almost never cried. A loving child from the start, and therefore easy prey for Howard. Oh, Alice was a bitch in her own right—Howard wasn't the only bad parent in the family. But it was Howard who manipulated Rhiannon most. "Daddy's feelings are hurt, sweetheart," and Rhiannon's eyes would grow wide, and she'd be sorry, and whatever Daddy wanted, Rhiannon would do. But this was normal, this was part of the pattern, this would have fit easily into all his life before except for last month.

And even now, after a day of grief at his own life, Howard could not face it. Could not but did. He unwillingly remembered walking by Rhiannon's almost-closed door, seeing just a flash of cloth moving quickly. He opened the door on impulse, just on impulse, as Rhiannon took off her brassiere and looked at herself in the mirror. Howard had never thought of his daughter with desire, not until that moment, but once the desire formed Howard had no strategy, no pattern in his mind to stop him from trying to get what he wanted. He was *uncomfortable*, and so he stepped into the room and closed the door behind him and Rhiannon knew no way to say no to her father. When Alice opened the door Rhiannon was crying softly, and Alice looked and after a moment Alice screamed and screamed and Howard got up from the bed and tried to smooth it all over but Rhiannon was still crying and Alice was still screaming, kicking at his crotch, beating him, raking at his face, spitting at him, telling him he was a monster, a monster, until at last he was able to flee the room and the house and, until now, the memory.

He screamed now as he had not screamed then, and threw himself against a plate glass window, weeping loudly as the blood gushed from a dozen glass cuts on his right arm, which had gone through the window. One large piece of glass stayed embedded in his forearm. He deliberately scraped his arm against the wall to drive the glass deeper. But the pain in his arm was no match for the pain in his mind, and he felt nothing.

They rushed him to the hospital, thinking to save his life, but the doctor was surprised to discover that for all the blood there were only superficial wounds, not dangerous at all. "I don't know why you didn't reach a vein or an artery," the doctor said. "I think the glass went everywhere it could possibly go without causing any important damage."

After the medical doctor, of course, there was the psychiatrist, but there were many suicidals at the hospital and Howard was not the dangerous kind. "I was insane for a moment, Doctor, that's all. I don't want to die, I didn't want to die then, I'm all right now. You can send me home." And the psychiatrist let him go home. They bandaged his arm. They did not know that his real relief was that nowhere in the hospital did he see the small, naked, child-shaped creature. He had purged himself. He was free.

Howard was taken home in an ambulance, and they wheeled him into the house and lifted him from the stretcher to the bed. Through it all Alice hardly said a word except to direct them to the bedroom. Howard lay still on the bed as she stood over him, the two of them alone for the first time since he had left the house a month ago.

"It was kind of you," Howard said softly, "to let me come back."

"They said there wasn't room enough to keep you, but you needed to be watched and taken care of for a few weeks. So lucky me, I get to watch you." Her voice was a low monotone, but the acid dripped from every word. It stung.

"You were right, Alice," Howard said.

"Right about what? That marrying you was the worst mistake of my life? No, Howard. *Meeting* you was my worst mistake."

Howard began to cry. Real tears that welled up from places in him that had once been deep but that now rested painfully close to the surface. "I've been a monster, Alice. I haven't had any control over myself. What I did to Rhiannon—Alice, I wanted to die, I wanted to die!"

Alice's face was twisted and bitter. "And I wanted you to, Howard. I have never been so disappointed as when the doctor called and said you'd be all right. You'll never be all right, Howard, you'll always be—"

"Let him be, Mother."

Rhiannon stood in the doorway.

"Don't come in, Rhiannon," Alice said.

Rhiannon came in. "Daddy, it's all right."

"What she means," Alice said, "is that we've checked her and she isn't pregnant. No little monster is going to be born."

Rhiannon didn't look at her mother, just gazed with wide eyes at her father. "You didn't need to—hurt yourself, Daddy. I forgive you. People lose control sometimes. And it was as much my fault as yours, it really was, you don't need to feel bad, Father."

It was too much for Howard. He cried out, shouted his confession, how he had manipulated her all her life, how he was an utterly selfish and rotten parent, and when it was over Rhiannon came to her father and laid her head on his chest and said softly, "Father, it's all right. We are who we are. We've done what we've done. But it's all right now. I forgive you."

When Rhiannon left, Alice said, "You don't deserve her."

I know.

"I was going to sleep on the couch, but that would be stupid. Wouldn't it, Howard?"

I deserve to be left alone, like a leper.

"You misunderstand, Howard. I need to stay here to make sure you don't do anything else. To yourself or to anyone."

Yes. Yes, please. I can't be trusted.

"Don't wallow in it, Howard. Don't enjoy it. Don't make yourself even more disgusting than you were before."

All right.

They were drifting off to sleep when Alice said, "Oh, when the doctor called he wondered if I knew what had caused those sores all over your arms and chest."

But Howard was asleep, and didn't hear her. Asleep with no dreams at all, the sleep of peace, the sleep of having been forgiven, of being clean. It hadn't taken that much, after all. Now that it was over, it was easy. He felt as if a great weight had been taken from him.

He felt as if something heavy was lying on his legs. He awoke, sweating even though the room was not hot. He heard breathing. And it was not Alice's low-pitched, slow breath, it was quick and high and hard, as if the breather had been exerting himself.

Itself.

Themselves.

One of them lay across his legs, the flippers plucking at the blanket. The other two lay on either side, their eyes wide and intent, creeping slowly toward where his face emerged from the sheets.

Howard was puzzled. "I thought you'd be gone," he said to the children. "You're supposed to be gone now."

Alice stirred at the sound of his voice, mumbled in her sleep.

He saw more of them stirring in the gloomy corners of the room, another writhing slowly along the top of the dresser, another inching up the wall toward the ceiling.

"I don't need you anymore," he said, his voice oddly high-pitched.

Alice started breathing irregularly, mumbling, "What? What?"

And Howard said nothing more, just lay there in the sheets, watching the creatures carefully but not daring to make a sound for fear Alice would wake up. He was terribly afraid she would wake up and not see the creatures, which would prove, once and for all, that he had lost his mind.

He was even more afraid, however, that when she awoke she *would* see them. That was the only unbearable thought, yet he thought it continuously as they relentlessly approached with nothing at all in their eyes, not even hate, not even anger, not even contempt. We are with you, they seemed to be saying, we will be with you from now on. We will be with you, Howard, forever.

And Alice rolled over and opened her eyes.

NARROW VALLEY

I n the year 1893, land allotments in severalty were made to the remaining eight hundred and twenty-one Pawnee Indians. Each would receive one hundred and sixty acres of land and no more, and thereafter the Pawnees would be expected to pay taxes on their land, the same as the White-Eyes did.

"Kitkehahke!" Clarence Big-Saddle cussed. "You can't kick a dog around proper on a hundred and sixty acres. And I sure am not hear before about this pay taxes on land."

Clarence Big-Saddle selected a nice green valley for his allotment. It was one of the half-dozen plots he had always regarded as his own. He sodded around the summer lodge that he had there and made it an all-season home. But he sure didn't intend to pay taxes on it.

So he burned leaves and bark and made a speech:

"That my valley be always wide and flourish and green and such stuff as that!" he orated in Pawnee chant style, "but that it be narrow if an intruder come."

He didn't have any balsam bark to burn. He threw on a little cedar bark instead. He didn't have any elder leaves. He used a handful of jack-oak leaves. And he forgot the word. How you going to work it if you forget the word?

"Petahauerat!" he howled out with the confidence he hoped would fool the fates.

"That's about the same long of a word," he said in a low aside to himself. But he was doubtful. "What am I, a White Man, a burr-tailed jack, a new kind of nut to think it will work?" he asked. "I have to laugh at me. Oh well, we see."

He threw the rest of the bark and the leaves on the fire, and he hollered the wrong word out again.

And he was answered by a dazzling sheet of summer lightning.

"Skidi!" Clarence Big-Saddle swore. "It worked. I didn't think it would."

Clarence Big-Saddle lived on his land for many years, and he paid no taxes. Intruders were unable to come down to his place. The land was sold for taxes three times, but nobody ever came down to claim it. Finally, it was carried as open land on the books. Homesteaders filed on it several times, but none of them fulfilled the qualification of living on the land.

Half a century went by. Clarence Big-Saddle called his son.

"I've had it, boy," he said. "I think I'll just go in the house and die."

"Okay, Dad," the son, Clarence Little-Saddle, said. "I'm going in to town to shoot a few games of pool with the boys. I'll bury you when I get back this evening."

So the son Clarence Little-Saddle inherited. He also lived on the land for many years without paying taxes.

There was a disturbance in the courthouse one day. The place seemed to be invaded in force, but actually there were but one man, one woman, and five children. "I'm Robert Rampart," said the man, "and we want the Land Office."

"I'm Robert Rampart, Junior," said a nine-year-old gangler, "and we want it pretty blamed quick."

"I don't think we have anything like that," the girl at the desk said. "Isn't that something they had a long time ago?"

"Ignorance is no excuse for inefficiency, my dear," said Mary Mabel Rampart, an eight-year-old who could easily pass for eight and a half. "After I make my report, I wonder who will be sitting at your desk tomorrow?"

"You people are either in the wrong state or the wrong century," the girl said.

"The Homestead Act still obtains," Robert Rampart insisted. "There is one tract of land carried as open in this county. I want to file on it."

Cecilia Rampart answered the knowing wink of a beefy man at a distant desk. "Hi," she breathed as she slinked over. "I'm Cecilia Rampart, but my stage name is Cecilia San Juan. Do you think that seven is too young to play ingenue roles?"

"Not for you," the man said. "Tell your folks to come over here."

"Do you know where the Land Office is?" Cecilia asked.

"Sure. It's the fourth left-hand drawer of my desk. The smallest office we got in the whole courthouse. We don't use it much anymore."

The Ramparts gathered around. The beefy man started to make out the papers.

"This is the land description—" Robert Rampart began, "—why, you've got it down already. How did you know?"

"I've been around here a long time," the man answered.

They did the paperwork, and Robert Rampart filed on the land.

"You won't be able to come onto the land itself, though," the man said.

"Why won't I?" Rampart demanded. "Isn't the land description accurate?"

"Oh, I suppose so. But nobody's ever been able to get to the land. It's become a sort of joke."

"Well, I intend to get to the bottom of that joke," Rampart insisted. "I will occupy the land, or I will find out why not."

"I'm not sure about that," the beefy man said. "The last man to file on the land, about a dozen years ago, wasn't able to occupy the land. And he wasn't able to say why he couldn't. It's kind of interesting, the look on their faces after they try it for a day or two, and then give it up."

The Ramparts left the courthouse, loaded into their camper, and drove out to find their land. They stopped at the house of a cattle and wheat farmer named Charley Dublin. Dublin met them with a grin which indicated he had been tipped off.

"Come along if you want to, folks," Dublin said. "The easiest way is on foot across my short pasture here. Your land's directly west of mine."

They walked the short distance to the border.

"My name is Tom Rampart, Mr. Dublin." Six-year-old Tom made conversation as they walked. "But my name is really Ramires, and not Tom. I am the issue of an indiscretion of my mother in Mexico several years ago."

"The boy is a kidder, Mr. Dublin," said the mother, Nina Rampart, defending herself. "I have never been in Mexico, but sometimes I have the urge to disappear there forever."

"Ah yes, Mrs. Rampart. And what is the name of the youngest boy here?" Charles Dublin asked.

"Fatty," said Fatty Rampart.

"But surely that is not your given name?"

"Audifax," said five-year-old Fatty.

"Ah well, Audifax, Fatty, are you a kidder too?"

"He's getting better at it, Mr. Dublin," Mary Mabel said. "He was a twin till last week. His twin was named Skinny. Mama left Skinny unguarded while she was out tippling, and there were wild dogs in the neighborhood. When Mama got back, do you know what was left of Skinny? Two neck bones and an ankle bone. That was all."

"Poor Skinny," Dublin said. "Well, Rampart, this is the fence and the end of my land. Yours is just beyond."

"Is that ditch on my land?" Rampart asked.

"That ditch *is* your land."

"I'll have it filled in. It's a dangerous deep cut even if it is narrow. And the other fence looks like a good one, and I sure have a pretty plot of land beyond it."

"No, Rampart, the land beyond the second fence belongs to Holister Hyde," Charley Dublin said. "That second fence is the *end* of your land."

"Now, just wait a minute, Dublin! There's something wrong here. My land is one hundred and sixty acres, which would be a half mile on a side. Where's my half-mile width?"

"Between the two fences."

"That's not eight feet."

"Doesn't look like it, does it, Rampart? Tell you what—there's plenty of throwing-sized rocks around. Try to throw one across it."

"I'm not interested in any such boys' games," Rampart exploded. "I want my land."

But the Rampart children *were* interested in such games. They got with it with those throwing rocks. They winged them out over the little gully. The stones acted funny. They hung in the air, as it were, and diminished in size. And they were small as pebbles when they dropped down, down into the gully. None of them could throw a stone across that ditch, and they were throwing kids.

"You and your neighbor have conspired to fence open land for your own use," Rampart charged.

"No such thing, Rampart," Dublin said cheerfully. "My land checks perfectly. So does Hyde's. So does yours, if we knew how to check it.

It's like one of those trick topological drawings. It really is a half mile
from here to there, but the eye gets lost somewhere. It's your land. Crawl
through the fence and figure it out."

Rampart crawled through the fence, and drew himself up to jump the
gully. Then he hesitated. He got a glimpse of just how deep that gully
was. Still, it wasn't five feet across.

There was a heavy fence post on the ground, designed for use as a
corner post. Rampart up-ended it with some effort. Then he shoved it
to fall and bridge the gully. But it fell short, and it shouldn't have. An
eight-foot post should bridge a five-foot gully.

The post fell into the gully, and rolled and rolled and rolled. It spun
as though it were rolling outward, but it made no progress except vertically. The post came to rest on a ledge of the gully, so close that Rampart
could almost reach out and touch it, but it now appeared no bigger than
a match stick.

"There is something wrong with that fence post, or with the world,
or with my eyes," Robert Rampart said. "I wish I felt dizzy so I could
blame it on that."

"There's a little game that I sometimes play with my neighbor Hyde
when we're both out," Dublin said. "I've a heavy rifle and I train it on
the middle of his forehead as he stands on the other side of the ditch
apparently eight feet away. I fire it off then (I'm a good shot), and I hear
it whine across. It'd kill him dead if things were as they seem. But Hyde's
in no danger. The shot always bangs into that little scuff of rocks and
boulders about thirty feet below him. I can see it kick up the rock dust
there, and the sound of it rattling into those little boulders comes back
to me in about two and a half seconds."

A bull-bat (poor people call it the night-hawk) raveled around in the
air and zoomed out over the narrow ditch, but it did not reach the other
side. The bird dropped below ground level and could be seen against the
background of the other side of the ditch. It grew smaller and hazier as
though at a distance of three or four hundred yards. The white bars on
its wings could no longer be discerned; then the bird itself could hardly
be discerned; but it was far short of the other side of the five-foot ditch.

A man identified by Charley Dublin as the neighbor Hollister Hyde
had appeared on the other side of the little ditch. Hyde grinned and
waved. He shouted something, but could not be heard.

"Hyde and I both read mouth," Dublin said, "so we can talk across
the ditch easy enough. Which kid wants to play chicken? Hyde will barrel

a good-sized rock right at your head, and if you duck or flinch you're chicken."

"Me! Me!" Audifax Rampart challenged. And Hyde, a big man with big hands, did barrel a fearsome jagged rock right at the head of the boy. It would have killed him if things had been as they appeared. But the rock diminished to nothing and disappeared into the ditch. Here was a phenomenon—things seemed real-sized on either side of the ditch, but they diminished coming out over the ditch either way.

"Everybody game for it?" Robert Rampart Junior asked.

"We won't get down there by standing here," Mary Mabel said.

"Nothing wenchered, nothing gained," said Cecilia. "I got that from an ad for a sex comedy."

Then the five Rampart kids ran down into the gully. Ran *down* is right. It was almost as if they ran down the vertical face of a cliff. They couldn't do that. The gully was no wider than the stride of the biggest kids. But the gully diminished those children, it ate them alive. They were doll-sized. They were acorn-sized. They were running for minute after minute across a ditch that was only five feet across. They were going deeper in it, and getting smaller. Robert Rampart was roaring his alarm, and his wife Nina was screaming. Then she stopped. "What am I carrying on so loud about?" she asked herself. "It looks like fun. I'll do it too."

She plunged into the gully, diminished in size as the children had done, and ran at a pace to carry her a hundred yards away across a gully only five feet wide.

That Robert Rampart stirred things up for a while then. He got the sheriff there, and the highway patrolmen. A ditch had stolen his wife and five children, he said, and maybe had killed them. And if anybody laughs, there may be another killing. He got the colonel of the State National Guard there, and a command post set up. He got a couple of airplane pilots. Robert Rampart had one quality: when he hollered, people came.

He got the newsmen out from T-Town, and the eminent scientists, Dr. Velikof Vonk, Arpad Arkabaranan, and Willy McGilly. That bunch turns up every time you get on a good one. They just happen to be in that part of the country where something interesting is going on.

They attacked the thing from all four sides and the top, and by inner and outer theory. If a thing measures a half mile on each side, and the sides are straight, there just has to be something in the middle of it. They took pictures from the air, and they turned out perfect. They proved that

Robert Rampart had the prettiest hundred and sixty acres in the country, the larger part of it being a lush green valley, and all of it being a half mile on a side, and situated just where it should be. They took ground-level photos then, and it showed a beautiful half-mile stretch of land between the boundaries of Charley Dublin and Holister Hyde. But a man isn't a camera. None of them could see that beautiful spread with the eyes in their heads. Where was it?

Down in the valley itself everything was normal. It really was a half mile wide and no more than eighty feet deep with a very gentle slope. It was warm and sweet, and beautiful with grass and grain.

Nina and the kids loved it, and they rushed to see what squatter had built that little house on their land. A house, or a shack. It had never known paint, but paint would have spoiled it. It was built of split timbers dressed near smooth with axe and draw knife, chinked with white clay, and sodded up to about half its height. And there was an interloper standing by the little lodge.

"Here, here, what are you doing on our land?" Robert Rampart Junior demanded of the man. "Now you just shamble off again wherever you came from. I'll bet you're a thief too, and those cattle are stolen."

"Only the black-and-white calf," Clarence Little-Saddle said. "I couldn't resist him, but the rest are mine. I guess I'll just stay around and see that you folks get settled all right."

"Is there any wild Indians around here?" Fatty Rampart asked.

"No, not really. I go on a bender about every three months and get a little bit wild, and there's a couple Osage boys from Gray Horse that get noisy sometimes, but that's about all," Clarence Little-Saddle said.

"You certainly don't intend to palm yourself off on us as an Indian," Mary Mabel challenged. "You'll find us a little too knowledgeable for that."

"Little girl, you as well tell this cow there's no room for her to be a cow since you're so knowledgeable. She thinks she's a short-horn cow named Sweet Virginia. I think I'm a Pawnee Indian named Clarence. Break it to us real gentle if we're not."

"If you're an Indian where's your war bonnet? There's not a feather on you anywhere."

"How you be sure? There's a story that we got feathers instead of hair on—Aw, I can't tell a joke like that to a little girl! How come you're not wearing the Iron Crown of Lombardy if you're a white girl? How you expect me to believe you're a little white girl and your folks came from Europe a couple hundred years ago if you don't wear it? There were six hundred tribes, and only one of them, the Oglala Sioux, had the war bonnet and only the big leaders, never more than two or three of them alive at one time, wore it."

"Your analogy is a little strained," Mary Mabel said. "Those Indians we saw in Florida and the ones at Atlantic City had war bonnets, and they couldn't very well have been the kind of Sioux you said. And just last night on the TV in the motel, those Massachusetts Indians put a war bonnet on the President and called him the Great White Father. You mean to tell me that they were all phonies? Hey, who's laughing at who here?"

"If you're an Indian where's your bow and arrow?" Tom Rampart interrupted. "I bet you can't even shoot one."

"You're sure right there," Clarence admitted. "I never shot one of those things but once in my life. They used to have an archery range in Boulder Park over in T-Town, and you could rent the things and shoot at targets tied to hay bales. Hey, I barked my whole forearm and nearly broke my thumb when the bowstring thwacked home. I couldn't shoot that thing at all. I don't see how anybody ever could shoot one of them."

"Okay, kids," Nina Rampart called to her brood. "Let's start pitching this junk out of the shack so we can move in. Is there any way we can drive our camper down here, Clarence?"

"Sure, there's a pretty good dirt road, and it's a lot wider than it looks from the top. I got a bunch of green bills in an old night charley in the shack. Let me get them, and then I'll clear out for a while. The shack hasn't been cleaned out for seven years, since the last time this happened. I'll show you the road to the top, and you can bring your car down it."

"Hey, you old Indian, you lied!" Cecilia Rampart shrilled from the doorway of the shack. "You *do* have a war bonnet. Can I have it?"

"I didn't mean to lie, I forgot about that thing," Clarence Little-Saddle said. "My son Clarence Bare-Back sent that to me from Japan for a joke a long time ago. Sure, you can have it."

All the children were assigned tasks carrying the junk out of the shack and setting fire to it. Nina Rampart and Clarence Little-Saddle ambled up to the rim of the valley by the vehicle road that was wider than it looked from the top.

"Nina, you're back! I thought you were gone forever," Robert Rampart jittered at seeing her again. "What—where are the children?"

"Why, I left them down in the valley, Robert. That is, ah, down in that little ditch right there. Now you've got me worried again. I'm going to drive the camper down there and unload it. You'd better go on down and lend a hand too, Robert, and quit talking to all these funny-looking men here."

And Nina went back to Dublin's place for the camper.

"It would be easier for a camel to go through the eye of a needle than for that intrepid woman to drive a car down into that narrow ditch," the eminent scientist Dr. Velikof Vonk said.

"You know how that camel does it?" Clarence Little-Saddle offered, appearing of a sudden from nowhere. "He just closes one of his own eyes and flops back his ears and plunges right through. A camel is mighty narrow when he closes one eye and flops back his ears. Besides, they use a big-eyed needle in the act."

"Where'd this crazy man come from?" Robert Rampart demanded, jumping three feet in the air. "Things are coming out of the ground now. I want my land! I want my children! I want my wife! Whoops, here she comes driving it. Nina, you can't drive a loaded camper into a little ditch like that! You'll be killed or collapsed!"

Nina Rampart drove the loaded camper into the little ditch at a pretty good rate of speed. The best of belief is that she just closed one eye and plunged right through. The car diminished and dropped, and it was smaller than a toy car. But it raised a pretty good cloud of dust as it bumped for several hundred yards across a ditch that was only five feet wide.

"Rampart, it's akin to the phenomenon known as looming, only in reverse," the eminent scientist Arpad Arkabaranan explained as he attempted to throw a rock across the narrow ditch. The rock rose very high in the air, seemed to hang at its apex while it diminished to the size of a grain of sand, and then fell into the ditch not six inches of the way across. There isn't anybody going to throw across a half-mile valley even if it looks five feet. "Look at a rising moon sometime, Rampart. It appears very large, as though covering a great sector of the horizon, but it only covers one half of a degree. It is hard to believe that you could set seven hundred and twenty of such large moons side by side around the horizon, or that it would take one hundred and eighty of the big things to reach from the horizon to a point overhead. It is also hard to believe that your valley is five hundred times as wide as it appears, but it has been surveyed, and it is."

"I want my land. I want my children. I want my wife," Robert chanted dully. "Damn, I let her get away again."

"I tell you, Rampy," Clarence Little-Saddle squared on him, "a man that lets his wife get away twice doesn't deserve to keep her. I give you till nightfall; then you forfeit. I've taken a liking to the brood. One of us is going to be down there tonight."

After a while a bunch of them were off in that little tavern on the road between Cleveland and Osage. It was only a half mile away. If the valley had run in the other direction, it would have been only six feet away.

"It is a psychic nexus in the form of an elongated dome," said the eminent scientist Dr. Velikof Vonk. "It is maintained subconsciously by the concatenation of at least two minds, the stronger of them belonging to a man dead for many years. It has apparently existed for a little less than a hundred years, and in another hundred years it will be considerably weakened. We know from our checking out of folk tales of Europe as well as Cambodia that these ensorcelled areas seldom survive for more than two hundred and fifty years. The person who first set such a thing in being will usually lose interest in it, and in all worldly things, within a hundred years of his own death. This is a simple thanato-psychic limitation. As a short-term device, the thing has been used several times as a military tactic.

"This psychic nexus, as long as it maintains itself, causes group illusion, but it is really a simple thing. It doesn't fool birds or rabbits or cattle or cameras, only humans. There is nothing meteorological about it. It is strictly psychological. I'm glad I was able to give a scientific explanation to it or it would have worried me."

"It is the continental fault coinciding with a noospheric fault," said the eminent scientist Arpad Arkabaranan. "The valley really is a half mile wide, and at the same time it really is only five feet wide. If we measured correctly, we would get these dual measurements. Of course it is meteorological! Everything including dreams is meteorological. It is the animals and cameras which are fooled, as lacking a true dimension; it is only humans who see the true duality. The phenomenon should be common along the whole continental fault where the earth gains or loses a half mile that has to go somewhere. Likely it extends through the whole sweep of the Cross Timbers. Many of those trees appear twice, and many do not appear at all. A man in the proper state of mind could farm that land or raise cattle on it, but it doesn't really exist. There is a clear parallel in the Luftspiegelungthal sector in the Black Forest of Germany which exists, or does not exist, according to the circumstances and to the attitude of the beholder. Then we have the case of Mad Mountain in Morgan County, Tennessee, which isn't there all the time, and also the Little Lobo Mirage south of Presidio, Texas, from which twenty thousand barrels of water were pumped in one two-and-a-half-hour period before the mirage reverted to mirage status. I'm glad I was able to give a scientific explanation to this or it would have worried me."

"I just don't understand how he worked it," said the eminent scientist Willy McGilly. "Cedar bark, jack-oak leaves, and the word 'Petahauerat.' The thing's impossible! When I was a boy and we wanted to make a hideout, we used bark from the skunk-spruce tree, the leaves of a box-elder, and the word was 'Boadicea.' All three elements are wrong here. I cannot find a scientific explanation for it, and it does worry me."

They went back to Narrow Valley. Robert Rampart was still chanting dully: "I want my land. I want my children. I want my wife."

Nina Rampart came chugging up out of the narrow ditch in the camper and emerged through that little gate a few yards down the fence row.

"Supper's ready and we're tired of waiting for you, Robert," she said. "A fine homesteader you are! Afraid to come onto your own land! Come along now, I'm tired of waiting for you."

"I want my land! I want my children! I want my wife!" Robert Rampart still chanted. "Oh, there you are, Nina. You stay here this time. I want my land! I want my children! I want an answer to this terrible thing."

"It is time we decided who wears the pants in this family," Nina said stoutly. She picked up her husband, slung him over her shoulder, carried him to the camper and dumped him in, slammed (as it seemed) a dozen doors at once, and drove furiously down into Narrow Valley, which already seemed wider.

Why, that place was getting normaler and normaler by the minute! Pretty soon it looked almost as wide as it was supposed to be. The psychic nexus in the form of an elongated dome had collapsed. The continental fault that coincided with the noospheric fault had faced facts and decided to conform. The Ramparts were in effective possession of their homestead, and Narrow Valley was as normal as any place anywhere.

"I have lost my land," Clarence Little-Saddle moaned. "It was the land of my father Clarence Big-Saddle, and I meant it to be the land of my son Clarence Bare-Back. It looked so narrow that people did not notice how wide it was, and people did not try to enter it. Now I have lost it."

Clarence Little-Saddle and the eminent scientist Willy McGilly were standing on the edge of Narrow Valley, which now appeared its true half-mile extent. The moon was just rising, so big that it filled a third of the sky. Who would have imagined that it would take 180 of such monstrous things to reach from the horizon to a point overhead, and yet you could sight it with sighters and figure it so.

"I had the little bear-cat by the tail and I let go," Clarence groaned. "I had a fine valley for free, and I have lost it. I am like that hard-luck guy in the funny-paper or Job in the Bible. Destitution is my lot."

Willy McGilly looked around furtively. They were alone on the edge of the half-mile-wide valley.

"Let's give it a booster shot," Willy McGilly said.

Hey, those two got with it! They started a snapping fire and began to throw the stuff onto it. Bark from the dog-elm tree—how do you know it won't work?

It *was* working! Already the other side of the valley seemed a hundred yards closer, and there were alarmed noises coming up from the people in the valley.

Leaves from a black locust tree—and the valley narrowed still more! There was, moreover, terrified screaming of both children and big people from the depths of Narrow Valley, and the happy voice of Mary Mabel Rampart chanting "Earthquake! Earthquake!"

"That my valley be always wide and flourish and such stuff, and green with money and grass!" Clarence Little-Saddle orated in Pawnee chant style, "but that it be narrow if intruders come, smash them like bugs!"

People, that valley wasn't over a hundred feet wide now, and the screaming of the people in the bottom of the valley had been joined by the hysterical coughing of the camper car starting up.

Willy and Clarence threw everything that was left on the fire. But the word? The word? Who remembers the word?

"Corsicanatexas!" Clarence Little-Saddle howled out with confidence he hoped would fool the fates.

He was answered, not only by a dazzling sheet of summer lightning, but also by thunder and raindrops.

"Chahiksi!" Clarence Little-Saddle swore. "It worked. I didn't think it would. It will be all right now. I can use the rain."

The valley was again a ditch only five feet wide.

The camper car struggled out of Narrow Valley through the little gate. It was smashed flat as a sheet of paper, and the screaming kids and people in it had only one dimension.

"It's closing in! It's closing in!" Robert Rampart roared, and he was no thicker than if he had been made out of cardboard.

"We're smashed like bugs," the Rampart boys intoned. "We're thin like paper."

"Mort, ruine, écrasement!" spoke-acted Cecilia Rampart like the great tragedienne she was.

"Help! Help!" Nina Rampart croaked, but she winked at Willy and Clarence as they rolled by. "This homesteading jag always did leave me a little flat."

"Don't throw those paper dolls away. They might be the Ramparts," Mary Mabel called.

The camper car coughed again and bumped along on level ground. This couldn't last forever. The car was widening out as it bumped along.

"Did we overdo it, Clarence?" Willy McGilly asked. "What did one flatlander say to the other?"

"Dimension of us never got around," Clarence said. "No, I don't think we overdid it, Willy. That car must be eighteen inches wide already, and they all ought to be normal by the time they reach the main road. The next time I do it, I think I'll throw wood-grain plastic on the fire to see who's kidding who."

THE DREAMSTONE

O f all possible paths to travel up out of Caerdale, that through the deep forest was the least used by Men. Brigands, outlaws, fugitives who fled mindless from shadows . . . men with dull, dead eyes and hearts which could not truly see the wood, souls so attainted already with the world that they could sense no greater evil nor greater good than their own—*they* walked that path; and if by broad morning, so that they had cleared the black heart of Ealdwood by nightfall, then they might perchance make it safe away into the new forest eastward in the hills, there to live and prey on the game and on each other.

But a runner by night, and that one young and wild-eyed and bearing neither sword nor blow, but only a dagger and a gleeman's harp, this was a rare venturer in Ealdwood, and all the deeper shadows chuckled and whispered in startlement.

Eld-born Arafel saw him, and she saw little in this latter age of earth, wrapped as she was in a passage of time different from the suns and moons which blink Men so startling-swift from birth to dying. She heard the bright notes of the harp which jangled on his shoulders, which companied his flight and betrayed him to all with ears to hear, in this world and the other. She saw his flight and walked into the way to meet him, out of the soft green light of her moon and into the colder white of his; and evils which had grown quite bold in the Ealdwood of latter earth suddenly felt the warm breath of spring and drew aside, slinking into dark places where neither moon cast light.

"Boy," she whispered. He startled like a wounded deer, hesitated, searching out the voice. She stepped full into his light and felt the dank wind of Ealdwood on her face. He seemed more solid then, ragged and torn by thorns in his headlong course, although his garments had been of fine linen and the harp at his shoulders had a broidered case.

She had taken little with her out of otherwhere, and yet did take—it was all in the eye which saw. She leaned against the rotting trunk of a dying tree and folded her arms unthreateningly, no hand to the blade she wore, propped one foot against a projecting root, and smiled. He looked on her with no less apprehension for that, seeing, perhaps, a ragged vagabond of a woman in outlaw's habit—or perhaps seeing more, for he did not look to be as blind as some. His hand touched a talisman at his breast and she, smiling still, touched that which hung at her own throat, which had power to answer his.

"Now where would you be going," she asked, "so recklessly through the Ealdwood? To some misdeed? Some mischief?"

"Misfortune," he said, breathless. He yet stared at her as if he thought her no more than moonbeams, and she grinned at that. Then suddenly and far away came a baying of hounds; he would have fled at once, and sprang to do so.

"Stay!" she cried, and stepped into his path a second time, curious what other venturers would come, and on the heels of such as he. "I do doubt they'll come this far. What name do you give, who come disturbing the peace of Eald?"

He was wary, surely knowing the power of names; and perhaps he would not have given his true one and perhaps he would not have stayed at all, but that she fixed him sternly with her eyes and he stammered out: "Fionn."

"Fionn." It was apt, for fair he was, tangled hair and first down of beard. She spoke it softly, like a charm. "Fionn. Come walk with me. I'd see this intrusion before others do. Come, come, have no dread of me; I've no harm in mind."

He did come, carefully, and much loath, heeded and walked after her, held by nothing but her wish. She took the Ealdwood's own slow time, not walking the quicker ways, for there was the taint of iron about him, and she could not take him there.

The thicket which degenerated from the dark heart of the Eald was an unlovely place . . . for the Ealdwood had once been better than it was, and there was yet a ruined fairness there; but these young trees had never been other than what they were. They twisted and tangled their roots among the bones of the crumbling hills, making deceiving and thorny barriers. Unlikely it was that Men could see the ways she found; but she was amazed by the changes the years had wrought—saw the slow work of root and branch and ice and sun, labored hard-breathing and scratched with thorns, but gloried in it, alive to the world. She turned from time to time when she sensed faltering behind her: he caught that look of hers and came on, pallid and fearful, past clinging thickets and over stones, as if he had lost all will or hope of doing otherwise.

The baying of hounds echoed out of Caerdale, from the deep valley at the very bounds of the forest. She sat down on a rock atop that last slope, where was prospect of all the great vale of the Caerbourne, a dark tree-filled void beneath the moon. A towered heap of stones had risen far across the vale on the hill called Caer Wiell, and it was the work of men: so much did the years do with the world.

The boy dropped down by the stone, the harp upon his shoulders echoing; his head sank on his folded arms and he wiped the sweat and the tangled hair from his brow. The baying, still a moment, began again, and he lifted frightened eyes.

Now he would run, having come as far as he would; fear shattered the spell. She stayed him yet again, a hand on his smooth arm.

"Here's the limit of *my* wood," she said. "And in it, hounds hunt that you could not shake from your heels, no. You'd do well to stay here by me, indeed you would. Is it yours, that harp?"

He nodded.

"Will you play for me?" she asked, which she had desired from the beginning; and the desire of it burned far more vividly than did curiosity about men and dogs: but one would serve the other. He looked at her as though he thought her mad; and yet took the harp from his shoulders and from its case. Dark wood starred and banded with gold, it sounded when he took it into his arms: he held it so, like something protected, and lifted a pale, resentful face.

And bowed his head again and played as she had bidden him, soft touches at the strings that quickly grew bolder, that waked echoes out of the depths of Caerdale and set the hounds to baying madly. The music drowned the voices, filled the air, filled her heart, and she felt now no faltering or tremor of his hands. She listened, and almost forgot which moon shone down on them, for it had been so long, so very long since the last song had been heard in Ealdwood, and that sung soft and elsewhere.

He surely sensed a glamour on him, that the wind blew warmer and the trees sighed with listening. The fear went from his eyes, and though sweat stood on his brow like jewels, it was clear, brave music that he made—suddenly, with a bright ripple of the strings, a defiant song, strange to her ears.

Discord crept in, the hounds' fell voices, taking the music and warping it out of tune. She rose as that sound drew near. The song ceased, and there was the rush and clatter of horses in the thicket below.

Fionn sprang up, the harp laid aside. He snatched at the small dagger at his belt, and she flinched at that, the bitter taint of iron. "No," she wished him, and he did not draw.

Then hounds and riders were on them, a flood of hounds black and slavering and two great horses, bearing men with the smell of iron about them, men glittering terribly in the moonlight. The hounds surged up baying and bugling and as suddenly fell back again, making wide their circle, whining and with lifting of hackles. The riders whipped them, but their horses shied and screamed under the spurs and neither could be driven further.

She stood, one foot braced against the rock, and regarded men and beasts with cold curiosity, for she found them strange, harder and wilder than Men she had known; and strange too was the device on them, that was a wolf's grinning head. She did not recall it—nor care for the manner of them.

Another rider clattered up the shale, shouted and whipped his unwilling horse farther than the others, and at his heels came men with bows. His arm lifted, gestured; the bows arched, at the harper and at her.

"Hold," she said.

The arm did not fall; it slowly lowered. He glared at her, and she stepped lightly up onto the rock so she need not look up so far, to him on his tall horse. The beast shied under him and he spurred it and curbed it cruelly; but he gave no order to his men, as if the cowering hounds and trembling horses finally made him see.

"Away from here," he shouted down at her, a voice to make the earth quake. "Away! or I daresay you need a lesson taught you too." And he drew his great sword and held it toward her, curbing the protesting horse.

"Me, lessons?" She set her hand on the harper's arm. "Is it on his account you set foot here and raise this noise?"

"My harper," the lord said, "and a thief. Witch, step aside. Fire and iron are answer enough for you."

In truth, she had no liking for the sword that threatened or for the iron-headed arrows which could speed at his lightest word. She kept her hand on Fionn's arm nonetheless, for she saw well how he would fare with them. "But he's mine, lord-of-men. I should say that the harper's no joy to you, or you'd not come chasing him from your land. And great joy he is to me, for long and long it is since I've met so pleasant a companion in Ealdwood. Gather the harp, lad, and walk away now; let me talk with this rash man."

"Stay!" the lord shouted; but Fionn snatched the harp into his arms and edged away.

An arrow hissed; the boy flung himself aside with a terrible clangor of the harp, and lost it on the slope and scrambled back for it, his undoing, for now there were more arrows ready, and these better-purposed.

"Do not," she said.

"What's mine is mine." The lord held his horse still, his sword outstretched before his archers, bating the signal; his face was congested with rage and fear. "Harp and harper are mine. And you'll rue it if you think any words of yours weigh with me. I'll have him and you for your impudence."

It seemed wisest then to walk away, and she did so—turned back the next instant, at a distance, at Fionn's side, and only half under his moon. "I ask your name, lord-of-men, if you aren't fearful of my curse."

Thus she mocked him, to make him afraid before his men. "Evald," he said back, no hesitating, with contempt for her. "And yours, witch?"

"Call me what you like, lord. And take warning, that these woods are not for human hunting and your harper is not yours anymore. Go away and be grateful. Men have Caerdale. If it does not please you, shape it until it does. The Ealdwood's not for trespass."

He gnawed at his mustaches and gripped his sword the tighter, but about him the drawn bows had begun to sag and the arrows to aim at the dirt. Fear was in the men's eyes, and the two riders who had come first hung back, free men and less constrained than the archers.

"You have what's mine," he insisted.

"And so I do. Go on, Fionn. Do go, quietly."

"You've what's *mine*," the valley lord shouted. "Are you thief then as well as witch? You owe me a price for it."

She drew in a sharp breath and yet did not waver in or out of the shadow. "Then do not name too high, lord-of-men. I may hear you, if that will quit us."

His eyes roved harshly about her, full of hate and yet of wariness as well. She felt cold at that look, especially where it centered, above her heart, and her hand stole to that moon-green stone that hung at her throat.

"The stone will be enough," he said. "*That.*"

She drew it off, and held it yet, insubstantial as she, dangling on its chain, for she had the measure of them and it was small. "Go, Fionn," she bade him; and when he lingered yet: "Go!" she shouted. At last he ran, fled, raced away like a mad thing, holding the harp to him.

And when the woods all about were still again, hushed but for the shifting and stamp of the horses and the complaint of the hounds, she let fall the stone. "Be paid," she said, and walked away.

She heard the hooves and turned, felt the insubstantial sword like a stab of ice into her heart. She recoiled elsewhere, bowed with the pain of it that took her breath away. But in time she could stand again, and had taken from the iron no lasting hurt: yet it had been close, and the feel of cold lingered even in the warm winds.

And the boy—she went striding through the shades and shadows in greatest anxiety until she found him, where he huddled hurt and lost within the deepest wood.

"Are you well?" she asked lightly, dropping to her heels beside him. For a moment she feared he might be hurt more than scratches, so tightly he was bowed over the harp; but he lifted his face to her. "You shall stay while you wish," she said, hoping that he would choose to stay long. "You shall harp for me." And when he yet looked fear at her: "You'd not like the new forest. They've no ear for harpers there."

"What is your name, lady?"

"What do you see of me?"

He looked swiftly at the ground, so that she reckoned he could not say the truth without offending her. And she laughed at that.

"Then call me Thistle," she said. "I answer sometimes to that, and it's a name as rough as I. But you'll stay. You'll play for me."

"Yes." He hugged the harp close. "But I'll not go with you. I've no wish to find the years passed in a night and all the world gone old."

"Ah. You know me. But what harm, that years should pass? What care of them or this age? It seems hardly kind to you."

"I am a man," he said, "and it's *my* age."

It was so; she could not force him. One entered otherwhere only by wishing it. He did not; and there was about him and in his heart still the taint of iron.

She settled in the moonlight, and watched beside him; he slept, for all his caution, and waked at last by sunrise, looking about him anxiously lest the trees had grown, and seeming bewildered that she was still there by day. She laughed, knowing her own look by daylight, that was indeed rough as the weed she had named herself, much-tanned and calloused and her clothes in want of patching. She sat plaiting her hair in a single silver braid and smiling sidelong at him, who kept giving her sidelong glances too.

All the earth grew warm. The sun did come here, unclouded on this day. He offered her food, such meager share as he had; she would have none of it, not fond of man-taint, or the flesh of poor forest creatures. She gave him instead of her own, the gift of trees and bees and whatsoever things felt no hurt at sharing.

"It's good," he said, and she smiled at that.

He played for her then, idly and softly, and slept again, for bright day in Ealdwood counseled sleep, when the sun burned warmth through the tangled branches and the air hung still, nothing breathing, least of all the wind. She drowsed too, for the first time since many a tree had grown, for the touch of the mortal sun did that kindness, a benison she had all but forgotten.

But as she slept she dreamed, of a close place of cold stone. In that dark hall she had a man's body, heavy and reeking of wine and ugly memories, such a dark fierceness she would gladly have fled if she might.

Her hand sought the moonstone on its chain and found it at his throat; she offered better dreams and more kindly, and he made bitter mock of them, hating all that he did not comprehend. Then she would have made the hand put the stone off that foul neck; but she had no power to compel, and *he* would not. He possessed what he owned, so fiercely and with such jealousy it cramped the muscles and stifled the breath.

And he hated what he did not have and could not have, that most of all; and the center of it was his harper.

She tried still to reason within this strange, closed mind. It was impossible. The heart was almost without love, and what little it had ever been given it folded in upon itself lest what it possessed escape.

"Why?" she asked that night, when the moon shed light on the Ealdwood and the land was quiet, no ill thing near them, no cloud above them. "Why does he seek you?" Though her dreams had told her, she wanted his answer.

Fionn shrugged, his young eyes for a moment aged; and he gathered against him his harp. "This," he said.

"You said it was yours. He called you thief. What did you steal?"

"It is mine." He touched the strings and brought forth melody. "It hung in his hall so long he thought it his, and the strings were cut and dead." He rippled out a somber note. "It was my father's and his father's before him."

"And in Evald's keeping?"

The fair head bowed over the harp and his hands coaxed sound from it, answerless.

"I've given a price," she said, "to keep him from it and you. Will you not give back an answer?"

The sound burst into softness. "It was my father's. Evald hanged him. Would hang me."

"For what cause?"

Fionn shrugged, and never ceased to play. "For truth. For truth he sang. So Evald hanged him, and hung the harp on his wall for mock of him. I came. I gave him songs he liked. But at winter's end I came down to the hall at night, and mended the old harp, gave it voice and a song he remembered. For that he hunts me."

Then softly he sang, of humankind and wolves, and that song was bitter. She shuddered to hear it, and bade him cease, for mind to mind with her in troubled dreams Evald heard and tossed, and waked starting in sweat.

"Sing more kindly," she said. Fionn did so, while the moon climbed above the trees, and she recalled elder-day songs which the world had not heard in long years, sang them sweetly. Fionn listened and caught up the words in his strings, until the tears ran down his face for joy.

There could be no harm in Ealdwood that hour: the spirits of latter earth that skulked and strove and haunted men fled elsewhere, finding nothing that they knew; and the old shadows slipped away trembling, for they remembered. But now and again the song faltered, for there came a touch of ill and smallness into her heart, a cold piercing as the iron, with thoughts of hate, which she had never held so close.

Then she laughed, breaking the spell, and put it from her, bent herself to teach the harper songs which she herself had almost forgotten, conscious the while that elsewhere, down in Caerbourne vale, on Caer Wiell, a man's body tossed in sweaty dreams which seemed constantly to mock him, with sound of eldritch harping that stirred echoes and sleeping ghosts.

With the dawn she and Fionn rose and walked a time, and shared food, and drank at a cold, clear spring she knew, until the sun's hot eye fell upon them and cast its numbing spell on all the Ealdwood.

Then Fionn slept; but she fought the sleep which came to her, for dreams were in it, her dreams while *he* should wake; nor would they stay at bay, not when her eyes grew heavy and the air thick with urging sleep. The dreams came more and more strongly. The man's strong legs bestrode a great brute horse, and hands plied whip and feet the spurs more than she would, hurting it cruelly. There was noise of hounds and hunt, a coursing of woods and hedges and the bright spurt of blood on dappled hide: he sought blood to wipe out blood, for the harping rang yet in his mind, and she shuddered at the killing her hands did, and at the fear that gathered thickly about him, reflected in his comrades' eyes.

It was better that night, when the waking was hers and her harper's, and sweet songs banished fear; but even yet she grieved for remembering, and at times the cold came on her, so that her hand would steal to her throat where the moon-green stone was not. Her eyes brimmed suddenly with tears: Fionn saw and tried to sing her merry songs instead. They failed, and the music died.

"Teach me another song," he begged of her. "No harper ever had such songs. And will *you* not play for *me?*"

"I have no art," she said, for the last harper of her folk had gone long ago: it was not all truth, for once she had known, but there was no more music in her hands, none since the last had gone and she had willed to stay, loving this place too well in spite of men. "Play," she asked of Fionn, and tried to smile, though the iron closed about her heart and the man raged at the nightmare, waking in sweat, ghost-ridden.

It was that human song Fionn played in his despair, of the man who would be a wolf and the wolf who was no man; while the lord Evald did not sleep again, but sat shivering and wrapped in furs before his hearth, his hand clenched in hate upon the stone which he possessed and would not, though it killed him, let go.

But she sang a song of elder earth, and the harper took up the tune, which sang of earth and shores and water, a journey, the great last journey, at men's coming and the dimming of the world. Fionn wept while he played, and she smiled sadly and at last fell silent, for her heart was gray and cold.

The sun returned at last, but she had no will to eat or rest, only to sit grieving, for she could not find peace. Gladly now she would have fled the shadow-shifting way back into otherwhere, to her own moon and softer sun, and persuaded the harper with her; but there was a portion of her heart in pawn, and she could not even go herself: she was too heavily bound. She fell to mourning bitterly, and pressed her hand often where the stone should rest. He hunted again, did Evald of Caer Wiell. Sleepless, maddened by dreams, he whipped his folk out of the hold as he did his hounds, out to the margin of the Ealdwood, to harry the creatures of woodsedge, having guessed well the source of the harping. He brought fire and axes, vowing to take the old trees one by one until all was dead and bare.

The wood muttered with whisperings and angers; a wall of cloud rolled down from the north on Ealdwood and all deep Caerdale, dimming the sun; a wind sighed in the face of the men, so that no torch was set to wood; but axes rang, that day and the next. The clouds gathered thicker and the wind blew colder, making Ealdwood dim again and dank. She yet managed to smile by night, to hear the harper's songs. But every stroke of the axes made her shudder, and the iron about her heart tightened day by day. The wound in the Ealdwood grew, and he was coming: she knew it well, and there remained at last no song at all, by day or night.

She sat now with her head bowed beneath the clouded moon, and Fionn was powerless to cheer her. He regarded her in deep despair, and touched her hand for comfort. She said no word to that, but gathered her cloak about her and offered to the harper to walk a time, while vile things stirred and muttered in the shadow, whispering malice to the winds, so that often Fionn started and stared and kept close beside her.

Her strength faded, first that she could not keep the voices away, and then that she could not keep from listening; and at last she sank upon his arm, eased to the cold ground and leaned her head against the bark of a gnarled tree.

"What ails?" he asked, and pried at her clenched and empty fingers, opened the fist which hovered near her throat as if seeking there the answer. "What ails you?"

She shrugged and smiled and shuddered, for the axes had begun again, and she felt the iron like a wound, a great cry going through the wood as it had gone for days; but he was deaf to it, being what he was. "Make a song for me," she asked.

"I have no heart for it."

"Nor have I," she said. A sweat stood on her face, and he wiped at it with his gentle hand and tried to ease her pain.

And again he caught and unclenched the hand which rested, empty, at her throat. "The stone," he said. "Is it *that* you miss?"

She shrugged, and turned her head, for the axes then seemed loud. He looked too—glanced back deaf and puzzled. " 'Tis time," she said. "You must be on your way this morning, when there's sun enough. The new forest will hide you after all."

"And leave you? Is that your meaning?"

She smiled, touched his anxious face. "I am paid enough."

"How paid? What did you pay? *What* was it you gave away?"

"Dreams," she said. "Only that. And all of that." Her hands shook terribly, and a blackness came on her heart too miserable to bear: it was hate, and aimed at him and at herself, and all that lived; and it was harder and harder to fend away. "Evil has it. He would do you hurt, and I would dream that too. Harper, it's time to go."

"Why would you give such a thing?" Great tears started from his eyes. "Was it worth such a cost, my harping?"

"Why, well worth it," she said, with such a laugh as she had left to laugh, that shattered all the evil for a moment and left her clean. "I have sung."

He snatched up the harp and ran, breaking branches and tearing flesh in his headlong haste, but not, she realized in horror, not the way he ought—but back again, to Caerdale.

She cried out her dismay and seized at branches to pull herself to her feet; she could in no wise follow. Her limbs which had been quick to run beneath this moon or the other were leaden, and her breath came hard. Brambles caught and held with all but mindful malice, and dark things which had never had power in her presence whispered loudly now, of murder.

And elsewhere the wolf-lord with his men drove at the forest, great ringing blows, the poison of iron. The heavy ironclad body which she sometimes wore seemed hers again, and the moonstone was prisoned within that iron, near a heart that beat with hate.

She tried the more to haste, and could not. She looked helplessly through Evald's narrow eyes and saw—saw the young harper break through the thickets near them. Weapons lifted, bows and axes. Hounds bayed and lunged at leashes.

Fionn came, nothing hesitating, bringing the harp, and himself. "A trade," she heard him say. "The stone for the harp."

There was such hate in Evald's heart, and such fear it was hard to breathe. She felt a pain to the depth of her as Evald's coarse fingers pawed at the stone. She felt his fear, felt his loathing of it. Nothing would he truly let go. But this—this he abhorred, and was fierce in his joy to lose it.

"Come," the lord Evald said, and held the stone, dangling and spinning before him, so that for that moment the hate was far and cold.

Another hand took it then, and very gentle it was, and very full of love. She felt the sudden draught of strength and desperation—sprang up then, to run, to save.

But pain stabbed through her heart, and such an ebbing out of love and grief that she cried aloud, and stumbled, blind, dead in that part of her.

She did not cease to run; and she ran now that shadowway, for the heaviness was gone. Across meadows, under that other moon she sped, and gathered up all that she had left behind, burst out again in the blink of an eye and elsewhere.

Horses shied and dogs barked; for now she did not care to be what suited men's eyes: bright as the moon she broke among them, and in her hand was a sharp blade, to meet with iron.

Harp and harper lay together, sword-riven. She saw the underlings start away and cared nothing for them; but Evald she sought. He cursed at her, drove spurs into his horse and rode at her, sword yet drawn, shivering the winds with a horrid slash of iron. The horse screamed and shied; he cursed and reined the beast, and drove it for her again. But this time the blow was hers, a scratch that made him shriek with rage.

She fled at once. He pursued. It was his nature that he must; and she might have fled otherwhere, but she would not. She darted and dodged ahead of the great horse, and it broke the brush and thorns and panted after, hard-ridden.

Shadows gathered, stirring and urgent on this side and on that, who gibbered and rejoiced for the way that they were tending, to the woods' blackest heart, for some of them had been Men; and some had known the wolf's justice, and had come to what they were for his sake. They reached, but durst not touch him, for she would not have it so. Over all, the trees bowed and groaned in the winds and the leaves went flying, thunder above and thunder of hooves below, scattering the shadows.

But suddenly she whirled about and flung back her cloak: the horse shied up and fell, cast Evald sprawling among the wet leaves. The shaken beast scrambled up and evaded his hands and his threats, thundered away on the moist earth, splashing across some hidden stream; and the shadows chuckled. She stepped full back again from otherwhere, and Evald saw her clear, moonbright and silver. He cursed, shifted that great black sword from hand to hand, for his right hand bore a scratch that now must trouble him. He shrieked with hate and slashed.

She laughed and stepped into otherwhere and back again, and fled yet farther, until he stumbled with exhaustion and sobbed and fell, forgetting now his anger, for the whispers came loud.

"Up," she bade him, mocking, and stepped again to here. Thunder rolled upon the wind, and the sound of horses and hounds came at a distance. A joyful malice came into his eyes when he heard it; his face grinned in the lightnings. But she laughed too, and his mirth died as the sound came on them, under them, over them, in earth and heavens.

He cursed then and swung the blade, lunged and slashed again, and she flinched from the almost-kiss of iron. Again he whirled it, pressing close; the lightning cracked—he shrieked a curse, and, silver-spitted—died.

She did not weep or laugh now; she had known him too well for either. She looked up instead at the clouds, gray wrack scudding before the storm, where other hunters coursed the winds and wild cries wailed—heard hounds baying after something fugitive and wild. She lifted then her fragile sword, salute to lord Death, who had governance over Men, a Huntsman too; and many the old comrades the wolf would find following in his train.

Then the sorrow came on her, and she walked the otherwhere path to the beginning and the end of her course, where harp and harper lay. There was no mending here. The light was gone from his eyes and the wood was shattered.

But in his fingers lay another thing, which gleamed like the summer moon amid his hand.

Clean it was from his keeping, and loved. She gathered it to her. The silver chain went again about her neck and the stone rested where it ought. She bent last and kissed him to his long sleep, fading then to otherwhere.

She dreamed at times then, waking or sleeping; for when she held close the stone and thought of him she heard a fair far music, for a part of his heart was there too, a gift of himself.

She sang sometimes, hearing it, wherever she walked.

That gift, she gave to him.

THE STORMING OF ANNIE KINSALE

I

t was on a rainy Thursday morning, just the odd speckles of rain
staining the front stoop, but the sky over Bantry Bay nearly black and
promising worse to come, that Annie Kinsale caught sight of the soldier's
ghost. She was standing at the kitchen window of her cottage, half-
listening to the radio, idly debating whether to add cheese or butter to
her shopping list—a body couldn't afford both what with prices these
days—when she saw the gray figure of a man waving a rifle and running,
stumbling, and then, as he passed the point where her primrose hedge
met the country lane, vanishing like smoke dispersed by a puff of wind.
Annie's heart went racing. There was no doubt in her mind that he had
been a ghost, and she had known him for a soldier by the curious shape
of his rifle. She crossed herself and peered once more out the window.
Gone, he was, and considering the paleness of his substance, the poor
soul had likely been at the end of his earthly term. Her first thought was
to hurry into the village of Gougane Barra and tell her best friend Eleanor
Downey what had happened; but on second thought she decided against
it. Though Eleanor was the only person in whom Annie had confided
her secret, though she was trustworthy in that regard, she would be quick
to spread the word of this, and Annie's reputation for being a "quare
one" would suffer an increase. Sure, and wasn't her name this moment

dancing on the tongues of those red-nosed layabouts who were welcoming
the morning in at Henry Shorten's pub.

"... livin' out in the midst of nowhere," that hulking stump of a man
Tom O'Corran was saying—his static-filled voice was issuing from Annie's transistor radio. "Six years, and nothin' warmin' her bed but that
damned cat! It ain't natural for a woman like herself."

" 'Twas the manner of Jake Kinsale's passin' what done her," said old
Matty, rheumy-eyed, with hardly a hair between the tips of his ears and
the porch of Heaven. "The heart is rarely wise, and violence will never
enlighten it. But I'll grant you she's a pretty woman."

Pretty, was she? Annie stared at her opaque reflection in the window
glass. Her skin was that milky white that turns easily to roses, and her
hair was a dark shawl falling to her shoulders, and her features—undis-
tinguished, except for large brown eyes aswim with lights—were at least
expressive. Pretty enough, she supposed, for a bump in the road such as
Gougane Barra. But thirty years old, she realized, was not the first bloom
of beauty, and lately she had accumulated a touch of what Eleanor—
with a giggle—had called her "secretarial spread."

"I'll not argue that she hasn't reason to grieve," said Tom. "Well I
know that the friction was hot and strong 'tween her and Jake, and he
was a soul worth grievin' over. But six years, man! That's time enough
for grief to go its rounds."

"It's not grief that's taken her," said Henry Shorten; his voice faded
into rock music, then swelled as Annie adjusted the tuning dial. "She's
settled into loneliness is all. Her mother and grandmother, and as I've
heard, her great-grandmother before them, were women who thrived on
loneliness."

"Och!" said old Matty. "I was only a scrapeen of a boy when her great-
grandmother was alive, but there was a force of a woman! 'Twas said she
had unearthly powers, and that the divil himself had tied a knot in her
petticoats. Maybe Annie Kinsale is not so alone as you're thinkin'."

"Well," said Tom, laughing, "be it diviltry or loneliness or grief that
keeps her shut away, before winter's end it'll be myself she's hearin' at
her bedroom door."

Irritated, Annie switched off the radio. That blustering fool! Then she
laughed. At the heart of Tom O'Corran's bluster was a great shyness,
and like as not, if he ever were to reach her bedroom door—a most
improbable event—she'd have to instruct him on how to insert the key.

———

For the remainder of the day Annie put aside all thought of ghosts and Tom O'Corran, and—also putting aside the idea of going shopping, because the storm that soon blew up from Bantry Bay was as thunderous and magical-seeming as the one that had carved the name of St. Kieran on the wall of Carrigadrohid Castle the year before—she went about cleaning the cottage. With muttered phrases and flicks of her fingers, she set the teakettle boiling and rags to polishing and the bed to making itself; and when the water had boiled, she sat herself down at the kitchen table with a steaming cup, her marmalade cat Diarmid curled beside her, and tuned in the radio to a Dublin station, hoping for some music to drown out the pelt and din of the storm. But there had been trouble in the North that day, and all she could find were reports of bombings and fires and pompous editorial expressions of concern. She switched it off. Ever since Jake had been cut down by an errant bullet on a Belfast street, she had not allowed any talk of war within the confines of her home. It was not that she was attempting to deny the existence of violence; it was only that she thought there should be one place in her life where such concerns did not enter in. The cottage, with its feather pillows and hand-me-down quilts and contented cat, was a fragment of a cozy, innocent time that had just faded around the corner of the world, and she meant to keep it so despite the ghosts of soldiers and bad news from the North.

A stroke of lightning illuminated the smears of rain on the window; beyond the glass, the lawn was momentarily drowned in yellow glare, and Annie saw a primrose torn from its stem and blown away into the night like a white coin thrown up to appease the Fates. It made her shiver to think the wind could be so particular, and she switched on the radio again, tuning not to the Dublin station but to the cottage belonging to Mrs. Borlin who—foul weather or fair—told the cards of an evening for those uncertain of their paths.

". . . faith," she was saying, "and isn't it a fine life I'm seein' before you! What's your name, girl?"

"Florence."

Thunder crashed, static obliterated their voices.

"Will you listen to that!" said Mrs. Borlin. "Praise be to God, at least the hay's in. Now, Florence, there's yourself there, the queen of hearts . . ."

And Annie, comforted by this telling of a golden future, sipped her tea and absently stroked Diarmid's back.

If you haven't yet guessed how it was that Annie accomplished her housework, how she eavesdropped on her neighbors, it was, simply stated, that she was a witch. Not a flamboyant witch of the sort typified by her mother, who had once caused the waters of Gougane Lake to rise into the air and assume the form of a dragon; nor was she a vengeful sort like her grandmother, who had once transformed an English banker's eyes into nuggets of silver; and she certainly was not as renowned as her great-grandmother, about whom it was said that an eagle-shaped rock had flown up from a mountain in Kerry to announce her death in Heaven. The witch blood was strong in Annie's veins—and hot blood it was, too, for an Irish witch is a creature of potent sexuality, her body serving as the ground upon which her spells are worked; but her mother had undergone a late conversion to the Church and had preached against witchery, infusing Annie with an enfeebling dose of Christian morality, and she had never developed her powers. She was—except for a spell she'd nurtured over the years, one she might use if someone more suitable than Tom O'Corran happened along—limited to feats of domestic management and the like. She had as well the gift of seeing into people's hearts (though not into her own), and she could sometimes catch the tag-ends of people's thoughts, an ability that came in handy when dealing with Mr. Spillane the grocer, a thoroughly larcenous individual. Yet she was content with these limits; she had no need for more, and what she did have sufficed to ease her loneliness. Mrs. Borlin's readings were a special balm to her—their uniform cheerfulness reinforced the atmosphere of the cottage.

"Don't be despairin', Florence," said the old woman. "A girl like yourself will soon be marchin' at the head of a regiment of suitors. You might have 'em all if that's your wish, and . . . "

Suddenly Diarmid sprang to his feet and let out a yowl, and at almost the same moment there came a thump on the door. Then another, and another yet. Slow, measured knocks, as if the hand that sounded them belonged to an oak-limbed Druid stiff from centuries of sleep. Annie lowered the volume of the radio, crept along the darkened hall, and put her ear to the door. All she heard were branches scraping the stone wall. She peeked through the window beside the door, but whoever it was must have been sheltering under the lintel, out of sight. If it *was* anyone. Chances were it had been a bump in the night, a spirit blown by the storm from its usual haunts and flapping there a moment. To make certain, she cracked the door. An eye was staring back at her. Lightning bloomed, and she saw that the eye was set into a man's haggard, bearded face. She screamed and tried to close the door; but the man's weight was against it, and as his eye fluttered shut, he slumped forward, forcing Annie to give ground, and pitched onto the carpet. His rifle was pinned beneath him.

Annie bolted for the kitchen and grabbed a carving knife, expecting him to follow and attack her. When he did not, she peeked out into the hall. He hadn't moved. The skeleton stock of his rifle made her wonder if he wasn't the soldier she had seen earlier—yet he was no ghost. She flicked on the lights, knelt beside him, and rolled him over. Blood came away on her fingers, and there was a mire of it soaking his right trouser leg above the knee. Without further speculation as to who he was, she dragged him into her bedroom and hoisted him onto the bed. She slit his trousers, ripped them up the seam, and Whssht! the sight of a livid scar running the length of his calf stopped her breath a moment. The new wound was drilled straight through the flesh, with—thank God—no bones or arteries involved; after cleaning and dressing it, she took his rifle and hid it under some logs in the woodshed. Then she came back and sat in a chair by the bed and applied cold compresses to his brow until his tossing and turning had abated.

Annie kept watch over him late into the night, easing him when he cried out, rearranging the blankets when he tossed them off, and while he slept she studied the puzzle he was. He was in his thirties, olive-skinned, with black hair, heavy-lidded eyes, a cruel mouth, and a blade of a nose. Written everywhere on his features were the signs of great good humor and equally great sadness. A face like that, she thought, was as uncommon around these parts as a rose in winter. He might be an immigrant, but that didn't wash—something about him failed to blend with the notion of dark northern winters and bitter springs. She tucked a blanket around her legs, preparing to sleep. The puzzle would be solved come morning, and if he was legal, she'd have him off to the county hospital. If not . . . well, she'd deal with that as events dictated. The last thing that crossed her mind before she slept was an odd feeling of satisfaction, of pleasure, in knowing that the morning would provide a chore more fulfilling than the composition of a shopping list.

Be they strangers or lovers, there's an artful process that goes on between two bodies sleeping in the same room, a subtle transfer of energies, and who's to say how much effect this process had upon Annie and the soldier. One thing was certain, though—Annie had not slept so soundly in years, and on waking, stretching out her arms to welcome the day, she felt her animal self uncoiling as it had long ago on waking after a night of love.

The rain had diminished to a dripping from the eaves, dawn hung gray in the folds of the curtains. It was to be a clear day. She pushed off her blanket, and as she stretched again, she saw that the soldier was watching her. His eyes looked all black in the half-light.

"*Quien eres?*" he said. "*Donde estoy?*"

Annie had a queer, chill feeling in her chest. "Don't you speak English?" she asked, laying her hand on his brow, which was cool.

He stared at her, bewildered, as if he had not understood. But after a second, he said, "Where are the others? Where is this place?"

"There weren't any others," said Annie. "And you're in Gougane Barra, County Cork." Then, the chill feeling intensifying, she added, "Ireland."

"Ireland?" He said it "Ay-er-lan," repeating it—the way you'd try out a new word, mulling over its peculiar sound. "That can't be true." Suspicion hardened his features. "Who are you?"

"I'm Annie Kinsale." She went to the window and pulled back the curtains and pointed out to the green hills rising into a silver haze. "And that's Ireland. Where did you think you were?"

He couldn't take his eyes off the window. "I was in the mountains above the village of Todos Santos." He shook his head, as if to clear it of a fog. "There was a storm. The fighting was very bad, and the government troops were all around us. I was running, and it seemed I was running just ahead of the lightning bursts, that they were striking at my heels. Then I was running in a place without light, without sound . . . not running, exactly. My legs were moving, and yet I felt as if I were falling, whirling. I thought I'd been hit again. . . . "

He had started to tremble. Annie sat beside him and tried to steady him with a consoling touch. "My grandmother used to tell us that storms and wars were sister and brother," she said. "Children of the same chaos. She said they had a way of interactin', creatin' a magical moment between them in which things could pass from place to place in the wink of an eye. I'll wager that's what happened to you." He wasn't listening, his trembling had increased. "What country are you from?" she asked.

"Chile." The answer seemed to give him strength—he cleared his throat and squared his shoulders, ordering himself.

"Chile, is it?" she said, affecting sunniness. "Well, now! That explains it further. Wasn't it an Irishman who freed your country from the Spanish? Bernardo O'Higgins. And wasn't it Chile that sent the first fuchsias to Ireland? There's many a connection between the two lands, both physical and spiritual, and maybe the storm was part of that."

"What year is it?" he said wildly, lunging up, then wincing in pain and falling back.

"1984," said Annie.

He looked relieved. "I thought that might have changed as well." He inched up on the pillows. "Is there a newspaper, a radio? I must learn what has happened."

"The local paper's more likely to have news of Cam Malloy's prize sow than of rebellion in Chile," said Annie. "And besides, though I'm glad to be of help to you, as long as you're here there's to be no talk of war in this house. I won't stand for it."

A flush of anger suffused his face. "Is it that you find the idea of war repulsive, or is it just that you're hiding from the realities of the world behind your riches?"

"Riches! You call this shoebox of a cottage riches?"

"You have warmth, food, health. In Chile these are riches."

"Well, here they're not, and I'm hidin' from nothin'! I've had a sufficiency of war in my life, and I'll not be takin' it into my bed!" She blushed, realizing what she had intimated, and, angry at herself, she lashed out. "If you won't obey that simple rule, then get the hell out of my house!"

"Very well," he said stonily. "In any case, I must get back to my men."

"Oh?" said Annie. "And I suppose you'll be catchin' the next bus for guerrilla headquarters?"

He stared at her a moment, dumbfounded, and then he burst into laughter. And Annie—never one to hold a grudge—joined in.

His name was Hugo Baltazar, and before becoming a soldier he had been a professor of comparative literature at the university in Santiago—thus his knowledge of English. Over the next two weeks as his wound mended, stormy, rainy weeks, he told Annie about his country, and she added each new detail to a picture she'd begun painting in her head. It was like one of those tourist maps with illustrations of parrots and golden beaches and cathedrals rearing up and dwarfing the little towns whose attractions they were—her version of Chile had so many attractions that it was less a map than a collage of brilliant colors. Of course she knew it was incomplete, that Chile was suffering a war the same as Ireland, probably a worse war, and that those terrible images might dwarf the ones she had pictured. But she liked thinking of Hugo as hailing from a land full of fiestas and shade trees, where an engraved and beaming sun rose out of a map-colored sea, and the four winds had smiling faces. War did not suit him. Not a man who carved flutes from twigs and sang and told stories about Indian ghosts and mysterious rites on Easter Island. He was, she thought, a born Irishman. Perhaps there had been some truth to that sauce she'd ladled about Ireland and Chile having a spiritual connection.

Be that as it may, shaved and washed and dressed in Jake's old clothes, he cut a fine figure. Now and again she would catch herself looking at him, watching, say, the muscles bunching in his jaw or his hair ruffling in the breeze; occasionally she would find him looking back at her, and then she would blush and duck her head and start peeling spuds or chopping lettuce or whatever chore was at hand. She knew very well what was happening, and even if she hadn't had the gift of seeing clear, she would have known by a dozen different signs—the way they passed each other in the hall, as stealthy as two cats on the prowl, being careful not to entangle their tails; the way he jerked back his hand after accidentally touching her, as if the prospect of touching her had been foremost on his mind; the way he tensed when she reached in front of him to set down his dinner plate. Yet she also knew that he was troubled by all he'd left behind, and one evening, while she was still trying to figure out how she could ease his mind, he brought up the subject on his own.

"Annie," he said, "I want to talk to you about . . . about the disturbance in my country."

They were standing at the kitchen sink, her washing, him drying, and Annie set down a plate so hard upon the counter that it split in two. "No!" she said. "I told you I won't have it!"

He balled up his towel and dropped it onto the broken plate. "If we can't talk here," he said, "then we'll go outside." He seized her by the arm, and, limping, fighting off her slaps, he dragged her into the garden behind the cottage. There he let loose of her arm, and she started to flounce back inside; but before she had taken three steps, he said, "I love you, Annie."

She stopped dead in her tracks but did not turn to face him; she could tell what was coming—it was spelled out in the drooping stalks of the primroses, in the angles of a broken ivy trellis, and in the stars that ignited cold and white like crystallized points of pure pain. "Do you?" she said. His hands fell on her hips, and they felt so heavy, they seemed to make her light, to drain away her strength. If he moved them, she would shatter.

"Yes," he said, "and I want to stay with you. But I can't. I have responsibilities I can't avoid. Friends who are suffering."

"Is it addicted you are to sufferin'?" Her anger became brighter and hotter with every word. "Is peace too stodgy a situation for your warlike soul?"

He tried to turn her, but she refused to budge. "I know you don't understand this kind of commitment," he said. "You haven't seen . . . "

"I've seen plenty, thank you very much! And one thing I've seen is that war changes nothin'. One dictator falls, and another pops right up."

"You can't stop trying," he said. "If you do, you risk losing your humanity."

She twisted free of his grasp and walked a few paces away. "How will you go?" she asked, her voice small and tight. "You've no money, and God knows I can't help. I'm barely scrapin' by."

He was silent a moment. "The other night during the squall, I had a feeling, a very strong feeling, that if the winds were blowing harder, if the lightning was striking down, I'd be able to walk out into it and find my way home. It sounds unreasonable, but it's as reasonable as my coming here." He moved up behind her and again put his hands on her hips. "You seem to have an understanding of these sorts of things. Do you think . . . "

"Yes, damn you!" She whirled around and pushed him away. "Go, if that's all you want of the world! Go, and good riddance to you!"

"Annie . . . "

"Leave me alone!"

"Please, Annie. I just want . . . "

"Will you for Jesus' sake quit tormentin' me!" Out of the corner of her eye, she watched him limp toward the door. She had an urge to call him back, but her temper got the best of her and she shouted at him instead. "All this time I thought I was givin' shelter to a man, and in truth I was just harborin' a Communist!"

"I should have known," he said angrily, pausing on the stoop. "I should have known you were the type to rationalize injustice, to cure a disease by sticking labels over the sores." He stepped inside and slammed the door.

Annie stood in the garden until the light in the guest room had been switched off and the moon—almost full—had risen over the roof of the cottage. She shivered a little with the night chill. She tried to hold everything inside her, to harden it into bitterness, but the bitterness caved in and she cried. The tears left cold, snaky tracks down her cheeks and blurred the sharp image of the moon—it seemed a weepy arch of moons was connecting her eyes and a distant point in the darkness beyond Bantry

Bay. Finally she blew her nose and wiped her cheeks. There was no use in moping. Things were as they were, and the question was what to do about them. What, indeed?

She went into the cottage and leaned against the wall beside the door of the guest room; her fingers strayed to the top button of her blouse. "Why not?" she said to the empty hall. "Better to know exactly what you're losin', if you're to lose it a'tall." In a matter of seconds her clothes were heaped on the carpet, and she was slipping through the door.

The room was ablaze with moonlight, so bright that she thought the arch of moons she'd seen must have been real, that they were beaming in from every angle. Hugo's head was a shadow on the pillow. He propped himself on an elbow, his breath sighing out. Annie came a step closer. She could feel the moonlight shining up her skin, and could see the shine of her skin reflected in his eyes, in all the stunned and stricken way he was staring at her; and she remembered a night twelve years before, how she'd stripped off her dress and gone dancing along the crest of a hill—a wild, slim girl taunting her first lover, Jake; and he'd stumbled after her, tripping over stones, afflicted with that same bedazzled look. She could almost believe she was that same girl, the years peeled away by grace of the moonlight. She knelt upon the edge of the bed and stretched out her hand to him.

"If you're really leavin' on the storm," she said, "we mustn't waste the calm weather."

Magic—at least the contemporary Irish brand—does not consist of a pair of golden thimbles or a book of spells or secret brews or of anything so rigid and bound to a single set of principles. Mainly it consists of having an eye for the materials appropriate to the moment, having the talent to weave them together, and having the power to spark them, to channel their own natural powers into a symmetry that fuses opportunity and intent. Annie had all these qualities, and by five o'clock the next morning, she had all the materials as well—hair, a silver thread, a ruby pinprick of her blood, and various other substances (which, for various reasons, are best left unmentioned). What she lacked, however, was the conviction that this was the proper course of action. Oh, she wanted Hugo right enough! Her senses were still stinging with him, and his smell was heavy on her skin. But her Christian upbringing was getting in the way. She wished now that her mother had let her develop her powers, that she had acquired a strong and helpful familiar rather than Diarmid—a fat old mouser with bad breath, a taste for porridge, and scarcely a flicker of animal cunning. She picked him up from the floor and gazed into his slitted yellow eyes. "What do you think, cat?" she said. "Will we have him, or should we let him fly?" Diarmid twisted his head to the side, trying to sniff the saucer that held the materials; he nudged it with his cheek, and the drop of blood slid down along the silver thread.

"Well," said Annie, deciding. "I imagine that's all the omen I'm likely to get."

She took the saucer and a lit candle and stole back into the guest room. Hugo was asleep, his breathing deep and regular. She knelt upon the floor, held the candle above the saucer, and searched her mind for words that—though they didn't have to be particularly meaningful—would give the spell sonority. She sang them softly, each phrase stirring the candleflame.

"May all white birds and unicorns
Here find shelter from the storm,
May man's light strand and woman's dark
Knit together in a spark,
Singe their spirits, steam the flood,
And bind this moment in our blood."

She touched the flame to the materials. They burned separately at first—the hair crisping, the thread shriveling, the rest sizzling and smoking—and then a web of cold white light united them, flared briefly, and was sucked into the ashes. Annie smeared the ashes on her lips, rubbing them in until her mouth began to tingle. Hurriedly, before the tingle could subside, she slipped into the bed. Hugo was lying on his side, facing her, and she pressed herself against him; she rested her knee on his hip, reached down and guided him between her legs, fitting him to her. He mumbled, waking to the touch. She kissed him, mixing the tingling ashes with their saliva. And as his hands gripped her hard and he eased inside, their mouths still clamped together, she felt the charge go out of her.

In the morning Hugo told her he would stay. He seemed happy, yet at the same time confused and a bit depressed. To take his mind off the confusion, Annie suggested they go on a trip, a honeymoon of sorts. She'd borrow Eleanor Downey's car and they'd drive out into the country. She'd show him Cork. Still confused, he agreed.

For the first four days it was as if the Emerald Isle were intent on proving the accuracy of its nickname, flashing a different facet of its beauty around every bend in the road. Near Glengariff they saw what appeared at a distance to be a river of milk flowing down a dark green hill; and as they drew near, it turned into a scene just as magical—a herd of sheep streaming over the hillside, with golden dogs barking, leaping, and men in bright sweaters shouting and running after. They picnicked in the Pass of Kimaneigh beneath steep, ivy-matted cliffs, the slopes thick with ferns and foxglove and honeysuckle, and they listened to an old man tell a story about a skeleton that ran nightly through the pass, carrying a ball of yellow flame in its hand. They walked along mossy bridges and tossed pennies into the still rivers for luck; they bought an armload of crimson fuchsias and decorated the car with them to symbolize the union of their souls and blood; they made love all night in a country inn as quaint as a picture on a teacup, and in the morning they watched the sunrise stripe a nearby lake with heliotrope, rose, and silver—like the markings of an enormous tropical fish. But by the end of the fifth day, despite the beauty of Cork, despite their own beauty, Annie realized that she had been wrong to work the spell. No amount of sightseeing and lovemaking could diminish Hugo's confusion. That night, lying awake beside him, she listened to the fringe of his thoughts—there were screams in Spanish, anguished faces, bursts of gunfire, gouts of flame rising from the midst of jungles. Those thoughts were part of him, permanent, untouchable by magic. She understood that sooner or later, bound together in this way, all their brightness would fade, and she determined to break the spell. It would be better to lose love quickly, she thought, than to watch it linger and die.

Now the breaking of a spell is the sole constant of Irish magic. Every spell worked successfully—it's said—causes pain to the Devil (not the Christian Devil, but the old Celtic demon whose back was broken by Cuchulain, whose splintered backbone props up the Irish hills), and the only way to reverse the process is to take back the Devil's pain. All this requires is the will and the strength to bear it, and a knowledge of those places where His bones lie close to the skin of the earth. Annie was not afraid of pain. She'd borne Jake's death, and nothing could hurt her worse. And so, that same night, she left Hugo asleep in their hotel outside the town of Schuul, and climbed to the top of a hill overlooking Bantry Bay, a spot dominated by a standing stone—a head-high cylinder of moss-stained granite, tufted around by weeds and carved deep with both pagan signs and crosses.

The moon was just past full, wisped by clouds; its light made the grass underfoot and the surrounding hills look dead and gray. The sea was the color of old iron, and the wind and wave-sound combined in a single mournful rush. Nothing seemed alive. Even the distant lights of Schuul might have only been flecks of moonstruck mica on a rock face. Annie shed her clothing, her skin pebbled by the chill, and embraced the standing stone, crushing her breasts against the largest cross, pressing her hips to one of the pagan signs. The stone's coldness pervaded her, but nothing happened. After a while, she realized that she did not want anything to happen, that she lacked the will. Determined, she began to talk sweetly to the stone, teasing and charming it, building up inside her the weight of self-loathing and perversity that was needed in order to contact the Devil. She crawled over the stone, grinding her hips into it, licking it, tracing the deep seams of its carvings with her fingers as if it were a live thing and she was giving it pleasure. Then she felt a trembling in the earth, felt also an eerie lustful joy that was both hers and another's, and heard a keening note within her skull. It seemed that the pain and her scream were one substance, a white cry issuing from the rock below, a column of pale fire pouring through her, reducing her to a white frequency that shrilled along the crisped pathways of her nerves. She fell back onto the tussocky ground. Her limbs were quaking, and the muscles of her abdomen were writhing like serpents beneath the milky skin. She tasted blood in her mouth.

She lay there for a long time, debased, ashamed, foul with the act. Dawn paled the sea with a dingy yellow light. At last she put on her dress and went back into Schuul. She brought Hugo coffee and cakes, kissed him as if nothing were out of the ordinary, and told him that she wasn't feeling well, that maybe after breakfast they had better get along home.

It went unspoken between them that he was leaving. He knew she knew and vice versa, so what was the point in talking? They made love sadly and spoke rarely and spent long hours staring at one object or another that they weren't really seeing at all. On the fourth night after their return, a mad black grandfather of a storm blew up off Bantry Bay, and Annie took shelter in her bedroom, lying on her back and gazing into nowhere. Every few seconds the walls were webbed with lightning flash and shadow; the porcelain vase on the bureau leaped forward from the dark like a plump little god garlanded with flowers, and evil energies winked in the facets of the crystal doorknob. Annie closed her eyes against the sight, against seeing in general. It wasn't long, though, before she heard Hugo enter. He stood in the door, holding his rifle.

"I'm leaving," he said.

"Leave, then." She turned away from him, wishing she was stone and trying to be so. "Mind you don't let out the cat."

"I can't part from you this way, Annie."

"Does that mean you'll stay if I keep up my sulkin'?"

"You know I can't." His footsteps came near. "For God's sake, Annie . . ."

"Is it for His sake you're leavin'? I thought it was to right the wrongs of the world that you were givin' me up." She sat up, tossing the hair from her eyes. "Don't expect me to be noble, to see you off down the garden path with a wave and a gentle tear. That's not the way I'm feelin'." She flung herself face down. "You'll be needin' all your concentration for the killin', so you'd do well to forget me. I'm startin' to forget you this very moment."

After a second, the door clicked—a vital, severing sound. She squeezed a handful of quilt hard as if she could make it cry out and lay motionless, heavy, full of dark thoughts. So this was to be her lot, was it? Growing old ungracefully in Gougane Barra, and, now that she'd wasted her one potent spell, settling for Tom O'Corran or some unsightly replica thereof, each night having the grand pleasure of watching his chin sink to meet his chest after a half dozen pints at Shorten's, and once a year—unless the weight of children was upon them—having a wild fling at the livestock fair in Killorglin. The storm lashed at the windows, raging, smearing the peaceful planes of her life with roaring light. God, what a fool she'd been to think she could shelter from it! It swept over the entire world, and whether by magic or bullet, it found you out and sucked you into its maw. There was no shelter from it, not in fortresses or mine shafts and least of all in a rosebud cottage on a country lane. . . . Then the real meaning of that thought penetrated her, startling her so that she jumped up from the bed and went into the hall without—at first—having any idea where she was going. There was no shelter, no hiding. But there was a more profound kind of shelter in doing and sharing. It shamed her to be learning it at such a late date. She took a step toward the door and felt a surge of insecurity; but the bonds tying her to Gougane Barra had suddenly grown frail—they were ancient Irish bonds of habit and hope-lessness, and she threw them off. She tore open the door and ran into the storm, with Diarmid streaking ahead of her.

Lightning was printing the world in negative, casting images of white electrified trees and palsied shrubs. Rain blinded her, thunder set her heart pounding. Where could he have gone? She spun in all directions, dizzy with the tumult. Then she spotted Diarmid prancing down the lane, his tail waving, as if the storm didn't exist in his universe. Shielding her eyes, she followed him. He turned off through a thicket, and Annie had to run to keep pace. Branches whipped her arms, eel-like strands of wet hair plastered to her cheeks, and she began to doubt Diarmid's instincts; but a few yards farther along she caught sight of Hugo standing on the slope of a hill, looking lost. A lightning flash showed his shocked face as she came stumbling up.

"What are you doing?" He grabbed her by the shoulders.

"I'm comin' with you!"

He shook his head and said something, but the words were drowned out by the thunder.

"What?"

"You don't know what it's like!" he yelled. "What'll you do there?"

"What am I doin' here? Nothin'!" She took his hand. "Come on!"

He pried her hand loose. "No!"

"All right! Be off with you! Or don't you know where to go?"

He didn't answer.

Another lightning burst lit the hillside, and Annie saw Diarmid perched on a stone farther up the slope. His tail was curled around his haunches, and he was licking a paw.

"This way!" she shouted, taking Hugo's hand and dragging him along.

Diarmid scampered off uphill. Beyond him, above the crest of the hill, the darkness was arched over by great forks of lightning that receded into the distance like the supports of an immense hallway. Shadows whirled through the air, briefly silhouetted by the flickering arches, and Annie saw that they were all bearing arms—rifles, pistols, knives. As she and Hugo drew near the crest, she felt the presence of these phantoms, the chill touch of their unreality, and it frightened her to think that she would become as insubstantial as they. But she kept walking. Ozone stung her nostrils, and the wind drove needles of rain into her cheeks. The darkness atop the hill now seemed to be flowing toward them, and though they were making a steady pace, they seemed to be moving faster, the toiling shapes of the bushes rushing past. She glanced at Hugo. His face was dissolving in a black medium; there were absences in his flesh— beneath his eyes, above his lip, in all the places where shadows might accumulate. And yet his hand was solid enough. He tightened his grip and pulled her around to face him.

"Are you sure?" he shouted. "Is this the right way?"

He didn't appear to notice anything out of the ordinary, and his dependence on her gave Annie confidence. She smiled and nodded. All the noise of the wind and rain and thunder was merging, resolving into a keening note that she heard inside her skull. The Devil's music. She wasn't surprised to learn that He was involved. She felt herself going dark, pressed thin and whirling by the union of two darknesses. Hugo took a step back, his face anxious.

"It's all right," she said, putting her lips close to his ear. "Like you told me—I've an understandin' for this sort of thing."

It was more than a year later in the dead of winter, a few weeks after the fall of the dictatorship in Chile—an event that had stirred barely a ripple on the still pond of Gougane Barra—when Eleanor Downey received a package from Annie Kinsale. There were exotic birds and Indian faces on the postage stamps, and inside was a letter, a newspaper clipping, and a vial of pinkish white powder. Eleanor read the clipping first. It was a sidebar to an article about the Chilean revolution, detailing the rash of minor upheavals that had afflicted the government and the military during the latter stages of the war—swindles disclosed, plots unmasked, infidelities revealed; two generals had been shot by their wives, and one of the wives—judged insane by the press—claimed to have been listening to a program of classical music on her radio, when suddenly she had heard instead her husband in intimate communion with his mistress. There were rumors of similar phenomena, all unsubstantiated. Eleanor laughed so hard that tears sprang to her eyes.

In the letter Annie said she was sorry to have run off without a word, but that she was happy with her marriage and work. Especially with her work—it was a joy to have a meaningful occupation. Things had improved immensely for her since leaving; even her powers were on the increase, what with the turmoil of war to stimulate them. And speaking of that, the one sight she wanted to see in Gougane Barra—aside from Eleanor, of course—was the expression on Tom O'Corran's face when he heard the news. If Eleanor would rub the powder on her eyelids and ears, and would read the pertinent parts of the letter to the boys at Shorten's, Annie would be able to see and hear all that transpired. Eleanor didn't waste a moment. She applied the powder and hurried through the snow to the pub, where she found Tom O'Corran, Henry Shorten, and old Matty gathered around a roaring fire and just lifting their first pints of the day.

"I thought she was dead," said Tom O'Corran after Eleanor had finished reading. His expression was that of a man who's swallowed something that didn't taste quite right.

"Chile!" said Henry Shorten. "She must have lost her wits to be runnin' off to a godforsaken place like that."

"True enough," said old Matty. "It's never the path of reason that leads you away from home, though. . . . "

His voice trailed away to a mutter, and he stared off into the malt-dark distance of his mug; Tom O'Corran sighed and lowered his head and scratched the back of his neck; Henry Shorten's eyes were misted and his Adam's apple worked; even Eleanor felt a bit gloomy, without knowing the reason why. It was a moment that comes often to Irishmen these days, when their souls understand what their minds will not—that Ireland is a poor, sad speck of greenery, pretty enough but losing its magic at a rapid rate, becoming a tourist map of unhaunted castles and mute stones and unhallowed darkness, lit only by the shining myths of its liars and the drunken glow of its poets.

"Well, she may be a fool, but still and all she's an Irish fool," said old Matty, recovering his spirits. He raised his glass, and the edges of his ears were made translucent and as red as fuchsias by the firelight behind them. "So here's to her!"

They all toasted her then, again and again, and before long the reminiscence was flowing. Hadn't she been a fine seamstress, and hadn't she had a grand touch with a tune, and couldn't you always count on her if you were a few pennies short of the necessary? And hadn't she been the prettiest flip of a girl in all of County Cork?

Halfway around the world, peering through the distanceless pour of the magical moment, Annie laughed at the way they talked about her—as if she were casketed, covered up, and on the verge of being canonized. As if they never expected to see her again. But Annie expected otherwise. Once things were more stable in Chile, she planned to go storming again, this time to Belfast where she would take up her new vocation. She had a score to settle there. Her story was far from over, and the radios of the world had just begun to tell their tales.

GREEN MAGIC

Howard Fair, looking over the relics of his great-uncle Gerald McIntyre, found a large ledger entitled:

WORKBOOK AND JOURNAL
Open at Peril!

Fair read the journal with interest, although his own work went far beyond ideas treated only gingerly by Gerald McIntyre.

"The existence of disciplines concentric to the elementary magics must now be admitted without further controversy," wrote McIntyre. "Guided by a set of analogies from the white and black magics (to be detailed in due course), I have delineated the basic extension of purple magic, as well as its corollary, Dynamic Nomism."

Fair read on, remarking the careful charts, the projections and expansions, the transpolations and transformations by which Gerald McIntyre had conceived his systemology. So swiftly had the technical arts advanced that McIntyre's expositions, highly controversial sixty years before, now seemed pedantic and overly rigorous.

"Whereas benign creatures: angels, white sprites, merrihews, sandestins—are typical of the white cycle; whereas demons, magners, trolls, and warlocks are evinced by black magic; so do the purple and green cycles sponsor their own particulars, but these are neither good nor evil, bearing, rather, the same relation to the black and white provinces that these latter do to our own basic realm."

Fair reread the passage. The "green cycle"? Had Gerald McIntyre wandered into regions overlooked by modern workers?

He reviewed the journal in the light of this suspicion, and discovered additional hints and references. Especially provocative was a bit of scribbled marginalia: "More concerning my latest researches I may not state, having been promised an infinite reward for this forbearance."

The passage was dated a day before Gerald McIntyre's death, which had occurred on March 21, 1898, the first day of spring. McIntyre had enjoyed very little of his "infinite reward," whatever had been its nature. . . . Fair returned to a consideration of the journal, which, in a sentence or two, had opened a chink on an entire new panorama. McIntyre provided no further illumination, and Fair set out to make a fuller investigation.

His first steps were routine. He performed two divinations, searched the standard indexes, concordances, handbooks, and formularies, evoked a demon whom he had previously found knowledgeable: all without success. He found no direct reference to cycles beyond the purple; the demon refused even to speculate.

Fair was by no means discouraged; if anything, the intensity of his interest increased. He reread the journal, with particular care to the justification for purple magic, reasoning that McIntyre, groping for a lore beyond the purple, might well have used the methods that had yielded results before. Applying stains and ultraviolet light to the pages, Fair made legible a number of notes McIntyre had jotted down, then erased.

Fair was immensely stimulated. The notes assured him that he was on the right track, and further indicated a number of blind alleys that Fair profited by avoiding. He applied himself so successfully that before the week was out he had evoked a sprite of the green cycle.

It appeared in the semblance of a man with green glass eyes and a thatch of young eucalyptus leaves in the place of hair. It greeted Fair with cool courtesy, would not seat itself, and ignored Fair's proffer of coffee.

After wandering around the apartment inspecting Fair's books and curios with an air of negligent amusement, it agreed to respond to Fair's questions.

Fair asked permission to use his tape recorder, which the sprite allowed, and Fair set the apparatus in motion. (When subsequently he replayed the interview, no sound could be heard.)

"What realms of magic lie beyond the green?" asked Fair.

"I can't give you an exact answer," replied the sprite, "because I don't know. There are at least two more, corresponding to the colors we call rawn and pallow, and very likely others."

Fair arranged the microphone where it would more directly intercept the voice of the sprite.

"What," he asked, "is the green cycle like? What is its physical semblance?"

The sprite paused to consider. Glistening mother-of-pearl films wandered across its face, reflecting the tinge of its thoughts. "I'm rather severely restricted by your use of the word 'physical.' And 'semblance' involves a subjective interpretation, which changes with the rise and fall of the seconds."

"By all means," Fair said hastily, "describe it in your own words."

"Well—we have four different regions, two of which floresce from the basic skeleton of the universe, and so subsede the others. The first of these is compressed and isthiated, but is notable for its wide pools of mottle which we use sometimes for deranging stations. We've transplanted club-mosses from Earth's Devonian and a few ice-fires from Perdition. They climb among the rods which we call devil-hair—" it went on for several minutes but the meaning almost entirely escaped Fair. And it seemed as if the question by which he had hoped to break the ice might run away with the entire interview. He introduced another idea.

" 'Can we freely manipulate the physical extensions of Earth?' " The sprite seemed amused. "You refer, so I assume, to the various aspects of space, time, mass, energy, life, thought, and recollection."

"Exactly."

The sprite raised its green cornsilk eyebrows. "I might as sensibly ask can you break an egg by striking it with a club. The response is on a similar level of seriousness."

Fair had expected a certain amount of condescension and impatience, and was not abashed. "How may I learn these techniques?"

"In the usual manner: through diligent study."

"Ah, indeed—but where could I study? Who would teach me?"

The sprite made an easy gesture, and whorls of green smoke trailed from its fingers to spin through the air. "I could arrange the matter, but since I bear you no particular animosity, I'll do nothing of the sort. And now, I must be gone."

"Where do you go?" Fair asked in wonder and longing. "May I go with you?"

The sprite, swirling a drape of bright green dust over its shoulders, shook its head. "You would be less than comfortable."

"Other men have explored the worlds of magic!"

"True: your uncle Gerald McIntyre, for instance."

"My uncle Gerald learned green magic?"

"To the limit of his capabilities. He found no pleasure in his learning. You would do well to profit by his experience and modify your ambitions." The sprite turned and walked away.

Fair watched it depart. The sprite receded in space and dimension, but never reached the wall of Fair's room. At a distance which might have been fifty yards, the sprite glanced back, as if to make sure that Fair was not following, then stepped off at another angle and disappeared.

Fair's first impulse was to take heed and limit his explorations. He was an adept in white magic, and had mastered the black art—occasionally he evoked a demon to liven a social gathering which otherwise threatened to become dull—but he had by no means illuminated every mystery of purple magic, which is the realm of Incarnate Symbols.

Howard Fair might have turned away from the green cycle except for three factors.

First was his physical appearance. He stood rather under medium height, with a swarthy face, sparse black hair, a gnarled nose, a small heavy mouth. He felt no great sensitivity about his appearance, but realized that it might be improved. In his mind's eye he pictured the personified ideal of himself: he was taller by six inches, his nose thin and keen, his skin cleared of its muddy undertone. A striking figure, but still recognizable as Howard Fair. He wanted the love of women, but he wanted it without the interposition of his craft. Many times he had brought beautiful girls to his bed, lips wet and eyes shining; but purple magic had seduced them rather than Howard Fair, and he took limited satisfaction in such conquests.

Here was the first factor which drew Howard Fair back to the green lore; the second was his yearning for extended, perhaps eternal, life; the third was simple thirst for knowledge.

The fact of Gerald McIntyre's death, or dissolution, or disappearance—whatever had happened to him—was naturally a matter of concern. If he had won a goal so precious, why had he died so quickly? Was the "infinite reward" so miraculous, so exquisite, that the mind failed under its possession? (If such were the case, the reward was hardly a reward.)

Fair could not restrain himself, and by degrees returned to a study of green magic. Rather than again invoke the sprite whose air of indulgent contempt he had found exasperating, he decided to seek knowledge by an indirect method, employing the most advanced concepts of technical and cabalistic science.

He obtained a portable television transmitter, which he loaded into his panel truck along with a receiver. On a Monday night in early May, he drove to an abandoned graveyard far out in the wooded hills, and there, by the light of a waning moon, he buried the television camera in graveyard clay until only the lens protruded from the soil.

With a sharp alder twig he scratched on the ground a monstrous outline. The television lens served for one eye, a beer bottle pushed neck-first into the soil the other.

During the middle hours, while the moon died behind wisps of pale cloud, he carved a word on the dark forehead; then recited the activating incantation.

The ground rumbled and moaned, the golem heaved up to blot out the stars.

The glass eyes stared down at Fair, secure in his pentagram.

"Speak!" called out Fair. "*Enteresthes, Akmai Adonai Bidemgir! Elohim, pa rahulli! Enteresthes, HVOI!* Speak!"

"Return me to earth, return my clay to the quiet clay from whence you roused me."

"First you must serve."

The golem stumbled forward to crush Fair, but was halted by the pang of protective magic.

"Serve you I will, if serve you I must."

Fair stepped boldly forth from the pentagon, strung forty yards of green ribbon down the road in the shape of a narrow V. "Go forth into the realm of green magic," he told the monster. "The ribbons reach forty miles; walk to the end, turn about, return, and then fall back, return to the earth from which you rose."

The golem turned, shuffled into the V of green ribbon, shaking off clods of mold, jarring the ground with its ponderous tread.

Fair watched the squat shape dwindle, recede, yet never reach the angle of the magic V. He returned to his panel truck, tuned the television receiver to the golem's eye, and surveyed the fantastic vistas of the green realm.

Two elementals of the green realm met on a spun-silver landscape. They were Jaadian and Misthemar, and they fell to discussing the earthen monster that had stalked forty miles through the region known as Cil; which then, turning in its tracks, had retraced its steps, gradually increasing its pace until at the end it moved in a shambling rush, leaving a trail of clods on the fragile moth-wing mosaics.

"Events, events, events," Misthemar fretted, "they crowd the chute of time till the bounds bulge. Or then again, the course is as lean and spare as a stretched tendon. . . . " He paused for a period of reflection, and silver clouds moved over his head and under his feet.

Jaadian remarked, "You are aware that I conversed with Howard Fair; he is so obsessed to escape the squalor of his world that he acts with recklessness."

"The man Gerald McIntyre was his uncle," mused Misthemar. "McIntyre besought, we yielded; as perhaps now we must yield to Howard Fair."

Jaadian uneasily opened his hand, shook off a spray of emerald fire. "Events press, both in and out. I find myself unable to act in this regard."

"I likewise do not care to be the agent of tragedy."

A Meaning came fluttering up from below: "A disturbance among the spiral towers! A caterpillar of glass and metal has come clinking; it has thrust electric eyes into the Portinone and broken open the Egg of Innocence. Howard Fair is the fault."

Jaadian and Misthemar consulted each other with wry disinclination. "Very well, both of us will go; such a duty needs two souls in support."

They impinged upon Earth and found Howard Fair in a wall booth at a cocktail bar. He looked up at the two strangers and one of them asked, "May we join you?"

Fair examined the two men. Both wore conservative suits and carried cashmere topcoats over their arms. Fair noticed that the left thumb-nail of each man glistened green.

Fair rose politely to his feet. "Will you sit down?"

The green sprites hung up their overcoats and slid into the booth. Fair looked from one to the other. He addressed Jaadian. "Aren't you he whom I interviewed several weeks ago?"

Jaadian assented. "You have not accepted my advice."

Fair shrugged. "You asked me to remain ignorant, to accept my stupidity and ineptitude."

"And why should you not?" asked Jaadian gently. "You are a primitive in a primitive realm; nevertheless not one man in a thousand can match your achievements."

Fair agreed, smiling faintly. "But knowledge creates a craving for further knowledge. Where is the harm in knowledge?"

Misthemar, the more mercurial of the sprites, spoke angrily. "Where is the harm? Consider your earthen monster! It befouled forty miles of delicacy, the record of ten million years. Consider your caterpillar! It trampled our pillars of carved milk, our dreaming towers, damaged the nerve-skeins which extrude and waft us our Meanings."

"I'm dreadfully sorry," said Fair. "I meant no destruction."

The sprites nodded. "But your apology conveys no guarantee of restraint."

Fair toyed with his glass. A waiter approached the table, addressed the two sprites. "Something for you two gentlemen?"

Jaadian ordered a glass of charged water, as did Misthemar. Fair called for another highball.

"What do you hope to gain from this activity?" inquired Misthemar. "Destructive forays teach you nothing!"

Fair agreed. "I have learned little. But I have seen miraculous sights. I am more than ever anxious to learn."

The green sprites glumly watched the bubbles rising in their glasses. Jaadian at last drew a deep sigh. "Perhaps we can obviate toil on your part and disturbance on ours. Explicitly, what gains or advantages do you hope to derive from green magic?"

Fair, smiling, leaned back into the red imitation-leather cushions. "I want many things. Extended life—mobility in time—comprehensive memory—augmented perception, with vision across the whole spectrum. I want physical charm and magnetism, the semblance of youth, muscular endurance. . . . Then there are qualities more or less speculative, such as—"

Jaadian interrupted. "These qualities and characteristics we will confer upon you. In return you will undertake never again to disturb the green realm. You will evade centuries of toil; we will be spared the nuisance of your presence, and the inevitable tragedy."

"Tragedy?" inquired Fair in wonder. "Why tragedy?"

Jaadian spoke in a deep reverberating voice. "You are a man of Earth. Your goals are not our goals. Green magic makes you aware of our goals."

Fair thoughtfully sipped his highball. "I can't see that this is a disadvantage. I am willing to submit to the discipline of instruction. Surely a knowledge of green magic will not change me into a different entity?"

"No. And this is the basic tragedy!"

Misthemar spoke in exasperation. "We are forbidden to harm lesser creatures, and so you are fortunate; for to dissolve you into air would end all the annoyance."

Fair laughed. "I apologize again for making such a nuisance of myself. But surely you understand how important this is to me?"

Jaadian asked hopefully, "Then you agree to our offer?"

Fair shook his head. "How could I live, forever young, capable of extended learning, but limited to knowledge which I already see bounds to? I would be bored, restless, miserable."

"That well may be," said Jaadian. "But not so bored, restless and miserable as if you were learned in green magic."

Fair drew himself erect. "I must learn green magic. It is an opportunity which only a person both torpid and stupid could refuse."

Jaadian sighed. "In your place I would make the same response." The sprites rose to their feet. "Come then, we will teach you."

"Don't say we didn't warn you," said Misthemar.

Time passed. Sunset waned and twilight darkened. A man walked up the stairs, entered Howard Fair's apartment. He was tall, unobtrusively muscular. His face was sensitive, keen, humorous; his left thumb-nail glistened green.

Time is a function of vital processes. The people of Earth had perceived the motion of their clocks. On this understanding, two hours had elapsed since Howard Fair had followed the green sprites from the bar.

Howard Fair had perceived other criteria. For him the interval had been seven hundred years, during which he had lived in the green realm, learning to the utmost capacity of his brain.

He had occupied two years training his senses to the new conditions. Gradually he learned to walk in the six basic three-dimensional directions, and accustomed himself to the fourth-dimensional short-cuts. By easy stages the blinds over his eyes were removed, so that the dazzling over-human intricacy of the landscape never completely confounded him.

Another year was spent training him to the use of a code-language— an intermediate step between the vocalizations of Earth and the meaning-patterns of the green realm, where a hundred symbol-flakes (each a flitting spot of delicate iridescence) might be displayed in a single swirl of import. During this time Howard Fair's eyes and brain were altered, to allow him the use of the many new colors, without which the meaning-flakes could not be recognized.

These were preliminary steps. For forty years he studied the flakes, of which there were almost a million. Another forty years was given to elementary permutations and shifts, and another forty to parallels, attenuation, diminishments, and extensions; and during this time he was introduced to flake patterns, and certain of the more obvious displays.

Now he was able to study without recourse to the code-language, and his progress became more marked. Another twenty years found him able to recognize more complicated Meanings, and he was introduced to a more varied program. He floated over the field of moth-wing mosaics, which still showed the footprints of the golem. He sweated in embarrassment, the extent of his wicked willfulness now clear to him.

So passed the years. Howard Fair learned as much green magic as his brain could encompass.

He explored much of the green realm, finding so much beauty that he feared his brain might burst. He tasted, he heard, he felt, he sensed, and each one of his senses was a hundred times more discriminating than before. Nourishment came in a thousand different forms: from pink eggs which burst into a hot sweet gas, suffusing his entire body; from passing through a rain of stinging metal crystals; from simple contemplation of the proper symbol.

Homesickness for Earth waxed and waned. Sometimes it was insupportable and he was ready to forsake all he had learned and abandon his hopes for the future. At other times the magnificence of the green realm permeated him, and the thought of departure seemed like the threat of death itself.

By stages so gradual he never realized them he learned green magic.

But the new faculty gave him no pride: between his crude ineptitudes and the poetic elegance of the sprites remained a tremendous gap—and he felt his innate inferiority much more keenly than he ever had in his old state. Worse, his most earnest efforts failed to improve his technique, and sometimes, observing the singing joy of an improvised manifestation by one of the sprites, and contrasting it to his own labored constructions, he felt futility and shame.

The longer he remained in the green realm, the stronger grew the sense of his own maladroitness, and he began to long for the easy environment of Earth, where each of his acts would not shout aloud of vulgarity and crassness. At times he would watch the sprites (in the gossamer forms natural to them) at play among the pearl-petals, or twining like quick flashes of music through the forest of pink spirals. The contrast between their verve and his brutish fumbling could not be borne and he would turn away. His self-respect dwindled with each passing hour, and instead of pride in his learning, he felt a sullen ache for what he was not and could never become. The first few hundred years he worked with the enthusiasm of ignorance, for the next few he was buoyed by hope. During the last part of his time, only dogged obstinacy kept him plodding through what now he knew for infantile exercises.

In one terrible bitter-sweet spasm, he gave up. He found Jaadian weaving tinkling fragments of various magics into a warp of shining long splines. With grave courtesy, Jaadian gave Fair his attention, and Fair laboriously set forth his meaning.

Jaadian returned a message. "I recognize your discomfort, and extend my sympathy. It is best that you now return to your native home."

He put aside his weaving and conveyed Fair down through the requisite vortices. Along the way they passed Misthemar. No flicker of meaning was expressed or exchanged, but Howard Fair thought to feel a tinge of faintly malicious amusement.

Howard Fair sat in his apartment. His perceptions, augmented and sharpened by his sojourn in the green realm, took note of the surroundings. Only two hours before, by the clocks of Earth, he had found them both restful and stimulating; now they were neither. His books: superstition, spuriousness, earnest nonsense. His private journals and workbooks: a pathetic scrawl of infantilisms. Gravity tugged at his feet, held him rigid. The shoddy construction of the house, which heretofore he had never noticed, oppressed him. Everywhere he looked he saw slipshod disorder, primitive filth. The thought of the food he must now eat revolted him.

He went out on his little balcony which overlooked the street. The air was impregnated with organic smells. Across the street he could look into windows where his fellow humans lived in stupid squalor.

Fair smiled sadly. He had tried to prepare himself for these reactions, but now was surprised by their intensity. He returned into his apartment. He must accustom himself to the old environment. And after all there were compensations. The most desirable commodities of the world were now his to enjoy.

Howard Fair plunged into the enjoyment of these pleasures. He forced himself to drink quantities of expensive wines, brandies, liqueurs, even though they offended his palate. Hunger overcame his nausea, he forced himself to the consumption of what he thought of as fried animal tissue, the hypertrophied sexual organs of plants. He experimented with erotic sensations, but found that beautiful women no longer seemed different from the plain ones, and that he could barely steel himself to the untidy contacts. He bought libraries of erudite books, glanced through them with contempt. He tried to amuse himself with his old magics; they seemed ridiculous.

He forced himself to enjoy these pleasures for a month; then he fled the city and established a crystal bubble on a crag in the Andes. To nourish himself, he contrived a thick liquid, which, while by no means as exhilarating as the substances of the green realm, was innocent of organic contamination.

After a certain degree of improvisation and make-shift, he arranged his life to its minimum discomfort. The view was one of austere grandeur; not even the condors came to disturb him. He sat back to ponder the chain of events which had started with his discovery of Gerald McIntyre's workbook. He frowned. Gerald McIntyre? He jumped to his feet, looked far off over the crags.

He found Gerald McIntyre at a wayside service station in the heart of the South Dakota prairie. McIntyre was sitting in an old wooden chair, tilted back against the peeling yellow paint of the service station, a straw hat shading his eyes from the sun.

He was a magnetically handsome man, blond of hair, brown of eyes whose gaze stung like the touch of icicles. His left thumb-nail glistened green.

Fair greeted him casually; the two men surveyed each other with wry curiosity.

"I see you have adapted yourself," said Howard Fair.

McIntyre shrugged. "As well as possible. I try to maintain a balance between solitude and the pressure of humanity." He looked into the bright blue sky where crows flapped and called. "For many years I lived in isolation. I began to detest the sound of my own breathing."

Along the highway came a glittering automobile, rococo as a hybrid goldfish. With the perceptions now available to them, Fair and McIntyre could see the driver to be red-faced and truculent, his companion a peevish woman in expensive clothes.

"There are other advantages to residence here," said McIntyre. "For instance, I am able to enrich the lives of passersby with trifles of novel adventure." He made a small gesture; two dozen crows swooped down and flew beside the automobile. They settled on the fenders, strutted back and forth along the hood, fouled the windshield.

The automobile squealed to a halt, the driver jumped out, put the birds to flight. He threw an ineffectual rock, waved his arms in outrage, returned to his car, proceeded.

"A paltry affair," said McIntyre with a sigh. "The truth of the matter is that I am bored." He pursed his mouth and blew forth three bright puffs of smoke: first red, then yellow, then blazing blue. "I have arrived at the estate of foolishness, as you can see."

Fair surveyed his great-uncle with a trace of uneasiness. McIntyre laughed. "No more pranks. I predict, however, that you will presently share my malaise."

"I share it already," said Fair. "Sometimes I wish I could abandon all my magic and return to my former innocence."

"I have toyed with the idea," McIntyre replied thoughtfully. "In fact I have made all the necessary arrangements. It is really a simple matter." He led Fair to a small room behind the station. Although the door was open, the interior showed a thick darkness.

McIntyre, standing well back, surveyed the darkness with a quizzical curl to his lip. "You need only enter. All your magic, all your recollections of the green realm will depart. You will be no wiser than the next man you meet. And with your knowledge will go your boredom, your melancholy, your dissatisfaction."

Fair contemplated the dark doorway. A single step would resolve his discomfort.

He glanced at McIntyre; the two surveyed each other with sardonic amusement. They returned to the front of the building.

"Sometimes I stand by the door and look into the darkness," said McIntyre. "Then I am reminded how dearly I cherish my boredom, and what a precious commodity is so much misery."

Fair made himself ready for departure. "I thank you for this new wisdom, which a hundred more years in the green realm would not have taught me. And now—for a time, at least—I go back to my crag in the Andes."

McIntyre tilted his chair against the wall of the service station. "And I—for a time, at least—will wait for the next passerby."

"Goodby then, Uncle Gerald."

"Goodby, Howard."

THE MARK
OF THE BEAST

Last of Suez, some hold, the direct control of Providence ceases; Man being there handed over to the power of the Gods and Devil of Asia, and the Church of England Providence only exercising an occasional and modified supervision in the case of Englishmen.

This theory accounts for some of the more unnecessary horrors of life in India: it may be stretched to explain my story.

My friend Strickland of the Police, who knows as much of natives of India as is good for any man, can bear witness to the facts of the case. Dumoise, our doctor, also saw what Strickland and I saw. The inference which he drew from the evidence was entirely incorrect. He is dead now; he died, in a rather curious manner, which has been elsewhere described.

When Fleete came to India, he owned a little money and some land in the Himalayas, near a place called Dharmsala. Both properties had been left him by an uncle, and he came out to finance them. He was a big, heavy, genial, and inoffensive man. His knowledge of natives was, of course, limited, and he complained of the difficulties of the language.

He rode in from his place in the hills to spend New Year in the station, and he stayed with Strickland. On New Year's Eve there was a big dinner at the club, and the night was excusably wet. When men foregather from the uttermost ends of the Empire, they have a right to be riotous. The Frontier had sent down a contingent o' Catch-'em-Alive-O's who had not seen twenty white faces for a year, and were used to ride fifteen miles to dinner at the next Fort at the risk of a Khyberee bullet where their drinks should lie. They profited by their new security, for they tried to play pool with a curled-up hedgehog found in the garden, and one of them carried the marker round the room in his teeth. Half a dozen planters had come in from the south and were talking "horse" to the Biggest Liar in Asia, who was trying to cap all their stories at once. Everybody was there, and there was a general closing up of ranks and taking stock of our losses in dead or disabled that had fallen during the past year.

It was a very wet night, and I remember that we sang "Auld Lang Syne" with our feet in the Polo Championship Cup, and our heads among the stars, and swore that we were all dear friends. Then some of us went away and annexed Burma, and some tried to open up the Soudan and were opened up by Fuzzies in that cruel scrub outside Suakim, and some found stars and medals, and some were married, which was bad, and some did other things which were worse, and the others of us stayed in our chains and strove to make money on insufficient experiences.

Fleete began the night with sherry and bitters, drank champagne steadily up to dessert, then raw, rasping Capri with all the strength of whisky, took Benedictine with his coffee, four or five whiskies and sodas to improve his pool strokes, beer and bones at half-past two, winding up with old brandy. Consequently, when he came out, at half-past three in the morning, into fourteen degrees of frost, he was very angry with his horse for coughing, and tried to leapfrog into the saddle. The horse broke away and went to his stables; so Strickland and I formed a Guard of Dishonor to take Fleete home.

Our road lay through the bazaar, close to a little temple of Hanuman, the Monkey-god, who is a leading divinity worthy of respect. All gods have good points, just as have all priests. Personally, I attach much importance to Hanuman, and am kind to his people—the great gray apes of the hills. One never knows when one may want a friend.

There was a light in the temple, and as we passed, we could hear voices of men chanting hymns. In a native temple, the priests rise at all hours of the night to do honor to their god. Before we could stop him, Fleete dashed up the steps, patted two priests on the back, and was gravely grinding the ashes of his cigar butt into the forehead of the red stone image of Hanuman. Strickland tried to drag him out, but he sat down and said solemnly:

"Shee that? 'Mark of the B—beasht! *I* made it. Ishn't it fine?"

In half a minute the temple was alive and noisy, and Strickland, who knew what came of polluting gods, said that things might occur. He, by virtue of his official position, long residence in the country, and weakness for going among the natives, was known to the priests and he felt unhappy. Fleete sat on the ground and refused to move. He said that "good old Hanuman" made a very soft pillow.

Then, without any warning, a Silver Man came out of a recess behind the image of the god. He was perfectly naked in that bitter, bitter cold, and his body shone like frosted silver, for he was what the Bible calls "a leper as white as snow." Also he had no face, because he was a leper of some years' standing and his disease was heavy upon him. We two stooped to haul Fleete up, and the temple was filling and filling with folk who seemed to spring from the earth, when the Silver Man ran in under our arms, making a noise exactly like the mewing of an otter, caught Fleete round the body and dropped his head on Fleete's breast before we could wrench him away. Then he retired to a corner and sat mewing while the crowd blocked all the doors.

The priests were very angry until the Silver Man touched Fleete. That nuzzling seemed to sober them.

At the end of a few minutes' silence one of the priests came to Strickland and said, in perfect English, "Take your friend away. He was done with Hanuman, but Hanuman has not done with him." The crowd gave room and we carried Fleete into the road.

Strickland was very angry. He said that we might all three have been knifed, and that Fleete should thank his stars that he had escaped without injury.

Fleete thanked no one. He said that he wanted to go to bed. He was gorgeously drunk.

We moved on, Strickland silent and wrathful, until Fleete was taken with violent shivering fits and sweating. He said that the smells of the bazaar were overpowering, and he wondered why slaughter-houses were permitted so near English residences. "Can't you smell the blood?" said Fleete.

We put him to bed at last, just as the dawn was breaking, and Strickland invited me to have another whisky and soda. While we were drinking he talked of the trouble in the temple, and admitted that it baffled him completely. Strickland hates being mystified by natives, because his business in life is to overmatch them with their own weapons. He has not yet succeeded in doing this, but in fifteen or twenty years he will have made some small progress.

"They should have mauled us," he said, "instead of mewing at us. I wonder what they meant. I don't like it one little bit."

I said that the Managing Committee of the temple would in all probability bring a criminal action against us for insulting their religion. There was a section of the Indian Penal Code which exactly met Fleete's offense. Strickland said he only hoped and prayed that they would do this. Before I left I looked into Fleete's room and saw him lying on his right side, scratching his left breast. Then I went to bed cold, depressed, and unhappy, at seven o'clock in the morning.

At one o'clock I rode over to Strickland's house to inquire after Fleete's head. I imagined that it would be a sore one. Fleete was breakfasting and seemed unwell. His temper was gone, for he was abusing the cook for not supplying him with an underdone chop. A man who can eat raw meat after a wet night is a curiosity. I told Fleete this and he laughed.

"You breed queer mosquitoes in these parts," he said. "I've been bitten to pieces, but only in one place."

"Let's have a look at the bite," said Strickland. "It may have gone down since this morning."

While the chops were being cooked, Fleete opened his shirt and showed us, just over his left breast, a mark, the perfect double of the black rosettes—the five or six irregular blotches arranged in a circle— on a leopard's hide. Strickland looked and said, "It was only pink this morning. It's grown black now."

Fleete ran to a glass.

"By Jove!" he said, "this is nasty. What is it?"

We could not answer. Here the chops came in, all red and juicy, and Fleete bolted three in a most offensive manner. He ate on his right grinders only, and threw his head over his right shoulder as he snapped the meat. When he had finished, it struck him that he had been behaving strangely, for he said apologetically, "I don't think I ever felt so hungry in my life. I've bolted like an ostrich."

After breakfast Strickland said to me, "Don't go. Stay here, and stay for the night."

Seeing that my house was not three miles from Strickland's, this request was absurd. But Strickland insisted, and was going to say something when Fleete interrupted by declaring in a shamefaced way that he felt hungry again. Strickland sent a man to my house to fetch over my bedding and a horse, and we three went down to Strickland's stables to pass the hours until it was time to go out for a ride. The man who has a weakness for horses never wearies of inspecting them; and when two men are killing time in this way they gather knowledge and lies the one from the other.

There were five horses in the stables, and I shall never forget the scene as we tried to look them over. They seemed to have gone mad. They reared and screamed and nearly tore up their pickets; they sweated and shivered and lathered and were distraught with fear. Strickland's horses used to know him as well as his dogs, which made the matter more curious. We left the stable for fear of the brutes throwing themselves in their panic. Then Strickland turned back and called me. The horses were still frightened, but they let us "gentle" and make much of them, and put their heads in our bosoms.

"They aren't afraid of us," said Strickland. "D'you know, I'd give three months' pay if Outrage here could talk."

But Outrage was dumb, and could only cuddle up to his master and blow out his nostrils, as is the custom of horses when they wish to explain things but can't. Fleete came up when we were in the stalls, and as soon as the horses saw him, their fright broke out afresh. It was all that we could do to escape from the place unkicked. Strickland said, "They don't seem to love you, Fleete."

"Nonsense," said Fleete; "my mare will follow me like a dog." He went to her; she was in a loose-box; but as he slipped the bars she plunged, knocked him down, and broke away into the garden. I laughed, but Strickland was not amused. He took his moustache in both fists and pulled at it till it nearly came out. Fleete, instead of going off to chase his property, yawned, saying that he felt sleepy. He went to the house to lie down, which was a foolish way of spending New Year's Day.

Strickland sat with me in the stables and asked if I had noticed anything peculiar in Fleete's manner. I said that he ate his food like a beast; but that this might have been the result of living alone in the hills out of the reach of society as refined and elevating as ours for instance. Strickland was not amused. I do not think that he listened to me, for his next sentence referred to the mark on Fleete's breast, and I said that it might have been caused by blister-flies, or that it was possibly a birthmark newly born and now visible for the first time. We both agreed that it was unpleasant to look at, and Strickland found occasion to say that I was a fool.

"I can't tell you what I think now," said he, "because you would call me a madman; but you must stay with me for the next few days, if you can. I want you to watch Fleete, but don't tell me what you think till I have made up my mind."

"But I am dining out tonight," I said.

"So am I," said Strickland, "and so is Fleete. At least if he doesn't change his mind."

We walked about the garden smoking, but saying nothing—because we were friends, and talking spoils good tobacco—till our pipes were out. Then we went to wake up Fleete. He was wide awake and fidgeting about his room.

"I say, I want some more chops," he said. "Can I get them?"

We laughed and said, "Go and change. The ponies will be round in a minute."

"All right," said Fleete. "I'll go when I get the chops—underdone ones, mind."

He seemed to be quite in earnest. It was four o'clock, and we had had breakfast at one; still, for a long time, he demanded those underdone chops. Then he changed into riding clothes and went out into the verandah. His pony—the mare had not been caught—would not let him come near. All three horses were unmanageable—mad with fear—and finally Fleete said that he would stay at home and get something to eat. Strickland and I rode out wondering. As we passed the temple of Hanuman, the Silver Man came out and mewed at us.

"He is not one of the regular priests of the temple," said Strickland. "I think I should peculiarly like to lay my hands on him."

There was no spring in our gallop on the racecourse that evening. The horses were stale, and moved as though they had been ridden out.

"The fright after breakfast has been too much for them," said Strickland.

That was the only remark he made through the remainder of the ride. Once or twice I think he swore to himself; but that did not count.

We came back in the dark at seven o'clock, and saw that there were no lights in the bungalow. "Careless ruffians my servants are!" said Strickland.

My horse reared at something on the carriage drive, and Fleete stood up under its nose.

"What are you doing, grovelling about the garden?" said Strickland.

But both horses bolted and nearly threw us. We dismounted by the stables and returned to Fleete, who was on his hands and knees under the orange bushes.

"What the devil's wrong with you?" said Strickland.

"Nothing, nothing in the world," said Fleete, speaking very quickly and thickly. "I've been gardening—botanizing you know. The smell of the earth is delightful. I think I'm going for a walk—a long walk—all night."

Then I saw that there was something excessively out of order somewhere, and I said to Strickland, "I am not dining out."

"Bless you!" said Strickland. "Here, Fleete, get up. You'll catch fever there. Come in to dinner and let's have the lamps lit. We'll all dine at home."

Fleete stood up unwillingly, and said, "No lamps—no lamps. It's much nicer here. Let's dine outside and have some more chops—lots of 'em and underdone—bloody ones with gristle."

Now a December evening in Northern India is bitterly cold, and Fleete's suggestion was that of a maniac.

"Come in," said Strickland sternly. "Come in at once."

Fleete came, and when the lamps were brought, we saw that he was literally plastered with dirt from head to foot. He must have been rolling in the garden. He shrank from the light and went to his room. His eyes were horrible to look at. There was a green light behind them, not in them, if you understand, and the man's lower lip hung down.

Strickland said, "There is going to be trouble—big trouble—tonight. Don't change your riding things."

We waited and waited for Fleete's reappearance, and ordered dinner in the meantime. We could hear him moving about his own room, but there was no light there. Presently from the room came the long-drawn howl of a wolf.

People write and talk lightly of blood running cold and hair standing up and things of that kind. Both sensations are too horrible to be trifled with. My heart stopped as though a knife had been driven through it, and Strickland turned white as the tablecloth.

The howl was repeated, and was answered by another howl far across the fields.

That set the gilded roof on the horror. Strickland dashed into Fleete's room. I followed, and we saw Fleete getting out of the window. He made beast-noises in the back of his throat. He could not answer us when we shouted at him. He spat.

I don't quite remember what followed, but I think that Strickland must have stunned him with the long boot-jack or else I should never have been able to sit on his chest. Fleete could not speak, he could only snarl, and his snarls were those of a wolf, not of a man. The human spirit must have been giving way all day and have died out with the twilight. We were dealing with a beast that had once been Fleete.

The affair was beyond any human and rational experience. I tried to say "hydrophobia," but the word wouldn't come, because I knew that I was lying.

We bound this beast with leather thongs of the punkah-rope, and tied its thumbs and big toes together, and gagged it with a shoehorn, which makes a very efficient gag if you know how to arrange it. Then we carried it into the dining room, and sent a man to Dumoise, the doctor, telling him to come over at once. After we had despatched the messenger and were drawing breath, Strickland said, "It's no good. This isn't any doctor's work." I, also, knew that he spoke the truth.

The beast's head was free, and it threw it about from side to side. Anyone entering the room would have believed that we were curing a wolf's pelt. That was the most loathsome accessory of all.

Strickland sat with his chin in the heel of his fist, watching the beast as it wriggled on the ground, but saying nothing. The shirt had been torn open in the scuffle and showed the black rosette mark on the left breast. It stood out like a blister.

In the silence of the watching we heard something without mewing like a she-otter. We both rose to our feet, and, I answer for myself, not Strickland, felt sick—actually and physically sick. We told each other, as did the men in *Pinafore*, that it was the cat.

Dumoise arrived, and I never saw a little man so unprofessionally shocked. He said that it was a heartrending case of hydrophobia, and that nothing could be done. At least any palliative measures would only prolong the agony. The beast was foaming at the mouth. Fleete, as we told Dumoise, had been bitten by dogs once or twice. Any man who keeps half a dozen terriers must expect a nip now and again. Dumoise could offer no help. He could only certify that Fleete was dying of hydrophobia. The beast was then howling, for it had managed to spit out the shoehorn. Dumoise said that he would be ready to certify to the cause of death, and that the end was certain. He was a good little man, and he offered to remain with us; but Strickland refused the kindness.

He did not wish to poison Dumoise's New Year. He would only ask him not to give the real cause of Fleete's death to the public.

So Dumoise left, deeply agitated; and as soon as the noise of the cartwheels had died away, Strickland told me, in a whisper, his suspicions. They were so wildly improbable that he dared not say them out aloud; and I, who entertained all Strickland's beliefs, was so ashamed of owning to them that I pretended to disbelieve.

"Even if the Silver Man had bewitched Fleete for polluting the image of Hanuman, the punishment could not have fallen so quickly."

As I was whispering this the cry outside the house rose again, and the beast fell into a fresh paroxysm of struggling till we were afraid that the thongs that held it would give way.

"Watch!" said Strickland. "If this happens six times I shall take the law into my own hands. I order you to help me."

He went into his room and came out in a few minutes with the barrels of an old shotgun, a piece of fishing-line, some thick cord, and his heavy wooden bedstead. I reported that the convulsions had followed the cry by two seconds in each case, and the beast seemed perceptibly weaker.

Strickland muttered, "But he can't take away the life! He can't take away the life!"

I said, though I knew that I was arguing against myself, "It may be a cat. It must be a cat. If the Silver Man is responsible, why does he dare to come here?"

Strickland arranged the wood on the hearth, put the gun barrels into the glow of the fire, spread the twine on the table and broke a walking stick in two. There was one yard of fishing-line, gut, lapped with wire, such as is used for *mahseer*-fishing, and he tied the two ends together in a loop.

Then he said, "How can we catch him? He must be taken alive and unhurt."

I said that we must trust in Providence, and go out softly with polo sticks into the shrubbery at the front of the house. The man or animal that made the cry was evidently moving round the house as regularly as a night watchman. We could wait in the bushes till he came by and knock him over.

Strickland accepted this suggestion, and we slipped out from a bathroom window into the front verandah and then across the carriage drive into the bushes.

In the moonlight we could see the leper coming round the corner of the house. He was perfectly naked, and from time to time he mewed and stopped to dance with his shadow. It was an unattractive sight, and thinking of poor Fleete, brought to such degradation by so foul a creature, I put away all my doubts and resolved to help Strickland from the heated gun barrels to the loop of twine—from the loins to the head and back again—with all tortures that might be needful.

The leper halted in the front porch for a moment and we jumped out on him with the sticks. He was wonderfully strong, and we were afraid that he might escape or be fatally injured before we caught him. We had an idea that lepers were frail creatures, but this proved to be incorrect. Strickland knocked his legs from under him and I put my foot on his neck. He mewed hideously, and even through my riding boots I could feel that his flesh was not the flesh of a clean man.

He struck at us with his hand and feet-stumps. We looped the lash of a dog whip round him, under the armpits and dragged him backwards into the hall and so into the dining room where the beast lay. There we tied him with trunk straps. He made no attempt to escape, but mewed.

When we confronted him with the beast the scene was beyond description. The beast doubled backwards into a bow as though he had been poisoned with strychnine, and moaned in the most pitiable fashion. Several other things happened also, but they cannot be put down here.

"I think I was right," said Strickland. "Now we will ask him to cure this case."

But the leper only mewed. Strickland wrapped a towel round his hand and took the gun barrels out of the fire. I put the half of the broken walking stick through the loop of fishing-line and buckled the leper comfortably to Strickland's bedstead. I understood then how men and women and little children can endure to see a witch burnt alive; for the beast was moaning on the floor, and though the Silver Man had no face, you could see horrible feelings passing through the slab that took its place, exactly as waves of heat play across red-hot iron—gun barrels for instance.

Strickland shaded his eyes with his hands for a moment and we got to work. This part is not to be printed.

The dawn was beginning to break when the leper spoke. His mewings had not been satisfactory up to that point. The beast had fainted from exhaustion and the house was very still. We unstrapped the leper and told him to take away the evil spirit. He crawled to the beast and laid his hand upon the left breast. That was all. Then he fell face down and whined, drawing in his breath as he did so.

We watched the face of the beast, and saw the soul of Fleete coming back into the eyes. Then a sweat broke out on the forehead and the eyes—they were human eyes—closed. We waited for an hour but Fleete still slept. We carried him to his room and bade the leper go, giving him the bedstead, and the sheet on the bedstead to cover his nakedness, the gloves and the towels with which we had touched him, and the whip that had been hooked round his body. He put the sheet about him and went out into the early morning without speaking or mewing.

Strickland wiped his face and sat down. A night-gong, far away in the city, made seven o'clock.

"Exactly four-and-twenty hours!" said Strickland. "And I've done enough to ensure my dismissal from the service, besides permanent quarters in a lunatic asylum. Do you believe that we are awake?"

The red-hot gun barrel had fallen on the floor and was singeing the carpet. The smell was entirely real.

That morning at eleven we two together went to wake up Fleete. We looked and saw that the black leopard-rosette on his chest had disappeared. He was very drowsy and tired, but as soon as he saw us, he said, "Oh! Confound you fellows. Happy New Year to you. Never mix your liquors. I'm nearly dead."

"Thanks for your kindness, but you're over time," said Strickland. "Today is the morning of the second. You've slept the clock round with a vengeance."

The door opened, and little Dumoise put his head in. He had come on foot, and fancied that we were laying out Fleete.

"I've brought a nurse," said Dumoise. "I suppose that she can come in for . . . what is necessary."

"By all means," said Fleete cheerily, sitting up in bed. "Bring on your nurses."

Dumoise was dumb. Strickland led him out and explained that there must have been a mistake in the diagnosis. Dumoise remained dumb and left the house hastily. He considered that his professional reputation had been injured, and was inclined to make a personal matter of the recovery. Strickland went out too. When he came back, he said that he had been to call on the Temple of Hanuman to offer redress for the pollution of the god, and had been solemnly assured that no white man had ever touched the idol and that he was an incarnation of all the virtues laboring under a delusion. "What do you think?" said Strickland.

I said, " 'There are more things . . . ' "

But Strickland hates that quotation. He says that I have worn it threadbare.

One other curious thing happened which frightened me as much as anything in all the night's work. When Fleete was dressed he came into the dining room and sniffed. He had a quaint trick of moving his nose when he sniffed. "Horrid doggy smell, here," said he. "You should really keep those terriers of yours in better order. Try sulphur, Strick."

But Strickland did not answer. He caught hold of the back of a chair, and, without warning, went into an amazing fit of hysterics. It is terrible to see a strong man overtaken with hysteria. Then it struck me that we had fought for Fleete's soul with the Silver Man in that room, and had disgraced ourselves as Englishmen forever, and I laughed and gasped and gurgled just as shamefully as Strickland, while Fleete thought that we had both gone mad. We never told him what we had done.

Some years later, when Strickland had married and was a church-going member of society for his wife's sake, we reviewed the incident dispassionately, and Strickland suggested that I should put it before the public.

I cannot myself see that this step is likely to clear up the mystery; because, in the first place, no one will believe a rather unpleasant story, and, in the second, it is well known to every rightminded man that the gods of the heathen are stone and brass, and any attempt to deal with them otherwise is justly condemned.

THE BIG DREAM

The lights of the car Davin was tailing suddenly swerved right and dropped out of sight: it had run off the road and down the embankment. Davin jerked his Chevy to a stop on the shoulder. A splintered gap in the white wooden retaining fence showed in his headlights, and beyond them the lights of Los Angeles lay spread across the valley.

He slid down the slope, kicking up dust and catching his jacket on the brush. The 1928 Chrysler roadster lay overturned at the bottom, its lights still on. He smelled gasoline as he drew near. The driver had been thrown from the wreck but was already trying to get up; he crouched a few yards away, touching a hand to his head. Davin got his arm around the man's shoulders and helped him stand.

"You all right?" he asked.

The man's voice was thick with booze. "Sure I'm all right. I always take this shortcut."

Davin smiled in the darkness. "Me, I couldn't take the wear and tear."

"You get used to it."

The man was able to walk and together they managed to get back to Davin's car. They climbed in and Davin started down the mountain again.

"The cops will spot that break in the fence within a couple of hours," he said. "You want to see a doctor?"

"No. Just take me home. 2950 Leeward. I'll call the police from there." Davin kept his eyes on the winding road; the Chevy needed its brakes tightened. His passenger seemed to sober remarkably quickly. He sat straighter in the seat and brushed his hair back with his hands like a college kid before a date. Maybe the fact that he'd almost killed himself had actually made an impression on him. "I'm lucky you happened along," the man said. "What's your name?"

"Michael Davin."

"Irish, huh?" There was a casual contempt in his voice.

"On my father's side."

"My father was a swine. Mother was Irish. Not Catholic, though." The contempt flashed again.

"Maybe you ought to go a little easier," Davin said.

The man tensed as if about to take a poke at Davin, then relaxed. He seemed completely sober now. "Perhaps you're right," he said.

Davin recognized the accent: British, faded from long residence in the U.S. The wife hadn't told him that. They rode in silence until they hit the outskirts of the city. Town, really. Despite what the Chamber of Commerce and the Planning Commission and the Police Department could do about it, the neighborhoods still had some of the sleepy feel of Hutchinson, Kansas. Davin sometimes felt right at home helping a businessman keep track of his partner—they would do that in Kansas, too; that would just be good town sense. And that reminded him that no matter how sick he got of LA, he couldn't stand to go back to the Midwest.

Davin knew that the address the man gave him was not his home. It was a Spanish-style bungalow court apartment in a middle-class neighborhood; Davin had begun trailing him at his real home on West Twelfth Street earlier that evening. He pulled over against the curb. The man hesitated before getting out.

"I'm sorry about that remark. The Irish, I mean. My grandmother was a terrible snob."

"Don't worry about it. You better have someone take a look at that bump on your head."

"I'll have my wife look at it." The man stood holding the door open, leaning in. His fine features were thrown into relief by the streetlight ahead of them. "Thank you," he said. "You might have saved my life."

Davin suddenly felt dizzy. He seemed to be outside himself, floating two feet above his own shoulder, listening to himself talk and think.

"All in a day's work," I said, and watched as the philanderer turned and strode up the walk to the door of bungalow number seven. He let himself in with his own key. An attractive young woman—his mistress— embraced him on the doorstep. They call LA the City of the Angels, but a private dick knows better.

It had started very quietly the day before, Friday. Before the knock on his door, there had been no dizziness, no feeling of doing things he did not want to say or do. Davin had been sitting in his office in the late afternoon, legs up on the scarred desk top and tie loosened against the stifling heat. Dust motes swirled in the sunlight slicing through the window over his shoulder. In the harsh light, the cheap sofa against the wall opposite him seemed to be radiating dust into the room. The blinds cut the light into parallel lances that slashed across the room like the tines of a fork.

It was the second week of the heat wave. The days seemed endless and thinking was more effort than his mind wanted to make. He had remembered waking one morning that week and imagining himself back in Wichita on one of those days that dawn warm and moist in early August and you know that by three o'clock there'll be reports of at least four old people dropping dead in airless apartments. That was how hot it had been in LA during the last two weeks.

He had the bottle of bootleg bourbon out and the glass beside it was half empty. Then the knock sounded on the door.

Davin drained the glass and stashed it and the bottle in the bottom desk drawer. "Come in," he said. "It's not locked."

A young woman entered.

Davin was tugging his tie straight when he realized the woman wasn't young after all. She sat in the chair opposite him and crossed her legs coquettishly, but worn hands and the tired line of her jaw gave her away. She wore a cloche hat and sunglasses—probably to mask crow's-feet around her eyes—and a white silk dress cut just above the knee. The hair curling out from under the hat was bleached blond. Maybe it didn't work anymore, but Davin could tell that she was a woman who had become used to men's attention at an early age.

"How may I help you, ma'am?"

She fluttered for about five seconds, then answered in a voice so alluring it made him shiver. He wanted to close his eyes and simply listen to the voice.

"I need to speak to you about my husband, Mr. Davin. I'm terribly worried about him. He's been behaving in a way I can only describe as destructive. He's threatening our marriage, and I am afraid that he may eventually hurt himself."

"What would you like me to do, Mrs. . . . "

"Chandler. Mrs. Raymond Chandler." She smiled, and more lines showed around her mouth. "You may call me Cecily."

"Keeping people's husbands from hurting themselves is not normally in my line of business, Mrs. Chandler."

"That's not exactly what I want you to do." She hesitated. "I want you to follow him and find out where he's going. Sometimes he disappears and I don't know where he is. I call his office and they say he isn't there. They say they don't know where he is."

So far it was something short of self-destruction. "How often does this happen, and how long is he gone?"

Cecily Chandler bit her lip. "It's been more and more frequent. Two or three times a month—in addition to the times he comes home late. Sometimes he's gone for days."

Davin reacted to her story as if she had handed him a script and told him to start reading.

I could have told her the problem was probably blond. "Where does he work?" I asked.

"The South Basin Oil Company. The office is on South Olive Street. He's the vice president."

I told myself to bump the fee to $25 a day. "Okay," I said. "I'll keep tabs on your husband for a week, Mrs. Chandler, but I'll be blunt with you. It's a common thing in this town for husbands to stray. There's too much bad money and too many eager starlets out for a percentage of the gross. One way or the other, no matter what I find out, you're going to have to work this problem out with him yourself."

Instead of taking offense, the woman smiled. "You don't need to treat me like an ingenue, Mr. Davin. . . . "

McKinley had been president when she was an ingenue.

"Wives stray, too," she continued, her voice like sunlight on silk. "I won't be surprised if you come to me with that kind of news. I only want Raymond to be happy."

Sure, I thought. Me too. Then I thought about my bank account. This smelled like divorce, but a couple of hundred dollars would go a long way toward sweetening my outlook on life. We talked terms and I asked a few more questions.

Somewhere in the middle of this conversation the script got lost, and bemused, Davin fell back into his own person.

"How long have you been married?"

"Five years."

"What kind of car does your husband drive?"

"He has two. A Hupmobile for business and a Chrysler roadster for his own."

"Do you have a picture of him?"

Cecily Chandler opened her tiny purse and pulled out a two-by-three Kodak. It showed a dark-haired man with a strong chin, lips slightly pursed, penetrating dark eyes. A good-looking man, maybe in his late thirties—at least fifteen years younger than the woman in Davin's office.

Davin sat in his car outside the Leeward bungalow and waited. He had driven off after Chandler went inside, cruised around the neighborhood for five minutes and come back to park down the street, in the dark between two streetlights, where he could watch the door to number seven and not be spotted easily.

It seemed that he spent a great deal of time watching things—people's houses, men at Santa Anita, an orange grove so far out Main Street you couldn't smell City Hall, people's cars, waitresses in restaurants, the light fixture over his bed, young men and women at the botanical gardens—and almost as much time making sure he wasn't spotted. That was how you found out things. You watched and waited and sometimes they came to you. Davin wondered why the hell he'd started acting wise to the Chandler woman. He didn't do that. He'd always been the type of man who became inconspicuous when the trouble started. Maybe all the watching was getting to him.

It hadn't taken long after Cecily Chandler had hired him for Davin to find out about the mistress in number seven. He had followed Chandler after he left work at the Bank of Italy building that afternoon. The woman had met him at a restaurant not far away and they had gone right to her bungalow.

So it was a simple case of infidelity, as he had known the minute the wife had talked about her husband's disappearances. Davin hated the smell of marriages going bad: tell her and let her get some other sucker to follow it up. That was the logical next step. But something kept Davin from writing it off at that. First, Chandler's wife had clearly known he was seeing some other woman before she came to see Davin. She had not hired him for that information.

A Ford with the top down and a couple of sailors in it drove by slowly, and Davin slid lower in his seat as the headlights flashed over the front seat of his car. The sailors seemed to be looking for an address. Maybe Chandler's girlfriend—M. Peterson according to the name on her mailbox—took in boarders.

Second, there was the question of why Chandler had married a woman old enough to be his mother. Money was the usual answer. But South Basin was one of the strongest companies to come out of the Signal Hill strikes, and a vice president had to have a lot of scratch in his own name. He could have married her for love. But there was another possibility: Cecily Chandler had something she could use against her husband, and that was how they got married. And that was why he wasn't faithful, and that led to the third thing that kept Davin from ending his investigation there.

Chandler *was* acting as if he wanted to kill himself. Davin had started following him again Saturday morning, had stuck with Chandler as he opened the day with lunch at a cheap restaurant and had gone home to Cecily in the afternoon. Davin ate a sandwich in his car. He'd picked Chandler up again as he'd headed to an airfield with another man of about his age and they went for an airplane ride. Someone in the family had to have money.

Davin had loitered around the hangar until they returned. A kid working on the oilpan of a Pierce Arrow told him that Chandler and his friend, Philleo, came out to go flying every month or so. When the plane landed the pilot jumped out, cussing Chandler, and stalked toward the office; Philleo was helping Chandler walk and Chandler was laughing. A mechanic asked what was going on, and the pilot told him loudly that Chandler had unbuckled himself when they were doing a series of barrel rolls and stood up in his seat.

Chandler got a bottle of gin out of the backseat of his roadster. Philleo tried to stop him but soon they were pals again. After that they'd driven up into the hills to a roadhouse speakeasy outside the city limits. When Chandler left in his white Chrysler, Davin had followed him down the winding road until he'd run through the fence.

The Ford with the sailors in it passed him going the other way, now. Other than that there was little traffic in the neighborhood. Chandler was sure to stay put for the night. Davin thought about getting something to eat. He thought about getting some sleep in a real bed. He was getting stiff from all the time he had spent sitting in his car. The heat made his shirt stick to his back. Worst of all, this kind of work got you in the kidneys. He tried to remember why he'd gotten into it.

After the war, being with the Pinkertons had been easy. At least until he'd gotten his fill of busting the heads of union organizers during the Red Scare. The city had to keep its good business reputation and Davin had done his part until one night when he caught a man in a railyard and realized that he liked using a club on an unconscious man. If one of the others had not pulled Davin off, he would have beaten the man to death. He'd woken up feeling great the next day and only began to tremble when he remembered why he felt so good. It scared him. He didn't want to kill anybody but after that night he realized that he could do it easily, and enjoy it. So he quit the Pinkertons, but he couldn't quite quit the work. He was his own agent now. He sat and watched and waited for that violence to happen again, and in the meantime stirred up other people's dirt at twenty bucks a day.

Davin had enough dirt for two days' work. As he was about to start the car, he noticed, in the rear-view mirror, the flare of light as someone lit a cigarette in a parked car some distance behind him on the other side of the street. The car had been there some time and he had neither heard nor seen anyone come or go.

Davin got out, crossed the street and walked down the sidewalk toward the car. A woman sat inside, leaning sideways against the door, smoking. She was watching the apartments where Chandler had met his girlfriend. She glanced briefly at Davin as he approached but made no effort to hide. As he came abreast of the car he pulled out a cigarette and fumbled in his jacket as if looking for a match.

"Say, miss, do you have a light?"

She looked up at him and without a word handed him a book of matches. He lit up.

"Thanks." Her hair looked black in the faint light of the street. It was cut very short; her lips were full and her nose straight. She looked serious.

"Are you waiting for someone?" Davin asked.

"Not you."

Davin took a guess. "Chandler's not going to be out again tonight, you know."

Bull's-eye. The girl looked from the bungalow toward him, upset. She ground out her cigarette.

"I don't know what you're talking about."

"Chandler and the Peterson woman are having a party right now. Too bad we weren't invited, though I bet you'd like to be. Maybe we ought to get a cup of coffee and figure out why."

The girl reached for the ignition and Davin put a hand through the open window to stop her. She tensed, then relaxed.

"All right," she said. "Get in."

She drove to an all-night diner on Wilshire. In the bright light Davin saw that she was small and very tired. Slender, well dressed, she did not look like a woman who was used to following married men around. Davin wondered if he looked like the kind of man who was.

"My name is Michael Davin, Miss . . . ?"

"Estelle Lloyd." She looked worried.

"Miss Lloyd. I have some business with Mr. Chandler and that makes me want to know why you're watching him."

"Cissy hired you." It was not a question.

Davin was momentarily surprised. "Who's Cissy?"

"Cissy is his wife. I know she wants to know what he's been doing. He's killing himself."

"What difference should that make to you?"

Estelle looked at him steadily for a few seconds. She was young, but she was no kid.

"I love him too," she said.

Estelle's father, Warren Lloyd, was a philosophy professor, and her uncle Ralph was a partner of Joseph Dabney, founder of the South Basin Oil Company. She told Davin that when she was just a girl her father and mother had been friends with Julian and Cissy Pascal, and that the two families had helped out a young man from England named Raymond Chandler when he arrived in California before the war.

Estelle had had a crush on the young man from the time she reached her teens, and he in turn had treated her like his favorite girl. It was all very romantic, the kind of play where men and women pretended there was no such thing as sex. When Chandler had gone away to the war, Estelle had worried and prayed, and when he came back she had not been the only one to expect a romance to develop. One did: between Chandler and Cissy Pascal, eighteen years his senior.

Cissy filed for divorce. Estelle was confused and hurt, and Chandler would have nothing to do with her. The minute she had become old enough for real love, he had abandoned her.

Chandler's mother did not like Cissy and so Raymond did not marry her right away. Instead he took an apartment for Cissy at Hermosa Beach and another for his mother in Redondo Beach. Despite the scandal, Estelle's uncle helped Chandler get a job in the oil business, and he rose rapidly in the company. Estelle kept her opinions to herself, but although she dated some nice young men, she was never serious. Davin wanted to like her. Looking into her open face, he wasn't sure he could keep himself from doing so.

"So why are you waiting around outside his girlfriend's apartment?"

Estelle looked at him speculatively. "Did Cissy hire you to watch him or do you like peeking in bedroom windows?"

He did like her. "*Touché.* I won't ask any more rude questions."

"I'll tell you anyway. I just don't want to see him hurt himself. I know there's no chance for me anymore—I knew it a long time ago." She hesitated, and when she spoke there was a trace of scorn in her voice. "There's something wrong with Raymond anyway. He's not made Cissy happy and he would be making me miserable too if I were in her place."

"What do you think the problem is?"

She smiled sadly. "I don't think he likes women. He uses them, gets disgusted because they let themselves get used, and calls it love."

"Now you sound bitter."

"I'm not, really. He's a good man at heart."

Davin finished his coffee. Everyone was worried about Chandler. "It's late," he said. "It's time for you to take me back."

It was no cooler in the street than it had been in the diner. Davin lit a cigarette while Estelle drove, and when she spoke the strange mood of the last two days was on him again.

Hesitantly, softly, in a voice that promised more heat than the California night, she said to me, "You don't have to stay there watching all night. I have an apartment at the Bryson."

It was like she'd pulled a thirty-eight on me. It was the last thing I expected. Her eyes flitted over me quickly as if she were measuring me for a suit of clothes. I could smell her faint perfume.

"No, thanks," I said. I almost gagged on the sweet scent of her. Ten minutes before, I had liked her, and now I saw her for what she really was. It was tough enough for a private eye to keep himself clean in this town; I'd expected better of this woman.

She let me off in the deserted street and drove away. I stood on the sidewalk watching the retreating lights of her car, inhaling deeply the scent of bougainvillea and night-blooming jasmine like overripe dreams, trying to figure out what Estelle's game might be.

A light was on in the Peterson bungalow. The curtains were partly drawn and the eucalyptus outside the window obscured his view. The night had cooled and a breeze that still held something of the sea rustled the trees as it wafted heavy, sweet air from the courtyard garden. A few clouds were sliding north toward the hills where Chandler's roadster lay at the bottom of an embankment; the high full moon turned Leeward Street into a scene in silver and black. Davin wondered at his own prudishness. He had not been propositioned so readily in a long time and had not turned down an offer like that in a longer one. As he reached his car he noticed a Ford with its top down parked in front of him. The sailors had found their address.

Something kept him from leaving. Instead he circled around the back of the bungalows until he reached number seven. The rear windows were unlit. Remembering Estelle's taunt, he crept to the side and looked in the lighted window. Through the gap in the curtains he could see a woman curled in the corner of a sofa beside a chintzy table lamp. She wore scarlet lounging pajamas. Her hair curled around her face in blond Mary Pickford ringlets; her lips were a bright red cupid's bow and she was painting her toenails fastidiously in the same color. Davin could not tell if there was anyone else in the room, but the woman did not act like she expected to be interrupted. Sometimes that was the best time to interrupt.

He walked around to the front and rang the bell. The scent of jasmine was even stronger. The door opened a crack, fastened by a chain, and the red lips spoke to him.

"Do you know what time it is? Who are you?"

"My name is Michael Davin. You're awake. I'd like to talk to you."

"We're talking."

"Pardon me. I thought we were playing peek-a-boo with a door between us."

The red lips smiled. The eyes—startling blue—didn't.

"All right, Davin. Come in and be a tough guy in the light where I can get a look at you." She unchained the door. That meant Chandler was gone. "Don't get the idea I'm in the habit of letting strange men in to see me in the middle of the night."

"Sure." She led him into the small living room. The pajamas were silk, with the name "May" stitched in gold over her left breast, and had probably cost more than the chair she offered Davin.

He sat on the sofa next to her instead. She ignored him and returned to painting her nails. The room was furnished with cheap imitations of expensive furniture: the curtains that looked like plush velvet the color of dark blood were too readily disturbed by the slight breeze through the window to be the real thing; the Spanish-style carpet was more Tijuana than Barcelona. May Peterson held her chin high to show off a fine profile and the clear white skin of her shoulders and breasts, but the blond hair had been brown once. The figure, however, was genuine.

"You like this color?" she asked him.

"It's very nice."

She shifted position, crossing her right foot in front of her, and leaned on his shoulder.

"Watch your balance," he said.

She pulled away and looked at him. "You're really here to talk? So talk." May's boldness surprised and attracted him. It was not just brass; she acted as if she knew what she was doing and had nothing to hide. As if she knew exactly who she was at every moment. As if she didn't have time for lying, as if the idea of lying never crossed her mind.

"Where's Chandler?" he asked her.

She did not flinch; her eyes were steady on his. "Gone. Sometimes he doesn't stay all night. You should try his wife."

"Maybe I should. Apparently he doesn't anymore."

"That's not my fault."

"Didn't say it was. But I bet you make it easier for him to forget where he lives."

May dipped the brush in the polish and finished off a perfect baby toe.

"You don't know Ray very well if you think I had to seduce him. Sure, he likes to think it was out of his control—lotsa men do. But before me he was all over half the girls in the office."

"You work in his office?"

"Six months in accounting. He hired me himself. Maybe he didn't think he hired me because I got a nice figure, but I figured out pretty quick that was in the back of his mind." She smiled. "Pretty soon it was in front."

If May was worried about what Davin was after, who he was or why he was asking questions, she did not show it. That didn't make sense. Maybe she was setting him up for some fall, or maybe he was in detective's paradise, where all the questions had answers and all the women wanted to go to bed.

May removed the cotton balls from between her toes and closed the bottle of polish. "There," she said, snuggling up against me. "Doesn't that look fine?"

Beneath the smell of the nail polish was the musky odor of woman and perfume. It seemed to be my night for propositions; I felt unclean. I needed to plunge into cold salt water to peel away the smell of my own flesh and hers. The world revolves by people rutting away like monkeys in the zoo, but I had enough self-respect to keep away from the cage. As much as I wanted to sometimes, I couldn't let myself be drawn down into the mire; I had to keep free because I had a job to do.

Wait a minute, Davin thought. Even if May knew he was a detective, she had to realize that bedding him wouldn't protect Chandler. So why be a monk? Cold salt water? Rutting in the zoo?

I didn't move an eyelash. The pajamas fit her like rainwater. Lloyd's of London probably carried the insurance on her perfect breasts. The nipples were beautifully erect. I got up.

"All right, May, pack it up for the night; I'm not in the market. Tell your friend Raymond that he's going to find himself in trouble if he keeps playing hooky. And you can bring your sailor pals back into the slip as soon as I leave."

"Sailor pals? What are you talking about?"

"Don't forget your manners, now. You're the hostess."

She looked at me as if I'd turned to white marble by an Italian master. Davin, rampant.

"Look, I'm not stupid," she said. "I figure you must be working for his wife. Big deal."

I looked down into her very blue eyes: maybe she was just a girl who worked in an office after all, one who got involved with the boss and didn't want any trouble. Maybe she was okay. But a voice whispered to me to see her the way she was—that a woman who looked like May, who said the things she said, was a whore.

"Sure, you're not stupid, May. Sure you're not. But some people take marriage seriously. Good night."

She stayed on the sofa, watching him; as soon as he closed the door behind him, he felt lost. He had just exited on some line about the sanctity of marriage. He'd pulled away from her as if she had leprosy, as if she had tempted him to jump off a cliff. He wasn't a kid and this wasn't some Boy Scout story. He had a job to do, but he wasn't a member of the Better Business Bureau. He was talking like a smart aleck and acting like an undergraduate at a Baptist college.

He drew a deep breath and fumbled in his pocket for his cigarettes. The moon was gone and morning would not be long in coming. It was as cool as it was going to get in any twenty-four hours and it still felt like ninety-five and climbing; the heat wave would not let up.

He started up the walk toward the street and a blow like someone dropping a cinder block on the back of his neck knocked him senseless.

The jasmine smelled good, but lying under a bush in a flower bed dimmed your appreciation. Davin rolled over and started to look for the back of his skull. It was not in plain sight. He got to his knees, then shakily stood. He didn't know how long he'd been out. It was still dark, but the eastern sky was smoked glass turning to mother-of-pearl. The door to May Peterson's bungalow was ajar and her light was still on. Head throbbing, Davin pushed the door slowly open and stepped in.

The lounging pajamas were torn open and she lay on the floor with one leg part way under the sofa and the other twisted awkwardly at the knee. Her neck had not gone purple from the bruises yet. All in all, she had died without putting up much of a struggle. The shade of the chintzy table lamp was awry but the bottle of nail polish was just where she'd left it. Someone had taken the trouble to pull the phony curtains completely closed.

Davin knelt over her and brushed the hair back from her forehead. Her hair was soft and thick and still fragrant. A deep cut on her scalp left the back of her head dark and wet with blood. The very blue eyes were open and staring as if she were trying to comprehend what had happened to her.

Davin shuddered. Light was beginning to seep in through the curtains. The small kitchen was in immaculate order, the two-burner gas stove spotless in the dim morning light; the bedclothes of the large bed in the back room were disordered but nothing else was disturbed. A cut-glass decanter of bourbon stood on the dressing table with its stopper and two glasses beside it. Davin felt a hundred years old. He rubbed the swelling at the back of his neck where he'd been slugged—the pain shot through his temples—and left May Peterson's apartment quietly and quickly.

He drove down to use the pay phone at the diner where he and Estelle had had coffee. Fumbling to find the number in his wallet—whoever had hit him hadn't bothered to rob him—he dialed the Chandler home. A sleepy woman answered the phone.

"Mrs. Chandler?"

"Yes?"

"This is Michael Davin. Is your husband at home?"

A pause. He could see her debating whether to try to save her pride. "No," she said. "I haven't seen him since he went out with Milton Philleo yesterday afternoon."

"Okay. Listen to me carefully. Your husband is in serious trouble, and he needs your help. The police are going to try to connect him with a murder. I don't think he had anything to do with it. Tell them the truth about him but don't tell them about me."

"Have you found out what Raymond has been involved in?"

Davin hesitated.

"Mr. Davin—I'm paying you for information. Don't leave me in the dark." The voice that had been so thrillingly sexy two days before was that of a worried old woman.

The light in the telephone booth seemed cruelly harsh; the air in the cramped space smelled of stale cigarette smoke. Behind the counter of the diner a waitress in white was refilling the stainless steel coffee urn.

"The less you know right now the easier it will go when the police call you," Davin said. There was no immediate answer. He felt sorry for her, and he thought about the hurt look in Estelle's eyes. "It's pretty much what I told you I suspected in my office."

"Oh."

Davin shook his head to dispel his weariness. "There's one more thing. Do you know of anyone who has it in for your husband? Anyone who'd like to see him in trouble?"

"John Abrams." There was certainty in her voice.

"Who is he?"

"He works for South Basin, in the Signal Hill field. He and Raymond have never gotten along. He's a petty man. He resents Raymond's ability."

"Do you know where he lives?"

"In Santa Monica. If you'll wait a minute I can see whether Raymond has his address in his book."

"Don't bother. Remember now—when the police call, say nothing about me. Raymond is not involved in this."

Davin hung up and opened the door of the booth, but did not get up immediately. It was full day outside; the waitress was drawing coffee for herself and the dayside short-order cook. Davin considered a cup. He decided against it but made himself eat two eggs over easy, with toast, then headed home for a couple of hours of sleep. He wished he were as certain that Chandler hadn't killed May as he'd told Cissy.

The sun was shining in his eyes when Davin woke the next morning; the sun never came in through his bedroom window that early. The sheets, sticky with sweat, were twisted around his legs. The air was stifling and his mouth felt like a dustpan. He fumbled for the clock on the bedside table and saw it was already one-thirty. The phone rang.

"Is this Mr. Michael Davin?"

"What is it, Cissy?"

"The police just left here a few minutes ago. I have to thank you for warning me. They told me about May Peterson."

She stopped as if waiting for some response. He was still half asleep and the back of his head was suing for divorce. After a moment she went on.

"I didn't tell them anything, as you suggested, but in the course of their questions they told me the neighbor who found Miss Peterson's body saw a man leave her apartment in the early morning. Was it Raymond? Do you know?"

"It was me," Davin said tiredly. "Have you heard anything from him?"

"No."

"Then why don't you let me do the investigating, Cissy—Mrs. Chandler."

There was an offended silence, then the phone clicked. Davin let the dial tone mock him for a moment before he hung up. He ought not to have been so blunt, but what did the woman expect? He wondered if Cissy had had any doubts before divorcing Pascal for Chandler. Pascal was a concert cellist, Estelle had told him. Older than Cissy. She had married for love that time. Davin imagined her a woman who had always been beautiful, bright, the center of attention. He supposed it was hard for such a woman to grow old: she would become reclusive, self-doubting, alternating between attempts to be youthful and knowledge that she wasn't anymore. He wondered what Chandler thought about her.

The speculations tasted worse than his cotton mouth. Men and women—over and over again Davin's job rubbed his nose in cases of them fouling each other up. Maybe beating up union men for a living was cleaner work after all. He pulled himself out of bed and into the bathroom. He felt hung over but without the compensation of having been drunk the night before.

A shower helped and a shave made him look almost alert. Measuring his narrow jaw and long nose in the mirror, he tried to imagine what had gotten those women so hot the previous night. What had moved May to let him into her apartment so easily? Maybe that had only been a pleasant fantasy; fantasies sometimes were called upon to serve for a sex life, as Cissy Chandler and Davin both knew. His revulsion toward both May and Estelle had been a less pleasant fantasy.

The memory of May Peterson's dead, bemused stare—that was neither pleasant nor fantasy.

While he dressed he turned on the radio and heard a report about the brutal murder that had taken place on Leeward Avenue the previous night. The weather forecast was for a high of 100 that afternoon. Davin pawed through the drawer in the table beside his bed until he found a black notebook and his phony horn-rimmed glasses. His Harold Lloyd glasses, he called them. He sat down and called the Santa Monica operator. There was a John Abrams on Harvard Street.

It was a white frame house that might have been shipped in from Des Moines. The wide porch was shaded by a slanting roof. Carefully tended poinsettias fronted the porch, and a lawn only slightly better kept than the Wilshire Country Club's sloped down to a sidewalk so white that the reflected sunlight hurt Davin's eyes. The leaded glass window in the front door was cut in a large oval with diamond-shaped prisms in the corners. Davin pressed the button and heard a bell ring inside.

The man who came to the door was large; his face was broad, with the high cheekbones and big nose of an Indian. He wore khaki pants with suspenders and a good dress shirt, collarless, the top buttons undone.

"Are you Mr. John Abrams? You work for the Dabney Oil Syndicate?" The blunt face stayed blunt. "Yes."

Davin held out his hand. "My name is Albert Parker, Mr. Abrams. I'm with Mutual Assurance of Hartford. We're running an investigation on another employee of South Basin Oil and would like to ask you a few questions. Anything you say will be held strictly confidential, of course."

"Who are you investigating?"

"A Mr. Raymond Chandler."

Abrams' eyebrows flicked a fraction of an inch. "Come in," he said. He ushered Davin into the living room. They sat down, Davin got out his notebook, and Abrams looked him over—the kind of look Davin suspected was supposed to make employees stiffen and try to look dependable.

Abrams leaned forward. "Is this about any litigation he's started lately? I wouldn't want to talk about anything that's in court."

"No. This is entirely a matter between Mutual and Mr. Chandler. We are seeking information about his character. In your opinion, is Mr. Chandler a reliable man?"

"I don't consider him reliable," Abrams said, watching for Davin's reaction. Davin gave him nothing.

"We've got a hundred wells out on Signal Hill and I'm the field manager," Abrams continued. "I like working for Mr. Dabney. He's a good man." He paused, and the silence stretched.

"Look, I don't know who told you to talk to me, but I'll tell you right now I don't like Chandler. He's a martinet and a hypocrite: he'll flatter Mr. Dabney on Tuesday morning and cuss him out for not backing one of his lawsuits on Tuesday afternoon. He runs that office like his little harem. If you'd watch him for a week you'd know."

"Yes."

Abrams got up and began pacing. "I've got no stomach for talking about a man behind his back," he said. "But Chandler is hurting the company and Mr. Dabney. He's dragged us into lawsuits just to prove how tough he is; he had us in court last year on a personal injury suit that the insurance company was ready to settle on, and then after he won—he did win—he turned around and canceled the policy. That soured a lot of people on South Basin Oil.

"The only reason he was hired was because he had an in with Ralph Lloyd. He started in accounting. So he sucks up to Bartlett, the auditor, and gets the reputation for being some kind of fair-haired college boy. A year later Bartlett gets arrested for embezzling thirty thousand dollars. Tried and convicted.

"Now it gets real interesting. Instead of promoting Chandler, Dabney goes out and hires a man named John Ballantine from a private accounting firm. This suits Chandler just fine because Ballantine's from Scotland and Chandler impresses the hell out of him with his British upper-crust manners. Ballantine makes Chandler his assistant. A year later Ballantine drops dead in the office. Chandler helps the coroner and the coroner decides it was a heart attack. Mr. Dabney gives up and makes Chandler the new auditor, and within another year he's office manager and vice president. Very neat, huh?"

Abrams had worked himself into a lather. Davin could have let him run on with just a few more neutral questions, but instead, as if someone else had taken over and was using his body like a ventriloquist's dummy, he said:

"You really hate him, don't you?"

Abrams froze. After a moment his big shoulders relaxed and his voice was back under control. "You've got to admit the story smells like a day-old mackerel."

"To hear you tell it."

"You don't have to believe me. Ask anyone on Olive Street. Check it with the coroner or the cops."

"If the cops thought there was anything to it I wouldn't have to check with them. Chandler would be spending his weekends in the exercise yard instead of with those girls you tell me about."

Abrams' brow furrowed. He looked like a theologian trying to fathom Aimee Semple McPherson. "Cops aren't always too smart," he said.

"A startling revelation." I was getting to like Abrams. He reduced the moral complexities of this case. He reminded me of a hand grenade ready to explode, and I was going to throw my body at him to save Raymond Chandler. "Mostly they aren't smart when somebody pays them not to be," I said. "Does the vice president of an oil company have that kind of money?"

"Don't overestimate a cop's integrity."

"Who, me? I'm just an insurance investigator. You're the one who knows what it costs to bribe cops."

The big shoulders were getting tense again, but the voice was under control. "Look, I didn't start this talk about bribes. You asked me my opinion. I gave it; let's leave it at that."

He was right; I should have left it at that. Instead I pushed on like a fighter who knows the fix is on and it's only a matter of time before the other guy takes a dive.

"So Chandler killed Ballantine?" I said. "What about May Peterson?" I felt good. I was baiting a man who could wring me out like a dishrag and who looked like he was about ready to.

"Peterson? Never heard of her. What kind of insurance man are you, anyway?"

"I'm investigating an accident. Maybe you were out a little late last night?"

Abrams took a step toward me. "Let's see your credentials, pal."

I got up. "You wouldn't hit a man with glasses on, Abrams. Let me turn my back."

"Get the hell out of here."

A woman wearing a gardening apron and gloves had come into the room. The house, which had seemed so cool when I'd entered, felt like an inferno. I slid the notebook into my pocket and left. The porch swing hung steady as a candle flame in a tomb; the sun on the sidewalk reawakened my headache. Abrams stood in the doorway watching as I walked down to the car. When I reached it he went back inside.

Davin shuddered convulsively, loosened his tie, leaned against the car. He squinted and focused on the street to keep the fear down: he was a sick man. He'd totally lost control of himself in Abrams' house. He wondered if that was what it felt like to go crazy—to do and say things as if you were drunk and watching yourself in a movie. He lifted his hand, looked at the hairy backs of his knuckles. He touched his thumb to each of his fingertips. His hand did exactly what he told it to. He seemed to be able to do whatever he wanted; he could call Cissy Chandler and tell her to sweat out her marriage by herself. He could drive home and sleep for twelve hours and wake up alone and free. What was to stop him?

Davin was about to get into the car when he noticed a piece of wire lying on the pavement below his running board. Just a piece of wire. The freshly clipped end glinted in the sunlight. He bent over and tried to pick it up: it was attached to something beneath the car. Getting down on one knee, he saw the trailing wires where someone had cut each of his brake cables.

He rode the interurban east on Santa Monica Boulevard. Along the way he enjoyed what little breeze the streetcar's passage gave to the hot, syrupy air. He got off at Cahuenga and walked north toward his office on Ivar and Hollywood Boulevard, trying to piece together what had happened.

Abrams could have told his wife to take the pruning shears and cut the cables as soon as he recognized Davin on the porch. Abrams would have recognized Davin only if he was the one who had slugged Davin and gone on to murder May Peterson. He might have done it out of some misplaced desire to get back at Chandler.

But there was a problem with this theory. Why would Abrams go on to slander Chandler so badly? It would look better if he hid any hostility he felt.

When Davin considered the picture of a middle-aged woman in gardening gloves crawling under a car on a residential street in broad daylight to cut brake cables, the whole card house collapsed. It couldn't be done, and not only that—Abrams simply had no reason to try such a stupid thing.

Then there was the question of why Davin had been slugged in the first place. Something about that had bothered him all day, and now he knew what it was: Whoever killed May had no reason to knock out Davin. Davin had been on his way out, and sapping him only meant he would be around to find her dead. It didn't make any sense.

Near the corner of Cahuenga and the boulevard he spotted a penny lying on the sidewalk. The bright copper shone in the late afternoon sun like a chip of heaven dropped at his feet. Normally he would have stopped to pick it up; one of the habits bred of a boyhood spent in a small town where a penny meant your pick of the best candies on display in Sudlow's Dry Goods. Instead he crossed the street.

But his mind, bemused by the puzzles of the cut brake cables and the senseless blow on the head, got stuck on this new mystery. If he'd paused to pick up the penny, he would have been a little later getting to the office. The whole sequence of events afterwards would be subtly different; it was as if stopping or not stopping marked a fork in the chain of happenings that made his life.

The strange frame of mind refused to leave him. Normally he *would* have stopped, so by not stopping he had set himself down a track of possibilities he would not normally have followed. Why hadn't he stopped? What had pushed him down this particular path? The incident expanded frighteningly in his mind until it swept away all other thoughts. Something had hold of him. It was just like the conversation with Abrams where he'd gone for the jugular—something was changing every decision he made, no matter how minor. With a conviction that chilled him on this hottest of days, he knew that he was being manipulated and that there was nothing he could do about it. He wondered how long it had been happening without his knowing it. He should have picked up that penny.

After a moment the conviction went away. No. To think that way was insane. He was tired and needed a drink. He could talk himself into all kinds of doubts if he let himself. He ought to take a good punch at the next passerby just to prove he could do whatever he wanted.

He didn't punch anybody.

Davin took the elevator up seven floors to his office. Quintanella and Sanderson from Homicide were in the waiting room.

"You don't keep your door locked," Sanderson said.

"I can't afford to turn away business."

Sanderson mashed his cigarette out in the standing ashtray and got up from the sofa. "Let's have a talk," he said.

Davin led them into the inner room. "What brings you two out to see me on a Sunday?"

"A dead woman," Quintanella said. His face, pocked with acne scars, was stiff as a pine board.

Davin lit a cigarette, shook out the wooden match, broke it in half and dropped the pieces into an ashtray. They pinged as they hit the glass. The afternoon sun was shooting into the room at the same angle it had taken when Cissy Chandler had come into his office.

I'd had about enough of them already.

"That's too bad," I said. "It's a rough business you're in. You going to try to find out who killed this one?"

Sanderson belched. "We are," he said. "And you're gonna help us. You're gonna start by telling us where Raymond Chandler is."

"Don't know the man. Sure you've got the right Davin? There's a couple in the book."

"Will you tell this guy to cut the crap, Dutch?" Quintanella said to Sanderson. "He makes me sick."

"I didn't think they ran to delicate stomachs down at Homicide," I said. "You have to swallow so many lies and keep your mouth shut."

"Tell him to shut up, Dutch."

"Calm down, Davin," Sanderson said.

"You tell me to talk, he tells me to shut up. Every time you guys get a burr in your paws, you make guys like me pull it out for you. Call me Androcles."

"We can do this downtown," Sanderson said. "It's a lot less comfortable down there."

"You got a subpoena in that ugly suit?" The words were rolling out now and I was riding them. "If you don't," I said, "save the back room and the hose for some poor greaser. You want any answers from me, you've got to tell me what's going on. I'm not going to get bruised telling you things you've got no business knowing."

Quintanella flexed his hands. "C'mon, Dutch, let's take him in."

"Shut up, Tony." Sanderson looked pained. "Don't try to kid us, Davin. We got a call from Mrs. Chandler this afternoon telling us she hired you last week. She said you knew about the murder of this call girl last night."

Call girl. The words momentarily shook Davin out of it. That was what Cissy would say, and guys like Sanderson would figure that was the only kind of woman who got murdered.

"Cissy Chandler's not the most reliable source," Davin said.

"That's why we came to you. The neighbor lady at the Rosinante Apartments said she saw a man who looked like you hanging around there last night. So why don't you tell us what's going on. Or should we let Tony take care of it?"

Davin watched them watch him. Quintanella was in the chair near the door, rubbing his left wrist with his other hand. This case was getting beyond him fast. He had no reason to protect Chandler when for all he knew the man had killed May.

"Jesus," Davin said. "You're crazy if you think I need this kind of heat. I'm not in this business to draw fire. I'll talk." He loosened his collar. "Will you let me get a drink out of this desk? No guns, just a little bourbon."

Sanderson came over behind the desk; Quintanella tensed. "You let me get it," Sanderson said. "Which drawer?"

"Bottom right."

Do it. Do it now. It was like Davin's blood talking to him, like the night in the freight yard with the club in his hand. He couldn't stop to pick up the penny.

When Sanderson opened the drawer and reached for the bottle, I punched him in the side of the throat. He fell back, hitting the corner of the desk, and Quintanella, fumbling for his gun, leapt toward me. I slipped around the other side of the desk and out the door before the big man could get the heater out. I was down the stairs and out the exit to the alley before they hit the lobby; I zigzagged half a block between the buildings that backed the alley, crossed the street and slipped into the rear of an apartment building on the opposite side of Ivar. I had just thrown away my investigator's license. I caught my breath and wondered what the hell I was going to do next.

Davin called Estelle from the lobby of the Bryson and she told him to come up. Although it was only early evening, she was in her robe. Her dark hair shone; her face was calm, with a trace of insouciance. She looked like Louise Brooks.

"I've got some trouble," Davin said. "Can I stay here for a while?"

"Yes."

She offered him coffee. They sat facing each other in the small living room. The two windows that fronted the street were open and a hot, humid wind waved the curtains like a tired maid shaking out bedsheets. The air smelled like coming rain. Maybe the heat wave would be broken. Davin told her about his talk with Abrams.

"You don't believe those things he said." There was an urgency in Estelle's voice that Davin supposed came from her love for Chandler. He realized that he didn't want her to care about Chandler at all.

"Did they happen?"

"Bartlett was convicted of embezzling. Ballantine died of a heart attack. Raymond had nothing to do with either of those things."

"He was just lucky."

Estelle exhaled cigarette smoke sharply. "I wouldn't use that word."

"I'm not trying to be sarcastic," Davin said. He hadn't had to try at all lately. "But you have to admit that it all has worked out nicely for him. He meets the right people, makes the right impression, and events break just the way you'd expect them to break if he was in the business of planning embezzlements and heart attacks. I can't blame a guy like Abrams for taking it the wrong way."

"Things don't always work out for Raymond. I know him better than you do. Look at his marriage."

"Okay, let's. Why did he marry her?"

Her brow knit. "He loved her, I guess."

"Why did he wait until his mother died?"

"She didn't approve."

"I'm not surprised. Age difference. But he was pretty old to still be listening to Mom."

Estelle took a last pull on her cigarette, then snuffed it out. Her dark eyes watched him. "I don't know. I don't know if I care anymore."

Davin wanted not to care about the whole case. But he had been hired to watch a man and he had lost that man. In the process a woman had been killed, and he couldn't bring himself to think she deserved it. *It was a matter of professional ethics.*

Ethics? He wasn't some white knight on a horse. The idea of ethics in his business was ludicrous; it made him mad that such an idea had worked its way into his head. Only a schoolboy would expect ethics from a private eye. Only a schoolboy would think less of May Peterson because she had slept with Chandler. Only a schoolboy would have turned Estelle down the previous night.

"I was surprised you asked me here last night," he said.

"That sounds sarcastic, too."

"Not necessarily."

The wind had strengthened and it was blissfully cool. With a sound of distant thunder, the rain started. Estelle got up to close the windows. She drew her robe tighter about her as she stood in the breeze; Davin watched her slender shoulders and hips as she pulled the windows shut. When she came back she folded her legs up under her on the sofa. The line of her neck and shoulders against the darkness of the next room was as pure as the sweep of a child's sparkler through a Fourth of July night. She spoke somberly.

"I used to be a good girl. Being in love with a married man made me think that over. I'm not a good or bad girl anymore; I'm not any kind of girl." She paused. "You don't look to me like you're really the kind of man you're supposed to be."

Davin felt free of compulsion for the first time in the last three days.

"I'm not," he said, in wonder. "I feel like I've been playing some kid's game—or more like dreaming some kid's dream. I feel like I'm just waking."

Estelle simply watched him.

"I'd like to stay with you tonight," Davin said.

She smiled. "Not a very romantic pickup line. Raymond would do it funnier, or more poetic."

"He would?"

"Certainly. He's very poetic. He even wrote poetry—still does, as far as I know. You didn't know that?"

"I haven't been on this case very long. Is it any good?"

"When I was nineteen I loved it. Now I think it'd be too sentimental for me."

"That's too bad."

Estelle came to Davin, sat on the arm of his chair, kissed him. She pulled away, a little out of breath.

"No it isn't," she said.

All during their lovemaking he felt something trying to make him pull away, like a voice whispering over and over, *get up and leave. Go now. She will push you, she will absorb you. Doesn't she smell bad? Isn't she an animal?*

It wasn't conscience. It was something outside him, alien, the same thing that had pulled him away from May Peterson. But Davin had finally picked up that penny, and he felt better, as he lay on the border of sleep, than he had in as long as he could remember. Being with Estelle was the first really good thing that he had done on his own since Friday afternoon. He felt that they were breaking a pattern merely by lying together, tired, limbs entwined. Estelle's breathing was regular, and Davin, listening to the rain, fell asleep.

Davin dreamt there had been a shipwreck and that he and the other passengers were floundering among the debris, trying to keep afloat. There was no sound. He knew the others in the water: Estelle was there, and

Cissy, and Abrams and May Peterson and some others he could not make out—and Chandler. Chandler could not swim, and he clutched at them, one after the other, as if they were pieces of wreckage that he could climb up on in order to keep afloat. They might have made it themselves, but they were all being shoved beneath the waves by the desperate man, and they would drown trying to save him. But Chandler never would drown, and would never understand the people dying around him. He could not even see them. He fumbled for Davin's head, his fingers in Davin's eyes, and Davin found he did not have the strength to shove him away. Davin coughed and sputtered and struggled toward the surface. Fighting against him in the salt sea, Davin saw that for Chandler, he was little more than a broken spar, an inanimate thing to be used without compunction because it was never alive. Drowning, Davin saw that Chandler had forced him under without even realizing what he had done.

He woke. It was still dark. Estelle still slept; some noise from the other room had stirred him. The rain had stopped and streetlights threw a pale wedge of light against the ceiling. Through the doorway, Davin saw something move. Two men slipped quietly into the room.

In the faint light Davin saw that they wore sailors' uniforms and that the smaller of the two had a sap in his hand. Davin snatched the bedside clock and threw it at him.

The man ducked and it glanced off his shoulder. Davin leapt out of the bed, dragging the bedclothes after him. He heard Estelle gasp behind him as he hit the smaller sailor full in the chest. They slammed into the wall and the man hit his head against the doorjamb. He slumped to the floor. Davin struggled to his feet, still tangled in the sheets, and turned to see that the big man had Estelle by the arm, a hand the size of a baseball glove smothering her cries. He dragged her out of bed.

"Quiet now, buddy," the big sailor said in a soft voice. "Else I wring the little girl's neck."

The man on the floor moaned.

"What's the deal?" Davin asked. Estelle's frightened eyes glinted in the dark.

"No deal. We just got some business to take care of."

Davin stood there naked, helpless. He was no Houdini. All he had to keep them alive was words.

"You killed May Peterson," he said. "Why?"

"We had to. To get at that bastard Chandler. He makes a good impression. We wanna see what kind of impression he makes on the cops."

Davin shifted his feet and stepped on something hard. The sap.

"What have you got against him?"

The big man seemed content to stand there all night with his arm around Estelle. He gasped, almost a chuckle. "Personal injury is what. Ten thousand bucks he cheated us outa. We hadda accident with one of his oil trucks. We had it as good as won until he made 'em go to court."

The man at Davin's feet rolled over, started to get up. "Be quiet, Lou," he said.

"What difference's it make," the big sailor said. "They're dead already."

"Be quiet and let's do it. There's other people in this place."

Davin's thoughts raced. "It makes no sense to kill us. I'm no friend of Chandler's. I've been tailing him."

"You was there last night," the small sailor said, poking around the floor in the dark for the sap. "That's good enough. We've got to get rid of you."

"Who says?"

Neither one answered.

"What the hell arc you looking for?" Davin asked.

"You'll know soon enough," the short one said.

"Damn, you guys are stupid. This doesn't make any sense. How do you expect to get away with this?"

Big Lou jerked back on his arm and Estelle struggled ineffectually. "It was you two that got caught in the bed together, right? Like a coupla animals? You don't deserve to live." He spoke with wounded innocence, as if he had explained everything. As if, Davin realized, he was hearing the same voice that had whispered to him. Davin trembled, furious, holding himself back, feeling himself ready to fight and afraid of what might happen if he did. Don't move, he thought.

Move.

The shorter sailor was still obsessed with finding his weapon, shuffling through the sheets on the floor, picking up Estelle's discarded camisole with two fingers as if it were a dead carp.

"Let me help," I said; I snatched the sap from beneath my foot and laid the sailor out with a blow across the temple. The small man hit the floor like the loser in a prelim. At the same time I heard Lou yell. Estelle had bitten his hand. Lou threw her aside, shook the pain away, and catlike, quickly for such a big man, moved toward me.

Lou wasn't too big. Tunney could have taken him in twelve. I tried to dance out of his way, but he cut me off and worked me toward the corner of the room. I swung the sap at his head; Lou caught the blow on his

forearm and I tried to knee him in the groin. He danced back a half-step.
I stumbled forward like a rodeo clown who missed the bull. As I tried to
get up I got hit in the ear with a fist that felt like a baseball bat. Just to
show there were no hard feelings, Lou kicked me in the ribs.

"Stop!" Estelle yelled. "I've got a gun."

Lou turned slowly. Estelle was kneeling on the bed, shaking. She had
a small automatic pointed at him.

Lou charged her. Two shots, painfully loud in the small room, sounded
before he got there. He knocked the gun away, grabbed Estelle's head in
one hand and smashed it against the brass bedstead once, twice, and she
was still. I was on him by then. Oh yes, I was real quick. Lou shook me
off his back and onto the floor, grunting now with the effort and the
realization that he was shot. He shook his head as if dazed and stumbled
toward me again. When he hit me I stood and heaved him over my shoulder.
There was a crash and a rush of air into the room: Lou had gone through
the window. Six stories to the street.

Davin shuddered with pain and rage—not at what Lou had done, but
at himself. The other sailor was still out. Estelle lay half off the bed, her
head hanging, mouth open. Her straight, short hair brushed the floor.
Davin lifted her onto the bed. He listened for her heartbeat and heard
nothing. He touched her throat and felt no pulse. He lay his cheek
against her lips and felt no wisp of breath.

A great anger, an anger close to despair, was building in him. He
knew who had killed Estelle, and why, and it was not the sailors.

No one had yet responded to the shots or the dead man in the street.
Davin pulled on his clothes and left.

Davin didn't know how much time he would have. He burned with
rage and impatience—and with fear. Estelle was dead. He shouldn't
have moved. He was not a hero. Somebody had made him. Somebody
had made him walk by that penny on the sidewalk, too, and as damp
night gave way to dawn his confusion gave way to cold certainty:
Chandler was his man. And, Davin realized, laughing aloud, he was
Chandler's.

He took the streetcar downtown, past the construction site of the new
civic center. He got off at Seventh and Hill and walked a block to South
Olive. He was hungry but would not eat; he wondered if it was Chandler
who decided whether he should become hungry. He watched the office-
workers come in for the beginning of the new week and wondered who
was trapped in Chandler's web and who wasn't. In the men's room of

the Bank of Italy building he washed the crusted trickle of blood from his ear, combed his hair, straightened his clothes.

Nothing that had happened in the last three days had made sense. Cissy hiring Davin, Chandler running off the road, Davin getting knocked out at May's apartment, the sailors killing May and then Estelle, the cutting of Davin's brake cables, Sanderson and Quintanella letting him get away so easily—and the crazy way things fit together, coincidence straight out of a bad novel. All of these things ought not to have happened in any sensible world. The only way they could have was if he were being pulled from his own life into a nightmare, and that was what Davin had realized. The nightmare was Chandler's.

Somehow, probably without his even knowing it, whatever Chandler wanted to happen, happened. Lives got jerked into new patterns, and his fantasies came true. Maybe it went back to Bartlett's embezzlement and Ballantine's heart attack; maybe it went back to Chandler's childhood. Whatever, the things that had been happening to Cissy and May and Estelle and even Big Lou and his partner, even the things Davin could not imagine any man consciously wanting to come true—were all what Chandler wanted to happen. Estelle was dead because of the situation the sailors and Davin had contrived to trap her in, and they had contrived this without knowing it because they were doing what Chandler wanted. There was no place in Chandler's world for women who liked sex and weren't afraid to go out and get it. There was no place in Chandler's world for the ordinary kind of private detective that Davin was. He had to find Chandler before the next disaster occurred.

He waited until he saw Philleo show up for work at South Basin Oil and followed him up to the fourth floor. Most of the staff was there already and talking about May Peterson. They stared at Davin as if he were an apparition—he felt like one—and Philleo turned to face him.

"May I help you?"

"Let's talk in your office, Mr. Philleo."

The man eyed him darkly, then motioned toward the corner room. They shut the door. Davin refused to sit down.

"Where's Raymond?" he asked.

"I talked to the police yesterday. You're no policeman."

"That's right. Where is he?"

"I have no idea," Philleo said. "And I'm not going—"

The phone rang. Philleo looked irritated, then picked it up. "Yes?" he said. There was a silence and Philleo looked as if he had swallowed a stone. "Put him on," he said.

Davin smiled grimly: yet another improbable coincidence. He had known the moment the phone rang who was calling. Philleo listened; he looked distressed. After a moment Davin took the receiver from his unresisting hand.

The man on the phone spoke in a voice choked with emotion and slurred by alcohol, with a trace of a British accent.

". . . swear to God I'll do it this time, Milt, I can't bear to think what a rat I am and what I'm doing to Cissy—"

"Where are you?" Davin said softly.

"Milt?"

"This isn't Milt. This is Michael Davin. I'm the man who helped you the other night when you ran off the road. Where are you?"

There was a pause, and Chandler's voice came back, more sober. "I want to talk to Milt."

"He doesn't want to talk to you anymore, Raymond. He's sick of you. He wants me to help you out instead."

Another silence.

"Well, you can tell that bastard that I'm in the Mayfair Hotel and if he wants to help me he can identify my body when they pull it off the sidewalk because I'm going to do it this time."

"No you won't. I'll be there in ten minutes." Davin gave the phone back to Philleo, who looked ashen. "He says he's going to kill himself."

"He's threatened before. I could tell you stories—"

"Just talk to him."

Davin ignored the elevator and ran down to the lobby, flagged a cab that took him speeding down Seventh Street. He didn't know what he was going to do when he got there, but he knew he had to reach Chandler. The ride seemed maddeningly slow. He peered out the window at the buildings and pedestrians, the sunlight flashing on storefronts and cars, searching for a sign that something had changed. Nothing happened. When Chandler died, would any of them who were controlled by him feel the difference? Would Davin collapse in the backseat of the taxi like a discarded puppet, leaving the driver with a ticking meter and a comatose man to pay the fare? Or would Chandler's death instead set Davin free? If Davin could only be sure of that, he would kill Chandler himself. Maybe he would kill him anyway. He needed to stay mad to keep from thinking about whether he could have saved Estelle. If Davin had walked out of her apartment instead of asking to stay, if she had kicked him out, then she would probably still be alive. She'd be a good girl, and he'd be a strong man. If May had slammed the door in his face—

They reached the Mayfair and Davin threw a couple of dollars at the driver. The desk clerk had a Mr. Chandler in room 712.

The door was not locked. The room stank of tobacco smoke and sweat and booze. Chandler had to have his own private bootlegger to stay drunk so consistently. The man was sitting in the opened window wearing rumpled trousers, shoes without socks, and a sleeveless T-shirt. He had his back against one side and one leg propped against the opposite. An almost-empty bottle stood on the sill in the crook of his knee. The phone lay on its side on the bedside table with the receiver dangling and a voice sounding tinnily from it. A book was opened face down on the bed, which looked as if it hadn't been made up in a couple of days. Beside the book lay a pulp magazine. *Black Mask.* Above a lurid picture of a man pointing a gun at another man who held a blond in front of him as a shield, was the slogan, "Smashing Detective Stories."

Chandler did not notice him enter. Davin crossed to the phone, stood it up, and quietly hung up the receiver. The silencing of the voice seemed to rouse Chandler. He lifted his head.

"Who are you?"

Davin's weariness suddenly caught up with him, and he sat down on the edge of the bed. He had felt some sympathy for Chandler even up to that moment, but seeing the man, and remembering Estelle's startled dead eyes, he now knew only disgust. Everyone who loved this man defended him, and he remained oblivious to it all, self-pitying and innocent when he ought to be guilty.

"You're the guy—" Chandler started.

"I'm the guy who pulled you out of the wreck. I'm the private detective hired by Cissy to keep you from hurting yourself. She didn't say anything about keeping you from hurting anyone else, and I was too stupid to catch on. Before Friday I had a life of my own, but now I'm the man you want me to be. I get beat up for twenty bucks a day and say please and thank you. I'm a regular guy and a strange one. I talk sex with the ladies and never follow through. I crack wise to the cops. I'm the best man in your world and good enough for any world. I go down these mean streets and don't get tarnished and I'm not afraid. I'm the hero."

"What are you talking about?"

"You're mystified, huh? Before Friday I could touch a woman and not have to worry about her getting killed for it. Now I'm busy taking care of a sleazy momma's boy."

Chandler pointed a shaking finger at him. "Don't you mock me," he said. "I know what I've done. I know—"

Davin was raging inside. "What have you done?" he said grimly. "You sound like you've got a big conscience. So tell me."

Chandler's weeping had turned into anger. "I've betrayed my wife. I'm not surprised she put you onto me—I would have told her to do that myself, in her situation. I've—" his voice became choked, "I've consorted with women who aren't any good. Women with death in their eyes and bedrooms that smell of too much cheap perfume."

"Are you serious?" Davin wanted to laugh but couldn't. "Where do you get all this malarkey? May and Estelle are dead. Really dead—not perfume dead."

Chandler jerked as if electrically shocked. He knocked the bottle out the window, and seconds later came the crash.

His face set in a sour expression. "I'm not surprised about May. She led a fast life." He paused, and his voice became philosophical. "Even Estelle—it doesn't surprise me. I finally figured out that she wasn't the innocent she pretended to be."

Davin's rage grew. He got up from the bed; the book beside him fell off and closed itself. *The Great Gatsby*, the cover read.

"May and Estelle were killed by those sailors you fought in the insurance suit. They said they were out to get revenge against you."

Chandler was shook again. "That makes no sense," he said. "May and Estelle had nothing to do with that. Anyone out to get me should come for me. There must have been some other reason they were killed."

Davin grabbed Chandler by the arm. He wanted to push him out the window; it would be easy, easier than the night in the railyard. Nobody would know. For the first time, Chandler looked him in the eye. Davin saw desperation there and something more frightening: Chandler seemed to know what he was thinking, was granting him permission, was making an appeal. He did not try to escape Davin's grasp. Davin fought the desire to give the one quick shove that would end it; the frustrated need, the rage of the years of keeping himself sane, pushed him toward it. The whole struggle was the matter of an instant. He pulled Chandler into the room.

"Quit the suicide act. What have you been doing since you left May?"

If Chandler had felt anything of the communication that had passed between them, he did not show it. "What does it look like?" he said. "I couldn't stay with her; when I first met her I thought she was innocent, defenseless, but I learned the kind she was quick. I couldn't go home and face Cissy. I came here."

He looked toward the window. "If I had any guts it wouldn't be an act."

"Those sailors had no reason to kill except you. They did it in the stupidest way possible. Not for revenge. Just so things could work out the way you want them to."

Chandler pushed by him and went into the bathroom; Davin heard the sound of running water. He was getting ready to shave. He seemed to be sobering fast.

"You're crazy," Chandler said as he lathered his face. "The way *I* wanted? Look, I feel like the bastard I am, but what did I have to do with any of this? Am I supposed to stop defending the company when we're in the right? I've got to try to do the right thing, don't I?"

Davin said nothing. After a few minutes, Chandler came out of the bathroom. Hair combed, freshly shaven, he seemed already to be on the way to becoming an executive again. The news of the deaths, the struggle on the windowsill, had knocked the booze out of him; knocked the guilt down in him, too. He picked up his shirt and began buttoning it.

Davin felt he was going to be sick.

"You know, that credo you spouted—you were just joking, I realize—but there's something to it," Chandler said seriously. " 'Down these mean streets.' I'd like to believe in that; I'd like to be able to live up to that code—if we could only get all the other bastards to."

Davin rushed into the bathroom and vomited into the toilet.

Chandler stuck his head into the room. "Are you all right?"

Davin gasped for breath. He wet a towel and rubbed his face.

Chandler had his tie knotted and put on the jacket of his rumpled summer suit. "You should take better care of yourself," he said. "You look awful. What's your name?"

"Michael Davin."

"Irish, huh?"

"I guess so."

"I'll bet being a private investigator is interesting work. There's a kind of honor to it. You ought to write up your experiences some day."

Estelle was dead, lying upside down with her hair brushing the dusty floor. Her mouth was open. "I don't want to," Davin said.

Chandler took the copy of *Black Mask* from the bed. Davin felt hollow, but the way Chandler held the magazine, so reverently, sparked his anger again.

"You actually read that junk?"

The other man ignored him. He bent over, a little unsteadiness the only evidence of his bender and the fact he'd been ready to launch himself out the window half an hour earlier. He picked up the copy of *Gatsby*.

"I've always wanted to be a writer," he said. "I used to write essays— even some poetry."

"Estelle told me that."

Chandler looked only momentarily uncomfortable. He motioned with the book in his hand. "So you don't like detective stories. Have you tried Fitzgerald?"

"No."

"Best damn writer in America. Best damn book. About a man chasing his dream."

"Does he catch it?"

Sadly, Chandler replied, "No. He doesn't."

"He ought to quit dreaming, then."

Chandler put his hand on Davin's shoulder. "We can't do that. We've got nothing else."

Davin wanted to tell him what a load of crap that was, but Chandler had turned his back and walked out of the room.

THE HOUSE OF COMPASSIONATE SHARERS

And he was there, and it was not far enough, not yet, for the Earth
hung overhead like a rotten fruit, blue with mold, crawling,
wrinkling, purulent and alive.

DAMON KNIGHT, "Masks"

In the Port Iranani Galenshall I awoke in the room Diderits liked to
call the "Black Pavilion." I was an engine, a system, a series of myoelectric
and neuromechanical components, and The Accident responsible for this
clean and enamel-hard enfleshing lay two full D-years in the past. This
morning was an anniversary of sorts. I ought by now to have adjusted.
And I had. I had reached an absolute accommodation with myself.
Narcissistic, one could say. And that was the trouble.

"Dorian? Dorian Lorca?"

The voice belonged to KommGalen Diderits, wet and breathy even
though it came from a small metal speaker to which the sable curtains
of the dome were attached. I stared up into the ring of curtains.

"Dorian, it's Target Day. Will you answer me, please?"

"I'm here, my galen. Where else would I be?" I stood up, listening
to the almost musical ratcheting that I make when I move, a sound like
the concatenation of tiny bells or the purring of a stope-car. The sound
is conveyed through the tempered porcelain plates, metal vertebrae, and
osteoid polymers holding me together, and no one else can hear it.

"Rumer's here, Dorian. Are you ready for her to come in?"

"If I agreed, I suppose I'm ready."

"Damn it, Dorian, don't feel you're bound by *honor* to see her! We've spent the last several brace-weeks preparing you for a resumption of normal human contact." Diderits began to enumerate: "Chameleodrene treatments . . . hologramic substitution . . . stimulus-response therapy . . . You ought to want Rumer to come in to you, Dorian."

Ought. My brain was—is—my own, but the body Diderits and the other kommgalens had given me had "instincts" and "tropisms" peculiar to itself, ones whose templates had a mechanical rather than a biological origin. What I ought to feel, in human terms, and what I in fact felt, as the inhabitant of a total prosthesis, were as dissimilar as blood and oil.

"Do you *want* her to come in, Dorian?"

"All right. I do." And I did. After all the biochemical and psychiatric preparation, I wanted to see what my reaction would be. Still sluggish from some drug, I had no exact idea how Rumer's presence would affect me.

At a parting of the pavilion's draperies, only two or three meters from my couch, appeared Rumer Montieth, my wife. Her garment of over-lapping latex scales, glossy black in color, was a hauberk designed to reveal only her hands, face, and hair. The way Rumer was dressed was one of Diderits's deceits, or "preparations": I was supposed to see my wife as little different from myself, a creature as intricately assembled and synapsed as the engine I had become. But the hands, the face, the hair— nothing could disguise their unaugmented humanity, and revulsion swept over me like a tide.

"Dorian?" And her voice—wet, breath-driven, expelled between parted lips . . .

I turned away from her. "No," I told the speaker overhead. "It hasn't worked, my galen. Every part of me cries out against this."

Diderits said nothing. Was he still out there? Or was he trying to give Rumer and me a privacy I didn't want?

"Disassemble me," I urged him. "Link me to the control systems of a delta-state vessel and let me go out from Diroste for good. You don't want a zombot among you, Diderits—an unhappy anproz. Damn you all, you're torturing me!"

"And you, us," Rumer said quietly. I faced her. "As you're very aware, Dorian, as you're very aware . . . Take my hand."

"No." I didn't shrink away; I merely refused.

"Here. Take it."

Fighting my own disgust, I seized her hand, twisted it over, showed her its back. "Look."

"I *see* it, Dor." I was hurting her.

"Surfaces, that's all you see. Look at this growth, this wen." I pinched the growth. "Do you see that, Rumer? That's sebum, fatty matter. And the smell, if only you could—"

She drew back, and I tried to quell a mental nausea almost as profound as my regret. . . . To go out from Diroste seemed to be the only answer. Around me I wanted machinery—thrumming, inorganic machinery— and the sterile, actinic emptiness of outer space. I wanted to be the probeship *Dorian Lorca*. It hardly seemed a step down from my position as "prince consort" to the Governor of Diroste.

"Let me out," Rumer commanded the head of the Port Iranani Galenshall, and Diderits released her from the "Black Pavilion."

Then I was alone again in one of the few private chambers of a surgical complex given over to adapting Civi Korps personnel to our leprotic little planet's fume-filled mine shafts. The Galenshall was also devoted to patching up these civkis after their implanted respirators had atrophied, almost beyond saving, the muscles of their chests and lungs.

Including administrative personnel, Kommfleet officials, and the Civi Korps laborers in the mines, in the year I'm writing of there were over a half-million people on Diroste. Diderits was responsible for the health of all of them not assigned to the outlying territories. Had I not been the husband of Diroste's first governor, he might well have let me die along with the seventeen "expendables" on tour with me in the Fetneh District when the roof of the Haft Paykar diggings fell in on us. Rumer, however, made Diderits's duty clear to him, and I am as I am because the resources were at hand in Port Iranani and Diderits saw fit to obey his governor.

Alone in my pavilion, I lifted a hand to my face and heard a caroling of minute copper bells. . . .

Nearly a month later I observed Rumer, Diderits, and a stranger by closed-circuit television as they sat in one of the Galenshall's wide conference rooms. The stranger was a woman, bald but for a scalplock, who wore gold silk pantaloons that gave her the appearance of a clown, and a corrugated green jacket that somehow reversed this impression. Even on my monitor I could see the thick sunlight pouring into their room.

"This is Wardress Kefa," Rumer informed me.

I greeted her through a microphone and tested the cosmetic work of Diderits's associates by trying to smile for her.

"She's from Earth, Dor, and she's here because KommGalen Diderits and I asked her to come."

"Forty-six lights," I murmured, probably inaudibly. I was touched and angry at the same time. To be constantly the focus of your friends' attentions, especially when they have more urgent matters to see to, can lead to either a corrosive cynicism or a humility just as crippling.

"We want you to go back with her on *Nizami*," Diderits said, "when it leaves Port Iranani tomorrow night."

"Why?"

"Wardress Kefa came all this way," Rumer responded, "because we wanted to talk to her. As a final stage in your therapy she's convinced us that you ought to visit her... her establishment there. And if this fails, Dorian, I give you up; if that's what you want, I relinquish you." Today Rumer was wearing a yellow sarong, a tasseled gold shawl, and a nun's hood of yellow and orange stripes. When she spoke she averted her eyes from the conference room's monitor and looked out its high windows instead. At a distance, I could appreciate the spare aesthetics of her profile.

"Establishment? What sort of establishment?" I studied the tiny Wardress, but her appearance volunteered nothing.

"The House of Compassionate Sharers," Diderits began. "It's located in Earth's western hemisphere, on the North American continent, nearly two hundred kilometers southwest of the gutted Urban Nucleus of Denver. It can be reached from Manitou Port by 'rail."

"Good. I shouldn't have any trouble finding it. But what is it, this mysterious house?"

Wardress Kefa spoke for the first time: "I would prefer that you learn its nature and its purposes from me, Mr. Lorca, when we have arrived safely under its several roofs."

"Is it a brothel?" This question fell among my three interlocutors like a heavy stone.

"No," Rumer said after a careful five-count. "It's a unique sort of clinic for treatment of unique emotional disorders." She glanced at the Wardress, concerned that she had revealed too much.

"Some would call it a brothel," Wardress Kefa admitted huskily. "Earth has become a haven of misfits and opportunists, a crossroads of Glaktik Komm influence and trade. The House, I must confess, wouldn't prosper if it catered only to those who suffer from rare dissociations of feeling. Therefore a few—a very few—of those who come to us are kommthors rich in power and exacting in their tastes. But these people are exceptions, Governor Montieth, KommGalen Diderits; they represent an uneasy compromise we must make in order to carry out the work for which the House was originally envisioned and built."

A moment later Rumer announced, "You're going, Dor. You're going tomorrow night. Diderits and I, well, we'll see you in three E-months." That said, she gathered in her cloak with both hands and rearranged it on her shoulders. Then she left the room.

"Goodbye, Dorian," Diderits said, standing.

Wardress Kefa fixed upon the camera conveying her picture to me a keen glance made more disconcerting by her small naked face. "Tomorrow, then."

"Tomorrow," I agreed. I watched my monitor as the galen and the curious-looking Wardress exited the conference room together. In the room's high windows Diroste's sun sang a cappella in the lemon sky.

They gave me a private berth on *Nizami*. I used my "nights," since sleep no longer meant anything to me, to prowl through those nacelles of shipboard machinery not forbidden to passengers. Although I wasn't permitted in the forward command module, I did have access to the computer-ringed observation turret and two or three corridors of auxiliary equipment necessary to the maintenance of a continuous probefield. In these places I secreted myself and thought seriously about the likelihood of an encephalic/neural linkage with one of Kommfleet's interstellar frigates.

My body was a trial. Diderits had long ago informed me that it—that I—was still "sexually viable," but this was something I hadn't yet put to the test, nor did I wish to. Tyrannized by morbidly vivid images of human viscera, human excreta, human decay, I had been rebuilt of metal, porcelain, and plastic *as if* from the very substances—skin, bone, hair, cartilage—that these inorganic materials derided. I was a contradiction, a quasi-immortal masquerading as one of the ephemera who had saved me from their own short-lived lot. Still another paradox was the fact that my aversion to the organic was itself a human (i.e., an organic) emotion. That was why I so fervently wanted out. For over a year and a half on Diroste I had hoped that Rumer and the others would see their mistake and exile me not only from themselves, but from the body that was a deadly daily reminder of my total estrangement.

But Rumer was adamant in her love, and I had been a prisoner in the Port Iranani Galenshall—with but one chilling respite—ever since the Haft Paykar explosion and cave-in. Now I was being given into the hands of a new wardress, and as I sat amid the enamel-encased engines of *Nizami* I couldn't help wondering what sort of prison the House of Compassionate Sharers must be. . . .

Among the passengers of a monorail car bound outward from Manitou Port, Wardress Kefa in the window seat beside me, I sat tense and stiff. Anthrophobia. Lorca, I told myself repeatedly, you must exercise self-control. Amazingly, I did. From Manitou Port we rode the sleek underslung bullet of our car through rugged, sparsely populated terrain toward Wolf Run Summit, and I controlled myself.

"You've never been 'home' before?" Wardress Kefa asked me.

"No. Earth isn't home. I was born on GK-world Dai-Han, Wardress. And as a young man I was sent as an administrative colonist to Diroste, where—"

"Where you were born again," Wardress Kefa interrupted. "Nevertheless, this is where we began."

The shadows of the mountains slid across the wraparound glass of our car, and the imposing white pylons of the monorail system flashed past us like the legs of giants. Yes. Like huge, naked cyborgs hiding among the mountains' aspens and pines.

"Where I met Rumer Montieth, I was going to say; where I eventually got married and settled down to the life of a bureaucrat who happens to be married to power. You anticipate me, Wardress." I didn't add that now Earth and Diroste were equally alien to me, that the probeship *Nizami* had bid fair to assume first place among my loyalties.

A 'rail from Wolf Run came sweeping past us toward Manitou Port. The sight pleased me; the vibratory hum of the passing 'rail lingered sympathetically in my hearing, and I refused to talk, even though the Wardress clearly wanted to draw me out about my former life. I was surrounded and beset. Surely this woman had all she needed to know of my past from Diderits and my wife. My annoyance grew.

"You're very silent, Mr. Lorca."

"I have no innate hatred of silences."

"Nor do I, Mr. Lorca—unless they're empty ones."

Hands in lap, humming bioelectrically, inaudibly, I looked at my tiny guardian with disdain. "There are some," I told her, "who are unable to engage in a silence without stripping it of its unspoken cargo of significance."

To my surprise the woman laughed heartily. "That certainly isn't true of you, is it?" Then, a wry expression playing on her lips, she shifted her gaze to the hurtling countryside and said nothing else until it came time to disembark at Wolf Run Summit.

Wolf Run was a resort frequented principally by Kommfleet officers and members of the administrative hierarchy stationed in Port Manitou. Civi Korps personnel had built quaint gingerbread châteaus among the trees and engineered two of the slopes above the hamlet for year-round skiing. "Many of these people," Wardress Kefa explained, indicating a crowd of men and women beneath the deck of Wolf Run's main lodge, "work inside Shays Mountain, near the light-probe port, in facilities built originally for satellite-tracking and missile-launch detection. Now they monitor the display boards for Kommfleet orbiters and shuttles; they program the cruising and descent lanes of these vehicles. Others are demographic and wildlife managers, bent on resettling Earth as efficiently as it may be done. Tedious work, Mr. Lorca. They come here to play." We passed below the lodge on a path of unglazed vitrofoam. Two or three of Wolf Run's bundled visitors stared at me, presumably because I was in my tunic sleeves and conspicuously undaunted by the spring cold. Or maybe their stares were for my guardian. . . .

"How many of these people are customers of yours, Wardress?"

"That isn't something I can divulge." But she glanced back over her shoulder as if she had recognized someone.

"What do they find at your establishment they can't find in Manitou Port?"

"I don't know, Mr. Lorca; I'm not a mind reader."

To reach the House of Compassionate Sharers from Wolf Run, we had to go on foot down a narrow path worked reverently into the flank of the mountain. It was very nearly a two-hour hike. I couldn't believe the distance or Wardress Kefa's stamina. Swinging her arms, jolting herself on stiff legs, she went down the mountain with a will. And in all the way we walked we met no other hikers.

At last we reached a clearing giving us an open view of a steep pine-peopled glen: a grotto that fell away beneath us and led our eyes to an expanse of smooth white sky. But the Wardress pointed directly down into the foliage.

"There," she said. "The House of Compassionate Sharers."

I saw nothing but afternoon sunlight on the aspens, boulders huddled in the mulch cover, and swaying tunnels among the trees. Squinting, I finally made out a geodesic structure built from the very materials of the woods. Like an upland sleight, a wavering mirage, the House slipped in and out of my vision, blending, emerging, melting again. It was a series of irregular domes as hard to hold as water vapor—but after several redwinged blackbirds flew noisily across the plane of its highest turret, the House remained for me in stark relief; it had shed its invisibility.

"It's more noticeable," Wardress Kefa said, "when its external shutters have been cranked aside. Then the House sparkles like a dragon's eye. The windows are stained glass."

"I'd like to see that. Now it appears camouflaged."

"That's deliberate, Mr. Lorca. Come."

When we were all the way down, I could see of what colossal size the House really was: it reared up through the pine needles and displayed its interlocking polygons to the sky. Strange to think that no one in a passing helicraft was ever likely to catch sight of it. . . .

Wardress Kefa led me up a series of plank stairs, spoke once at the door, and introduced me into an antechamber so clean and military that I thought "barracks" rather than "bawdyhouse." The ceiling and walls were honeycombed, and the natural flooring was redolent of the outdoors. My guardian disappeared, returned without her coat, and escorted me into a much smaller room shaped like a tapered well. By means of a wooden hand-crank she opened the shutters, and varicolored light filtered in upon us through the room's slant-set windows. On elevated cushions that snapped and rustled each time we moved, we sat facing each other.

"What now?" I asked the Wardress.

"Just listen: The Sharers have come to the House of their own volition, Mr. Lorca; most lived and worked on extrakomm worlds toward Glaktik Center before being approached for duty here. The ones who are here accepted the invitation. They came to offer their presences to people very like yourself."

"Me? Are they misconceived machines?"

"I'm not going to answer that. Let me just say that the variety of services the Sharers offer is surprisingly wide. As I've told you, for some visitants the Sharers are simply a convenient means of satisfying exotically aberrant tastes. For others they're a way back to the larger community. We take whoever comes to us for help, Mr. Lorca, in order that the Sharers not remain idle nor the House vacant."

"So long as whoever comes is wealthy and influential?"

She paused before speaking. "That's true enough. But the matter's out of my hands, Mr. Lorca. I'm an employee of Glaktik Komm, chosen for my empathetic abilities. I don't make policy. I don't own title to the House."

"But you *are* its madam. Its 'wardress,' rather."

"True. For the last twenty-two years. I'm the first and only wardress to have served here, Mr. Lorca, and I love the Sharers. I love their devotion to the fragile mentalities who visit them. Even so, despite the time I've lived among them, I still don't pretend to understand the source of their transcendent concern. That's what I wanted to tell you."

"You think me a 'fragile mentality'?"

"I'm sorry—but you're here, Mr. Lorca, and you certainly aren't fragile of *limb*, are you?" The Wardress laughed. "I also wanted to ask you to . . . well, to restrain your crueler impulses when the treatment itself begins."

I stood up and moved away from the little woman. How had I borne her presence for as long as I had?

"Please don't take my request amiss. It isn't *specifically* personal, Mr. Lorca. I make it of everyone who comes to the House of Compassionate Sharers. Restraint is an unwritten corollary of the only three rules we have here. Will you hear them?"

I made a noise of compliance.

"First, that you do not leave the session chamber once you've entered it. Second, that you come forth immediately upon my summoning you . . . "

"And third?"

"That you do not kill the Sharer."

All the myriad disgusts I had been suppressing for seven or eight hours were now perched atop the ladder of my patience, and, rung by painful rung, I had to step them back down. Must a rule be made to prevent a visitant from murdering the partner he had bought? Incredible. The Wardress herself was just perceptibly sweating, and I noticed too how grotesquely distended her earlobes were.

"Is there a room in this establishment for a wealthy and influential patron? A private room?"

"Of course," she said. "I'll show you."

It had a full-length mirror. I undressed and stood in front of it. Only during my first "period of adjustment" on Diroste had I spent much time looking at what I had become. Later, back in the Port Iranani Galenshall, Diderits had denied me any sort of reflective surface at all—looking glasses, darkened windows, even metal spoons. The waxen perfection of my features ridiculed the ones another Dorian Lorca had possessed before the Haft Paykar Incident. Cosmetic mockery. Faintly corpselike, speciously paradigmatic, I was both more than I was supposed to be and less.

In Wardress Kefa's House the less seemed preeminent. I ran a finger down the inside of my right arm, scrutinizing the track of one of the intubated veins through which circulated a serum that Diderits called hematocybin: an efficient "low-maintenance" blood substitute, combative of both fatigue and infection, which requires changing only once every six D-months. With a proper supply of hematocybin and a plastic recirculator I can do the job myself, standing up. That night, however, the ridge of my vein, mirrored only an arm's length away, was more horror than miracle. I stepped away from the looking glass and closed my eyes.

Later that evening Wardress Kefa came to me with a candle and a brocaded dressing gown. She made me put on the gown in front of her, and I complied. Then, the robe's rich and symbolic embroidery on my back, I followed her out of my first-floor chamber to a rustic stairwell seemingly connective to all the rooms in the House.

The dome contained countless smaller domes and five or six primitive staircases, at least. Not a single other person was about. Lit flickeringly by Wardress Kefa's taper as we climbed one of these sets of stairs, the House's mid-interior put me in mind of an Escheresque drawing in which verticals and horizontals become hopelessly confused and a figure who from one perspective seems to be going up a series of steps, from another seems to be coming down them. Presently the Wardress and I stood on a landing above this topsy-turvy well of stairs (though there were still more stairs above us), and, looking down, I experienced an unsettling reversal of perspectives. Vertigo. Why hadn't Diderits, against so human a susceptibility, implanted tiny gyrostabilizers in my head? I clutched a railing and held on.

"You can't fall," Wardress Kefa told me. "It's an illusion. A whim of the architects."

"Is it an illusion behind this door?"

"Oh, the Sharer's real enough, Mr. Lorca. Please. Go on in." She touched my face and left me, taking her candle with her.

After hesitating a moment I went through the door to my assignation, and the door locked of itself. I stood with my hand on the butterfly shape of the knob and felt the night working in me and the room. The only light came from the stove-bed on the opposite wall, for the fitted polygons overhead were still blanked out by their shutters and no candles shone here. Instead, reddish embers glowed behind an isinglass window beneath the stove-bed, strewn with quilts, on which my Sharer awaited me.

Outside, the wind played harp music in the trees.

I was trembling rhythmically, as when Rumer had come to me in the

"Black Pavilion." Even though my eyes adjusted rapidly, automatically, to the dark, it was still difficult to see. Temporizing, I surveyed the dome. In its high central vault hung a cage in which, disturbed by my entrance, a bird hopped skittishly about. The cage swayed on its tether.

Go on, I told myself.

I advanced toward the dais and leaned over the unmoving Sharer who lay there. With a hand on either side of the creature's head, I braced myself. The figure beneath me moved, moved weakly, and I drew back. But because the Sharer didn't stir again, I reassumed my previous stance: the posture of either a lover or a man called upon to identify a disfigured corpse. But identification was impossible; the embers under the bed gave too feeble a sheen. In the chamber's darkness even a lover's kiss would have fallen clumsily. . . .

"I'm going to touch you," I said. "Will you let me do that?"

The Sharer lay still.

Then, willing all of my senses into the cushion of synthetic flesh at my forefinger's tip, I touched the Sharer's face.

Hard, and smooth, and cool.

I moved my finger from side to side; and the hardness, smoothness, coolness, continued to flow into my pressuring fingertip. It was like touching the pate of a death's-head, the cranial cap of a human being: bone rather than metal. My finger distinguished between these two possibilities, deciding on bone; and, half-panicked, I concluded that I had traced an arc on the skull of an intelligent being who bore his every bone on the outside, like an armor of calcium. Could that be? If so, how could this organism—this entity, this *thing*—express compassion?

I lifted my finger away from the Sharer. Its tip hummed with a pressure now relieved and emanated a faint warmth.

A death's-head come to life . . .

Maybe I laughed. In any case, I pulled myself onto the platform and straddled the Sharer. I kept my eyes closed, though not tightly. It didn't seem that I was straddling a skeleton.

"Sharer," I whispered. "Sharer, I don't know you yet."

Gently, I let my thumbs find the creature's eyes, the sockets in the smooth exoskeleton, and both thumbs returned to me a hardness and a coldness that were unquestionably metallic in origin. Moreover, the Sharer didn't flinch—even though I'd anticipated that probing his eyes, no matter how gently, would provoke at least an involuntary pulling away. Instead, the Sharer lay still and tractable under my hands.

And why not? I thought. *Your eyes are nothing but two pieces of sophisticated optical machinery. . . .*

It was true. Two artificial light-sensing image-integrating units gazed up at me from the sockets near which my thumbs probed, and I realized that even in this darkness my Sharer, its vision mechanically augmented beyond my own, could *see* my blind face staring down in a futile attempt to create an image out of the information my hands had supplied me. I opened my eyes and held them open. I could see only shadows, but my thumbs could *feel* the cold metal rings that held the Sharer's photosensitive units so firmly in its skull.

"An animatronic construct," I said, rocking back on my heels. "A soulless robot. Move your head if I'm right."

The Sharer continued motionless.

"All right. You're a sentient creature whose eyes have been replaced with an artificial system. What about that? Lord, are we brothers then?"

I had a sudden hunch that the Sharer was very old, a senescent being owing its life to prosthetics, transplants, and imitative organs of laminated silicone. Its life, I was certain, had been *extended* by these contrivances, not saved. I asked the Sharer about my feeling, and very, very slowly it moved the helmetlike skull housing its artificial eyes and its aged, compassionate mind. Uncharitably I then believed myself the victim of a deception, whether the Sharer's or Wardress Kefa's I couldn't say. Here, after all, was a creature who had chosen to prolong its organic condition rather than to escape it, and it had willingly made use of the same materials and methods Diderits had brought into play to save me.

"You might have died," I told it. "Go too far, Sharer—go too far with these contrivances and you may forfeit suicide as an option."

Then, leaning forward again, saying, "I'm still not through, I still don't know you," I let my hands come down the Sharer's bony face to its throat. Here a shield of cartilage graded upward into its jaw and downward into the plastically silken skin covering the remainder of its body, internalizing all but the defiantly naked skull of the Sharer's skeletal structure. A death's-head with the body of a man . . .

That was all I could take. I rose from the stove-bed and, cinching my dressing gown tightly about my waist, crossed to the other side of the chamber. There was no furniture in the room but the stove-bed (if that qualified), and I had to content myself with sitting in a lotus position on the floor. I sat that way all night, staving off dreams.

Diderits had said that I needed to dream. If I didn't dream, he warned, I'd be risking hallucinations and eventual madness; in the Port Iranani

Galenshall he'd seen to it that drugs were administered to me every two days and my sleep period monitored by an ARC machine and a team of electroencephalographers. But my dreams were almost always night-mares, descents into klieg-lit charnel houses, and I infinitely preferred the risk of going psychotic. There was always the chance someone would take pity and disassemble me, piece by loving piece. Besides, I had lasted two E-weeks now on nothing but grudging catnaps, and so far I still had gray matter upstairs instead of scrambled eggs. . . .

I crossed my fingers.

A long time after I'd sat down, Wardress Kefa threw open the door. It was morning. I could tell because the newly canted shutters outside our room admitted a singular roaring of light. The entire chamber was illuminated, and I saw crimson wall-hangings, a mosaic of red and purple stones on the section of the floor, and a tumble of scarlet quilts. The bird in the suspended cage was a redwinged blackbird.

"Where is it from?"

"You could use a more appropriate pronoun."

"*He? She?* Which is the more appropriate, Wardress Kefa?"

"Assume the Sharer masculine, Mr. Lorca."

"My sexual proclivities have never run that way, I'm afraid."

"Your sexual proclivities," the Wardress told me stingingly, "enter into this only if you persist in thinking of the House as a brothel rather than a clinic and the Sharers as whores rather than therapists!"

"Last night I heard two or three people clomping up the stairs in their boots, that and a woman's raucous laughter."

"A visitant, Mr. Lorca, *not* a Sharer."

"I didn't think she was a Sharer. But it's difficult to believe I'm in a 'clinic' when that sort of noise disrupts my midnight meditations, Wardress."

"I've explained that. It can't be helped."

"All right, all right. Where is *he* from, this 'therapist' of mine?"

"An interior star. But where he's from is of no consequence in your treatment. I matched him to your needs, as I see them, and soon you'll be going back to him."

"Why? To spend another night sitting on the floor?"

"You won't do that again, Mr. Lorca. And you needn't worry. Your reaction wasn't an uncommon one for a newcomer to the House."

"Revulsion?" I cried. "Revulsion's therapeutic?"

"I don't think you were as put off as you believe."

"Oh? Why not?"

"Because you talked to the Sharer. You addressed him directly, not once but several times. Many visitants never get that far during their first session, Mr. Lorca."

"Talked to him?" I said dubiously. "Maybe. Before I found out what he was."

"Ah. Before you found out what he was." In her heavy green jacket and swishy pantaloons the tiny woman turned about and departed the well of the sitting room.

I stared bemusedly after her for a long time.

Three nights after my first "session," the night of my conversation with Wardress Kefa, I entered the Sharer's chamber again. Everything was as it had been, except that the dome's shutters were open and moonlight coated the mosaic work on the floor. The Sharer awaited me in the same recumbent, unmoving posture, and inside its cage the redwinged blackbird set one of its perches to rocking back and forth.

Perversely, I had decided not to talk to the Sharer this time—but I did approach the stove-bed and lean over him. *Hello,* I thought, and the word very nearly came out. I straddled the Sharer and studied him in the stained moonlight. He looked just as my sense of touch had led me to conclude previously . . . like a skull, oddly flattened and beveled, with the body of a man. But despite the chemical embers glowing beneath his dais the Sharer's body had no warmth, and to know him more fully I resumed tracing a finger over his alien parts.

I discovered that at every conceivable pressure point a tiny scar existed, or the tip of an implanted electrode, and that miniature canals into which wires had been sunk veined his inner arms and legs. Just beneath his sternum a concave disc about eight centimeters across, containing neither instruments nor any other surface features, had been set into the Sharer's chest like a stainless-steel brooch. It seemed to hum under the pressure of my finger as I drew my nail silently around the disc's circumference. What was it for? What did it mean? Again, I almost spoke.

I rolled toward the wall and lay stretched out beside the unmoving Sharer. Maybe he *couldn't* move. On my last visit he had moved his dimly phosphorescent head for me, of course, but that only feebly, and maybe his immobility was the result of some cybergamic dysfunction. I had to find out. My resolve not to speak deserted me, and I propped myself up on my elbow.

"Sharer . . . Sharer, can you move?"

The head turned toward me slightly, signaling . . . well, what?

"Can you get off this platform? Try. Get off this dais under your own power."

To my surprise the Sharer nudged a quilt to the floor and in a moment stood facing me. Moonlight glinted from the photosensitive units serving the creature as eyes and gave his bent, elongated body the appearance of a piece of Inhodlef Era statuary, primitive work from the extrakomm world of Glaparcus.

"Good," I praised the Sharer; "very good. Can you tell me what you're supposed to share with me? I'm not sure we have as much in common as our Wardress seems to think."

The Sharer extended both arms toward me and opened his tightly closed fists. In the cups of his palms he held two items I hadn't discovered during my tactile examination of him. I accepted these from the Sharer. One was a small metal disc, the other a thin metal cylinder. Looking them over, I found that the disc reminded me of the larger mirrorlike bowl set in the alien's chest, while the cylinder seemed to be a kind of penlight.

Absently, I pulled my thumb over the head of the penlight; a ridged metal sheath followed the motion of my thumb, uncovering a point of ghostly red light stretching away into the cylinder seemingly deeper than the penlight itself. I pointed this instrument at the wall, at our bedding, at the Sharer himself—but it emitted no beam. When I turned the penlight on my wrist, the results were predictably similar: not even a faint red shadow appeared along the edge of my arm. Nothing. The cylinder's light existed internally, a beam continuously transmitted and retransmitted between the penlight's two poles. Pulling back the sheath on the instrument's head had in no way interrupted the operation of its self-regenerating circuit.

I stared wonderingly into the hollow of redness, then looked up. "Sharer, what's this thing for?"

The Sharer reached out and took from my other hand the disc I had so far ignored. Then he placed this small circle of metal in the smooth declivity of the larger disc in his chest, where it apparently adhered—for I could no longer see it. That done, the Sharer stood distressingly immobile, even more like a statue than he had seemed a moment before, one arm frozen across his body and his hand stilled at the edge of the sunken plate in which the smaller disc had just adhered. He looked dead and self-commemorating.

"Lord!" I exclaimed. "What've you done, Sharer? Turned yourself off? That's right, isn't it?"

The Sharer neither answered nor moved.

Suddenly I felt sickeningly weary, opiate-weary, and I knew that I wouldn't be able to stay on the dais with this puzzle-piece being from an anonymous sun standing over me like a dark angel from my racial subconscious. I thought briefly of manhandling the Sharer across the room, but didn't have the will to touch this catatonically rigid being, this sculpture of metal and bone, and so dismissed the idea. Nor was it likely that Wardress Kefa would help me, even if I tried to summon her with murderous poundings and cries—a bitterly amusing prospect. Wellaway, another night propped against the chamber's far wall, keeping sleep at bay . . .

Is this what you wanted me to experience, Rumer? The frustration of trying to piece together my own "therapy"? I looked up through one of the dome's unstained polygons in lethargic search of the constellation Auriga. Then I realized that I wouldn't recognize it even if it happened to lie within my line of sight. Ah, Rumer, Rumer . . .

"You're certainly a pretty one," I told the Sharer. Then I pointed the penlight at his chest, drew back the sheath on its head, and spoke a single onomatopoeic word: "*Bang.*"

Instantly a beam of light sang between the instrument in my hand and the plate in the Sharer's chest. The beam died at once (I had registered only its shattering brightness, not its color), but the disc continued to glow with a residual illumination.

The Sharer dropped his frozen arm and assumed a posture more limber, more suggestive of life. He looked . . . expectant.

I could only stare. Then I turned the penlight over in my hands, pointed it again at the Sharer, and waited for another coursing of light. To no purpose. The instrument still burned internally, but it wouldn't relume the alien's inset disc, which, in any case, continued to glow dimly. Things were all at once interesting again. I gestured with the penlight.

"You've rejoined the living, haven't you?"

The Sharer acknowledged this with a slight turn of the head.

"Forgive me, Sharer, but I don't want to spend another night sitting on the floor. If you can move again, how about over there?" I pointed at the opposite wall. "I don't want you hovering over me."

Oddly, he obeyed. But he did so oddly, without turning around. He cruised backward as if on invisible coasters—his legs moving a little, yes, but not enough to propel him so smoothly, so quickly, across the chamber. Once against the far wall, the Sharer settled into the motionless but expectant posture he had assumed after his "activation" by the penlight. I could see that he still had some degree of control over his own movements, for his long fingers curled and uncurled and his skull nodded eerily in the halo of moonlight pocketing him. Even so, I realized that he had truly moved only at my voice command and my simultaneous gesturing with the penlight. And what did *that* mean?

Well, that the Sharer had relinquished control of his body to the man-machine Dorian Lorca, retaining for himself just those meaningless reflexes and stirrings that convince the manipulated of their own autonomy. It was an awesome prostitution, even if Wardress Kefa would have frowned to hear me say so. Momentarily I rejoiced in it, for it seemed to free me from the demands of an artificial eroticism, from the need to figure through what was expected of me. The Sharer would obey my simplest wrist-turning, my briefest word; all I had to do was *use* the control he had literally handed to me.

This virtually unlimited power, I thought then, was a therapy whose value Rumer would understand only too well. This was a harsh assessment, but penlight in hand, I felt that I too was a kind of marionette. . . .

Insofar as I could, I tried to come to grips with the physics of the Sharer's operation. First, the disc-within-a-disc on his chest apparently broke the connections ordinarily allowing him to exercise the senile powers that were still his. And, second, the penlight's beam restored and amplified these powers but delivered them into the hands of the speaker of imperatives who wielded the penlight. I recalled that in Earth's lunar probeship yards were crews of animatronic laborers programmed for fitting and welding. A single trained supervisor could direct from fifteen to twenty receiver-equipped laborers with one penlight and a microphone.

"Sharer," I commanded, blanking out his reverie, pointing the penlight, "go there. . . . No, no, not like that. Lift your feet. March for me. . . . That's right, a *goosestep.*"

While Wardress Kefa's third rule rattled in the back of my mind like a challenge, for the next several hours I toyed with the Sharer. After the marching I set him to calisthenics and interpretative dance, and he obeyed, moving more gracefully than I would have imagined possible. Here—then there—then back again. All he lacked was Beethoven's piano sonatas for an accompaniment.

At intervals I rested, but always the fascination of the penlight drew me back, almost against my will, and I once again played puppetmaster.

"Enough, Sharer, enough." The sky had a curdled quality suggestive of dawn. Catching sight of the cage overhead, I was taken by an irresistible impulse. I pointed the penlight at the cage and commanded, "Up, Sharer. Up, up, up."

The Sharer floated up from the floor and glided effortlessly toward the vault of the dome: a beautiful aerial walk. Without benefit of hawsers or scaffolds or wings the Sharer levitated. Hovering over the stove-bed he had been made to surrender, hovering over everything in the room, he reached the cage and swung before it with his hands touching the scrolled iron work on its little door. I dropped my own hands and watched him. So tightly was I gripping the penlight, however, that my knuckles must have resembled the caps of four tiny bleached skulls.

A great deal of time went by, the Sharer poised in the gelid air awaiting some word from me.

Morning began coming in the room's polygonal windows.

"Take the bird out," I ordered the Sharer, moving my penlight. "Take the bird out of the cage and kill it." This command, sadistically heartfelt, seemed to me a foolproof, indirect way of striking back at Rumer, Diderits, the Wardress, and the Third Rule of the House of Compassionate Sharers. More than anything, against all reason, I wanted the redwinged blackbird dead. And I wanted the Sharer to kill it.

Dawn made clear the cancerous encroachment of age in the Sharer's legs and hands, as well as the full horror of his cybergamically rigged death's-head. He looked like he had been unjustly hanged. And when his hands went up to the cage, instead of opening its door the Sharer lifted the entire contraption off the hook, fastening it to its tether, and then accidentally lost his grip on the cage.

I watched the cage fall—land on its side—bounce—bounce again. The Sharer stared down with his bulging silver-ringed eyes, his hands still spread wide to accommodate the fallen cage.

"Mr. Lorca," Wardress Kefa was knocking at the door. "Mr. Lorca, what's going on, please?"

I arose from the stove-bed, tossed my quilt aside, straightened my heavy robes. The Wardress knocked again. I looked at the Sharer swaying in the half-light like a sword or a pendulum, an instrument of severance. The night had gone faster than I liked.

Again, the purposeful knocking.

"Coming," I barked.

In the dented cage there was a flutter of crimson, a stillness, and then another bit of melancholy flapping. I hurled my penlight across the room. When it struck the wall, the Sharer rocked back and forth for a moment without descending so much as a centimeter. The knocking continued.

"You have the key, Wardress. Open the door."

She did, and stood on its threshold taking stock of the games we had played. Her eyes were bright but devoid of censure, and I swept past her wordlessly, burning with shame and bravado.

I slept that day—all that day—for the first time since leaving my own world. And I dreamed. I dreamed that I was connected to a mechanism pistoning away on the edge of the Haft Paykar diggings, siphoning deadly gases out of the shafts and perversely recirculating them through the pump with which I shared a symbiomechanic linkage. Amid a series of surreal turquoise sunsets and intermittent gusts of sand, this pistoning went on, and on, and on. When I awoke I lifted my hands to my face, intending to scar it with my nails. But a moment later, as I had known it would, the mirror in my chamber returned me a perfect, unperturbed Dorian Lorca. . . .

"May I come in?"

"I'm the guest here, Wardress. So I suppose you may."

She entered and, quickly intuiting my mood, walked to the other side of the chamber. "You slept, didn't you? And you dreamed?"

I said nothing.

"You dreamed, didn't you?"

"A nightmare, Wardress. A long and repetitious nightmare, notable only for being different from the ones I had on Diroste."

"A start, though. You weren't monitored during your sleep, after all, and even if your dream *was* a nightmare, Mr. Lorca, I believe you've managed to survive it. Good. All to the good."

I went to the only window in the room, a hexagonal pane of dark blue through which it was impossible to see anything. "Did you get him down?"

"Yes. And restored the birdcage to its place." Her tiny feet made pacing sounds on the hardwood. "The bird was unharmed."

"Wardress, what's all this about? Why have you paired me with . . . with this particular Sharer?" I turned around. "What's the point?"

"You're not estranged from your wife only, Mr. Lorca. You're—"

"I know that. I've *known* that."

"And I know that you know it. Give me a degree of credit. . . . You also know," she resumed, "that you're estranged from yourself, body and soul at variance—"

"Of course, damn it! And the argument between them's been stamped into every pseudo-organ and circuit I can lay claim to!"

"Please, Mr. Lorca, I'm trying to explain. This interior 'argument' you're so aware of . . . it's really a metaphor for an attitude you involuntarily adopted after Diderits performed his operations. And a metaphor can be taken apart and explained."

"Like a machine."

"If you like." She began pacing again. "To take inventory you have to surmount that which is to be inventoried. You go outside, Mr. Lorca, in order to come back in." She halted and fixed me with a colorless, lopsided smile.

"All of that," I began cautiously, "is clear to me. 'Know thyself,' saith Diderits and the ancient Greeks. . . . Well, if anything, my knowledge has *increased* my uneasiness about not only myself, but others—and not only others, but the very phenomena permitting us to spawn." I had an image of crimson-gilled fish firing upcurrent in a roiling, untidy barrage. "What I know hasn't cured anything, Wardress."

"No. That's why we've had you come here. To extend the limits of your knowledge and to involve you in relationships demanding a recognition of others as well as self."

"As with the Sharer I left hanging up in the air?"

"Yes. Distance is advisable at first, perhaps inevitable. You needn't feel guilty. In a night or two you'll be going back to him, and then we'll just have to see."

"Is this the only Sharer I'm going to be . . . working with?"

"I don't know. It depends on the sort of progress you make."

But for the Wardress Kefa, the Sharer in the crimson dome, and the noisy midnight visitants I had never seen, there were times when I believed myself the only occupant of the House. The thought of such isolation, although not unwelcome, was an anchoritic fantasy: I knew that breathing in the chambers next to mine, going about the arcane business of the lives they had bartered away, were humanoid creatures difficult to imagine; harder still, once lodged in the mind, to put out of it. To what number and variety of beings had Wardress Kefa indentured her love . . . ?

I had no chance to ask this question. We heard an insistent clomping on the steps outside the House and then muffled voices in the antechamber.

"Who's that?"

The Wardress put up her hand to silence me and opened the door to my room. "A moment," she called. "I'll be with you in a moment." But her husky voice didn't carry very well, and whoever had entered the House set about methodically knocking on doors and clomping from apartment to apartment, all the while bellowing the Wardress's name. "I'd better go talk with them," she told me apologetically.

"But who is it?"

"Someone voice-coded for entrance, Mr. Lorca. Nothing to worry about." And she went into the corridor, giving me a scent of spruce needles and a vision of solidly hewn rafters before the door swung to.

But I got up and followed the Wardress. Outside I found her face to face with two imposing persons who looked exactly alike in spite of their being one a man and the other a woman. Their faces had the same lantern-jawed mournfulness, their eyes a hooded look under prominent brows. They wore filigreed pea jackets, ski leggings, and fur-lined caps bearing the interpenetrating-galaxies insignia of Glaktik Komm. I judged them to be in their late thirties, E-standard, but they both had the domineering, glad-handing air of high-ranking veterans in the bureaucratic establishment, people who appreciate their positions just to the extent that their positions can be exploited. I knew. I had once been an official of the same stamp.

The man, having been caught in midbellow, was now trying to laugh. "Ah, Wardress, Wardress."

"I didn't expect you this evening," she told the two of them.

"We were granted a proficiency leave for completing the Salous blueprint in advance of schedule," the woman explained, "and so caught a late 'rail from Manitou Port to take advantage of the leave. We hiked down in the dark." Along with her eyebrows she lifted a hand lantern for our inspection.

"We *took* a proficiency leave," the man said, "even if we *were* here last week. And we deserved it too." He went on to tell us that "Salous" dealt with reclaiming the remnants of aboriginal populations and pooling them for something called integrative therapy. "The Great Plains will soon be our bordello, Wardress. There, you see: you and the Orhas are in the same business . . . at least until we're assigned to stage-manage something more prosaic." He clapped his gloved hands together and looked at me. "You're new, aren't you? Who are you going to?"

"Pardon me," the Wardress interjected wearily. "Who do *you* want tonight?"

The man looked at his partner with a mixture of curiosity and concern. "Cleva?"

"The mouthless one," Cleva responded at once. "Drugged, preferably."

"Come with me, Orhas," the Wardess directed. She led them first to her own apartment and then into the House's midinterior, where the three of them disappeared from my sight. I could hear them climbing one of the sets of stairs.

Shortly thereafter the Wardress returned to my room.

"They're twins?"

"In a manner of speaking, Mr. Lorca. Actually they're clonemates: Cleva and Cleirach Orha, specialists in Holosyncretic Management. They do abstract computer planning involving indigenous and alien populations, which is why they know of the House at all and have an authorization to come here."

"Do they always appear here together? Go upstairs together?"

The Wardress's silence clearly meant yes.

"That's a bit kinky, isn't it?"

She gave me an angry look whose implications immediately silenced me. I started to apologize, but she said: "The Orhas are the only visitants to the House who arrive together, Mr. Lorca. Since they share a common upbringing, the same genetic material, and identical biochemistries, it isn't surprising that their sexual preferences should coincide. In Manitou Port, I'm told, is a third clonemate who was permitted to marry, and her I've never seen either here or in Wolf Run Summit. It seems there's a *degree* of variety even among clonal siblings."

"Do these two come often?"

"You heard them in the House several days ago."

"They have frequent leaves, then?"

"Last time was an overnighter. They returned to Manitou Port in the morning, Mr. Lorca. Just now they were trying to tell me that they intend to be here for a few days."

"For treatment," I said.

"You know better. You're baiting me, Mr. Lorca." She had taken her graying scalplock into her fingers and was holding its fan of hair against her right cheek. In this posture, despite her preoccupation with the arrival of the Orhas, she looked very old and very innocent.

"Who is the 'mouthless one,' Wardess?"

"Good night, Mr. Lorca. I only returned to tell you good night." And with no other word she left.

It was the longest I had permitted myself to talk with her since our first afternoon in the House, the longest I had been in her presence since our claustrophobic 'rail ride from Manitou Port. Even the Orhas, bundled to the gills, as vulgar as sleek bullfrogs, hadn't struck me as altogether insufferable.

Wearing neither coat nor cap, I took a walk through the glens below the House, touching each wind-shaken tree as I came to it and trying to conjure out of the darkness a viable memory of Rumer's smile. . . .

"Sex as weapon," I told my Sharer, who sat propped on the stove-bed amid ten or twelve quilts of scarlet and off-scarlet. "As prince consort to the Governor of Diroste, that was the only weapon I had access to. . . . Rumer employed me as an emissary, Sharer, an espionage agent, a protocol officer, whatever state business required. I received visiting representatives of Glaktik Komm, mediated disputes in the Port Iranani business community, and went on biannual inspection tours of the Fetneh and Furak District mines. I did a little of everything, Sharer."

As I paced, the Sharer observed me with a macabre, but somehow not unsettling, penetration. The hollow of his chest was exposed, and, as I passed him, an occasional metallic wink caught the corner of my eye.

I told him the story of my involvement with a minor official in Port Iranani's department of immigration, a young woman whom I had never called by anything but her maternal surname, Humay. There had been others besides this woman, but Humay's story was the one I chose to tell. Why? Because alone among my ostensible "lovers," Humay I had never lain with. I had never chosen to.

Instead, to her intense bewilderment, I gave Humay ceremonial pendants, bracelets, earpieces, brooches, necklaces, and die-cut cameos of gold on silver, all from the collection of Rumer Montieth, Governor of Diroste—anything, in short, distinctive enough to be recognizable to my wife at a glance. Then, at those state functions requiring Rumer's attendance upon a visiting dignitary, I arranged for Humay to be present; sometimes I accompanied her myself, sometimes I found her an escort among the unbonded young men assigned to me as aides. Always I ensured that Rumer should see Humay, if not in a reception line then in the promenade of the formal recessional. Afterward I asked Humay, who never seemed to have even a naive insight into the purposes of my game, to hand back whatever piece of jewelry I had given her for ornament, and she did so. Then I returned the jewelry to Rumer's sandalwood box before my wife could verify what her eyes had earlier that evening tried to tell her. Everything I did was designed to create a false impression of my relationship with Humay, and I wanted my dishonesty in the matter to be conspicuous.

Finally, dismissing Humay for good, I gave her a cameo of Rumer's that had been crafted in the Furak District. I learned later that she had flung this cameo at an aide of mine who entered the offices of her department on a matter having nothing to do with her. She created a disturbance, several times raising my name. Ultimately (in two days' time), she was disciplined by a transfer to the frontier outpost of Yagme, the administrative center of the Furak District, and I never saw her again.

"Later, Sharer, when I dreamed of Humay, I saw her as a woman with mother-of-pearl flesh and ruby eyes. In my dreams she *became* the pieces of jewelry with which I'd tried to incite my wife's sexual jealousy— blunting it even as I incited it."

The Sharer regarded me with hard but sympathetic eyes.

Why? I asked him. Why had I dreamed of Humay as if she were an expensive clockwork mechanism, gilded, beset with gemstones, invulnerably enameled? And why had I so fiercely desired Rumer's jealousy?

The Sharer's silence invited confession.

After the Haft Paykar Incident (I went on, pacing), after Diderits had fitted me with a total prosthesis, my nightmares often centered on the young woman who'd been exiled to Yagme. Although in Port Iranani I hadn't once touched Humay in an erotic way, in my monitored nightmares I regularly descended into either a charnel catacomb or a half-fallen quarry—it was impossible to know which—and there forced myself, without success, on the bejeweled automaton she had become. In every instance Humay waited for me underground; in every instance she turned me back with coruscating laughter. Its echoes always drove me upward to the light, and in the midst of nightmare I realized that I wanted Humay far less than I did residency in the secret subterranean places she had made her own. The klieg lights that invariably directed my descent always followed me back out, too, so that Humay was always left kilometers below exulting in the dark. . . .

My Sharer got up and took a turn around the room, a single quilt draped over his shoulders and clutched loosely together at his chest. This was the first time since I had been coming to him that he had moved so far of his own volition, and I sat down to watch. Did he understand me at all? I had spoken to him as if his understanding were presupposed, a certainty—but beyond a hopeful *feeling* that my words meant something to him I'd had no evidence at all, not even a testimonial from Wardress Kefa. All of the Sharer's "reactions" were really nothing but projections of my own ambiguous hopes.

When he at last returned to me, he extended both hideously canaled arms and opened his fists. In them, the disc and the penlight. It was an offering, a compassionate, selfless offering, and for a moment I stared at his open hands in perplexity. What did they want of me, this Sharer, Wardress Kefa, the people who had sent me here? How was I supposed to buy either their forbearance or my freedom? By choosing power over impotency? By manipulation? . . . But these were altogether different questions, and I hesitated.

The Sharer then placed the small disc in the larger one beneath his sternum. Then, as before, a thousand esoteric connections severed, he froze. In the hand still extended toward me, the penlight glittered faintly and threatened to slip from his insensible grasp. I took it carefully from the Sharer's fingers, pulled back the sheath on its head, and gazed into its red-lit hollow. I released the sheath and pointed the penlight at the disc in his chest.

If I pulled the sheath back again, he would become little more than a fully integrated, *external* prosthesis—as much at my disposal as the hands holding the penlight.

"No," I said. "Not this time." And I flipped the penlight across the chamber, out of the way of temptation. Then, using my fingernails, I pried the small disc out of its electromagnetic moorings above the Sharer's heart.

He was restored to himself.

As was I to myself. As was I.

A day later, early in the afternoon, I ran into the Orhas in the House's midinterior. They were coming unaccompanied out of a lofty, seemingly sideways-canted door as I stood peering upward from the access corridor. Man and woman together, mirror images ratcheting down a Moebius strip of stairs, the Orhas held my attention until it was too late for me to slip away unseen.

"The new visitant," Cleirach Orha informed his sister when he reached the bottom step. "We've seen you before."

"Briefly," I agreed. "The night you arrived from Manitou Port for your proficiency leave."

"What a good memory you have," Cleva Orha said. "We also saw you the day *you* arrived from Manitou Port. You and the Wardress were just setting out from Wolf Run Summit together. Cleirach and I were beneath the ski lodge, watching."

"You wore no coat," her clonemate said in explanation of their interest. They both stared at me curiously. Neither was I wearing a coat in the well of the House of Compassionate Sharers—even though the temperature inside hovered only a few degrees above freezing and we could see our breaths before us like the ghosts of ghosts. . . . I was a queer one, wasn't I? My silence made them nervous and brazen.

"No coat," Cleva Orha repeated, "and the day cold enough to fur your spittle. 'Look at that one,' Cleirach told me; 'thinks he's a polar bear.' We laughed about that, studling. We laughed heartily."

I nodded, nothing more. A coppery taste of bile, such as I hadn't experienced for several days, flooded my mouth, and I wanted to escape the Orhas' warty good humor. They were intelligent people, otherwise they would never have been cloned, but face to face with their flawed skins and their loud, insinuative sexuality I began to feel my newfound stores of tolerance overbalancing like a tower of blocks. It was a bitter test, this meeting below the stairs, and one I was on the edge of failing.

"We seem to be the only ones in the House this month," the woman volunteered. "Last month the Wardress was gone, the Sharers had a holiday, and Cleirach and I had to content ourselves with incestuous buggery in Manitou Port."

"Cleva!" the man protested, laughing.

"It's true." She turned to me. "It's true, studling. And that little she-goat—Kefa, I mean—won't even tell us why the Closed sign was out for so long. Delights in mystery, that one."

"That's right," Cleirach went on. "She's an exasperating woman. She begrudges you your privileges. You have to tread lightly on her patience. Sometimes you'd like to take *her* into a chamber and find out what makes her tick. A bit of exploratory surgery, heyla!" Saying this, he showed me his trilling tongue.

"She's a maso-ascetic, brother."

"I don't know. There are many mansions in this House, Cleva, several of which she's refused to let us enter. Why?" He raised his eyebrows suggestively, as Cleva had done the night she lifted her hand lantern for our notice. The expressions were the same.

Cleva Orha appealed to me as a disinterested third party: "What do you think, studling? Is Wardress Scalplock at bed and at bone with one of her Sharers? Or does she lie by herself, maso-ascetically, under a hide of untanned elk hair? What do you think?"

"I haven't really thought about it." Containing my anger, I tried to leave. "Excuse me, Orha-clones."

"Wait, wait, wait," the woman said mincingly, half-humorously. "You know our names and a telling bit of our background. That puts you up, studling. We won't have that. You can't go without giving us a name."

Resenting the necessity, I told them my name.

"From where?" Cleirach Orha asked.

"Colony World GK-11. We call it Diroste."

Brother and sister exchanged a glance of sudden enlightenment, after which Cleva raised her thin eyebrows and spoke in a mocking rhythm: "Ah ha, the mystery solved. Out and back our Wardress went and therefore closed her House."

"Welcome, Mr. Lorca. Welcome."

"We're going up to Wolf Run for an afterbout of toddies and P-nol. What about you? Would you like to go? The climb wouldn't be anything to a warm-blooded studling like you. Look, Cleirach. Biceps unbundled and his sinuses still clear."

In spite of the compliment I declined.

"Who have *you* been with?" Cleirach Orha wanted to know. He bent forward conspiratorially. "We've been with a native of an extrakomm world called Trope. That's the local name. Anyhow, there's not another such being inside of a hundred light-years, Mr. Lorca."

"It's the face that intrigues us," Cleva Orha explained, saving me from an immediate reply to her brother's question. And then she reached out, touched my arm, and ran a finger down my arm to my hand. "Look. Not even a goose bump. Cleirach, you and I are suffering the shems and trivs, and our earnest Mr. Lorca's standing here bareboned."

Brother was annoyed by this analysis. There was something he wanted to know, and Cleva's non sequiturs weren't advancing his case. Seeing that he was going to ask me again, I rummaged about for an answer that was neither informative nor tactless.

Cleva Orha, meanwhile, was peering intently at her fingertips. Then she looked at my arm, again at her fingers, and a second time at my arm. Finally she locked eyes with me and studied my face as if for some clue to the source of my reticence.

Ah, I thought numbly, she's recognized me for what I am. . . .

"Mr. Lorca can't tell you who he's been with, Cleirach," Cleva Orha told her clonemate, "because he's not a visitant to the House at all and he doesn't choose to violate the confidences of those who are."

Dumbfounded, I said nothing.

Cleva put her hand on her brother's back and guided him past me into the House's antechamber. Over her shoulder she bid me good afternoon in a toneless voice. Then the Orha-clones very deliberately let themselves out the front door and began the long climb to Wolf Run Summit.

What had happened? It took me a moment to figure it out. Cleva Orha had recognized me as a human-machine and from this recognition drawn a logical but mistaken inference: she believed me, like the "mouthless one" from Trope, a slave of the House. . . .

During my next tryst with my Sharer I spoke for an hour, two hours, maybe more, of Rumer's infuriating patience, her dignity, her serene ardor. I had moved her—maneuvered her—to the expression of these qualities by my own hollow commitment to Humay and the others before Humay who had engaged me only physically. Under my wife's attentions, however, I preened sullenly, demanding more than Rumer—than any woman in Rumer's position—had it in her power to give. My needs, I wanted her to know, my needs were as urgent and as real as Diroste's.

And at the end of one of these vague encounters Rumer seemed both to concede the legitimacy of my demands and to decry their intemperance by removing a warm pendant from her throat and placing it like an accusation in my palm.

"A week later," I told the Sharer, "was the inspection tour of the diggings at Haft Paykar."

These things spoken, I did something I had never done before in the Wardress's House: I went to sleep under the hand of my Sharer. My dreams were dreams rather than nightmares, and clarified ones at that, shot through with light and accompanied from afar by a peaceful funneling of sand. The images that came to me were haloed arms and legs orchestrated within a series of shifting yellow, yellow-orange, and subtly red discs. The purr of running sand behind these movements conferred upon them the benediction of mortality, and that, I felt, was good.

I awoke in a blast of icy air and found myself alone. The door to the Sharer's apartment was standing open on the shaft of the stairwell, and I heard faint, angry voices coming across the emptiness between. Disoriented, I lay on my stove-bed staring toward the door, a square of shadow feeding its chill into the room.

"*Dorian!*" a husky voice called. "*Dorian!*"

Wardress Kefa's voice, diluted by distance and fear. A door opened, and her voice hailed me again, this time with more clarity. Then the door slammed shut, and every sound in the House took on a smothered quality, as if mumbled through cold semiporous wood.

I got up, dragging my bedding with me, and reached the narrow porch on the stairwell with a clear head. Thin starlight filtered through the unshuttered windows in the ceiling. Nevertheless, looking from stairway to stairway to stairway inside the House, I had no idea behind which door the Wardress now must be.

Because there existed no connecting stairs among the staggered landings of the House, my only option was to go down. I took the steps two at a time, very nearly plunging.

At the bottom I found my Sharer with both hands clenched about the outer stair rail. He was trembling. In fact, his chest and arms were quivering so violently that he seemed about to shake himself apart. I put my hands on his shoulders and tightened my grip until the tremors racking him threatened to rack my systems, too. Who would come apart first?

"Go upstairs," I told the Sharer. "Get the hell upstairs."

I heard the Wardress call my name again. Although by now she had squeezed some of the fear out of her voice, her summons was still distance-muffled and impossible to pinpoint.

The Sharer either couldn't or wouldn't obey me. I coaxed him, cursed him, goaded him, tried to turn him around so that he was heading back up the steps. Nothing availed. The Wardress, summoning me, had inadvertently called the Sharer out as my proxy, and he now had no intention of giving back to me the role he'd just usurped. The beautifully faired planes of his skull turned toward me, bringing with them the stainless-steel rings of his eyes. These were the only parts of his body that didn't tremble, but they were helpless to countermand the agues shaking him. As inhuman and unmoving as they were, the Sharer's features still managed to convey stark, unpitiable entreaty. . . .

I sank to my knees, felt about the insides of the Sharer's legs, and took the penlight and the disc from the two pocketlike incisions tailored to these instruments. Then I stood and used them.

"Find Wardress Kefa for me, Sharer," I commanded, gesturing with the penlight at the windows overhead. "Find her."

And the Sharer floated up from the steps through the midinterior of the House. In the crepuscular starlight, rocking a bit, he seemed to pass through a knot of curving stairs into an open space where he was all at once brightly visible.

"Point to the door," I said, jabbing the penlight uncertainly at several different landings around the well. "Show me the one."

My words echoed, and the Sharer, legs dangling, inscribed a slow half-circle in the air. Then he pointed toward one of the nearly hidden doorways.

I stalked across the well, found a likely seeming set of stairs, and climbed them with no notion at all of what was expected of me.

Wardress Kefa didn't call out again, but I heard the same faint, somewhat slurred voices that I'd heard upon waking and knew that they belonged to the Orhas. A burst of muted female laughter, twice repeated, convinced me of this, and I hesitated on the landing.

"All right," I told my Sharer quietly, turning him around with a turn of the wrist, "go on home."

Dropping through the torus of a lower set of stairs, he found the porch in front of our chamber and settled upon it like a clumsily handled puppet. And why not? I was a clumsy puppetmaster. Because there seemed to be nothing else I could do, I slid the penlight into a pocket of my dressing gown and knocked on the Orhas' door.

"Come in," Cleva Orha said. "By all means, Sharer Lorca, come in."

I entered and found myself in a room whose surfaces were all burnished as if with beeswax. The timbers shone. Whereas in the other chambers I had seen nearly all the joists and rafters were rough-hewn, here they were smooth and splinterless. The scent of sandalwood pervaded the air, and opposite the door was a carven screen blocking my view of the chamber's stove-bed. A tall wooden lamp illuminated the furnishings and the three people arrayed around the lamp's border of light like iconic statues.

"Welcome," Cleirach Orha said. "Your invitation was from the Wardress, however, not us." He wore only a pair of silk pantaloons drawn together at the waist with a cord, and his right forearm was under Wardress Kefa's chin, restraining her movement without quite cutting off her wind.

His disheveled clonemate, in a dressing gown very much like mine, sat cross-legged on a cushion and toyed with a wooden stiletto waxed as the beams of the chamber were waxed. Her eyes were too wide, too lustrous, as were her brother's, and I knew this was the result of too much placenol in combination with too much Wolf Run small-malt in combination with the Orhas' innate meanness. The woman was drugged, and drunk, and, in consequence of these things, malicious to a turn. Cleirach didn't appear quite so far gone as his sister, but all he had to do to strangle the Wardress, I understood, was raise the edge of his forearm into her trachea. I felt again the familiar sensation of being out of my element, gill-less in a sluice of stinging salt water. . . .

"Wardress Kefa—" I began.

"She's all right," Cleva Orha assured me. "Perfectly all right." She tilted her head so that she was gazing at me out of her right eye alone, and then barked a hoarse, deranged-sounding laugh.

"Let the Wardress go," I told her clonemate.

Amazingly, Cleirach Orha looked intimidated. "Mr. Lorca's an an-proz," he reminded Cleva. "That little letter opener you're cleaning your nails with, it's not going to mean anything to him."

"Then let her go, Cleirach. Let her go."

Cleirach released the Wardress, who, massaging her throat with both hands, ran to the stove-bed. She halted beside the carven screen and beckoned me with a doll-like hand. "Mr. Lorca . . . Mr. Lorca, please . . . will you see to him first? I beg you."

"I'm going back to Wolf Run Summit," Cleirach informed his sister, and he slipped on a night jacket, gathered up his clothes, and left the room. Cleva Orha remained seated on her cushion, her head tilted back as if she were tasting a bitter potion from a heavy metal goblet.

Glancing doubtfully at her, I went to the Wardress. Then I stepped around the wooden divider to see her Sharer.

The Tropeman lying there was a slender creature, almost slight. There was a ridge of flesh where his mouth ought to be, and his eyes were an organic variety of crystal, uncanny and depthful stones. One of these brandy-colored stones had been dislodged in its socket by Cleva's "letter opener"; and although the Orhas had failed to pry the eye completely loose, the Tropeman's face was streaked with blood from their efforts. The streaks ran down into the bedding under his narrow, fragile head and gave him the look of an aborigine in war paint. Lacking external genitalia, his sexless body was spread-eagled atop the quilts so that the burn marks on his legs and lower abdomen cried out for notice as plangently as did his face.

"Sweet light, sweet light," the Wardress chanted softly, over and over again, and I found her locked in my arms, hugging me tightly above her beloved, butchered ward, this Sharer from another star.

"He's not dead," Cleva Orha said from her cushion. "The rules . . . the rules say not to kill 'em, and we go by the rules, brother and I."

"What can I do, Wardress Kefa?" I whispered, holding her. "What do you want me to do?"

Slumped against me, the Wardress repeated her consoling chant and held me about the waist. So, fearful that this being with eyes like precious gems would bleed to death as we delayed, each of us undoubtedly ashamed of our delay, we delayed—and I held the Wardress, pressed her head to my chest, gave her a warmth I hadn't before believed in me. And she returned this warmth in undiluted measure.

Wardress Kefa, I realized, was herself a Compassionate Sharer; she was as much a Sharer as the bleeding Tropeman on the stove-bed or that obedient creature whose electrode-studded body and luminous death's-head had seemed to mock the efficient mechanical deadness in myself— a deadness that, in turning away from Rumer, I had made a god of. In the face of this realization my disgust with the Orhas was transfigured into something very unlike disgust: a mode of perception, maybe; a means of adapting. An answer had been revealed to me, and, without its being either easy or uncomplicated, it was still, somehow, very simple: I, too, was a Compassionate Sharer. Monster, machine, anproz, the designation didn't matter any longer. Wherever I might go, I was forevermore a ward of this tiny woman's House—my fate, inescapable and sure.

The Wardress broke free of my embrace and knelt beside the Trope-man. She tore a piece of cloth from the bottom of her tunic. Wiping the blood from the Sharer's face, she said, "I heard him calling me while I was downstairs, Mr. Lorca. Encephalogoi. 'Brain words,' you know. And I came up here as quickly as I could. Cleirach took me aside. All I could do was shout for you. Then, not even that."

Her hands touched the Sharer's burns, hovered over the wounded eye, moved about with a knowledge the Wardress herself seemed unaware of.

"We couldn't get it all the way out," Cleva Orha laughed. "Wouldn't come. Cleirach tried and tried."

I found the cloned woman's pea jacket, leggings, and tunic. Then I took her by the elbow and led her down the stairs to her brother. She reviled me tenderly as we descended, but otherwise didn't protest.

"You . . . " she predicted once we were down, "you we'll never get."

She was right. It was a long time before I returned to the House of Compassionate Sharers, and, in any case, upon learning of their sadistic abuse of one of the wards of the House, the authorities in Manitou Port denied the Orhas any future access to it. A Sharer, after all, was an expensive commodity.

But I did return. After going back to Diroste and living with Rumer the remaining forty-two years of her life, I applied to the House as a novitiate.

I am here now. In fact as well as in metaphor, I am today one of the Sharers.

My brain cells die, of course, and there's nothing anyone can do to stop utterly the depredations of time—but my body seems to be that of a middle-aged man and I still move inside it with ease. Visitants seek comfort from me, as once, against my will, I sought comfort here; and I try to give it to them . . . even to the ones who have only a muddled understanding of what a Sharer really is. My battles aren't really with these unhappy people; they're with the advance columns of my senility (I don't like to admit this) and the shock troops of my memory, which is still excessively good. . . .

Wardress Kefa has been dead seventeen years, Diderits twenty-three, and Rumer two. That's how I keep score now. Death has also carried off the gem-eyed Tropeman and the Sharer who drew the essential Dorian Lorca out of the prosthetic rind he had mistaken for himself.

I intend to be here a while longer yet. I have recently been given a chamber into which the light sifts with a painful white brilliance reminiscent of the sands of Diroste or the snows of Wolf Run Summit. This is all to the good. Either way, you see, I die at home. . . .

THE FALLEN COUNTRY

H e had blank, sky-blue eyes and confused blond hair. He had a wry, dry voice with just a lemon twist of longing in it. He was small for his age, almost as though he had willed himself not to grow. As I closed the door behind us, my hand brushed against his and he flinched away violently in the split second before willing himself to smile; from this I pegged him as a victim of child abuse.

"Hi," I said, answering him. "My name is Dora Marx." I eased him into the brown, wombish chair that faced my desk. "You may call me—" I sat down myself, with the stuck-record-in-a-groove smoothness that comes from seeing a thousand children a year for twenty years, "—either Dora, or Mrs. Marx. Whichever makes you feel more comfortable."

"I think I'd prefer Mrs. Marx," he said. "But," he added, "you can call me Billy." Touché.

He didn't look at me. I went to the window to slam out the eleven o'clock yelling from the schoolyard. God damn it, they should never make you work under these conditions. . . .

I said, "You're the one who—"

"They found at five in the morning, clinging to the steeple of Santa Maria's. You read the papers?"

"Sometimes," I said, flicking the clipping out of his file.

BILLY BINDER, AGE 12—

"Where'd you get that scar?"—*like an albino earth-worm, wriggling into the sleeve of his T-shirt.*

"Fell off my bike." Sure.

—FOUND HALF-DEAD ON THE LEDGE, HIS ARMS AROUND THE STEEPLE ON THE SIDE OVERLOOKING ANGEL PLAZA. FATHER EP-STEIN, SUMMERTIME PASTOR STANDING IN FOR FATHER SAN-TINI, WHILE TRYING TO RING THE BELL—

"It says here," I said, "that you were suffering from severe frostbite."

"Yes. From the snow."

"It doesn't snow in Florida in the middle of August—" No point trying to argue with him yet. My job was to listen, only to listen. I wasn't trained to root out traumas. It wasn't up to me to pronounce the kid an attempted suicide either, or to solve the mystery of how he got to the topmost turret of a locked historical monument, or to elucidate the medical wonder of frostbite in a hundred-degree heat wave. I was only a counselor in a parochial school too poor and stupid to afford an expert.

I wouldn't get anywhere by questioning his story. Perhaps I should start with something else. "How often do they beat you up?" I said.

"What?" Terror flecked his eyes for a second. Then they went dead. He said, "Almost every day." It was in the same tone of voice.

"Who?"

"Pete, my Mom's boyfriend."

"What?"

He told me about it, never raising his voice. I had been doing this for twenty years. After a while you grow iron railings round your brains. Nothing hurts anymore. I listened, staring at my hands and wishing a ton of Porcelana on them. I knew I would sit there and endure until the catalogue of beltings and poundings had dissolved into incoherence, into tears, into hysteria, and then I would flow into the cracks in the kid's soul like epoxy glue and make him seem whole for a while . . . but he didn't give me a chance. He went on in that same monotone, detail after detail, until it was I who was ready to crack. I held up my hand. He stopped.

"Don't you ever cry?" I said.

"Not anymore," he said. "I've promised."

"What do you mean, you promised?"

"The Snow Dragon."

"Tell me about him."

"I knew it!" he cried. Now he was exultant, taunting. I wasn't prepared for the change in mood; I started most unprofessionally. "You're supposed to be trying to help me or something, but all you want to do is listen to me lie!"

Shifting gears to accommodate his outburst: "Is that why he hits you?"

"Yes! Yes! But I won't stop!"

"It's all right," I said. "You can lie if you want. You can tell all the lies you want in this room. Nothing will ever escape from here. . . . "

"Like a confessional? Like a black hole?"

"Yes." Imaginative imagery, at least. This kid was no dummy. "Like a black hole." He looked me in the eye for the first time. His eyes were clear as glass; I could read no deceit in them.

"Good," he said firmly. I waited. I think he had begun to trust me.

"So what were you really doing, then, up there. Straddling the steeple, I mean."

"Rescuing a princess."

That's how he started telling me the stories. The stories! They would have been the envy of any clinical psychiatrist with a pet theory and a deadline and a paper to be churned out in a fury. To me they were only stories. Of course I did not believe them; but my job was to listen, not to judge.

Billy had been fostered by one set of parents after another. He couldn't remember the first few. After the divorcees had played musical chairs for a while he had settled with the third or fourth mother, Joan, and they'd moved to our town, a spiderweb of brash fast food places that circled the eighteenth-century Spanish church that was the town's one attraction. Billy shed pasts like a snake sloughing its skin or a duck shaking off canal water. The only thing he kept was the name, Billy Binder. He'd always been adamant about his name. He'd always gotten his way about it somehow: throwing tantrums, whining, running away. It was the only part of him he'd ever kept successfully. Days his mother typed accounts in a doctor's office; nights she went to school, dreaming vaguely of a softer future. As I grew to know Billy I would go over and meet her sometimes at the doctor's. She was a dark-haired, tired, cowering, rake-thin woman; I never got much of a feel for her. And somehow I never met Pete. I never went to their house, except once, at the end of my association with Billy; and I shall never return there.

Pete came on a motorcycle and took over their lives. He and Billy exchanged a single glance and understood each other to the core: *enemy*. But Pete was the stronger, physically anyway. He wielded his leather belt like a lion tamer in a circus. Nights, after it was over—and it almost always happened, every night—Billy went to his closet of a room and lay down choked with anger. He never tried to disguise his weals. He flaunted them in school, never offering any explanation for them. And no one dared ask him for one. They saw him shrouded in anger as in a burning forceshield, and they were afraid to touch his loneliness.

A night came when the anger burst at last. It was long past midnight and the pain had died down a little. Billy got out of bed, wriggled into some old cutoffs, pulled on a T-shirt, wincing as it raked against new welts. He tiptoed out of the house. He found his old bike leaning against the front door, and then he biked like a maniac into the burning night. He did not know what drove him. A quick twisty path rounded some shadowy palms and crossed an empty highway and skirted the beach for some miles. It was a night without stars, the heat wringing moisture from the blackness. At first he heard the sea, but the surf-shatter faded quickly. In the distance rose a wall of luxury hotels, distant giants' tombstones. In a while he made a left turn into the town. He was not biking with any particular purpose. It began to snow.

He didn't take it in at first. His anger was everything. But it didn't stop. Fragments of cold were pelting his face, and then great sheets of white, but Billy had never seen snow before, and he was too busy being angry to realize that this was a blizzard. . . .

(*I'll kill him!* he was thinking, forcing the pedals against the ever-piling snow. . . .)

And then it thinned. He came to a stop, stuck against a rock or a drift. A dead, sourceless light played over vistas of whiteness. It didn't feel like the world at all. The snow didn't stop. Sometimes it tickled his face. Sometimes it swirled in the sky, its flakes like stars in a nebula. There was no sun or moon. Misty in the horizon, an impossibly far horizon, Billy saw white crenellated castle walls that ran behind a white hill and emerged from the other side of it; they went on as far as he could see, twisting like marble serpents. Billy began walking toward the hill. He did not wonder at where he was. The cold didn't touch him, not like sticking your hand in the freezer. He walked. By a strange foreshortening or trick of perspective he found himself facing the hill—

The hill's wings flapped, eyes flared briefly, fire-brilliant blue. It was a dragon. Again the eyes flared, dulled, flared, dulled. . . . Billy gazed at the dragon for a long time. In a rush that sent the wind sighing, the dragon spread its wings, sweeping the snow into fierce sudden flurries. Billy saw that the dragon had no scales, but little mosaic-things of interlocking snowflakes; when the dragon's eyes flashed, the flakes caught rainbow fire and sparkled for a few seconds.

The dragon said, "Billy Binder, welcome to the fallen country."

Billy was afraid at last. "Send me home!" he cried. And then he remembered Pete and said nothing.

When the dragon spoke, its voice was piping clear, emotionless, like the voice of a child's ghost. It wasn't a booming, threatening voice at all.

"What are you thinking?" he said. "That I don't sound fierce and threatening the way a dragon should? That I don't roar?" He did roar then, a tinny, buzzing roar like an electric alarm clock.

Billy said, "Who has stolen your roar?" He felt a twinge of pity for the dragon; but then his anger slapped it down.

"This is the fallen country, Billy. Here there is no emotion at all. We cannot love or hate. We cannot utter great thunderous cries of joy or terror. . . . The world is muted by perpetual snow. That is why you are here."

"What do you mean?" Billy was scared and wanted to go back to his bike. He looked behind him and saw it, impossibly far away; it seemed strange that he could have walked this far, through the trudge-thick snowdrifts, in only a few minutes. Perhaps time was different here. He knew that time was different in different countries.

The dragon said, "You are here because you are full of anger, Billy Binder. In the fallen country we need such anger as yours. Anger is strength here. . . . If I could feel such anger, such love, such hatred as you can feel, I would die, Billy. . . . "

Wrenching his feet out of the knee-deep coldless snow, Billy forced himself to walk toward the dragon. Even the dread he had been feeling had passed away now. "But who has done this to you? Who has stolen your feelings?"

"You know. You have touched his shadow. His shadow has come pursuing you. The Ringmaster. With his whip of burning cold."

Pete! "You should kill him!" Whiteness burned all around him, making the tears run.

"He cannot be killed. He slips from world to world as easily as you have done." Again the pitiful whinebuzz that passed for a roar. "But we can work against him. Slowly, slowly we can sap him of his strength. Your anger is powerful here. Your anger can build bridges, can burn pathways through the snow. Try it, Billy."

Billy clenched himself, feeling the rage course through him, and when he opened his eyes he saw greenery poking through the snow for a few seconds, but then it was misted over by white again.

"Do you see?" the dragon said. "You are Binder."

"That's my name," said Billy, "but—"

"Your roots are in the fallen country. That is why you have never felt truly at home in your world, why you have been tossed from household to household, taking only the name *Binder* with you."

Thunder shuddered through the cloud-haze. For a moment the sky parted. A whip cracking, halving the sky, retracting into the grayness, a burst of sound that could have been applause or a circus band starting up or a crowd deriding a fallen clown—

"*Pete!*" he blurted out.

"No," said the dragon, "only the shadow; the Ringmaster has a thousand shadows, and it is only a shadow of his shadow that has followed you all the way to your distant world."

Billy nodded, understanding suddenly.

Then he saw a red weal open on the dragon's neck, blood trickling in slow motion onto the snow, blood that stained the whiteness like a poppy-cluster—"He's hurt you!" he said. They were akin then, he and this alien creature. Both were at the mercy of—"Can't you cry out?" he cried into the howling wind. "Can't you feel anything?"

"No." The dragon's voice did not change. "Here one need feel no pain at all. It's better to feel nothing, isn't it? Come now. Ride me."

He extended a wing; it fanned out into a diamond-speckled staircase. When Billy stepped onto it he realized that he felt no cold at all. He should be freezing to death through his worn sneakers, but he felt only numbness. It was less real than a dream.

"Let's go now. We'll have adventures, rescuing princesses, fighting monsters and such. Isn't that what every child wants to do? A lot of children find their way into the fallen country. And they find a use for themselves here. . . . One day we'll have a whole army of them."

"But I want to find the Ringmaster himself! I don't want him to hurt you and me anymore. I want to kill him."

The dragon only laughed, a wretched ghost of a laugh. Billy clambered up the wing.

"Every child who comes here dreams of reaching the Ringmaster. Of shaping his anger into a bridge that will touch the very heart of the Ringmaster and topple the circus where he wields his whip. They learn better, Billy."

"*I want to kill him!*"

Again a specter of a laugh. Billy settled on the dragon's back; it was ridged with soft dunes of snow. The dragon flapped his wings, not resoundingly, but with a thud like a cellar door slamming shut in a next-door house.

The dragon said, "You'll never need to cry again, Billy. From now on you will have to save your grief, your anger, save it for here where it will be of some use. Listen! I am the Snow Dragon, the last surviving dragon of the fallen country. I survived by purging myself of all that made me dragon: my fire, my rage, my iridescing, sparkle-flashing scales that gleamed silver in the moon and gold in the sun. Now sun and moon are gone. And I have waited for a thousand years, so long that I have lost the capacity to feel any joy at your coming. . . . I, the Snow Dragon, tell you to dry your tears for the last time. Promise me."

"I promise." Billy found himself acceding, on impulse, without think-ing it out. Already his eyes felt drained. Only the melting snowflakes moistened his cheeks. He felt no motion, but saw the ground fall from the dragon's claws. They were rising.

They flew through snowstorms into landscapes overcast and lightly puffed with snow: here and there the outlines of castles, here and there a spire poking through the whiteness. There were oceans frosted with vanilla icing. There were cities full of silent people, trudging listlessly, never pausing to watch the dragon swooping in the sky, never lifting their glazed-dead eyes from the snow. At times the sky opened, the whip cracked once, twice, thunderclap-swift, raising fresh welts in the dragon's hide. They flew on; and the Snow Dragon never seemed to notice the Ringmaster's capricious punishments.

"Do you still want to kill him?" said the dragon. The air streamed past Billy's face, and yet he felt nothing, as though he carried around him a bubble of utter stillness. "After what you've seen he can do—"

"Yes! Yes!" Billy cried fiercely. Anger pounded inside him. "I see what I have to do now; I see why I was brought here!" And he closed his eyes, thinking of the bridge of anger. And again and again the light-ning-whip cracked. Although he didn't feel its wetness he saw he was sitting in a pool of congealing blood. Dragon's blood. Purple, smoking in the chill air.

I pushed myself into a nice, controlled, professional posture. "I liked your story," I said, noting from the silence through the window that the forty-five minutes were over.

How can he sit there and spin such a haunting web of dreams—I was shivering in my chair. So was Billy, as though from terrible cold. I thought, *He has plucked, out of the septic tank of the human unconscious, an image of such precision, such startling profundity, an image of the dark country we all carry inside us.* . . . I checked myself, knowing I was beginning to sound like a pretentious academic paper. *Get a grip on yourself.*

"Billy," I said, trying to gauge my tone, to show just the right blend of concern and unconcern. His story cried out for involvement, for belief, the way poetry does even when it lies. But my job was not to sit back and revel in the mystery and the beauty of his delusions. It was to help him find reality . . . to shatter the crystal goblet with my sledgehammer of platitudes. "I liked it," I repeated.

"It wasn't a story."

"Of course not."

Pause. "See you next week." I tried a noncommittal half-smile.

"Sure." And suddenly he was gone, leaving me alone to hunt for shadows in the shadowless sunshine.

The following week, Billy said, "I wait until it builds up, until I can't stand it anymore. And then it bursts out of me and I'm free to enter the fallen country. And afterwards, I'll find myself in bed or maybe in some strange place, and sometimes I'll be blue with cold and my joints will feel like icicles and I'll be shaking all over. . . . "

I found the mother, Joan, at a desk in an office in a huge building, coffined in by expanses of naked glass, always reaching for the phone.

I said, "You know there's at least one way of ending the problem, don't you?"

She said, "Yes." When she looked at me she reminded me of myself, and I was unnerved by this. She was a dark-haired, slight woman, who didn't look like Billy at all—well, that was only to be expected. Unlike her stepson, she did not hide her feelings well. I saw her guilt very clearly.

I said, "Then why don't you get rid of the man?"

She paused to take an appointment. A crisp, mediciny odor wisped by for a moment. Outside, palm-fringed concrete paths crisscrossed a carpet of harsh, brash green. But I was thinking of snow, of cold, numbing snow. Finally she answered me, speaking with difficulty.

"I can't, I can't!" She was crying a little, and I found myself turning away, embarrassed. "What can I do, Mrs. Marx? He's a force, not a person—he's not human. And what about Billy's lies? Will they suddenly end?"

"By imagining that Pete is not human," I said cruelly, "you make it
a lot easier on yourself, don't you?" *Mustn't lose control . . .*
Feeling very foolish, I turned around and walked out. I don't know
what I was trying to accomplish. All I knew was that I was well past my
good years, and that I longed for the snow, for the fallen country that
we all keep locked in our hearts. I wanted to be like Billy. I was looking
forward to his next appointment, even as I felt guilty, because I had been
spying on another's pain.

Then there were the princesses: Some were in dungeons, buried neck-
deep in the snow; others were chained in the topmost turrets of candy-
cane castles of intertwisting tourmaline and olivine, half-veiled by the
clinging whiteness. Billy saved a princess the second or third time he
came to the fallen country.
They were swooping down from where the sun should have shone,
and Billy saw the castle, a forest of ice-caked spires, mist-shrouded, dull
gray in the unchanging cold light of the fallen country.
"Time to rescue a princess!" said the dragon.
They circled the tower; for a minute Billy reveled in the rushing of
the wing-made wind. The dragon's flight was a dance that almost seemed
like joy. But when Billy asked the dragon, "Are you happy, Snow Dragon?
Has my coming done this to you, then?" the dragon's swooping seemed
to lose its passion.
The dragon said, "Now, Billy, isn't rescuing princesses one of the
oldest compulsions of your world? Isn't it what every earth creature longs
to do?"
"I wouldn't know," said Billy, who didn't always do too well in school,
and did not know of such things as myths. "Where's the princess?"
"In the castle, of course. And now—" they were skimming the turret's
edge, almost, and the windrush had become still—"you must do what
you know best how to do."
"I don't know what you mean!"
"Your anger, Billy . . . "
And Billy understood, then, what he was capable of doing. He took
the anger inside him, he thought of Pete and of terrible nights lying
awake and burning for vengeance, he concentrated all this anger until it
took shape, took form. . . . A bridge sprang up where the dragon had
hovered, clawing the emptiness—a bridge of thin ice, as though someone
had sliced up a skating rink and slung it into the sky. The bridge ran all

the way to a round window, gaping with serrations like a monster's mouth, at the top of the tower. Billy sprang lightly from the dragon's back. He looked down for a moment, thinking, *I should be scared but I'm not, I'm too angry.*

Beneath him the whiteness stretched limitlessly. He could not be scared; you could not gauge the distance of things at all, the ground seemed cushiony-soft, not a death trap at all. He took a couple of steps on the bridge. It was slippery. He looked at the dark yawning jaws of the window, feeling no fear, fueled instead by his terrible anger, and he began walking.

He leapt gingerly from the bridge into the room; he expected it to be dark but it was lit by the same depressing sourceless light that illuminated the world outside. The princess was chained to the wall. He closed his eyes and shattered the chains with a swift spurt of anger, and the princess came toward him. She was a typical blond, boyish, unvoluptuous princess like the ones in Disney cartoons, with kohl-darkened eyelashes fluttering over expressionless glittering eyes that seemed almost faceted like an insect's. She did not smile, but walked toward him stiffly and thanked him.

"That's all I get?" he said.

"What did you expect?" said the princess. Her voice was like the dragon's voice: thin, toneless, uninterested.

"But I expected—"

The princess laughed. "Expected what? Something strange and beautiful and romantic? How can that be, with *him* up there, watching, watching? He'll catch me again, don't you fret."

I want to kill him!

"I know you want to kill him," the princess said, seeming to read his mind. "But you won't, you know. He is more real than you will ever be."

And then she stepped out of the window and left him stranded; for the bridge was gone, melted into the air. And it was because he had lain aside his anger for a moment.

"That's how I ended up on top of the church," Billy told me. But how could I believe such a thing? And yet it was so neat, so cleverly paradigmaticized. That the real world and the fantasy should have such interfaces of confluence: the church, the castle. Piety and passion, authority and rebellion, father-shadow and princess-anima, superego and id. An amateur analyst's dream.

I said to Billy, "Let's work together now, you and I. Let's come out of the fallen country into the real world, let's fight this inner grief of yours." The words sounded so false. They *were* false.

"You know what he told me?" said Billy. "The Snow Dragon, I mean."

"What?"

"He told me that I would never have to leave if I didn't want to."

That bastard Pete! But it's people like him who pay my rent. I too am a vampire, feeding myself on children's emotions. Would Billy understand, if I told him, how we all have a piece of Pete inside us?

Billy said, "Our time's up, Mrs. Marx."

"Wait a moment—" I had no business going on longer than the allotted time. "Billy, won't you stop and just let me help?"

He paused at the door. We confronted each other for a moment, an innocent child who daily harrowed hell and a middle-aged, middle-class, middle-grade couselor jaded with trivialities who must supposedly know all the answers. His face was trusting. He was a pathological liar, a liar of frightening vividness, but all I saw was a frightened kid who yearned for something I did not have to give. He said, "How can I let you help me if you won't even believe me?"

I said—I couldn't lie, even to reassure him—"No, I don't believe you."

"But until you believe me, Mrs. Marx, we'll never get anywhere."

To my surprise I found myself longing to agree with him.

When I looked up he was gone. I saw that carefully, methodically, I had been shredding his file with my fingernails. Hating the sunlight, I found myself walking through the schoolyard, wishing it would snow.

I live in a luxury condominium—there are dozens such in our town—where children cannot come. There the old people hide. There I am protected from the nightmares that I must face every day.

Usually I do not remember any dreams; but of that night's—the fourth week of Billy's visits with me—I do remember things: dragons' wings, leathery, hung with icicles. . . . Did my father ever beat me? I couldn't even remember, damn it!

Waking up. Outside—a hurricane building up? Beating of giant wings?

I sat up on the bed. Through the mosquito netting of the open window I heard night-sounds, insects, the ocean hidden by a dozen Hiltons and Ramada Inns. I thought of calling Pop, whom I hadn't thought about in years, but I knew it was too late to patch up my life now—

There was a knock on the door.

Not the buzzer, not the little loudspeaker I use to force strangers to admit that they came in peace. I did not move. It came again, and then that voice, that heart-wringing voice: "I'm cold, Mrs. Marx."

Children may not enter this domain.

How had he gotten past the security? Unless he had just materialized, like in his stories . . . I pulled on a bathrobe and went, through the dusty little living room, to the door, opened it—

He collapsed into my arms. It was like . . . when I was a kid, hugging a snowman. "For God's sake, Billy."

"I killed a monster today!" His voice frail, defiant. "But now I'm ready for *him!*"

"Don't try to attack Pete, he's too strong for you—"

"Pete? Screw Pete. I mean *him.*"

He's going into fugue. Got to keep him here, got to keep him warm, or God knows what he'll try—

"Look at me, you bitch!" He ripped his T-shirt open. I saw blood. I saw scars. I saw blue bruises. Red, white and blue, like the goddamn American flag. But his eyes were dry. And blazing. "Now try to believe. You're all I have, Mrs. Marx. I'm going back like the Snow Dragon says, maybe forever. Or until I kill the Ringmaster."

"No!" I tried to hold on to him, but he twisted away from me. Somehow he had warmed up, as though the very fever of his anger could melt away the cold. I knew how unbearable the real world was, I knew the cold hard beauty of his imaginary one, but I couldn't let him run away from reality, I couldn't let him hide inside himself, I was conditioned to helping the children face the truth—

"Believe me!" he shouted. "Come with me!"

Grasping at straws, "All right. All right." Quickly I was pulling on an old dress, not caring that he could see my sagging breasts—we had come too close for modesty now—I was shepherding him out of the door, down the steps, into the car, thinking, *Hospital, doctor, shrink, anything, just anything . . .*

I am ashamed to admit that I was also afraid that walking through the condo grounds at midnight would jeopardize my rental agreement, would force me out of my own fallen country.

As we pulled out onto the highway, it began to snow.

I panicked, fumbling for the wipers. Billy watched me solemnly, with a kind of I-told-you-so superiority. The snow grew from powder-fluffy to blizzard sheets; I stomped on the accelerator and slithered, I couldn't see the road at all.

"I knew it," Billy was saying softly, "I knew you had it in you to come with me."

He understands, I thought suddenly. *About my secret fears, about the pain I think I hide so successfully. And all the while I thought I was taking the lead.* We ploughed through the thick whiteness, until—

I stalled out. I pushed hard on the door handle, cursing old clunkers. When I got the door open the snow flew in, whipping my face and flooding the car floor with chalky ice.

"Out of the car now," Billy said.

"We'll freeze!" I didn't want to lose control of the fantasy, didn't want to relinquish myself into the hands of a demented kid.

"No we won't," he said firmly. He scooted over me, a bony breadcrust of a boy, and then he was walking out into the billowing whiteness, was striding, oblivious to the cold, had become a gray shadowghost streaked with white.

I tried to remember the things he'd told me. *Be angry!* I told myself. *Anger will warm you.*

Why didn't I pinch myself? Why didn't I think I was going mad? I must have known all along, the realness of Billy's fantasy must have touched me all along. . . .

I followed the kid cautiously. Soon I too felt nothing. The wind lashed my face and I could have been in a shopping mall buying shoes. I called out the kid's name but he was too intent to answer. I fell into the fallen country's strange detachment; it lured me, it drugged my pain, I knew that I could live there forever.

The snow whirled around me and I saw nothing but eye-smarting toothpaste-commercial dazzlewhite, and then, through the burning white, two pinpoints of blue fire.

The Snow Dragon!

The storm subsided a little. There he hovered. I watched him, believing in him completely. The wings were not leathery—my nightmares had lied to me—but like a thousand layers of crystal-stitched gauze. He landed, shook a snowdrift from his back—whiteness peppering whiteness—and I saw the sky open and the whip crack and I saw the blood trickle down him, and he did not even tense in pain. I called his name, "Snow Dragon."

"You have brought another one?" The dragon spoke only to Billy. I was here only as an observer, then.

"She's been hurt, too, Snow Dragon! Only she doesn't see it; sometimes she hides it too well."

"You are back too soon. Something is wrong with things. The fallen country is all disordered."

"This time I've come to kill him!"

"You cannot kill him." He sounded resigned. "You haven't energy enough."

"I *am* energy enough! She's seen! She can tell you!"

The dragon seemed not to hear. The wing came down, lashing the snow and making it dance for a moment. Without hesitating Billy leapt up. I followed, searching in vain for my fear.

And then we broke through the thick mist, and still there was no sunlight, only a kind of gray clarity in the air. I sat hunched into a ridge on the dragon's spine, my shapeless blotchy dress fluttering a little. I saw the castles blanketed with white; I saw the distant ice-sea, the snow-forts ringing the snow-hills.

"My bridge of anger," Billy said. His voice did not waver. The dragon circled slowly. I felt the kind of unease you feel on a plane in a holding pattern, but only for a second; then I felt nothing again. It was good to feel nothing.

Billy stood. The dragon braked in midair, an eerie, weightless feeling. And then Billy began to dream his bridge into being.

At first nothing. Then the whip, cracking in the sky, over and over, the dragon shivering himself into stillness as though concentrating the pain deep inside himself, and I was sitting in fast-hardening purple blood, and the dragon's breath came harder, clouding the chill wind. And as the cloud cleared I saw that a bridge was growing in the air, a suspension bridge with great columns of ice sprouting up from the mistiness below, pathway of living ice, thrusting in a rainbow-curve across the sky, reaching for the crack in the sky where the whip still cracked, from which great thunder-howls of laughter burst forth now, shrieks of a blood-lusty crowd.

The bridge hung there. Girders, rainbow-fringed from the sourceless light, a boy-wide road that thinned in the distance into a point.

"Your anger," the dragon said, "you are exhausting your anger, see, it will soon be gone, Billy Binder."

"Never!" the boy cried resolutely. "Only when he dies, *that'll* kill my anger, only that." He stepped out onto the ice. Again I felt a second's anxiety, and then the fallen country's spell drug-dragged it from me.

"Let me come too!" I yelled after him. Already he was tiny in the distance. Space and time seemed to work differently in this country. An adventuress now, this old woman who had made nothing of her life, I ran after him, my low heels clicking like castanets on the thin ice. I had to be with him. I was angry too, angry because of all the times I'd listened to the kids and done nothing while they bawled their guts out onto the floor of my little office. I was going to kill one child abuser in my lifetime! I was going to crush this dream-Pete that Billy had created, to throttle him to death with my twenty years of rage! Already I felt my fury fueling the bridge, making it firmer, easier to run on.

I was getting tired fast. But Billy still ran ahead, relentless as a wind. With a burst of anger I caught up with him, we ran neck and neck for a moment, and I saw that he wasn't even tired yet, and I knew I was wrong to think I could help or that I had anger enough in me— I who had never been hurt like that, who experienced the hurt only vicariously. The bridge soared up, steep in the strange foreshortening, and now even Billy was gasping. Then I was lurching forward, seeing the bridge telescope contact between my eyes, seeing the splitting sky.

A circus tent now, walls of flapping canvas painted sun moon stars shivering sheep-cloudlets, floors of mist-steaming packed snow, countless rings where bone-bare children leapt through fire-hoops, their faces tense with terror, frightened seals with planets whirling on their noses, scared to drop them, elephants trampling with earthquake feet, toppling skyscraper building-blocks, trumpeting thunderstorms. . . .

I stood there, panting, exhausted, couldn't take anything in. But Billy . . . he strode through the chaos, single-minded, seeking the center of things. And then I saw him, a little man with a whip, and he was dancing as he waved the whip, his eyes were as cold and expressionless as tundra-snow that has never thawed. And I knew his face. My face, Pete's face, even Billy's face, a template of human faces, always changing. I even saw Pop. I swear it, even Pop . . . Pop whom I couldn't remember beating me, until tonight.

The Ringmaster bowed to the audience. The cacklebuzz that had been a constant background, soft-brush percussion to the raucous band music, died down. He spoke very quietly. I recognized a little of Snow Dragon in his voice, and I was chilled by it.

The Ringmaster stepped out of his ring. He advanced toward Billy; again I saw that I was being ignored, that I was a watcher in another's confrontation, that I might as well have been sitting at the desk in the office listening to the screaming children in the yard.

The Ringmaster cracked his whip. Once. Worlds whirled! Children leapt! Blood spattered the sand! And then, like clockwork winding down, they sank into slow motion.

"You came, Billy Binder," said the Ringmaster. "I've been expecting you."

"You bastard!" Billy cried. "But I'm strong enough to get you!" Laughter echoed from the stands; I spun round to watch, and I saw that they all had his face, his face that was also mine and Billy's and Pop's and everyone else's, and they all laughed in unison, as though animated by a single hand.

"So come and get me!"

Billy reached out with his rage, a fireball burning tracks in the snow. I saw grass for a split second.

"You've got it all wrong!" the Ringmaster said. "You haven't come here to kill me at all! I sent for you. I bred you to be another shadow, another Ringmaster even—that's how you were able to find me. I granted you this gift of anger so you could build a way to me."

"No!" he shrieked.

"A shadow of my shadow," said the Ringmaster, raising his whip but never his voice. "You too are to become a shadow of my shadow, like Pete, like all the others.

"Billy, Billy . . . " the Ringmaster said. "You could be just like me, I have no pain, I only *give* pain now; I've been freed. . . . Hate me, Billy. Hate me! Your anger only makes me greater, only binds you more to me! For you are my son, Billy Binder; be free, Billy, be free, like me. . . . "

Billy stood, catapulting firedarts of anger, and the Ringmaster absorbed them all and grew tall, and snow-tempests swept around him, blurring him. Once I tried to step in, to add to Billy's store of rage, but I was frozen to the floor of snow.

The Ringmaster went on, "Oh, Billy, how can you turn your back on this? We are alike, you and I. You too can wield the whip and make a thousand universes dance with pain, and never feel the pain yourself."

"I'll never be like you! Never never never—" Billy screamed, and then I saw a final blast of rage explode from him and the canvas wall split open for a moment and I saw for an instant another whip, and another face of another Ringmaster up in the sky above us, and behind him another and another.

Then I looked at Billy, saw him shrunken, spent, the anger burned from him. I looked at the Ringmaster, panicking, thinking: *We're stranded*

here now, we'll never get back to the real world; we'll stay and rescue
princesses and fight monsters and see the princesses get recaptured and
the monsters get reborn, for ever and ever.

I began to yell hysterically at the Ringmaster. He stood for everything
I'd ever been angry about. I shouted: "I hate you! There's no reason for
you to be; you're senseless, you screw up the whole universe!"

But Billy said, very quietly, "I don't have any anger left." And the
Ringmaster's face grew pale, and he said, "But you *must* hate me! I bred
you to hate me! I followed you and beat the hatred into you. . . ."

Billy turned and spoke to me at last. "Don't you see?" he said. "I could
have been like that. He's not the real Ringmaster at all. You glimpsed
it, didn't you? I was so angry that I opened up . . . another country, the
fallen country behind the fallen country, and I saw that the Ringmaster
was only a shadow himself, that he danced to the whip of a higher
ringmaster. . . . How can I hate him?"

"Don't . . . " the Ringmaster said. I saw anguish cross his face for the
first time. Or maybe I was just imagining it. It was only for a second.

Deliberately, quietly, Billy turned his back on him.

I followed the boy like an idiot. The dragon waited by the bridge, the
bridge was already dissipating into mist, the dismal, cold light was brightening into sunlight, and—

By the car, patches of green.

Billy said to the dragon, "It's true, isn't it? What he said. That he's
my father."

The dragon said nothing. I knew, though, that he did not disagree.
And then Billy said, "It's strange, isn't it, how he plants in all his kids a
little shred of something . . . that could destroy him, like he was dancing
for his Ringmaster and secretly working to sabotage him at the same
time."

The dragon said, "I too am part of the shadow, Billy, the part that
seeks the shadow's own death, the left hand that does what the right hand
dares not know about. You have killed us both: him by your compassion,
me by compelling me to feel love for you. . . .

"The snow is melting. The fallen country will be closed to you now."

He did not speak again, but uttered a roar that rent the sky as sunlight
broke the cloud-veils, a cry both of heartache and of joy, and he spread
his wings and soared upwards with a heart-stopping whistlerush of wind.
And then he was gone, disintegrated like a windgust, like a dream, like
a half-stirred memory.

There was the car. I drove like a madwoman, churning up snow, bursting suddenly into the known world of concrete roads and forests of hotels and condominiums bleached lifeless by loneliness—

Police sirens! Lights! "The house!" Billy cried. We rounded a turn, he sprang out and sprinted toward the house, red blur of revolving sirens everywhere, swirling . . . We watched, silently. They brought Joan out, shaking, and then a stretcher, a covered one. I heard the onlookers muttering, looking curiously at Billy, avoiding his eyes, heard them say how Pete had gone crazy and just gone and crashed his motorbike into the house.

"I killed him," Billy said softly, for me alone. And I believed him. For he had found the way into Pete's soul, and in understanding it, in giving it peace, had destroyed it. The inner and outer worlds are congruent in a thousand places. Wherever we stand, we are within a hair's breadth of the fallen country.

Billy had understood things that I had never understood, I, whose job was understanding. I'd been so sure of myself, coaxing traumas out of children, beating on their little minds until they danced out their pain for me in my office. But where was *my* peace? My suffering was trivial, and so was my reward—to be beset by little things only, to be a watcher, not one who can compress the shadow-substance of her dreams until they become diamond-hard, like truth.

I moved closer to him, trying irrationally to shield him from the screaming sirens. Quietly, but openly, without shame, he had begun to cry.

If only we could wear our griefs as lightly as the snow wears the sneakerprints of children's dreams.

I went closer to him, almost touching him now, and began to do what I am trained to do. At first no words would come. *Damn it, Dora Marx,* I thought. *Who has stolen your roar?* I groped—

"Sure," I murmured. "Sure." I wondered if he would flinch if I tried to hug him.

STRATA

Six hundred million years in thirty-two miles. Six hundred million years in fifty-one minutes. Steve Mavrakis traveled in time—courtesy of the Wyoming Highway Department. The epochs raveled between Thermopolis and Shoshoni. The Wind River rambled down its canyon with the Burlington Northern tracks cut into the west walls and the two-lane blacktop, U.S. 20, sliced into the east. Official signs driven into the verge of the highway proclaimed the traveler's progress:

DINWOODY FORMATION
TRIASSIC
185–225 MILLION YEARS

BIG HORN FORMATION
ORDOVICIAN
440–500 MILLION YEARS

FLATHEAD FORMATION
CAMBRIAN
500–600 MILLION YEARS

The mileposts might have been staked into the canyon rock under the pressure of millennia. They were there for those who could not read the stone. Tonight Steve ignored the signs. He had made this run many times before. Darkness hemmed him. November clawed when he cracked the window to exhaust Camel smoke from the Chevy's cab. The CB crackled occasionally and picked up exactly nothing.

The wind blew—that was nothing unusual. Steve felt himself hypnotized by the skiff of snow skating across the pavement in the glare of his brights. The snow swirled only inches above the blacktop, rushing across like surf sliding over the black packed sand of a beach.

Time's predator hunts.

Years scatter before her like a school of minnows surprised. The rush of her passage causes eons to eddy. Wind sweeps down the canyon with the roar of combers breaking on the sand. The moon, full and newly risen, exerts its tidal force.

Moonlight flashes on the slash of teeth.

And Steve snapped alert, realized he had traversed the thirty-two miles, crossed the flats leading into Shoshoni, and was approaching the junction with U.S. 26. Road hypnosis? he thought. Safe in Shoshoni, but it was scary. He didn't remember a goddamned minute of the trip through the canyons! Steve rubbed his eyes with his left hand and looked for an open cafe with coffee.

It hadn't been the first time.

All those years before, the four of them had thought they were beating the odds. On a chill night in June, high on a mountain edge in the Wind River Range, high on more than mountain air, the four of them celebrated graduation. They were young and clear-eyed: ready for the world. That night they knew there were no other people for miles. Having learned in class that there were 3.8 human beings per square mile in Wyoming, and as *four*, they thought the odds outnumbered.

Paul Onoda, eighteen. He was second-generation Wyoming; the great-grandson of Japanese immigrants. In 1942, before he was conceived, his parents were removed with eleven hundred thousand other Japanese Americans from California to the Heart Mountain Relocation Center in northern Wyoming. Twelve members and three generations of the Onodas shared one of four hundred and sixty-five crowded, tar-papered barracks for the next four years. Two died. Three more were born. With their fellows, the Onodas helped farm eighteen hundred acres of virgin agricultural land. Not all of them had been Japanese gardeners or truck farmers in California; so the pharmacists and the teachers and the carpenters learned agriculture. They used irrigation to bring in water. The crops flourished. The Nisei not directly involved with farming were dispatched from camp to be seasonal farm laborers. A historian later laconically noted that "Wyoming benefited by their presence."

Paul remembered the Heart Mountain camps only through the memories of his elders, but those recollections were vivid. After the war, most of the Onodas stayed on in Wyoming. With some difficulty, they bought farms. The family invested thrice the effort of their neighbors, and prospered.

Paul Onoda excelled in the classrooms and starred on the football field of Fremont High School. Once he overheard the president of the school board tell the coach, "By God but that little Nip can run!" He thought about that, and kept on running even faster.

More than a few of his classmates secretly thought he had it all. When prom time came in his senior year, it did not go unnoticed that Paul had an extraordinarily handsome appearance to go with his brains and athlete's body. In and around Fremont, a great many concerned parents admonished their white daughters to find a good excuse if Paul asked them to the prom.

Carroll Dale, eighteen. It became second nature early on to explain to people first hearing her given name that it had two r's and two l's. Both sides of her family went back four generations in this part of the country, and one of her bequests had been a proud mother. Cordelia Carroll had pride, one daughter, and the desire to see the Hereford Carrolls retain *some* parity with the Charolais Dales. After all, the Carrolls had been ranching on Bad Water Creek before John Broderick Okie illuminated his Lost Cabin castle with carbide lights. That was when Teddy Roosevelt had been President, and it was when all the rest of the cattlemen in Wyoming, including the Dales, had been doing their accounts at night by kerosene lanterns.

Carroll grew up to be a good roper and a better rider. Her apprenticeship intensified after her older brother, her only brother, fatally shot himself during deer season. She wounded her parents when she neither married a man who would take over the ranch nor decided to take over the ranch herself.

She grew up slim and tall, with ebony hair and large, dark, slightly oblique eyes. Her father's father, at family Christmas dinners, would overdo the whisky in the eggnog and make jokes about Indians in the woodpile until her paternal grandmother would tell him to shut the hell up before she gave him a goodnight the hard way, with a rusty sickle and knitting needles. It was years before Carroll knew what her grandmother meant.

In junior high, Carroll was positive she was eight feet tall in Lilliput. The jokes hurt. But her mother told her to be patient, that the other girls would catch up. Most of the girls didn't; but in high school the boys did, though they tended to be tongue-tied in the extreme when they talked to her.

She was the first girl president of her school's National Honor Society. She was a cheerleader. She was the valedictorian of her class and earnestly quoted John F. Kennedy in her graduation address. Within weeks of graduation, she eloped with the captain of the football team.

It nearly caused a lynching.

Steve Mavrakis, eighteen. Courtesy allowed him to be called a native despite his birth eighteen hundred miles to the east. His parents, on the other hand, had settled in the state after the war when he was less than a year old. Given another decade, the younger native-born might grudgingly concede their adopted roots; the old-timers, never.

Steve's parents had read Zane Grey and *The Virginian*, and had spent many summers on dude ranches in upstate New York. So they found a perfect ranch on the Big Horn River and started a herd of registered Hereford. They went broke. They refinanced and aimed at a breed of inferior beef cattle. The snows of '49 killed those. Steve's father determined that sheep were the way to go—all those double and triple births. Very investment-effective. The sheep sickened, or stumbled and fell into creeks where they drowned, or panicked like turkeys and smothered in heaps in fenced corners. It occurred then to the Mavrakis family that wheat doesn't stampede. All the fields were promptly hailed out before what looked to be a bounty harvest. Steve's father gave up and moved into town where he put his Columbia degree to work by getting a job managing the district office for the Bureau of Land Management.

All of that taught Steve to be wary of sure things.

And occasionally he wondered at the dreams. He had been very young when the blizzards killed the cattle. But though he didn't remember the National Guard dropping hay bales from silver C-47s to cattle in twelve-foot-deep snow, he did recall, for years after, the nightmares of herds of nonplussed animals futilely grazing barren ground before towering, slowly grinding, bluffs of ice.

The night after the crop duster terrified the sheep and seventeen had expired in paroxysms, Steve dreamed of brown men shrilling and shaking sticks and stampeding tusked, hairy monsters off a precipice and down hundreds of feet to a shallow stream.

Summer nights Steve woke sweating, having dreamed of reptiles slithering and warm waves beating on a ragged beach in the lower pasture. He sat straight, staring out the bedroom window, watching the giant ferns waver and solidify back into cottonwood and box elder.

The dreams came less frequently and vividly as he grew older. He willed that. They altered when the family moved into Fremont. After a while Steve still remembered he had had the dreams, but most of the details were forgotten.

At first the teachers in Fremont High School thought he was stupid. Steve was administered tests and thereafter was labeled an underachiever. He did what he had to do to get by. He barely qualified for the college-bound program, but then his normally easygoing father made threats. People asked him what he wanted to do, to be, and he answered honestly that he didn't know. Then he took a speech class. Drama fascinated him and he developed a passion for what theater the school offered. He played well in *Our Town* and *Arsenic and Old Lace* and *Harvey*. The drama coach looked at Steve's average height and average looks and average brown hair and eyes, and suggested at a hilarious cast party that he become either a character actor or an FBI agent.

By this time, the only dreams Steve remembered were sexual fantasies about girls he didn't dare ask on dates.

Ginger McClelland, seventeen. Who could blame her for feeling out of place? Having been born on the cusp of the school district's regulations, she was very nearly a year younger than her classmates. She was short. She thought of herself as a dwarf in a world of Snow Whites. It didn't help that her mother studiously offered words like "petite" and submitted that the most gorgeous clothes would fit a wearer under five feet, two inches. Secretly she hoped that in one mysterious night she would bloom and grow great, long legs like Carroll Dale. That never happened.

Being an exile in an alien land didn't help either. Though Carroll had befriended her, she had listened to the president of the pep club, the queen of Job's Daughters, and half the girls in her math class refer to her as "the foreign exchange student." Except that she would never be repatriated home; at least not until she graduated. Her parents had tired of living in Cupertino, California, and thought that running a coast-to-coast hardware franchise in Fremont would be an adventurous change of pace. They loved the open spaces, the mountains and free-flowing streams. Ginger wasn't so sure. Every day felt like she had stepped into a time machine. All the music on the radio was old. The movies that turned up at the town's one theater—forget it. The dancing at the hops was grotesque.

Ginger McClelland was the first person in Fremont—and perhaps in all of Wyoming—to use the adjective "bitchin'." It got her sent home from study hall and caused a bemused and confusing interview between her parents and the principal.

Ginger learned not to trust most of the boys who invited her out on dates. They all seemed to feel some sort of perverse mystique about California girls. But she did accept Steve Mavrakis's last-minute invitation to the prom. He seemed safe enough.

Because Carroll and Ginger were friends, the four of them ended up double-dating in Paul's father's old maroon DeSoto that was customarily used for hauling fence posts and wire out to the pastures. After the dance, when nearly everyone else was heading to one of the sanctioned after-prom parties, Steve affably obtained from an older intermediary an entire case of chilled Hamms. Ginger and Carroll had brought along jeans and Pendleton shirts in their overnight bags and changed in the restroom at the Chevron station. Paul and Steve took off their white jackets and donned windbreakers. Then they all drove up into the Wind River Range. After they ran out of road, they hiked. It was very late and very dark. But they found a high mountain place where they huddled and drank beer and talked and necked.

They heard the voice of the wind and nothing else beyond that. They saw no lights of cars or outlying cabins. The isolation exhilarated them. They *knew* there was no one else for miles.

That was correct so far as it went.

Foam hissed and sprayed as Paul applied the church key to the cans. Above and below them, the wind broke like waves on the rocks.

"Mavrakis, you're going to the university, right?" said Paul.

Steve nodded in the dim moonlight, added, "I guess so."

"What're you going to take?" said Ginger, snuggling close and burping slightly on her beer.

"I don't know; engineering, I guess. If you're a guy and in the college-bound program, you end up taking engineering. So I figure that's it."

Paul said, "What kind?"

"Don't know. Maybe aerospace. I'll move to Seattle and make spaceships."

"That's neat," said Ginger. "Like in *The Outer Limits*. I wish we could get that here."

"You ought to be getting into hydraulic engineering," said Paul. "Water's going to be really big business not too long from now."

"I don't think I want to stick around Wyoming."

Carroll had been silently staring out over the valley. She turned back toward Steve and her eyes were pools of darkness. "You're really going to leave?"

"Yeah."

"And never come back?"

"Why should I?" said Steve. "I've had all the fresh air and wide-open spaces I can use for a lifetime. You know something? I've never even seen the ocean." *And yet he had* felt *the ocean.* He blinked. "I'm getting out."

"Me too," said Ginger. "I'm going to stay with my aunt and uncle in LA. I think I can probably get into the USC journalism school."

"Got the money?" said Paul.

"I'll get a scholarship."

"Aren't you leaving?" Steve said to Carroll.

"Maybe," she said. "Sometimes I think so, and then I'm not so sure."

"You'll come back even if you do leave," said Paul. "All of you'll come back."

"Says who?" Steve and Ginger said it almost simultaneously.

"The land gets into you," said Carroll. "Paul's dad says so."

"That's what he says." They all heard anger in Paul's voice. He opened another round of cans. Ginger tossed her empty away and it clattered down the rocks, a noise jarringly out of place.

"Don't," said Carroll. "We'll take the empties down in the sack."

"What's wrong?" said Ginger. "I mean, I . . ." Her voice trailed off and everyone was silent for a minute, two minutes, three.

"What about you, Paul?" said Carroll. "Where do you want to go? What do you want to do?"

"We talked about—" His voice sounded suddenly tightly controlled. "Damn it, I don't know now. If I come back, it'll be with an atomic bomb—"

"What?" said Ginger.

Paul smiled. At least Steve could see white teeth gleaming in the night.

"As for what I want to do—" He leaned forward and whispered in Carroll's ear.

She said, "Jesus, Paul! We've got witnesses."

"What?" Ginger said again.

"Don't even ask you don't want to know." She made it one continuous sentence. Her teeth also were visible in the near-darkness. "Try that and I've got a mind to goodnight you the hard way."

"What're you talking about?" said Ginger.

Paul laughed. "Her grandmother."

"Charlie Goodnight was a big rancher around the end of the century," Carroll said. "He trailed a lot of cattle up from Texas. Trouble was, a lot of his expensive bulls weren't making out so well. Their testicles—"

"Balls," said Paul.

"—kept dragging on the ground," she continued. "The bulls got torn up and infected. So Charlie Goodnight started getting his bulls ready for the overland trip with some amateur surgery. He'd cut into the scrotum and shove the balls up into the bull. Then he'd stitch up the sack and there'd be no problem with high-centering. That's called goodnighting."

"See," said Paul. "There are ways to beat the land."

Carroll said, "'You do what you've got to.' That's a quote from my father. Good pioneer stock."

"But not to me." Paul pulled her close and kissed her.

"Maybe we ought to explore the mountain a little," said Ginger to Steve. "You want to come with me?" She stared at Steve who was gawking at the sky as the moonlight suddenly vanished like a light switching off.

"Oh my God."

"What's wrong?" she said to the shrouded figure.

"I don't know—I mean, nothing, I guess." The moon appeared again. "Was that a cloud?"

"I don't see a cloud," said Paul, gesturing at the broad belt of stars. "The night's clear."

"Maybe you saw a UFO," said Carroll, her voice light.

"You okay?" Ginger touched his face. "Jesus, you're shivering." She held him tightly.

Steve's words were almost too low to hear. "It swam across the moon."

"What did?"

"I'm cold too," said Carroll. "Let's go back down." Nobody argued. Ginger remembered to put the metal cans into a paper sack and tied it to her belt with a hair ribbon. Steve didn't say anything more for a while, but the others all could hear his teeth chatter. When they were halfway

down, the moon finally set beyond the valley rim. Farther on, Paul
stepped on a loose patch of shale, slipped, cursed, began to slide beyond
the lip of the sheer rock face. Carroll grabbed his arm and pulled him
back.

"Thanks, Irene." His voice shook slightly, belying the tone of the
words.

"Funny," she said.

"I don't get it," said Ginger.

Paul whistled a few bars of the song.

"Good night," said Carroll. "You do what you've got to."

"And I'm grateful for that." Paul took a deep breath. "Let's get down
to the car."

When they were on the winding road and driving back toward Fremont, Ginger said, "What did you see up there, Steve?"

"Nothing. I guess I just remembered a dream."

"Some dream." She touched his shoulder. "You're still cold."

Carroll said, "So am I."

Paul took his right hand off the wheel to cover her hand. "We all
are."

"I feel all right." Ginger sounded puzzled.

All the way into town, Steve felt he had drowned.

The Amble Inn in Thermopolis was built in the shadow of Round Top
Mountain. On the slope above the inn, huge letters formed from white-
washed stones proclaimed: WORLD'S LARGEST MINERAL HOT SPRING.
Whether at night or noon, the inscription invariably reminded Steve of
the Hollywood sign. Early in his return from California, he realized the
futility of jumping off the second letter "O." The stones were laid flush
with the steep pitch of the ground. Would-be suicides could only roll
down the hill until they collided with the log side of the inn.

On Friday and Saturday night, the parking lot of the Amble Inn
was filled almost exclusively with four-wheel-drive vehicles and conventional pickups. Most of them had black-enameled gun racks up in
the rear window behind the seat. Steve's Chevy had a rack, but that
was because he had bought the truck used. He had considered buying
a toy rifle, one that shot caps or rubber darts, at a Penney's Christmas
catalog sale. But like so many other projects, he never seemed to get
around to it.

Tonight was the first Saturday night in June, and Steve had money
in his pocket from the paycheck he had cashed at Safeway. He had no

reason to celebrate, but then he had no reason not to celebrate. So a little after nine he went to the Amble Inn to drink tequila hookers and listen to the music.

The inn was uncharacteristically crowded for so early in the evening, but Steve secured a small table close to the dance floor when a guy threw up and his girl had to take him home. Dancing couples covered the floor though the headline act, The Radford & Lewis Band, wouldn't be on until eleven. The warmup group was a Montana band called the Great Falls Dead. They had more enthusiasm than talent, but they had the crowd dancing.

Steve threw down the shots, sucked limes, licked the salt, intermittently tapped his hand on the table to the music, and felt vaguely melancholy. Smoke drifted around him, almost as thick as the special-effects fog in a bad horror movie. The inn's dance floor was in a dim, domed room lined with rough pine.

He suddenly stared, puzzled by a flash of near-recognition. He had been watching one dancer in particular, a tall woman with curly raven hair, who had danced with a succession of cowboys. When he looked at her face, he thought he saw someone familiar. When he looked at her body, he wondered whether she wore underwear beneath the wide-weave red knit dress.

The Great Falls Dead launched into "Good-hearted Woman" and the floor was instantly filled with dancers. Across the room, someone squealed, "Willieee!" This time the woman in red danced very close to Steve's table. Her high cheekbones looked hauntingly familiar. Her hair, he thought. If it were longer—She met his eyes and smiled at him.

The set ended, her partner drifted off toward the bar, but she remained standing beside his table. "Carroll?" he said. "*Carroll?*"

She stood there smiling, with right hand on hip. "I wondered when you'd figure it out."

Steve shoved his chair back and got up from the table. She moved very easily into his arms for a hug. "It's been a long time."

"It has."

"Fourteen years? Fifteen?"

"Something like that."

He asked her to sit at his table, and she did. She sipped a Campari-and-tonic as they talked. He switched to beer. The years unreeled. The Great Falls Dead pounded out a medley of country standards behind them.

"... I never should have married, Steve. I was wrong for Paul. He was wrong for me."

"... *thought* about getting married. I met a lot of women in Hollywood, but nothing ever seemed . . ."

"... all the wrong reasons . . ."

"... did end up in a few made-for-TV movies. Bad stuff. I was always cast as the assistant manager in a holdup scene, or got killed by the werewolf right near the beginning. I think there's something like ninety percent of all actors who are unemployed at any given moment, so I said . . ."

"You really came back here? How long ago?"

"... to hell with it . . ."

"How long ago?"

"... and sort of slunk back to Wyoming. I don't know. Several years ago. How long were you married, anyway?"

"... a year, more or less. What do you do here?"

"... beer's getting warm. Think I'll get a pitcher . . ."

"What do you do here?"

"... better cold. Not much. I get along. You . . ."

"... lived in Taos for a time. Then Santa Fe. Bummed around the Southwest a lot. A friend got me into photography. Then I was sick for a while and that's when I tried painting . . ."

"... landscapes of the Tetons to sell to tourists?"

"Hardly. A lot of landscapes, but trailer camps and oil fields and perspective vistas of I-80 across the Red Desert . . ."

"I tried taking pictures once . . . kept forgetting to load the camera."

"... and then I ended up half-owner of a gallery called Good Stuff. My partner throws pots."

"... must be dangerous . . ."

"... located on Main Street in Lander . . ."

"... going through. Think maybe I've seen it . . ."

"What do you do here?"

The comparative silence seemed to echo as the band ended its set. "Very little," said Steve. "I worked a while as a hand on the Two-bar. Spent some time being a roughneck in the fields up around Buffalo. I've got a pickup—do some short-hauling for local businessmen who don't want to hire a trucker. I ran a little pot. Basically I do whatever I can find. You know."

Carroll said, "Yes, I do know." The silence lengthened between them. Finally she said, "Why did you come back here? Was it because—"

"—because I'd failed?" Steve said, answering her hesitation. He looked at her steadily. "I thought about that a long time. I decided that I could fail anywhere, so I came back here." He shrugged. "I love it. I love the space."

"A lot of us have come back," Carroll said. "Ginger and Paul are here."

Steve was startled. He looked at the tables around them.

"Not tonight," said Carroll. "We'll see them tomorrow. They want to see you."

"Are you and Paul back—" he started to say.

She held up her palm. "Hardly. We're not exactly on the same wavelength. That's one thing that hasn't changed. He ended up being the sort of thing you thought you'd become."

Steve didn't remember what that was.

"Paul went to the School of Mines in Colorado. Now he's the chief exploratory geologist for Enerco."

"Not bad," said Steve.

"Not good," said Carroll. "He spent a decade in South America and the Middle East. Now he's come back home. He wants to gut the state like a fish."

"Coal?"

"And oil. And uranium. And gas. Enerco's got its thumb in a lot of holes." Her voice had lowered, sounded angry. "Anyway, we *are* having a reunion tomorrow, of sorts. And Ginger will be there."

Steve poured out the last of the beer. "I thought for sure she'd be in California."

"Never made it," said Carroll. "Scholarships fell through. Parents said they wouldn't support her if she went back to the West Coast—you know how one-hundred-and-five-percent converted immigrants are. So Ginger went to school in Laramie and ended up with a degree in elementary education. She did marry a grad student in journalism. After the divorce five or six years later, she let him keep the kid."

Steve said, "So Ginger never got to be an ace reporter."

"Oh, she did. Now she's the best writer the Salt Creek *Gazette*'s got. Ginger's the darling of the environmental groups and the bane of the energy corporations."

"I'll be damned," he said. He accidentally knocked his glass off the table with his forearm. Reaching to retrieve the glass, he knocked over the empty pitcher.

"I think you're tired," Carroll said.

"I think you're right."

"You ought to go home and sack out." He nodded. "I don't want to drive all the way back to Lander tonight," Carroll said. "Have you got room for me?"

When they reached the small house Steve rented off Highway 170, Carroll grimaced at the heaps of dirty clothes making soft moraines in the living room. "I'll clear off the couch," she said. "I've got a sleeping bag in my car."

Steve hesitated a long several seconds and lightly touched her shoulders. "You don't have to sleep on the couch unless you want to. All those years ago . . . You know, all through high school I had a crush on you? I was too shy to say anything."

She smiled and allowed his hands to remain. "I thought you were pretty nice too. A little shy, but cute. Definitely an underachiever."

They remained standing, faces a few inches apart, for a while longer. "Well?" he said.

"It's been a lot of years," Carroll said. "I'll sleep on the couch."

Steve said disappointedly, "Not even out of charity?"

"Especially not for charity." She smiled. "But don't discount the future." She kissed him gently on the lips.

Steve slept soundly that night. He dreamed of sliding endlessly through a warm, fluid current. It was not a nightmare. Not even when he realized he had fins rather than hands and feet.

Morning brought rain.

When he awoke, the first thing Steve heard was the drumming of steady drizzle on the roof. The daylight outside the window was filtered gray by the sheets of water running down the pane. Steve leaned off the bed, picked up his watch from the floor, but it had stopped. He heard the sounds of someone moving in the living room and called, "Carroll? You up?"

Her voice was a soft contralto. "I am."

"What time is it?"

"Just after eight."

Steve started to get out of bed, but groaned and clasped the crown of his head with both hands. Carroll stood framed in the doorway and looked sympathetic. "What time's the reunion?" he said.

"When we get there. I called Paul a little earlier. He's tied up with some sort of meeting in Casper until late afternoon. He wants us to meet him in Shoshoni."

"What about Ginger?"

They both heard the knock on the front door. Carroll turned her head away from the bedroom, then looked back at Steve. "Right on cue," she said. "Ginger didn't want to wait until tonight." She started for the door, said back over her shoulder, "You might want to put on some clothes."

Steve pulled on his least filthy jeans and a sweatshirt labeled AMAX TOWN—LEAGUE VOLLEYBALL across the chest. He heard the front door open and close, and words murmured in his living room. When he exited the bedroom he found Carroll talking on the couch with a short blond stranger who only slightly resembled the long-ago image he'd packed in his mind. Her hair was long and tied in a braid. Her gaze was direct and more inquisitive than he remembered.

She looked up at him and said, "I like the mustache. You look a hell of a lot better now than you ever did then."

"Except for the mustache," Steve said, "I could say the same."

The two women seemed amazed when Steve negotiated the disaster area that was the kitchen and extracted eggs and Chinese vegetables from the refrigerator. He served the huge omelet with toast and freshly brewed coffee in the living room. They all balanced plates on laps.

"Do you ever read the Gazoo?" said Ginger.

"Gazoo?"

"The Salt Creek *Gazette*," said Carroll.

Steve said, "I don't read any papers."

"I just finished a piece on Paul's company," said Ginger.

"Enerco?" Steve refilled all their cups.

Ginger shook her head. "A wholly owned subsidiary called Native American Resources. Pretty clever, huh?" Steve looked blank. "Not a poor damned Indian in the whole operation. The name's strictly sham while the company's been picking up an incredible number of mineral leases on the reservation. Paul's been concentrating on an enormous new coal field his teams have mapped out. It makes up a substantial proportion of the reservation's best lands."

"Including some sacred sites," said Carroll.

"Nearly a million acres," said Ginger. "That's more than a thousand square miles."

"The land's never the same," said Carroll, "no matter how much goes into reclamation, no matter how tight the EPA says they are."

Steve looked from one to the other. "I may not read the papers," he said, "but no one's holding a gun to anyone else's head."

"Might as well be," said Ginger. "If the Native American Resources deal goes through, the mineral royalty payments to the tribes'll go up precipitously."

Steve spread his palms. "Isn't that good?"

Ginger shook her head vehemently. "It's economic blackmail to keep the tribes from developing their own resources at their own pace."

"Slogans," said Steve. "The country needs the energy. If the tribes don't have the investment capital—"

"They *would* if they weren't bought off with individual royalty payments."

"The tribes have a choice—"

"—with the prospect of immediate gain dangled in front of them by NAR."

"I can tell it's Sunday," said Steve, "even if I haven't been inside a church door in fifteen years. I'm being preached at."

"If you'd get off your ass and think," said Ginger, "nobody'd have to lecture you."

Steve grinned. "I don't think with my ass."

"Look," said Carroll. "It's stopped raining."

Ginger glared at Steve. He took advantage of Carroll's diversion and said, "Anyone for a walk?"

The air outside was cool and rainwashed. It soothed tempers. The trio walked through the fresh morning along the cottonwood-lined creek. Meadowlarks sang. The rain front had moved far to the east; the rest of the sky was bright blue.

"Hell of a country, isn't it?" said Steve.

"Not for much longer if—" Ginger began.

"Gin," Carroll said warningly.

They strolled for another hour, angling south where they could see the hills as soft as blanket folds. The tree-lined draws snaked like green veins down the hillsides. The earth, Steve thought, seemed gathered, somehow expectant.

"How's Danny?" Carroll said to Ginger.

"He's terrific. Kid wants to become an astronaut." A grin split her face. "Bob's letting me have him for August."

"Look at that," said Steve, pointing.

The women looked. "I don't see anything," said Ginger.

"Southeast," Steve said. "Right above the head of the canyon."

"There—I'm not sure." Carroll shaded her eyes. "I thought I saw something, but it was just a shadow."

"Nothing there," said Ginger.

"Are you both blind?" said Steve, astonished. "There was something in the air. It was dark and cigar-shaped. It was there when I pointed."

"Sorry," said Ginger, "didn't see a thing."

"Well, it *was* there," Steve said, disgruntled.

Carroll continued to stare off toward the pass. "I saw it too, but just for a second. I didn't see where it went."

"Damnedest thing. I don't think it was a plane. It just sort of cruised along, and then it was gone."

"All I saw was something blurry," Carroll said. "Maybe it was a UFO."

"Oh, you guys," Ginger said with an air of dawning comprehension. "Just like prom night, right? Just a joke."

Steve slowly shook his head. "I really saw something then, and I saw this now. This time Carroll saw it too." She nodded in agreement. He tasted salt.

The wind started to rise from the north, kicking up early spring weeds that had already died and begun to dry.

"I'm getting cold," said Ginger. "Let's go back to the house."

"Steve," said Carroll, "you're shaking."

They hurried him back across the land.

PHOSPHORIC FORMATION
PERMIAN
225–270 MILLION YEARS

They rested for a while at the house; drank coffee and talked of the past, of what had happened and what had not. Then Carroll suggested they leave for the reunion. After a small confusion, Ginger rolled up the windows and locked her Saab, and Carroll locked her Pinto.

"I hate having to do this," said Carroll.

"There's no choice anymore," Steve said. "Too many people around now who don't know the rules."

The three of them got into Steve's pickup. In fifteen minutes they had traversed the doglegs of U.S. 20 through Thermopolis and crossed the Big Horn River. They passed the massive mobile-home park with its trailers and RVs sprawling in carapaced glitter.

The flood of hot June sunshine washed over them as they passed between the twin bluffs, red with iron, and descended into the miles and years of canyon.

TENSLEEP FORMATION
PENNSYLVANIAN
270–310 MILLION YEARS

On both sides of the canyon, the rock layers lay stacked like sections from a giant meat slicer. In the pickup cab, the passengers had been listening to the news on KTWO. As the canyon deepened, the reception faded until only a trickle of static came from the speaker. Carroll clicked the radio off.

"They're screwed," said Ginger.

"Not necessarily." Carroll, riding shotgun, stared out the window at the slopes of flowers the same color as the bluffs. "The BIA's still got hearings. There'll be another tribal vote."

Ginger said again, "They're screwed. Money doesn't just talk—it makes obscene phone calls, you know? Paul's got this one bagged. You know Paul—I know him just about as well. Son of a bitch."

"Sorry there's no music," said Steve. "Tape player busted a while back and I've never fixed it."

They ignored him. "Damn it," said Ginger. "It took almost fifteen years, but I've learned to love this country."

"I know that," said Carroll.

No one said anything for a while. Steve glanced to his right and saw tears running down Ginger's cheeks. She glared back at him defiantly. "There's Kleenexes in the glove box," he said.

MADISON FORMATION
MISSISSIPPIAN
310–350 MILLION YEARS

The slopes of the canyon became more heavily forested. The walls were all shades of green, deeper green where the runoff had found channels. Steve felt time collect in the great gash in the earth, press inward.

"I don't feel so hot," said Ginger.

"Want to stop for a minute?"

She nodded and put her hand over her mouth.

Steve pulled the pickup over across both lanes. The Chevy skidded slightly as it stopped on the graveled turnout. Steve turned off the key, and in the sudden silence they heard only the light wind and the tickings as the Chevy's engine cooled.

"Excuse me," said Ginger. They all got out of the cab. Ginger quickly moved through the Canadian thistle and the currant bushes and into the beyond. Steve and Carroll heard her throwing up.

"She had an affair with Paul," Carroll said casually. "Not too long ago. He's an extremely attractive man." Steve said nothing. "Ginger ended it. She still feels the tension." Carroll strolled over to the side of the thistle patch and hunkered down. "Look at this."

Steve realized how complex the ground cover was. Like the rock cliffs, it was layered. At first he saw among the sunflowers and dead dandelions only the wild sweetpeas with their blue blossoms like spades with the edges curled inward.

"Look closer," said Carroll.

Steve saw the hundreds of tiny purple moths swooping and swarming only inches from the earth. The creatures were the same color as the low purple blooms he couldn't identify. Intermixed were white, bell-shaped blossoms with leaves that looked like primeval ferns.

"It's like going back in time," said Carroll. "It's a whole, nearly invisible world we never see."

The shadow crossed them with an almost subliminal flash, but they both looked up. Between them and the sun had been the wings of a large bird. It circled in a tight orbit, banking steeply when it approached the canyon wall. The creature's belly was dirty white, muting to an almost-black on its back. It seemed to Steve that the bird's eye was fixed on them. The eye was a dull black, like unpolished obsidian.

"That's one I've never seen," said Carroll. "What is it?"

"I don't know. The wingspread's got to be close to ten feet. The markings are strange. Maybe it's a hawk? An eagle?"

The bird's beak was heavy and blunt, curved slightly. As it circled, wings barely flexing to ride the thermals, the bird was eerily silent, pelagic, fishlike.

"What's it doing?" said Carroll.

"Watching us?" said Steve. He jumped as a hand touched his shoulder.

"Sorry," said Ginger. "I feel better now." She tilted her head back at the great circling bird. "I have a feeling our friend wants us to leave."

They left. The highway wound around a massive curtain of stone in which red splashed down through the strata like dinosaur blood. Around the curve, Steve swerved to miss a deer dead on the pavement—half a deer, rather. The animal's body had been truncated cleanly just in front of its haunches.

"Jesus," said Ginger. "What did that?"

"Must have been a truck," said Steve. "An eighteen-wheeler can really tear things up when it's barreling."

Carroll looked back toward the carcass and the sky beyond. "Maybe that's what our friend was protecting."

GROS VENTRE FORMATION

CAMBRIAN

500–600 MILLION YEARS

"You know, this was all under water once," said Steve. He was answered only with silence. "Just about all of Wyoming was covered with an ancient sea. That accounts for a lot of the coal." No one said anything. "I think it was called the Sundance Sea. You know, like in the Sundance Kid. Some Exxon geologist told me that in a bar."

He turned and looked at the two women. And stared. And turned back to the road blindly. And then stared at them again. It seemed to Steve that he was looking at a double exposure, or a triple exposure, or— he couldn't count all the overlays. He started to say something, but could not. He existed in a silence that was also stasis, the death of all motion. He could only see.

Carroll and Ginger faced straight ahead. They looked as they had earlier in the afternoon. They also looked as they had fifteen years before. Steve saw them *in process*, lines blurred. And Steve saw skin merge with feathers, and then scales. He saw gill openings appear, vanish, reappear on textured necks.

And then both of them turned to look at him. Their heads swiveled slowly, smoothly. Four reptilian eyes watched him, unblinking and incurious.

Steve wanted to look away.

The Chevy's tires whined on the level blacktop. The sign read:

SPEED ZONE AHEAD

35 MPH

"Are you awake?" said Ginger.

Steve shook his head to clear it. "Sure," he said. "You know that reverie you sometimes get into when you're driving? When you can drive miles without consciously thinking about it, and then suddenly you realize what's happened?"

Ginger nodded.

"That's what happened."

The highway passed between modest frame houses, gas stations, motels. They entered Shoshoni.

There was a brand new WELCOME TO SHOSHONI sign, as yet without bullet holes. The population figure had again been revised upward. "Want to bet on when they break another thousand?" said Carroll.

Ginger shook her head silently.

Steve pulled up to the stop sign. "Which way?"

Carroll said, "Go left."

"I think I've got it." Steve saw the half-ton truck with the Enerco decal and NATIVE AMERICAN RESOURCES DIVISION labeled below that on the door. It was parked in front of the Yellowstone Drugstore. "Home of the world's greatest shakes and malts," said Steve. "Let's go."

The interior of the Yellowstone had always reminded him of nothing so much as an old-fashioned pharmacy blended with the interior of the cafe in *Bad Day at Black Rock*. They found Paul at a table nursing a chocolate malted.

He looked up, smiled, said, "I've gained four pounds this afternoon. If you'd been any later, I'd probably have become diabetic."

Paul looked far older than Steve had expected. Ginger and Carroll both appeared older than they had been a decade and a half before, but Paul seemed to have aged thirty years in fifteen. The star quarterback's physique had gone a bit to pot. His face was creased with lines emphasized by the leathery curing of skin that has been exposed for years to wind and hot sun. Paul's hair, black as coal, was streaked with firn-lines of glacial white. His eyes, Steve thought, looked tremendously old.

He greeted Steve with a warm handclasp. Carroll received a gentle hug and a kiss on the cheek. Ginger got a warm smile and a hello. The four of them sat down, and the fountain man came over. "Chocolate all around?" Paul said.

"Vanilla shake," said Ginger.

Steve sensed a tension at the table that seemed to go beyond dissolved marriages and terminated affairs. He wasn't sure what to say after all the years, but Paul saved him the trouble. Smiling and soft-spoken, Paul gently interrogated him.

So what have you been doing with yourself?

Really?

How did that work out?

That's too bad; then what?

What about afterward?

And you came back?

How about since?

What do you do now?

Paul sat back in the scrolled-wire ice-cream parlor chair, still smiling, playing with the plastic straw. He tied knots in the straw and then untied them.

"Do you know," said Paul, "that this whole complicated reunion of the four of us is not a matter of chance?"

Steve studied the other man. Paul's smile faded to impassivity. "I'm not that paranoid," Steve said. "It didn't occur to me."

"It's a setup."

Steve considered that silently.

"It didn't take place until after I had tossed the yarrow stalks a considerable number of times," said Paul. His voice was wry. "I don't know what the official company policy on such irrational behavior is, but it all seemed right under extraordinary circumstances. I told Carroll where she could likely find you and left the means of contact up to her."

The two women waited and watched silently. Carroll's expression was, Steve thought, one of concern. Ginger looked apprehensive. "So what is it?" he said. "What kind of game am I in?"

"It's no game," said Carroll quickly. "We need you."

"You know what I thought ever since I met you in Miss Gorman's class?" said Paul. "You're not a loser. You've just needed some—direction."

Steve said impatiently, "Come on."

"It's true." Paul set down the straw. "Why we need you is because you seem to see things most others can't see."

Time's predator hunts.

Years scatter before her like a school of minnows surprised. The rush of her passage causes eons to eddy. Wind sweeps down the canyon with the roar of combers breaking on the sand. The moon, full and newly risen, exerts its tidal force.

Moonlight flashes on the slash of teeth.

She drives for the surface not out of rational decision. All blunt power embodied in smooth motion, she simply is what she is.

Steve sat without speaking. Finally he said vaguely, "Things."

"That's right. You see things. It's an ability."

"I don't know. . . ."

"We think *we* do. We all remember that night after the prom. And there were other times, back in school. None of us has seen you since we all played scatter-geese, but I've had the resources, through the corporation, to do some checking. The issue didn't come up until recently. In the last month, I've read your school records, your psychiatric history."

"That must have taken some trouble," said Steve. "Should I feel flattered?"

"Tell him," said Ginger. "Tell him what this is all about."

"Yeah," said Steve. "Tell me."

For the first time in the conversation, Paul hesitated. "Okay," he finally said. "We're hunting a ghost in the Wind River."

"Say again?"

"That's perhaps poor terminology." Paul looked uncomfortable. "But what we're looking for is a presence, some sort of extranatural phenomenon."

" 'Ghost' is a perfectly good word," said Carroll.

"Better start from the beginning," said Steve.

When Paul didn't answer immediately, Carroll said, "I know you don't read the papers. Ever listen to the radio?"

Steve shook his head. "Not much."

"About a month ago, an Enerco mineral-survey party in the Wind River got the living daylights scared out of them."

"Leave out what they saw," said Paul. "I'd like to include a control factor."

"It wasn't just the Enerco people. Others have seen it, both Indians and Anglos. The consistency of the witnesses has been remarkable. If you haven't heard about this at the bars, Steve, you must have been asleep."

"I haven't been all that social for a while," said Steve. "I did hear that someone's trying to scare the oil and coal people off the reservation."

"Not someone," said Paul. "Some *thing*. I'm convinced of that now."

"A ghost," said Steve.

"A presence."

"There're rumors," said Carroll, "that the tribes have revived the Ghost Dance—"

"Just a few extremists," said Paul.

"—to conjure back an avenger from the past who will drive every white out of the county."

Steve knew of the Ghost Dance, had read of the Paiute mystic Wovoka who, in 1888, had claimed that in a vision the spirits had promised the return of the buffalo and the restoration to the Indians of their ancestral lands. The Plains tribes had danced assiduously the Ghost Dance to ensure this. Then in 1908 the U.S. government suppressed the final Sioux uprising and, except for a few scattered incidents, that was that. Discredited, Wovoka survived to die in the midst of the Great Depression.

"I have it on good authority," said Paul, "that the Ghost Dance was revived *after* the presence terrified the survey crew."

"That really doesn't matter," Carroll said. "Remember prom night? I've checked the newspaper morgues in Fremont and Lander and Riverton. There've been strange sightings for more than a century."

"That was then," said Paul. "The problem now is that the tribes are infinitely more restive, and my people are actually getting frightened to go out into the field." His voice took on a bemused tone. "Arab terrorists couldn't do it, civil wars didn't bother them, but a damned ghost is scaring the wits out of them—literally."

"Too bad," said Ginger. She did not sound regretful.

Steve looked at the three gathered around the table. He knew he did not understand all the details and nuances of the love and hate and trust and broken affections. "I can understand Paul's concern," he said. "But why the rest of you?"

The women exchanged glances. "One way or another," said Carroll, "we're all tied together. I think it includes you, Steve."

"Maybe," said Ginger soberly. "Maybe not. She's an artist. I'm a journalist. We've all got our reasons for wanting to know more about what's up there."

"In the past few years," said Carroll, "I've caught a tremendous amount of Wyoming in my paintings. Now I want to capture this too."

Conversation languished. The soda-fountain man looked as though he were unsure whether to solicit a new round of malteds.

"What now?" Steve said.

"If you'll agree," said Paul, "we're going to go back up into the Wind River to search."

"So what am I? Some sort of damned occult Geiger counter?"

Ginger said, "It's a nicer phrase than calling yourself bait."

"Jesus," Steve said. "That doesn't reassure me much." He looked from one to the next. "Control factor or not, give me some clue to what we're going to look for."

Everyone looked at Paul. Eventually he shrugged and said, "You know the Highway Department signs in the canyon? The geological time chart you travel when you're driving U.S. 20?"

Steve nodded.

"We're looking for a relic of the ancient inland sea."

After the sun sank in blood in the west, they drove north and watched dusk unfold into the splendor of the night sky.

"I'll always marvel at that," said Paul. "Do you know, you can see three times as many stars in the sky here as you can from any city?"

"It scares the tourists sometimes," said Carroll.

Ginger said, "It won't after a few more of those coal-fired generating plants are built."

Paul chuckled humorlessly. "I thought they were preferable to your nemesis, the nukes."

Ginger was sitting with Steve in the backseat of the Enerco truck. Her words were controlled and even. "There are alternatives to both those."

"Try supplying power to the rest of the country with them before the next century," Paul said. He braked suddenly as a jackrabbit darted into the bright cones of light. The rabbit made it across the road.

"Nobody actually *needs* air conditioners," said Ginger.

"I won't argue that point," Paul said. "You'll just have to argue with the reality of all the people who think they do."

Ginger lapsed into silence. Carroll said, "I suppose you should be congratulated for the tribal council vote today. We heard about it on the news."

"It's not binding," said Paul. "When it finally goes through, we hope it will whittle the fifty-percent jobless rate on the reservation."

"It sure as hell won't!" Ginger burst out. "Higher mineral royalties mean more incentive not to have a career."

Paul laughed. "Are you blaming me for being the chicken, or the egg?"

No one answered him.

"I'm not a monster," he said.

"I don't think you are," said Steve.

"I know it puts me in a logical trap, but I think I'm doing the right thing."

"All right," said Ginger. "I won't take any easy shots. At least, I'll try."

From the backseat, Steve looked around his uneasy allies and hoped to hell that someone had brought aspirin. Carroll had aspirin in her handbag, and Steve washed it down with beer from Paul's cooler.

GRANITE

PRE-CAMBRIAN

600+ MILLION YEARS

The moon had risen by now, a full, icy disk. The highway curved around a formation that looked like a vast, layered birthday cake. Cedar provided spectral candles.

"I've never believed in ghosts," said Steve. He caught the flicker of Paul's eyes in the rearview mirror and knew the geologist was looking at him.

"There are ghosts," said Paul, "and there are ghosts. In spectroscopy, ghosts are false readings. In television, ghost images—"

"What about the kind that haunt houses?"

"In television," Paul continued, "a ghost is a reflected electronic image arriving at the antenna some interval after the desired wave."

"And are they into groans and chains?"

"Some people are better antennas than others, Steve."

Steve fell silent.

"There is a theory," said Paul, "that molecular structures, no matter how altered by process, still retain some sort of 'memory' of their original form."

"Ghosts."

"If you like." He stared ahead at the highway and said, as if musing, "When an ancient organism becomes fossilized, even the DNA patterns that determine its structure are preserved in the stone."

GALLATIN FORMATION

CAMBRIAN

500–600 MILLION YEARS

Paul shifted into a lower gear as the half-ton began to climb one of the long, gradual grades. Streaming black smoke and bellowing like a great saurian lumbering into extinction, an eighteen-wheel semi with oil field gear on its back passed them, forcing Paul part of the way onto the right shoulder. Trailing a dopplered call from its airhorn, the rig disappeared into the first of three short highway tunnels quarried out of the rock.

"One of yours?" said Ginger.

"Nope."

"Maybe he'll crash and burn."

"I'm sure he's just trying to make a living," said Paul mildly.

"Raping the land's a living?" said Ginger. "Cannibalizing the past is a living?"

"Shut up, Gin." Quietly, Carroll said, "Wyoming didn't do anything to your family, Paul. Whatever was done, people did it."

"The land gets into the people," said Paul.

"That isn't the only thing that defines them."

"This always has been a fruitless argument," said Paul. "It's a dead past."

"If the past is dead," Steve said, "then why are we driving up this cockamamie canyon?"

AMSDEN FORMATION
PENNSYLVANIAN
270–310 MILLION YEARS

Boysen Reservoir spread to their left, rippled surface glittering in the moonlight. The road hugged the eastern edge. Once the crimson taillights of the oil field truck had disappeared in the distance, they encountered no other vehicle.

"Are we just going to drive up and down Twenty all night?" said Steve. "Who brought the plan?" He did not feel flippant, but he had to say something. He felt the burden of time.

"We'll go where the survey crew saw the presence," Paul said. "It's just a few more miles."

"And then?"

"Then we walk. It should be at least as interesting as our hike prom night."

Steve sensed that a lot of things were almost said by each of them at that point.

I didn't know then . . .

Nor do I know for sure yet.

I'm seeking . . .

What?

Time's flowed. I want to know where now, finally, to direct it.

"Who would have thought . . . " said Ginger.

Whatever was thought, nothing more was said.

The headlights picked out the reflective green-and-white Highway Department sign. "We're there," said Paul. "Somewhere on the right, there ought to be a dirt access road."

SHARKTOOTH FORMATION
CRETACEOUS
100 MILLION YEARS

"Are we going to use a net?" said Steve. "Tranquilizer darts? What?"

"I don't think we can catch a ghost in a net," said Carroll. "You catch a ghost in your soul."

A small smile curved Paul's lips. "Think of this as the Old West. We're only a scouting party. Once we observe whatever's up here, we'll figure out how to get rid of it."

"That won't be possible," said Carroll.

"Why do you say that?"

"I don't know," she said. "I just feel it."

"Woman's intuition?" He said it lightly.

"*My* intuition."

"Anything's possible," said Paul.

"If we really thought you could destroy it," said Ginger, "I doubt either of us would be up here with you."

Paul had stopped the truck to lock the front hubs into four-wheel drive. Now the vehicle clanked and lurched over rocks and across potholes eroded by the spring rain. The road twisted tortuously around series of barely graded switchbacks. Already they had climbed hundreds of feet above the canyon floor. They could see no lights anywhere below.

"Very scenic," said Steve. If he had wanted to, he could have reached out the right passenger's side window and touched the porous rock. Pine branches whispered along the paint on the left side.

"Thanks to Native American Resources," said Ginger, "this is the sort of country that'll go."

"For Christ's sake," said Paul, finally sounding angry. "I'm *not* the Antichrist."

"I know that." Ginger's voice softened. "I've loved you, remember? Probably I still do. Is there no way?"

The geologist didn't answer.

"Paul?"

"We're just about there," he said. The grade moderated and he shifted to a higher gear.

"Paul—" Steve wasn't sure whether he actually said the word or not. He closed his eyes and saw glowing fires, opened them again and wasn't sure what he saw. He felt the past, vast and primeval, rush over him like a tide. It filled his nose and mouth, his lungs, his brain. It—

"Oh my God!"

Someone screamed.

"Let go!"

The headlight beams twitched crazily as the truck skidded toward the edge of a sheer dark drop. Both Paul and Carroll wrestled for the wheel. For an instant, Steve wondered whether both of them or, indeed, either of them were trying to turn the truck back from the dark.

Then he saw the great, bulky, streamlined form coasting over the slope toward them. He had the impression of smooth power, immense and inexorable. The dead stare from flat black eyes, each one inches across, fixed them like insects in amber.

"Paul!" Steve heard his own voice. He heard the word echo and then it was swallowed up by the crashing waves. He felt unreasoning terror, but more than that, he felt—awe. What he beheld was juxtaposed on this western canyon, but yet it was not out of place. Genius loci, guardian, the words hissed like the surf.

It swam toward them, impossibly gliding on powerful gray-black fins.

Brakes screamed. A tire blew out like a gunshot.

Steve watched its jaws open in front of the windshield; the snout pulling up and back, the lower jaw thrusting forward. The maw could have taken in a heifer. The teeth glared white in reflected light, white with serrated, razor edges. Its teeth were as large as shovel blades.

"Paul!"

The Enerco truck fishtailed a final time; then toppled sideways into the dark. It fell, caromed off something massive and unseen, and began to roll.

Steve had time for one thought. *Is it going to hurt?*

When the truck came to rest, it was upright. Steve groped toward the window and felt rough bark rather than glass. They were wedged against a pine.

The silence astonished him. That there was no fire astonished him. That he was alive—"Carroll?" he said. "Ginger? Paul?" For a moment, no one spoke.

"I'm here," said Carroll, muffled, from the front of the truck. "Paul's on top of me. Or somebody is. I can't tell."

"Oh God, I hurt," said Ginger from beside Steve. "My shoulder hurts."

"Can you move your arm?" said Steve.

"A little, but it hurts."

"Okay." Steve leaned forward across the front seat. He didn't feel anything like grating, broken bone-ends in himself. His fingers touched flesh. Some of it was sticky with fluid. Gently he pulled who he assumed was Carroll from beneath Paul. She moaned and struggled upright.

"There should be a flashlight in the glove box," he said.

The darkness was almost complete. Steve could see only vague shapes inside the truck. When Carroll switched on the flashlight, they realized the truck was buried in thick, resilient brush. Carroll and Ginger stared back at him. Ginger looked as if she might be in shock. Paul slumped on the front seat. The angle of his neck was all wrong.

His eyes opened and he tried to focus. Then he said something. They couldn't understand him. Paul tried again. They made out, "Goodnight, Irene." Then he said, "Do what you have." His eyes remained open, but all the life went out of them.

Steve and the women stared at one another as though they were accomplices. The moment crystallized and shattered. He braced himself as best he could and kicked with both feet at the rear door. The brush allowed the door to swing open one foot, then another. Carroll had her door open at almost the same time. It took another few minutes to get Ginger out. They left Paul in the truck.

They huddled on a naturally terraced ledge about halfway between the summit and the canyon floor. There was a roar and bright lights for a few minutes when a Burlington Northern freight came down the tracks on the other side of the river. It would have done no good to shout and wave their arms. So they didn't.

No one seemed to have broken any bones. Ginger's shoulder was apparently separated. Carroll had a nosebleed. Steve's head felt as though he'd been walloped with a two-by-four.

"It's not cold," he said. "If we have to, we can stay in the truck. No way we're going to get down at night. In the morning we can signal people on the road."

Ginger started to cry and they both held her. "I saw something," she said. "I couldn't tell—what was it?"

Steve hesitated. He had a hard time separating his dreams from Paul's theories. The two did not now seem mutually exclusive. He still heard the echoing thunder of ancient gulfs. "I'm guessing it's something that lived here a hundred million years ago," he finally said. "It lived in the inland sea and died here. The sea left, but it never did."

"A native . . . " Ginger said and trailed off. Steve touched her forehead; it felt feverish. "I finally saw," she said. "Now I'm a part of it." In a smaller voice, "Paul." Starting awake like a nightmare, "Paul?"

"He's—all right now," said Carroll, her even tone plainly forced.

"No, he's not," said Ginger. "He's not." She was silent for a time. "He's dead." Tears streamed down her face. "It won't stop the coal leases, will it?"

"Probably not."

"Politics," Ginger said wanly. "Politics and death. What the hell difference does any of it make now?"

No one answered her.

Steve turned toward the truck in the brush. He suddenly remembered from his childhood how he had hoped everyone he knew, everyone he loved, would live forever. He hadn't wanted change. He hadn't wanted to recognize time. He remembered the split-second image of Paul and Carroll struggling to control the wheel. "The land," he said, feeling the sorrow. "It doesn't forgive."

"That's not true." Carroll slowly shook her head. "The land just *is*. The land doesn't care."

"I care," said Steve.

Amazingly, Ginger started to go to sleep. They laid her down gently on the precipice, covered her with Steve's jacket, and cradled her head, stroking her hair. "Look," she said. "Look." As the moon illuminated the glowing sea.

Far below them, a fin broke the dark surface of the forest.

AND NOW
THE NEWS . . .

The man's name was MacLyle, which by looking at you can tell wasn't his real name, but let's say this is fiction, shall we? MacLyle had a good job in—well—a soap concern. He worked hard and made good money and got married to a girl called Esther. He bought a house in the suburbs and after it was paid for he rented it to some people and bought a home a little farther out and a second car and a freezer and a power mower and a book on landscaping, and settled down to the worthy task of giving his kids all the things he never had.

He had habits and he had hobbies, like everybody else, and (like everybody else) his were a little different from anybody's. The one that annoyed his wife the most, until she got used to it, was the news habit, or maybe hobby. MacLyle read a morning paper on the 8:14 and an evening paper on the 6:10, and the local paper his suburb used for its lost dogs and auction sales took up forty after-dinner minutes. And when he read a paper he read it, he didn't mess with it. He read page 1 first and page 2 next, and so on all the way through. He didn't care too much for books but he respected them in a mystical sort of way, and he used to say a newspaper was a kind of book, and so would raise particular hell if a section was missing or in upside down, or if the pages were out of line. He also heard the news on the radio. There were three stations in town with hourly broadcasts, one on the hour, one on the half-hour, and one five minutes before the hour, and he was usually able to catch them all. During these five-minute periods he would look you right in the eye while you talked to him and you'd swear he was listening to you, but he wasn't. This was a particular trial to his wife, but only for five years or so. Then she stopped trying to be heard while the radio talked about floods and murders and scandal and suicide. Five more years, and she went back to talking right through the broadcasts, but by the time people are married ten years, things like that don't matter; they talk in code anyway, and nine tenths of their speech can be picked up anytime like ticker-tape. He also caught the 7:30 news on Channel 2 and the 7:45 news on Channel 4 on television.

Now it might be imagined from all this that MacLyle was a crotchety character with fixed habits and a neurotic neatness, but this was far from the case. MacLyle was basically a reasonable guy who loved his wife and children and liked his work and pretty much enjoyed being alive. He laughed easily and talked well and paid his bills. He justified his preoccupation with the news in a number of ways. He would quote Donne: "... any man's death diminishes me, because I am involved in mankind..." which is pretty solid stuff and hard to argue down. He would point out that he made his trains and his trains made him punctual, but that because of them he saw the same faces at the same time day after endless day, before, during, and after he rode those trains, so that his immediate world was pretty circumscribed, and only a constant awareness of what was happening all over the earth kept him conscious of the fact that he lived in a bigger place than a thin straight universe with his house at one end, his office at the other, and a railway track in between.

It's hard to say just when MacLyle started to go to pieces, or even why, though it obviously had something to do with all that news he exposed himself to. He began to react, very slightly at first; that is, you could tell he was listening. He'd shh! you, and if you tried to finish what you were saying he'd run and stick his head in the speaker grille. His wife and kids learned to shut up when the news came on, five minutes before the hour until five after (with MacLyle switching stations) and every hour on the half-hour, and from 7:30 to 8:00 for the TV, and during the forty minutes it took him to read the local paper. He was not so obvious about it when he read his paper, because all he did was freeze over the pages like a catatonic, gripping the top corners until the sheets shivered, knotting his jaw and breathing from his nostrils with a strangled whistle.

Naturally all this was a weight on his wife Esther, who tried her best to reason with him. At first he answered her, saying mildly that a man has to keep in touch, you know; but very quickly he stopped responding altogether, giving her the treatment a practiced suburbanite gets so expert in, as when someone mentions a lawn mower just too damn early on Sunday morning. You don't say yes and you don't say no, you don't even grunt, and you don't move your head or even your eyebrows. After a while your interlocutor goes away. Pretty soon you don't hear these ill-timed annoyances any more than you appear to.

It needs to be said again here that MacLyle was, outside his peculiarity, a friendly and easygoing character. He liked people and invited them and visited them, and he was one of those adults who can really listen to a first-grade child's interminable adventures and really care. He never forgot things like the slow leak in the spare tire or antifreeze or anniversaries, and he always got the storm windows up in time, but he didn't rub anyone's nose in his reliability. The first thing in his whole life he didn't take as a matter of course was this news thing that started so small and grew so quickly.

So after a few weeks of it his wife took the bull by the horns and spent the afternoon hamstringing every receiver in the house. There were three radios and two TV sets, and she didn't understand the first thing about them, but she had a good head and she went to work with a will and the can-opening limb of a pocket knife. From each receiver she removed one tube, and one at a time, so as not to get them mixed up, she carried them into the kitchen and meticulously banged their bases against the edge of the sink, being careful to crack no glass and bend no pins, until she could see the guts of the tube rolling around loose inside. Then she replaced them and got the back panels on the sets again.

MacLyle came home and put the car away and kissed her and turned on the living-room radio and then went to hang up his hat. When he returned the radio should have been warmed up but it wasn't. He twisted the knobs a while and bumped it and rocked it back and forth a little, grunting, and then noticed the time. He began to feel a little frantic, and raced back to the kitchen and turned on the little ivory radio on the shelf. It warmed up quickly and cheerfully and gave him a clear sixty-cycle hum, but that was all. He behaved badly from then on, roaring out the information that the sets didn't work, either of them, as if that wasn't pretty evident by that time, and flew upstairs to the boys' room, waking them explosively. He turned on their radio and got another sixty-cycle note, this time with a shattering microphonic when he rapped the case, which he did four times, whereupon the set went dead altogether.

Esther had planned the thing up to this point, but no further, which was the way her mind worked. She figured she could handle it, but she figured wrong. MacLyle came downstairs like a pallbearer, and he was silent and shaken until 7:30, time for the news on TV. The living-room set wouldn't peep, so up he went to the boys' room again, waking them just as they were nodding off again, and this time the little guy started to cry. MacLyle didn't care. When he found out there was no picture on the set, he almost started to cry too, but then he heard the sound come in. A TV set has an awful lot of tubes in it and Esther didn't know audio from video. MacLyle sat down in front of the dark screen and listened to the news. *"Everything seemed to be under control in the riot-ridden border country in India,"* said the TV set. Crowd noises and a background of Beethoven's *"Turkish March." "And then—"* Cut music. Crowd noise up: gabble-wurra and a scream. Announcer over: *"Six hours later, this was the scene."* Dead silence, going on so long that MacLyle reached out and thumped the TV set with the heel of his hand. Then, slow swell, Ketelbey's *"In a Monastery Garden." "On a more cheerful note, here are the six finalists in the Miss Continuum contest."* Background music, *"Blue Room,"* interminably, interrupted only once, when the announcer said through a childish chuckle, *"... and she meant it!"* MacLyle pounded himself on the temples. The little guy continued to sob. Esther stood at the foot of the stairs wringing her hands. It went on for thirty minutes like this. All MacLyle said when he came downstairs was that he wanted the paper—that would be the local one. So Esther faced the great unknown and told him frankly she hadn't ordered it and wouldn't again, which of course led to a full and righteous confession of her activities of the afternoon.

Only a woman married better than fourteen years can know a man well enough to handle him so badly. She was aware that she was wrong but that was quite overridden by the fact that she was logical. It would not be logical to continue her patience, so patience was at an end. That which offendeth thee, cast it out, yea, even thine eye and thy right hand. She realized too late that the news was so inextricably part of her husband that in casting it out she cast him out too. And out he went, while whitely she listened to the rumble of the garage door, the car door speaking its sharp syllables, clear as *Exit* in a play script; the keen of a starter, the mourn of a motor. She said she was glad and went in the kitchen and tipped the useless ivory radio off the shelf and retired, weeping.

And yet, because true life offers few clean cuts, she saw him once more. At seven minutes to three in the morning she became aware of faint music from somewhere; unaccountably it frightened her, and she tiptoed about the house looking for it. It wasn't in the house, so she pulled on MacLyle's trench coat and crept down the steps into the garage. And there, just outside in the driveway, where steel beams couldn't interfere with radio reception, the car stood where it had been all along, and MacLyle was in the driver's seat dozing over the wheel. The music came from the car radio. She drew the coat tighter around her and went to the car and opened the door and spoke his name. At just that moment the radio said "... and now the news" and MacLyle sat bolt upright and shh'd furiously. She fell back and stood a moment in a strange transition from unconditional surrender to total defeat. Then he shut the car door and bent forward, his hand on the volume control, and she went back into the house.

After the news report was over and he had recovered himself from the stab wounds of a juvenile delinquent, the grinding agonies of a derailed train, the terrors of the near-crash of a C-119, and the fascination of a cabinet officer, charter member of the We Don't Trust Nobody Club, saying in exactly these words that there's a little bit of good in the worst of us and a little bit of bad in the best of us, all of which he felt keenly, he started the car (by rolling it down the drive because the battery was almost dead) and drove as slowly as possible into town.

At an all-night garage he had the car washed and greased while he waited, after which the automat was open and he sat in it for three hours drinking coffee, holding his jaw set until his back teeth ached, and making occasional, almost inaudible noises in the back of his throat. At 9:00 he pulled himself together. He spent the entire day with his astonished attorney, going through all his assets, selling, converting, establishing, until when he was finished he had a modest packet of cash and his wife would have an adequate income until the children went to college, at which time the house would be sold, the tenants in the older house evicted, and Esther would be free to move to the smaller home with the price of the larger one added to the basic capital. The lawyer might have entertained fears for MacLyle except for the fact that he was jovial and loquacious throughout, behaving like a happy man—a rare form of insanity, but acceptable. It was hard work but they did it in a day, after which MacLyle wrung the lawyer's hand and thanked him profusely and checked into a hotel.

When he awoke the following morning he sprang out of bed, feeling years younger, opened the door, scooped up the morning paper and glanced at the headlines.

He couldn't read them.

He grunted in surprise, closed the door gently, and sat on the bed with the paper in his lap. His hands moved restlessly on it, smoothing and smoothing until the palms were shadowed and the type hazed. The shouting symbols marched across the page like a parade of strangers in some unrecognized lodge uniform, origins unknown, destination unknown, and the occasion for marching only to be guessed at. He traced the letters with his little finger, he measured the length of a word between his index finger and thumb and lifted them up to hold them before his wondering eyes. Suddenly he got up and crossed to the desk, where signs and placards and printed notes were trapped like a butterfly collection under glass—the breakfast menu, something about valet service, something about checking out. He remembered them all and had an idea of their significance—but he couldn't read them. In the drawer was stationery, with a picture of the building and no other buildings around it, which just wasn't so, and an inscription which might have been in Cyrillic for all he knew. Telegram blanks, a bus schedule, a blotter, all bearing hieroglyphs and runes, as far as he was concerned. A phone book full of strangers' names in strange symbols.

He requested of himself that he recite the alphabet. "A," he said clearly, and "Eh?" because it didn't sound right and he couldn't imagine what would. He made a small foolish grin and shook his head slightly and rapidly, but grin or no, he felt frightened. He felt glad, or relieved—mostly happy anyway, but still a little frightened.

He called the desk and told them to get his bill ready, and dressed and went downstairs. He gave the doorman his parking check and waited while they brought the car round. He got in and turned the radio on and started to drive west.

He drove for some days, in a state of perpetual, cold, and (for all that) happy fright—roller-coaster fright, horror-movie fright—remembering the significance of a stop sign without being able to read the word STOP across it, taking caution from the shape of a railroad-crossing notice. Restaurants look like restaurants, gas stations like gas stations; if Washington's picture denotes a dollar and Lincoln's five, one doesn't need to read them. MacLyle made out just fine. He drove until he was well into one of those square states with all the mountains and cruised until he recognized the section where, years before he was married, he had spent a hunting vacation. Avoiding the lodge he had used, he took back roads

until, sure enough, he came to that deserted cabin in which he had
sheltered one night, standing yet, rotting a bit but only around the edges.
He wandered in and out of it for a long time, memorizing details because
he could not make a list, and then got back into his car and drove to the
nearest town, not very near and not very much of a town. At the general
store he bought shingles and flour and nails and paint—all sorts of paint,
in little cans, as well as big containers of house paint—and canned goods
and tools. He ordered a knockdown windmill and a generator, eighty
pounds of modeling clay, two loaf pans and a mixing bowl, and a war-
surplus jungle hammock. He paid cash and promised to be back in two
weeks for the things the store didn't stock, and wired (because it could
be done over the phone) his lawyer to arrange for the predetermined
eighty dollars a month which was all he cared to take for himself from
his assets. Before he left he stood in wonder before a monstrous piece of
musical plumbing called an ophicleide which stood, dusty and majestic,
in a corner. (While it might be easier on the reader to make this a French
horn or a sousaphone—which would answer narrative purposes quite as
well—we're done telling lies here. MacLyle's real name is concealed,
his home town cloaked, and his occupation disguised, and dammit, it
really was a twelve-keyed, 1824, fifty-inch, obsolete brass ophicleide.)
The storekeeper explained how his great-grandfather had brought it over
from the old country and nobody had played it for two generations except
an itinerant tuba player who had turned pale green on the first three
notes and put it down as if it were full of percussion caps. MacLyle asked
how it sounded and the man told him, terrible. Two weeks later MacLyle
was back to pick up the rest of his stuff, nodding and smiling and saying
not a word. He still couldn't read, and now he couldn't speak. Even
more, he had lost the power to understand speech. He paid for the
purchases with a hundred-dollar bill and a wistful expression, and then
another hundred-dollar bill, and the storekeeper, thinking he had turned
deaf and dumb, cheated him roundly but at the same time felt so sorry
for him that he gave him the ophicleide. MacLyle loaded up his car
happily and left. And that's the first part of the story about MacLyle's
being in a bad way.

MacLyle's wife Esther found herself in a peculiar position. Friends and
neighbors offhandedly asked her questions to which she did not know
the answers, and the only person who had any information at all—
MacLyle's attorney—was under bond not to tell her anything. She had
not, in the full and legal sense, been deserted, since she and the children

were provided for. She missed MacLyle, but in a specialized way; she missed the old reliable MacLyle, and he had, in effect, left her long before that perplexing night when he had driven away. She wanted the old MacLyle back again, not this untrolleyed stranger with the grim and spastic preoccupation with the news. Of the many unpleasant facets of this stranger's personality, one glowed brightest, and that was that he was the sort of man who would walk out the way he did and stay away as long as he had. Ergo, he was that undesirable person just as long as he stayed away, and tracking him down would, if it returned him against his will, return to her only a person who was not the person she missed.

Yet she was dissatisfied with herself, for all that she was the injured party and had wounds less painful than the pangs of conscience. She had always prided herself on being a good wife, and had done many things in the past which were counter to her reason and her desires purely because they were consistent with being a good wife. So as time went on she gravitated away from the "what shall I do?" area into the "what ought a good wife to do?" spectrum, and after a great deal of careful thought, went to see a psychiatrist.

He was a fairly intelligent psychiatrist, which is to say he caught on to the obvious a little faster than most people. For example, he became aware in only four minutes of conversation that MacLyle's wife Esther had not come to him on her own behalf, and further decided to hear her out completely before resolving to treat her. When she had quite finished and he had dug out enough corroborative detail to get the picture, he went into a long silence and cogitated. He matched the broad pattern of MacLyle's case with his reading and his experience, recognized the challenge, the clinical worth of the case, the probable value of the heirloom diamond pendant worn by his visitor. He placed his fingertips together, lowered his fine young head, gazed through his eyebrows at MacLyle's wife Esther, and took up the gauntlet. At the prospect of getting her husband back safe and sane, she thanked him quietly and left the office with mixed emotions. The fairly intelligent psychiatrist drew a deep breath and began making arrangements with another headshrinker to take over his other patients, both of them, while he was away, because he figured to be away quite a while.

It was appallingly easy for him to trace MacLyle. He did not go near the lawyer. The solid foundation of all skip tracers and Bureaus of Missing Persons, in their *modus operandi*, is the piece of applied psychology which dictates that a man might change his name and his address, but he will seldom—can seldom—change the things he does, particularly the things he does to amuse himself. The ski addict doesn't skip to Florida, though he might make Banff instead of an habitual Mont Tremblant. A philatelist is not likely to mount butterflies. Hence when the psychiatrist found, among MacLyle's papers, some snapshots and brochures, dating from college days, of the towering Rockies, of bears feeding by the roadside, and especially of season after season's souvenirs of a particular resort to which he had never brought his wife and which he had not visited since he married her, it was worth a feeler, which went out in the form of a request to that state's police for information on a man of such-and-such a description driving so-and-so with out-of-state plates, plus a request that the man not be detained nor warned, but only that he, the fairly intelligent psychiatrist, be notified. He threw out other lines, too, but this is the one that hooked his fish. It was a matter of weeks before a state patrol car happened by MacLyle's favorite general store: after that it was a matter of minutes before the information was in the hands of the psychiatrist. He said nothing to MacLyle's wife Esther except good-bye for a while, and this bill is payable now, and then took off, bearing with him a bag of tricks.

He rented a car at the airport nearest MacLyle's hideout and drove a long, thirsty, climbing way until he came to the general store. There he interviewed the proprietor, learning some eighteen hundred items about how bad business could get, how hot it was, how much rain hadn't fallen and how much was needed, the tragedy of being blamed for high markups when anyone with the brains God gave a goose ought to know it cost plenty to ship things out here, especially in the small quantities necessitated by business being so bad and all; and betwixt and between, he learned eight or ten items about MacLyle—the exact location of his cabin, the fact that he seemed to have turned into a deaf-mute who was also unable to read, and that he must be crazy because who but a crazy man would want eighty-four different half-pint cans of house paint or, for that matter, live out here when he didn't have to?

The psychiatrist got loose after a while and drove off, and the country got higher and dustier and more lost every mile, until he began to pray that nothing would go wrong with the car, and sure enough, ten minutes later he thought something had. Any car that made a noise like the one he began to hear was strictly a shotrod, and he pulled over to the side to worry about it. He turned off the motor and the noise went right on, and he began to realize that the sound was not in the car or even near it, but came from somewhere uphill. There was a mile and a half more of the hill to go, and he drove it in increasing amazement, because that sound got louder and more impossible all the time. It was sort of like music, but like no music currently heard on this or any other planet. It was a solo voice, brass, with muscles. The upper notes, of which there seemed to be about two octaves, were wild and unmusical, the middle was rough, but the low tones were like the speech of these mountains themselves, big up to the sky, hot, and more natural than anything ought to be, basic as a bear's fang. Yet all the notes were perfect—their intervals were perfect—this awful noise was tuned like an electronic organ. The psychiatrist had a good ear, though for a while he wondered how long he'd have any ears at all, and he realized all these things about the sound, as well as the fact that it was rendering one of the more primitive fingering studies from Czerny, Book One, the droning little horror that goes: *do mi fa sol la sol fa mi, re fa sol la ti la sol fa, mi sol la* . . . etcetera, inchworming up the scale and then descending hand over hand.

He saw blue sky almost under his front tires and wrenched the wheel hard over, and found himself in the grassy yard of a made-over prospector's cabin, but that he didn't notice right away because sitting in front of it was what he described to himself, startled as he was out of his professional detachment, as the craziest-looking man he had ever seen.

He was sitting under a parched, wind-warped Engelmann spruce. He was barefoot up to the armpits. He wore the top half of a skivvy shirt and a hat the shape of one of those conical Boy Scout tents when one of the Boy Scouts has left the pole home. And he was playing, or anyway practicing, the ophicleide, and on his shoulders was a little moss of spruce-needles, a small shower of which descended from the tree every time he hit on or under the low B-flat. Only a mouse trapped inside a tuba during band practice can know precisely what it's like to stand that close to an operating ophicleide.

It was MacLyle all right, looming well-fed and filled-out. When he saw the psychiatrist's car he went right on playing, but, catching the psychiatrist's eye, he winked, smiled with the small corner of lip that showed from behind the large cup of the mouthpiece, and twiddled three fingers of his right hand, all he could manage of a wave without stopping. And he didn't stop, either, until he had scaled the particular octave he was working on and let himself down the other side. Then he put the ophicleide down carefully and let it lean against the spruce tree, and got up. The psychiatrist had become aware, as the last stupendous notes rolled away down the mountain, of his extreme isolation with this offbeat patient, of the unconcealed health and vigor of the man, and of the presence of the precipice over which he had almost driven his car a moment before, and had rolled up his window and buttoned the door lock and was feeling grateful for them. But the warm good humor and genuine welcome on MacLyle's sunburned face drove away fright and even caution, and almost before he knew what he was doing the psychiatrist had the door open and was stooping up out of the car, thinking, merry is a disused word but that's what he is, by God, a merry man. He called him by name but either MacLyle did not hear him or didn't care; he just put out a big warm hand and the psychiatrist took it. He could feel hard flat calluses in MacLyle's hand, and the controlled strength an elephant uses to lift a bespangled child in its trunk; he smiled at the image, because after all MacLyle was not a particularly large man, there was just that feeling about him. And once the smile found itself there it wouldn't go away.

He told MacLyle that he was a writer trying to soak up some of this magnificent country and had just been driving wherever the turn of the road led him, and here he was; but before he was half through he became conscious of MacLyle's eyes, which were in some indescribable way very much on him but not at all on anything he said; it was precisely as if he had stood there and hummed a tune. MacLyle seemed to be willing to listen to the sound until it was finished, and even to enjoy it, but that enjoyment was going to be all he got out of it. The psychiatrist finished anyway and MacLyle waited a moment as if to see if there would be any more, and when there wasn't he gave out more of that luminous smile and cocked his head toward the cabin. MacLyle led the way, with his visitor bringing up the rear with some platitudes about nice place you got here. As they entered, he suddenly barked at that unresponsive back, "Can't you hear me?" and MacLyle, without turning, only waved him on.

They walked into such a clutter and clabber of colors that the psychiatrist stopped dead, blinking. One wall had been removed and replaced with glass panes; it overlooked the precipice and put the little building afloat on haze. All the walls were hung with plain white chenille bedspreads, and the floor was white, and there seemed to be much more light indoors here than outside. Opposite the large window was an oversized easel made of peeled poles, notched and lashed together with baling wire, and on it was a huge canvas, most nonobjective, in the purest and most uncompromising colors. Part of it was unquestionably this room, or at least its air of colored confusion here and all infinity yonder. The ophicleide was in the picture, painstakingly reproduced, looking like the hopper of some giant infernal machine, and in the foreground some flowers; but the central figure repulsed him—more, it repulsed everything that surrounded it. It did not look exactly like anything familiar and, in a disturbed way, he was happy about that.

Stacked on the floor on each side of the easel were other paintings, some daubs, some full of ruled lines and overlapping planes, but all in this achingly pure color. He realized what was being done with the dozens of colors of house paint in little cans which had so intrigued the storekeeper.

In odd places around the room were clay sculptures, most mounted on pedestals made of sections of tree trunks large enough to stand firmly on their sawed ends. Some of the pedestals were peeled, some painted, and in some the bark texture or the bulges or clefts in the wood had been carried right up into the model, and in others clay had been knived or pressed into the bark all the way down to the floor. Some of the clay was painted, some not, some ought to have been. There were free-forms and gollywogs, a marsupial woman and a guitar with legs, and some, but not an overweening number, of the symbolisms which preoccupy even fairly intelligent psychiatrists. Nowhere was there any furniture per se. There were shelves at all levels and of varying lengths, bearing nail kegs, bolts of cloth, canned goods, tools, and cooking utensils. There was a sort of table but it was mostly a workbench, with a vise at one end and at the other, half-finished, a crude but exceedingly ingenious foot-powered potter's wheel.

He wondered where MacLyle slept, so he asked him, and again MacLyle reacted as if the words were not words, but a series of pleasant sounds, cocking his head and waiting to see if there would be any more. So the psychiatrist resorted to sign language, making a pillow of his two hands, laying his head on it, closing his eyes. He opened them to see MacLyle nodding eagerly, then going to the white-draped wall. From behind the chenille he brought a hammock, one end of which was fastened to the wall. The other end he carried to the big window and hung on a hook screwed to a heavy stud between the panes. To lie in that hammock would be to swing between heaven and earth like Mahomet's tomb, with all that sky and scenery virtually surrounding the sleeper. His admiration for this idea ceased as MacLyle began making urgent indications for him to get into the hammock. He backed off warily, expostulating, trying to convey to MacLyle that he only wondered, he just wanted to know; no, *no*, he wasn't tired, dammit; but MacLyle became so insistent that he picked the psychiatrist up like a child sulking at bedtime and carried him to the hammock. Any impulse to kick and quarrel was quenched by the nature of this and all other hammocks to be intolerant of shifting burdens, and by the proximity of the large window, which he now saw was built leaning outward, enabling one to look out of the hammock straight down a minimum of four hundred and eighty feet. So all right, he concluded, if you say so. I'm sleepy.

So for the next two hours he lay in the hammock watching MacLyle putter about the place, thinking more or less professional thoughts.

He doesn't or can't speak (he diagnosed): aphasia, motor. He doesn't or can't understand speech: aphasia, sensory. He won't or can't read and write: alexia. And what else?

He looked at all that art—if it *was* art, and any that was, was art by accident—and the gadgetry: the chuntering windmill outside, the sash-weight door-closer. He let his eyes follow a length of clothesline dangling unobtrusively down the leaning centerpost to which his hammock was fastened, and the pulley and fittings from which it hung, and its extension clear across the ceiling to the back wall, and understood finally that it would, when pulled, open two long, narrow horizontal hatches for through ventilation. A small door behind the chenille led to what he correctly surmised was a primitive powder room, built to overhang the precipice, the most perfect no-plumbing solution for that convenience he had ever seen.

He watched MacLyle putter. That was the only word for it, and his actions were the best example of puttering he had ever seen. MacLyle lifted, shifted, and put things down, backed off to judge, returned to lay an approving hand on the thing he had moved. Net effect, nothing tangible—yet one could not say there was no effect, because of the intense satisfaction the man radiated. For minutes he would stand, head cocked, smiling slightly, regarding the half-finished potter's wheel, then explode into activity, sawing, planing, drilling. He would add the finished piece to the cranks and connecting rods already completed, pat it as if it were an obedient child, and walk away, leaving the rest of the job for some other time. With a woodrasp he carefully removed the nose from one of his dried clay figures, and meticulously put on a new one. Always there was this absorption in his own products and processes, and the air of total reward in everything. And there was time, there seemed to be time enough for everything, and always would be.

Here is a man, thought the fairly intelligent psychiatrist, in retreat, but in a retreat the like of which my science has not yet described. For observe: He has reacted toward the primitive in terms of supplying himself with his needs with his own hands and by his own ingenuity, and yet there is nothing primitive in those needs themselves. He works constantly to achieve the comforts that his history has conditioned him to in the past—electric lights, cross-ventilation, trouble-free waste disposal. He exhibits a profound humility in the low rates he pays himself for his labor: he is building a potter's wheel apparently in order to make his own cooking vessels, and, since wood is cheap and clay free, his vessel can only cost him less than engine-turned aluminum by a very low evaluation of his own efforts.

His skills are less than his energy (mused the psychiatrist). His carpentry, like his painting and sculpture, shows considerable intelligence, but only moderate training; he can construct but not beautify, draw but not draft, and reach the artistically pleasing only by not erasing the random shake, the accidental cut; so that real creation in his work is, like any random effect, rare and unpredictable. Therefore his reward is in the area of satisfaction—about as wide a generalization as one can make.

What satisfaction? Not in possessions themselves, for this man could have bought better for less. Not in excellence in itself, for he obviously could be satisfied with less than perfection. Freedom, perhaps, from routine, from dominations of work? Hardly, because for all the complexity of this cluttered cottage, it had its order and its system; the presence of an alarm clock conveyed a good deal in this area. He wasn't dominated by regularity—he used it. And his satisfaction? Why, it must lie in this closed circle, himself to himself, and in the very fact of noncommunication!

Retreat... retreat. Retreat to savagery and you don't engineer your cross-ventilation or adjust a five-hundred-foot gravity flush for your john. Retreat into infancy and you don't design and build a potter's wheel. Retreat from people and you don't greet a stranger like...

Wait.

Maybe a stranger who had something to communicate, or some way of communication, wouldn't be so welcome. An unsettling thought, that. Running the risk of doing something MacLyle didn't like would be, possibly, a little more unselfish than the challenge warranted.

MacLyle began to cook.

Watching him, the psychiatrist reflected suddenly that this withdrawn and wordless individual was a happy one, in his own matrix; further, he had fulfilled all his obligations and responsibilities and was bothering no one.

It was intolerable.

It was intolerable because it was a violation of the prime directive of psychiatry—at least, of that school of psychiatry that he professed, and he was not going to confuse himself by considerations of other, less-tried theories—*It is the function of psychiatry to adjust the aberrant to society, and to restore or increase his usefulness to it.* To yield, to rationalize this man's behavior as balance, would be to fly in the face of science itself; for this particular psychiatry finds its most successful approaches in the scientific method, and it is unprofitable to debate whether or not it is or is not a science. To its practitioner it is, and that's that; it has to be. Operationally speaking, what has been found true, even statistically, must be Truth, and all other things, even Possible, kept the hell out of the toolbox. No known Truth allowed a social entity to secede this way, and, for one, this fairly intelligent psychiatrist was not going to give this—this *suicide* his blessing.

He must, then, find a way to communicate with MacLyle, and when he had found it, he must communicate to him the error of his ways. Without getting thrown over the cliff.

He became aware that MacLyle was looking at him, twinkling. He smiled back before he knew what he was doing, and obeyed MacLyle's beckoning gesture. He eased himself out of the hammock and went to the workbench, where a steaming stew was set out in earthenware bowls. The bowls stood on large plates and were surrounded by a band of carefully sliced tomatoes. He tasted them. They were obviously vine-ripened and had been speckled with a dark-green paste which, after studious attention to its aftertaste, he identified as fresh basil mashed with fresh garlic and salt. The effect was symphonic.

He followed suit when MacLyle picked up his own bowl and they went outside and squatted under the old Engelmann spruce to eat. It was a quiet and pleasant occasion, and during it the psychiatrist had plenty of opportunity to size up his man and plan his campaign. He was quite sure now how to proceed, and all he needed was opportunity, which presented itself when MacLyle rose, stretched, smiled, and went indoors. The psychiatrist followed him to the door and saw him crawl into the hammock and fall almost instantly asleep.

The psychiatrist went to his car and got out his bag of tricks. And so it was that late in the afternoon, when MacLyle emerged stretching and yawning from his nap, he found his visitor under the spruce tree, hefting the ophicleide and twiddling its keys in a perplexed and investigatory fashion. MacLyle strode over to him and lifted the ophicleide away with a pleasant I'll-show-you smile, got the monstrous contraption into position, and ran his tongue around the inside of the mouthpiece, large as a demitasse. He had barely time to pucker up his lips at the strange taste there before his irises rolled up completely out of sight and he collapsed like a grounded parachute. The psychiatrist was able only to snatch away the ophicleide in time to keep the mouthpiece from knocking out MacLyle's front teeth.

He set the ophicleide carefully against the tree and straightened MacLyle's limbs. He concentrated for a moment on the pulse, and turned the head to one side so saliva would not drain down the flaccid throat, and then went back to his bag of tricks. He came back and knelt, and MacLyle did not even twitch at the bite of the hypodermics: a careful blend of the nonsoporific tranquilizers Frenquel, chlorpromazine, and Reserpine, and a judicious dose of scopolamine, a hypnotic.

The psychiatrist got water and carefully sponged out the man's mouth, not caring to wait out another collapse the next time he swallowed. Then there was nothing to do but wait, and plan.

Exactly on schedule, according to the psychiatrist's wristwatch, MacLyle groaned and coughed weakly. The psychiatrist immediately and in a firm quiet voice told him not to move. Also not to think. He stayed out of the immediate range of MacLyle's unfocused eyes and explained that MacLyle must trust him, because he was there to help, and not to worry about feeling mixed-up or disoriented. "You don't know where you are or how you got here," he informed MacLyle. He also told MacLyle, who was past forty, that he was thirty-seven years old, but he knew what he was doing.

MacLyle just lay there obediently and thought these things over and waited for more information. He knew he must trust this voice, the owner of which was here to help him; that he was thirty-seven years old; and his name. In these things he lay and marinated. The drugs kept him conscious, docile, submissive, and without guile. The psychiatrist observed and exulted: oh you azacyclonol, he chanted silently to himself, you pretty piperidyl, handsome hydrochloride, subtle Serpasil. . . . Confidently he left MacLyle and went into the cabin where, after due search, he found some decent clothes and some socks and shoes and brought them out and wrapped the supine patient in them. He helped MacLyle across the clearing and into his car, humming as he did so, for there is none so happy as an expert faced with excellence in his specialty. MacLyle sank back into the cushions and gave one wondering glance at the cabin and at the blare of late light from the bell of the ophicleide; but the psychiatrist told him firmly that these things had nothing to do with him, nothing at all, and MacLyle smiled relievedly and fell to watching the scenery. As they passed the general store MacLyle stirred, but said nothing about it. Instead he asked the psychiatrist if the Ardsmere station was open yet, whereupon the psychiatrist could barely answer him for the impulse to purr like a cat: the Ardsmere station, two stops before MacLyle's suburban town, had burned down and been rebuilt almost six years ago; so now he knew for sure that MacLyle was living in a time preceding his difficulties—a time during which, of course, MacLyle had been able to talk. All of this the psychiatrist kept to himself, and answered gravely that yes, they had the Ardsmere station operating again. And did he have anything else on his mind?

MacLyle considered this carefully, but since all the immediate questions were answered—unswervingly, he *knew* he was safe in the hands of this man, whoever he was; he knew (he thought) his correct age and that he was expected to feel disoriented; he was also under a command not to think—he placidly shook his head and went back to watching the road unroll under their wheels. "Fallen Rock Zone," he murmured as they passed a sign. The psychiatrist drove happily down the mountain and across the flats, back to the city where he had hired the car. He left it at the railroad station ("Rail Crossing Road," murmured MacLyle) and made reservations for a compartment on the train, aircraft being too open and public for his purposes and far too fast for the hourly rate he suddenly decided to apply.

They had time for a silent and companionable dinner before train time, and then at last they were aboard.

The psychiatrist turned off all but one reading lamp and leaned forward. MacLyle's eyes dilated readily to the dimmer light, and the psychiatrist leaned back comfortably and asked him how he felt. He felt fine and said so. The psychiatrist asked him how old he was and MacLyle told him, thirty-seven, but he sounded doubtful.

Knowing that the scopolamine was wearing off but the other drugs, the tranquilizers, would hang on for a bit, the psychiatrist drew a deep breath and removed the suggestion; he told MacLyle the truth about his age, and brought him up to the here and now. MacLyle just looked puzzled for a few minutes and then his features settled into an expression that can only be described as not unhappy. "Porter," was all he said, gazing at the push button, and announced that he could read now.

The psychiatrist nodded sagely and offered no comment, being quite willing to let a patient stew as long as he produced essence.

MacLyle abruptly demanded to know why he had lost the powers of speech and reading. The psychiatrist raised his eyebrows a little, smiled one of those "You-tell-me" smiles, and then got up and suggested they sleep on it. He got the porter in to fix the beds and as an afterthought told the man to come back with the evening papers. Nothing can orient a cultural expatriate better than the evening papers. The man did. MacLyle paid no attention to this, one way or the other. He just climbed into the psychiatrist's spare pajamas thoughtfully and they went to bed.

The psychiatrist didn't know if MacLyle had awakened him on purpose or whether the train's slowing had done it, anyway he awoke about three in the morning to find MacLyle standing beside his bunk looking at him fixedly. He noticed, too, that MacLyle's reading lamp was lit and the papers were scattered all over the floor. MacLyle said, "You're some kind of a doctor," in a flat voice.

The psychiatrist admitted it.

MacLyle said, "Well, this ought to make some sense to you. I was skiing out here years ago when I was a college kid. Accident, fellow I was with broke his leg. Compound. Made him comfortable as I could and went for help. Came back, he'd slid down the mountain, thrashing around, I guess. Crevasse, down in the bottom; took two days to find him, three days to get him out. Frostbite. Gangrene."

The psychiatrist tried to look as if he was following this.

MacLyle said, "The one thing I always remember, him pulling back the bandages all the time to look at his leg. Knew it was gone, couldn't keep himself from watching the stuff spread around and upward. Didn't like to; *had* to. Tried to stop him, finally had to help him or he'd hurt himself. Every ten, fifteen minutes all the way down to the lodge, fifteen hours, looking under the bandages."

The psychiatrist tried to think of something to say and couldn't.

MacLyle said, "That Donne, that John Donne I used to spout, I always believed that."

The psychiatrist began to misquote the thing about send not to ask for whom the bell . . .

"Yeah, that, but especially '*any man's death diminishes me, because I am involved in mankind.*' I believed that," MacLyle repeated. "I believed more than that. Not only death. Damn foolishness diminishes me because I am involved. People all the time pushing people around diminishes me. Everybody hungry for a fast buck diminishes me." He picked up a sheet of newspaper and let it slip away; it flapped off to the corner of the compartment like a huge gravemoth. "I was getting diminished to death and I had to watch it happening to me like that kid with the gangrene, so that's why." The train, crawling now, lurched suddenly and yielded.

MacLyle's eyes flicked to the window, where neon beer signs and a traffic light were reluctantly being framed. MacLyle leaned close to the psychiatrist. "I just had to get uninvolved with mankind before I got diminished altogether, everything mankind did was my fault. So I did and now here I am involved again." MacLyle abruptly went to the door. "And for that, thanks."

The psychiatrist asked him what he was going to do.

"Do?" asked MacLyle cheerfully. "Why, I'm going out there and diminish mankind right back." He was out in the corridor with the door closed before the psychiatrist so much as sat up. He banged it open again and leaned in. He said in the sanest of all possible voices, "Now mind you, doctor, this is only one man's opinion," and was gone. He killed four people before they got him.

THE WHITE
HORSE CHILD

When I was seven years old, I met an old man by the side of the dusty road between school and farm. The late afternoon sun had cooled and he was sitting on a rock, hat off, hands held out to the gentle warmth, whistling a pretty song. He nodded at me as I walked past. I nodded back. I was curious, but I knew better than to get involved with strangers. Nameless evils seemed to attach themselves to strangers, as if they might turn into lions when no one but a little kid was around.

"Hello, boy," he said.

I stopped and shuffled my feet. He looked more like a hawk than a lion. His clothes were brown and gray and russet, and his hands were pink like the flesh of some rabbit a hawk had just plucked up. His face was brown except around the eyes, where he might have worn glasses; around the eyes he was white, and this intensified his gaze. "Hello," I said.

"Was a hot day. Must have been hot in school," he said.

"They got air-conditioning."

"So they do, now. How old are you?"

"Seven," I said. "Well, almost eight."

"Mother told you never to talk to strangers?"

"And Dad, too."

"Good advice. But haven't you seen me around here before?"
I looked him over. "No."
"Closely. Look at my clothes. What color are they?"
His shirt was gray, like the rock he was sitting on. The cuffs, where
they peeped from under a russet jacket, were white. He didn't smell bad,
but he didn't look particularly clean. He was smooth-shaven, though.
His hair was white and his pants were the color of the dirt below the
rock. "All kinds of colors," I said.
"But mostly I partake of the landscape, no?"
"I guess so," I said.
"That's because I'm not here. You're imagining me, at least part of
me. Don't I look like somebody you might have heard of?"
"Who are you supposed to look like?" I asked.
"Well, I'm full of stories," he said. "Have lots of stories to tell little
boys, little girls, even big folk, if they'll listen."
I started to walk away.
"But only if they'll listen," he said. I ran. When I got home, I told
my older sister about the man on the road, but she only got a worried
look and told me to stay away from strangers. I took her advice. For some
time afterward, into my eighth year, I avoided that road and did not speak
with strangers more than I had to.
The house that I lived in, with the five other members of my family
and two dogs and one beleaguered cat, was white and square and comfortable. The stairs were rich, dark wood overlaid with worn carpet. The
walls were dark oak paneling up to a foot above my head, then white
plaster, with a white plaster ceiling. The air was full of smells—bacon
when I woke up, bread and soup and dinner when I came home from
school, dust on weekends when we helped clean.
Sometimes my parents argued, and not just about money, and those
were bad times; but usually we were happy. There was talk about selling
the farm and the house and going to Mitchell where Dad could work in
a computerized feed-mixing plant, but it was only talk.
It was early summer when I took to the dirt road again. I'd forgotten
about the old man. But in almost the same way, when the sun was
cooling and the air was haunted by lazy bees, I saw an old woman.
Women strangers are less malevolent than men, and rarer. She was sitting
on the gray rock, in a long green skirt summer-dusty, with a daisy-colored
shawl and a blouse the precise hue of cottonwoods seen in a late hazy
day's muted light. "Hello, boy," she said.
"I don't recognize you, either," I blurted, and she smiled.

"Of course not. If you didn't recognize him, you'd hardly know me."

"Do you know him?" I asked. She nodded. "Who was he? Who are you?"

"We're both full of stories. Just tell them from different angles. You aren't afraid of us, are you?"

I was, but having a woman ask the question made all the difference. "No," I said. "But what are you doing here? And how do you know—?"

"Ask for a story," she said. "One you've never heard of before." Her eyes were the color of baked chestnuts, and she squinted into the sun so that I couldn't see her whites. When she opened them wider to look at me, she didn't have any whites.

"I don't want to hear stories," I said softly.

"Sure you do. Just ask."

"It's late. I got to be home."

"I knew a man who became a house," she said. "He didn't like it. He stayed quiet for thirty years, and watched all the people inside grow up, and be just like their folks, all nasty and dirty and leaving his walls to flake, and the bathrooms were unbearable. So he spit them out one morning, furniture and all, and shut his doors and locked them."

"What?"

"You heard me. Upchucked. The poor house was so disgusted he changed back into a man, but he was older and he had a cancer and his heart was bad because of all the abuse he had lived with. He died soon after."

I laughed, not because the man had died but because I knew such things were lies. "That's silly," I said.

"Then here's another. There was a cat who wanted to eat butterflies. Nothing finer in the world for a cat than to stalk the grass, waiting for black and pumpkin butterflies. It crouches down and wriggles its rump to dig in the hind paws, then it jumps. But a butterfly is no sustenance for a cat. It's practice. There was a little girl about your age—might have been your sister, but she won't admit it—who saw the cat and decided to teach it a lesson. She hid in the taller grass with two old kites under each arm and waited for the cat to come by stalking. When it got real close, she put on her mother's dark glasses, to look all bug-eyed, and she jumped up flapping the kites. Well, it was just a little too real, because in a trice she found herself flying, and she was much smaller than she had been, and the cat jumped at her. Almost got her, too. Ask your sister about that sometime. See if she doesn't deny it."

"How'd she get back to be my sister again?"

"She became too scared to fly. She lit on a flower and found herself crushing it. The glasses broke, too."

"My sister did break a pair of Mom's glasses once."

The woman smiled.

"I got to be going home."

"Tomorrow you bring me a story, okay?"

I ran off without answering. But in my head, monsters were already rising. If she thought I was scared, wait until she heard the story I had to tell! When I got home my oldest sister, Barbara, was fixing lemonade in the kitchen. She was a year older than I, but acted as if she were grown-up. She was a good six inches taller and I could beat her if I got in a lucky punch, but no other way—so her power over me was awesome. But we were usually friendly.

"Where you been?" she asked, like a mother.

"Somebody tattled on you," I said.

Her eyes went doe-scared, then wizened down to slits. "What're you talking about?"

"Somebody tattled about what you did to Mom's sunglasses."

"I already been whipped for that," she said nonchalantly. "Not much more to tell."

"Oh, but *I* know more."

"Was *not* playing doctor," she said. The youngest, Sue-Ann, weakest and most full of guile, had a habit of telling the folks somebody or other was playing doctor. She didn't know what it meant—I just barely did— but it had been true once, and she held it over everybody as her only vestige of power.

"No," I said, "but I know what you were doing. And I won't tell anybody."

"You don't know nothing," she said. Then she accidentally poured half a pitcher of lemonade across the side of my head and down my front. When Mom came in I was screaming and swearing like Dad did when he fixed the cars, and I was put away for life plus ninety years in the bedroom I shared with younger brother Michael. Dinner smelled better than usual that evening, but I had none of it. Somehow, I wasn't brokenhearted. It gave me time to think of a scary story for the country-colored woman on the rock.

School was the usual mix of hell and purgatory the next day. Then the hot, dry winds cooled and the bells rang and I was on the dirt road again, across the southern hundred acres, walking in the lees and shadows of the big cottonwoods. I carried my Road Runner lunch pail and my pencil box and one book—a handwriting manual I hated so much I tore pieces out of it at night, to shorten its lifetime—and I walked slowly, to give my story time to gel.

She was leaning up against a tree, not far from the rock. Looking back, I can see she was not so old as a boy of eight years thought. Now I see her lissome beauty and grace, despite the dominance of gray in her reddish hair, despite the crow's-feet around her eyes and the smile-haunts around her lips. But to the eight-year-old she was simply a peculiar crone. And he had a story to tell her, he thought, that would age her unto graveside.

"Hello, boy," she said.

"Hi." I sat on the rock.

"I can see you've been thinking," she said.

I squinted into the tree shadow to make her out better. "How'd you know?"

"You have the look of a boy that's been thinking. Are you here to listen to another story?"

"Got one to tell, this time," I said.

"Who goes first?"

It was always polite to let the woman go first so I quelled my haste and told her she could. She motioned me to come by the tree and sit on a smaller rock, half-hidden by grass. And while the crickets in the shadow tuned up for the evening, she said, "Once there was a dog. This dog was a pretty usual dog, like the ones that would chase you around home if they thought they could get away with it—if they didn't know you, or thought you were up to something the big people might disapprove of. But this dog lived in a graveyard. That is, he belonged to the caretaker. You've seen a graveyard before, haven't you?"

"Like where they took Grandpa."

"Exactly," she said. "With pretty lawns, and big white and gray stones, and for those who've died recently, smaller gray stones with names and flowers and years cut into them. And trees in some places, with a mortuary nearby made of brick, and a garage full of black cars, and a place behind the garage where you wonder what goes on." She knew the place, all right. "This dog had a pretty good life. It was his job to keep the grounds clear of animals at night. After the gates were locked, he'd be set loose, and he wandered all night long. He was almost white, you see. Anybody human who wasn't supposed to be there would think he was a ghost, and they'd run away.

"But this dog had a problem. His problem was, there were rats that didn't pay much attention to him. A whole gang of rats. The leader was a big one, a good yard from nose to tail. These rats made their living by burrowing under the ground in the old section of the cemetery."

That did it. I didn't want to hear any more. The air was a lot colder than it should have been, and I wanted to get home in time for dinner and still be able to eat it. But I couldn't go just then.

"Now the dog didn't know what the rats did, and just like you and I, probably, he didn't much care to know. But it was his job to keep them under control. So one day he made a truce with a couple of cats that he normally tormented and told them about the rats. These cats were scrappy old toms and they'd long since cleared out the competition of other cats, but they were friends themselves. So the dog made them a proposition. He said he'd let them use the cemetery any time they wanted, to prowl or hunt in or whatever, if they would put the fear of God into a few of the rats. The cats took him up on it. 'We get to do whatever we want,' they said, 'whenever we want, and you won't bother us.' The dog agreed.

"That night the dog waited for the sounds of battle. But they never came. Nary a yowl." She glared at me for emphasis. "Not a claw scratch. Not even a twitch of tail in the wind." She took a deep breath, and so did I. "Round about midnight the dog went out into the graveyard. It was very dark and there wasn't wind, or bird, or speck of star to relieve the quiet and the dismal, inside-of-a-box-camera blackness. He sniffed his way to the old part of the graveyard, and met with the head rat, who was sitting on a slanty, cracked wooden grave marker. Only his eyes and a tip of tail showed in the dark, but the dog could smell him. 'What happened to the cats?' he asked. The rat shrugged his haunches. 'Ain't seen any cats,' he said. 'What did you think—that you could scare us out with a couple of cats? Ha. Listen—if there had been any cats here tonight, they'd have been strung and hung like meat in a shed, and my young'uns would have grown fat on—' "

"No-o-o!" I screamed, and I ran away from the woman and the tree until I couldn't hear the story anymore.

"What's the matter?" she called after me. "Aren't you going to tell me your story?" Her voice followed me as I ran.

It was funny. That night, I wanted to know what happened to the cats. Maybe nothing had happened to them. Not knowing made my visions even worse—and I didn't sleep well. But my brain worked like it had never worked before.

The next day, a Saturday, I had an ending—not a very good one in retrospect—but it served to frighten Michael so badly he threatened to tell Mom on me.

"What would you want to do that for?" I asked. "Cripes, I won't ever tell you a story again if you tell Mom!"

Michael was a year younger and didn't worry about the future. "You never told me stories before," he said, "and everything was fine. I won't miss them."

He ran down the stairs to the living room. Dad was smoking a pipe and reading the paper, relaxing before checking the irrigation on the north thirty. Michael stood at the foot of the stairs, thinking. I was almost down to grab him and haul him upstairs when he made his decision and headed for the kitchen. I knew exactly what he was considering—that Dad would probably laugh and call him a little scaredy cat. But Mom would get upset and do me in proper.

She was putting a paper form over the kitchen table to mark it for fitting a tablecloth. Michael ran up to her and hung onto a pants leg while I halted at the kitchen door, breathing hard, eyes threatening eternal torture if he so much as peeped. But Michael didn't worry about the future much.

"Mom," he said.

"Cripes!" I shouted, high-pitching on the i. Refuge awaited me in the tractor shed. It was an agreed-upon hiding place. Mom didn't know I'd be there, but Dad did, and he could mediate.

It took him a half-hour to get to me. I sat in the dark behind a workbench, practicing my pouts. He stood in the shaft of light falling from the unpatched chink in the roof. Dust motes maypoled around his legs. "Son," he said, "Mom wants to know where you got that story."

Now, this was a peculiar thing to be asked. The question I'd expected had been, "Why did you scare Michael?" or maybe, "What made you think of such a thing?" But no. Somehow, she had plumbed the problem, planted the words in Dad's mouth, and impressed upon him that father-son relationships were temporarily suspended.

"I made it up," I said.

"You've never made up that kind of story before."

"I just started."

He took a deep breath. "Son, we get along real good, except when you lie to me. We know better. Who told you that story?"

This was uncanny. There was more going on than I could under-stand—there was a mysterious, adult thing happening. I had no way around the truth. "An old woman," I said.

Dad sighed even deeper. "What was she wearing?"

"Green dress," I said.

"Was there an old man?"

I nodded.

"Christ," he said softly. He turned and walked out of the shed. From outside, he called me to come into the house. I dusted off my overalls and followed him. Michael sneered at me.

" 'Locked them in coffins with old dead bodies,' " he mimicked. "Phhht! You're going to get it."

The folks closed the folding door to the kitchen with both of us outside. This disturbed Michael, who'd expected instant vengeance. I was too curious and worried to take my revenge on him, so he skulked out the screen door and chased the cat around the house. "Lock you in a coffin!" he screamed.

Mom's voice drifted from behind the louvered doors. "Do you hear that? The poor child's going to have nightmares. It'll warp him."

"Don't exaggerate," Dad said.

"Exaggerate what? That those filthy people are back? Ben, they must be a hundred years old now! They're trying to do the same thing to your son that they did to your brother . . . and just look at *him!* Living in sin, writing for those hell-spawned girlie magazines."

"He ain't living in sin, he's living alone in an apartment in New York City. And he writes for all kinds of places."

"They tried to do it to you, too! Just thank God your aunt saved you."

"Margie, I hope you don't intend—"

"Certainly do. She knows all about them kind of people. She chased them off once, she can sure do it again!"

All hell had broken loose. I didn't understand half of it, but I could feel the presence of Great-Aunt Sybil Danser. I could almost hear her crackling voice and the shustle of her satchel of Billy Grahams and Zondervans and little tiny pamphlets with shining light in blue offset on their covers.

I knew there was no way to get the full story from the folks short of listening in, but they'd stopped talking and were sitting in that stony kind of silence that indicated Dad's disgust and Mom's determination. I was mad that nobody was blaming me, as if I were some idiot child not capable of being bad on my own. I was mad at Michael for precipitating the whole mess.

And I was curious. Were the man and woman more than a hundred years old? Why hadn't I seen them before, in town, or heard about them from other kids? Surely I wasn't the only one they'd seen on the road and told stories to. I decided to get to the source. I walked up to the louvered doors and leaned my cheek against them. "Can I go play at George's?"

"Yes," Mom said. "Be back for evening chores."

George lived on the next farm, a mile and a half east. I took my bike and rode down the old dirt road going south.

They were both under the tree, eating a picnic lunch from a wicker basket. I pulled my bike over and leaned it against the gray rock, shading my eyes to see them more clearly.

"Hello, boy," the old man said. "Ain't seen you in a while."

I couldn't think of anything to say. The woman offered me a cookie and I refused with a muttered, "No, thank you, ma'am."

"Well then, perhaps you'd like to tell us your story."

"No, ma'am."

"No story to tell us? That's odd. Meg was sure you had a story in you someplace. Peeking out from behind your ears maybe, thumbing its nose at us."

The woman smiled ingratiatingly. "Tea?"

"There's going to be trouble," I said.

"Already?" The woman smoothed the skirt in her lap and set a plate of nut bread into it. "Well, it comes sooner or later, this time sooner. What do you think of it, boy?"

"I think I got into a lot of trouble for not much being bad," I said. "I don't know why."

"Sit down then," the old man said. "Listen to a tale, then tell us what's going on."

I sat down, not too keen about hearing another story but out of politeness. I took a piece of nut bread and nibbled on it as the woman sipped her tea and cleared her throat. "Once there was a city on the shore of a broad, blue sea. In the city lived five hundred children and nobody else, because the wind from the sea wouldn't let anyone grow old. Well, children don't have kids of their own, of course, so when the wind came up in the first year the city never grew any larger."

"Where'd all the grownups go?" I asked. The old man held his fingers to his lips and shook his head.

"The children tried to play all day, but it wasn't enough. They became frightened at night and had bad dreams. There was nobody to comfort them because only grownups are really good at making nightmares go away. Now, sometimes nightmares are white horses that come out of the sea, so they set up guards along the beaches, and fought them back with wands made of blackthorn. But there was another kind of nightmare, one that was black and rose out of the ground, and those were impossible to guard against. So the children got together one day and decided to tell all the scary stories there were to tell, to prepare themselves for all the nightmares. They found it was pretty easy to think up scary stories, and every one of them had a story or two to tell. They stayed up all night spinning yarns about ghosts and dead things, and live things that shouldn't have been, and things that were neither. They talked about death and about monsters that suck blood, about things that live way deep in the earth and long, thin things that sneak through cracks in doors to lean over the beds at night and speak in tongues no one could understand. They talked about eyes without heads, and vice versa, and little blue shoes that walk across a cold empty white room, with no one in them, and a bunk bed that creaks when it's empty, and a printing press that produces newspapers from a city that never was. Pretty soon, by morning, they'd told all the scary stories. When the black horses came out of the ground the next night, and the white horses from the sea, the children greeted them with cakes and ginger ale, and they held a big party. They also invited the pale sheet-things from the clouds, and everyone ate hearty and had a good time. One white horse let a little boy ride on it, and took him wherever he wanted to go. So there were no more bad dreams in the city of children by the sea."

I finished the piece of bread and wiped my hands on my crossed legs. "So that's why you tried to scare me," I said.

She shook her head. "No. I never had a reason for telling a story, and neither should you."

"I don't think I'm going to tell stories anymore," I said. "The folks get too upset."

"Philistines," the old man said, looking off across the fields.

"Listen, young man. There is nothing finer in the world than the telling of tales. Split atoms if you wish, but splitting an infinitive—and getting away with it—is far nobler. Lance boils if you wish, but pricking pretensions is often cleaner and always more fun."

"Then why are Mom and Dad so mad?"

The old man shook his head. "An eternal mystery."

"Well, I'm not so sure," I said. "I scared my little brother pretty bad and that's not nice."

"Being scared is nothing," the old woman said. "Being bored, or ignorant—now that's a crime."

"I still don't know. My folks say you have to be a hundred years old. You did something to my uncle they didn't like, and that was a long time ago. What kind of people are you, anyway?"

The old man smiled. "Old, yes. But not a hundred."

"I just came out here to warn you. Mom and Dad are bringing out my great-aunt, and she's no fun for anyone. You better go away." With that said, I ran back to my bike and rode off, pumping for all I was worth. I was between a rock and a hard place. I loved my folks but I itched to hear more stories. Why wasn't it easier to make decisions?

That night I slept restlessly. I didn't have any dreams, but I kept waking up with something pounding at the back of my head, like it wanted to be let in. I scrunched my face up and pressed it back.

At Sunday breakfast, Mom looked across the table at me and put on a kind face. "We're going to pick up Auntie Danser this afternoon, at the airport," she said.

My face went like warm butter.

"You'll come with us, won't you?" she asked. "You always did like the airport."

"All the way from where she lives?" I asked.

"From Omaha," Dad said.

I didn't want to go, but it was more a command than a request. I nodded and Dad smiled at me around his pipe.

"Don't eat too many biscuits," Mom warned him. "You're putting on weight again."

"I'll wear it off come harvest. You cook as if the whole crew was here, anyway."

"Auntie Danser will straighten it all out," Mom said, her mind elsewhere. I caught the suggestion of a grimace on Dad's face, and the pipe wriggled as he bit down on it harder.

The airport was something out of a TV space movie. It went on forever, with stairways going up to restaurants and big smoky windows which looked out on the screaming jets, and crowds of people, all leaving, except for one pear-shaped figure in a cotton print dress with fat ankles and glasses thick as headlamps. I knew her from a hundred yards.

When we met, she shook hands with Mom, hugged Dad as if she didn't want to, then bent down and gave me a smile. Her teeth were yellow and even, sound as a horse's. She was the ugliest woman I'd ever seen. She smelled of lilacs. To this day lilacs take my appetite away.

She carried a bag. Part of it was filled with knitting, part with books and pamphlets. I always wondered why she never carried a Bible—just

Billy Grahams and Zondervans. One pamphlet fell out and Dad bent to pick it up.

"Keep it, read it," Auntie Danser instructed him. "Do you good." She turned to Mom and scrutinized her from the bottom of a swimming pool. "You're looking good. He must be treating you right."

Dad ushered us out the automatic doors into the dry heat. Her one suitcase was light as a mummy and probably just as empty. I carried it and it didn't even bring sweat to my brow. Her life was not in clothes and toiletry but in the plastic knitting bag.

We drove back to the farm in the big white station wagon. I leaned my head against the cool glass of the rear seat window and considered puking. Auntie Danser, I told myself, was like a mental dose of castor oil. Or like a visit to the dentist. Even if nothing was going to happen her smell presaged disaster, and like a horse sniffing a storm, my entrails worried.

Mom looked across the seat at me—Auntie Danser was riding up front with Dad—and asked, "You feeling okay? Did they give you anything to eat? Anything funny?"

I said they'd given me a piece of nut bread. Mom went, "Oh, Lord."

"Margie, they don't work like that. They got other ways." Auntie Danser leaned over the backseat and goggled at me. "Boy's just worried. I know all about it. These people and I have had it out before."

Through those murky glasses, her flat eyes knew me to my young, pithy core. I didn't like being known so well. I could see that Auntie Danser's life was firm and predictable, and I made a sudden commitment. I liked the man and woman. They caused trouble, but they were the exact opposite of my great-aunt. I felt better, and I gave her a reassuring grin. "Boy will be okay," she said. "Just a colic of the upset mind."

Michael and Barbara sat on the front porch as the car drove up. Somehow a visit by Auntie Danser didn't bother them as much as it did me. They didn't fawn over her but they accepted her without complaining—even out of adult earshot. That made me think more carefully about them. I decided I didn't love them any the less, but I couldn't trust them, either. The world was taking sides and so far on my side I was very lonely. I didn't count the two old people on my side, because I wasn't sure they were—but they came a lot closer than anybody in my family.

Auntie Danser wanted to read Billy Graham books to us after dinner, but Dad snuck us out before Mom could gather us together—all but Barbara, who stayed to listen. We watched the sunset from the loft of the old wood barn, then tried to catch the little birds that lived in the rafters. By dark and bedtime I was hungry, but not for food. I asked Dad if he'd tell me a story before bed.

"You know your mom doesn't approve of all that fairy-tale stuff," he said.

"Then no fairy tales. Just a story."

"I'm out of practice, son," he confided. He looked very sad. "Your mom says we should concentrate on things that are real and not waste our time with make-believe. Life's hard. I may have to sell the farm, you know, and work for that feed-mixer in Mitchell."

I went to bed and felt like crying. A whole lot of my family had died that night, I didn't know exactly how, or why. But I was mad.

I didn't go to school the next day. During the night I'd had a dream, which came so true and whole to me that I had to rush to the stand of cottonwoods and tell the old people. I took my lunch box and walked rapidly down the road.

They weren't there. On a piece of wire braided to the biggest tree they'd left a note on faded brown paper. It was in a strong, feminine hand, sepia-inked, delicately scribed with what could have been a goose-quill pen. It said: "We're at the old Hauskopf farm. Come if you must."

Not "Come if you can." I felt a twinge. The Hauskopf farm, abandoned fifteen years ago and never sold, was three miles farther down the road and left on a deep-rutted fork. It took me an hour to get there.

The house still looked deserted. All the white paint was flaking, leaving dead gray wood. The windows stared. I walked up the porch steps and knocked on the heavy oak door. For a moment I thought no one was going to answer. Then I heard what sounded like a gust of wind, but inside the house, and the old woman opened the door. "Hello, boy," she said. "Come for more stories?"

She invited me in. Wildflowers were growing along the baseboards and tiny roses peered from the brambles that covered the walls. A quail led her train of inch-and-a-half fluffball chicks from under the stairs, into the living room. The floor was carpeted but the flowers in the weave seemed more than patterns. I could stare down and keep picking out detail for minutes. "This way, boy," the woman said. She took my hand. Hers was smooth and warm but I had the impression it was also hard as wood.

A tree stood in the living room, growing out of the floor and sending its branches up to support the ceiling. Rabbits and quail and a lazy-looking brindle cat looked at me from tangles of roots. A wooden bench surrounded the base of the tree. On the side away from us, I heard someone breathing. The old man poked his head around and smiled at me, lifting his long pipe in greeting. "Hello, boy," he said.

"The boy looks like he's ready to tell us a story, this time," the woman said.

"Of course, Meg. Have a seat, boy. Cup of cider for you? Tea? Herb biscuit?"

"Cider, please," I said.

The old man stood and went down the hall to the kitchen. He came back with a wooden tray and three steaming cups of mulled cider. The cinnamon tickled my nose as I sipped.

"Now. What's your story?"

"It's about two hawks," I said. I hesitated.

"Go on."

"Brother hawks. Never did like each other. Fought for a strip of land where they could hunt."

"Yes?"

"Finally, one hawk met an old, crippled bobcat that had set up a place for itself in a rockpile. The bobcat was learning itself magic so it wouldn't have to go out and catch dinner, which was awful hard for it now. The hawk landed near the bobcat and told it about his brother, and how cruel he was. So the bobcat said, 'Why not give him the land for the day? Here's what you can do.' The bobcat told him how he could turn into a rabbit, but a very strong rabbit no hawk could hurt."

"Wily bobcat," the old man said, smiling.

" 'You mean, my brother wouldn't be able to catch me?' the hawk asked. 'Course not,' the bobcat said. 'And you can teach him a lesson. You'll tussle with him, scare him real bad—show him what tough animals there are on the land he wants. Then he'll go away and hunt somewheres else.' The hawk thought that sounded like a fine idea. So he let the bobcat turn him into a rabbit and he hopped back to the land and waited in a patch of grass. Sure enough, his brother's shadow passed by soon, and then he heard a swoop and saw the claws held out. So he filled himself with being mad and jumped up and practically bit all the tail feathers off his brother. The hawk just flapped up and rolled over on the ground, blinking and gawking with his beak wide. 'Rabbit,' he said, 'that's not natural. Rabbits don't act that way.'

" 'Round here they do,' the hawk-rabbit said. 'This is a tough old land, and all the animals here know the tricks of escaping from bad birds like you.' This scared the brother hawk, and he flew away as best he could, and never came back again. The hawk-rabbit hopped to the rock-pile and stood up before the bobcat, saying, 'It worked real fine. I thank you. Now turn me back and I'll go hunt my land.' But the bobcat only grinned and reached out with a paw and broke the rabbit's neck. Then he ate him, and said, 'Now the land's mine, and no hawks can take away the easy game.' And that's how the greed of two hawks turned their land over to a bobcat."

The old woman looked at me with wide, baked-chestnut eyes and smiled. "You've got it," she said. "Just like your uncle. Hasn't he got it, Jack?" The old man nodded and took his pipe from his mouth. "He's got it fine. He'll make a good one."

"Now, boy, why did you make up that story?"

I thought for a moment, then shook my head. "I don't know," I said. "It just came up."

"What are you going to do with the story?"

I didn't have an answer for that question, either.

"Got any other stories in you?"

I considered, then said, "Think so."

A car drove up outside and Mom called my name. The old woman stood and straightened her dress. "Follow me," she said. "Go out the back door, walk around the house. Return home with them. Tomorrow, go to school like you're supposed to do. Next Saturday, come back and we'll talk some more."

"Son? You in there?"

I walked out the back and came around to the front of the house. Mom and Auntie Danser waited in the station wagon. "You aren't allowed out here. Were you in that house?" Mom asked. I shook my head.

My great-aunt looked at me with her glassed-in flat eyes and lifted the corners of her lips a little. "Margie," she said, "go have a look in the windows."

Mom got out of the car and walked up the porch to peer through the dusty panes. "It's empty, Sybil."

"Empty, boy, right?"

"I don't know," I said. "I wasn't inside."

"I could hear you, boy," she said. "Last night. Talking in your sleep. Rabbits and hawks don't behave that way. You know it, and I know it. So it ain't no good thinking about them that way, is it?"

"I don't remember talking in my sleep," I said.

"Margie, let's go home. This boy needs some pamphlets read into him."

Mom got into the car and looked back at me before starting the engine. "You ever skip school again, I'll strap you black and blue. It's real embarrassing having the school call, and not knowing where you are. Hear me?"

I nodded.

Everything was quiet that week. I went to school and tried not to dream at night, and did everything boys are supposed to do. But I didn't feel like a boy. I felt something big inside, and no amount of Billy Grahams and Zondervans read at me could change that feeling.

I made one mistake, though. I asked Auntie Danser why she never read the Bible. This was in the parlor one evening after dinner and cleaning up the dishes. "Why do you want to know, boy?" she asked.

"Well, the Bible seems to be full of fine stories, but you don't carry it around with you. I just wondered why."

"Bible is a good book," she said. "The only good book. But it's difficult. It has lots of camouflage. Sometimes—" She stopped. "Who put you up to asking that question?"

"Nobody," I said.

"I heard that question before, you know," she said. "Ain't the first time I been asked. Somebody else asked me, once."

I sat in my chair, stiff as a ham.

"Your father's brother asked me that once. But we won't talk about him, will we?"

I shook my head.

Next Saturday I waited until it was dark and everyone was in bed. The night air was warm but I was sweating more than the warm could cause as I rode my bike down the dirt road, lamp beam swinging back and forth. The sky was crawling with stars, all of them looking at me. The Milky Way seemed to touch down just beyond the road, like I might ride straight up it if I went far enough.

I knocked on the heavy door. There were no lights in the windows and it was late for old folks to be up, but I knew these two didn't behave like normal people. And I knew that just because the house looked empty from the outside didn't mean it was empty within. The wind rose up and beat against the door, making me shiver. Then it opened. It was dark for a moment and the breath went out of me. Two pairs of eyes stared from the black. They seemed a lot taller this time. "Come in, boy," Jack whispered.

Fireflies lit up the tree in the living room. The brambles and wild-flowers glowed like weeds on a sea floor. The carpet crawled, but not to my feet. I was shivering in earnest now and my teeth chattered.

I only saw their shadows as they sat on the bench in front of me. "Sit," Meg said. "Listen close. You've taken the fire and it glows bright. You're only a boy but you're just like a pregnant woman now. For the rest of your life you'll be cursed with the worst affliction known to humans. Your skin will twitch at night. Your eyes will see things in the dark. Beasts will come to you and beg to be ridden. You'll never know one truth from another. You might starve, because few will want to encourage you. And if you do make good in this world, you might lose the gift and search forever after, in vain. Some will say the gift isn't special. Beware them. Some will say it is special and beware them, too. And some—"

There was a scratching at the door. I thought it was an animal for a moment. Then it cleared its throat. It was my great-aunt.

"Some will say you're damned. Perhaps they're right. But you're also enthused. Carry it lightly, and responsibly."

"Listen in there. This is Sybil Danser. You know me. Open up."

"Now stand by the stairs, in the dark where she can't see," Jack said. I did as I was told. One of them—I couldn't tell which—opened the door and the lights went out in the tree, the carpet stilled, and the brambles were snuffed. Auntie Danser stood in the doorway, outlined by star glow, carrying her knitting bag. "Boy?" she asked. I held my breath.

"And you others, too."

The wind in the house seemed to answer. "I'm not too late," she said. "Damn you, in truth, damn you to hell! You came to our towns, and you plague us with thoughts no decent person wants to think. Not just fairy stories, but telling the way people live, and why they shouldn't live that way! Your very breath is tainted! Hear me?" She walked slowly into the empty living room, feet clonking on the wooden floor. "You make them write about us, and make others laugh at us. Question the way we think. Condemn our deepest prides. Pull out our mistakes and amplify them beyond all truth. What right do you have to take young children and twist their minds?"

The wind sang through the cracks in the walls. I tried to see if Jack or Meg was there, but only shadows remained.

"I know where you come from, don't forget that! Out of the ground! Out of the bones of old, wicked Indians! Shamans and pagan dances and worshiping dirt and filth! I heard about you from the old squaws on the reservation. Frost and Spring, they called you, signs of the turning year. Well, now you got a different name! Death and demons, I call you, hear me?"

She seemed to jump at a sound but I couldn't hear it. "Don't you argue with me!" she shrieked. She took her glasses off and held out both hands. "Think I'm a weak old woman, do you? You don't know how deep I run in these communities! I'm the one who had them books taken off the shelves. Remember me? Oh, you hated it—not being able to fill young minds with your pestilence. Took them off high school shelves, and out of lists—burned them for junk! Remember? That was me. I'm not dead yet! Boy, where are you?"

"Enchant her," I whispered to the air. "Magic her. Make her go away. Let me live here with you."

"Is that you, boy? Come with your aunt, now. Come with me, come away!"

"Go with her," the wind told me. "Send your children this way, years from now. But go with her."

I felt a kind of tingly warmth and knew it was time to get home. I snuck out the back way and came around to the front of the house. There was no car. She'd followed me on foot all the way from the farm. I wanted to leave her there in the old house, shouting at the dead rafters, but instead I called her name and waited.

She came out crying. She knew.

"You poor, sinning boy," she said, pulling me to her lilac bosom.

PRINCE
SHADOWBOW

Prince Shadowbow of Faerie believed that time was fairly done for princes. "I am an anachronism," he said to his reflection in the pallid pool of stars that had the peculiar property of reflecting everything, even thoughts, whether at noon or midnight. Moons, moods, faeries, feelings—all were the same in the pool of stars, and it rippled now at the Prince's dramatic expression of despair as he turned to his companion of the court and demanded, "Am I not, Georges?"

"I am not sure Your Highness is old enough to be an anachronism," replied the old man, keeping a carefully straight face.

"One need not be old. Eighteen is quite old enough. Besides, it is the Princeness of me that is out of time, not the age of the Prince in question. I was an anachronism when I was born." This approached a forbidden subject rather more closely than was considered appropriate, and the Prince noted a slight tightening in Georges's expression. He peered out, therefore, at the limits of vision—as though seeking someone to agree with him—to the mist-veiled edges of Faerie, which were tattered now, fringed with time-mold and that strange rust that eats at the delicate borders of dreams. "I see the place fading around me, Georges. Day by day it tarnishes and dwindles. The colors are not as bright as when I was very young. The songs of the nymphs are not as sweet. The whole place is an anachronism."

"It has that quality, Your Highness. However, from time to time it can have that quality and still be restored to what it . . . was. One might say that what was, will be. One might say that the fragility is . . . intentional." The old courtier let the words trail into silence as the moody youth took them up.

"I've heard the argument, Georges. Since Faerie may have that quality intentionally, may we not say that the World outside is more truly the anachronism? Sorry, Georges. That would be a case of the flea defining the dog, would it not? I have been carefully reared not to think overmuch, but even such a mist-brain as I can see that the outside is much more . . . vital than the inside. Are we not only a drifting dream waiting to be experienced and forgotten?"

"Are we indeed, Your Highness? That would much surprise your mother, our Queen. And, who is to do the forgetting?"

The youth sighed. "Sometimes I am tempted to turn myself inside out and do it myself, just to end the agony of suspense. Oh, I know. Such moebian conduct would not become a Prince. My Royal mother would be distressed. Still, Georges, sometimes I feel this tension, this oddness, a wanting to run away, to be elsewhere. . . . "

"A condition, if I may say so, Your Highness, which is not untypical of youth."

"Even in this untypical place, eh, Georges? Well, this is no time to flirt with irresponsibility. The ceremony is tonight, isn't it?"

"It is, Your Highness." As both of them knew well enough and had known well for as long as both could remember. The ceremony would take place at dusk on the ides of autumn, which would occur when Shadowbow was eighteen. The season had been advancing for some time now. He could scarcely remember the springtime of his birth. Even the summer of his childhood had faded—he remembered it as a tapestry in which the colors had gone and only the lovely workmanship remained to testify to beauty long past. And now the autumn, and the ides of it upon him, and then—either spring again or . . . Either the slow rot at the borders would be stayed, the gradual paling and fading of the fabric of Faerie would be stopped, or . . .

Well, nothing could be done until the ceremony. All would be wagered, then, on one attempt. Thinking of it, Shadowbow flushed, bit nervously at his lower lip and tried to think of anything else, anything else at all.

"We'll walk back through Trollwood," he offered, turning from the pool of stars and strolling into the copses that lined the clearing. They walked on leaf-strewn paths, passing the gnarled shapes of ancient trees and the dark pits of the Trolls who leered and menaced from the entrances. Though they groveled at the sight of the Prince, he did not deign to notice them. Trolls were among the least favored of Faerie's inhabitants. They tended to snivel, the Prince thought, rather more than was necessary to be in keeping with their roles.

He turned his back on them and went down a side path to the Unicorn Glade. The single unicorn on duty was allowing itself to be used as a quoit target by three centaurs pitching wreaths of flowers.

"Pretty," called the Prince in a sarcastic tone. "Very pretty." Only one of the centaurs had the grace to flush; the other two only grinned as they galloped away.

He walked into the Glade, reaching out to the unicorn, burying his fingers in the silken mane. "Farewell," he whispered, overcome by nostalgia. "I will not be able to hold you so again, lovely one."

The unicorn sighed, rubbing her silken head upon the Prince's cheek. Then she stepped back, touched the needle point of her horn to his forehead and pressed, lightly, until the bright blood started through, falling like dew upon his cheek. "Lovely one," he sighed, fingering the mark. It would leave a tiny, puckered scar, like a kiss. His mother carried such a scar. Presumably her . . . progenitors had done so as well.

The centaurs had returned, galloping around the edges of the Glade as though the unicorn were only another like themselves. "Common," remarked the Prince with some disgust. "Common."

"It is still some time until dusk," murmured Georges, his voice soothing. "They seek to distract themselves from what lies ahead. They are only playing. . . . "

"I know, Georges. Believe me, I do know. I would sometimes prefer that they play for *me*, too. Is that selfish of me?"

"You pay no attention when the Trolls play for you."

"That's because the Trolls aren't playing. They're so dreadfully sincere. Every grovel a sincere grovel. Oh, Georges, forgive me. I'm nervous, touchy, and I know it's unbecoming. Don't pay attention to me. Ignore me."

Georges nodded, somewhat ironically, at this command as he opened the wicket gate leading through the great hedge into the stable yard. Here a dozen grooms were currying the dragons while stable boys mucked out the stalls. A dragonet amused itself by puffing fiery breath into the dragon trough, sending clouds of steam puffing into the slanting sunlight. The grooms nudged one another to attention as the Prince walked by. He smiled, making an effort to appear pleasant and calm. Poor little sods. What must it be like to be a dragon groom and know that no matter what happened in Faerie or the World outside, one would still be a dragon groom? On the other hand, it wasn't that bad a life. At least they could stay in Faerie. There were no ceremonies hanging in their futures to make them all grim and fevered with duty and despair.

"I should hurry," he murmured, not hurrying. "Did you lay out my clothes, Georges?"

"I did, Your Highness. The suit of pearl, of course, as is traditional. Your seven-league boots and the cloak of invisibility. It came back from the cleaners only yesterday." Georges coughed, the dry, wry cough of a valued retainer who may indulge himself in a little carefully veiled sarcasm. "Your Highness may remember the episode during which it became . . . soiled."

The Prince blushed.

"Her Majesty, your mother, will give you your bow, of course."

"Of course."

There were murmurs behind them as they went from the stable yard into the orchards. At one time Georges would have hurried the boy through these pleasant reaches, but he did not presume to hurry the youth. The nymphs of the trees had laughed no more seductively for the five-year-old Prince than they did now, but one did not presume to protect the Prince of the Royal Line on the eve of his great trial. Georges allowed himself one curious glance at the Prince's face, but there was no lust there. Instead, he was gazing up through the scarlet trees to the castle wall where ivory towers blossomed with pennants against the rosy sky.

"It is very beautiful," he admitted in the voice of one who would rather have criticized but could not.

"It is certainly very beautiful," assented the old man. "There is nothing more beautiful; there can be nothing more beautiful. As is intended, Your Highness."

"I know," sighed Shadowbow, with a little laugh.

That laughter was echoed by the nymphs, and that laughter in turn faded behind them as they approached the gate, open upon the solemn quiet of the courts. From one shimmering tower a bell rang, plangent and marvelous, echoing in sound the brilliance and sadness of the sunset. Along the corridors, the servitors stood in their hundreds, bowing as he passed, line on endless line, their voices following him.

"Bring us to springtime, Your Highness."

"Grant strength to Your Highness for the ides."

He nodded, smiled, smiled and nodded, coming at last to his own tower room where body servants waited to bathe him, where the suit of pearl lay inexorably splendid upon his bed.

In the largest audience hall of the castle the nobility of Faerie had gathered. The floors were tessellated in sardonyx and chrysoberyl, amethyst and topaz. The lanterns were of gold, filled with exotic oils and rare resins upon which the pale flames danced. Through the tall, western windows the last light fell into the glory of the place, not more glorious than those assembled there glistening in samite, scintillating in jewels. The Queen, pale as ivory, stood upon the dais among her coterie, her laughter falling into the pool of their attention like drops of molten silver, hissing into heavy silences. Prince Shadowbow stopped this careening metaphor. He had seen her so ten thousand times, so high, so royal, so beyond his callow youthfulness. And yet, and yet they were one blood, one line, and he loved her in desperation and silence. Over her shoulder he saw the shadowy face of King Cloak-of-Mist, the Queen's father and mate, Shadowbow's father. Beyond the King stood Queen Morning-Glory, the King's mother and mate, mother of the Queen. One line, doubly mated within itself, to rule—to rule if...

"Oh, let it all pass away," he told himself, "if only she might live. . . ." She could not, of course. If Faerie passed, she would pass with it, and this knowledge alone was enough to hold him to his duty, however foul and gross it seemed when compared to her grace. He knew that if he turned quickly, he would surprise an expression of gentle concern in Georges's eyes. He sought a distraction, a bit of misdirection.

"I am thinking," he said, trying to sound lightly humorous, "that it is all very *intentionally* melancholy."

"No less enchanting for that," whispered Georges.

Somewhere a signal was given. Trumpeters filled the room with silver tumult, and the Prince walked behind tabarded escorts to the dais where his mother fixed him with a stare of oracular perspicacity. "She knows," he thought, suddenly astounded by that knowledge. "She is not so far removed from her own youth. She remembers when she turned eighteen. Did she feel this same fear? This shame?" In the fullness of that thought he was overtaken by embarrassment and chagrin. He could have borne his own feelings, but to know she had borne them as well! He knelt, which was all he could have done. Neither of them would have wished to weep before the court.

"Prince Shadowbow," cried the Queen. "We see Faerie fade around us. Our lives run chill into autumn. Time creeps upon us as the night-slugs creep upon the delphinium spires, eating them to nothing. I call upon you, heir to the Throne of Faerie, Master of the Mists, Lastborn son of the Line of Oberon, Lord of the Borderlands, Prince Shadowbow of the Golden Arrows, to say whether you will risk your very soul in our renewal, or will you remain with us, beloved . . . son . . . and dwindle with us into silence?"

Behind her on the high, marble wall hung the lip-curved shapes of the bows which the ancestors of the line had carried, a thousand shadow-kisses upon that wall. Beside the Queen upon the dais lay her own bow. The Prince looked upon the wall and choked down cowardice. What they had done, he could do. What she had done, he could do. He turned to make the affirmation.

"I, Prince Shadowbow, last of my lineage yet alive, swear unto everlasting time my joy and my duty, to venture into the World that the strength that is there shall be brought to my people and my line-age. . . . " He turned, hands held out, palms upward, to take upon them the thing he had seen but never touched until then, the great Shadowbow of the Borderlands. Even as he held it, felt its delicate weight upon his hands, he heard the glad cry of the Queen as she hung her own bow upon the marble wall, hers retired into honorable place from which she never need take it again—as her father's before her, as his mother's before him, into time past remembering.

Only the minor ceremonies remained; the incantation over the arrows, the dedication of the quiver which held them, the censing of the cloak. Then came the processional ride to the Borderlands, all in company, the Prince first among his gentlemen and the Queen riding in a light carriage behind them. It hurt him to see her riding so, she who had been first in every hunt, no centaur more part of his steed than she. Now—now she had taken a new role, and he bit his lip again as she came down from the carriage at the border saying that no hands but hers should fix the boots upon his feet or clasp the cloak about his throat. There at the border she kissed him, bidding him farewell and safe re-turn, and their eyes met in a mutual understanding at once pungent and achingly sweet.

"So we say farewell to innocence," she whispered. "My love will not be less on the morning when it is done."

He bowed before her, holding her tiny hands in his own. He could not bring himself to believe her, but doubt would have seemed discourteous. What could he have said? "Until that morning, then." Something more lengthy and equivocal? No, better to say nothing and go; go and hope to return, no matter how one dreaded it or despaired of being able at that last instant to do what one had to do. He felt weak and ill, empty. There had been no feast. Who could have eaten before this? Who could believe her love would not be less on the morrow? After this betrayal, this infidelity?

Except, he reminded himself, that in her time, she too—she, too . . .

He merely bowed, therefore, and was silent as he turned and stepped across the border into the World.

To emerge invisibly onto a grimy street in the afternoon. The evenings and mornings of Faerie did not coincide with the times of the World. He knew this, but the transition left him disoriented for the moment. The place stank of chemical fumes, which he had been prepared for, counted on. Georges had said that the disgust he felt at the smells might be his best—perhaps his only—protection. Nervously he checked the bow, the arrows. Everything he needed was with him. He stepped forward in the seven-league boots, a tiptoeing step that brought him to the center of the city, motion and sound boiling around him, unquiet and impatient, full of fury and disenchantment.

He clutched the cloak high above his throat, drew it across his mouth and nose. The disenchantment was like acid air, eating away at him, draining purpose and vigor. There were stories of some who had come into the World and had not returned, who had succumbed. He could not delay. Delay would increase the danger. Summoning all his concentration, he listened for the tug—the tug.

It came, a kind of harsh pulling, a half-pleasurable pain, and he went toward it, in tiny steps, stopping between them to look and listen. With each step the sensation grew stronger. He stopped at last near a green lawn to the wild cacophony of bells where *they* poured from a building in their hundreds, their thousands.

He staggered, overwhelmed by the mad, wild pulsing of his blood, the thundering of his heart. They were all around him, in twos and threes, their arms about one another, in crowds and clots, singly, flowing away in all directions, girls, Worldly girls, the beast scent of them filling the air in clouds so that he could not breathe except of that smell.

Oh, he cried to himself, but they are graceless. Look at the things they wear upon their feet. The crude, high clogs which cripple their walk so that they prance like the back half of a cow. Look at their hair.

Like briars, tangled, like rope, frizzled. Oh. Look, look at their eyes, daubed like those of a chimney sweep. They are trolls, trolls. . . .

And they did resemble the Trolls more than he had expected, but it did not matter, for the smell of them was in his nostrils. It would not have mattered if they had appeared as Afrits or Demons, as witches of the depths, with that smell in his head, he could not have let them go. Even as his body turned to follow a group of them, however, his mind said cold, harsh things to him, bending his discrimination toward them. "Pick with some sense," he told himself. "Pick with some chance of success. . . . " And he dropped behind them a little way so that he should not be so maddened by the smell of them.

There were one or two in the group who looked less Troll-like than the others. They seemed cleaner, with less soot around their eyes, with hair that was more like silk than rope. These two or three he followed with his eyes, finding the places they went, remembering them. Then he left the place, as quickly as he could. When it was dark, he would return.

He sped the boots from the city to a more rural place, one saddened with trash and indiscriminate filth, but removed from the smell that had maddened him and the noise that had disgusted him. He waited for night, brooding upon the needs of Faerie.

"I am an anachronism," he said again. "Is it worth this? Would we not do better to fade into time as the older Gods have done, forgotten and long gone? Oh, in the ancient times when the Borderlands were permeable, when the World and Faerie lay like lovers at one another's side, yes, oh, yes, then it was right. But now? Now, when one must come into a place totally strange, totally inimical? When one must risk everything to break that border so much as a hair's width—only a hair's width—to let the rude vigor flow through?"

And his memories swept over him, the loveliness and glory of his home, the beauties of the Queen, and he answered himself. "Yes. Though it is to open only a hair's width to the door of life, though I risk everything, still it would be worth it, for if Faerie fades, nothing would be left but *this*." And he put his head into his hands, summoned up a memory of the well of the naiads and their coruscating fountain and to the memory of that music he listened until darkness came.

In the town once more he was glad to see that much of the ugliness was decently hidden by the dark. He began at the first house among those he had identified, searching for the spoor Georges had taught him to recognize, holding his breath not to smell them. He moved into rooms where girls slept, searched there, left there to lean weakly upon a fence or porch railing, sick and heaving. Romance novels. Movie magazines. Rock music. Caches of dried herbs—drugs of some kind or other.

Pictures of loose-lipped, meaty boys. Records of their voices shouting in a primitive, rhythmic chant words the Prince could not understand. That, too, was Troll-like. They did a great deal of that.

Finally only one house remained. He tottered toward it, weak and febrile. Far in the east the false dawn lit the sky with a fluorescent glow, and he shivered at the sight, an omen of failure. If he could not find the traces Georges had told him to find, then he must take one of the others, for he did not think he could survive another day in this place or another night of search. Almost weeping, he went into the room where the last girl slept.

He remembered her. Of the little group he had followed, she had been the silent one, the one with lips pursed tight as though they closed over a delicious secret. Her forehead was slightly bulbous over level brows, and in sleep her face was drained of the day's dross to gleam with almost porcelain smoothness. He began the search. . . .

And found them almost at once. The notebooks into which paragraphs had been distilled slow word by slow word. The verses, crossed out and a hundred times rewritten. The little box, sticky with much handling, which held yellowed newspaper clippings announcing the winners of a writing contest. Upon her bookshelves were the names he had been told to seek.

The Prince steadied himself, then took the great Shadowbow from his shoulder and notched a golden arrow. With a fervent appeal to all the strength remaining in Faerie, he shot her through the heart.

Thus enchanted she could be carried to the Borderlands. Thus bewitched she could be laid upon the velvet mosses while he blew his horn in signal that he had returned and was not alone. He was fighting very hard to keep from sneezing. The scent of her, even while it fevered his loins almost unbearably, was very difficult to bear. He divested himself of cloak and boots. Then, fully visible and in the glory of his youth he knelt beside her as the nymphs began the much-rehearsed chorus.

Even he, who had heard their song from his cradle, was moved. Upon the heights trumpets blew, the sound of joyous bells wafted from the castle. "Play, people," he murmured to himself as he prepared to wake her with a kiss. "Play, for Faerie depends upon it."

The eyes of Elsbeth Blodge opened and she beheld Prince Shadowbow kneeling at her side, resplendent in the suit of pearl.

Thereafter it was as it had been rehearsed a hundred times.

There were declarations in enchanted forests, abductions by Trolls, Ogres, Demons. She was set free from ensorcelled towers, dungeons, caves, only to be captured again. They fled together on unicorns, dragons, on winged horses. Skies loomed dark with fantastic clouds, cleared into crepuscular twilight, dawned with roseate charm. Nymphs chorused in the background except during the more martial episodes. Only he, who knew the language of Faerie, understood their bawdy lyrics. To Elsbeth Blodge, late of the World, it could have been a caroling of angels.

Days fled in mixed terror and glory. Romantic dusk was succeeded by passionate night until at last . . . at last only that final, ultimate act remained. Prince Shadowbow fixed his mind upon duty, brought determination to fever pitch, and accomplished that impregnation which left him exhausted and ill. He lay where they had coupled, breathing raggedly into the graying mosses.

The golden arrow that had transfixed her heart was melting. She had to be returned to the World before it was altogether gone. Georges, efficient as always, and as kind, donned the seven-league boots and the cloak of invisibility to carry her home. The sound of their exit through the border was as of a delicate fabric ripped. It alerted the servitors who sought their Prince, brought a soft litter on which to carry him to the castle, stripped him of the suit of pearl, washed him in water from the well of the nymphs, and let him go on sleeping. It was all they could do to stay awake until this last duty was done. They slept. All of Faerie slept. The last strength had been used, the last enchantment spent. Now it was left to time, time and Elsbeth Blodge.

Time.

The evenings and mornings of Faerie are not those of the World. The seasons of the World are not those of Faerie. Who knows how many of the one were slept away, how many of the other shaped clangingly upon the anvil of Time. Who was Elsbeth Blodge, after all? Whose child was she? What power resided in her that all of Faerie slept on her account, knowing it might never wake again?

Until one morning.

Prince Shadowbow wakened to see the east alive with rose and amber, heard the sound of singing from the green chasms among the orchard trees, felt the blood of Faerie boil along his veins in a surging flood. On the castle roof outside his window ruby-footed pigeons danced intricate minuets. Wind scurried among the leaves, bringing a scent of flowers. High against a backdrop of cloud, dragons chased one another, and from the Troll forest came the thunder of drums and the rattle of bones.

"Oh," laughed Prince Shadowbow, "this is how it was when I was young, so young. . . . "

"This is how it is when we are young, so young. . . . " It was the Queen, standing in his door clad in boots and trousers, looking no more than fourteen in the rosy light. "This is how it is, my son, my love, my husband, my Shadowbow."

"Then she . . . she did it . . . she . . . "

"Shhh," said the Queen with a moue of distaste. "We will not speak of it."

He frowned, obscurely disappointed by this. "I would like—I would like to have seen it."

She looked at him, perhaps a trifle annoyed, perhaps with only a flicker of foolish jealousy. "Very well, my love. I believe I, too, felt much the same. We will send Georges."

So, faithful Georges went out into the World once more to return bearing a small burden. He found the Prince eating pears in the orchard, his head in the Queen's lap, while they watched the dryads dance. Georges put the burden down upon the grass, swaddled as he had carried it.

The Prince looked long at it, somewhat doubtfully. "Is it really mine, Georges? You're sure?"

"Your firstborn," said Georges, fondly and sadly at once. "Your firstborn, Your Majesty."

He knelt to unwrap it there upon the lawn of Faerie, and they stared at it when the wraps came away. It was only a slender thing, a little enough thing with its name upon its cover.

" 'The Trollwood,' " read Prince Shadowbow. " 'By Elsbeth Bouvier.' Was that her name, Georges? I don't recall."

The Queen made a face. Georges, who was wise about many things, removed the book. He took it to the deep and hidden place he had taken all the others. Even the earliest lay there still. The foundations of Faerie rest upon them.

THE GIRL WHO WENT TO THE RICH NEIGHBORHOOD

There was once a widow who lived with her six daughters in the poorest neighborhood in town. In summer the girls all went barefoot, and even in winter they often had to pass one pair of shoes between them as they ran through the street. Even though the mother got a check every month from the welfare department, it never came to enough, despite their all eating as little as possible. They would not have survived at all if the supermarkets hadn't allowed the children to gather behind the loading gates at the end of the day and collect the crushed or fallen vegetables.

Sometimes, when there was no more money, the mother would leave her left leg as credit with the grocer. When her check came, or one of the children found a little work, she would get back her leg and be able to walk without the crutch her oldest daughter had made from a splintery board. One day, however, after she'd paid her bill, she found herself stumbling. When she examined her leg she discovered that the grocery had kept so many legs and arms jumbled together in their big metal cabinet that her foot had become all twisted. She sat down on their only chair and began to cry, waving her arms over her head.

Seeing her mother so unhappy the youngest girl, whose name was Rose, walked up and announced, "Please don't worry. I'll go to the rich neighborhood." Her mother kept crying. "And I'll speak to the mayor. I'll get him to help us." The widow smiled and stroked her daughter's hair.

She doesn't believe me, Rose thought. Maybe she won't let me go. I'd better sneak away. The next day, when the time came to go to the supermarket Rose took the shoes she shared with her sisters and slipped them in her shopping bag. She hated doing this, but she would need the shoes for the long walk to the rich neighborhood. Besides, maybe the mayor wouldn't see her if she came barefoot. Soon, she told herself, she'd bring back shoes for everyone. At the supermarket she filled her bag with seven radishes that had fallen off the bunch, two sticks of yellowed celery, and four half-blackened bananas. Well, she thought, I guess I'd better get started.

As soon as she left the poor neighborhood Rose saw some boys shoving and poking a weak old lady who was trying to cross the street. What a rotten thing to do, the girl thought, and hoped the children in the rich neighborhood weren't all like that. She found a piece of pipe in the street and chased them away.

"Thank you," wheezed the old woman, who wore a yellow dress and had long blond hair that hung, uncombed, down to her knees. She sat down in the middle of the road, with cars going by on every side. Rose said, "Shouldn't we get out of the street? We could sit on the pavement."

"I can't," said the old woman, "I must eat something first. Don't you have anything to eat?"

Rose reached in her basket to give the old woman a radish. In a moment the shriveled red thing had vanished and the woman held out her hand. Rose gave her another radish, and then another, until all the radishes had slid down the old woman's densely veined throat. "Now we can go," she said, and instantly jumped to her feet to drag Rose across the road.

Rose told herself that maybe she wouldn't need them. She looked down at the silver pavement and then up at the buildings that reached so far above her head the people in the windows looked like toys. "Is this the rich neighborhood?" she asked.

"Hardly," the woman said, "you have to go a long way to reach the rich neighborhood." Rose thought how she'd better be extra careful with the rest of her food. The old woman said, "But if you really want to go there I can give you something to help you." She ran her fingers through her tangled gold hair and when she took them out she was holding a lumpy yellow coin. "This token will always get you on or off the underground railway."

What a strange idea, thought Rose. How could you use a token more than once? And even if you could, everyone knew that you didn't need anything to get off the underground. But she put the coin in the bag and thanked the old woman.

All day she walked and when night came she crawled under a fire escape beside some cardboard cartons. She was very hungry but she thought she had better save her celery and bananas for the next day. Trying not to think of the warm mattress she shared with two of her sisters, she went to sleep.

The next morning the sound of people marching to work woke her up. She stretched herself, thinking how silver streets may look very nice but didn't make much of a bed. Then she rubbed her belly and stared at the celery. I'd better get started first, she told herself. But when she began to walk her feet hurt, for her sisters' shoes, much too big for her, had rubbed the skin raw the day before.

Maybe she could take the tube train. Maybe the old woman's token would work at least once. She went down a subway entrance where a guard with a gun walked back and forth, sometimes clapping his hands or stamping his feet. As casually as she could Rose walked up and put her token in the slot. I hope he doesn't shoot me, she thought. But then the wooden blades of the gate turned and she passed through.

A moment later, she was walking down the stairs when she heard a soft clinking sound. She turned around to see the token bouncing on its rim along the corridor and down the stairs until it bounced right into the shopping bag. Rose looked to see if the guard was taking his gun out but he was busy staring out the entrance.

All day she traveled on the tube train, but whenever she tried to read the signs she couldn't make out what they said beneath the huge black marks drawn all over them. Rose wondered if the marks formed the magic that made the trains go. She'd sometimes heard people say that without magic the underground would break down forever. Finally she decided she must have reached the rich neighborhood. She got off the train, half expecting to have to use her token. But the exit door swung open with no trouble and soon she found herself on a gold pavement, with buildings that reached so high the people looked like birds fluttering around in giant caves.

Rose was about to ask someone for the mayor's office when she saw a policeman with a gold mask covering his face slap an old woman. Rose hid in a doorway and made a sound like a siren, a trick she'd learned in the poor neighborhood. The policeman ran off waving his gold truncheon.

"Thank you, thank you," said the old woman, whose tangled red hair reached down to her ankles. "I'm so hungry now, could you give me something to eat?" Trying not to cry Rose gave the woman first one piece of celery and then the other. Then she asked, "Is this the rich neighborhood?"

"No, no, no," the woman laughed, "but if you're planning to go there I can give you something that might help you." She ran her fingers through her hair and took out a red feather. "If you need to reach something and cannot, then wave this feather." Rose couldn't imagine how a feather could help her reach anything but she didn't want to sound rude so she put the feather in her bag.

Since it was evening and Rose knew that gangs sometimes ran through the streets after dark she thought she'd better find a place to sleep. She saw a pile of wooden crates in front of a store and lay down behind them, sadly thinking how she'd better save her four bananas for the next day.

The next morning the sound of opening and closing car doors woke her up, and she stretched painfully. The gold streets had hurt her back even more than the silver ones the night before. With a look at her bananas, now completely black, she got to her feet and walked back to the underground.

All day she rode on the train, past underground store windows showing clothes that would tear in a day, and bright flimsy furniture, and strange machines with rows of black buttons. The air became very sweet, but thick, as if someone had sprayed the tunnels with perfume. Finally Rose decided she couldn't breathe and had to get out.

She came up to a street made all of diamond, and buildings so high she couldn't see anything at all in the windows, only flashes of colors. The people walking glided a few inches above the ground, while the cars moved so gently on their white tires they looked like swimmers floating in a pool.

Rose was about to ask for the mayor's office when she saw an old woman surrounded by manicured dogs and rainbow-dyed cats whose rich owners had let them roam the street. Rose whistled so high she herself couldn't hear it, but the animals all ran away, thinking their owners had called them for dinner.

"Thank you so much," the woman said, dusting off her long black dress. Her black hair trailed the ground behind her. "Do you suppose you could give me something to eat?"

Biting back her tears Rose held out the four bananas. The woman laughed and said, "One is more than enough for me. You eat the others." Rose had to stop herself shoving all three bananas into her mouth at once. She was glad she did, for each one tasted like a different food, from chicken to strawberries. She looked up amazed.

"Now," said the woman, "I suppose you want the mayor's house." Her mouth open, Rose nodded yes. The woman told her to look for a street so bright she had to cover her eyes to walk on it. Then she said, "If you ever find the road too crowded blow on this." She ran her fingers through her hair and took out a black whistle shaped like a pigeon. The girl said, "Thank you," though she didn't think people would get out of the street just for a whistle.

When the woman had gone, Rose looked around at the diamond street. I'd break my back sleeping here, she thought, and decided to look for the mayor's house that evening. Up and down the streets she hobbled, now and then running out of the way of dark-windowed cars or lines of children dressed all in money and holding hands as they ran screaming through the street.

At one point she saw a great glow of light and thought she must have found the mayor's house, but when she came close she saw only an empty road where bright balls of light on platinum poles shone on giant fountains spouting liquid gold into the air. Rose shook her head and walked on.

Several times she asked people for the mayor's house but no one seemed to hear or see her. As night came Rose thought that at least the rich neighborhood wouldn't get too cold; they probably heated the streets. But instead of warm air a blast of cold came up from the damned pavement. The people in the rich neighborhood chilled the streets so they could use the personal heaters built into their clothes.

For the first time Rose thought she would give up. It was all so strange, how could she ever think the mayor would even listen to her? About to look for a subway entrance she saw a flash of light a few blocks away and began to walk toward it. When she came close the light became so bright she automatically covered her eyes, only to find she could see just as well as before. Scared now that she'd actually found the mayor she slid forward close to the buildings.

The light came from a small star that the mayor's staff had captured and set in a lead cage high above the street. A party was going on, with people dressed in all sorts of costumes. Some looked like birds with beaks instead of noses, and giant feathered wings growing out of their backs; others had become lizards, their heads covered in green scales. In the middle, on a huge chair of black stone, sat the mayor looking very small in a white fur robe. Long curved fingernails hooked over the ends of his chair. All around him advisers floated in the air on glittery cushions.

For a time Rose stayed against the wall, afraid to move. Finally she told herself she could starve just standing there. Trying not to limp, she marched forward and said, "Excuse me."

No one paid any attention. And no wonder. Suspended from a helicopter a band played on peculiar horns and boxes. "Excuse me," Rose said louder, then shouted, the way she'd learned to shout in the poor neighborhood when animals from outside the city attacked the children.

Everything stopped. The music sputtered out, the lizards stopped snatching at the birds who stopped dropping jeweled "eggs" on the lizards' heads. Two policemen ran forward. Masks like smooth mirrors covered their heads so that the rich people would only see themselves if they happened to glance at a policeman. They grabbed Rose's arms, but before they could handcuff her the mayor boomed (his voice came through a microphone grafted onto his tongue), "Who are you? What do you want? Did you come to join the party?"

Everyone laughed. Even in the rich neighborhood, they knew, you had to wait years for an invitation to the mayor's party.

"No, sir," said Rose. "I came to ask for help for the poor neighborhood. Nobody has any money to buy food and people have to leave their arms and legs at the grocery just to get anything. Can you help us?"

The laughter became a roar. People shouted ways the mayor could help the poor neighborhood. Someone suggested canning the ragged child and sending her back as charity dinners. The mayor held up his hand and everyone became silent. "We could possibly help you," he said. "But first you will have to prove yourself. Will you do that?"

Confused, Rose said yes. She didn't know what he meant. She wondered if she needed a welfare slip or some other identification. "Good," the mayor said. "We've got a small problem here and maybe you could help us solve it." He waved a hand and a picture appeared in the air in front of Rose. She saw a narrow metal stick about a foot long with a black knob at one end and a white knob at the other. The mayor told Rose that the stick symbolized the mayor's power, but the witches had stolen it.

"Why don't you send the police to get it back?" Rose asked. Again the mayor had to put up his hand to stop the laughter. He told the girl that the witches had taken the stick to their embassy near the United Nations, where diplomatic immunity kept the police from following them.

"I have to go to the witches' embassy?" Rose asked. "I don't even know where it is. How will I find it?" But the mayor paid no attention to her. The music started and the birds and lizards went back to chasing each other.

Rose was walking away when a bird woman flapped down in front of her. "Shall I tell you the way to the witches' embassy?"

"Yes," Rose said. "Please." The woman bent over laughing. Rose thought she would just fly away again, but no, in between giggles she told the girl exactly how to find the witches. Then she wobbled away on her wingtips, laughing so hard she bumped into buildings whenever she tried to fly.

With her underground token Rose arrived at the embassy in only a few minutes. The iron door was so tall she couldn't even reach the bell, so she walked around looking for a servants' entrance. Shouts came from an open window. She crept forward.

Wearing nothing but brown oily mud all over their bodies the witches were dancing before a weak fire. The whole embassy house smelled of damp moss. Rose was about to slip away when she noticed a charred wooden table near the window, and on top of it the mayor's stick.

She was about to climb over the sill, grab the stick and run, when she noticed little alarm wires strung across the bottom of the window. Carefully she reached in above the wires toward the table. No use. The stick lay a good six inches out of reach.

An image of the woman in red came to her. "If you need to reach something and cannot, then wave this feather." Though she still couldn't see how the feather could help her, especially with something so heavy, she fluttered it toward the table.

The red-haired woman appeared behind the witches, who nevertheless seemed not to notice her. "I am the East Wind," she said, and Rose saw that her weakness had vanished and her face shone as bright as her hair waving behind her. "Because you helped me and gave me your food when you had so little I will give you what you want." She blew on the table and a gust of wind carried the stick over the wires into Rose's hands.

The girl ran off with all the speed she'd learned running away from trouble in the poor neighborhood. Before she could go half a block, however, the stick cried out, "Mistresses! This little one is stealing me."

In an instant the witches were after her, shrieking and waving their arms as they ran, leaving drops of mud behind them. Soon, however, Rose reached the underground where her token let her inside while the witches, who hadn't taken any money, let alone tokens, could only stand on the other side of the gate and scream at her.

Rose could hardly sit she was so excited. The tube train clacked along, and only the silly weeping of the stick in her bag kept her from jumping up and down. She imagined her mother's face when she came home in the mayor's car piled so high with money and food.

At the stop for the mayor's house Rose stepped off the train swinging her bag. There, lined up across the exit, stood the witches. They waved their muddy arms and sang peculiar words in warbly, high-pitched voices. The stick called, "Mistresses, you found me."

Rose looked over her shoulder at the underground. She could run back, but suppose they were waiting for her in the tunnel? And she still had to get to the mayor. Suddenly she remembered the old woman saying that the token could get her off the underground as well as on. She grabbed it from her bag and held it up.

The woman in yellow appeared before her. "I am the South Wind," she said, "and because you helped me I will help you." Gently she blew on Rose and a wind as soft as an old bed carried the girl over the heads of the witches and right out of the underground to the street.

As fast as she could she ran to the mayor's house. But as soon as she turned the corner to the street with the captured star she stopped and clutched her bag against her chest. The mayor was waiting for her, wrapped in a head to toe cylinder of bullet-proof glass, while behind him, filling the whole street, stood a giant squad of police. Their mirrored heads bounced the starlight back to the sky. "Give me the witches' stick," the mayor said.

"The witches? You said—"

"Idiot child. That stick contains the magic of the witches' grandmothers." He then began to rave about smashing the witches' house and putting them to work in the power stations underneath the rich neighborhood. Rose tried to back away. "Arrest her," the mayor said.

What had the old woman in black said? "If you ever find the road too crowded, blow on this." Rose grabbed the pigeon whistle and blew as hard as she could. The woman appeared, her hair wider than the whole wave of police. "I am the North Wind," she told the girl, and might have said more but the squad was advancing. The North Wind threw out her arms and instead of a gust of air a huge flock of black pigeons flew from her dress to pick up the mayor and all the police. Ferociously beating their wings the pigeons carried them straight over the wall into the Northern Borough, where they were captured by burglars and never heard from again.

"Thank you," Rose said, but the old woman was gone. With a sigh Rose took out the witches' stick. "I'm sorry," she told it. "I just wanted to help the poor neighborhood."

"May I go home now?" the stick asked sarcastically. Before the girl could answer the stick sprang out of her hands and flew end over end through the air, back to the witches' embassy.

Rose found herself limping along the riverside, wondering what she would tell her mother and her sisters. Why didn't I help the West Wind? she said to herself. Maybe she could've done something for me.

A woman all in silver appeared on the water. Her silver hair tumbled behind her into the river. "I do not need to test you to know your goodness," she said. She blew on the river and a large wave rose up to drench the surprised girl.

But when Rose shook the water off she found that every drop had become a jewel. Red, blue, purple, green, stones of all shapes and colors, sapphires in the shape of butterflies, opals with sleeping faces embedded in the center, they all covered Rose's feet up to her ankles. She didn't stop to look at them. With both hands she scooped them up into her basket, and then her shoes. Hurry, she told herself. She knew that no matter how many police you got rid of there were always more. And wouldn't the rich people insist the jewels belonged to them?

So full of jewels she could hardly run Rose waddled to the underground entrance. Only when she got there did she notice that the streets had lost their diamond paving. All around her the rich people stumbled or fell on the lumpy gray concrete. Some of them had begun to cry or to crawl on all fours, feeling the ground like blind people at the edge of a cliff. One woman had taken off all her clothes, her furs and silks and laces, and was spreading them all about the ground to hide its ugliness.

Fascinated, Rose took a step back toward the street. She wondered if anything had happened to the star imprisoned in its cage above the mayor's house. But then she remembered how her mother had limped when the grocer had gotten her foot all twisted. She ran downstairs to use her magic token for the last time.

Though the tube train was crowded Rose found a seat in the corner where she could bend over her treasures to hide them from any suspicious eyes. What does a tax collector look like, she wondered.

As the rusty wheels of the train shrieked through the gold neighborhood and then the silver one Rose wondered if she'd ever see the old ladies again. She sighed happily. It didn't matter. She was going home, back to her mother and her sisters and all her friends in the poor neighborhood.

CONSEQUENCES

White sails cut precise arcs against a background of vivid color: green sea, blue sky, black volcanic sand. Spindrift shone like diamonds as it spattered over the weather rail. *Birdwing* heeled in the strong gust; timber and cordage groaned as they took the strain. Captain Derec SuPashto adjusted his stance to the increased tilt of the deck: his mind was on other things.

Birdwing and its convoy was about to be attacked by the Liavekan navy.

"My compliments to the ship's wizard, Facer," he said. "Ask him if he can veer this wind two or four points."

"Sir."

A veering wind would be useful, Derec thought, if Levett could conjure one up. But whatever happened, let it stay strong.

"Starboard a point, Sandor."

"Starboard a point, aye aye."

"Break out our colors, SuKrone."

"Sir."

Derec's first reaction on seeing the three Liavekan warships was not one of anxiety, but rather relief. *Birdwing* would finally have a chance to prove itself to Ka Zhir, and that chance was desperately needed.

As the streaming black-and-gold Zhir ensign broke out overhead, Derec studied the enemy with narrowed eyes: three bright ships on a shallow sea the color of green baize. The lead galleass was a big one, thirty oars or more per side, white foam curling from its massive ramming prow. It was painted purple with scarlet trim; a rear admiral's blue pennant fluttered from its maintop and gold leaf winked from the carved arabesques that decorated the stern. The second galleass, three cables astern, was smaller and lighter, its rigging more delicate: it would be at a disadvantage in this strong wind, this choppy sea. It hadn't been painted; its sides were the bright color of varnished wood. Astern of the second enemy was a small xebec—its military value was negligible unless it could get under an enemy's stern in a dead calm, in which case it could pound away with its bow chaser until its opponent was nothing but driftwood. Likely it served as a tender, or was used for chasing down unarmed merchantmen. Derec's impulse was to discount it.

A brave sight, these three, on the green ocean. They seemed entirely in their element.

Derec knew that appearances were deceiving.

He wondered what the Liavekan admiral was thinking as he stood on his fine gingerbread poop. The Liavekan squadron had been lurking along the coast between Ka Zhir and Gold Harbor for the obvious purpose of attacking a convoy; and now a convoy had appeared, twelve caravels and two huge carracks, all crammed to the gunnels with trade goods. The Liavekan squadron, waiting behind a barren, palm-covered islet, had duly sprung their ambush and were now driving toward their prey. But what in hell, they must wonder, was the escort?

A ship of *Birdwing*'s type had never been seen in these waters. The stout masts and heavy standing rigging marked her as northern-built, a Farlander ship able to stand up to winter gales in the high latitudes, but even in the north she would cut an odd figure. She was too narrow, flat-sided, and low for a carrack. The forward-tilting mainmast and bonaventure mizzen would have marked her as a galleon, but if she was a galleon, where were the high forecastles and sterncastles? And where were the billowing, baglike square sails the Liavekans had come to associate with those heavy, sluggish northern ships? *Birdwing*'s square sails were cut flat, curved gently like a bird's wing, hence her name.

To the Liavekan admiral, Derec wondered, how did this all add up? A galleon with its upper decks razed, perhaps, in an effort to make it lighter, and furthermore cursed with an eccentric sailmaker. Some kind of bastard ship at any rate, neither fish nor fowl, with a broadside to beware of, but a military value easily enough discounted. Everyone knew that northern ships couldn't sail to weather—unlike the oar-driven galleys and galleasses of the Levar's navy, galleons were doomed to sail only downwind. And the Liavekan's tactics were clearly aimed at getting the escort to leeward of its convoy, where it couldn't possibly sail upwind again to protect it.

You're in for a surprise, milord admiral, Derec thought. Because *Birdwing* is going to make those wormy hulks of yours obsolete, and all in the next turn of the glass.

"Wizard's compliments, sir." Lieutenant Facer had returned, sunlight winking from his polished brass earrings; he held his armored cap at the salute. "He might venture a spell to veer the wind, but it would take twenty minutes or more."

Within twenty minutes they'd be in gunshot. Weather spells were delicate things, consuming enormous amounts of power to shift the huge kinetic energies that made up a wind front, and often worked late or not at all.

"Compliments to the wizard, Facer. Tell him we'll make do with the wind we've got."

"Sir." Facer dropped his hat back on his peeling, sunburned head. For a sailor he had a remarkably delicate complexion, and these southern latitudes made things worse: his skin was forever turning red and flaking off. He was openly envious of Derec's adaptation to the climate: the sun had just browned the captain's skin and bleached his graying hair almost white.

Facer turned and took two steps toward the poop companionway, then stopped. "Sir," he said. "I think our convoy has just seen the enemy."

"Right. Cut along, Facer."

"Sir."

The Zhir convoy, arrayed in a ragged line just downwind of *Birdwing*, was now showing belated signs of alarm. Five minutes had passed before any of them noticed an entire enemy squadron sweeping up from two miles away. Derec had no illusions about the quality of the merchant captains: the convoy would scatter like chaff before a hailstorm. None of them was capable of outrunning a squadron of warships: their only chance was to scatter in all directions and hope only a few would fall victim to the enemy. Still, Derec should probably try to do something, at least to show the Zhir he'd tried to protect their cities' shipping.

"Signal to the convoy, Randem," he said. "Close up, then tack simultaneously."

The boy's look was disbelieving. "As you like, sir."

Derec gave him a wry grin. "For form's sake, Random."

"Aye aye, sir. For form's sake."

Signal flags rose on the halyards, but none of the convoy bothered an acknowledgment: the merchanters had no confidence in the ship's fighting abilities and were looking out for themselves. Derec shrugged. This was nothing more than he expected. At least they were clearing out and leaving an empty sea between *Birdwing* and the enemy.

Birdwing gave a shuddering roll as it staggered down the face of a wave; Derec swayed to compensate and almost lost his balance. His heavy breastplate and helmet were adding unaccustomed weight to his upper body. The helmet straps were pressing uncomfortably on his brass earrings, and the helmet was warming in the sun, turning into an oven.

Carefully Derec calculated his course and the enemy's. The wind was holding a point north of west: the convoy had been moving roughly north along the general trend of land. The enemy squadron was racing under oars and sail as close to the wind as their characteristics permitted: they were trying to gain as much westing as possible so as not to be pinned between *Birdwing* and the coast. Their course was more or less northwest: *Birdwing* was moving nor'-nor'east on a converging tack. Unless something prevented it, the ships would brush at the intersection of their paths; and then the enemy would be to windward of the *Birdwing*, which was just where they wanted to be.

At which point, Derec thought confidently, they were going to suffer a terrible surprise.

Birdwing's crew were already at quarters; they'd been doing a gun drill when the enemy appeared. There was nothing to do but wait.

"Wizard's compliments, sir." Facer was back, his leather-and-iron cap doffed at the salute. "The enemy is attempting a spell."

"Thank you, Facer." Suddenly the brisk warm breeze blew chill on Derec's neck. He turned to face the enemy, touched his amulet of Thurn Bel, and summoned his power.

Awareness flooded his mind. He could feel the protective shields that Levett, *Birdwing*'s wizard, had wound around the ship; from eastward he could feel a strong attempt to penetrate those shields. Derec called his power to him, but held it in reserve in case the onslaught was a feint. The attack faded grudgingly before Levett's persistent defense, then disappeared. Whatever it was, the probe had failed. Levett's protective spells remained intact, on guard.

That was the strategy Derec and Levett had formed weeks ago. The wizard's magic would remain defensive, and *Birdwing's* bronze cannon would bring the war to the enemy.

Derec let his hand fall from his amulet. He saw his officers standing around him expectantly; he gave them a smile. "Done," he said. "We're safe for the moment." He saw them breathe easier.

He looked at the enemy. Brightness winked from the enemy's decks: marines in their polished armor. He could hear the thud of kettledrums and crash of cymbals as the enemy quartermasters beat time for the rowers. A mile to leeward, in deeper, bluer water now, the galleasses were laboring in the steep sea, the smaller one having a particularly hard time of it.

Derec's awareness tingled: the enemy wizard was making another attempt. Derec monitored the assault and Levett's efforts to parry it. Once again the enemy was repulsed.

There was a flash from the flagship's fo'c'sle, then a gush of blue smoke that the wind tore into streamers across her bows. The thud came a half second later, followed by a shrieking iron ball that passed a half cable to larboard. The range was long for gunshot from the pitching deck of a ship beating to windward. Jeers rose from *Birdwing's* crew.

Another thud, this time from the smaller galleass, followed by another miss, this one coming close to clipping *Birdwing's* stern. The enemy were giving their gun crews something to do, Derec thought, rather than stand and think about what might come, their own possible mutilation and death.

There was a bump and a mild bang from *Birdwing's* maindeck, followed by a hoarse bellow. Derec stepped forward to peer over the poop rail; he saw one of the marines had stumbled and dropped his firelock, and the thing had gone off. Marcoyn, the giant marine lieutenant, jerked the man to his feet and smashed him in the face. The marine staggered down the gangway, arms windmilling: Marcoyn followed, driving another punch into the marine's face. Derec clenched his teeth. Hatred roiled in his belly.

"Marcoyn!" he bellowed. The lieutenant looked up at him, his pale eyes savage under the brim of his boarding helmet. His victim clutched the hammock nettings and moaned.

"No interference with the sojers!" Marcoyn roared. "We agreed that, *Captain!*" He almost spat the word.

Derec bit back his anger. "I was going to suggest, Marcoyn, that you blacken the man's eyes later. We may need him in this fight."

"I'll do more than blacken his eyes, by Thurn Bel!"

"Do as you think best, Marcoyn." Derec spoke as tactfully as possible;

but still he held Marcoyn's eyes until the marine turned away, muttering under his breath, his fists clenched at the ends of his knotted arms.

Marcoyn's strange pale eyes never seemed to focus on anything, just glared out at the world with uncentered resentment. He was a brute, a drunk, illiterate, and very likely mad, but he represented an element of *Birdwing*'s crew that Derec couldn't do without. Marcoyn was the living penalty, Derec thought, for the crimes he had committed for the ship he loved.

Derec remembered Marcoyn's massive arms twisting the garrote around young Sempter's neck, the way the boy's eyes had started out of his head, feet kicking helplessly against the mizzen pinrail, shoes flying across the deck. Derec standing below, helpless to prevent it, his shoes tacky with Lieutenant Varga's blood . . .

His mouth dry, Derec glanced at the mizzen shrouds, then banished the memory from his mind. The enemy had fired their bow chasers once more.

The smaller galleass fired first this time, followed a half second later by the flagship. Interesting, Derec thought. The smaller ship had the better crew.

A strong gust heeled the galleon and drove it through the sea. The waves' reflection danced brightly on the enemy's lateen sails. The enemy squadron was half a mile away. If the ships continued on their present courses, *Birdwing* would soon be alongside the enemy flagship in a yard-arm-to-yardarm fight, a situation ideal for the northern galleon.

Another pair of bangs, followed by a buzzing and a smack: the smaller galleass's ball had pitched right through *Birdwing*'s main topsail. Derec saw blond and redheaded countrymen looking up in surprise, heard nervous laughter. This was the first time most of them had been under fire. Derec realized he should probably say something now, offer an inspiring comment to drive any thoughts of fear out of his sailors' heads. He could think of nothing.

"Run out the starboard chaser!" he finally called. "We'll answer that!"

There were some scattered cheers, but Derec could see puzzled expressions. The enemy were within range of the broadside guns: why not open fire with the whole battery? Derec kept his counsel. He was saving the first broadside for close range.

The bronze starboard demiculverin rumbled as it thrust its muzzle from the port. Derec could see the gun captain bent low over the chaser's barrel, timing the ship's motion, linstock in his hand. There was a gush of fire from the priming, then a roar; the gun flung itself back like a monstrous bronze beast. Derec turned to leeward and saw the nine-pound ball skip on the waves like a dancer twenty yards ahead of the enemy's prow. A groan of disappointment went up from *Birdwing*'s crew.

"Chaser crew, fire at will!" Derec called.

The chasers banged at each other for another three or four rounds apiece. The Liavekans showed no sign of changing course: were they really going to let Derec lay alongside and fight exactly the kind of battle he wanted? Ignoring the artillery duel, Derec studied the enemy, the changing relationship between the ships. Tried to get into his enemy's head, wondered what the enemy admiral was thinking.

The sound of kettledrums and cymbals was very loud now, carrying clearly upwind. The enemy sweeps moved in beautiful synchrony, the blue water boiling at their touch. The distance between *Birdwing* and the lead enemy narrowed, and Derec was considering running out his starboard battery when flame blossomed from the enemy's sides and the air was full of shrieking. Derec's heart turned over at the sound of a slamming noise from below—a shot lodged home—followed by another smack as a ball tore through the fore topsail. The enemy had fired its full broadside, maybe ten guns in all.

His nerves wailing in surprise, Derec bit his lip and frowned at the enemy. Something had changed, but he couldn't say what. Something in the pattern of drumbeats and cymbals. Another level of his awareness sensed the enemy's magician attempting a spell. With a start he realized what the enemy intended.

"Hard a-starboard!" he roared, and ran to the break in the poop. Just below him, sheltered by the poop overhang, Sandor the timoneer controlled the ship's whipstaff. "Hard a-starboard!" Derec shrieked again, and he felt the change in the ship's motion that meant the timoneer had flung his weight against the whipstaff and the galleon was beginning to respond to its big rudder. Derec suddenly felt the nature of the enemy spell—it was an attempt to paralyze them for a few seconds, but Levett had parried it, again without the need for Derec's assistance. Derec glanced at the surprised faces of his crew.

"Both broadsides, load and run out! Starboard guns, load with double-shot! Larboard guns, load with roundshot!" He glanced at the enemy to confirm what he suspected, and found it true—the bright silhouettes were narrowing as one set of sweeps backed water while the other continued driving forward. Lateen sails billowed and snapped as the yards were dropped to the deck. The enemy were changing course, driving straight into the wind under the power of their sweeps alone.

Birdwing lurched as the waves caught it at a new angle. "Braces, there!" Derec shouted. "Rudder amidships!" The galleon filled with shouting and stamping as the crews bent to their work. Heart in his mouth, Derec gazed at the enemy.

The relationship between the ships had changed drastically. The enemy vessels had simultaneously turned straight into the wind while preserving their relationship to one another, from a line ahead into a line of bearing. They had attempted to cut behind the Farlander galleon, head upwind and into the convoy without the necessity of a fight. *Birdwing* had just turned downwind and within the next two minutes would pass along the flagship's starboard side. The ships would exchange broadsides on the run, and then race past one another.

If *Birdwing* were a caravel or high-charged galleon, that would have been the end of the fight: Derec could never have turned into the wind to pursue the enemy. The Liavekan admiral would have got between him and his convoy, a master stroke. But *Birdwing* was something the Liavekan hadn't seen, and savage exultation filled Derec as he realized he had the enemy in his hand.

There was a massive rumbling as the guns were run out, all fifty-four of them, heavy demicannon on the lower deck and lighter, longer culverins on the maindeck. Derec stood on the break in the poop and shouted through cupped hands.

"Larboard gun captains and second captains remain with your guns! All extra crew to the starboard guns!" Bare feet drummed the planks—the crew had practiced this many times. *Birdwing* didn't carry enough crew to efficiently fight both sides, and Derec wanted his starboard guns served well.

Enemy kettledrums thundered over the water. The purple-and-scarlet galleass was frighteningly close.

"Starboard broadside, make ready!" Derec shouted. "Fire on my order! Sail trimmers, stand by the braces! Timoneer—starboard a bit!" He'd pass alongside the enemy and drive *Birdwing* right through their starboard bank of sweeps if he could.

But abruptly the kettledrums made a flourish, then fell silent. The enemy sweeps rose like white teeth from the water, and then drew inward. The Liavekans were prepared for Derec's maneuver.

" 'Midships!" he called. And suddenly there was eerie silence—no kettledrums, no shouted orders, no guns running out, only the whisper of the wind and the deafening beat of Derec's pulse in his ears.

The galleass came alongside, and the guns spoke. The enemy fo'c'sle guns bellowed first, so close their fires licked *Birdwing*'s timbers, and the air filled with splinters and moaning shot. Then Derec shrieked "Fire!" and the galleon lurched as all its guns went off more or less together, from the demicannon on the lower decks to the little sakers and minions used by the marines. Abruptly there was a chorus of screams from the galleass as shot and splinters tore through the close-packed oarsmen— the weird and awful cries sounded clearly even to Derec's deafened ears. The enemy quarterdeck guns went off last, massive iron cannon firing fifty-pound stone shot that burst on impact and laid low a score of Marcoyn's marines.

But all that was anticlimax: as soon as *Birdwing*'s guns fired, Derec was shouting new orders. "Hard a-starboard! Starboard guns, reload! Larboard guns, fire as you bear!"

Kettledrums and cymbals punctuated Derec's cries: the enemy admiral's galleass was losing momentum, beginning to swing in the wind. They had to get under way, and quickly. Derec saw sweeps beginning to run out, and saw also that his salvo had blown gaping holes in the galleass's sides. The row-deck must be a shambles. Triumph filled his heart.

Suddenly he was aware of the pressure of an enemy spell. Levett seemed to be handling it; but suddenly there was another strike, moving fast as lightning, a white-hot flare in Derec's mind. Derec's own power lashed out without his conscious effort, turning the spell away. A hollow feeling overtook him as he realized the spell's nature: the enemy wizard had tried to set off the powder cartridges on the gundeck. The powder magazine itself was well guarded by spells renewed yearly, but the powder was vulnerable as the ship's boys carried it to the guns, as the gun crews ladled the cartridges into the breeches and rammed shot atop them. This closely engaged, explosions on the gundeck would be disastrous.

The purple galleass fell off the wind a bit before its sweeps finally struck the water. *Birdwing* turned like a dolphin under the enemy stern, the starboard guns running out again, barking as they drove iron lengthwise through the enemy, wreaking hideous destruction on the narrow enemy vessel. Derec pounded the taffrail, roaring encouragement to the guncrews. *Birdwing* was now close-hauled between the two enemy galleasses, and the larboard guns—manned inefficiently by two men apiece—fired as the smaller vessel came into line: the range was much longer, but Derec saw the foremast come down. The fully crewed starboard guns ran out again, driving another broadside into the admiral's port quarter. The kettledrums fell silent. Sweeps flailed the water in panic.

"Stations for tacking! Helm's a-lee!" Derec's heart beat fire: a blood-thirsty demon howled in his soul. He wanted the enemy smashed.

Birdwing pivoted on its heel like a dancer, running along the purple ship's larboard side. Two full broadsides lashed out; the enemy timbers moaned to the impact of shot. The mainmasts and mizzenmasts fell: the enemy rudder hung useless from its gudgeons. Nothing but small arms replied: the Liavekans hadn't reloaded their larboard guns after the first broadside, either because they hadn't the crew or hadn't thought it was necessary. Now they paid for their neglect.

The enemy flagship was left astern, a near-wreck pouring blood from its scuppers. *Birdwing* tacked again, heading for the smaller enemy; the lighter galleass had bravely turned toward the fight in an effort to succor its admiral. Useless: *Birdwing* forged ahead and yawed to fire one broad-side, then the other. The guns smashed enough enemy sweeps to stagger the galleass in the water; the next broadside brought the mainmast down along with the enemy colors.

Derec saw the third enemy vessel's colors coming down—the xebec had surrendered, even though it had stood away from the battle and might have got away.

Then there was silence, filled only with the gusting wind and the eerie sounds of the dying. Wreckage littered the sea: broken sweeps, jagged splinters, torn bodies of the dead. The enemy were drifting toward land: Derec would have to order them to drop an anchor, till he could jury-rig masts and get them under way.

Suddenly the silence was broken by cheers, *Birdwing*'s crew sending roar upon defiant roar into the sky.

Derec looked down at the capering men, laughing and dancing in the waist of the ship, dancing in the blood of their crewmates who lay where the enemy's shot had flung them.

Then he remembered the mutiny, the way the men had danced in the blood of their countrymen, and the taste of victory turned to bitterness in his mouth.

"Ah," said Prince Jeng. "My mutineer."

"Your serene and glorious Highness," Derec said, and fell to his knees, bowing low and raising his hands to his forehead.

Jeng was a balding man in his late thirties, tall for a Zhir, bearded and portly; he was heir to the throne, and head of the Regency Council while his father the king was ill and recuperating at the Obsidian Palace inland. It was Jeng who had intensified the undeclared naval war against

Liavek, and who as a means of forwarding his policy had welcomed *Birdwing* to Ka Zhir. This was Derec's first lone audience with the Prince—he had met Jeng twice before, but only as one petitioner among many.

Jeng seemed a bit surprised at Derec's submission.

"Rise, Captain SuPashto. This is an informal audience, after all. Would you like a sherbet on the terrace?"

"Thank you, Your Highness." Derec rose and suppressed a feeling of discomfort. Back in the Twin Kingdoms, on the continent the Zhir called Farland, he'd never had any dealings with high nobility, and despite Prince Jeng's hospitality he was not at home here. Derec was also uncomfortable in Prince Jeng's language: his tongue was rough, and he desperately wished for an interpreter.

Jeng's cool summer silks whispered on marble as Derec followed him to the terrace. The sherbets were already laid on a wrought-iron serving table: obviously the Prince had not expected Derec to refuse an offer of refreshment. Below the terrace, cliffs fell away to reveal the Inner Harbor of Ka Zhir.

A strong sea breeze blew through the palace, but below the harbor was windless. A hundred ships of burden stood on their perfect reflections in the still blue water. Among them, small guard boats scuttled like water spiders under oars. Thirty war galleys were drawn up on the shelving pebble beach of Great Kraken Island, safe beneath the guns and curtain walls of Fort Shzafakh, which was perched atop the old volcanic dome. Beyond, between the Inner and Outer harbors, thousands of slaves were toiling to build the New Mole, at the end of which a new defensive fortification would rise, one from which a massive chain could be raised to block the channel and keep the Inner Harbor safe. The new fort was coming to be known as Jeng's Castle, just as the intensified conflict with Liavek was gaining the name of Jeng's War. Neither term was official; but language was, in its inevitable fashion, reflecting the realities of power.

Jeng scooped up his sherbet in one broad paw and walked to a brass telescope set on the terrace. Touching it gingerly—the metal had grown hot in the sun—he adjusted the instrument and peered through it.

"Your conquests, Captain," he said. He stepped back from the telescope and, with a graceful gesture, offered Derec a look. Derec nodded his thanks and put his eye to the instrument.

The bright varnished galleass leaped into view, anchored in the Outer Harbor next to the xebec. The Zhir ensign floated over both, black-and-gold raised over the Liavekan blue. The admiral's purple galleass was just behind, drawn up on the shelving beach where it had been run aground to keep from sinking. *Birdwing*'s distinctive silhouette, a total contrast to every other vessel in the harbor, shimmered in a patch of bright, reflective water.

"I understand the xebec surrendered without a fight," Jeng commented. Derec straightened and faced the Prince. The sea breeze tugged at the Prince's cloth-of-gold silks.

"Yes, Your Highness. The xebec captain witnessed the loss of the two larger vessels and concluded that mighty wizardry was at work. He surrendered rather than be blasted to the bottom."

"But wizardry was not at work, was it?"

Derec shook his head. "Nay, sir. We had a wizard, and so did they; but the magics canceled each other out."

Jeng raised his delicate silver spoon to his mouth. "We have interrogated Tevvik, their wizard," he said, sipping sherbet as if it were wine, "and he confirms this. In return for his testimony, we have released him on parole."

Derec shrugged: the wizard's fate meant nothing to him.

"A pity that Admiral Bandur was killed in the fight. He might have brought you a large ransom."

"With Your Highness's blessing," Derec said slowly, staggering through the foreign phrases, "we will capture more admirals."

Prince Jeng smiled catlike and licked his spoon. "So you shall, Thung willing."

"If Your Highness will modify our privateer's license to permit us to cruise alone against the enemy . . . " Derec began, but Jeng frowned and held up a hand.

"There are those on the Council who say your victory was a fluke," Jeng said. "They say the winds were kind to you. What should I answer, Captain?"

Derec hesitated, an array of technical terms running through his head. How much did Jeng know of the sea? Ka Zhir depended on ships and trade for its livelihood, and Jeng was an intelligent man who took an interest in the affairs of the kingdom; but how much practical seamanship did the Prince know?

"Your Highness has seen galleons from the Two Kingdoms before, and from Tichen?"

Jeng nodded. "They come with the annual trading convoys, yes. My mariners do not think well of them."

"They are slow, yes. And cannot sail into the wind."

Jeng finished his sherbet and scoured the dish with his spoon. The sound grated on Derec's nerves. "So my advisors tell me. You say your ship is different."

"It is, Your Highness. We call it a *race-built* galleon," stumbling, having to fall into his own language, "to distinguish it from the old style, which we call *high-charged.*"

Jeng reached for a bell on the table and rang it. "Race-built?" he said. "Because it is faster?"

Derec was surprised at Jeng's conclusion: the Prince understood Derec's language better than he'd suspected.

"With respect, Your Highness, the root of the word is *razor,*" Derec said. "Because the upper decks, the high sterncastles and forecastles, are *razored* off. The race-built galleon is lower in profile, and also lighter, without the weight of the castles."

A servant appeared. The Prince ordered more sherbet, then looked at Derec and frowned. "The castles, my advisors tell me, are the galleon's great advantage in combat. The castles can hold many soldiers, and the soldiers can fire down into enemy ships."

"The castles also make a high profile, and a high profile can catch the wind. The wind catches the ship and tries to push it to leeward. This is called *leeway.* . . . "

Prince Jeng's eyes flashed. "Any Zhir child knows this, Captain. Please do not inform me of matters I learned at my mother's knee."

Derec's heart skipped a beat. He lowered his eyes and looked at Jeng's feet. "Your pardon, Your Highness. I was merely trying to make the point that with a lower profile, the race-built galleon makes much less leeway and is therefore able to point higher into the wind."

"Yes." Curtly. "Very well. I understand."

"Also, Your Highness, we have a new form of square sail called the birdwing. It's flatter, rather like your own lateen sail. Although it holds less air, it's somehow able to drive a ship nearer the wind."

Prince Jeng's sternness dropped away, replaced by frank curiosity. "Is that so? How can that be?"

Derec shrugged helplessly. "I do not know, Your Highness. It appears to be a property of the wind that we do not yet understand."

"It works, but you don't know why?" Jeng considered this. "I shall have to inquire of my philosophers. We know why the lateen works so well, of course—it's the triangular shape, which reflects the universality of the Triple Unities of Heart, Wit, and Spirit."

"Perhaps Captain-General Collerne understands these matters," Derec said, "I don't know. The birdwing sail had been in use on some of our smaller craft for two or three generations, but it was Captain-General Collerne who thought to use it on a warship. It was also his idea to raze the upper decks, after he noticed that some old ships that had their castles removed became better sailers." A fire kindled in Derec as he thought of his old captain and teacher. "He wanted to create a fleet taking its orders from *sailors*, not generals appointed to command at sea. A fleet that fights with broadside guns instead of rapiers and firelocks, that uses the wind and water to its own advantage . . . " His thick northern tongue stumbled on the Zhir words.

"Yes, yes," Jeng said. "That's all very well, but it's practical issues I'm concerned with." A servant arrived with another bowl of sherbet. He gave his catlike smile as he tasted the treat. Derec understood how the man had grown so stout.

"I am trying to speak practically, Your Highness," Derec said. "Your galleys and galleasses are built lightly, so they can be driven through the water by muscle power. Because they must have so many rowers, they must water and victual frequently, and they must stop and let the rowers off every few days, so that they won't sicken and die. If the enemy attacks while your ships are beached, your fleet is in grave jeopardy. Your ships can carry only a limited number of guns, because they are built lightly.

"Because it is powered by the wind, *Birdwing* is built stoutly and can resist punishment that would sink one of your galleys. Our holds are deeper and our crews are smaller, so that we can carry more provision and stay at sea much longer. *Birdwing* carries twenty-seven guns on each broadside, twice as many as your largest ship—and that's not counting sakers and minions. The Liavekans simply won't be able to stand up to a race-built ship, and a fleet of race-built craft will sweep them from the Sea of Luck. I'll stake my life on that, Your Highness."

Prince Jeng looked at him darkly. "You may have to, Captain Su-Pashto." Derec felt a cold touch on his neck. Prince Jeng took a deliberate sip of sherbet. "You are from a northern land, where political realities are somewhat different. Your King Torn is bound by custom and by the House of Nobles. There *is* no law of custom in Ka Zhir, Captain. The King is the law here, and in the absence of the King, the Regent."

"I understand, Your Highness."

Jeng's eyes were cold. "I think not, Captain. I think you do not comprehend the . . . *necessities* . . . of life in Ka Zhir." He turned, facing the Inner Harbor, and pointed with his silver spoon, an oddly delicate gesture in such a big man. "You see the New Mole, Captain? I ordered

that. One order, and thousands of slaves were set to work. Many of them
will die. I didn't have to apply to the Regency Council, I didn't have to
speak to a treasurer, I didn't have to get the permission of a House of
Nobles. I merely gave an order one fine morning—and behold, the slaves
die, and the mole is built."

"Yes, Your Highness."

"Perhaps our political character," Jeng said, turning philosophical, "is
derived from our volcanoes. They are unpredictable, inclined to sudden
violence, and prone to massacre. So are the Zhir. So is my family.

"I am a tyrant, Captain," he said. He turned back to Derec, and his
smile sent a chill through the northern man. "My very whim is law. I
am an educated man and am considered an enlightened tyrant by my
philosophers"—his smile was cynical—"but I would scarcely expect them
to say anything else, as I would then be compelled to have them crucified.
That is the problem with being a tyrant, you see—I can't *stop* being
tyrannical, even if inclined otherwise, because that would encourage
other would-be tyrants to take my place, and they would be worse. I am
not as great a tyrant as my father—he had his unsuccessful commanders
beheaded, and I only have them whipped, or make slaves of them. But
I promise *you*, Captain SuPashto," and here he pointed his spoon at
Derec, and the gesture could not have been more threatening if the
Prince had held a sword. "I promise you that if you fail me I will have
you killed."

Prince Jeng fell silent, and slowly ate two bites of sherbet. Derec said
nothing. From the moment he had entered into conspiracy with Marcoyn
and the two of them had raised the crew, he had expected nothing but
death.

Jeng looked at him curiously. "You do not fear death, northern man?
I can make the death unpleasant if I wish."

"My life is in your hands," Derec said. "I have always known this."

"Then you understand the essential character of our relationship."
Prince Jeng smiled. He finished his sherbet and put the bowl down, then
put his arm around Derec's shoulders and began to walk with him back
into the palace. "I have in mind to give you a squadron, Captain," he
said. "It will be under the nominal orders of a Zhir, but it will be yours
to command, and my admiral will understand this. Bring me back lots
of the Levar's ships, and I will favor you. You will be able to replace
those old brass earrings with rings of gold, and diamonds and emeralds
will gleam like reflective water on your fingers. Fail me, and . . . well,
why be morbid on such a lovely day?"

Derec's mind whirled. "Thank you, Your Highness," he stammered.
"I will send some slaves aboard to replace your casualties."
Derec hesitated. "I thank you, Your Highness. Could I not have
freemen? They—"
Jeng's tones were icy. "Slaves can pull ropes as well as anyone."
Derec sighed inwardly. Jeng would send his slaves aboard and collect
their share of the pay and prize money. The slaves would not work hard
and would prove cowardly, because they hadn't anything to fight for. It
was a persistent evil here, one Derec had hoped to avoid—but now he
must concede.
"I thank you, Your Highness. Strong men, if you please."
"No women? Not one?"
"Women are not as strong. On a galleon, the sailors must move heavy
cannon, and fight the yards when the sails are filled with wind. . . ."
"Really? But surely there are less physical tasks. Scrubbing the planks,
or cooking, or serving the officers."
"Then there are discipline problems, Your Highness. If you will look
at the complaints in your navy, I'm sure you'll find more than half
having to do with officers playing favorites among their prettier
crewmates."
"But how do your sailors keep warm at night?"
Derec smiled. "Abstinence makes them . . . fiercer fighters, Your
Highness."
Prince Jeng looked shocked. "I would never deprive my men and
women of their pleasures, Captain. They're prone enough to disobedience
as it is. But if you *insist* on your barbaric customs . . ." He shrugged.
"The least I can do is rescue *you* from this cold regime—one of my
commanders must learn to enjoy life, yes? Until your ship is ready, you
will stay in the palace and accept my hospitality. I will send a woman
to your room tonight." He hesitated. "You *do* like women, yes?"
"Ah. Yes, Your Highness."
"You *did* make me wonder, Captain. Perhaps you would prefer more
than one?"
Derec was surprised. "One is generally sufficient."
Jeng laughed. "I'm unused to such modesty. Very well. One it
is."
"Thank you, Your Highness. For everything."
The Prince had steered Derec back to the audience chamber, and he
dropped his arm and stepped back. "The majordomo will show you to
an apartment."

"Thank you, Your Highness." Derec knelt again, raising his hands to his forehead.

"One more thing, SuPashto."

"Your Highness?"

Prince Jeng was smiling his catlike smile. "No more mutinies, Captain."

A day later, coming aboard *Birdwing*, Derec was surprised to meet the Liavekan wizard, Tevvik, at the entry port. The pleasant-looking young man smiled and bowed, his expression cheerful. Derec nodded curtly and stepped below to his own wizard's hot, airless cabin. He rapped on the flimsy partition.

"Enter." Derec stepped in to find Levett sitting in his bunk, reading a Zhir grammar by the light of a tallow candle. Derec stood over him.

"I've come for my lesson, wizard," he said.

Levett was a short, thin man. Though he was young, his hair and beard were white. Diamond chips glittered in his hoop earrings. His green eyes studied Derec.

"As you like, Captain. I was just chatting with a colleague. Tevvik's an interesting man. Shall we go to your cabin?"

Derec turned and moved down the passageway to his cabin. The stern windows were open, providing relief from the heat. Flitting reflections danced on the deckhead above.

"I have been comparing notes with Tevvik," Levett offered.

"The Liavekan."

"He's Tichenese, actually. That's why he's so dark. It was a matter of chance that he was in the Liavekan navy—it might as easily have been Ka Zhir, or the Two Kingdoms. He's seeking adventure and foreign lands; he doesn't care whom he serves. He's on parole; now he'll set up on his own, here in town. Of course," Levett said rather deliberately, "he has no family. No one depending on him. He can afford to wander."

Derec sat at his table and held the wizard's eyes for a long moment. The wizard looked away.

"I have promised you your liberty, wizard. As soon as I know your weather spells."

"I have never doubted your word, Captain."

"Just my ability to keep it."

Levett said nothing.

"This situation was not of my making, Levett," Derec said. "I'm sorry you are without your wife and family; I know you love them dearly. As soon as I can spare you, you will be free to take the first ship north. With money in your pocket."

Levett licked his lips. "They will call me a mutineer."

"The mutiny was mine, wizard."

"I understand. You were left no choice. I had no choice myself—when the fighting broke out, I wrapped myself in illusion and hid."

"You had no part in the mutiny, true enough."

"Those in authority at home . . . may not understand."

"There would have been a mutiny in any case. My choice was to try to control it, lest everyone die."

The finest ship in the Two Kingdoms' fleet, Derec thought bitterly, and the man who had conceived it, fought for its building, sweated through its construction—Captain-General Collerne—had been denied command. Instead *Birdwing* received a courtier from the capital, Captain Lord Fors, and his venomous lieutenant, Grinn . . . and within two months, with their policy of vicious punishments mixed with capricious favoritism, they had destroyed the morale of the crew and driven them to the brink of violence. Derec—who as a commoner had risen to the highest rank available to the lowborn, that of sailing master—had tried to stand between the captain and his crew, had tried to mitigate the punishments and hold the crew in check, but had only been mocked for his pains and threatened by Grinn with a beating. A sailing master, the senior warrant officer on the ship, flogged . . . the threat was unheard of, even in a service accustomed to violence.

After that, Derec knew that mutiny was only a matter of time. Derec approached Marcoyn first—the man was constantly in trouble, but he was a fighter. Derec then chose his moment, and as an officer had the keys to the arms chests: Fors and Grinn both died screaming, begging for their lives as maddened crewmen hacked at them with swords and pikes. Lieutenant Varga, a good officer who had been appalled by his captain's conduct, had nonetheless tried to rescue Fors, and was stabbed and flung bodily into the sea for his pains.

Derec had tried to hold the killings to three, but the mutineers got into the liquor store and things soon ran out of control. The ship's corporal died, bludgeoned to death in the hold; another dozen, known captain's favorites or those suspected of being informers, were killed. Marcoyn had led the blood-maddened crewmen on their hunt for enemies, had hung the remaining lieutenants and a fourteen-year-old midshipman, Sempter, from the mizzen shrouds, and there garroted them one by one. Derec had stood by underneath, watching the starting eyes and kicking heels, helpless to prevent it—he was the ship's sailing master, another officer, and if he'd objected he would have danced in the shrouds with the others.

After the crew had sobered, Derec had been able to reassert his authority. Levett, who had hidden during the mutiny, had lent supernatural influence to Derec's command. Now Derec was captain, and had chosen his officers from among the bosun's and master's mates. Marcoyn, who was illiterate and could not navigate, had been given the marines, whose morale and efficiency he was in the process of ruining with a brutality and capriciousness as hardened as that of Captain Lord Fors.

"You have done as well as you could, Captain," Levett said. "But now that you possess the royal favor, can you not do without me?"

Derec looked up at him. "Not yet, wizard. You are the best windspeller I know."

Levett was silent for a time, then shrugged. "Very well. Let us go about our lessons, then."

Derec reached inside his shirt for his amulet of Thurn Bel. The wizard seated himself. "Clear your mind, Captain," he said, "and summon your power. We shall try again."

Drained, his lesson over, Derec stepped onto the poop and nodded briskly to Random, the officer of the watch. Moaning through the rigging and rattling the windsails was the fitful wind that he had, at great effort, succeeded in summoning. Not much to show for three hours' effort.

He stepped to the stern and gazed over the taffrail at the lights of Ka Zhir. His eyes moved to the cliffs above, where his apartment and his harlot waited in Jeng's palace. She would be disappointed tonight, he thought; the wizardry had exhausted him.

Time to call his barge and head ashore. The order poised on his lips, he turned to head back for the poop companion. He froze in his tracks, terror lurching in his heart.

Dark forms dangled from the mizzen shrouds, their legs stirring in the wind. Tongues protruded from blackened lips. Pale eyes rolled toward Derec, glowing with silent accusation.

Wrenching his eyes from the sight, Derec looked at Random, at the other men on deck. They were carrying on as normal. The ghosts were invisible to them.

Derec looked again at the dead and stared in horror at young Sempter, the boy swinging from the shrouds with the garrote still knotted about his neck.

The dead had risen, risen to curse him.
He was doomed.

Drums and cymbals beat time as Derec's rowing squadron backed gracefully onto the shelving pebble beach of Ka Zhir's Outer Harbor. *Birdwing*,
a damaged galleass in tow, dipped its ensign to its nominal Zhir admiral.
The galleass had lost its rudder in an autumn storm, had broached-to
and been pounded before the rowers got it under way again. *Birdwing*
was continuing to the Inner Harbor, to deliver its crippled charge to the
Royal Dockyard.

"Keep the Speckled Tower right abeam till the octagonal tower comes
in line," the Zhir pilot said. "Then alter course three points to larboard
to clear the New Mole."

"Aye aye, sir," said the timoneer.

The sound of anchors splashing echoed over the bay, followed by the
roar of cable. The squadron's three prizes, all round-bowed merchantmen, had just come to rest. Derec, looking out over the taffrail, saw the
crippled galleass slew sideways in a gust, then come to a sharp check at
the end of the hawser. *Birdwing* gave a brief lurch as the cripple's weight
came onto the line.

The bonaventure flapped overhead as *Birdwing* turned gracefully to
larboard. A ghastly stench passed over the quarterdeck, and Derec hawked
and spat. Ka Zhir used slaves in some of their ships, and they were
chained to the benches and lay in their own filth—the smell was incredible. Derec turned away from the galleass and faced forward, his eyes
automatically giving a guilty glance to the mizzen shrouds. His mind
eased as he saw the clear, tarred black hawser cutting through the bright
blue tropical sky.

Over his voyages of the last six months, the ghosts had returned many
times, every few days, sometimes in broad daylight. Usually Derec saw
them hanging in the mizzen rigging, but on occasion he'd see them elsewhere: Lieutenant Varga, his wounds pouring blood, his hair twined with
seaweed as he watched Derec from amid the crew as the hands witnessed
punishment; the ship's corporal, his skull beaten in, sitting on the main
crosstrees and laughing through broken teeth as the ship went through gun
drill; and once, most horribly, Derec had entered his cabin at dinnertime
only to find Midshipman Sempter sitting at his place, gazing at him over
his meal, his mouth working silently as he tried to speak past the garrote.
Derec's steward had watched in amazement as the captain bolted the
room, then returned later, sweating and trembling, to find the ghost gone.

Nothing untoward had ever happened: Derec's luck on his voyages had been good. Admiral Zhi-Feng, Derec's nominal superior, was an intelligent man, and on Prince Jeng's orders had diffidently followed Derec's advice; he was learning quickly, and had recommended that *Birdwing*'s lines be taken by draftsmen so that an entire squadron of race-built galleons might rise on the Royal Dockyard's stocks. Five galleons were a-building and would be ready by spring. Derec had fought three engagements with Liavekan squadrons and won them all, capturing two galleasses, four galleys, and a number of smaller craft; he had sent in over forty merchant ships as prizes. Corrupt and slow though Ka Zhir's prize courts were, they had made Derec a wealthy man: the strongbox he kept beneath the planks in his sleeping cabin was crammed with gold and jewels. Prince Jeng's War was proving successful, much to the discomfort of Liavek. With an entire squadron of galleons, Derec had no doubt the Liavekan navy would be swept from the seas.

Derec glanced up at the royal palace, the white walls on the tall brown cliffs, and frowned at the sight of the flag that flapped from its staff. Something was wrong there. He stepped to the rack, took a glass, and trained it on the flag. The Royal Standard leaped into view. Derec took a breath.

So King Thelm was back, having presumably recovered from his illness. Jeng would no longer be Regent; absolute power had now passed to his father. He wondered at the alteration's implication for himself, for *Birdwing*, and decided there would be little change. Thelm might negotiate an end to the war, but still *Birdwing* and Derec had proven themselves over and over again: Thelm wouldn't throw away such a strategic asset.

"Bel's sandals!" SuKrone's curse brought Derec's eyes forward. Amazement crackled in his mind.

Birdwing had rounded the fortification at the end of the New Mole, and the entire Inner Harbor was opened to view. The harbor was full of the tall masts and dark rigging of a northern fleet, the huge round-bellied caravels that brought metals, pitch, and turpentine to Ka Zhir every autumn, returning with sugar, kaf, and spices; and riding to anchor were northern warships, three high-charged galleons and one leaner, lower shape, a race-built galleon like *Birdwing*, but longer, showing thirty gunports each side.

Floating above each ship was a green ensign with two gold crowns, the flag of Derec's homeland.

They had come early this year, and caught Derec unprepared.

The scent of death swept over the poop. It was just the smell of the galleass, Derec thought; but still his spine turned chill.

"What do we *do*, Captain?" Marcoyn's mad eyes were wild. Drunkenly, he shook his fist in Derec's face. "What the piss do we *do?* They're going to have us kicking in the rigging by nightfall!"

Birdwing was still moving toward the Inner Harbor, a party of men standing in the forecastle ready to drop the best bower. Derec was looking thoughtfully over the rail. One of the big galleons—Derec recognized the *Sea Troll*—had storm damage: one topmast was gone. The *Double Crowns* was missing its castles: they had presumably been razored in an effort to make it as light and handy as *Birdwing*. *Monarch*, the other high-charged galleon, stood closest, towering over every ship in harbor and carrying eighty guns. But it was the other race-built ship that had an admiral's red pennant flying from its maintruck, and it was to this ship that Derec's eyes turned. *Torn II*, he thought: so they had built her, and sent her here to find her precursor.

"Captain! Answer, damn you!" Marcoyn staggered, not from the heave of the deck but from his liquor.

Derec turned his eyes on the man and tried to control the raging hatred he felt. "We will wait, Mr. Marcoyn," he said.

"You've got to *do* something!" Marcoyn raged. "You know Prince Jeng! *Talk* to him!"

Derec looked at Marcoyn for a long moment. Marcoyn dropped his unfocused eyes, then his fist.

"We fight under the flag of Ka Zhir," Derec said, indicating the ensign flying overhead. "We have Zhir protection. The trading fleet is here, aye, but it's under the two hundred guns of Fort Shzafakh and another two hundred on the mainland. They *daren't* attack us, Marcoyn. Not openly."

Marcoyn chewed his nether lip as he thought this over. "Very well, SuPashto," he said.

Derec stiffened. "*Captain* SuPashto, if you please, Mr. Marcoyn."

Marcoyn's eyes blazed dull hatred. "*Captain*," he spat. He saluted and turned away.

The other crewmen, the small, dark Zhir standing beside the tall, fair Farlanders, had watched the confrontation, trying hard to conceal their rising fear. Derec's quiet tones had seemed to calm them. He stepped forward to the break in the poop.

"They daren't touch us, boys!" he shouted. "Not openly. But there

will be Two Kingdoms men ashore on leave, and for now we'll have no
shore parties. When we *must* send parties ashore, we will go armed and
in large groups. Now," he ventured a ragged grin, "let's show them what
we've learned. As soon as our anchor's down, I want those sails harbor-
furled, without a dead man in 'em; I want our old chafing-gear down;
and I'll have some parties detailed to renew our gilding. Mr. Facer, see
to it."

"Yes, sir."

Derec nodded curtly and stepped to the weather rail. He watched the
northern fleet grow closer.

The admiral's summons came at sunset. Derec was half expecting it; he'd
seen Zhi-Feng's barge take him ashore to his quarters in the Lower Town.
Derec put on his best clothes, strapped on his rapier, and thrust a pair
of pistols in his belt. He called for his gig and had himself rowed to the
admiral's apartments.

The admiral was dressed in a gorgeous silk robe, and his hair and
beard had been curled and perfumed. Gemstones clustered on his fingers.
He drank wine from a crystal goblet as big as his head. His belt had scales
of gold.

Derec scarcely noted this magnificence, his attention instead riveted
on the admiral's other visitor, a portly man plainly dressed. He fell to
his knees and raised his palms to his forehead.

"Rise, Captain," said Prince Jeng. "Forgive this melodrama, but I
thought it best not to let anyone know we had met." He sat in a heavy
cushioned chair, eating red licorice. Derec rose. Jeng looked at him and
frowned.

"Problems are besetting the two of us, Captain SuPashto," he said.
"The same problems, actually. My father, and the trading fleet."

"I trust in your guidance, Highness."

Jeng seemed amused. "That's more than *I* can say, Captain. Neither
I nor anyone else really expected His Encompassing Wisdom to recover,
and I'm afraid the old man's found my regency a bit... premature...
in diverting from his policies. He didn't want a naval war with Liavek
in his old age, and now he's got one, and if the war hadn't been so
successful, half the Council would have got the chop." Jeng grimly raised
the edge of his hand to his throat. "But since we're winning," he added,
"he's not sure what to do. At this point I think we'll fight on, so long as
we stay ahead." He picked up a stick of licorice and pointed it at Derec
like a royal scepter. "That makes you valuable to him, and so you may

thank your victories for the fact that you and Zhi-Feng haven't been beheaded on your own quarterdecks."

"I owe my victories to your kindness and support," Derec said. "May Thung preserve Your Highness."

"Thank you for your concern, SuPashto, but I doubt I'm in real danger," Jeng said. "I'm the only heir the old man's got left. The first went mad, the second died trying to invest his luck, the third played a losing game with His Scarlet Eminence and got his neck severed for losing. . . . There's no one left but me. The worst that will happen to me, I think, is exile to an island. It's everyone around me who'll lose his head." He smiled. "His Encompassing Wisdom might want to perpetrate a massacre just to show everyone he's back."

Zhi-Feng looked a little green. "Gods keep us from harm," he murmured.

Jeng chewed meditatively on his licorice wand. "The problem presented by my shining and beloved ancestor, may Thung preserve him, may be finessed," he said. "The problem of your trading fleet is not so easily dealt with. Briefly, they want you dead."

"I expect no less, Highness."

"They have demanded that you and your ship be turned over to them. This demand has thus far been refused. You are too valuable to the war effort."

Derec felt his tension ease. "I thank Your Highness."

Jeng's eyebrows rose. "I had little to do with it, Captain. His Encompassing Wisdom cares little for my counsel these days. We may thank the old man's common sense for that—he's not going to throw away the war's biggest asset, not without some thought, anyway. No, the problem is that your northern admiral is proving damnably clever."

"May I ask which admiral, Your Highness?"

"I have heard you speak of him. One Captain-General Collerne."

A cold wind touched Derec's spine. For the first time in this interview he felt fear. "Aye," he said. "A clever man indeed."

"You know him well?"

"My first captain. Brilliant. He designed *Birdwing* and taught me everything I've learned about the sea. He got me my master's warrant. He's the best sailor I know."

Jeng looked at Derec coldly. "I'd advise you to leave off this admiration and learn to hate him, Captain SuPashto. He wants your hide, and he won't leave the Sea of Luck without it."

Yes, Derec thought, that was Collerne. Brilliant, unforgiving, a demon for discipline. He would not countenance mutiny, not even against the evil man who had supplanted him in his longed-for command.

"I must trust to Your Highness's protection," Derec said simply.

Jeng's eyes were shards of ice. "My protection is worth little. Let me tell you what your damned captain-general did. Once he realized we wouldn't give you up because of your value to the war, he offered to fight in your place. In exchange for you and the other ringleaders, he's offered us his two best ships, *Torn II* and *Double Crowns*, to fight under our license and flag for the next year. Collerne himself has offered to command them." Jeng sucked his licorice wand. "The implication, I believe, is that if we refuse him, he'll offer his ships to Liavek instead."

Derec's mouth turned dry. "Can he do that, Your Highness? Does his commission extend that far?"

"If it doesn't, he's taking a remarkable amount of initiative. The fact is, he's made the offer, and the King's considering it."

"Highness," the admiral said. There was sweat on his perfumed brow. "We—Captain SuPashto and I—we have experience in this war. We've fought together for six months. Our crews are well drilled and every man is worth three of this Collerne's."

Jeng looked bleak. "I shall attempt to have some friends on the Council point this out to His Encompassing Wisdom. But in the meantime I'll try to get you both out of the harbor. If Collerne can't find you, he can't kill you."

"Very well, Your Highness," said Zhi-Feng. He looked somewhat less anxious.

"Your fleet is ready?"

"We need only take on water," Derec said. "*Birdwing* has six months' provision. The rowing fleet carries victuals only for six weeks, but we can take food from captured ships if necessary. Or buy it ashore."

"I will have water-lighters alongside at dawn," Jeng said. He threw down his licorice and straightened. "I'll try to . . . persuade the harbor master to send you a pilot. If he's not aboard by nightfall, warp your way out the back channel. I'm afraid now the New Mole's completed, the chain bars the main channel at sunset, so you can't escape that way."

"Your Highness is wise." The admiral bowed.

Jeng's face turned curious. He looked at Derec. "How do they treat mutineers in your navy, SuPashto?" he asked.

"They are tied to the mast of a small boat," Derec said, "rowed to each ship in the squadron and flogged in view of each ship's company. Then they are taken to the admiral's ship, hung from the mizzen shrouds, and disemboweled. Before they can die they are garroted. Then their bodies are preserved with salt and hung in an iron cage till they weather away."

"That sounds most unpleasant," Jeng said mildly. "Were I you, I would provide myself with poison. When the time comes, you can cheat your countrymen out of some of their fun." He shrugged. "Life is full of experiences, my philosophers tell me, but I think I can attest that some are best avoided."

Desolation stirred in Derec like a rising autumn gale. "I will follow your advice in all things, Highness," he said.

When he returned to the ship, Derec didn't look up. He knew the ghosts were there, dark shadows that smiled at his approaching doom.

The water-lighters arrived just before dawn, and just afterward a messenger from the palace. *Birdwing* was to remain at anchor in the Inner Harbor until the complication with the Two Kingdoms fleet was resolved. If the galleon moved, she would be fired on by every gun on Great Kraken Island.

There was a hush on the *Birdwing* after that. Derec bought fresh food and wine from lighters offering wares alongside—he never let the hucksters aboard, fearing Two Kingdoms agents—and he kept the crew at their tasks, brightening the ship's paint and overhauling the running rigging; but the men were subdued, expectant. Dark shapes hung in the shrouds, filling the air with the stench of death. Red stains bubbled silently on the white holystoned planks. Derec kept his eyes fixed firmly on the horizon and sent the wizard ashore to buy poison. Levett returned with a vial of something he said was strong enough to kill half the crew.

On the evening of the second day, the summons from court arrived. Derec was ready. He spoke briefly with his officers concerning what was to be done after he left, put on his best clothing, and dropped two small pistols in his pockets.

With an escort of the Zhir Guard, quaintly old-fashioned in their ancient plumed helmets, he was rowed to the quay, then taken in a palankeen up the steep cliffs to the palace. There were new heads above the gate, illuminated by torches: a pair of the Council had died just that afternoon. The wall beneath them was stained with red. Local witches clustered beneath, hoping to catch the last of the ruddy drops in order to make their potions. A chamberlain took Derec through the halls to an anteroom.

"Wait within," the chamberlain said, raising his palms to his forehead.

"His Everlasting and All-Encompassing Wisdom will grant you audience as soon as the Council meeting has concluded."

"May Thung protect His Majesty," Derec answered. He turned to the door.

"I shall send refreshment," the chamberlain said. Derec opened the door, stepped inside, and froze.

Glowing eyes turned their cold light on him. The ghosts were there, Varga with blood and seawater dripping from his clothes, the corporal with brains spattered over his clothing, the others with blackened faces and starting eyes, the garrotes twisted about their necks. Terror poured down Derec's spine.

Young Sempter stood before Derec, five paces away. His brass-buttoned jacket, too big for him, hung limply on his boyish frame. His feet, the feet that had kicked their shoes off as he died, were bare. There was a hole in one stocking. Sempter's mouth worked in his beardless face, and he took a step forward. Derec shrank back. The boy took a step, and another. His pale hand came up, and it closed around Derec's amulet of Thurn Bel. He tugged, and the thong cut into Derec's neck like a garrote. Derec smelled death on the boy's breath. The boy tugged again, and the amulet came free.

"Take him," Sempter said, and smiled as he stepped back.

Strong hands closed on Derec's arms. His pistols and his vial of poison were pulled from his pockets. His rapier was drawn from its sheath.

The image of Sempter twisted like that in a distorting mirror, faded, became that of Levett. The others were Zhir Guard. Their officer was holding Derec's sword.

Levett held up the amulet of Thurn Bel. "Never let another mage know where you keep your power, Captain," he said. He pocketed the amulet. "The rest of his men will surrender easily enough. They're fools or boys, all of them."

Derec's mind whirled as cuffs were fastened before him on his wrists. A chain was passed from the shackles between Derec's legs. The Guard officer unfolded a scroll and began to read.

"By order of King Thelm and the Council, Captain Derec SuPashto is placed under arrest. The Royal Authority is shocked"—she was remarkably straight-faced in conveying the King's surprise—"to discover that Derec SuPashto is a mutineer and rebel. He is commanded to the Tiles Prison under close guard, until he can be turned over to Two Kingdoms justice." She rolled up the scroll and placed it in her pocket. Her face was expressionless. "Take the prisoner away."

Derec looked at Levett. Mist seemed to fill his mind. "There were never any ghosts," he said dully.

Levett looked at him. "Illusions only," he said.

The man behind Derec tugged on the chain. Derec ignored it. "You planned this," Derec said. "All along."

"Something like it." Levett looked at him from three paces away, the distance beyond which Derec could not manipulate any power stored in the amulet. "I regret this, Captain. Necessity compelled me, as it compelled you during the mutiny. I want to return to our homeland and to live in peace with my family. Collerne can guarantee that, and you can't."

The guard, impatient, tugged hard on Derec's chain. Pain shot through Derec's groin. He bent over, tears coming to his eyes.

"This way," the guard said. Stumbling, Derec let himself be dragged backward out of the room. A push sent him staggering forward. With five of the Guard and Levett, he was marched from the palace, beneath the dripping heads of traitors and into the night.

No palankeen waited: he would walk down the long switchback path to the Lower Town, then through town to the prison. The cool night breeze revived him. The officer lit a torch and gave it to one of her men. The party was silent save for the clink of the guards' chain coifs as they walked.

The Lower Town was growing near, tall buildings shuttered against the violence of the streets. Anyone with sense went armed here, and in company. Derec began to murmur under his breath. The party passed into the shadows of the crowded buildings. The street lamps were out, smashed by vandals. Derec's heart beat like a galley's kettledrum.

A pike lunged from an alley and took the Guard officer in the side. A dark body of men boiled from the darkness. The shackles dropped from Derec's wrists, and he lunged for the guard to his right, drew the main gauche from the man's belt, and slid it up under the chain coif to cut the astonished man's throat. Feet pounded the cobbles. Steel thudded into flesh. The torch fell and went out. Derec spun, seeing in the starlight the stunned look on the guard who was suddenly holding an empty chain where once a prisoner had been. The dagger took him in the heart, and he died without a sound.

A dark figure reeled back: Levett, already dead from a rapier thrust through both lungs. Marcoyn's bulk followed him, boarding axe raised high; and then the axe came down. Derec turned away at the sound of the wizard's head being crushed. Facer stepped out of the darkness, his face sunburned beneath his leather-and-iron cap, his sword bloody.

"Are you well, Captain?"

"Aye. Good work. Drag the bodies into the alleys where the City Runners won't find them."

"Fucking traitor." There were more thudding sounds as Marcoyn drove the axe into Levett again and again. Finally the big man drew back, grinning as he wiped a spatter of blood from his face. Liquor was on his breath.

"Got to make sure a wizard's dead," he grunted. "They're tricky."

"Best to be certain," Derec said, his mind awhirl. He'd posted the men here and knew what was coming, but the fight had been so swift and violent that he needed a moment to take his bearings. He looked at the dead wizard and saw, in the starlight, the amulet of Thurn Bel lying in the dust of the alleyway. He bent and picked it up. *Never let another mage know where you keep your power*, Levett had said; and Derec had always followed this prescription, though Levett never knew it. He'd invested his power in one of his brass earrings, one so old and valueless that no captor looting valuables would ever be tempted to tear it from his ear.

The bodies were dragged into the alley, piled carelessly atop one another. Wind ruffled Derec's graying hair: somewhere in the melee, he'd lost his cap. "To the ship, Captain?" Facer asked. He held out Derec's sword and the Guard officer's brace of wheellock pistols.

Derec passed the sword belt over his shoulder and rammed the pistols in his waistband. "Not yet," he said. "We have another errand first." He grinned at Facer's anxiety. "We have to wait an hour for the tide in any case, Lieutenant."

"Yes, sir." Doubtfully.

He led them through the empty streets of the Lower Town. Even the taverns were shut. Working people lived here, dockworkers and warehousemen: they didn't roister long into the night. Derec searched for one narrow apartment, found it, knocked on the door.

"Who is it?" A young, foreign voice.

"Captain SuPashto of the *Birdwing*."

"A moment."

The Tichenese wizard, Tevvik, opened the door, a lamp in his hand. His long hair was coiled on his head, held in place by a pin in the shape of a blue chipmunk. He recognized Derec and smiled. "An unexpected pleasure, Captain," he said. His Zhir was awkward.

"We're sailing for Liavek immediately. You're to accompany us."
Tevvik looked surprised. "I'm to be exchanged?"
"Something like that."
Tevvik thought about this for a moment, and shrugged. "I think I'd rather stay, Captain. I've developed a profitable business here."
From over his shoulder, Derec heard Marcoyn's growl. Derec was tempted to echo it. Instead he decided to be frank. "We're escaping arrest," he said. "You're accompanying us because you're a water wizard."
Tevvik's eyes widened. "You mean I'm being *abducted?*" He seemed delighted by the news.
"Aye. You are."
The wizard laughed. "That puts a different complexion on matters, Captain. Of course I'll accompany you. Do I have time to fetch my gear?"
"I'm afraid not."
Tevvik shrugged, then blew out his lamp. "As you like, Captain."
The waterfront district was a little more lively: music rang from taverns, whores paraded the streets, and drunken sailors staggered in alleyways looking to be relieved of their money. Derec and his party moved purposefully to the quay, then took the waiting barge to the galleon.
"Everything's prepared, Captain," Facer said. "We've cleared for action and the men are at quarters. The yards are slung with chains, the cable's ready to slip, the sails can be sheeted home in an instant, and we aren't showing any lights."
"Has the other party found our pilot?"
"SuKrone's got her under guard in the gunroom."
"Very good."
The boatmen tossed oars and Derec jumped for the entry port. He stepped onto the maindeck and sensed rather than saw his crew massed beneath the stars. He mounted the poop, then turned to face them. "We're running for Liavek, men," he said. "I have reason to believe they will welcome us."
There was a stirring ended swiftly by the petty officers' voices calling for silence.
"Those of you who were slaves," Derec said, "are now free."
Now there was an excited chattering that took the officers some time to quiet. Derec held up a hand.
"You may have to fight to keep that freedom, and that within the hour. Now—quietly—go to your stations. No drums, no noise. Facer, fetch me the pilot."

Derec leaned against the poop rail, pulled the big horse pistols from his waistband, and carefully wound the spring-driven locks. He was aware of the Tichenese wizard standing by, watching him. "Do you know weather magic, wizard?"

"Some. It is not my specialty."

"What is?"

"Fireworks. Explosions. Illusion."

"Can you make *Birdwing* look like something else?"

"Your ship is a little large for that. Perhaps I could cloak it in darkness. The darkness will not be absolute, but it may make its outlines less clear."

"Very well. Do so."

Facer and SuKrone pushed the pilot up the poop ladder. She was a small, dark woman, her head wrapped in a kind of turban. She was dressed in the house robe she'd been wearing when SuKrone's men had kidnapped her. Derec pointed one of his pistols at her, and he heard her intake of breath.

"Take us out by the back channel," he said coldly. "If you fail me, I will shoot you twice in the belly. Follow my instructions, and I'll put you over the side in a small boat once we're clear."

The pilot bowed, raising her palms to her forehead. "I understand, Your Excellency. But we must await the tide."

"Half an hour."

"Thereabouts, yes."

"Do not fail me." He gestured with the pistol. "Stand over there."

"Your obedient servant, Excellency."

"Wizard, Facer, come with me." Derec stepped forward off the poop, along the gangway, climbed the fo'c'sle. The land breeze brought the sound of music and laughter from the town. Derec looked to starboard, where the twisting back channel between Great Kraken Island and the mainland was invisible in the darkness. Glowing softly in the night, masthead riding lights stood out against the black.

"There's our problem," he said. "*Double Crowns* is moored right near the entrance to the passage. We'll have to pass within half a cable."

Facer pursed his lips, blew air hesitantly. "They've lookouts set for us, I'm sure. They know we want to run. And if they give the alarm, Shzafakh's bastions will blow us to bits."

"My darkness won't cover us *that* well, Captain," the wizard said. He was speaking easily in Derec's own language, and with a native accent: apparently he'd spent time in the Two Kingdoms.

"We can't fire on them without raising an alarm," Derec mused. "We can't run aboard them without calling attention to ourselves." He shook his head. "We'll just have to run past and hope for a miracle."

"Captain . . . " Tevvik's tone was meditative. "If we can't pass without being noticed, perhaps we can make people notice something other than ourselves."

"What d'ye mean, wizard?"

"Perhaps I can cause an explosion aboard *Double Crowns*. Then maybe the gunners in Shzafakh will think we're running from a fire, not for freedom."

Derec scowled. "The magazine is protected against spells."

"I'm sure. But powder in the open is not."

"They would not have cartridges in the open—it's all held in the magazine till needed. Don't waste my time with these notions, wizard."

"I was suggesting a boat full of powder nestled under that ship's stern. I can make *that* go off well enough."

Astonishment tingled in Derec's nerves. He tried not to show it; instead he stroked his chin and frowned. "With a little sorcerous wind to push it where it's needed, aye," he said. He pretended to consider. "Very well, wizard," he said. "We'll do it. Facer, fetch the gunner."

Tevvik smiled. "I wish you wouldn't use the word 'wizard' that way, Captain. The word's not a curse."

Derec looked at him. "That's a matter of opinion, Mr. Tevvik."

He led the Tichenese back to the quarterdeck and gave the orders for men to file to the magazine and bring up ten casks of powder. "Barefoot only, mind," he said. "No hobnails to strike a spark. Belts and weapons are to be laid aside. Scarves tied over their ears so their earrings won't strike a spark." He drew his pistols and pointed them at Tevvik.

"Don't set them off when they're alongside," he said, "or I'll serve you as I'd serve the pilot."

The wizard raised his hands and grinned. "I have no intention of blowing myself up, Captain."

"Maintain those intentions," Derec said, "and we'll have no trouble."

The barge was loaded with powder, and canvas thrown over the barrels to avoid getting them wet. The boat's small mast was raised, its lateen set, its tiller lashed. The boat was warped astern and Derec concentrated, summoning his power, keeping it ready. A small wind to blow his thirty-foot barge was fully within his capabilities.

"Tide's turning, Captain."

"Very well. Prepare to slip the cable and sheet home."

"Aye aye, sir."

There was a murmur of bare feet as men took their stations. Derec took a careful breath. "Sheet home the main tops'l. Set the spritsail and bonaventure."

The heavy canvas topsail fell with a rumble, then rumbled again as it filled with wind. *Birdwing* tilted, surged, came alive. Water chuckled under the counter.

"Slip the cable."

The cable murmured from the hawsehole, then there was a splash as its bitter end fell into the sea. A pity, Derec thought, to lose the best bower anchor.

"Helm answers, sir," said the steersman.

"Larboard two points. There. Amidships."

Derec glanced over the stern, saw phosphorescence glinting from the bone in the teeth of the powder boat.

Birdwing was barely moving. The back channel was dangerous and twisting; he needed maneuverability there, not speed.

"Pilot," he said. The woman stepped forward.

"Sir."

"Take command. No shouting, now. Pass your orders quietly."

"Yes, sir."

The pistols were growing heavy in Derec's hands. He ignored the tension in his arms and stepped to the weather rail, peering for sight of *Double Crowns*. The masthead lights were growing nearer. Five cables. Four. Three. He summoned his power.

"Cast off the boat."

Derec's heart leaped to his throat as the boat lurched wildly to the first puff of wind and threatened to capsize, but the barge steadied onto its course, passing to weather of *Birdwing*. He guided the boat with little tugs of his mind, aimed it toward *Double Crowns*.

Two cables. Now one, and from across the water a shout. More shouts. The barge thudded against the razee galleon's tumblehome near the stern. A drum began beating. Alarm pulsed in Derec: on this still night, that drum would be heard all over town. Derec steeled his mind to the necessity of what was to come.

"Give us fire, wizard," he said.

"Your obedient servant." Tevvik pursed his lips in concentration and made an elegant gesture with his hand. Derec remembered at the last second to close his eyes and preserve his night vision.

Even through closed lids he saw the yellow flash. A burst of hot wind gusted through his hair. He could hear shouts, screams, and, from his own ship, gasps of awe. He opened his eyes.

Double Crowns seemed unchanged, but he could hear the sound of water pouring like a river into her hold. The drum was silenced; in its place were cries of alarm. As Derec watched, the razee began to list. Crewmen poured from the hatches in a storm of pounding feet. The galleon's list grew more pronounced; Derec could hear things rolling across the deck, fetching up against the bulwarks. Then came a sound that was a seaman's nightmare, a noise that half paralyzed Derec with fear—the rumble of a gun broken loose, roaring across the tilting deck like a blind, maddened bull before it punched clean through the ship's side, making another hole through which the sea could enter.

He couldn't stand to watch anymore. He moved to the other side of the poop, but the sounds still pursued him, more guns breaking free, timbers rending, men screaming, the desperate splashing of drowning crewmen. Then, mercifully, *Birdwing* was past, heeled to the wind, and entering the channel.

The pilot negotiated two turns before the first challenge came from one of Fort Shzafakh's bastions. The island rose steeply here, and *Birdwing* ghosted with its sails luffing for lack of wind. The fort was perched right overhead—from its walls the garrison could as easily drop cannonballs on *Birdwing* as fire them from cannon.

"Hoy, there! What ship is that!"

Derec was ready. He cupped his hands and shouted upward in his accented Zhir. "Two Kingdoms ship *Sea Troll!*" he roared. "A warship blew up in harbor and started fires on other ships! We're trying to run clear!"

"Holy Thung! So that's what we heard." There was an awed pause. "Good luck, there."

"Much obliged."

Birdwing ghosted on. Derec could see grins on the faces of his officers, on the wizard. In his mind he could only hear the sounds of *Double Crowns* filling with water, men dying and timbers rending. He barely noticed when the channel opened up and ahead lay the dark and empty sea.

An hour after dawn the land breeze died. The pilot had been put ashore long since, and even the old cone of Great Kraken Island was below the horizon: *Birdwing* was running northwest along the coast in the clear, broad, shallow channel between the mainland and Ka Zhir's stretch of low boundary islands. Winds were often uncertain in the morning, particularly near the coast and especially during the transition between the nightly land breeze and the daytime sea breeze: there was nothing unusual about it. Derec dropped the second bower anchor and let the galleon swing to and fro in the little puffs that remained. The crew drowsed at their stations. Fretfully Derec looked southward. *Sea Troll*, he thought, was damaged: it could not pursue without raising a new main-topmast. But *Monarch* and the new race-built ship were fully seaworthy. Were they becalmed as well? He suspected not. Derec looked at the Tichenese.

"Master Tevvik, do you think we can whistle up a wind between the two of us?"

The wizard spread his hands. "I am willing to try, Captain. I am not an expert."

Derec called for a pot of kaf, ordered breakfast for the crew, and the two went to his day cabin. The partitions separating the cabin from the maindeck had been broken down when *Birdwing* was cleared for action, providing a long, unbroken row of guns from the stern windows to the bow, and Derec's table was hastily brought up from the orlop, and blankets to screen him from the curious eyes of the crew.

"You're planning on privateering for Liavek now, I take it?" the wizard asked. "There will be a Two Kingdoms fleet in harbor, you know."

"I'll find a small harbor somewhere along the coast. Come in under a flag of truce, negotiate with the Levar's government."

"I can speak for you." Derec looked up in surprise. The wizard smiled again. "I know a man named Pitullio—he worked for His Scarlet Eminence."

"I thank you," Derec said. "I'll consider that."

For two and a half hours he and the wizard tried to raise a wind, preferably a strong westerly that *Birdwing* could tack into and *Monarch*, the old-fashioned high-charged galleon, could not. The puffs continued, the ship dancing at the end of its cable, sails slatting.

"Captain." Facer's voice. "The lookouts see a squall coming up from the south."

Derec sighed. He could feel sweat dotting his brow: he had been concentrating hard. The wizard looked at him with amused eyes, grin white in his dark face.

"It's not *our* wind," Tevvik said, "but I hope it will do."

Derec rose wordlessly and pushed aside the curtain. His body was a mass of knots. "Ready a party at the capstan," he ordered. "I don't want to lose another anchor." He climbed to the poop.

It was a black squall, right enough, coming up from the south with deliberate speed. Ten minutes of stiff wind, at least, and with luck the squall might carry *Birdwing* with it for hours, right into the stronger ocean breezes. Derec had the second bower broken out. The galleon drifted, waiting for the squall.

Derec looked into the darkness, hoping to gauge its strength, and his heart sank.

Right in the center of the squall, he saw, were two ships. He didn't need his glass to know they were *Monarch* and *Torn II*, driving after him on a sorcerous breeze. Perhaps their wizards had even been responsible for his being becalmed.

"Quarters, gentlemen," he said. "We are being pursued. Have my steward fetch my armor, and send the wizard to the orlop."

He stopped himself, just in time, from glancing up into the mizzen shrouds. The ghosts of his slaughtered countrymen, he knew, had been an illusion.

But now, more than ever, he felt their gaze on the back of his head.

They were coming down together, Derec saw, straight down the eight-mile slot between the mainland and the sandy barrier isles. *Monarch* was to starboard of the race-built ship, three or four cables apart. There was a black line drawn in the azure sea a mile before them where the squall was pushing up a wave.

"We'll try to outrun them," Derec said. "We may prove their match in speed." He tried to sound confident, but he knew his assurances were hollow: the conditions were ideal for *Monarch*, booming straight downwind with her baggy sails full of sorcery. "If we lose the race," Derec went on, "I'll try to get the weather gage. If we're to windward, *Monarch* at least will be out of the fight."

A sigh of wind ruffled *Birdwing*'s sails. The ship stirred on the water. The sails filled, then died again. Derec strapped on his armor and watched as the darkness approached.

And then the squall hit, and the sun went dark. The sails boomed like thunder as they flogged massively in the air; the ship tilted; rain spattered Derec's breastplate. Then the sails were sheeted home, the yards braced—the helm answered, and *Birdwing* was racing straight downwind, a white bone in its teeth, sails as taut as the belly of a woman heavy with child. Magic crackled in Derec's awareness, a seething chaos of storm and wind. Desperately he looked astern.

Monarch seemed huge, castles towering over its leaner consort, its masts bending like coachwhips in the force of the wind. Derec gauged its speed, and a cold welling of despair filled him. *Birdwing* seemed to be maintaining its lead over *Torn II*, but *Monarch* was surging ahead as studding sails blossomed on its yards. *Birdwing*'s own studding sails were useless in this wind; the stuns'l booms would snap like toothpicks.

Derec stiffened at the sound of a gun: the big ship was trying its chasers. *Monarch* was pitching too much in this following sea, and Derec never saw the fall of shot.

Yard by yard the great ship gained, its black hull perched atop a boil of white water. Derec hoped for a miracle, and none came. Hollow anguish filled him.

"Take in the t'gallants," he ordered. "We will await them." Diligently he fought down despair. "Don't send down the t'gallantyards," he said. "We may yet be able to show them our heels."

Monarch's stuns'ls began coming in as they perceived Derec's shortening sail. The maneuver was not done well, and sheets began to fly, spilling wind from sails, a last-ditch method of slowing *Monarch* so that it would not overshoot its target.

Derec watched nervously, gnawing his lip, trying to summon his power and weave a defensive net around his ship. He could feel Tevvik's energies joining his, strengthening his shields. Another gust of rain spattered the deck; gun captains shielded their matches with their bodies. *Monarch* looked as if it was coming up on *Birdwing*'s larboard side, but that might be a feint. Would the huge ship alter course at the last minute and try for a raking shot across *Birdwing*'s stern? If so, Derec had to be ready to turn with her. Plans flickered through Derec's mind as he gauged possible enemy moves and his own responses.

"Load the guns. Roundshot and grape. Run out the larboard battery." Maybe the guns running out would prod *Monarch*'s captain into making his move.

But no. The man seemed eager to get to grips, and disdained maneuver. He had almost thirty guns more than Derec; he could afford to let them do his thinking for him. The black ship came closer, its little scraplike sprit topsail drawing even with *Birdwing*'s stern. Derec could hear officers' bellowed commands as they struggled to reduce sail.

Anxiety filled Derec as the ship rumbled to the sound of gun trucks running out. *Monarch* was pulling up within fifty yards. *Torn II* was

CONSEQUENCES 321

eclipsed behind the big ship, but now that *Birdwing* had shortened sail he could expect her shortly. He glanced again at the men, seeing the gun captains crouched over the guns with their slow matches, the officers pacing the deck with rapiers drawn, ready to run through any crewman who left his station. "No firing till my order!" Derec bellowed. "There may be a few premature shots—ignore them!" And then inspiration struck. He turned to one of Marcoyn's marines, a blond man sighting down the length of a swivel gun set aft of the mizzen shrouds. "Blow on your match, man," Derec said. "I'm going to try a little trick."

The marine looked at him uncertainly, then grinned through his curling blond beard, leaned forward over his matchlock, and blew. The match brightened redly. "You other marines, stand ready," Derec said. He looked at the black ship, and fear shivered down his spine as he saw himself looking straight into the muzzle of a demicannon. Each enemy gunport had been decorated with the snarling brass head of a leopard: now guns were running out the beasts' mouths. *Monarch*'s foremast was even with *Birdwing*'s mizzen. Derec waited, his pulse beating in his ears, as *Monarch* crawled forward with glacial speed.

"Pick your target," Derec told the marine. "Steady now! Fire."

The four-pound mankiller barked and the air filled with a peculiar whirring noise as grapeshot and a handful of scrap iron flew toward the enemy. "Fire the murderers!" Derec spat. "Now!"

Another three minions banged out, and then there was a massive answering roar as every enemy gun went off, flinging their iron toward *Birdwing*. The smaller ship shuddered as balls slammed home. Derec took an involuntary step backward at the awesome volume of fire, but then he began to laugh. He'd tricked *Monarch* into firing prematurely, before all her guns bore. They'd wasted their first and most valuable broadside, half the shot going into the sea.

"Reload, you men! Helmsman, larboard a point!" Derec cupped his hands to carry down the ship's well to the gundeck below. "Fire on my command! Ready, boys!" *Birdwing* began a gentle curve toward the giant ship.

"Fire!" The deck lurched as the big guns went off, the long fifteen-foot maindeck culverins leaping inboard on their carriages. Derec could hear crashing from the enemy ship as iron smashed through timbers. "Reload!" Derec shrieked. "Fire at will! Helmsman, starboard a point!"

Enemy guns began crashing. Derec saw a piece of bulwark dissolve on the maindeck and turn to a storm of white fifteen-inch splinters that mowed down half a dozen men. Shot wailed overhead or thudded into planking. Musketry twittered over Derec's head: the enemy castles were full of marines firing down onto *Birdwing*'s decks. The smaller ship's guns replied. For the first time Derec felt a magic probe against his defenses; he sensed Tevvik parrying the strike. There was a crash, a deadly whirl of splinters, and the yellow-bearded marine was flung across the deck like a sack, ending up against the starboard rail, head crushed by a grapeshot. Derec, still in his haze of concentration, absently sent a man from the starboard side to service the gun.

Guns boomed, spewing powder smoke. *Birdwing*'s practiced crews were loading and firing well. Derec smiled; but then his ship rocked to a storm of fire and his heart lurched. His crews were faster in loading and firing, but still the enemy weight was overwhelming. Derec's smaller vessel couldn't stand this pounding for long. He gnawed his lip as he peered at the enemy through the murk. His next move depended on their not seeing him clearly.

The deck jarred as half a dozen gundeck demicannon went off nearly together. Smoke blossomed between the ships, and at once Derec ran for the break in the poop.

"Sailtrimmers, cast off all tacks and sheets!" he roared. "Gun crews shift to the starboard broadside! Smartly, now!" He could see crewmen's bewildered heads swiveling wildly: man the *starboard* guns? Had *Torn II* run up to starboard and caught them between two fires?

"Cast off all sheets! *Fly 'em!* Run out the starboard battery!"

Topsails boomed as the great sails spilled wind. *Birdwing*'s purposeful driving slowed as if stopped by a giant hand. The flogging canvas roared louder than the guns. The galleon staggered in the sea, the black ship pulling ahead. Frantically Derec gauged his ship's motion.

"Hard a-larboard, Sandor! Smartly, there!"

Losing momentum, *Birdwing* rounded onto its new tack. A rumble sounded from the gundeck as the demicannon began thrusting from the ports. "Sheet home! Sailtrimmers to the braces! Brace her up sharp, there!"

There; he'd done it: checked his speed and swung across the black ship's stern. He could see the big stern windows, the heraldic quarterings of the Two Kingdoms painted on the flat surface of the raised poop, officers in armor running frantically atop the castle, arms waving. . . .

"Fire as you bear! Make it count, boys!"

Birdwing trembled as the first culverin spat fire. The whole broadside followed, gun by gun, and Derec exulted as he saw the enemy's stern dissolve in a chaos of splinters and roundshot, a great gilt lantern tumbling into the sea, the white triangle of the bonaventure dancing as grape pockmarked the canvas. . . . He'd raked her, firing his whole broadside the length of the ship without the enemy being able to reply with a single shot. Derec laughed aloud. "We've got upwind of them!" he shouted. "They'll not catch us now!"

"Holy Thung! Look ahead!" Random's young voice was frantic. Derec ran to the weather rail and peered out.

Torn II was bearing down on them, bow to bow, within a cable's distance. She'd been trying to weather *Monarch* so as to attack *Birdwing* from her unengaged side, and now the two race-built ships were on a collision course.

"Hands to the braces! Stations for tacking! Starboard guns load double-shot and grape! Put the helm down!"

Birdwing, barely under way again, staggered into the wind. Canvas slatted wildly. *Torn II* was bearing down on her beam, its royal figurehead glowering, waving a bright commanding sword.

"Fire as you bear!" Derec pounded the rail with a bleeding fist. "Run out and fire!"

The marines' murderers spat their little balls and scrap iron. Then a demicannon boomed, and another, then several of the long maindeck culverins. *Birdwing* hung in the eye of the wind, all forward momentum lost, the gale beating against her sails, driving her backward. More guns went off. *Torn*'s spritsail danced as a roundshot struck it. Captain-General Collerne was curving gently downwind, about to cross *Birdwing*'s stern at point-blank range.

"Starboard your helm! Help her fall off!"

Too late. Captain-General Collerne's scarlet masthead pennant coiled over the waves like a serpent threatening to strike. "Lie down!" Derec shouted. "Everyone lie down!"

He flung himself to the planks as the world began to come apart at the seams. The ship staggered like a toy struck by a child's hand as an entire rippling broadside smashed the length of *Birdwing*'s hull. Gun-smoke gushed over the quarterdeck. The taffrail dissolved. The bona-venture mizzen collapsed, draping the poop in pockmarked canvas. Yards of sliced rigging coiled down on the deck. Below there was a metallic gong as a cannon was turned over on its shrieking crew.

Then there was a stunned silence: *Torn* had passed by. Through the clouds of gunsmoke Derec could see Marcoyn standing, legs apart, on the fo'c'sle, sword brandished at the enemy, an incoherent, lunatic bellow of rage rising from his throat. "What a madman," Derec muttered, his ears ringing, and then he got to his feet.

"Brace the spritsail to larboard!" he called. "Clear that wreckage!" The tattered remains of the bonaventure were turning red: there were bodies underneath. As the canvas was pulled up, Derec saw one of them was Facer, the sunburned man cut in half by his homeland's iron. Derec turned away. He would pray for the man later.

Slowly *Birdwing* paid off onto the larboard tack. The sails filled and the galleon lost sternway. Water began to chuckle along the strakes as the ship slowly forged ahead. Canvas boomed as *Torn II*, astern, began to come about. Derec looked anxiously over the shattered taffrail.

Monarch was only now lumbering into the wind: she was almost a mile away and had no hope of returning to the fight unless the wind shifted to give her the weather gage once again. But *Torn II* was the ship that had worried Derec all along, and she was right at hand, completing her tack, moving onto the same course as *Birdwing*. If she was faster sailing upwind, she could overhaul the fugitive ship. Derec gave a worried glance at the set of his sails.

"Keep her full, Sandor. Let her go through the water."

"Full an' bye, sir."

"Set the t'gallants." He was suddenly glad he hadn't sent down the topgallant yards.

"Aye aye, sir."

"All hands to knot and splice."

The topgallants rumbled as they were smoothly sheeted home. *Birdwing* heeled to starboard, foam spattering over the fo'c'sle like handfuls of dark jewels tossed by the spirits of the sea. She was drawing ahead, fast as a witch as she drove through the black gale. Water drizzled from the sky, washing Facer's blood from the planks. The water tasted sweet on Derec's tongue, washed away the powder that streaked his face.

Torn's topgallant yards were rising aloft, a swarm of men dark on her rigging. *Birdwing* made the most of her temporary advantage; she'd gained over a mile on her adversary before *Torn's* topgallant bloomed and the larger ship began to race in earnest.

Derec felt his heart throbbing as he slitted his eyes to look astern, judging the ships' relative motion. *Birdwing* had lost her bonaventure: would that subtract from the ship's speed? He continued staring astern. His face began to split in a smile.

"We're pulling ahead!" he roared. "We've got the heels of her, by Thurn Bel!"

A low cheer began to rise from the crew, then, as the word passed, it grew deafening. *Birdwing* was going to make her escape. Nothing could stop her now.

Two miles later, as *Birdwing* neared a half-mile-wide channel between a pair of boundary isles, the wind died away entirely.

The sails fell slack, booming softly as the ship rocked on the waves.

From astern, traveling clearly from the two enemy vessels, Derec could hear the sound of cheering.

"Sway out the longboat! Ready to lower the second bower! We'll kedge her!"

The words snapped from Derec's mouth before the enemy cheering had quite ended. There was a rush of feet as the crew obeyed. Derec wanted to keep them busy, not occupied with thinking about their predicament.

"Send a party below to splice every anchor cable together. Fetch the wizard. A party to the capstan. Bring up the tackles and the spare t'gallant yards. We're going to jury a bonaventure. SuKrone, help me out of this damned armor."

One of the two longboats was swung out and set in the water. Carefully, the remaining bower anchor was lowered into it, and the boat moved under oars to the full length of the spliced anchor cables. Then the anchor was pitched overboard into the shallow sea and crewmen began stamping around the capstan, dragging the ship forward by main force until it rested over its anchor.

Tevvik appeared on deck to Derec's summons. He looked haggard.

"Hot work, Captain," he said. "Their wizards are good."

"I felt only one assault."

"Good. That means I was keeping them off."

"We're going to need wind."

Tevvik seemed dead with weariness. "Aye, Captain. I'll try."

"I'll work with you. Stand by the rail; I'll be with you in a moment."

The sound of clattering capstan pawls echoed from astern. *Torn* and *Monarch* were kedging as well.

"Up and down, sir." *Birdwing* was resting over its anchor.

"Bring her up smartly."

"Aye aye."

Birdwing lurched as the anchor broke free of the bottom. Derec moved toward the poop ladder, then frowned as he saw the two stream anchors lashed to the main chains. A shame, Derec considered, that so much time was wasted getting the anchor up, then rowing it out again. Capstan pawls whirred in accompaniment to Derec's thoughts.

"Swing out the other longboat," he said. "We'll put one of the stream anchors on the other end of the cable. Have one anchor going out while the other's coming in." He grinned at SuKrone's startled expression. "See to it, man!"

"Sir."

Crewmen rushed to the remaining longboat. Derec walked to where the Tichenese was waiting, propped against the lee rail where he'd be out of the way.

"We shall try to bring a wind, wizard," Derec said. "A westerly, as before. Ready?"

"I'll do what I can."

Wearily Derec summoned his power, matched it to the wizard's, and called the elements for a wind. Meanwhile a spare topgallant mast was dropped in place of the broken bonaventure mizzen, a lateen yard hoisted to its top, a new bonaventure set that hung uselessly in the windless air. Derec and Tevvik moved into its shade. Capstan pawls clattered, drawing the race-built ship forward, through the channel between barrier islands, the two longboats plying back and forth with their anchors. The pursuers were using only one anchor at a time and were falling behind. The water began to deepen, turn a profounder blue. *Torn II* crawled through the island passage. *Monarch's* topgallant masts loomed above the nearer island.

The heat of the noon sun augured a hot afternoon. Pitch bubbled up between the deck seams and stuck to crewmen's feet. Weary sailors were relieved at the capstan and fed.

"Deck, there! Captain! Right ahead! *See what's happening!*"

Derec glanced up from his summoning, and his heart lurched as he saw the wind itself appear, visible as a dim swirling above the water; and then the sea itself rose, a wall of curling white foam. Desperate energy filled him.

"Clew up the t'gallants! Close the gunports! Call the boats back! Clew up the fores'l!"

The sea was coming with a growing hiss, a furious rank of white horsemen galloping over an azure plain. Tevvik looked at the wave with a dazed expression. "It's all coming at once," he said. "It's been building out there, everything we've been summoning since dawn, and now it's all on us at once."

"Helmsman! A point to starboard! Use what way you can!"

Sails were clewed up in a squeal of blocks. The entry port filled with frantic sailors as one of the boats came alongside. There was a cry of wind in the rigging, an anticipation of what was to come. Derec ran to the mizzen shrouds and wrapped his arm around a stout eight-inch tarred line. He looked at Tevvik.

"I suggest you do likewise, wizard."

And then the summoning was on them. The bow rose to the surge of white water and suddenly the air was full of spray as the frothing sea boiled around the ship. Canvas crashed as it filled with wind, bearing *Birdwing* back till suddenly she came up short at the end of her anchor cable, and with a plank-starting shudder the galleon was brought up short, burying her beak in foam, a wave sweeping the decks fore and aft, carrying crewmen and capstan bars and everything not lashed down in a frantic, clawing spill for the stern. . . . Derec closed his eyes and mouth and tried to hang on, his shoulders aching as the water tore at his clothing and body. His mind still registered what was happening to the ship, the jarring and checking that meant the anchor was dragging, the demon shriek of wind in the rigging, the thrumming tautness of the shroud around which Derec wrapped his arms. . . .

Just as suddenly, the white water was gone, past. A strong sea breeze hummed in the rigging. Half-drowned crewmen lay on the planks like scattered driftwood, gasping for air. Exultation filled Derec.

"Hands to the capstan! Prepare to set the fores'l and t'gallants! Lively, there, lively—we've got a wind!"

The stunned survivors raised a feeble cheer and dragged wearily to their work. The other longboat—miraculously it had survived, bobbing on the wave like a twig—picked up a few swimmers who had been carried overboard, then came to the entry port in a mad thrash of oars. Wind whipping his hair, Derec gazed astern to see the wall of white as it drove toward his enemies.

Torn II had seen it coming and had had time to prepare. Her boats were in, her anchor catted home; and Derec suppressed a surge of admiration for the proud way her head tossed to the wave, the clean manner in which she cut the water and kept her head to the wind. Then the wave was past, and she began setting sails. Derec's gaze shifted to *Monarch*. The wave was almost on her.

She hadn't seen it coming; that much was clear. She'd just kedged clear of the southern tip of the island, and the white water was within two cables' lengths before *Monarch* was aware of it. Suddenly there was frantic movement on her decks, sails drawing up, the boats thrashing water; but the white water hit her broadside, driving her over. She staggered once, then was gone, only wreckage and the tips of her masts visible on the rushing water. Derec blinked: it had happened so fast he could scarce believe the sight of it. He looked again. His eyes had spoken truly: *Monarch* was gone.

"Thurn Bel protect them," Derec said, awed, reaching automatically for his amulet and finding nothing. He knew precisely what had happened. The gunports had been open on this hot afternoon, and the wind and water had pushed her lower ports under; she'd filled and gone down in seconds. Six hundred men, their lives snuffed out in an instant. Derec shook his head, sorrow filling him. Why was he fated to kill his countrymen so?

"The sea trolls will feed well tonight," Tevvik said solemnly. His hairpins had been torn from his head, and his long dark hair hung dripping to his shoulders.

SuKrone's voice broke into Derec's reverie. "Cable's up and down, sir."

"Break the anchor free. Lay her on the larboard tack."

The anchor came free with a lurch, the yards were braced round, the birdwing sails set and filled with wind. *Birdwing* heeled gracefully in the stiff ocean breeze.

"This isn't over yet," Derec said as he watched *Torn II* flying after them. "The captain-general's lost two ships, half his squadron, with nothing to show for it. He's got to bring us back or he's done for. He'll never have another command."

"We're faster than he on this tack."

"That won't end it. He'll spend the rest of his life in the Sea of Luck if he has to."

"Let us hope," Tevvik said, his eyes hardening, "he will not live long."

Derec shook his head: he couldn't wish Collerne dead, not Collerne who had been such a friend to him, who had raised him to the highest rank to which a non-noble could aspire.

The brisk wind carried *Birdwing* smartly over the water, the bow rising to each ocean wave. But then the wind dropped little by little and *Torn II* began closing the distance, her red admiral's pennant snapping in the breeze like a striking serpent. *Birdwing* was faster only in stiffer winds: *Torn* had the advantage here. Derec's heart sank.

"We shall have to fight, then. Gun captains to draw their cartridges and replace them with fresh—they may have got wet. All hands check their powder."

Derec donned his cuirass—the helmet had been washed overboard—and reloaded his pistols. Tevvik returned to the safety of the orlop. There was no cheer among the crew as they went to their tasks, only a kind of grim despair.

They had labored all day, escaped death so many times. Were they cursed, to be so forced into yet another struggle?

"Stations for tacking," Derec said. "We'll see how badly the captain-general wants to fight us." He still could not bring himself to speak of the man disrespectfully.

Birdwing came across the wind easily. "Ease her a bit," Derec ordered. "Keep her full." He ordered the guns loaded with roundshot and gauged his distance carefully. "Back the main tops'l," he said finally. "Run out the larboard battery." He was going to give Collerne a hard choice. "Ready, boys!" he called. "Aim carefully, now!" The ship's motion altered as the main topsail backed, as the ship's speed checked and its corkscrew shudder ended. Carefully Derec gauged the ship's motion. Tops'l aback, *Birdwing* was a far steadier platform.

"Fire!" The deck shuddered to the salvo. White feathers leaped from the sea around *Torn*. "Fill the tops'l! Reload and run out! Helm down!"

Derec looked at the other race-built ship, eyes narrowing. His main-deck culverins, longer though with a smaller bore than the demicannon on the gundeck, were ideal at this range. He would claw to windward, fall off, fire, then claw to windward again while his crews reloaded: he was going to punish *Torn II* mercilessly on the approach, make her pay for every fathom gained. The enemy couldn't reply, not without luffing out of the wind to present her broadside.

Collerne had two choices now, Derec knew. He could continue beating toward *Birdwing*, paying for every inch with lives, or he could luff and open the battle at this range. The battle wouldn't be decisive at a half mile's distance—the two ships would fire off their ammunition at this range, fail to do mortal damage, and that would be the end of it. Derec prayed Collerne would choose the latter outcome.

"Back the main tops'l! Run out!"

Another broadside crashed out. "Fill the tops'l! Load! Helm down!"

Luff, Derec thought fiercely as he looked at the enemy. Luff, damn you.

The enemy were determined to stand Derec's fire. His heart sank at the thought of killing more of his countrymen.

Having no choice, he did what he must. He fired another broadside, tacked, fired the larboard guns. *Torn*'s bow chasers replied, pitching a ball at *Birdwing* every few minutes; but *Torn II* had to be taking punishment as she came into the culverins' ideal range. Her sails were as pitted by shot holes as the cheeks of a whore with the Great Pox.

Five hundred yards. *"Fire!"* He could hear the sound of shot striking home. Four hundred. *"Fire!"* Three. *"Fire!"*

The wind blew the ocean clear of smoke. Derec stared to leeward, hoping to see a mast fall, a sail flog itself to bits, anything that might allow him to slip away. Nothing. Reluctantly he gave the orders. "Fill the mains'l. Clew up the t'gallants. We'll give the captain-general the fight he's come for."

The guns lashed out once more and then *Torn* luffed elegantly, the bronze guns running out the square ports, two lines of teeth that shone in the bright southern sun. There were gaps in the rows of teeth; two ports beaten into one, another empty port where a gun may have been disabled. Derec's breath caught in his throat.

Fire lapped the surface of the ocean. *Torn*'s crew had waited hours for this and it seemed as if every shot struck home, a rapid series of crashes and shudders that rocked the deck beneath Derec's feet. There was a cry as a half dozen of Marcoyn's marines were scattered in red ruin over the fo'c'sle, then a shriek, sounding like the very sky being torn asunder, as a ball passed right over Derec's head to puncture the mizzen lateen. He was too startled to duck.

Birdwing's guns gave their answering roars. Derec gave the command to fire at will. He could sense the magic shields Tevvik wove about the ship; felt a probe, felt it easily rebuffed. There was only one enemy wizard now; he was as tired as everyone else. The range narrowed and the marines' murderers began to bark. Gunfire was continuous, a neverending thunder. A musket ball gouged wood from the mizzen above Derec's head; he began to pace in hope of discouraging marksmen.

Derec's ship seemed to be pulling ahead as the range narrowed and *Birdwing* stole *Torn*'s wind. Derec didn't want that, not yet; he had the foretops'l laid aback, allowed *Torn* to forge ahead slightly, then filled the sail and resumed his course.

Fifty yards: here they would hammer it out, guns double-shotted with a round of grape choked down each barrel for good measure. A maindeck culverin tipped onto its crew, its carriage wrecked by a ball. There was a crash, a massive rumble followed by a human shriek. Derec stared: the main topgallant had been shot away and come roaring down, a tangle of rigging and canvas and broken timber. Marcoyn already had a party hacking at the wreckage and tossing it overboard. Derec clenched his teeth and waited. Thunder smote his ears. Gunpowder coated his tongue in layers, like dust on a dead man.

The wreckage was clear: good. The enemy was falling a bit behind. "Set the fore t'gallant!" Derec roared; the seamen gave him puzzled glances, and he repeated the order.

Canvas boomed as the topgallant was sheeted home; Derec could feel the surge of speed, the lift it gave his nimble ship. He peered over the bulwark, squinting through the smoke that masked the enemy. With his added speed, he'd try to cross her bows and let her run aboard: he'd have his every gun able to rake down the enemy's length with scarce a chance of reply.

"Put up the helm!" A musket ball whirred overhead; two quarterdeck murderers barked in reply. The marines were cursing without cease as they loaded and fired, a constant drone of obscenity. Derec wondered where they found the energy.

Birdwing curved downwind like a bird descending on its prey, Derec staring anxiously at the enemy. He felt his heart sink: the blue sky between the enemy's masts was widening. Collerne had been ready for him, and was matching *Birdwing*'s turn with his own.

"Helm hard to weather!" Frantic energy pulsed through Derec. "Hands to the larboard guns! Run 'em out! Braces, there! Brace her around!"

If he made his turn quick enough, he might be able to slide across Collerne's stern and deliver a raking shot with his fresh larboard broadside, a stroke as devastating as that which *Torn* had fired into *Birdwing*'s stern that morning.

Sails boomed and slatted overhead. The firing trailed off as the guns no longer bore. Derec ran frantically for the larboard rail and saw, too late, a tantalizing glimpse of *Torn*'s stern, a glimpse lasting only a few seconds before it slid away. Derec beat a fist on the rail. The maneuver hadn't worked at all—Collerne had anticipated everything. The ships had just changed places, larboard tack to starboard, like dancers at a ball. And *Torn* was firing with a new broadside now, not the one he'd punished for the last few hours.

"Luff her! Gun crews, fire as you bear!" He'd get in one unopposed broadside, at least.

The unused broadside blasted away into *Torn*'s starboard quarter.

Derec could see splinters flying like puffs of smoke. He filled his sails and surged on.

Now they were yardarm to yardarm again, the guns hammering at point-blank range. The crews were weary, taking casualties, and the rate of fire had slowed: the deadly iron thunderstorm was blowing itself out. A whirring charge of grape caught SuKrone in the side and flung him to weather like a doll, already dead; a musket ball whanged off Derec's breastplate and made him take a step back, his heart suddenly thundering in panic. Frantically he began pacing, his feet slipping in pools of blood.

Who was winning? *Torn* had been hard hit, but her weight of armament was superior; she had a larger crew, having probably taken men off the damaged *Sea Troll;* and Derec was forced to admit she had the better captain. *Birdwing* had been hit hard in the first fight, and her crew were exhausted. Everywhere he looked Derec saw blood, death, smoke, and ruin.

He'd try his trick one more time, Derec thought. He couldn't think of anything else. If it didn't work, he'd just fight it out toe to toe until there was nothing left to fight with. He wouldn't surrender. If *Birdwing* lost, he'd take one of his stolen pistols and blow his own brains out.

Birdwing was forging ahead, the topgallant still set. Very well. He'd try to do it better.

"Hands to tacks and sheets! Hands to the braces! Ready, there? Helm to weather!"

Birdwing lurched as the rudder bit the water. Bullets twittered overhead. The enemy wizard made some kind of strike, and Derec felt it deep in his awareness; his mind lanced out and parried. He could sense Tevvik there, feel a part of the foreigner's mind merge with his own.

If you ever do anything, he begged, *do it now.*

The answer came. *Very well.*

Derec looked up again, saw the blue space between the enemy's masts increasing. Damn: he'd been anticipated *again.*

"Hard a-weather! Sheets, there! Man the starboard guns!"

They were dancing round again, just changing places. The bonaventure and mizzen lateen boomed as the wind slammed them across the deck. Derec saw the enemy stern and knew he could never cross it, knew it for certain—and then there was a yellow flash, *Torn's* windows blowing out in rainbow splinters, bright light winking from each gunpoint along the maindeck. Guns boomed, firing at empty sea. Derec's mouth dropped as he saw an enemy marine, standing with his firelock in the mizzen chains, suddenly fling his arms back as each of the powder flasks he carried across his chest went off, little dots of fire that knocked him into the shrouds . . .

Tevvik, Derec thought. He specialized in fireworks. But now Derec was screaming, his throat a raw agony.

"Fire as you bear!" *Birdwing* was going to win the race: the maindeck explosion had paralyzed the enemy, possibly blown the helmsmen away from the whipstaff.

The guns went off, flinging hundreds of pounds of metal into the helpless ship's stern. *Torn* wallowed, the wind pushing her away. Derec could hear her crewmen screaming for water buckets. Tevvik must have set off a pile of cartridges on the maindeck, spreading fire, making guns go off prematurely while their crews were still ramming shots home. . . .

Birdwing followed, firing shot after shot; *Torn*'s crew were desperately fighting fires and could not reply. Derec sensed a new energy in his gunners; they were firing faster than they had since the enemy's approach. They knew this was victory and wanted to hasten it.

"Captain." It was one of the surgeon's assistants, a boy in a bloody apron. Derec glared at him.

"What is it?"

"The wizard's unconscious, sir. The Liavekan, what's-his-name. He just yelled something in his heathen tongue and collapsed. Surgeon thought you'd need to know."

Derec put his hand on the boy's arm. "Compliments to the surgeon. Thank you, boy."

The guns roared on. *Torn* got her fires under control, but the explosion had devastated the crew: they didn't have the heart to continue. When all the gun crews dribbled away, heading for the hatches, the officers conceded the inevitable and hauled down their colors. *Birdwing* came alongside to take possession.

Collerne, leading his surviving officers, surrendered in person, a tall, white-haired man in beautifully crafted muscled armor, a splinter wound on one cheek, both hands blackened where he'd beat at the fire. Derec looked into the man's eyes, hoping to see some sign of friendship, of understanding for what Derec had had to do. There was nothing there, no understanding, no friendship, not even hate. Derec took his patron's sword wordlessly.

"We've done it, SuPashto! Beaten 'em!" Marcoyn was by Derec's side now, his pale, unfocused eyes burning fire. "We're *free!*" Marcoyn saw Collerne standing mute by the poop rail; he turned to the captain-general, stared at him for a long moment, then deliberately spat in his face.

"Free, d'ye hear, Collerne?" he roared. "You thought you'd strangle us all, but now I'll throttle you myself. And now I'll be captain of your ship as well."

The spittle hung on Collerne's face. He said nothing, but his deep gray eyes turned to Derec, and Derec's blood turned chill.

Derec put a hand on Marcoyn's armored shoulder. "He's worth more in ransom alive," he said. "You and your people take possession of the other ship."

Marcoyn considered this, the taunting grin still on his face. "Aye," he said. "Maybe I'd like their money more than their lives." He gave a laugh. "I'll have to give it some thought. While I enjoy my new cabin on my new ship."

He turned to his men and roared orders. There were cheers from the marines as they swarmed aboard *Torn II* and began looting the enemy survivors. Collerne's eyes turned away from Derec. There was no gratitude there, just an emptiness as deep as the ocean. Despair filled Derec. The rapier in his hand felt as heavy as a lead weight.

"Go to my cabin, Captain-General," he said. "Wait for me there. I'll send the surgeon to tend to your hands." In silence, Collerne obeyed. Derec sent the other officers below to the cable tier and had them put under guard.

Suddenly Derec was aware of Tevvik standing by the break of the poop. How long had the wizard been there? His face showed strain and exhaustion, but he'd heard everything; his hooded expression demonstrated that well enough.

Derec glanced up at the mizzen shrouds. There wasn't room any longer for all the countrymen he'd killed; the ghosts, he thought, would have to stand in line.

It wasn't over yet, Derec knew. The Two Kingdoms trading fleets came to the Sea of Luck every year, and sailors had long memories. Squadrons would hunt for *Birdwing*, and even if Derec received the protection of one of the cities, there would still be kidnappers and assassins. No end to this killing, Derec thought, not until I'm dead. Will the gods forgive me, he wondered, for not killing myself and ending this slaughter?

The two race-built ships spun in the wind, locked together like weary prizefighters leaning against each other for support. Wreckage and bodies bobbed in the water. From *Torn II* came a smell of burning.

Derec realized he was the only man remaining who could navigate. He ordered his charts to be brought up from the safety of the hold. "Secure the guns," he said. "I'll chart a course north, to Liavek."

The sea was kind that night; a moderate wind, a moderate swell. The two ships traveled under easy sail and echoed to the sound of repairs.

Near staggering with weariness, Derec paced *Birdwing's* weather rail. Collerne still waited in Derec's cabin. Marcoyn was probably drunk and unconscious in the admiral's cabin aboard *Torn*. Only Derec was without a place to sleep.

There was a tread on the poop companion, and Derec saw Tevvik approaching him.

"You have recovered?" Derec asked. His tongue was thick. No matter how much kaf he consumed his mouth still tasted of powder.

"Somewhat." The wizard's voice was as weary as his own. "May I join you, Captain?"

"If you like." Exhaustion danced in Derec's brain. He swayed, put a hand on the bulwark to steady himself.

Tevvik's voice was soft. "You will have to make a choice, Captain," he said.

"Not now, wizard."

"Soon, Captain."

Derec said nothing. Tevvik stepped closer, pitched his voice low. "If Marcoyn gets his way, you will all die. His Scarlet Eminence won't make a deal with a butcher."

"This is my affair, wizard. None of yours."

"Only the thought of ransom kept him from another massacre. What will happen when he realizes the ransom will never come? Liavek isn't at war with the Two Kingdoms—their prize courts will never permit you to ransom a neutral. When Marcoyn thinks things through, there will be trouble." Tevvik's easy smile gleamed in his dark face. "I can deal with Marcoyn, Captain. He will have gone overboard while drunk, and that's all anyone will ever know."

Derec glared at the foreigner and clenched his fists. "I'll have my own discipline on my own ship," he grated. "I don't need wizard's tricks, and I won't be a party to conspiracies."

"It's far too late for that, Captain."

Derec jerked as if stung. "It's not too late to stop."

"Events generate their own momentum. You of all people should know that." He leaned closer, put a hand on Derec's shoulder. "Marcoyn's marines have the firelocks, Captain. He has possession of one ship already, and he can take yours anytime he wants."

"He needs me. The man can't navigate."

"Once he turns pirate, he can capture all the navigators he needs."

"*I can deal with him, wizard!*" Derec's voice roared out over the still ship. Tevvik took a step back from the force of his rage.

His mind ablaze, Derec stormed down the poop ladder, past the startled helmsman, and down the passage that led to his cabin. The guard at the door straightened in surprise as Derec flung open the door.

Collerne looked up. He was out of his armor and seated in one of Derec's chairs, trying to read a Zhir book on navigation with his bandaged hands. Derec hesitated before the man's depthless gaze.

"I want you off my ship, Captain-General," he said.

Collerne's eyes flickered. "Why is that, Mr. SuPashto?" He spoke formally, without expression.

"I'm going to put you and your officers in a boat and let you make your way to Gold Harbor. You'll have food and water for the trip. A backstaff so you can find your latitude."

With a careful gesture, Collerne closed his book and held it between bandaged hands. "You are running for Liavek, are you not? Can you not let us off there?"

Derec looked at him. "It's for your safety, Captain-General."

Collerne took a moment to absorb this. "Very well, Mr. SuPashto. I understand that you might have difficulty controlling your people now that they've had a taste of rebellion."

Suddenly Derec hated the man, hated his superiority, the cold, relentless precision of his intelligence. "You would have strangled and eviscerated every man on this ship!" he said.

Collerne's voice was soft. "That was my duty, Mr. SuPashto," he said. "Not my pleasure. That's the difference between me and your Mr. Marcoyn."

"Marcoyn had a good teacher," Derec said. "His name was Captain Lord Fors. Marcoyn's an amateur in cruelty compared to him."

Collerne stiffened. Mean satisfaction trickled into Derec's mind; he'd got a reaction from the man at last. He wondered if it was because he'd scored a point or simply had the bad taste to criticize one officer in front of another.

"The only order I've ever had questioned," Derec said, "is the one that would prevent my people doing to you what you fully intended to do to them. Now"—he nodded—"you will follow me, Captain-General, and from this point onward you will address me as captain. Maybe I wasn't born to the rank, but I think I've earned it."

Collerne said nothing, just rose from his chair and followed. Perhaps, Derec thought, he would say nothing at all rather than have to call Derec by his stolen title. Derec collected the rest of the officers in the cable tier and then climbed to the maindeck. *Birdwing's* remaining small boat had been warped astern after the fight, and Derec had it brought alongside. He put a stock of food and water aboard, made certain the boat had mast, cordage, sail, and backstaff, then sent the prisoners into it. Collerne was last. The captain-general turned in the entry port, prepared to lower himself to the boat, curled his fingers around the safety line. His bandaged hand slipped uselessly, and Collerne gave a gasp of pain as he began to topple backward into the boat.

Derec leaned out and took the captain-general's arm, steadying him. Collerne looked at him with dark, fathomless eyes.

"I acted to preserve the ship, Captain-General," Derec said. "There was no other way. *Birdwing* was your dream, and it is alive, thanks to me."

Collerne's face hardened. He turned away, and with Derec's assistance lowered himself into the boat.

"Cast off," said Derec. He stepped up to the poop and watched the fragment of darkness as it fell astern, as it vanished among the gentle swells of the Sea of Luck.

He'd said what he'd had to, Derec thought. If Collerne refused to understand, that was naught to do with Derec.

"What now, Captain?" Tevvik's voice. Derec turned to the wizard.

"Sleep," he said. "I'll deal with Marcoyn in the morning."

Derec rose at dawn. He wound his two pistols and put them in his belt, then reached for his sword. He stepped on deck, scanned the horizon, found it empty save for *Torn II* riding two miles off the starboard quarter. He brought *Birdwing* alongside, shouted at the other ship to heave to, then backed *Birdwing's* main topsail and brought her to rest a hundred yards from the other ship. He armed a party of *Birdwing's* sailors and had them ready at the entry port. Derec told *Torn's* lookout to give Mr. Marcoyn his compliments and ask him to come aboard *Birdwing*.

Out of the corner of his eye, Derec saw Tevvik mounting the poop ladder. The Tichenese seemed unusually subdued; his expression was hooded, his grin absent entirely.

Marcoyn arrived with a party of half a dozen marines, all dressed grandly in plundered clothing and armor. The big man looked savage; he was probably hung over. A brace of pistols had been shoved into his bright embroidered sash.

Derec could feel tension knotting his muscles. He tried to keep his voice light. "I need you to resume your duties aboard *Birdwing*, Mr. Marcoyn," Derec told him. "I'm sending Sandor to take charge of the prize."

There was a pause while Marcoyn absorbed this. He gave an incredulous laugh. "Th' piss you will," he said. "The prize is mine!"

Derec's nerves shrieked. Ignoring the sharp scent of liquor on Marcoyn's breath, he stepped closer to the big man. His voice cracked like a whip. "By whose authority? I'm captain here."

Marcoyn stood his ground. His strange pale eyes were focused a thousand yards away.

"The prize is mine!" he barked. "I'm in charge of the sojers here!"

Hot anger roared from Derec's mouth like fire from a cannon. "And *I* am in charge of *you!*" he shouted. He thrust his face within inches of Marcoyn's. "*Birdwing* is mine! The prize is mine! And *you* and your sojers are mine to command! D'you dispute that, Marcoyn?"

Do it, Marcoyn, he thought. Defy me and I'll pistol your brains out the back of your head.

Marcoyn seemed dazed. He glanced over the poop, his hands flexing near his weapons. Derec felt triumph racing through his veins. If Marcoyn made a move he was dead. Derec had never been more certain of anything in his life.

Marcoyn hesitated. He took a step back.

"Whatever you say, Captain," he said.

Readiness still poised in Derec. Marcoyn was not safe yet, not by any means. "You are dismissed, Marcoyn," Derec said. "I'd advise you to get some sleep."

"Aye aye, sir." The words were mumbled. Marcoyn raised his helmet in a sketchy salute, then turned away and was lost.

Tension poured from Derec like an ebbing tide. He watched the burly marine descend the poop ladder, then head for his cabin. He looked at Marcoyn's marines.

"Return your firelocks to the arms locker," he said. "Then report to Randem's repair party."

"Sir."

Derec sent Sandor and some of the armed sailors to the *Torn*, then looked up at the sails. "Hands to the main braces," he said. "Set the main tops'l. Steer nor'-nor'west."

Men tailed onto the braces, fighting the wind as they heaved the big mainyards around. Canvas boomed as it filled, as *Birdwing* paid off and began to come around, a bone growing in its teeth.

Relief sang in Derec's mind. He had managed it somehow, managed not to have to become Marcoyn in order to defeat him.

"Well done, sir." Tevvik's voice came quietly in Derec's ear. "But you should have let me handle him. Marcoyn's still a danger."

"To no one but himself." Flatly.

"I disagree, Captain. What will happen when he discovers you've set Collerne and the others free?"

"Nothing will happen. He will drink and mutter and that will be the end of it."

"I pray you are right, Captain."

Derec looked at him. "I won't have a man killed because he *might* be a problem later. That was Lord Fors's way, and Marcoyn's way, and I'll have none of it."

Tevvik shook his head and offered no answer. Derec glanced aloft to check the set of the sails.

Suddenly he felt his heart ease. He was free.

No more mutinies, he thought.

Birdwing heeled to a gust, then rose and settled into its path, forging ahead through a bright tropical dawn.

THE STONE FEY

She was out near twilight one evening, looking for a strayed lamb and muttering under her breath about the stupidity of sheep; truly they were the stupidest creatures ever created. It was a great misfortune that wool was so useful an item, and mutton so nourishing. Her dog, terribly embarrassed that he had not noticed the lamb's absence earlier, slunk along at her heels. "Anyone would think you went in fear of a beating," she said to him, and he flattened his ears humbly. She sighed. Aerlich was an admirable sheepdog, but he took himself very seriously.

It would soon be too dark to see anything, but a succulent young lamb would not survive the night in the wild rocky scree beyond the farm; if a folstza didn't get him, a yerig would. Damn. And she needed all her lambs; there had been several stillborns in her small flock this year, and none of the ewes had thrown twins; she was already short her usual market count.

Aerlich paused, raised his head and pricked his ears. He tried to growl, or thought about growling, or started to growl and then changed his mind, dropped his head again, and looked confused.

Something had appeared from the twilight, from the low scrub trees, from the rocky foothills of the Horfels where they stood; something stood on the faint deer trail they had been following, and faced them, holding a lamb—her lamb—in his arms.

He walked toward them. The lamb seemed quite content where it lay cuddled next to his breast. Aerlich growled again, stopped again, sighed, and sat tightly down by her feet. She could feel how tense he was, for what came to them, cuddling their sleepy lamb, was not human. If he had turned away, tried to run; if the lamb had bleated or struggled, Aerlich would have been on him at once. Aerlich, who was afraid of almost everything, was fearless as a sheepdog. He had once almost gotten them both killed trying to take on a whole pack of yerig by himself, and she, with as little foresight as her dog, had gone to help him. They both still wore the scars, but the yerig hadn't been hungry enough to take the victory they could have had, and she and Aerlich had been permitted to save their sheep.

What walked toward them now walked silently, on bare feet; she stood her ground, but she found her knees were trembling. Aerlich pressed against her nearer knee as the walker drew close to them. He stopped only when he was an arm's length away, so that he could hold the lamb out to her; and she, bemused, accepted it into her own arms. It gave a little grunt of annoyance at being so disturbed, but settled again straight away, its head on her shoulder, its stupid, gentle eye glazed with drowsy contentment.

He was just her height; she looked into black eyes, the iris as black as the pupil.

"Thank you," she said; her voice sounded so unnatural that Aerlich stirred, and growled again, audibly this time, but the half-man before them never glanced at the dog. He looked into her eyes for a long moment, and her heart beat in her throat; and then he smiled, or only seemed to smile as the night shadows moved across his face; and then he turned away, and disappeared again into the fast-lowering twilight.

It was deep dark by the time she got back to the farm. Partly from weariness, partly from the dark, partly from bewilderment at the strange meeting with the creature that had given her back her lamb, she stumbled several times. The successive jerks in their progress eventually woke her prodigal. It noticed perhaps that it had missed its dinner, and grew irritable. Aerlich, trotting at her side, looked up at her anxiously as it began to kick and baa aggrievedly. "If you don't be good, I'll make you walk," she said to it, and tripped over another rough spot in the ground.

The bereaved mother had made herself hysterical over her loss, and having gotten so far into her hysteria it took a while before she could be convinced that she was no longer bereaved. The animals were all restless with her fretting, and by the time the barn was quiet and the doors shut for the night, she and Aerlich were both exhausted. She leaned against the barn door and looked at the sky; it was vaster here, she believed, than anywhere else on earth, and she had never had any desire to discover empirically if this were true or not. The stars were coming out, white and shining, over the crowns of the Horfels; there were the merest wisps of clouds drifting, high and far away, across the midnight blue: fair weather again tomorrow. It was a windless night, and almost silent. Her shepherd's ear—and Aerlich's relaxed body sprawled beside her—told her that none of the small rustlings she heard were dangerous to sheep.

A breath of cooking smell crept to her from the farmhouse; dear Ifgold, she'd told him she might be out late after her lost lamb, though he'd only scowled. It was almost worth the aggravation—at least since she'd found it, or it had been found for her—not to cook dinner an extra night, and Ifgold was never mean about return favors.

She sighed, and Aerlich raised his head from the ground and looked up at her, and stirred his plumy tail when she smiled at him, but it was only a very little stir, because, after all, he had not found the lamb himself. Aerlich's mother had been one of the merriest beings she had ever known; how could such a charming mother have given birth to so solemn a son? But he had inherited her sheep sense, which was the important thing.

The food smells tickled her and her stomach rumbled, but she wasn't ready to go inside yet. She slid down the barn door and sat on the ground next to her dog, who looked at her earnestly a moment, and then, tentatively, put his chin on her knee. His mother would have jumped onto her lap at once, and then scrabbled up to put her forepaws on her mistress' shoulders. On a whim she leaned over and picked Aerlich up as she would a lamb, and set him on her lap. He started to scramble off again in alarm—whether it was his dignity or hers that he felt had been outraged she couldn't begin to guess—and paused with his hindquarters still across her thighs. He bent his head around and looked seriously into her face, and visibly changed his mind. He didn't fit in her lap any more than his mother had, but he scooted around again, slid down her out-stretched legs, let his forepaws trail over her hips, and rested his head on her stomach. He half shut his eyes and sighed profoundly.

She looked up at the sky again, her fingers trailing through Aerlich's silky hair. She had lived in this farmhouse all her life. When her mother, Thassie, had married Tim, she had brought him here to the farm, where she and her mother before her had lived all their lives. Tim had contentedly built a short wing off the kitchen for his jewelry-making, and took his pieces to town occasionally when his wife or his eldest daughter went on market-day. But the outside world didn't impinge too much on Tim; she was surprised he'd bestirred himself enough even to marry her bustling mother. And while Thassie was Mother, Tim had always been Tim, even to the littlest of them.

He was good with babies—better than Mother, really—and was happy to nurse the very young ones while Mother tended her vegetables; but as soon as they were old enough to start learning their letters and doing useful chores, he lost interest. Ifgold had said to her once, sadly, that he thought Tim had to remember his name every time he looked at him, his only son.

"He's that way with all of us, you know," she said, offering what comfort she could.

"I know," Ifgold said slowly. "I don't know why it still bothers me. . . . At least you have market-day; he has to recognize you then."

She smiled faintly. "Not true. He looks surprised when I come to his stall and tell him it's time to go home. It takes him a minute to realize I have the right to say it."

If anyone was to see strange things in their Hills, it should be Tim, dreamy Tim, who made such necklaces that one was even bought by a sola to give his lady in the great City of the king. His daughter was only a shepherd.

She knew what it was that she had seen; she remembered her grandmother's tales, for her grandmother was a little less matter-of-fact than her mother. Perhaps there was a little more of Tim in her than she realized, for she remembered those tales far more vividly than a shepherd need, of the wild things that lived in their Hills; there was even supposed to be a wizard who had lived for thousands of years somewhere to the south of them. But she had spent too much time alone with her dog, wandering the low wild foothills, not to know that there were creatures that lived there that she could not call by name; things besides the yerig and the folstza, the small shy orobog, the sweet-singing britti; things that were not birds or beasts, or lizards or fish or spiders.

Things like what had brought her back her lamb. She recognized him from one of her grandmother's stories: he was a stone fey. They were shorter and burlier than the other feys, with broad shoulders and heavy bones; in her childhood she had imagined them as shambling and clumsy, but she knew now it was not so. It was his skin that had told her for sure, for his skin was gray, the gray of rocks, and yet it was obvious—as her grandmother's story had told her it was obvious—that it was not the color of ill-health, and there was a rose-quartz flush across his cheekbones.

The smell of dinner would not let her sit any longer. She patted Aerlich and said, "We must go." He skittered off her lap at once and groveled, certain that he wasn't supposed to have been there in the first place, and she laughed. "You are impossible," she told him. "Come along; you must be hungry too."

Ifgold looked up from his work at once when he heard the door; Tim, staring dreamily into the fire, didn't look up at all. Thassie didn't raise her eyes from the piecework on her lap, but she got that listening look on her face that all her children knew well. Berry sat frowning over a book at the end of the long kitchen table; she looked up briefly with a smile for her big sister as sweet and vague as Tim's, and then went back to her book. The littlest ones were already in bed.

"I found the lamb," she said.

"Good," said Ifgold.

Thassie smiled. Her tidy fingers seemed to spin the thread through the neat hems and corners; between her quilts and her vegetables the farm needed no extra income. Her daughter's sheep were her own idea. The farm had had sheep in her grandmother's day, but Thassie was an only child, and it had taken her brood to begin to push the farm's productivity back up to what it had been. But Thassie was firm about where her children's profits went: Ifgold and Berry needed more schooling than the small village school could give them, and everything that could be spared from seed and fenceposts and shingles and sheep-dip went into the small but plump linen bag in the bottom of the wardrobe in Thassie and Tim's bedroom. Kitchet complained regularly that she had picked enough vegetables and dug enough holes and pulled enough weeds to have earned three ponies and she only wanted one, but no one stood up long to Thassie. Or almost no one. Her eldest daughter smiled a little wryly.

Ifgold would be going to a school in the south soon, and she would miss him, not only for the dinners he cooked out of turn, but because he was the only one of them all she could talk to. Mother was inimically businesslike, dispensing sympathy as neatly as she added up columns of figures; and Berry was as impossible to talk to as Tim was, or nearly; and the others were too young.

She bent to kiss her mother and then Tim. "Lamb?" he said. "I did tell him," Thassie said.

She shrugged. "Lamb. One strayed. I was lucky to find it."

Tim, who barely recognized his daughter from the rest of the people on market-day, heard something in her voice, and looked up at her almost sharply; but Ifgold said innocently, "Luck indeed. But you could use a little." Ifgold knew—unlike Tim—that ewes should have twins sometimes, and that none of hers had this season. Thassie murmured something in agreement, and Ifgold got up from his books—Berry took the opportunity to reach across the table and grab whatever it was he had been reading—and dipped up some of his stew on a plate. She sat down gratefully and let him serve her.

He put a bowl on the floor as well for Aerlich. "Everyone else has eaten." Looking across the table he said in sudden outrage, "You're supposed to be doing your schoolwork!" He glowered, but Berry ignored him, absorbed in the stolen book.

Curious, she reached out and delicately raised the book in Berry's hands till she could read the spine: *Tales of the Feys*. She dropped it as if it burnt her fingers, and Berry, startled, said, "I have done my schoolwork."

Embarrassed, she muttered, "I'm sorry. I didn't mean to disturb you."

From the fireside, Thassie said, "Finish the chapter, Berry, and off to bed with you."

Berry left, grumbling, and Ifgold reclaimed his book. He turned it over to look at the back, and then looked measuringly at his older sister; but she refused to meet his eyes, concentrating on her food. "I can at least do the washing-up," she said.

"I was hoping you'd say that," Ifgold said.

Tim drifted over to dry the dishes for her, but she had to put them away if they were to go anywhere that anyone could find them again. It was not usual for him to do any of the homely chores unless they involved a hammer or saw, and she had not liked the sudden intent look he'd given her when she'd come in.

"The lamb," he said, as she hung the dishrag over the edge of the sink and prepared to blow out the lamp that hung beside it. "It was all right when you found it?"

"Yes," she said. "I—" She wanted to tell him about the stone fey; Tim might even understand. But something stopped her words. She stood staring into the sink a moment, but she did not see the sink or the rag or her white-knuckled hands; she saw a gray-skinned face framed in black hair, and the intense black eyes that had looked into her own. When she looked up, Tim was still watching her with the same sharpness so unlike him. "I think I'm just tired," she said.

She climbed the stairs to her bedroom. She had fought and won the right to have a private bedroom; she was the eldest, and earned the most money—after Thassie—and she had to keep strange hours during lambing season. In exchange her room was the smallest, no more than a closet with a crack of window, but she didn't mind; it had a door on it that closed her in and the rest of the world out. Except Aerlich, who slept on the narrow bit of rug between her bed and the wall.

She hung her clothes on their peg, and leaned her elbows a moment on the windowsill—which was just about two elbows wide—and looked up again at her Hills. Even on cloudy nights she could look out her window and see in her mind's eye what the weather obscured; but tonight it wasn't necessary. Even the last faint shreds of cloud had left, and the sky was ablaze with stars. She wondered where the stone fey was, if he looked at the sky before he slept; if he slept out-of-doors or in some secret, stony cavern; if he slept. Perhaps at night he walked far over the Hills on his bare silent feet; perhaps he had been walking far this evening, when he found her lamb, and would never come this way again. She shook her head.

When she had trouble sleeping, she counted over in her mind the little pile of coins that was going to buy her own farm some day soon, the farm for herself and Donal; a little pile that when she had first wrested the right to it from her mother was small enough to fit under her thin mattress without discomfort. But it had grown bigger, slowly, and it lived now in another linen bag, smaller than the one in her parents' wardrobe, in a spare boot under her bed. With Donal's little pile they would soon be able to buy what they needed to settle on the bit of land they had chosen—that she had found one day, wandering far afield with her sheep—not too far from here, not so far that the Hills and the sky would look different from their new windows.

Donal had hired himself out this year as a logger, far away in the western mountains, near the mines; he had been gone only three months, and she would not see him again for another nine. She missed him bitterly, for while their parents' farms were far enough apart that they did not see each other daily nor at busy times even weekly, they had grown up together, had been good friends since she was eleven and he was ten and a half, when she'd met him at a market-day, trying to steal one of her first sheep. He hadn't realized it was one of hers—he said—

and by the time they had it sorted out (involving several bruises and one black eye—his) they were well on their way to becoming excellent friends. But as friendship had turned to love and thoughts of a life together and a farm of their own, they had discussed their chances, over and over again. She had finally, reluctantly, agreed to his plan to go away; his salary for a year was worth three times what she could earn by her flock— and probably more than that, this year.

She might not have had the strength of will, finally, to push it to the end with her mother, had she not had Donal to help her. Donal, youngest of six as she was eldest, was as determined as she, for perhaps precisely the opposite reasons, to have a life independent of his family—and he had had little choice, for the fourth and fifth children had already been afterthoughts, and there was little left for the sixth but kindness. Donal was the last person to be willing to plunge himself into another overflowing family, another family where he would always feel slightly superfluous. . . . She had wondered more than once if that had not been part of his initial attraction for her: someone to remind her when she wavered of how splendid it would be to be making their own fresh, new, individual mark on a piece of land unaccustomed to human feet and hands, and ploughs and scythes.

The only time she had ever seen her mother upset to the point of complete physical stillness was when she told her that she and Donal wanted their own farm. The eldest daughter had always brought her husband here; for generations it had been that way, back almost to Aerin's day, so her grandmother had said. She didn't know why it meant so much to her that she should leave, that her land should be new land, land that had not been farmed for generations of her own blood; perhaps she hadn't known till she met Donal. But that wasn't true, for she hadn't known Donal when Berry was born, and she was glad even then that there was another daughter, that even if it wouldn't be the eldest daughter, there would be another girl to grow up and take Thassie's place on the farm.

It wouldn't be Berry, though. Berry would be a scholar, or perhaps a teacher; she could hardly weed. Sometimes the little ones were a nuisance, but at least they provided three more girls, and Lonnie already was a passionate farmer.

But tonight she was too tired to think, and there seemed to be a cloud over her mind that was more than just tiredness; and the knowledge of the contents of a spare boot under the bed did not cheer her, nor the consciousness that every night was one day sooner that she would see

Donal again give her any pleasure. She went to bed and fell asleep at once.

She saw the stone fey again only a sennight later. Since she had a smaller flock this year, she had taken the opportunity to range a little further than she usually did—which was how she almost lost a lamb—looking for new pasture. Their country was stony, and all the local farmers with livestock were perennially occupied with keeping them fed. Her and Donal's farm would be little different; nowhere near the Hills was there rich land, but the Hills were the Hills. In the south, it was said, the trees were so lush they covered the sky in some places, and they could even grow oranges; but the Hills were her flesh and bone.

Her mother's farm was the furthest out. In Dockono, on market-day, she was the only one who came from the east. There was one other farmer whose land lay in as inhospitable a spot, to the north of her, and several from the south, but most of the farms lay west. It was a joke among those who met on the market-day streets that her farm and Nerra's must be blessed by the mountain wizard, for there was no other reason for there to be farms there at all.

Her and Donal's valley lay even further away from the market at Dockono than her mother's farm, but it would be worth it for her, living in the Hills instead of only in their shadow; and by its individual geography its land was a little more arable than much of what lay near it, which pleased Donal. It had been in a year of drought that she'd found it; she'd had a small flock that year, too, even smaller than this year, and even so she had had to range far, often gone from home for several nights together, to find enough fodder for her growing lambs.

But she had no drought as excuse this year. After she lost the lamb she should perhaps have gone back to her usual ways. But she didn't. She told herself that she would be extra watchful; she knew that Aerlich, still smarting in shame, was being extra watchful; and she told herself further that there was indeed no reason that her mother's farm did thrive— had thrived for several hundred years—and that if she could find new pasturage she should. For Lonnie's sake, perhaps, or Kitchet's. Kitchet liked animals better than vegetables too, and might want to have sheep. She did not think of the stone fey. So she told herself.

But she was not surprised when she saw him. She looked up, one afternoon, and he was sitting on a rock; near her, but not too near. She had no idea if he had been there all along, or if he had only just arrived, stepping so softly that even Aerlich—intent, at present, in facing down one of the oldest ewes, who felt she was beyond having to pay attention to a young whippersnapper of a sheepdog—had not noticed him; or if he had materialized out of air, or out of the rock he sat on.

He turned his head slowly to meet her gaze. He did not look surprised; he did not look anything at all. He merely looked back at her as she looked at him. The angles of his face cast queer, inhuman shadows over his stone-gray features, and his black eyes gave her no clue of what he might be thinking.

She dropped her eyes first; then, remembering herself, glanced over to see if Aerlich needed any help with his ewe. He did not. She did not want to look up at the fey again—they were on a hill, and he sat a little above her—but her eyes were drawn to him in spite of herself. How often did a mortal see a fey, after all, particularly a stone fey, who were supposed to be the shyest of all the feys? Why should she not look?

He was still looking down at her, and she felt an unaccustomed flush rising to her face. Should she say something? Could she just get up and leave? Aerlich would justifiably feel put-upon if, just as he got the herd settled for the day, she decided to move. She found, suddenly, that she was sitting uncomfortably, and had to rearrange herself. But the stone she was on obstinately remained uncomfortable, and at last she got up and found another rock, higher on the hillside. When she glanced at the fey again he was still there and still watching her, but she was now even with him. No closer, but she did not have to look up anymore.

"What is your name?"

The sound of his voice startled her, as if a stone had spoken; yet her grandmother's tales had informed her that feys did speak when they chose to. She blinked at him while her surprise subsided; it was the choosing that startled her, not the speaking, although his voice was not, somehow, what she would have expected. A stone fey should have a deep, harsh voice, a rumbling, stony voice; his voice was none of these things.

"Maddy," she said.

Silence fell. She stared out over her herd. They were grazing across a little plateau, and the Hill fell away below them as it rose at her back. When she looked for the fey again, he was gone.

Two days later she found an "M" in a beautiful mosaic of shimmering grays, nestled at the threshold of her sheep barn. No one ever came to the barn but herself and Aerlich; she cleaned it herself, and even replaced fallen shingles herself. She would far rather shovel sheep dung than ever come near a seed or a plough; her mother's other children could help her there. Hating vegetable duty was how she got started on sheep.

She saw the stones gleaming from the ground even as the sheep pattered over them and disappeared into the twilight inside, milling and protesting as they felt obliged to do each evening. Aerlich got them neatly into their pen and waited for her to close the gate and bestow upon him the words of praise he deserved. He looked around, astonished at her absence. She was standing by the outer door, staring down. He whined, a tiny, questioning whine, and her head snapped up. She came inside, and closed the gate, and told Aerlich he was the finest sheepdog in Damar. He looked up into her face worriedly, however, even as his tail dutifully wagged, for her voice lacked conviction.

She went back outside, Aerlich at her heels, and looked at the shimmering gray stones again. They were both subtle and conspicuous; the gleam of the gray looked as if it were only a trick of the light, as if at just a slightly different time of day they would not show at all. They looked, most particularly, like things of twilight, like the uneasy ghosts one was supposed to be able to see only during that grayest of daylight; as if, when the sun set, they would fall back into being pebbles of no particular heritage and in no particular order. They were set so perfectly into the low stone-flagged ramp at the door of the barn that they looked as if they had been there always, though she knew they had not. They had not been there even so recently as that morning—and yet the barn was in clear sight of the house and most of the fields around it. How—?

Staring at the silver "M" was making her head ache. It lay just where she had sat, Aerlich in her lap, the evening she had lost the lamb, and had it found for her.

There was nothing to do; nothing to say. She went indoors to start dinner.

She saw him again the next day. He seemed to be waiting for her; and yet she had not known, till she arrived at the little half valley on a knee of one of the foothills, that it would look good to her, and she would decide to stay.

Aerlich happily began to dispose of the sheep as suited him, and she flopped onto the ground. It was a good thing she raised her sheep primarily for their fleece; they were doing far too much walking, lately, to make them at all appetizing as mutton. Even the lambs must be getting thin and stringy. She watched while several of them at once sprang straight into the air, as young sheep will do, coming down again in a series of more or less graceful arcs, all now facing in different directions. They then pelted off, whichever way they were headed, apparently for no more reason than the pleasure of doing something dumb so often gives sheep of any age. Even a year ago such behavior still occasionally made Aerlich slightly hysterical, when he wasn't yet entirely accustomed to being the only sheepdog, and was first learning to do without his mother's somewhat overbearing direction. Maddy had had to help him sometimes, setting an example of placid resignation to the whimsies of their charges. Aerlich knew all about this sort of thing now, and was proud that he was in charge alone. The look of weary acquiescence on his face now as he trotted off to head the wanderers back toward the flock again was a precise canine version of Maddy's own expression under similar circumstances.

She started to laugh, and from nowhere, in this wild place, she had the feeling she was being watched. She swallowed her laughter and looked around, and there he was, sitting on a rock near her as he had sat on another rock in another stretch of rough Hill-grass a few days before. Perhaps he spends all his days sitting on rocks in the foothills, she thought lightheadedly; and picked herself up from her sprawl on the ground, and tried to sit with dignity. But she wasn't used to having to do anything with reference to dignity (except Aerlich's) when she was out with her sheep, and she scowled and fidgeted, and eventually got to her feet and went toward her unexpected visitor—except, she thought, I suppose I'm his unexpected visitor. I really have no reason at all to be coming so far. . . .

She paused a few steps from his rock, first startled by her own presumption and then held by the thought that he might run away from her, like a stzik or deer or any wild thing; or turn into a rock, or vanish, or whatever the feys did. She looked into his face, timidly, and his eyes looked back at her, as inscrutable as any deer's. She did not receive the impression that her arrival was unexpected; rather, and for no good reason, except for the patient, quiet grace of his sitting and the slow way he turned his head to follow her with his eyes, that he had been expecting her for quite some time, and that she was late. Her stomach felt funny, and she decided to sit down where she was.

She wasn't prepared for him to get up from his rock and come so near to her that the little breeze of his motion brushed her face. He sat down beside her, and she tried to look at the ground around her feet, at the small rocks, spotted or plain, rough or smooth, at the grasses, short and sharp and yet a hundred different shades of green; but she saw nothing, for while her eyes looked her mind was wholly taken up with the sound of his breathing.

He smelled of green things, of the sorts of green things that grow in still, shady places, of mosses and ferns, with a background sharpness like a stream-washed rock, or herbs trodden underfoot. It was a cool sort of smell, and she wanted to reach out for him, to see if his skin was cool to the touch; and then she wanted merely to touch him, for any reason whatsoever, and she clasped her hands tightly together, and stared miserably at her lap. He turned toward her and breathed something that might have been her name, and she raised her shoulders as if against a blow; and then felt his fingers, their touch only a little cooler than her own, on the nape of her neck, stroke up to her hairline, run along the curve of her jaw, and turn her face toward his.

Going home that night, she had little idea of where she was or where she was going; the sun was still in her eyes, the feeling of his black hair and smooth gray skin under her fingers, the taste of his mouth in hers. She even thought she might jump straight into the air for no reason, and dash off in whatever direction she found herself in when she came down again, only for the pleasure of doing something dumb. When Aerlich had safely brought his mistress and his sheep home, she blinked up at the barn for a minute as if she didn't recognize it; and then she had to think for another minute to remember how to lift the bar down and open the doors.

There were more "M"s wound around the stones of the little hard-packed yard in front of the sheep barn over the next few weeks. They twined together like vines, like the tiny stitches of her mother's quilting; they seemed to make a larger pattern she could never quite grasp. And they seemed to say her name aloud to her when she stepped over them, echo her name under the small sheep hooves, murmur her name after her as she walked away. In the evenings, the sheep safely penned for the night, she wanted to pause at the edge of the ramp, to listen to the whispering she might or might not be imagining; but Aerlich no longer enjoyed lingering anywhere in the barn's vicinity, and he would trot determinedly toward the farmhouse, his white tail-tip gleaming in the gathering twilight. He'd pause about halfway and turn, his white chest shining at her, though she could not see the reproachful look in his eyes; and she would pull herself away with a sigh, and follow him.

She tried to tease him about being over-anxious for his supper, but he only looked at her sidelong, and she realized, for the first time in the four years of his life, that he did have a sense of humor; that he had teased her with his earnestness as she teased him for it—and she missed it now, because he would no longer play. He worried about her as he worried about his sheep, harried her as best he could for her own good— and, she thought, no longer credited her with much intelligence. She started to get angry with him one evening for this, and then realized how idiotic it was, to yell at your sheepdog for disapproving of your private life; perhaps she didn't entirely know what she was doing.

And yet she had always known exactly what she was doing; as the eldest of six children it was a central fact of her sanity, if not her survival. She always knew what she was doing, and she made her choices clearheadedly.

She grew vague with her family, more like Tim or Berry than Ifgold or Thassie. She was asked, finally, if she were ill—after several conversations had stopped when she entered the room. She smiled, a smile they seemed not to like, and said that she was not. But Ifgold and her mother each asked her again, separately, drawing her aside, as if she might admit to something if she were alone. But she shook off their hands and their prying questions; she was not sick, and nothing else was any of their business. Even Tim asked her, one evening when she had come in particularly late and had had no reason to tell for it.

This at last made her angry, and she said sharply, "I am not ill. Do I look ill?" Aerlich crept away from her and disappeared behind Tim's chair. Tim was staring at her, a wrinkle between his brows that she couldn't remember ever having seen there before, and his eyes seemed darker than usual as he watched her, and she had the unpleasant feeling that since he looked at any of his children so rarely, perhaps when he did look at them he could see more. She turned abruptly away, and her mother was just at her shoulder, and laid a hand across her forehead. She started to jerk away, and then sighed and stood still.

"No," Thassie said. "You don't look ill, and I don't believe you have any fever. But you don't look like Maddy either."

"She looks haunted," Berry said. "Maybe she has a—"

"Hush," their mother said, fiercely for her. "Hush."

"It's what Grandmother would have said," Berry persisted. "You remember, her story about cousin whatever, third cousin forty times removed or something, Regh her name was? She went too far into the Hills to gather herbs, and—"

"Berry," said Tim, and Berry stopped in shock. She looked at her father with an expression suitable to one who has just heard a piece of furniture speak and give orders.

"I don't care what your grandmother would have said," Thassie said, and the tone of voice was so odd that Maddy was almost drawn back from wherever she'd wandered, these last weeks, to ask her mother if she were telling the truth. But she didn't.

"All I care is that she stop burning dinner," said Igard, one of the little ones. "You used to be able to trust Maddy. But she's as bad as Berry now."

"I don't burn dinner," Berry said irritably. "Hardly ever."

"Only about once a week," Igard said doggedly. "And you only have to cook once a week."

"That's enough," Thassie said.

"Yes, but—"

"Enough."

Silence fell, and Maddy permitted herself to wonder if she had changed so much. There was the way Aerlich watched her, even as her family did, unhappily; and the sheep began to shy away from her hands, which had never happened before. She did most of her own doctoring; she had to. The nearest healer who knew as much about sheep as she did lived on the other side of Dockono and by the time he got to the farm, or she got to him, it was often too late. She had an assortment of nasty little bottles and jars for most common ailments, and she knew how to pin a sheep in almost any position to get at whatever portion of its anatomy she needed to get at (with occasional help from Ifgold); but lately they seemed to flinch away from her in a way that had little to do with ordinary sheeply brainlessness.

That night when she went to bed she sat down on the floor and put her arms around Aerlich. He pulled his head free to lick her face—sadly, she thought, almost as if he were saying good-bye. "Is it truly so terrible?" she said. "It doesn't mean anything—I'm still Maddy. I *am* still Maddy. And it will all be over soon. I know it will be over soon." She shivered as she said that and put her face down on Aerlich's shoulder, and he sat very still, pressed up against her.

She asked her fey what his name was and he told her, Fel. She asked him if he had parents, brothers and sisters; he said he did, but he preferred solitude and saw them seldom; he did not volunteer any more. She wondered if all stone feys were solitary, or if he was unusual, but she did not ask him. She did not know what she might ask him, and feared to anger him; it was too important, too desperately important, that she be permitted to go on seeing him.

He never smiled when he saw her; her heart always paused, just for the moment when their eyes first met, in the hope that he would; and then, disappointed but obedient, took up its patient work again. She remembered that he never smiled only so long as it took him to come to her and put his arms around her; and then it no longer mattered, and till the afternoon, when she had to take her sheep home, it did not matter, till the next day.

He told her the fey names of different rocks and herbs; stone feys did not care much for trees or large animals, but they had names for each stage in a fern's life, and for the individual flavors of different waters, dependent on what minerals were dissolved in them and what plants might trail their leaves through them. Through him she saw her Hills as she had never seen them, and loved them as she had never loved them; but this new love had an ache in it. He smiled sometimes, briefly, over his rocks and ferns, but his eyes were always calm. He showed her how to walk quietly in the woods, for there were woods higher up on the sides of the Hills, and as the season progressed she found herself drawn higher and higher; and he taught her to move secretly even through the lower lands where there was little but rock and scree.

Or at least he taught her as much as he could; she was aware that she was not a very good pupil, however hard she tried. He did not scold her, any more than he praised her, or than he smiled at her. But she did not quite dare ask him about this either—even to ask him why he taught her. It was perhaps simply that what she offered him was enough—or so she told herself. What her sheep offered her was enough, too, because she knew they were sheep.

She left the sheep-tending to Aerlich, who was perfectly competent to do it; and fortunately they did not run into any more yerigs. But when, occasionally, during the days, she checked to see that Aerlich was still in command, she often caught him looking back at her with a puzzled, lonesome gaze that irritated her; what was a sheepdog for but to take care of sheep? He and Fel ignored each other; politely but implacably.

They never arranged to meet, but when she set out in the morning she seemed to know which way to go; and once they'd climbed well away from the farm she began to look eagerly around each bend in the path and over each boulder for him to appear. Occasionally it was a long time before she saw him, and she would go on, faster and a little faster, and a little faster yet, her breath coming a little too quickly for the climb, and the sheep beginning to protest the hurrying, till he did appear. And occasionally she did not get back home till after dark, which was foolish of her, for it was tricky enough to keep the sheep together and aimed in the right direction in daylight; and she dared not lose even one this year, for the sake of her farm. Her and Donal's farm. Her mind shied away from thoughts of Donal, though she preserved memory of him carefully, like an heirloom quilt in an old wooden chest, dried flowers tucked in its folds; something she wanted kept near her, something she might want to take out and shake free, and use, some time in the future; just not right now.

And Ifgold was no longer there to cook for her when she was late. She had forgotten that he was to leave so soon; or perhaps more time had passed than she realized. Ifgold had tried the hardest to talk to her in the first weeks of her meetings with Fel, but she had told him that she had nothing to say, and smiled her new, dreamy smile; and then, when he persisted, she grew short with him, and began to avoid him. And then it was too late, for he was leaving.

"Will you write to me?" he said, a little desperately.

"Of course," she said, but they both knew she lied.

Ifgold shook his head. "I don't know what to do," he said, and his voice cracked; but he was still at an age when boys' voices do sometimes crack, and his eldest sister patted him on the shoulder and told him not to worry. His face crumpled like a much younger child's, and he turned away from her. Thassie was taking him to Dockono in the wagon, since he was lugging a box of his precious books with him, where he would meet with one other southbound scholar, that they might travel together. Ifgold turned once, when he was seated in the wagon; Maddy raised her hand in a final farewell, and he, reluctantly, raised his hand in response.

She almost ran up the Hills that day, for waiting to see her brother off had made her late getting started; and a few days later, when she took the early lambs to market, she failed to get as good a price for them as she should have, because she could not concentrate on her bargaining.

One of the nights that she should have made dinner she got back very late to be greeted by a furious Berry, who'd been impressed into duty in her absence—and who had contrived that there should not be enough dinner left for the latecomer. Maddy had to do with bread and apples, which wasn't nearly enough. As she bit slowly into her third apple, it occurred to her suddenly that she missed Ifgold. She had been thinking that she might justly complain to Thassie about Berry's behavior; she always paid back a dinner out of turn, and after a long day following sheep, she needed a hot supper, especially since her noon meal was always cold. It used to be that she took a tinderbox with her occasionally, and something that wanted cooking; Aerlich particularly liked those days. But Fel shied away from fires and hot food, and so she had not done so for a long time.

She took a second bite of the apple. But it probably wasn't worth complaining about; very little seemed to be worth much lately, except counting the hours till she saw Fel again. Funny about missing Ifgold; he was only her brother.

That night she dreamed, terribly, of Donal. She dreamed that he was caught under a falling tree, and he held his hands out to her, and called her, weeping, to help him; but Fel was waiting for her, if not around this bend in the path, then around just this next one. . . . She woke up, but the tears on her face were her own. It was still deep night. She crept to her windowsill, but there was no space to lean her elbows anymore, for she put the pebbles and small stones that she found in Fel's company there, to remind her of him during those long hours they were parted; and she drew back now as if they might burn her.

"We will not go high into the Hills today," she told Aerlich in the morning; and the silver stones under their feet as they left the barn lay silent. When the sheep were rounded up and moving, she set out in a direction that was not the direction she wished to go. They grazed that day across ground she had once often used, and it had grown almost lush—as lush as sheep-nibbled Hill-turf can ever grow—for its rest. Aerlich was as dutiful as ever, but, he did look often over his shoulder as if to check that she was still there; and when he felt he had a minute free he would rush over to her, to press his jaw up against her legs, and gaze adoringly into her face—and then dash off again, back to his flock. She couldn't eat her noon meal, and her hands shook, and she found herself irrationally annoyed that Aerlich no longer expected her to have anything to do with herding sheep.

The second day was the same, except that the call to climb into the Hills was stronger, and on the third day she answered it. Aerlich understood at once as she chose the path that led them away from their once-familiar trails, and his head and tail drooped, though he kept the sheep no less snugly together for it.

Fel was sitting on a rock, waiting, as he had waited so many other days. He did not ask her where she had been; he gave her no words of reproach, but looking into his smooth, undisturbed face, she knew he had none to give. Their day together was shadowed, for her, by this knowledge, and before they parted that evening she took his face between her hands and stared long at him, at the strong straight nose, the curl of the black eyelashes. "The gods save me," she said hopelessly. "I love you." Fel did not reply, and she turned away, to follow her sheep.

She did not go into the Hills again. After the first few days she found it difficult to sleep, for she heard that call—whatever it was—even at night, and she trembled, and thrashed under her blanket, and her head ached, and in the morning her eyes were heavy. The call became something that she oriented herself by; it told her where not to go; it reminded her why she felt so awful all the time; it gave her suddenly empty life meaning by its existence. She dreamed no more of Donal, and she managed to be interested when the family received Ifgold's first letter. His journey had been uneventful; he was finding his feet with his peers, a few of whom were from even as vast a sweep of nowhere as himself; the masters were kind but the work was appalling. "Appalling" was his word, but it was obvious that he was delighted with it.

She held the letter in her hands to read it over to herself, after Thassie had read it aloud to everyone, and the memory of Ifgold and their friend- ship was very strong; he wrote just the way he talked, and she could hear him, and she missed him. She was free of the Hill call, for a moment, as she remembered her brother.

She wrote back. He answered almost at once, a letter just for her, although Igard and Lonnie nagged her into reading it aloud to everyone; and Ifgold must have guessed they would, for he said nothing that she need disguise. At the same time the relief in him was written larger than any of the words on the page, even as he spoke of harmless things, the work he was set, a boy he grew to be friends with. She read the letter several times. Her hands did not shake so much as they had.

She still could not sleep a night through; she still heard the call to come into the Hills, to leave her foolish sheep and her humorless dog and her dull family, and come to the Hills. She thought the call said *forever*. She thought: if he truly wanted me, he would come for me, and she squeezed her eyes shut.

He did not come, and the silver stones by the barn grew gray with use.

It came easier as the weeks passed, and the seasons turned again; and she no longer burnt the food she cooked, and she was very rarely home late, and then only for a very good reason. The rest of the lambs were sold, and as everyone's flocks this year were short, she got a good price for them, and did not lose so much as she had feared; and this time she bargained hard. The sheep lost their skittishness around her, except insofar as sheep are always skittish, and occasionally she took tinder and flint with her, and food to cook, and had a hot meal in the lee of a boulder, and shared it with Aerlich, who began occasionally to let her make decisions about the sheep again. When she thought of Fel she thought only to wonder why what had happened had happened at all; and if the call still came from the Hills, she ignored it, as she learned to ignore a certain place beneath her breastbone, which had once not been empty, and now was.

A full year came round, and Donal came home. He came to her first, even before his family. They'd written few letters in the past year; that had been part of their agreement, that neither would feel slighted while each was buried in work, in earning the money for their life together. She had found it only too easy to write rarely, and then in haste, and briefly, about sheep and weather; and she could not have said, beyond the very first ones, what Donal's letters to her had contained. But he had written that he was coming; and, almost against her will, she felt a rising excitement as the last few days of their long separation passed. She woke up in the mornings almost happy, and she recognized the sense of expectancy before she remembered why she felt it; and in the resultant storm of conflicting emotions she finally tried only to put all of it out of her mind. But it wouldn't leave her; and Donal was coming home.

She heard unfamiliar hoofbeats in the yard early one evening, and knew who it must be; and her mind had no part in the decision, for her feet picked her up and flung her out the door. Donal hugged her hard and then lifted her and swung her around.

"You're thinner," he said, just as she breathlessly said, "You're stronger." They were both right. Donal had never been burly, but a year's hard labor had filled him out, neck, chest, shoulders and thighs; it was as if the old Donal had a new shadow. She looked at him a little fearfully, for he suddenly reminded her of someone else, someone who no longer existed for her; and she grabbed at his newly broad upper arms to steady herself, and stared into his face; he was very little taller than she. He looked back at her, puzzled and then hurt by her expression. "Aren't you happy to see me?"

"Of course I am," she said, and threw her arms around his neck and kissed him, and his arms closed eagerly around her. When he let her go she looked into his face again, and cupped her hands around it; his hair was brown, and his eyes brown too, warm against the black iris, and his skin was a warm ruddy brown from the sun. She felt her face relax, and more easily she slipped back into his arms, and kissed him again, and his mouth smiled against hers.

When they turned, the rest of the family had come out, and Thassie had Lonnie's shoulder in a firm grip and gave her a shake as she was inclined to snigger. Kitchet had already gone to pet Donal's horse; they were having a low snuffly conversation off to one side. Maddy's eye met her mother's, and a little hard look went between them; and Maddy snuggled against Donal's side and put her arm around his waist, and Thassie smiled.

Donal refused to be parted from her, and so swept her off with him to visit his parents. Her family sent her with him willingly—a little too willingly, she thought, but she did not pursue it. Everyone treats me like a convalescent, she thought more than once: they welcome me back as if from the gates of death, after an illness they had despaired of. The thought was bitter, and mixed of several bitternesses. And Donal, she saw, watched her anxiously when he thought she did not see; and she wondered if perhaps her mother had said something to him, but decided it was unlikely. Thassie was too grateful that her strayed daughter looked like coming back to the fold to risk the coming back by unnecessary words about the straying. And little does she know the truth of it, her daughter thought grimly.

But Maddy's determination to behave as she should, as if what had happened had not happened, or had not mattered, held her in good stead till she found that Donal's kindness, and obvious pleasure in her company, began truly to bring her back to what she once had been. She did not ask him what he guessed, and tried to pass it off lightly when he, too, treated her as gently as a recent invalid, and teased him that they had only been parted for a year—really, she was still Maddy. He searched her face with his eyes—and at night, when they lay together, with his lips and fingers—hoping to find the truth of her words; she did not know if he thought he had succeeded.

They were gone to his family a fortnight. Maddy had not argued when Donal insisted that she go with him, only arranged that Lonnie and Kitchet should go together with Aerlich and the sheep; not that Aerlich needed human companions, particularly not young almost useless ones, but even Lonnie should enjoy a break from her usual farm chores, and

Kitchet idolized her biggest sister, and was delighted to get to do what Maddy did.

Kitchet was full of the wonders of sheep-grazing when they got back: the views from her favorite hillsides, the cleverness of Aerlich, the personalities of sheep. "Personalities!" Maddy said, laughing. "You give them more credit than I ever have. Well! You will grow up to be our next shepherd. I'm glad. I agree, wandering alone over the Hills is like nothing else. . . . " Her voice trailed off, and the adults grew very still; but Lonnie said in her blunt way, "It's *boring*. Nothing but rocks and scrub and more rocks and scrub, and sheep are stupid and they smell, and Aerlich does everything." Everyone laughed, and the tension was blown away.

And then at last she and Donal went off to look at their farmsite. She had wheedled him into staying an extra day with her family—their chosen valley was less than a day's brisk march from her mother's farm—saying that the weather promised rain, and she didn't want to come trailing into their new home dripping wet and miserable. Donal laughed and agreed to wait. They spent one cloudy day on a little knoll close enough to her mother's farm to look down on the buildings from where they sat watching the sheep. Aerlich seemed exhausted, and let Maddy do more of the work than he had since . . . she stopped the thought abruptly. But it didn't rain, and on the next day dawn arrived with a glad blue sky, and she had no further excuses, though a sense of oppression weighed her spirit more and more.

But she put a bright face on it and after a quick breakfast she and Donal set out. At the last minute she decided to take Aerlich too. The sheep would be content in their small outdoor pen, with plenty of silage; and she awarded Kitchet the task of keeping an eye on them. She and Donal would return the next day.

Aerlich was surprised when she whistled him away from the sheep pen. He looked at her, and he looked at the sheep, nosing through their fodder, rubbing along the fence for splintery spots that might catch at their fleece so they could bolt away in terror, and running blindly into each other so that they could complain about it—and the weight on her spirit lifted long enough to let her laugh at him. "Come along, silly," she said. "It's a holiday."

He stiffened all over and turned his face away because she'd called him silly, and she smiled, and the oppression lifted a little more, because she remembered the days when he had treated her humorlessly, as a burden. She said gently, "Come, Aerlich," and he came.

But he didn't seem to know what to do with himself, and for most of the day kept close to Maddy's heels, bumping into her if she stopped suddenly. But she was almost as dumbly following Donal, who strode out confidently. He called over his shoulder sometimes about this bird, "I haven't seen one of those in a year!" or that fall of rock, "Isn't it ever going to fall down the rest of the way?" or general cheerful nothings she didn't bother to hear. For her own breath came short, and the Hills, her Hills, gave her no joy, neither the rock and turf underfoot nor the bird-speckled sky overhead; nor the rough green smell of the hardy Hill-grass and the low sturdy trees; and she knew at last some measure of her real loss, and the reason her heart beat so hollowly.

She hurried Donal on when he would have stopped for lunch, and he fell in with her haste willingly, misinterpreting it as eagerness to reach the end of their journey. But when they came down over the little rocky shoulder that heralded the gap in the Hill's side that gave into their valley, her feet slowed involuntarily, and Donal went on alone. He was out of sight around the spur when he missed her; but as he turned back to call she came round it herself and stood beside him.

There was grass in their valley, real grass, and a few real trees, for the Hill curved around it on three sides, and the entrance to it was southwest. It was sheltered from the bitter winter wind, and from the irresponsible summer wind that sometimes knocked down half-grown crops and scoured the thin topsoil away from the rock that always lay near beneath the earth of the Hills. A little stream watered it, and spread out to become a pool before it parted again into several rivulets that ran in all directions; it had been a joke in her family that this tiny lake fed the stream that ran near her mother's farm, and that she would be able to send messages, once she and Donal had made their own farm beside it, by wrapping notes around stones and dropping them in the water. Kitchet—very young then—had believed it.

She looked at her valley, at its green spring promise of the fulfillment of her and Donal's dreams, at everything they had worked for the last six years, and she burst into tears. Donal said, "My own darling, whatever is wrong?" But he saw at once that she was beyond speech, and so took her in his arms and rocked her gently, while she held onto him as she might a tree in a storm; and Aerlich sat at their feet and whined, a tiny, anxious, high-pitched whine.

She quieted at last, and they walked hand in hand to the pool where she washed her face—and gasped, for it was brutally cold—and then they sat down together, and he put an arm around her and she rested her tired head on his shoulder and gave a long shuddering sigh. The tears seemed to have washed away her ability to think; what could she say? She was not sure she could explain anything satisfactorily even to herself; so what could she say to Donal, when there was so much she could not say to him, and would not say to herself?

"I can't stay here," she said at last, dully, and there was a silence, and Aerlich put his head on her leg and looked up at her.

"I—I think I have guessed that much," Donal said. "I—perhaps I guessed it some time ago." There was something in his voice she could not identify.

"I'm sorry."

His shoulder lifted briefly under her cheek. "This valley was always more yours than mine. I only want to farm. It's you who has Hillrock for bones."

"We could go somewhere else," she said tentatively; and he caught her up at once, sharply: "We?"

Then she knew what she heard in his voice: fear. His *we* hung in the air between them, as cold as the mountain water, and she said, "If—if you wish to come with me," and heard fear in her own voice.

He sighed, and his breath caught in his chest halfway. "I do wish it. Perhaps I wish it as desperately as you wish not to stay here. . . . I'm sorry. I thought you loved the Hills best of all; better than me, better certainly than your sheep, which I've always believed were only an excuse to let you run free up here. I want to farm—somewhere—and I want you, and I don't—I don't want to have to choose between you."

She said, muffled by his shoulder, "My brother has written of the land around his school; he can't altogether stop being a farmer for all he's a scholar now. He says it's good land, rich, and underused." She heard her voice speaking, as if from very far away; it sounded vague and unconvincing. She remembered Ifgold's words in his letter, and wondered if he had written them just for this occasion. She remembered, from even longer ago, the tales that many of the local farmers told about the southlands; how, very far away, farther even than Ifgold's school, there were orange groves. But she had heard the tales with indifference, and remembered them little; for she had Hillrock for bones. "He says they've only begun to learn to irrigate, but . . . "

Donal laughed. "If it weren't for you I would never have thought of staying in the Hills. It's wild land here—not farmland. But I was afraid to say anything. Afraid that you'd decide I was too dull and ordinary a fellow, too tame, for you and your Hills. . . . This valley would have been fine," he went on hastily; "there is some real earth here. But south, to Illya, where your brother is—to grow something besides korf and a few vegetables! Yes, I should like it above all things. I'm sorry. If I'd known— if I'd guessed—I'd have spoken long ago."

She looked up into his face, transformed with happiness, and a new little glow began to bloom in her own heart, and she realized that he would be tender with her always about his mistake; and that since she would for long need the tenderness she would let him go on thinking the mistake was his.

"We can set out as soon as you like," he went on, eagerly. "We'll not need to take much with us; it will make better sense to start fresh when we arrive."

"I'll write Ifgold, so that he can look us out a place to stay," she said slowly, and her voice sounded less hollow, and she smiled timidly at Donal. "He lives in a boarding house near the school; perhaps there's even room there, while we look around us."

After a moment she went on, "I'll sell the rest of my damn sheep; Kitchet can start her own flock if she wants to, when she's old enough."

"The sheep are your problem," Donal said firmly. "I refuse to have anything to do with anything that doesn't have roots and isn't green."

Maddy was suddenly conscious of the weight across her leg, and she looked down into a black and white face with hopeful brown eyes. "Aerlich will come with us. If we decide—if I decide—not to have sheep, I'll buy him some geese to herd."

CLOSE OF NIGHT

I

t had finished raining by the time they drove through the first suburbs of Edinburgh, and a slate, disconsolate sky yawned hugely over the car, glimmers of sick yellow tearing the clouds to the west. Usually the wedges of Arthur's Seat, truculent slabs massing into view over the tall buildings, cheered Eva. Not this time, however—they seemed withdrawn a little from her, and less clear-edged. She felt uncertain of the city's welcome.

The Pentlands brooded over the coming night; and further north, the gaunt Highland line hunched its shoulders over the gray spears of the retreating rain, which had been chilly, whining, persistent, not easily cleared by a red evening sun.

Eva wanted nothing so much as to get to the hotel, and retreat over dinner from James's tireless, clacking, instructing tongue, which reckoned up business deals over the miles of travel.

They had stayed the night before at Carlisle. Later on this afternoon, the first meeting of the conference would begin, full of introductions and mistrustful back-patting. There was an evening sherry reception, to which wives were invited. "Commanded" would be a more appropriate word. Not for the first time in fifteen years, Eva wondered why she had married a businessman, to become almost a necessary part of an entourage. She

had been a social worker, scurrying about desiccated city streets in constant trails of crises, too tired to eat, often; too discouraged by her environment to bother to dress well. Tall and slender, with a mass of floppy,
bright-brown curls, she looked well when she could trouble herself to
search out something that suited her. She had done just that on the
evening when she decided to accept the invitation to the party at which
she had met James. He was somebody's cousin, up from the country on
a family inspection of the girl's lodgings, and invited only by hasty
accident.

He was extremely presentable, but quite out of his depth, both in talk
and attitudes. She felt sorry for him. He recognized it and was grateful.
He invited her to leave the party and have dinner; she accepted, amused
at his need to find a social substitute for his instinctive rejection by the
party-goers, and somehow the meetings turned into a habit, while he
remained in the town.

She had married him within the year, still not knowing quite why.
Something to do with his more vulnerable spots, his need of a listening
wife—his delightful manners played a part in it, too. She found herself
honestly charmed by the habits of a man who always opened a car door,
or any other door, for her, who pulled her chair back, helped her off
with her coat. It was later on in their married life, and after they had
discovered that they could not have children, that she also found out
that charming manners cannot replace absorption—the absorption that
stems from genuine concern with another, and intense interest in that
being's every thought, movement, or action. She had had lovers, and if
James had known of them, he had never said anything. But she had
never found another person who looked into her face and watched her
soul looking back at him, and waited for it to explain itself in speech and
deed.

Perhaps there weren't many of them. Wealth formed a good cushion,
she enjoyed traveling, and they traveled a great deal and in comfort.

She could concern herself with housework or not, as she pleased, for
there was plenty of money to hire servants; she could work, if she wanted,
voluntary, charitable work—as long as she was available to be presented
as James's assured token of marital success and security.

She was a great deal better off than many wives. She was also bored,
discontented, unhappy, and a little frightened.

"I know you're tired," said James. He prided himself, perhaps rather
pathetically, on his perceptiveness. But who wouldn't be tired, after three
hundred miles?

Eva shrugged, and regretted it—her neck ached badly, a series of sad, tenuous threads of pain that wound their way up into her brain.

"I think I'm probably hungry. I always feel like eating a lot when I'm in Edinburgh."

"Good food here, particularly the bakeries," agreed James. But Eva sometimes felt uneasily that it was because there had been so much hunger here in the past—whenever she entered the city, it was as if old odors called her to recognize them and include them with her own feelings. Odors of fear and hunger and sly passion without fulfillment and cruelty and blank incomprehension. She knew too much of the history of the place; she thought of no one famous or infamous individual—John Knox, Brodie, Queen Margaret—but of a nameless buzzing tumult of little people who had watched and suffered from the wings, while the great players strode and plotted and bargained.

"Walk-on parts," she said aloud, and James turned to look at her with concern.

"Having hallucinations, darling?" He chose jocularity rather than anxiety, and certainly he was perceptive about what irritated her. She smiled back, and he drew the car to a halt in one of the side streets. The Argonne was one of the better small hotels, but not the best. This meant that at off-peak seasons they often had it nearly to themselves, and the excellent, unobtrusive care of the proprietor and his wife, John and Ellen Dobree, was centered mostly on her while James was at meetings. She liked these journeys for no other reason than that she was lightly spoiled by a couple who knew nothing about her, but had been trained, and had practiced to give as much attention to guests as the guests themselves desired. She liked, too, the well-bred, shabby, dark furniture, and the unostentatious but plentiful comfort of the hangings and carpets. The walls were exceedingly thick, and it was very quiet, although the city center was quite close.

The food was excellent, as the best English home cooking can be, with recipes handed down over a dozen generations. There were not many Scottish dishes, but always superb bread, cakes, and oatcakes, and the best fish she had ever eaten.

There was time for a very hurried tea before James went off to his five o'clock session of introductions. She was to join him at the Great Britain at about half-past six—she was glad he had not booked them into the conference's main hotel. It would have meant more of the normal, rather tedious, social chores of joining women without common interests for coffee and shopping.

She unpacked efficiently, chose a green silk dress with a high curly neckline lined with peach, changed, and decided to walk into town, rather than catch a bus or call a taxi. Her shoes were not entirely practical for the purpose, glossy bronze with small thin heels, but they were comfortable enough, and it wasn't cold.

She arrived on the North Bridge with enough time to spare to look around her for a little while; she decided to visit St. Giles's Cathedral, and absorb darkness and grave silence for a while, before being thrust into the overlighted, high-pitched gaiety of the sherry party.

The Cathedral was nearly empty, and she sat at the back, trying not to think, and above all, not to hear the sound of the car's remorseless engine, which was always so hard to get out of one's head after a long journey.

She thought someone whispered to her, and brushed her elbow, but turning she saw that her nearest neighbor was not only rapt in silent prayer, but many yards away. She read the notices near her—an organ recital, a string quartet from London, an appeal for those interested to take part in street theater on the church's behalf. She noted the day of that, and thought that she might find an opportunity to watch it. She became aware that someone was watching her, and turned, half-smiling, to anticipate a remark from some friendly stranger—one of the vergers, perhaps. Did they call them vergers here? She must find out. Irritated and confused, she found that she had made that most familiar of mistakes—a dark old clothes-press, standing upright in a corner, had seemed to her, with her shoulder turned, to be leaning toward her like a human being.

There was a small metal plate set into the wall by her, and she read that, too. Jhonet Cowrey, it said, 1678, and nothing else. The clothes-press looked old enough to have belonged to one Jhonet Cowrey, too, though it was undoubtedly used for vestments, now.

A door creaked, and she saw the woman she had thought deep in prayer was slipping out of the Cathedral. A deep ray of light struck a tangle of red-gold curls above her neck, and the handwoven cloth that hid the rest of her hair was a warm blending of purple and green, soft and blurred, like wet heather.

Eva thought it beautiful, and determined to try to buy one like it in one of the smaller, more expensive shops. It would not be anything like so attractive in a cheap make. Probably Princes Street would be better than the Royal Mile. She would ask Ellen Dobree.

As she rose to leave, an odd moment of half-suffocation overtook her, and for a moment she felt the Cathedral close its walls around her, with singing, and a rose and gold haze of bright candles, and a press of dark garments and dropped heads smelling of hurry and unwashed human flesh. It was as if her knowledge and her imagination had temporarily worked together to cast her back into some earlier time, when the life of mankind was the life of the church, and without the church there was not any authority or law or comfort.

The Royal Mile was almost as dark as the Cathedral had been, for a whole strip of street-lighting had failed, and she quickened her step, partly through nervousness, and partly because she had lost a few minutes during her dizziness in the Cathedral.

It was while she was passing the entry to a small dark flight of steps, quite close to a wine bar she had often visited with James, that she heard a voice and this time certainly a touch on her elbow.

"Ye're late out," said a boy's voice, and a lad of about twelve went past her, turning to smile (but his face was half-hidden), and disappeared down the steps. She had not thought children so badly clothed still lived in Edinburgh—he was out at the elbows, and, she was almost sure, barefooted. She had seen the marks of some great burns on his hands as he moved—he must have scorched himself badly at home or school.

"I'll soon be indoors," she called after him, but he had gone. Moved by curiosity, she went down the steps a little way, and looked into the close where the boy had vanished.

She could not see very much, only enough to tell her that it was one of the unrestored old closes, not like the cleaned, renewed stone of Lady Stair's House, but dank and slimed, with pools between filthy cobbles, and strings of washing hanging high between the rooms.

There were obviously people in the houses, for many lights showed, and there was a smell of fish cooking, and whispers from a doorway, perhaps from a courting couple. Eva shuddered fastidiously at the thought of anyone sitting or lying on such stones. There was one single lamp in the close, tall and beckoning, like an iron lily. It shone with no warmth, but its light was singularly powerful, and lay in puddles of yellow beneath it.

As she turned back to go up the steps again, she felt her gaze drawn upwards, and found it met by a grossly fat old man who was sitting motionless in a bare window embrasure. He wore nothing on his arms— some kind of filthy white sleeveless shirt covered his bloated belly—and she could not tell whether he could see her. His eyes were white-blue, filmed all over with what might have been cataracts. It was like some

obscene parody of the balcony scene from *Romeo and Juliet*, and she
leant sickly against the damp wall, for the dizziness had come over her
mind again.

In the whitewash, scored deeply in black, near her hand, she saw
letters:

Morag—gudewife—spaewife

and then much further down, large and hastily written:

Nae wife

She went out, wondering what the unknown Morag had done to attract
praise and criticism of such different kinds on the same piece of wall. A
strange place, Edinburgh—some of the stories were so well-known, and
some so hidden. Had Jhonet Cowrey, perhaps, known a Morag? It was
a common enough name. That was nonsense, though—they need not
have lived at anything like the same time.

When she arrived at the Great Britain, the party had already overflowed
from the conference suite and slopped into the bars. She could see James
almost immediately, holding a drink, with another by his side on the
table, and talking earnestly to a fat woman with too much makeup. He
looked anxious and irritated, and his eyes constantly left her to roam
round the room, and then returned to pay painful attention. So this must
be somebody powerful and important, and undoubtedly he had asked
her to meet his wife who would soon be here, and was already wondering
how to explain her lateness. Eva felt annoyed, but contrite—this was
what she disliked so much about James and his business—her part-
accountability for so many things.

She went and made her apologies, and was astonished to discover that
she had somehow lost another fifteen minutes—she was now nearly half
an hour late for the sherry party, and James was obviously exasperated,
if worried. He introduced her to Mrs. Ferolstein, and was rather obviously
careful not to ask her what she had been doing, and how she had taken
so long doing it.

Mrs. Ferolstein proved unexpectedly pleasant and perceptive. Whatever business connections, she was a devoted live-in lover, as the dailies
would have it, of Edinburgh.

"You were enjoying your little trek round the streets, were you?" she asked, in a soft rich voice, warmed with small Scottish inflections. "I never tire of her myself, the mysterious old lady of a town that she is!"

Eva smiled briefly, thinking of the night and the unexpected, unwelcome appearances.

"It's intriguing. . . . I won't say I enjoyed it. I was lost for a while," she ended, looking apologetically at James, who merely shrugged, exasperated, before he set off to get them all another drink and some canapés.

Over dinner, Mrs. Ferolstein talked to her on one side about the historic glories of Edinburgh, and James lectured on the other about the dangers of getting lost in the dark and menace of the old town.

Eva had a sudden thought. "Mrs. Ferolstein, do you know anything about the plates set into the walls of the Cathedral?" she asked, ignoring one of James's more vivid descriptions of a recent court case concerning a late woman walker and a mugger.

Mrs. Ferolstein appeared to have an encyclopedic knowledge of the antiquities of St. Giles' Cathedral.

"Oh, Jhonet Cowrey!" she exclaimed, when Eva had enlightened her. "Poor woman!"—as if she were talking about some distant and unfortunate relative—"Yes, they put her on trial for her husband's death—it seems she'd been worried about his health, and lack of—lack of energy," said Mrs. Ferolstein delicately, "and she'd apparently asked for help from some woman in the neighborhood who had the reputation of being able to help in odd matters like this . . . some kind of a white witch, you may say. It was quite a celebrated case in the seventeenth century. The wretched man died, and of course, if you know the kind of thing that the herbal leeches of the day thought good for a complaint of that kind, you wouldn't wonder. There was some doubt, because she came from a good family, though they were poor, and everyone knew she was fond of him—naturally, or she wouldn't have been asking for the remedy. Nevertheless, they hanged poor Jhonet—the neighborhood woman was never known. I daresay there were a good many people who wanted to help Jhonet. She was well liked. But no one would risk their necks or the enmity of the medical-lady busybody who had put a good man into the next world out of kindness of heart, and out of a desire to save his wife from seeking consolation from someone more potent. So no one opened a mouth in the wrong place—after all, they might have had a need of their own one day, and a good spaewife is not all that easy to come by."

"Spaewife?" Eva mused. "I've heard it before—a fortune-telling woman or something of the kind. Would she deal in herbs and potions, too?"

"Oh, for sure! And no doubt she would give a bit of good counsel, and along with a few charms, she'd explain to the nagging wife how to use the right words to her husband, or the timid young girl how to find confidence and make the best of herself for the boys."

Eva laughed. "A sort of primitive social worker-cum-psych too, then? Apart from the herbs and charms I've had to do some of that sort of talking in my time."

"Oh, were you a social worker, then?" Mrs. Ferolstein's bright black eyes snapped with curiosity, and the talk turned to the rights or wrongs of the welfare state, and the ability of families in more ancient times to stand on their own feet, as compared with their acquired modern skill in knowing exactly what state body could be most easily called upon. "It's all a matter of survival," insisted Mrs. Ferolstein, "only they have different tools and weapons now. They used to survive at all costs, on Nature's whim or bounty, or on their own sheer hard work. Now—" she shrugged off the indigent masses.

Before they left, however, Eva said, "It still seems odd that there should be a memorial in the Cathedral—how could that happen if she was actually hanged? Surely—"

"Her family was a good one, as I've said. They couldn't prevail upon the authorities of the kirk to let her be buried in consecrated ground. But the family waited, with its long memories, until most of the elders were dead, and the cause of Jhonet's posthumous banishment nigh forgotten. Then they asked for the plate, and gave a generous sum with it, for the rest of the souls of the poor of St. Giles. Nobody seems to have raised even the slightest demur. The date on the plate had to be the one that the rector allowed them to place it there—none of them wished to commemorate the day of her hanging. That might have been a bit too obvious, even for a church grown more easygoing. So the metal in the Cathedral may well be the only resting place her poor forgotten soul has to cling to."

As they walked down to the car, parked in a back street not far from Holyrood Palace, Eva pointed out the close to James. At least, she tried to—she was not absolutely sure, among the many, but she thought she remembered the marks on the walls nearby, and the colors of the paving stones and the patterns of the cobbles. A drift of seagulls rose up over their heads as they peered closely together through the iron trellis-work that someone had drawn across the entrance.

Eva had not realized that entrances like this might be closed off at night—James said that it didn't usually happen.

"The place looks derelict to me," he remarked. "I should think they're rebuilding it—they're doing that with many of the really old places. Extraordinary to think they used to be the lodgings of large and noble families—ugh, look at that!"

Eva had seen nothing.

"A rat," James informed her, moving distastefully away from the wall, "slipping along through the refuse as if it owned the place. There's no one there, you know. Most of the windows are broken or boarded up. I doubt if you really saw any inhabitants. There could be some still left, I suppose. But it's pretty unlikely."

Eva still saw vividly the gross white old man and his statuelike corpulence—a pallid Buddha—and heard the whispers and rustles and giggles, perhaps of lovers. But it was with the eyes of her mind, and she took James's arm obediently, and left the stairs to darkness and the night wind.

As they turned into the street in which the car was parked, a woman brushed against Eva's shoulder. She stopped, and James, irritated, stopped with her.

A pale, wrinkled face looked back at her, the patient smile on it belonging to someone who was not old, but wrung through by years of trial and near-hunger, and a whisper dropped through the rising mists, as the woman went up to the higher part of the road: "She said to come by tomorrow or the night after. He's no just so weel—and my own bairns, if ye can. They're but poorly."

"What on earth was all that about?" asked James, and Eva could not answer, although she felt already that she might know something more than her mind would bring to the surface.

"Must have mistaken you for someone local," James answered himself. "One of the panel doctors, perhaps."

"Doctors aren't the answer to every difficulty," said Eva, unaccountably annoyed.

"What an extraordinary thing to say!" James's eyebrows arched in some displeasure. "I never suggested that they were. Aren't you rather touchy this evening, Eva? And that was an odd time to arrive at a function that you knew very well was important to me. Mrs. Ferolstein's a very powerful and a very intelligent lady—fortunately she seemed to take rather a fancy to you."

Eva snapped, "And you find that odd?"

James sighed. "There you go again—and once more, I never suggested that. No, my dear, you do have an air of quiet self-sufficient competence sometimes. That would attract her attention. She likes people who can do things—solve problems, for instance. Perhaps it's because you used to do exactly that so much, at one time. She likes answers, without uneven ends hanging out."

"But I didn't know I gave that impression!" Eva laughed ruefully. "It's probably because I often feel lost in the kind of conversation your people have. So I sit quietly. Perhaps they mistake that for enigmatic knowledge. They must be rather stupid if they do."

"My kind of people," said James stiffly, "don't converse in such widely different terms from the rest of humanity. They go to plays and concerts, sometimes, like other people. Sometimes they even make jokes. It's simply that when they are engrossed in professionalism, they find it absorbing to the exclusion of everything else."

"Obviously." Eva's tone was slightly waspish, and they drove home to the hotel in a rather sulky silence.

James elected to have a whisky and ginger at the small hotel bar, which kept open till the most uncanny hours, and Eva cornered Ellen, who had been helping her husband serve, but was now quietly putting empty bottles in a basket, with one tired eye on the clock. Ellen at first professed no knowledge of the close which Eva had visited; but after a brief description of the shops in its neighborhood, some light dawned in her eyes.

"Oh, that's the Stirk Close—it was Butcher's Wynd, but there's a tale that one of the animals got loose from the slaughterer's, this'll be many years back, and rampaged round and got into the close, and couldn't get back up the stairs again. So round and round he goes, until he's tramped two-three bairns nigh to death. My, that was aye an unlucky place. My granny lived on the opposite side from them, at the start of this century, and she used to tell us about the sheer black fortune that seemed to hang on those folks' sleeve, and had for more years than any of them could remember. If it was hunger, there was always more there that were starving than anywhere else. If it was the sickness, they'd be down in droves. When it was bitter in the rest of the city, it was the Stirk Close that had snow piled up so they could barely get out, and there it stayed freezing, till it was gone from everywhere else. Some trick of the wind, maybe, that brought in the dust and the germs and the frost. But once people left the place, they vowed never to go back, and they always found themselves better off elsewhere."

"I know." Eva found herself suddenly thinking of some of the past families she had thought of as "hers," with the sheer aching pity she had always had for those who, bewildered, never did well, and could never seem to get the knack of it, somehow. There was always the next court case, or the next filthy disease, or the next bastard—they could never get clear of it, and they could never get away from their background. Call it what you would, unwillingness, lack of caring, inability to cope, the desire to yield, she had never been able to believe that it was entirely the fault of "her" families.

"Some of them said it was like a curse on it, my granny told me," said Ellen cheerfully enough, tipping up a bottle in which a tiny dram of cherry brandy remained, and licking it off her finger.

A full bluish moon had risen, and was edging the velvet curtains of the bar with watered silver. Eva looked from the warmth and smoky orange comfort of the small lamp-lit room to the austere fields of the sky, ridden by steely cloud bands, and felt a sudden yearning to be out in the night, breathing cold air.

James was affronted and astonished. "But where are you going? You won't walk, will you? It would be stupid."

"Just a quick turn in the car, round the road at the foot of Arthur's Seat, maybe as far as the water, and then quickly back," lied Eva.

"D'you want me—?" James persisted.

"No, no!" cried Eva, in almost hysterical impatience, as if someone was waiting for her who might soon be gone. She ran out of the hotel, fingering the car keys impatiently, and ducked into the driver's seat with a sigh of relief, while James stood on the steps, gazing at her with bewilderment.

As soon as she was moving, she felt a calm move into her excited veins, soothing down the blood that had been flowing at too hot a pace.

She drove rather slowly, knowing and savoring where she was bound, not the place so much as the adventure of assailing it by moonlight. The idea gave her short tremors of intense excitement at the pit of her belly, like the shivers that had shot through the depth of her being, sometimes, when she had looked down over high walls, and not quite been able to contain an unreasonable fear, yet longing, at the deep well of air and space that could so easily pull down her falling body.

The street was almost deserted as she drove down the steep slope, jouncing over the cobbles. Certainly the police would not trouble her, if she stopped just for a short while to see how the moon fell on the horrible place where so many of the poor had mourned and suffered, and asked vainly for help. But perhaps not always vainly—for there had been someone, had there not? Someone who cared, someone who was interested, who had tried to help Jhonet, even if it had been in error? The spaewife?

She stood by the steps, looking in and down, and, to her surprise, the gate had gone, the iron fretwork no longer interfered between her and what she looked for.

The stones were washed by the moon, and looked paler, and leprous, with trails as if slugs had been climbing them. But the windows, like wide open orange and yellow eyes, looked at her, fully alive and clustered with people. She could almost see what some of them were doing—washing, putting children to bed, poring over pots or clothes and, in one window, a great old book with brass on its back and corners. There was faint noise, too, quarreling and crying, and fat gouts of obscene laughter from one room where a whore fondled a customer.

But it was the streetlamp that took her eye. It drowned out the moon, blooming yellow as a giant, stalked lemon stuck out in the middle of the close, a wrecking beacon for the dazzled eyes.

Its peaked head stood out belligerently, and round its foot was a magic circle of sharp-edged light, defined territory where nothing could creep or move, outside which there was indecision, chaos, dirt, and sickliness. Inside that circle, felt Eva, order and action functioned effectively and hygienically, like the functioning within the lights of a surgical ward.

The night closed off her excitement, and she felt suddenly sick and drowsy. She heard the voices, and they seemed to have some relationship to her, and to what she was feeling; but she turned from them and the lamp, and went back to the car.

"What are you doing with yourself today?" asked James at breakfast. The morning was clear and lovely, and sun gilded the caps of the small autumn flowers in Ellen's neat garden.

Eva liked the autumn versions of plants that bloomed more opulently in the hot weather. They showed restraint and a vivacious economy, like poor Frenchwomen attempting chic on small budgets. And the leaves smelt more spicy, especially the chrysanthemums. There was a brisk, herbal, curative effect about an autumn garden.

Ellen brought more oatcakes and smiled at them. "Good weather for a picnic, now—they say Cramond is lovely just now, and the wind not cold yet at all."

"It's an idea," said James. "You'll weary of the city if you stay in it all the time." Eva thought not; but she could see the sense of a trip to Cramond, as a time-waster. Did she really want a time-waster? She had an urgent sense of pressing hurry in her chest, as if there were something she had left undone, and that really ought to be done quickly. It affected her breathing, too, and she felt as if the fresh sea-wind off the harbor at Cramond might help her to relax and breathe more smoothly.

"The zoo's out in the same direction," said James doubtfully, "isn't it? I suppose you won't want to—" he stopped. Eva was shaking her head, as he knew she might. She did not care for restraints for human beings or animals, even if they knew no better. Freedom ought always to be an option, even if it were only to be refused.

Ellen put her up a picnic: cake, and a couple of bridies, the pasties she liked so well, and fruit, and she bought herself a can of lager, and drove out toward the harbor. It was as she struggled with the twists of road and traffic at the bottom of Princes Street, that she caught a glimpse of red-gold hair, curling under a kerchief, and saw a pair of hands stretched out beseechingly toward her, and the anxious profile of a woman's face, and knew that she could not go out of the city that day.

James would not be home until late, and there was no party or reception, but she knew of other things she could do.

She was not needed just yet, but she must be within reach; it was a long time since she had planned her day to be within earshot, or telephone call, or walking distance of someone in just that way. Or on call? It was, again, a long time since she had heard or used that phrase. But she could go shopping for a while. At least part of the day was free to her; and nightfall was not yet.

The day passed remarkably quickly, as if it had simply hovered near her, and then been withdrawn. She bought a head-scarf of nearly the weave she had already seen twice, and ate her lunch in the gardens below the Scott Memorial; she watched the patient queue to ascend it, and the fuzz of black dots at the top that were heads peering over, and she listened to a band.

She went into the gallery and looked at pictures, she visited the Camera Obscura and saw gray, dizzying windswept scenes, a panorama of half-real towers and houses; but she did not go near the Royal Mile. The time for that would soon be near, and she wished to feel the waiting and the excitement.

An elderly woman talked to her for quite a long time about the difficulties she was having with the nephew who lived with her—the illogicalities and thoughtlessness of the young, and the expense of having to feed them; and Eva answered so politely and sensibly that no one would have guessed that she heard hardly anything of what was said.

At last the sun sank, and grape-dark shadows bloomed in doorways, and thin mists began twining up from the long dank grass on the castle slopes, and stars pricked luminous patches in the evening sky, and Eva rose and stretched herself, from the bench she had been sitting on, and began to walk toward her close.

There were more houses than she remembered, and in better repair, and she missed the women carrying water, and the cries of the street-sellers, but she was content to be going back to the tasks she had to do, and to the people who needed her, every one.

She paused in the entry, and rubbed her hand lovingly over the inscription: "gudewife—spaewife"; they had loved her, that had scrawled that over the stone. And never mind the spite of yon man whom she would not have in wedlock! She had better things to do with her time than to marry—look where it had led poor Jhonet. The healing gift was the greatest honor, and the greatest burden a woman could carry, whether it were of body or spirit.

The windows shone their usual homely good cheer to her, and she could hear the whispers of young Nan lying with her Willie, in the darkest patch, where the shadows were thickest. And what that child's clothing would be like the morrow, dear only knew!

The only man who saw her come in was old Master attie, who had been the best of all tailors, until he lost the use of his hand—she could help with the pain, but not the loss of movement. He inclined his head to her, and she knew others would soon hear of her coming home— those whose bairns were sick of the wasting disease, or the men whose warts and blains were made worse by their work in the mills, or the girls who wanted a love-spell, or something that would just disfigure a rival, not too badly, for a wee while. So, before she took up her abode again, behind one of those welcoming windows, she must sit at her old spot, and ply her old trade, and take care of their lives, for those that could not care for themselves.

The lamp pulled her, as it always did, into the safety of its covering glow, and all the faces came silently to the windows and watched her, as she sat down inside its limits, held safely and bound within the bourn and path of its globe; while outside the chatter and clutter of some other world, with which she had no longer anything to do, passed on and away from her.

HOGFOOT RIGHT
AND BIRD-HANDS

FOR LISA

There lived, high above the empty streets in a tall building, an old woman whose pet cat had recently died. In those days cats were rare and the old woman had not the means to purchase another. So she called for the machine whose duty it was to look after the welfare of lost and lonely people.

The welfare machine came to her apartment in the middle of the night, and when she explained her plight it suggested that the old woman replace her cat with a pet fashioned from a part of her body. It said it could remove and modify one of her feet to resemble a piglet, and the old woman agreed to this scheme. Since she spent all her time in the mobile bed-chair that saw to all her needs, she did not require the use of her feet, nor any other part of her body for that matter, apart from her brain, to which the bed-chair and other appliances were connected. The old woman was not sick, unless apathy and idleness be looked upon as an illness, but she had no desire to take part in any physical activity of any sort. She merely went from one gray day to the next, sleeping, eating, and watching a device called wallscreen, on which she could witness the lives of others, long since dead, over and over again.

Thus, her right foot was removed and roughly shaped and given a life of its own. This appendage she called Hogfoot Right, and it gave her much pleasure to see the creature scuttling around the floor and nosing in the corners of the rooms the way such creations did. However, Hogfoot Right was not one of those pets that liked to be stroked and fussed over, the way the old woman's cat had been when it was alive, and eventually she grew tired of its company, wanting something more. Watching the creature grub around the carpet was interesting enough at first, but when she had seen it done once or twice the novelty began to pall. So she called her welfare machine again and had her other foot removed. This one she called Basil, in the hope that giving it a proper name would make it more affectionate toward its mistress.

Basil turned out to be such a sweet creature. He would sit on the old woman's lap and let her stroke him for hours, his little hog nose twitching in ecstasy as she ran her hands over his dozing form.

Hogfoot Right, however, was moody and irritable and would skulk around in the darker corners of the house and cower away from the old woman when she approached him. He did not actually hiss or spit at her, but his bad temper was evident in the expression on his blunted face and in the sour line of his crudely fashioned mouth.

However, Hogfoot Right was Basil's good companion and in that respect the old woman had no complaint. He served his brother well, snuggling up with him at night and making sure he did not get too excited when something happened to amuse him. Sometimes even Hogfoot Right would join in with his brother's antics, and the two of them would butt each other's rumps and roll around the carpet like six-month-old piglets. Then suddenly, Hogfoot Right would become resentful of something and would sidle away to frequent the edges of the room, glowering at both his brother and the old woman if they tried to entice him to play again. The old woman despaired of this temperamental pet and eventually gave up on the beast.

It was because of her great success with Basil that she decided to increase her menagerie. The welfare machine called one day to see how she was faring and she asked for more surgery. She told it she wanted to lose her hands and her ears. Her bed-chair responded to brain impulses, and she said she could not see what use both these sets of her appendages were to her anymore.

The welfare machine was all in favor of the idea. The ears were fused together to make a moth, and the hands became a beautiful pale birdlike creature that soared gracefully around the room and was really the most delicate, delightful pet the old woman had ever set eyes on. She loved it from the first moment she saw it. It would perch on the back of the bed-chair and flutter its fingerfeathers with more dignity than a fantailed dove, and though it remained aloof from the other creatures in the room it would often sit and watch their games from a suitable place above their heads.

Moth-ears was a bit of a disappointment. She fluttered here and there occasionally and was best seen floating past the window with the light shining through her translucent form, but mostly she hung from the old woman's collar with her wings closed. It was almost as if she were trying to get back to her original positions on the old woman's head. She was nervous and shy and tended to start at sudden, loud noises and was really quite useless as a pet. Yet the old woman was happy to keep her, seeing in her an aspect of her own personality.

Bird-hands liked to perch on the light fittings or sit on the windowsill with folded wings, looking out at the sky. She would watch the house martins—the way they swooped before alighting on the outer sill—and she would copy their flight patterns. Since the old woman could not fondle her pets anymore, Bird-hands would stroke her instead, running her fingerwings along the old woman's shoulders and down her neck. At night she nestled in her warm lap while the others slept. The old woman loved her dearly.

Bird-hands seemed the most contented of the group of creatures. There was a musical instrument in the apartment that could be played manually if required, and this the creature would do, running her fingerwings over the keys and producing the most delightful melodies. Occasionally she would switch the instrument to automatic and fly to the rhythm of the tune, adding that extra dimension to the unfolding of the notes with her graceful motion.

The group prospered. Even when Snake-arm came along the harmony remained, though at times the sinuous movements alarmed the old woman when she caught sight of it suddenly out of the corner of her eye.

Thus, they all lived together in a harmonious group, apart from the unsociable Hogfoot Right. The old woman could not thank the welfare machine enough, pouring praises on its mechanical parts whenever it came to see how she was getting along. Sometimes the machine would sit with Bird-hands and squeak at it in its high-pitched language, always ending in a rattling laugh. Once, it brought a pair of satin gloves, white, with lace around the cuffs, which Bird-hands wore to fly around the room while the old woman exclaimed upon the beauty of the creature.

Another time, the welfare machine brought an old leather boot, and forced Hogfoot Right to wear it, making the foot clump around the room while the old woman sniggered at such a humorous sight. The welfare machine carefully watched her heartbeat monitor at times like these, intently observant for any variation in its pace and strength.

It was a very happy time for the old woman.

Until, one night, it all went wrong.

A terrible noise woke the old woman. It was the sound of crashing furniture and struggling bodies. A glass ornament smashed against a wall, spraying her legs with fragments. There was a life-and-death struggle going on somewhere in the room. A standard lamp fell across a table and shattered the ceramic stem. The old woman was too frightened even to turn on the light. She was sure that an android had entered her apartment: a rogue machine whose brain had suffered a malfunction and was on the rampage. All she could do was quietly guide her bed-chair to the corner of the room and stay there until the ruckus was over.

The fighting, she was sure, was between her pets and the intruder, and since there was little she could do she had to await the outcome without interfering.

Finally, after a long while, there was silence, and she ordered the light switch on. The scene that met her eyes was horrific.

In the center of the room were Bird-hands and Hogfoot Right, obviously squaring up to one another. Around them, bleeding, broken, and bruised, were the other pets. Moth-ears had been torn and crushed and was obviously dead. Snake-arm had been pierced by a long ceramic splinter that protruded from its head. It, too, was deathly still. Basil was black with bruises, having been beaten, fatally it seemed.

The old woman had not the slightest doubt that Hogfoot Right had gone berserk. There was no sign of any android intruder, and Hogfoot Right looked as though he were now about to attack Bird-hands.

The two combatants fell upon one another. There was a frenzied scrambling and clawing. The old woman began yelling like crazy for Bird-hands, telling her to dig her claws in, while the seemingly mad hog was butting her round and round the walls with its heel-hard head.

It was a vicious battle.

Furniture was scattered this way and that, and twice the old woman had to move her bed-chair to get out of their path as they rolled across the floor, locked in a tight ball. Once, she thought Hogfoot had had enough, as he backed away into a corner, but again he went forward, just when Bird-hands was trying to recover.

Finally, Bird-hands picked him up by the hindquarters and flung him at the exposed end of the standard lamp. It was bristling with live contacts. With a bouncing arc of his body he twisted in agony as the shock went through him. He lay broken and still, across the sputtering wires.

Bird-hands fluttered to the middle of the room.

"Well done," cried the old woman. "Well fought."

Bird-hands just sat there, her thumb-head turned toward the window, through which the dawn was just beginning to emerge. Then suddenly the creature launched herself into the air and began throwing her body at the glass panes in a seemingly desperate attempt to smash her way through, like a wild bird that is trapped in a closed room.

Then the old woman understood. It had not been Hogfoot Right, but Bird-hands. She had seen the martins cutting through the blue sky outside and she wanted to be free too. She wanted to be out amongst those of her own kind. Maybe she had run amok amongst the others because they refused or were unable to understand her desire for escape? Perhaps she had tried to get them to open the window—something only the old woman could do with a brain command—only to find they could not help her? Anyway, she had killed them all. Even little Moth-ears. And Hogfoot Right, the bad-tempered one, had given her the toughest opposition of all.

Poor Hogfoot, misjudged right to the end.

Now Bird-hands sat on the ledge, her nails dripping with blood. She seemed to be waiting for the old woman to open the window, which could only be done by direct order. There came, in the silence, the sound of real birds chirruping outside, and Bird-hands displayed restlessness. The old woman, still in a state of shock, refused to respond.

Bird-hands carefully wiped the gore from her fingerwings on one of the curtains. By this time the old woman had recovered a little but she had much of the stubbornness of her erstwhile right foot and she made it obvious that she was not going to comply.

Finally, Bird-hands flew from the ledge and settled on the old woman's neck. The creature began to stroke the withered throat sensuously, hoping perhaps to persuade her mistress to do what she wished. The woman sat rigidly still, grim-faced. Gradually the stroking became firmer. At the last, the fingerwings tightened and squeezed, slowly but effectively. There were a few minutes during which the old woman convulsed. Then the body went slack.

Bird-hands, after a long while, released her grip and fluttered down to the floor. She crabbed her way amongst the dead creatures, inspecting them for signs of life. Then she came to Hogfoot Right, lying across the electrified strands of the light socket. Bird-hands observed her victim with seeming dispassion. She inched forward, close to the hog's head, looking down.

Suddenly there was a jerk from Hogfoot Right, as his head flashed out and his jaws clamped on a little finger. A brilliant shower of blue-white sparks rained around the pair, and then the stillness in the room was complete.

Later, the welfare machine came to call and surveyed the scene with mechanical surprise. It made a careful note of all the damage and recorded a verdict of suicide. Just as it was about to leave, it sensed some vibrations coming from somewhere in the room. One of the creatures had stirred. Suddenly something snapped at its metal leg and then went careering through the open doorway and along the corridor. . . .

LONGTOOTH

My word is good. How can I prove it? Born in Darkfield, wasn't I? Stayed away thirty more years after college, but when I returned I was still Ben Dane, one of the Darkfield Danes, Judge Marcus Dane's eldest. And they knew my word was good. My wife died and I sickened of all cities; then my bachelor brother Sam died too, who'd lived all his life here in Darkfield, running his one-man law office over in Lohman— our nearest metropolis, pop. 6,437. A fast coronary at fifty; I had loved him. Helen gone, then Sam—I wound up my unimportances and came home, inheriting Sam's housekeeper Adelaide Simmons, her grim stability and celestial cooking. Nostalgia for Maine is a serious matter, late in life: I had to yield. I expected a gradual drift into my childless old age playing correspondence chess, translating a few of the classics. I thought I could take for granted the continued respect of my neighbors. I say my word is good.

I will remember again that middle of March a few years ago, the snow skimming out of an afternoon sky as dirty as the bottom of an old aluminum pot. Harp Ryder's back road had been plowed since the last snowfall; I supposed Bolt-Bucket could make the mile and a half in to his farm and out again before we got caught. Harp had asked me to get him a book if I was making a trip to Boston, any goddamn book that told about Eskimos, and I had one for him, De Poncins's *Kabloona*. I saw the midget devils of white running crazy down a huge slope of wind, and recalled hearing at the Darkfield News Bureau, otherwise Cleve's General Store, somebody mentioning a forecast of the worst blizzard in forty years. Joe Cleve, who won't permit a radio in the store because it pesters his ulcers, inquired of his Grand Inquisitor who dwells ten yards behind your right shoulder: "Why's it always got to be the worst in so-and-so many years, that going to help anybody?" The Bureau was still analyzing this difficult inquiry when I left, with my cigarettes and as much as I could remember of Adelaide's grocery list after leaving it on the dining table. It wasn't yet three when I turned in on Harp's back road, and a gust slammed at Bolt-Bucket like death with a shovel.

I tried to win momentum for the rise to the high ground, swerved to avoid an idiot rabbit and hit instead a patch of snow-hidden melt-and-freeze, skidding to a full stop from which nothing would extract us but a tow.

I was fifty-seven that year, my wind bad from too much smoking and my heart (I now know) no stronger than Sam's. I quit cursing—gradually, to avoid sudden actions—and tucked *Kabloona* under my parka. I would walk the remaining mile to Ryder's, stay just to leave the book, say hello, and phone for a tow; then, since Harp never owned a car and never would, I could walk back and meet the truck.

If Leda Ryder knew how to drive, it didn't matter much after she married Harp. They farmed it, back in there, in almost the manner of Harp's ancestors of Jefferson's time. Harp did keep his two hundred laying hens by methods that were considered modern before the poor wretches got condemned to batteries, but his other enterprises came closer to antiquity. In his big kitchen garden he let one small patch of weeds fool themselves for an inch or two, so he'd have it to work at; they survived nowhere else. A few cows, a team, four acres for market crops, and a small dog Droopy, whose grandmother had made it somehow with a dachshund. Droopy's only menace in obese old age was a wheezing bark. The Ryders must have grown nearly all vital necessities except chewing tobacco and once in a while a new dress for Leda. Harp could snub the twentieth century, and I doubt if Leda was consulted about it in spite of his obsessive devotion for her. She was almost thirty years younger, and yes, he should not have married her. Other side up just as scratchy: she should not have married him, but she did.

Harp was a dinosaur perhaps, but I grew up with him, he a year the younger. We swam, fished, helled around together. And when I returned to Darkfield growing old, he was one of the few who acted glad to see me, so far as you can trust what you read in a face like a granite promontory. Maybe twice a week Harp Ryder smiled.

I pushed on up the ridge, and noticed a going-and-coming set of wide tire-tracks already blurred with snow. That would be the egg-truck I had passed a quarter-hour since on the main road. Whenever the west wind at my back lulled, I could swing around and enjoy one of my favorite prospects of birch and hemlock lowland. From Ryder's Ridge there's no sign of Darkfield two miles southwest except one church spire. On clear days you glimpse Bald Mountain and his two big brothers, more than twenty miles west of us.

The snow was thickening. It brought relief and pleasure to see the black shingles of Harp's barn and the roof of his Cape Codder. Foreshortened, so that it looked snug against the barn; actually house and barn were connected by a two-story shed fifteen feet wide and forty feet long—woodshed below, hen-loft above. The Ryders' sunrise-facing bedroom window was set only three feet above the eaves of that shed roof. They truly went to bed with the chickens. I shouted, for Harp was about to close the big shed door. He held it for me. I ran, and the storm ran after me. The west wind was bouncing off the barn; eddies howled at us. The temperature had tumbled ten degrees since I left Darkfield. The thermometer by the shed door read 15 degrees, and I knew I'd been a damn fool. As I helped Harp fight the shed door closed, I thought I heard Leda, crying.

A swift, confused impression. The wind was exploring new ranges of passion, the big door squawked, and Harp was asking: "Ca' break down?" I do still think I heard Leda wail. If so, it ended as we got the door latched and Harp drew a newly fitted two-by-four bar across it. I couldn't understand that: the old latch was surely proof against any wind short of a hurricane.

"Bolt-Bucket never breaks down. Ought to get one, Harp—lots of company. All she did was go in the ditch."

"You might see her again come spring." His hens were scratching overhead, not yet scared by the storm. Harp's eyes were small gray glitters of trouble. "Ben, you figure a man's getting old at fifty-six?"

"No." My bones (getting old) ached for the warmth of his kitchen-dining-living-everything room, not for sad philosophy. "Use your phone, okay?"

"If the wires ain't down," he said, not moving, a man beaten on by other storms. "Them loafers didn't cut none of the overhang branches all summer. I told 'em, of course, I told 'em how it would be. . . . I meant, Ben, old enough to get dumb fancies?" My face may have told him I thought he was brooding about himself with a young wife. He frowned, annoyed that I hadn't taken his meaning. "I meant, *seeing* things. Things that can't be so, but—"

"We can all do some of that at any age, Harp."

That remark was a stupid brush-off, a stone for bread, because I was cold, impatient, wanted in. Harp had always a tense one-way sensitivity. His face chilled. "Well, come in, warm up. Leda ain't feeling too good. Getting a cold or something."

When she came downstairs and made me welcome, her eyes were reddened. I don't think the wind made that noise. Droopy waddled from her basket behind the stove to snuff my feet and give me my usual low passing mark.

Leda never had it easy there, young and passionate with scant mental resources. She was twenty-eight that year, looking tall because she carried her firm body handsomely. Some of the sullenness in her big mouth and lucid gray eyes was sexual challenge, some pure discontent. I liked Leda; her nature was not one for animosity or meanness. Before her marriage the Darkfield News Bureau used to declare with its customary scrupulous fairness that Leda had been covered by every goddamn thing in pants within thirty miles. For once the Bureau may have spoken a grain of truth in the malice, for Leda did have the smoldering power that draws men without word or gesture. After her abrupt marriage to Harp—Sam told me all this; I wasn't living in Darkfield then and hadn't met her— the garbage-gossip went hastily underground: enraging Harp Ryder was never healthy.

The phone wires weren't down, yet. While I waited for the garage to answer, Harp said, "Ben, I can't let you walk back in that. Stay over, huh?"

I didn't want to. It meant extra work and inconvenience for Leda, and I was ancient enough to crave my known safe burrow. But I felt Harp wanted me to stay for his own sake. I asked Jim Short at the garage to go ahead with Bolt-Bucket if I wasn't there to meet him. Jim roared: "Know what it's doing right now?"

"Little spit of snow, looks like."

"Jesus!" He covered the mouthpiece imperfectly. I heard his enthusiastic voice ring through cold-iron echoes: "Hey, old Ben's got that thing into the ditch again! Ain't that something . . . ? Listen, Ben, I can't make no promises. Got both tow trucks out already. You better stop over and praise the Lord you got that far."

"Okay," I said. "It wasn't much of a ditch."

Leda fed us coffee. She kept glancing toward the landing at the foot of the stairs where a night-darkness already prevailed. A closed-in stairway slanted down at a never-used front door; beyond that landing was the other ground floor room—parlor, spare, guest room—where I would sleep. I don't know what Leda expected to encounter in that shadow. Once when a chunk of firewood made an odd noise in the range, her lips clamped shut on a scream.

The coffee warmed me. By that time the weather left no loophole for argument. Not yet three-thirty, but west and north were lost in furious black. Through the hissing white flood I could just see the front of the barn forty feet away. "Nobody's going no place into that," Harp said. His little house shuddered, enforcing the words. "Leda, you don't look too brisk. Get you some rest."

"I better see to the spare room for Ben."

Neither spoke with much tenderness, but it glowed openly in him when she turned her back. Then some other need bent his granite face out of its normal seams. His whole gaunt body leaning forward tried to help him talk. "You wouldn't figure me for a man'd go off his rocker?" he asked.

"Of course not. What's biting, Harp?"

"There's something in the woods, got no right to be there." To me that came as a letdown of relief: I would not have to listen to another's marriage problems. "I wish, b' Jesus Christ, it would hit somebody else once, so I could say what I know and not be laughed at all to hell. I *ain't* one for dumb fancies."

You walked on eggs, with Harp. He might decide any minute that *I* was laughing. "Tell me," I said. "If anything's out there now it must feel a mite chilly."

"Ayah." He went to the north window, looking out where we knew the road lay under white confusion. Harp's land sloped down on the other side of the road to the edge of mighty evergreen forest. Katahdin stands more than fifty miles north and a little east of us. We live in a withering shrinkworld, but you could still set out from Harp's farm and, except for the occasional country road and the rivers—not many large ones—you could stay in deep forest all the way to the tundra, or Alaska. Harp said, "This kind of weather is when it comes."

He sank into his beat-up kitchen armchair and reached for *Kabloona*. He had barely glanced at the book while Leda was with us. "Funny name."

"Kabloona's an Eskimo word for white man."

"He done these pictures . . . ? Be they good, Ben?"

"I like 'em. Photographs in the back."

"Oh." He turned the pages hastily for those, but studied only the ones that showed the strong Eskimo faces, and his interest faded. Whatever he wanted was not here. "These people, be they—civilized?"

"In their own way, sure."

"Ayah, this guy looks like he could find his way in the woods."

"Likely the one thing he couldn't do, Harp. They never see a tree unless they come south, and they hate to do that. Anything below the Arctic is too warm."

"That a fact . . . ? Well, it's a nice book. How much was it?" I'd found it second-hand; he paid me to the exact penny. "I'll be glad to read it." He never would. It would end up on the shelf in the parlor with the Bible, an old almanac, a Longfellow, until some day this place went up for auction and nobody remembered Harp's way of living.

"What's this all about, Harp?"

"Oh . . . I was hearing things in the woods, back last summer. I'd think, fox, then I'd know it wasn't. Make your hair stand right on end. Lost a cow, last August, from the north pasture acrosst the rud. Section of board fence tore out. I mean, Ben, the two top boards was *pulled out from the nail holes*. No hammer marks."

"Bear?"

"Only track I found looked like bear except too small. You know a bear wouldn't *pull* it out, Ben."

"Cow slamming into it, panicked by something?"

He remained patient with me. "Ben, would I build a cow-pasture fence nailing the cross-pieces from the outside? Cow hit it with all her weight she might bust it, sure. And kill herself doing it, be blood and hair all over the split boards, and she'd be there, not a mile and a half away into the woods. Happened during a big thunderstorm. I figured it had to be somebody with a spite ag'inst me, maybe some son of a bitch wanting the prop'ty, trying to scare me off that's lived here all my life and my family before me. But that don't make sense. I found the cow a week later, what was left. Way into the woods. The head and the bones. Hide tore up and flang around. Any *person* dressing off a beef, he'll cut whatever he wants and take off with it. He don't sit down and chaw the meat off the *bones*, b' Jesus Christ. He don't tear the thighbone out of the joint. . . . All right, maybe bear. But no bear did that job on that fence and then driv old Nell a mile and a half into the woods to kill her. Nice little Jersey, clever's a kitten. Leda used to make over her, like she don't usually do with the stock. . . . I've looked plenty in the woods since then, never turned up anything. Once and again I did smell something. Fishy, like bear-smell but—*different*."

"But Harp, with snow on the ground—"

"Now you'll really call me crazy. When the weather is clear, I ain't once found his prints. I hear him then, at night, but I go out by daylight where I think the sound was, there's no trail. Just the usual snow tracks. I know. He lives in the trees and don't come down except when it's storming, I got to believe that? Because then he does come, Ben, when the weather's like now, like right now. And old Ned and Jerry out in the stable go wild, and sometimes we hear his noise under the window. I shine my flashlight through the glass—never catch sight of him. I go out with the ten-gauge if there's any light to see by, and there's prints around the house—holes filling up with snow. By morning there'll be maybe some marks left, and they'll lead off to the north woods, but under the trees you won't find it. So he gets up in the branches and travels that away? . . . Just once I have seen him, Ben. Last October. I better tell you one other thing first. A day or so after I found what was left of old Nell, I lost six roaster chickens. I made over a couple box stalls, maybe you remember, so the birds could be out on range and roost in the barn at night. Good doors, and I always locked 'em. Two in the morning, Ned and Jerry go crazy. I got out through the barn into the stable, and they was spooked, Ned trying to kick his way out. I got 'em quiet, looked all over the stable—loft, harness room, everywhere. Not a thing. Dead quiet night, no moon. It had to be something the horses smelled. I come back into the barn, and found one of the chicken-pen doors open—*tore* out from the lock. Chicken thief would bring along something to pry with— wouldn't he be a Christly idjut if he didn't . . . ? Took six birds, six nice eight-pound roasters, and left the heads on the floor—bitten off."

"Harp—some lunatic. People *can* go insane that way. There are old stories—"

"Been trying to believe that. Would a man live the winter out there? Twenty below zero?"

"Maybe a cave—animal skins."

"I've boarded up the whole back of the barn. Done the same with the hen-loft windows—two-by-fours with four-inch spikes driv slantwise.

They be twelve feet off the ground, and he ain't come for 'em, not yet. . . .
So after that happened I sent for Sheriff Robart. Son of a bitch happens
to live in Darkfield, you'd think he might've took an interest."

"Do any good?"

Harp laughed. He did that by holding my stare, making no sound,
moving no muscle except a disturbance at the eye corners. A New England art; maybe it came over on the *Mayflower*. "Robart he come by,
after a while. I showed him that door. I showed him them chicken heads.
Told him how I'd been spending my nights out there on my ass, with
the ten-gauge." Harp rose to unload tobacco juice into the range fire; he
has a theory it purifies the air. "Ben, I might've showed him them chicken
heads a shade close to his nose. By the time he got here, see, they wasn't
all that fresh. He made out he'd look around and let me know. Mid-
September. Ain't seen him since."

"Might've figured he wouldn't be welcome?"

"Why, he'd be welcome as shit on a tablecloth."

"You spoke of—seeing it, Harp?"

"Could call it seeing. . . . All right. It was during them Indian summer
days—remember? Like June except them pretty colors, smell of wind-
falls—God, I like that, I like October. I'd gone down to the slope acrosst
the rud where I mended my fence after losing old Nell. Just leaning
there, guess I was tired. Late afternoon, sky pinking up. You know how
the fence cuts acrosst the slope to my east wood lot. I've let the bushes
grow free—lot of elder, other stuff the birds come for. I was looking
down toward that little break between the north woods and my wood lot,
where a bit of old growed-up pasture shows through. Pretty spot. Painter
fella come by a few years ago and done a picture of it, said the place
looked like a coro, dunno what the hell that is, he didn't say."

I pushed at his brown study. "You saw it there?"

"No. Off to my right in them elder bushes. Fifty feet from me, I guess.
By God I didn't turn my head. I got it with the tail of my eye and turned
the other way as if I meant to walk back to the rud. Made like busy with
something in the grass, come wandering back to the fence some nearer.
He stayed for me, a brownish patch in them bushes by the big yellow
birch. Near the height of a man. No gun with me, not even a stick . . .
Big shoulders, couldn't see his goddamn feet. He don't stand more'n five
feet tall. His hands, if he's got real ones, hung out of my sight in a tangle
of elder branches. He's got brown fur, Ben, reddy-brown fur all over
him. His face too, his head, his big thick neck. There's a shine to fur
in sunlight, you can't be mistook. So—I did look at him direct. Tried

to act like I still didn't see him, but he knowed. He melted back and got the birch between him and me. Not a sound." And then Harp was listening for Leda upstairs. He went on softly: "Ayah, I ran back for a gun, and searched the woods, for all the good it did me. You'll want to know about his face. I ain't told Leda all this part. See, she's scared, I don't want to make it no worse, I just said it was some animal that snuck off before I could see it good. A big face, Ben. Head real human except it sticks out too much around the jaw. Not much nose—open spots in the fur. Ben, the—the *teeth!* I seen his mouth drop open and he pulled up one side of his lip to show me them stabbing things. I've seen as big as that on a full-growed bear. That's what I'll hear, I ever try to tell this. They'll say I seen a bear. Now I shot my first bear when I was sixteen and Pa took me over toward Jackman. I've got me one maybe every other year since then. I know 'em, all their ways. But that's what I'll hear if I tell the story."

I am a frustrated naturalist, loaded with assorted facts. I know there aren't any monkeys or apes that could stand our winters except maybe the harmless Himalayan langur. No such beast as Harp described lived anywhere on the planet. It didn't help. Harp was honest; he was rational; he wanted reasonable explanation as much as I did. Harp wasn't the village atheist for nothing. I said, "I guess you will, Harp. People mostly won't take the—unusual."

"Maybe you'll hear him tonight, Ben."

Leda came downstairs, and heard part of that. "He's been telling you, Ben. What do you think?"

"I don't know what to think."

"Led', I thought, if I imitate that noise for him—"

"No!" She had brought some mending and was about to sit down with it, but froze as if threatened by attack. "I couldn't stand it, Harp. And—it might bring them."

"Them?" Harp chuckled uneasily. "I don't guess I could do it that good he'd come for it."

"Don't *do* it, Harp!"

"All right, hon." Her eyes were closed, her head drooping back. "Don't git nerved up so."

I started wondering whether a man still seeming sane could dream up such a horror for the unconscious purpose of tormenting a woman too young for him, a woman he could never imagine he owned. If he told her a fox bark wasn't right for a fox, she'd believe him. I said, "We shouldn't talk about it if it upsets her."

He glanced at me like a man floating up from under water. Leda said in a small, aching voice: "I wish to God we could move to Boston."

The granite face closed in defensiveness. "Led', we been over all that. Nothing is going to drive me off of my land. I got no time for the city at my age. What the Jesus would I do? Night watchman? Sweep out somebody's back room, b' Jesus Christ? Savings'd be gone in no time. We been all over it. We ain't moving nowhere."

"I could find work." For Harp of course that was the worst thing she could have said. She probably knew it from his stricken silence. She said clumsily, "I forgot something upstairs." She snatched up her mending and she was gone.

We talked no more of it the rest of the day. I followed through the milking and other chores, lending a hand where I could, and we made everything as secure as we could against storm and other enemies. The long-toothed furry thing was the spectral guest at dinner, but we cut him, on Leda's account, or so we pretended. Supper would have been awkward anyway. They weren't in the habit of putting up guests, and Leda was a rather deadly cook because she cared nothing about it. A Darkfield girl, I suppose she had the usual twentieth-century mishmash of television dreams until some impulse or maybe false signs of pregnancy tricked her into marrying a man out of the nineteenth. We had venison treated like beef and overdone vegetables. I don't like venison even when it's treated right.

At six Harp turned on his battery radio and sat stone-faced through the day's bad news and the weather forecast—"a blizzard which may prove the worst in 42 years. Since three P.M., eighteen inches have fallen at Bangor, twenty-one at Boston. Precipitation is not expected to end until tomorrow. Winds will increase during the night with gusts up to seventy miles per hour." Harp shut it off, with finality. On other evenings I had spent there he let Leda play it after supper only kind of soft, so there had been a continuous muted bleat and blatter all evening. Tonight Harp meant to listen for other sounds. Leda washed the dishes, said an early good night, and fled upstairs.

Harp didn't talk, except as politeness obliged him to answer some blah of mine. We sat and listened to the snow and the lunatic wind. An hour of it was enough for me; I said I was beat and wanted to turn in early. Harp saw me to my bed in the parlor and placed a new chunk of rock maple in the pot-bellied stove. He produced a difficult granite smile, maybe using up his allowance for the week, and pulled out

a bottle from a cabinet that had stood for many years below a parlor print—George Washington, I think, concluding a treaty with
some offbeat sufferer from hepatitis who may have been General Corn-
wallis if the latter had two left feet. The bottle contained a brand of rye
that Harp sincerely believed to be drinkable, having charred his gullet
forty-odd years trying to prove it. While my throat healed Harp said,
"Shouldn't've bothered you with all this crap, Ben. Hope it ain't going
to spoil your sleep." He got me his spare flashlight, then let me be, and
closed the door.

I heard him drop back into his kitchen armchair. Under too many
covers, lamp out, I heard the cruel whisper of the snow. The stove
muttered, a friend, making me a cocoon of living heat in a waste of outer
cold. Later I heard Leda at the head of the stairs, her voice timid, tired,
and sweet with invitation: "You comin' up to bed, Harp?" The stairs
creaked under him. Their door closed; presently she cried out in that
desired pain that is brief release from trouble.

I remembered something Adelaide Simmons had told me about this
house, where I had not gone upstairs since Harp and I were boys. Adelaide, one of the very few women in Darkfield who never spoke unkindly
of Leda, said that the tiny west room across from Harp's and Leda's
bedroom was fixed up for a nursery, and Harp wouldn't allow anything
in there but baby furniture. Had been so since they were married seven
years before.

Another hour dragged on, in my exasperations of sleeplessness.

Then I heard Longtooth.

The noise came from the west side, beyond the snow-hidden vegetable
garden. When it snatched me from the edge of sleep, I tried to think it
was a fox barking, the ringing, metallic shriek the little red beast can
belch dragonlike from his throat. But wide awake, I knew it had been
much deeper, chestier. Horned owl?—no. A sound that belonged to
ancient times when men relied on chipped stone weapons and had full
reason to fear the dark.

The cracks in the stove gave me firelight for groping back into my
clothes. The wind had not calmed at all. I stumbled to the west window,
buttoning up, and found it a white blank. Snow had drifted above the
lower sash. On tiptoe I could just see over it. A light appeared, dimly
illuminating the snowfield beyond. That would be coming from a lamp
in the Ryders' bedroom, shining through the nursery room and so out,
weak and diffused, into the blizzard chaos.

Yaaarrhh!

Now it had drawn horribly near. From the north windows of the parlor I saw black nothing. Harp squeaked down to my door. "'Wake, Ben?"

"Yes. Come look at the west window."

He had left no night light burning in the kitchen, and only a scant glow came down to the landing from the bedroom. He murmured behind me, "Ayah, snow's up some. Must be over three foot on the level by now."

Yaaarrhh!

The voice had shouted on the south side, the blinder side of the house, overlooked only by one kitchen window and a small one in the pantry where the hand pump stood. The view from the pantry window was mostly blocked by a great maple that overtopped the house. I heard the wind shrilling across the tree's winter bones.

"Ben, you want to git your boots on? Up to you—can't ask it. I might have to go out." Harp spoke in an undertone as if the beast might understand him through the tight walls.

"Of course." I got into my knee boots and caught up my parka as I followed him into the kitchen. A .30-caliber rifle and his heavy shotgun hung on deerhorn over the door to the woodshed. He found them in the dark.

What courage I possessed that night came from being shamed into action, from fearing to show a poor face to an old friend in trouble. I went through the Normandy invasion. I have camped out alone, when I was younger and healthier, in our moose and bear country, and slept nicely. But that noise of Longtooth stole courage. It ached along the channel of the spine.

I had the spare flashlight, but knew Harp didn't want me to use it here. I could make out the furniture, and Harp reaching for the gun rack. He already had on his boots, fur cap, and mackinaw. "You take this'n," he said, and put the ten-gauge in my hands. "Both barrels loaded. Ain't my way to do that, ain't right, but since this thing started—"

Yaaarrhh!

"Where's he got to now?" Harp was by the south window. "Round this side?"

"I thought so. . . . Where's Droopy?"

Harp chuckled thinly. "Poor little shit! She come upstairs at the first sound of him and went under the bed. I told Led' to stay upstairs. She'd want a light down here. Wouldn't make sense."

Then, apparently from the east side of the hen-loft and high, booming off some resonating surface: *Yaaarrhh!*

"He can't! Jesus, that's twelve foot off the ground!" But Harp plunged out into the shed, and I followed. "Keep your light on the floor, Ben." He ran up the narrow stairway. "Don't shine it on the birds, they'll act up."

So far the chickens, stupid and virtually blind in the dark, were making only a peevish tut-tutting of alarm. But something was clinging to the outside of the barricaded east window, snarling, chattering teeth, pounding on the two-by-fours. With a fist?—it sounded like nothing else. Harp snapped, "Get your light on the window!" And he fired through the glass.

We heard no outcry. Any noise outside was covered by the storm and the squawks of the hens scandalized by the shot. The glass was dirty from their continual disturbance of the litter; I couldn't see through it. The bullet had drilled the pane without shattering it, and passed between the two-by-fours, but the beast could have dropped before he fired. "I got to go out there. You stay, Ben." Back in the kitchen he exchanged rifle for shotgun. "Might not have no chance to aim. You remember this piece, don't y'?—eight in the clip."

"I remember it."

"Good. Keep your ears open." Harp ran out through the door that gave on a small paved area by the woodshed. To get around under the east loft window he would have to push through the snow behind the barn, since he had blocked all the rear openings. He could have circled the house instead, but only by bucking the west wind and fighting deeper drifts. I saw his big shadow melt out of sight.

Leda's voice quavered down to me: "He—get it?"

"Don't know. He's gone to see. Sit tight. . . . "

I heard that infernal bark once again before Harp returned, and again it sounded high off the ground; it must have come from the big maple. And then moments later—I was still trying to pierce the dark, watching for Harp—a vast smash of broken glass and wood, and the violent bang of the door upstairs. One small wheezing shriek cut short, and one scream such as no human being should ever hear. I can still hear it.

I think I lost some seconds in shock. Then I was groping up the narrow stairway, clumsy with the rifle and flashlight. Wind roared at the opening of the kitchen door, and Harp was crowding past me, thrusting me aside. But I was close behind him when he flung the bedroom door open. The blast from the broken window that had slammed the door had also blown out the lamp. But our flashlights said at once that Leda was not there. Nothing was, nothing living.

Droopy lay in a mess of glass splinters and broken window sash, dead from a crushed neck—something had stamped on her. The bedspread had been pulled almost to the window—maybe Leda's hand had clenched on it. I saw blood on some of the glass fragments, and on the splintered sash, a patch of reddish fur.

Harp ran back downstairs. I lingered a few seconds. The arrow of fear was deep in me, but at the moment it made me numb. My light touched up an ugly photograph on the wall, Harp's mother at fifty or so, petrified and acid-faced before the camera, a puritan deity with shallow, haunted eyes. I remembered her.

Harp had kicked over the traces when his father died, and quit going to church. Mrs. Ryder "disowned" him. The farm was his; she left him with it and went to live with a widowed sister in Lohman, and died soon, unreconciled. Harp lived on as a bachelor, crank, recluse, until his strange marriage in his fifties. Now here was Ma still watchful, puckerfaced, unforgiving. In my dullness of shock I thought: Oh, they probably always made love with the lights out.

But now Leda wasn't there.

I hurried after Harp, who had left the kitchen door to bang in the wind. I got out there with rifle and flashlight, and over across the road I saw his torch. No other light, just his small gleam and mine.

I knew as soon as I had forced myself beyond the corner of the house and into the fantastic embrace of the storm that I could never make it. The west wind ground needles into my face. The snow was up beyond the middle of my thighs. With weak lungs and maybe an imperfect heart, I could do nothing out here except die quickly to no purpose. In a moment Harp would be starting down the slope to the woods. His trail was already disappearing under my beam. I drove myself a little further, and an instant's lull in the storm allowed me to shout: "Harp! I can't follow!"

He heard. He cupped his mouth and yelled back: "Don't try! Git back to the house! Telephone!" I waved to acknowledge the message and struggled back.

I only just made it. Inside the kitchen doorway I fell flat, gun and flashlight clattering off somewhere, and there I stayed until I won back enough breath to keep myself living. My face and hands were ice-blocks, then fires. While I worked at the task of getting air into my body, one thought continued, an inner necessity: *There must be a rational cause. I do not abandon the rational cause.* At length I hauled myself up and stumbled to the telephone. The line was dead.

I found the flashlight and reeled upstairs with it. I stepped past poor Droopy's body and over the broken glass to look through the window space. I could see that snow had been pushed off the shed roof near the bedroom window; the house sheltered that area from the full drive of the west wind, so some evidence remained. I guessed that whatever came must have jumped to the house roof from the maple, then down to the shed roof, and then hurled itself through the closed window without regard for it as an obstacle. Losing a little blood and a little fur.

I glanced around and could not find that fur now. Wind must have pushed it out of sight. I forced the door shut. Downstairs, I lit the table lamps in kitchen and parlor. Harp might need those beacons—if he came back. I refreshed the fires, and gave myself a dose of Harp's horrible whisky. It was nearly one in the morning. If he never came back?

It might be days before they could plow out the road. When the storm let up I could use Harp's snowshoes, maybe. . . .

Harp came back, at one-twenty, bent and staggering. He let me support him to the armchair. When he could speak he said, "No trail. No trail." He took the bottle from my hands and pulled on it. "Christ Jesus! What can I do? Ben . . . ? I got to go to the village, get help. If they got any help to give."

"Do you have an extra pair of snowshoes?"

He stared toward me, battling confusion. "Hah? No, I ain't. Better you stay anyhow. I'll bring yours from your house if you want, if I can git there." He drank again and slammed in the cork with the heel of his hand. "I'll leave you the ten-gauge."

He got his snowshoes from a closet. I persuaded him to wait for coffee. Haste could accomplish nothing now; we could not say to each other that we knew Leda was dead. When he was ready to go, I stepped outside with him into the mad wind. "Anything you want me to do before you get back?" He tried to think about it.

"I guess not, Ben. . . . God, ain't I *lived* right? No, that don't make sense. God? That's a laugh." He swung away. Two or three great strides and the storm took him.

That was about two o'clock. For four hours I was alone in the house. Warmth returned, with the bedroom door closed and fires working hard. I carried the kitchen lamp into the parlor, and then huddled in the nearly total dark of the kitchen with my back to the wall, watching all the windows, the ten-gauge near my hand, but I did not expect a return of the beast, and there was none.

The night grew quieter, perhaps because the house was so drifted in that snow muted the sounds. I was cut off from the battle, buried alive.

Harp would get back. The seasons would follow their natural way, and somehow we would learn what had happened to Leda. I supposed the beast would have to be something in the human pattern—mad, deformed, gone wild, but still human.

After a time I wondered why we had heard no excitement in the stable. I forced myself to take up gun and flashlight and go look. I groped through the woodshed, big with the jumping shadows of Harp's cordwood, and into the barn. The cows were peacefully drowsing. In the center alley I dared to send my weak beam swooping and glimmering through the ghastly distances of the hayloft. Quiet, just quiet; natural rustling of mice. Then to the stable, where Ned whickered and let me rub his brown cheek, and Jerry rolled a humorous eye. I suppose no smell had reached them to touch off panic, and perhaps they had heard the barking often enough so that it no longer disturbed them. I went back to my post, and the hours crawled along a ridge between the pits of terror and exhaustion. Maybe I slept.

No color of sunrise that day, but I felt paleness and change; even a blizzard will not hide the fact of dayshine somewhere. I breakfasted on bacon and eggs, fed the hens, forked down hay and carried water for the cows and horses. The one cow in milk, a jumpy Ayrshire, refused to concede that I meant to be useful. I'd done no milking since I was a boy, the knack was gone from my hands, and relief seemed less important to her than kicking over the pail; she was getting more amusement than discomfort out of it, so for the moment I let it go. I made myself busy-work shoveling a clear space by the kitchen door. The wind was down, the snowfall persistent but almost peaceful. I pushed out beyond the house and learned that the stuff was up over my hips.

Out of that, as I turned back, came Harp in his long, snowshoe stride, and down the road three others. I recognized Sheriff Robart, overfed but powerful; and Bill Hastings, wry and ageless, a cousin of Harp's and one of his few friends; and last, Curt Davidson, perhaps a friend to Sheriff Robart but certainly not to Harp.

I'd known Curt as a thick-witted loudmouth when he was a kid; growing to man's years hadn't done much for him. And when I saw him I thought, irrationally perhaps: Not good for our side. A kind of absurdity, and yet

Harp and I were joined against the world simply because we had experienced together what others were going to call impossible, were going to interpret in harsh, even damnable ways; and no help for it.

I saw the white thin blur of the sun, the strength of it growing. Nowhere in all the white expanse had the wind and the new snow allowed us any mark of the visitation of the night.

The men reached my cleared space and shook off snow. I opened the woodshed. Harp gave me one hopeless glance of inquiry and I shook my head.

"Having a little trouble?" That was Robart, taking off his snowshoes.

Harp ignored him. "I got to look after the chores." I told him I'd done it except for that damn cow. "Oh, Bess, ayah, she's nervy. I'll see to her." He gave me my snowshoes that he had strapped to his back. "Adelaide, she wanted to know about your groceries. Said I figured they was in the ca'."

"Good as an icebox," says Robart, real friendly.

Curt had to have his pleasures too. "Ben, you sure you got hold of old Bess by the right end, where the tits was?" Curt giggles at his own jokes, so nobody else is obliged to. Bill Hastings spat in the snow.

"Okay if I go in?" Robart asked. It wasn't a simple inquiry: he was present officially and meant to have it known. Harp looked him up and down.

"Nobody stopping you. Didn't bring you here to stand around, I suppose."

"Harp," said Robart pleasantly enough, "don't give me a hard time. You come tell me certain things has happened, I got to look into it is all." But Harp was already striding down the woodshed to the barn entrance. The others came into the house with me, and I put on water for fresh coffee. "Must be your ca' down the rud a piece, Ben? Heard you kind of went into a ditch. All's you can see now is a hump in the snow. Deep freeze might be good for her, likely you've tried everything else." But I wasn't feeling comic, and never had been on those terms with Robart. I grunted, and his face shed mirth as one slips off a sweater. "Okay, what's the score? Harp's gone and told me a story I couldn't feed to the dogs, so what about it? Where's Mrs. Ryder?"

Davidson giggled again. It's a nasty little sound to come out of all that beef. I don't think Robart had much enthusiasm for him either, but it seems he had sworn in the fellow as a deputy before they set out. "Yes, sir," said Curt, "that was *really* a story, that was."

"Where's Mrs. Ryder?"

"Not here," I told him. "We think she's dead."

He glowered, rubbing cold out of his hands. "Seen that window. Looks like the frame is smashed."

"Yes, from the outside. When Harp gets back you'd better look. I closed the door on that room and haven't opened it. There'll be more snow, but you'll see about what we saw when we got up there."

"Let's look right now," said Curt.

Bill Hastings said, "Curt, ain't you a mite busy for a dep'ty? Mr. Dane said when Harp gets back." Bill and I are friends; normally he wouldn't mister me. I think he was trying to give me some flavor of authority.

I acknowledged the alliance by asking: "You a deputy too, Bill?" Giving him an opportunity to spit in the stove, replace the lid gently, and reply: "Shit no."

Harp returned and carried the milk pail to the pantry. Then he was looking us over. "Bill, I got to try the woods again. You want to come along?"

"Sure, Harp. I didn't bring no gun."

"Take my ten-gauge."

"Curt here'll go along," said Robart. "Real good man on snowshoes. Interested in wildlife."

Harp said, "That's funny, Robart. I guess that's the funniest thing I heard since Cutler's little girl fell under the tractor. You joining us too?"

"Fact is, Harp, I kind of pulled a muscle in my back coming up here. Not getting no younger neither. I believe I'll just look around here a little. Trust you got no objection? To me looking around a little?"

"Coffee's dripped," I said.

"Thing of it is, if I'd've thought you had any objection, I'd've been obliged to get me a warrant."

"Thanks, Ben." Harp gulped the coffee scalding. "Why, if looking around the house is the best you can do, Sher'f, I got no objection. Ben, I shouldn't be keeping you away from your affairs, but would you stay? Kind of keep him company? Not that I got much in the house, but still— you know—"

"I'll stay." I wished I could tell him to drop that manner; it only got him deeper in the mud.

Robart handed Davidson his gun belt and holster. "Better have it, Curt, so to be in style."

Harp and Bill were outside getting on their snowshoes; I half heard some remark of Harp's about the sheriff's aching back. They took off. The snow had almost ceased. They passed out of sight down the slope to the north, and Curt went plowing after them. Behind me Robart said, "You'd think Harp believed it himself."

"That's how it's to be? You make us both liars before you've even done any looking?"

"I got to try to make sense of it is all." I followed him up to the bedroom. It was cruelly cold. He touched Droopy's stiff corpse with his foot. "Hard to figure a man killing his own dog."

"We get nowhere with that kind of idea."

"Ben, you got to see this thing like it looks to other people. And keep out of my hair."

"That's what scares me, Jack. Something unreasonable did happen, and Harp and I were the only ones to experience it—except Mrs. Ryder."

"You claim you saw this—animal?"

"I didn't say that. I heard her scream. When we got upstairs this room was the way you see it." I looked around, and again couldn't find that scrap of fur, but I spoke of it, and I give Robart credit for searching. He shook out the bedspread and blankets, examined the floor and the closet. He studied the window space, leaned out for a look at the house wall and the shed roof. His big feet avoided the broken glass, and he squatted for a long gaze at the pieces of window sash. Then he bore down on me, all policemen personified, a massive, rather intelligent, conventionally honest man with no patience for imagination, no time for any fact not already in the books. "Piece of fur, huh?" He made it sound as if I'd described a Jabberwock with eyes of flame. "Okay, we're done up here." He motioned me downstairs—all policemen who'd ever faced a crowd's dangerous stupidity with their own.

As I retreated I said, "Hope you won't be too busy to have a chemist test the blood on that sash."

"We'll do that." He made move-along motions with his slab hands. "Going to be a pleasure to do that little thing for you and your friend."

Then he searched the entire house, shed, barn, and stable. I had never before watched anyone on police business; I had to admire his zeal. I got involved in the farce of holding the flashlight for him while he rooted in the cellar. In the shed I suggested that if he wanted to restack twenty-odd cords of wood he'd better wait till Harp could help him; he wasn't amused. He wasn't happy in the barn loft either. Shifting tons of hay to find a hypothetical corpse was not a one-man job. I knew he was capable of returning with a crew and machinery to do exactly that. And by his lights it was what he ought to do. Then we were back in the kitchen, Robart giving himself a manicure with his jackknife, and I down to my last cigarette, almost the last of my endurance.

Robart was not unsubtle. I answered his questions as temperately as I could—even, for instance: "Wasn't you a mite sweet on Leda yourself?" I didn't answer any of them with flat silence; to do that right you need an accompanying act like spitting in the stove, and I'm not a chewer. From the north window he said: "Comin' back. It figures." They had been out a little over an hour.

Harp stood by the stove with me to warm his hands. He spoke as if alone with me: "No trail, Ben." What followed came in an undertone: "Ben, you told me about a friend of yours, scientist or something, professor—"

"Professor Malcolm?" I remembered mentioning him to Harp a long while before; I was astonished at his recalling it. Johnny Malcolm is a professor of biology who has avoided too much specialization. Not a really close friend. Harp was watching me out of a granite despair as if he had asked me to appeal to some higher court. I thought of another acquaintance in Boston too, whom I might consult—Dr. Kahn, a psychiatrist who had once seen my wife Helen through a difficult time. . . .

"Harp," said Robart, "I got to ask you a couple, three things. I sent word to Dick Hammond to get that goddamn plow of his into this road as quick as he can. Believe he'll try. Whiles we wait on him, we might 's well talk. You know I don't like to get tough."

"Talk away," said Harp, "only Ben here he's got to get home without waiting on no Dick Hammond."

"That a fact, Ben?"

"Yes. I'll keep in touch."

"Do that," said Robart, dismissing me. As I left he was beginning a fresh manicure, and Harp waited rigidly for the ordeal to continue. I felt morbidly that I was abandoning him.

Still—corpus delicti—nothing much more would happen until Leda Ryder was found. Then if her body were found dead by violence, with no acceptable evidence of Longtooth's existence—well, what then?

I don't think Robart would have let me go if he'd known my first act would be to call Short's brother Mike and ask him to drive me in to Lohman where I could get a bus for Boston.

———

Johnny Malcolm said, "I can see this is distressing you, and you wouldn't lie to me. But, Ben, as biology it won't do. Ain't no such animile. You know that."

He wasn't being stuffy. We were having dinner at a quiet restaurant, and I had of course enjoyed the roast duckling too much. Johnny is a rock-ribbed beanpole who can eat like a walking famine with no regrets. "Suppose," I said, "just for argument and because it's not biologically inconceivable, that there's a basis for the Yeti legend."

"Not inconceivable. I'll give you that. So long as any poorly known corners of the world are left—the Himalayan uplands, jungles, tropic swamps, the tundra—legends will persist and some of them will have little gleams of truth. You know what I think about moon flights and all that?" He smiled; privately I was hearing Leda scream. "One of our strongest reasons for them, and for the biggest flights we'll make if we don't kill civilization first, is a hunt for new legends. We've used up our best ones, and that's dangerous."

"Why don't we look at the countries inside us?" But Johnny wasn't listening much.

"Men can't stand it not to have closed doors and a chance to push at them. Oh, about your Yeti—he might exist. Shaggy anthropoid able to endure severe cold, so rare and clever the explorers haven't tripped over him yet. Wouldn't have to be a carnivore to have big ugly canines— look at the baboons. But if he was active in a Himalayan winter, he'd have to be able to use meat, I think. Mind you, I don't believe any of this, but you can have it as a biological not-impossible. How'd he get to Maine?"

"Strayed? Tibet—Mongolia—Arctic ice."

"Maybe." Johnny had begun to enjoy the hypothesis as something to play with during dinner. Soon he was helping along the brute's passage across the continents, and having fun till I grumbled something about alternatives, extraterrestrials. He wouldn't buy that, and got cross. Still hearing Leda scream, I assured him I wasn't watching for little green men.

"Ben, how much do you know about this—Harp?"

"We grew up along different lines, but he's a friend. Dinosaur, if you like, but a friend."

"Hardshell Maine bachelor picks up dizzy young wife—"

"She's not dizzy. Wasn't. Sexy, but not dizzy."

"All right. Bachelor stewing in his own juices for years. Sure he didn't get up on that roof himself?"

"Nuts. Unless all my senses were more paralyzed than I think, there wasn't time."

"Unless they were more paralyzed than you think."

"Come off it! I'm not senile yet. . . . What's he supposed to have done with her? Tossed her into the snow?"

"Mph," said Johnny, and finished his coffee. "All right. Some human freak with abnormal strength and the endurance to fossick around in a Maine blizzard stealing women. I liked the Yeti better. You say you suggested a madman to Ryder yourself. Pity if you had to come all the way here just so I could repeat your own guesswork. To make amends, want to take in a bawdy movie?"

"Love it."

The following day Dr. Kahn made time to see me at the end of the afternoon, so polite and patient that I felt certain I was keeping him from his dinner. He seemed undecided whether to be concerned with the traumas of Harp Ryder's history or those of mine. Mine were already somewhat known to him. "I wish you had time to talk all this out to me. You've given me a nice summary of what the physical events appear to have been, but—"

"Doctor," I said, "it *happened*. I heard the animal. The window *was* smashed—ask the sheriff. Leda Ryder did scream, and when Harp and I got up there together, the dog had been killed and Leda was gone."

"And yet, if it was all as clear as that, I wonder why you thought of consulting me at all, Ben. I wasn't there. I'm just a headshrinker."

"I wanted . . . Is there any way a delusion could take hold of Harp *and* me, disturb our senses in the same way? Oh, just saying it makes it ridiculous."

Dr. Kahn smiled. "Let's say, difficult."

"Is it possible Harp could have killed her, thrown her out through the window of the *west* bedroom—the snow must have drifted six feet or higher on that side—and then my mind distorted my time sense? So I might've stood there in the dark kitchen all the time it went on, a matter of minutes instead of seconds? Then he jumped down by the shed roof, came back into the house the normal way while I was stumbling upstairs? Oh, hell."

Dr. Kahn had drawn a diagram of the house from my description, and peered at it with placid interest. "Benign" was a word Helen had used for him. He said, "Such a distortion of the time sense would be— unusual. . . . Are you feeling guilty about anything?"

"About standing there and doing nothing? I can't seriously believe it was more than a few seconds. Anyway that would make Harp a monster out of a detective story. He's not that. How could he count on me to freeze in panic? Absurd. I'd've heard the struggle, steps, the window of the west room going up. Could he have killed her and I known all about it at the time, even witnessed it, and then suffered amnesia for that one event?"

He still looked so patient I wished I hadn't come. "I won't say any trick of the mind is impossible, but I might call that one highly improbable. Academically, however, considering your emotional involvement—"

"I'm not emotionally involved!" I yelled that. He smiled, looking much more interested. I laughed at myself. That was better than poking him in the eye. "I'm upset, Doctor, because the whole thing goes against reason. If you start out knowing nobody's going to believe you, it's all messed up before you open your mouth."

He nodded kindly. He's a good joe. I think he'd stopped listening for what I didn't say long enough to hear a little of what I did say. "You're not unstable, Ben. Don't worry about amnesia. The explanation, perhaps some human intruder, will turn out to be within the human norm. The norm of possibility does include such things as lycanthropic delusions, maniacal behavior, and so on. Your police up there will carry on a good search for the poor woman. They won't overlook that snowdrift. Don't underestimate them, and don't worry about your own mind, Ben."

"Ever seen our Maine woods?"

"No, I go away to the Cape."

"Try it some time. Take a patch of it, say about fifty miles by fifty, that's twenty-five hundred square miles. Drop some eager policemen into it, tell 'em to hunt for something they never saw before and don't want to see, that doesn't want to be found."

"But if your beast is human, human beings leave traces. Bodies aren't easy to hide, Ben."

"In those woods? A body taken by a carnivorous animal? Why not?" Well, our minds didn't touch. I thanked him for his patience and got up. "The maniac responsible," I said. "But whatever we call him, Doctor, he was *there*."

Mike Short picked me up at the Lohman bus station, and told me something of a ferment in Darkfield. I shouldn't have been surprised. "They're all scared, Mr. Dane. They want to hurt somebody." Mike is Jim Short's younger brother. He scrapes up a living with his taxi service and occasional odd jobs at the garage. There's a droop in his shaggy ringlets, and I believe thirty is staring him in the face. "Like, old Harp he wants to tell it like it happened and nobody buys. That's sad, man. You been away what, three days? The fuzz was pissed off. You better connect with Mister Sheriff Robart like soon. He climbed all over my ass just for driving you to the bus that day, like I should've known you shouldn't."

"I'll pacify him. They haven't found Mrs. Ryder?"

Mike spat out the car window, which was rolled down for the mild air. "Old Harp he never got such a job of snow-shoveling done in all his days. By the c'munity, for free. No, they won't find her." In that there was plenty of I-want-to-be-asked, and something more, a hint of the mythology of Mike's generation.

"So what's your opinion, Mike?"

He maneuvered a fresh cigarette against the stub of the last and drove on through tiresome silence. The road was winding between ridged mountains of plowed, rotting snow. I had the window down on my side too for the genial afternoon sun, and imagined a tang of spring. At last Mike said, "You prob'ly don't go along . . . Jim got your ca' out, by the way. It's at your place. . . . Well, you'll hear 'em talking it all to pieces. Some claim Harp's telling the truth. Some say he killed her himself. They don't say how he made her disappear. Ain't heard any talk against you, Mr. Dane, nothing that counts. The sheriff's peeved, but that's just on account you took off without asking." His vague, large eyes watched the melting landscape, the ambiguous messages of spring. "Well, I think, like, a demon took her, Mr. Dane. She was one of his own, see? You got to remember, I knew that chick. Okay, you can say it ain't scientific, only there is a science to these things, I read a book about it. You can laugh if you want."

I wasn't laughing. It wasn't my first glimpse of the contemporary medievalism and won't be my last if I survive another year or two. I wasn't laughing, and I said nothing. Mike sat smoking, expertly driving his twentieth-century artifact while I suppose his thoughts were in the seventeenth, sniffing after the wonders of the invisible world, and I recalled what Johnny Malcolm had said about the need for legends. Mike and I had no more talk.

Adelaide Simmons was dourly glad to see me. From her I learned that the sheriff and state police had swarmed all over Harp's place and the surrounding countryside, and were still at it. Result, zero. Harp had repeatedly told our story and was refusing to tell it anymore. "Does the chores and sets there drinking," she said, "or staring off. Was up to see him yesterday, Mr. Dane—felt I should. Couple days they didn't let him alone a minute, maybe now they've eased off some. He asked me real sharp, was you back yet. Well, I redd up his place, made some bread, least I could do."

When I told her I was going there, she prepared a basket, while I sat in the kitchen and listened. "Some say she busted that window herself, jumped down and run off in the snow, out of her mind. Any sense in that?"

"Nope."

"And some claim she deserted him. Earlier. Which'd make you a liar. And they say whichever way it was, Harp's made up this crazy story because he can't stand the truth." Her clever hands slapped sandwiches into shape. "They claim Harp got you to go along with it, they don't say how."

"Hypnotized me, likely. Adelaide, it all happened the way Harp told it. I heard the thing too. If Harp is ready for the squirrels, so am I."

She stared hard, and sighed. She likes to talk, but her mill often shuts off suddenly, because of a quality of hers which I find good as well as rare: I mean that when she has no more to say she doesn't go on talking.

I got up to Ryder's Ridge about suppertime. Bill Hastings was there. The road was plowed slick between the snow ridges, and I wondered how much of the litter of tracks and crumpled paper and spent cigarette packages had been left by sightseers. Ground frost had not yet yielded to the mud season, which would soon make normal driving impossible for a few weeks. Bill let me in, with the look people wear for serious illness. But Harp heaved himself out of that armchair, not sick in body at least. "Ben, I heard him last night. Late."

"What direction?"

"North."

"You hear it, Bill?" I set down the basket.

My pint-size friend shook his head. "Wasn't here." I couldn't guess how much Bill accepted of the tale.

Harp said, "What's the basket?—oh. Obliged. Adelaide's a nice woman." But his mind was remote. "It was north, Ben, a long way, but I think I know about where it would be. I wouldn't've heard it except the night was so still, like everything had quieted for me. You know, they been a-deviling me night and day. Robart, state cops, mess of smart little buggers from the papers. I couldn't sleep, I stepped outside like I was called. Why, he might've been the other side of the stars, the sky so full of 'em and nothing stirring. Cold . . . You went to Boston, Ben?"

"Yes. Waste of time. They want it to be something human, anyhow something that fits the books."

Whittling, Bill said neutrally, "Always a man for the books yourself, wasn't you, Ben?"

I had to agree. Harp asked, "Hadn't no ideas?"

"Just gave me back my own thoughts in their language. We have to find it, Harp. Of course some wouldn't take it for true even if you had photographs."

Harp said, "Photographs be goddamned."

"I guess you got to go," said Bill Hastings. "We been talking about it, Ben. Maybe I'd feel the same if it was me. . . . I better be on my way or supper'll be cold and the old woman raising hellfire." He tossed his stick back in the woodbox.

"Bill," said Harp, "you won't mind feeding the stock couple, three days?"

"I don't mind. Be up tomorrow."

"Do the same for you some time. I wouldn't want it mentioned anyplace."

"Harp, you know me better'n that. See you, Ben."

"Snow's going fast," said Harp when Bill had driven off. "Be in the woods a long time yet, though."

"You wouldn't start this late."

He was at the window, his lean bulk shutting off much light from the time-seasoned kitchen where most of his indoor life had been passed. "Morning, early. Tonight I got to listen."

"Be needing sleep, I'd think."

"I don't always get what I need," said Harp.

"I'll bring my snowshoes. About six? And my carbine—I'm best with a gun I know."

He stared at me a while. "All right, Ben. You understand, though, you might have to come back alone. I ain't coming back till I get him, Ben. Not this time."

At sunup I found him with Ned and Jerry in the stable. He had lived eight or ten years with that team. He gave Ned's neck a final pat as he turned to me and took up our conversation as if night had not intervened.

"Not till I get him. Ben, I don't want you drug into this ag'inst your inclination."

"Did you hear it again last night?"

"I heard it. North."

The sun was at the point of rising when we left on our snowshoes, like morning ghosts ourselves. Harp strode ahead down the slope to the woods without haste, perhaps with some reluctance. Near the trees he halted, gazing to his right where a red blaze was burning the edge of the sky curtain; I scolded myself for thinking that he was saying good-bye to the sun.

The snow was crusted, sometimes slippery even for our web feet. We entered the woods along a tangle of tracks, including the fat tire-marks of a snow-scooter. "Guy from Lohman," said Harp. "Hired the goddamn thing out to the state cops and hisself with it. Goes pootin' around all over hell, fit to scare everything inside eight, ten miles." He cut himself a fresh plug to last the morning. "I b'lieve the thing is a mite further off than that. They'll be messing around again today." His fingers dug into my arm. "See how it is, don't y'? They ain't looking for what we are. Looking for a dead body to hang onto my neck. And if they was to find her the way I found—the way I found—"

"Harp, you needn't borrow trouble."

"I know how they think," he said. "Was I to walk down the road beyond Darkfield, they'd pick me up. They ain't got me in shackles because they got no—no body, Ben. Nobody needs to tell me about the law. They got to have a body. Only reason they didn't leave a man here overnight, they figure I can't go nowhere. They think a man couldn't travel in three, four foot of snow. . . . Ben, I mean to find that thing and shoot it down. . . . We better slant off thisaway."

He set out at a wide angle from those tracks, and we soon had them out of sight. On the firm crust our snowshoes left no mark. After a while we heard a grumble of motors far back, on the road. Harp chuckled viciously. "Bright and early like yesterday." He stared back the way we had come. "They'll never pick that up, without dogs. That son of a bitch Robart did talk about borrying a hound somewhere, to sniff Leda's clothes. More likely give 'em a sniff of mine, now."

We had already come so far that I didn't know the way back. Harp would know it. He could never be lost in any woods, but I have no mental compass such as his. So I followed him blindly, not trying to memorize our trail. It was a region of uniform old growth, mostly hemlock, no recent lumbering, few landmarks. The monotony wore down native patience to a numbness, and our snowshoes left no more impression than our thoughts.

An hour passed, or more; after that the sound of motors faded. Now and then I heard the wind move peacefully overhead. Few bird calls, for most of our singers had not yet returned. "Been in this part before, Harp?"

"Not with snow on the ground, not lately." His voice was hushed and careful. "Summers. About a mile now, and the trees thin out some. Stretch of slash where they was taking out pine four, five years back and left everything a Christly pile of shit like they always do."

No, Harp wouldn't get lost here, but I was well lost, tired, sorry I had come. Would he turn back if I collapsed? I didn't think he could, now, for any reason. My pack with blanket roll and provisions had become infernal. He had said we ought to have enough for three or four days. Only a few years earlier I had carried heavier camping loads than this without trouble, but now I was blown, a stitch beginning in my side. My wrist watch said only nine o'clock.

The trees thinned out as he had promised, and here the land rose in a long slope to the north. I looked up across a tract of eight or ten acres where the devastation of stupid lumbering might be healed if the hurt region could be let alone for sixty years. The deep snow, blinding out here where only scrub growth interfered with the sunlight, covered the worst of the wreckage. "Good place for wild ras'berries," Harp said quietly. "Been time for 'em to grow back. Guess it was nearer seven years ago when they cut here and left this mess. Last summer I couldn't hardly find their logging road. Off to the left—"

He stopped, pointing with a slow arm to a blurred gray line that wandered up from the left to disappear over the rise of ground. The nearest part of that gray curve must have been four hundred feet away, and to my eyes it might have been a shadow cast by an irregularity of the snow surface; Harp knew better. Something had passed there, heavy enough to break the crust. "You want to rest a mite, Ben? Once over that rise I might not want to stop again."

I let myself down on the butt of an old log that lay tilted toward us, cut because it had happened to be in the way, left to rot because they happened to be taking pine. "Can you really make anything out of that?"

"Not enough," said Harp. "But it could be him." He did not sit by me but stood relaxed with his load, snowshoes spaced so he could spit between them. "About half a mile over that rise," he said, "there's a kind of gorge. Must've been a good brook, former times, still a stream along the bottom in summer. Tangle of elders and stuff. Couple, three caves in the bank at one spot. I guess it's three summers since I been there. Gloomy goddamn place. There was foxes into one of them caves. Natural caves, I b'lieve. I didn't go too near, not then."

I sat in the warming light, wondering whether there was any way I could talk to Harp about the beast—if it existed, if we weren't merely a pair of aging men with disordered minds. Any way to tell him the creature was important to the world outside our dim little village? That it ought somehow to be kept alive, not just shot down and shoveled aside? How could I say this to a man without science, who had lost his wife and also the trust of his fellow-men?

Take away that trust and you take away the world.

Could I ask him to shoot it in the legs, get it back alive? Why, to my own self, irrationally, that appeared wrong, horrible, as well as beyond our powers. Better if he shot to kill. Or if I did. So in the end I said nothing, but shrugged my pack into place and told him I was ready to go on.

With the crust uncertain under that stronger sunshine, we picked our way slowly up the rise, and when we came at length to that line of tracks, Harp said matter-of-factly, "Now you've seen his mark. It's him."

Sun and overnight freezing had worked on the trail. Harp estimated it had been made early the day before. But wherever the weight of Longtooth had broken through, the shape of his foot showed clearly down there in its pocket of snow, a foot the size of a man's but broader, shorter. The prints were spaced for the stride of a short-legged person. The arch of the foot was low, but the beast was not actually flat-footed. Beast or man. I said, "This is a man's print, Harp. Isn't it?"

He spoke without heat. "No. You're forgetting, Ben. I seen him."

"Anyhow there's only one."

He said slowly, "Only one set of tracks."

"What d'you mean?"

Harp shrugged. "It's heavy. He could've been carrying something. Keep your voice down. That crust yesterday, it would've held me without no web feet, but he went through, and he ain't as big as me." Harp checked his rifle and released the safety. "Half a mile to them caves. B'lieve that's where he is, Ben. Don't talk unless you got to, and take it slow."

I followed him. We topped the rise, encountering more of that lumberman's desolation on the other side. The trail crossed it, directly approaching a wall of undamaged trees that marked the limit of the cutting.

Here forest took over once more, and where it began, Longtooth's trail
ended. "Now you seen how it goes," Harp said. "Any place where he
can travel above ground he does. He don't scramble up the trunks, seems
like. Look here—he must've got aholt of that branch and swung hisself
up. Knocked off some snow, but the wind knocks off so much too you
can't tell nothing. See, Ben, he—he figures it out. He knows about trails.
He'll have come down out of these trees far enough from where we are
now so there ain't no chance of us seeing the place from here. Could
be anywhere in a half-circle, and draw it as big as you please."

"Thinking like a man."

"But he ain't a man," said Harp. "There's things he don't know. How
a man feels, acts. I'm going on to them caves." From necessity, I followed
him. . . .

I ought to end this quickly. Prematurely I am an old man, incapacitated
by the effects of a stroke and a damaged heart. I keep improving a little—
sensible diet, no smoking, Adelaide's care. I expect several years of tol-
erable health on the way downhill. But I find, as Harp did, that it is
even more crippling to lose the trust of others. I will write here once
more, and not again, that my word is good.

It was noon when we reached the gorge. In that place some melancholy
part of night must always remain. Down the center of the ravine between
tangles of alder, water murmured under ice and rotting snow, which here
and there had fallen in to reveal the dark brilliance. Harp did not enter
the gorge itself but moved slowly through tree-cover along the left edge,
eyes flickering for danger. I tried to imitate his caution. We went a
hundred yards or more in that inching advance, maybe two hundred. I
heard only the occasional wind of spring.

He turned to look at me, with a sickly triumph, a grimace of disgust
and of justification, too. He touched his nose and then I got it also, a
rankness from down ahead of us, a musky foulness with an ammoniacal
tang and some smell of decay. Then on the other side of the gorge, off
in the woods but not far, I heard Longtooth.

A bark, not loud. Throaty, like talk.

Harp suppressed an answering growl. He moved on until he could
point down to a black cave mouth on the opposite side. The breeze blew
the stench across to us. Harp whispered, "See, he's got like a path. Jumps
down to that flat rock, then to the cave. We'll see him in a minute."
Yes, there were sounds in the brush. "You keep back." His left palm
lightly stroked the underside of his rifle barrel.

So intent was he on the opening where Longtooth would appear, I may have been first to see the other who came then to the cave mouth and stared up at us with animal eyes. Longtooth had called again, a rather gentle sound. The woman wrapped in filthy hides may have been drawn by that call or by the noise of our approach.

Then Harp saw her.

He knew her. In spite of the tangled hair, scratched face, dirt, and the shapeless deer pelt she clutched around herself against the cold, I am sure he knew her. I don't think she knew him, or me. An inner blindness, a look of a beast wholly centered on its own needs. I think human memories had drained away. She knew Longtooth was coming. I think she wanted his warmth and protection, but there were no words in the whimper she made before Harp's bullet took her between the eyes.

Longtooth shoved through the bushes. He dropped the rabbit he was carrying and jumped down to that flat rock snarling, glancing sidelong at the dead woman who was still twitching. If he understood the fact of death, he had no time for it. I saw the massive overdevelopment of thigh and leg muscles, their springy motions of preparation. The distance from the flat rock to the place where Harp stood must have been fifteen feet. One spear of sunlight touched him in that blue-green shade, touched his thick red fur and his fearful face.

Harp could have shot him. Twenty seconds for it, maybe more. But he flung his rifle aside and drew out his hunting knife, his own long tooth, and had it waiting when the enemy jumped.

So could I have shot him. No one needs to tell me I ought to have done so.

Longtooth launched himself, clawed fingers out, fangs exposed. I felt the meeting as if the impact had struck my own flesh. They tumbled roaring into the gorge, and I was cold, detached, an instrument for watching.

It ended soon. The heavy brownish teeth clenched in at the base of Harp's neck. He made no more motion except the thrust that sent his blade into Longtooth's left side. Then they were quiet in that embrace, quiet all three. I heard the water flowing under the ice.

I remember a roaring in my ears, and I was moving with slow care, one difficult step after another, along the lip of the gorge and through mighty corridors of white and green. With my hard-won detached amusement I supposed this might be the region where I had recently followed poor Harp Ryder to some destination or other, but not (I thought) one of those we talked about when we were boys. A band of iron had closed around my forehead, and breathing was an enterprise needing great effort and caution, in order not to worsen the indecent pain that clung as another band around my diaphragm. I leaned against a tree for thirty seconds or thirty minutes, I don't know where. I knew I mustn't take off my pack in spite of the pain, because it carried provisions for three days. I said once: "Ben, you are lost."

I had my carbine, a golden bough, staff of life, and I recall the shrewd management and planning that enabled me to send three shots into the air. Twice.

It seems I did not want to die, and so hung on the cliff-edge of death with a mad stubbornness. They tell me it could not have been the second day that I fired the second burst, the one that was heard and answered— because, they say, a man can't suffer the kind of attack I was having and then survive a whole night of exposure. They say that when a search party reached me from Wyndham Village (eighteen miles from Dark-field), I made some garbled speech and fell flat on my face.

I woke immobilized, without power of speech or any motion except for a little life in my left hand, and for a long time memory was only a jarring of irrelevancies. When that cleared I still couldn't talk for another long deadly while. I recall someone saying with exasperated admiration that with cerebral hemorrhage on top of coronary infarction, I had no damn right to be alive; this was the first sound that gave me any pleasure. I remember recognizing Adelaide and being unable to thank her for her presence. None of this matters to the story, except the fact that for months I had no bridge of communication with the world; and yet I loved the world and did not want to leave it.

One can always ask: What will happen next?

Some time in what they said was June my memory was (I think) clear. I scrawled a little, with the nurse supporting the deadened part of my arm. But in response to what I wrote, the doctor, the nurses, Sheriff Robart, even Adelaide Simmons and Bill Hastings, looked—sympathetic. I was not believed. I am not believed now, in the most important part of what I wish I might say: that there are things in our world that we do not understand, and that this ignorance ought to generate humility. People find this obvious, bromidic—oh, they always have!—and there-fore they do not listen, retaining the pride of their ignorance intact.

Remnants of the three bodies were found in late August, small thanks to my efforts, for I had no notion what compass direction we took after the cut-over area, and there are so many such areas of desolation I couldn't tell them where to look. Forest scavengers, including a pack of dogs, had found the bodies first. Water had moved them too, for the last of the big snow melted suddenly, and for a couple of days at least there must have been a small river raging through that gorge. The head of what they are calling the "lunatic" got rolled downstream, bashed against rocks, partly buried in silt. Dogs had chewed and scattered what they speak of as "the man's fur coat."

It will remain a lunatic in a fur coat, for they won't have it any other way. So far as I know, no scientist ever got a look at the wreckage, unless you glorify the coroner by that title. I believe he was a good vet before he got the job. When my speech was more or less regained, I was already through trying to talk about it. A statement of mine was read at the inquest—that was before I could talk or leave the hospital. At this ceremony society officially decided that Harper Harrison Ryder, of this township, shot to death his wife Leda and an individual, male, of unknown identity, while himself temporarily of unsound mind, and died of knife injuries received in a struggle with the said individual of unknown, and so forth.

I don't talk about it because that only makes people more sorry for me, to think a man's mind should fail so, and he not yet sixty.

I cannot even ask them: "What is truth?" They would only look more saddened, and I suppose shocked, and perhaps find reasons for not coming to see me again.

They are kind. They will do anything for me, except think about it.

MY ROSE AND
MY GLOVE

J

ames Huberman began collecting things in his earliest youth. He had
an incredible sense of the future. When we were no more than nine or
ten, he told me, "Someday my childhood will be worth a fortune. My
father's toys already sell in antique shops for tremendous prices. My
mother's old clothes are collector's items. I'm not going to make the
mistake they made."

Of course, Huberman was a strange lad and the butt of many terrible
jokes. When there was nothing else to do, it became the fashion to torture
him in small ways. Once he was painted orange. Once an attempt was
made to tattoo a picture of Hitler on his ass. Once his parakeet was held
for a ransom of five hero sandwiches. Once he was locked in the school
toilet over Washington's Birthday while the police searched for his body.
Once a suicide note was "signed" by him and left, along with his underwear and raincoat, near a raging river. Huberman made the most of
those woeful experiences. He not only pledged to remember his assassins,
he actually preserved mementos. He saved what was left of the orange
paint, he sat for hours on a warm cloth to transfer Hitler's picture and
succeeded in creating a kind of Nazi Shroud of Turin, and when the
parakeet died of exposure he stuffed it himself. While he was locked in
the school toilet, he copied and filed the graffiti he found on the walls.

The suicide note, the underwear, the raincoat, and a specimen from the river, along with an article from the local paper denying the incident, became an exhibit in Huberman's own Museum of Indignities.

I was Huberman's only friend—at least, his only active nonenemy. I had a premonition about him. I was afraid of his vengeance. Don't ask me why.

After high school, we all went our separate ways. Unlike Huberman, I was not a collector of either things or people. I dropped my roots into hostile soil . . . the communications business. After a few years in public relations, I realized that the essence of communications was noncommunication. I started out writing clear prose and making direct statements on behalf of my clients. Then I changed my style in favor of obfuscation and made it big. I grew moderately rich.

From time to time, I revisited my hometown. I always asked about Huberman, but nobody seemed to know his fate. He had opened an antique shop, predictably, then sold it and moved away. It must have been difficult for Huberman to sell anything, if ever he did sell anything. In the yearbook, under Huberman's picture, the caption read, "He has one saving grace . . . " with *saving* in italics. Clever. I wrote that.

Things went well for me. One afternoon—it was in winter, a silver snow was falling over New York—I remembered my Rosebud, a toy motorcycle given to me by an uncle now dead. I had sold it to Huberman, or exchanged it for a Howdy Doody ring. He got the better of the bargain. He always did. The ring was rusty. Now, twenty years later, at the top of my profession, I wanted my motorcycle. I wanted it. And I assumed that Huberman must still have it. Huberman kept his dandruff. But I did not know where Huberman was to be found.

My desire for the motorcycle became an obsession. I began checking information listings in cities I thought might appeal to Huberman. He would enjoy old cities suffering population loss with growing slum problems. As buildings crumbled, Huberman would be there snapping up parapets and door frames for pennies. As populations emigrated, Huberman would wait by the road to buy up their leavings. I found Huberman in a suburb of Cleveland, a small city named Wyet that once manufactured carbon paper. They still had a small plant that turned out the stuff—maybe one box a year—and the Japs were threatening even that company. When I heard about Wyet, I couldn't wait to call information. Sure enough, Huberman, James, was listed.

I dialed the number slowly, enjoying the anticipation. Huberman looked so funny painted orange, so serious stuffing his bird. A voice grunted on the telephone—conserving energy, not wasting it on *hello*. That was promising.

"I want my motorcycle back."

"It'll cost you," said Huberman, and it was James Huberman beyond any doubt.

"Huberman, how are you?" I said. "How the hell have you been?"

"How should I be?"

"What are you up to?"

"The same. You?"

"The same. Nothing has changed. So, it's good to talk to you."

"Ah. The motorcycle?"

"I really do want it. Ask me not why."

"Who asked?"

"Well, I'm not surprised that you still have it. Nor that you knew me by my opening remark."

"So what?"

"Just conversing, Huberman. Listen, I'll tell you what. I have a client in Cleveland. Usually I don't make house calls, not anymore, but maybe I'll come on out there to visit his plant, and while I'm there I can run over to Wyet. We can lift a glass and talk about days gone by."

"I don't know. I'm busy," Huberman said.

"Listen, *friend*," I said, "I'm quite anxious to see you."

"You are?"

"I most certainly am. And I'm equally serious about my motorcycle."

"I'll be glad to give you a price," Huberman said. "But it will reflect the market."

"Did I call for a bargain? You know the trouble I went to to find you?"

"Trouble?"

"Trouble. Incredible anguish. I've talked with information operators in forty states."

"Mmm. Come then."

It was arranged. I flew to Cleveland and met with my client. When business was done, I called Huberman and we made plans for our reunion.

Once I called a girl I knew at college some fifteen years after the fact. She agreed to meet for a drink. On the way to our meeting place, I became very nervous. I suddenly felt the presence of time as weight. She must have felt the same. When we finally met, there was a split-second taking of inventory—we both looked thicker and older. She said, "Anything new?" and I said, "Not really, you?" And she said, "Not really."

Meeting Huberman was different. I had always felt superior to him; everybody did. My career had blossomed into a fat and desirable flower. Huberman was stuck in Wyet, Ohio, still the man with the broom following a parade, Chaplinesque but unfunny. His pratfalls hurt. The very pleasure of comparing Huberman's track record with my own flooded me with guilt. I would offer him a large sum of money for the toy motorcycle. It would be a blatant handout, a bribe to lower his accusing eyes.

Reaching his street had a Dante-esque quality. Wyet, the carbon-paper capital of America, had no lush houses left. On the main street, mannequins in new clothes looked like bag ladies. The town had the feeling of an abandoned spiderweb. And that was the classy neighborhood. The farther I got from the glittering center of Wyet, the worse it got. The web was torn. I found Huberman's "house." Not a house. A gigantic warehouse, certainly a relic of the days when every secretary carbon-copied to a long list. No more.

Of course Huberman, James, would have a warehouse. He had out-grown drawers and closets by the time he was fifteen. The warehouse would be bulging, and Huberman would know where every item could be found. That was Huberman.

Inches from the door, I nearly turned back. But I pressed the buzzer. After a wait, I heard boxes moving, pots clanging, and the slow progress of a presence moving through impossible obstacles. Then the knob turned.

"Yes? Ah. So you did come."

There he was, much different from before, yet the same. Huberman seemed taller and much fatter, yet he had a short, thin appearance. If that sounds confusing, it is because the man emitted conflicting signals. He had a huge belly but a thin face. He had long legs, but crotch to head he reminded me of a golf ball. He wore shoes made for bad feet, striped gray pants that must have come from some executive's annual-meeting suit, a sweatshirt with a faded picture of the Beatles, and an Army fatigue cap. His face hung in space, a planet without promise. But his eyes glittered. He was actually glad to see me. I held out my hand. Huberman looked at it; then he grabbed it and pumped.

"Come in. How are you? I'll make tea."

"Not necessary, Huberman. I can't stay too long. I thought it would be nice to touch base. A lot of years under the bridge."

"Years and years. You look well. Are you doing well?"

"I make a living. And you've got quite a place here."

"Six floors."

The floor was a garden of used TVs, bicycles, sleds, washing machines, sofas, chairs, tables, whatever. Bare bulbs hanging from twisted wires lit the place. I saw a pile of newspapers and magazines and another pile of song sheets and comic books. The piles were immense, as high as pyramids. I sang, "Give me my rose and my glove. . . . "

"Why are you singing that?"

"It's from a song called 'People Will Say We're in Love.' About a man who saves souvenirs of a developing romance. The girl attempts to warn him—"

"I know the song," Huberman said. "*Oklahoma!* Rodgers and Hammerstein. I bought the costumes from the original production. I have the *Playbill.* And one of Hammerstein's shoes."

"I always thought that song should be your theme, Huberman."

"I'm not sure I follow you."

"Forget it. A bit of whimsy."

We began walking upstairs. It was like navigating to the center of a hive. The walls were hung with posters of former presidents and film stars. We had to climb over a hill of manual typewriters and through a tunnel of radios in wooden cabinets.

"Be careful," Huberman said.

"Aren't you worried about fire?" I said.

Huberman stopped and turned. His face was almost purple. "I'm very worried about fire," he said.

I winced. Of course. It was the kind of question that didn't need asking. Are you worried about cancer? What else would Huberman be worried about, if not fire? With his luck he must know that someday a spark from something or a lightning bolt would start a tiny flame that would grow and devour his spectacular hoard. Some prankster might throw a firecracker or cigarette. He *should* worry. Especially him.

On the third floor, Huberman kept his living quarters. In the center of his mounds and piles was a clear area that held a bed, a table, two chairs, a TV, a sink connected to rubber tubes that led into the darkness to some source of water, and a hot plate wired to one of the ceiling fixtures.

"Home is where you hang your heart," Huberman said. That was very frivolous for him, and I chuckled. He laughed back at me. Huberman turned on his hot plate and filled a kettle made of chipped porcelain. He gathered up five or six used tea bags that had dried into knots and put them into a brown bag. He put the bag in a drawer. Then he took a new bag from a Lipton's package. One bag. He kept sugar in a tin that once held marshmallows, and powdered milk in a jar.

"This is cozy," I said.

"It serves the purpose," he said.

I sat and waited while he made tea. The tea was brewed from the single bag in large mugs with pictures of the young Queen Elizabeth. Huberman gave me the mug he dipped first. *One saving grace . . .*

"So, Huberman, here we are," I said.

"Long time, no see," Huberman said.

"And you seem content."

"I am. Are you?"

"Reasonably. So tell me: Any wife? Any kiddies?"

"I'm thinking seriously about marriage," Huberman said. "I have a girlfriend."

"Congratulations," I said. "I was married for a time. No children, though. Tell me about your girlfriend."

"She's smart, and she's got tits."

"Listen, nowadays that's plenty."

"I know. She's rich. Her father was a doctor. He left her well fixed. She loves me."

"I'm really glad."

"Why?"

"Why? Because. On general principles."

"Thank you. But I'm not sure yet."

"Risk. That's what life is about, Huberman. Don't hesitate because she's a doctor's daughter, smart, rich, and with tits. I mean, just because you're in the junk business. It's an honorable profession."

"Junk business?"

"Whatever. Antiques. Collectibles."

"I am a curator," Huberman said deliberately. "I am building a museum of art and artifacts. I live among priceless and beautiful things."

"Oh. Right."

"You think this is a temple of crap?"

"I never said that."

"The temple of crap is outside."

"I get your point, Huberman."

"You came for your cycle. We traded fairly. I gave you a Howdy Doody ring."

"The ring was rusty. It broke."

"Risk. That's what life is about, eh?"

"Score one for you, Huberman. I had my eyes open. It's curious. I was sitting in my office one day, and I began to think about that motorcycle. That's weird."

"It begins that way."

"I realized how much I wanted it. I also realize I shouldn't be telling you. That's not how I usually bargain."

"You can't have the motorcycle. You have nothing to trade. No wife. No children. Nothing."

"I have cash, Huberman."

"Cash? Are you serious? Cash? Now tell me you have stock certificates and municipal bonds." Huberman roared. He spilled his tea and coughed. He was really having himself a good time.

"I don't get the joke," I said.

"Finish your cup of tea. Come with me," Huberman said.

I finished my tea and followed Huberman up two more flights. We went through a fire door to another landscape of "art and artifacts." There, sorting through yellowing dentures in an Ivory Soap carton, was a hunched little man.

"He's cataloging," Huberman said. "Do you recognize him?"

"Should I?"

"He once painted me orange," Huberman said.

"Bill Vanderweil? The football player?"

"The very same."

"What's he doing here?"

"He wanted his skates. We'd done a fair trade. I gave him lollipops. He liked lollipops. He gave me his skates. Then he wanted his skates."

"Bill Vanderweil. He must have really wanted his skates," I said.

"He did. Very much. He works here now. Very reasonably. He's been an enormous help. Look over there."

In the shadows, I saw a slender woman wiping thick dust off a grandfather clock. It stood among a graveyard of grandfather clocks. There were hundreds.

"Jinny Sue Ellenbogel," Huberman said.

"The majorette?"

"Remember how she twirled her baton? Wasn't it elevating?"

"Jinny Sue. I had such a crush on her."

"She traded her baton for a rhinestone brooch, the silly bitch. Then she wanted her baton. It took time, but she understood that she needed her baton. Now she's employed here. Nonunion, I might add. Her boyfriend, Lobster Hallmark, killed my parakeet. He exposed it to the elements."

"Lobster Hallmark. The one with the convertible."

"The convertible is upstairs. He sits in it on his day off. He shifts the gears. I don't allow him to blow the horn except on Christmas."

"Listen, Huberman," I said, "I'm prepared to offer you twenty-five dollars for my motorcycle, but that's it."

"No deal. Come back when you're ready to do business."

"Thirty dollars. Not a penny more. I can live without the motorcycle. The driver's head is loose. The rear wheel is bent. Thirty is my final offer."

"Of course it is," Huberman said. "Would you like more tea? Some time to think?"

"No more tea," I said. "I drink Earl Grey. Not Lipton's."

"I'm sorry," Huberman said.

On the way down, we passed several children carrying boxes up the stairs. Their faces looked familiar. But I didn't ask about their parents.

"Tell me something," Huberman said on the bottom landing. "What do you feel about the neutron bomb?"

"What do I feel? I hate it. How can you feel about a bomb that saves property and kills people?"

"Affectionate," said Huberman. "Let's lay it on the line. You're in public relations. The neutron bomb is getting a lot of god-awful publicity. The other side of the story should be told."

"What other side of the story?"

"The good side. The positive side. The life of objects. Objects are a life form, you know. A campaign could be mounted. People believe that plants have feelings, even consciousness. They need to be educated about things."

"You want me to mount a campaign that celebrates the neutron bomb?"

"We were friends, after a fashion. You never stomped on me. If you agree to the campaign, I'll give you your motorcycle. If not . . . well, what are friends for?"

"Never," I said. "Besides, my best client is a coal company with no involvement in nukes. How do you think they would feel if my organization—"

"The ball is in your court."

"Sixty dollars," I said. "The new tax laws exempt collectibles from Individual Retirement Accounts and Keogh Plans. Remember that, Huberman."

"Please consider," Huberman said, "the realities. There is every chance that life on earth will be destroyed or rendered senseless. Even if there is no war, a mechanized world with consequent leisure will destroy the population. Look what's happened to love. It's become sensation, hardly competitive with video games. And take video games. The most popular one features the perfect cannibal. It devours everything. Winning is consuming. But winning is losing. Because everything becomes nothing. So they come to me. And even when people cease to come for their batons, skates, convertibles—yes, motorcycles—*others* will come. What will *they* find? What I have collected and collated. This building is a time capsule. The only real history. Books lie. Film and tape can be edited. But my objects *are*. When *they* come here they will fondle real *things*: ratty mattresses, stained pillows, cups with rings at the bottom—glorious things. And *they* will play with my toys. *They* will ask themselves about the man who stocked this lode. His birthday will become a holiday."

"Like Washington. Huberman, you've never forgotten that incident in the toilet."

"If you want your motorcycle, it's going to cost you, my friend. But because you were my friend, I'm willing to let you share in this splendid adventure. A modest campaign, possibly some television, some print, a speech here and there. I'm not asking for billboards. Just explain that the shadow burned on a wall is as important as the shadow's father or mother. You know. Neutrons are your friends. Like that. All I want is equal time."

"Huberman, you're mad, but I want that motorcycle. One hundred dollars."

"Done."

"You'll take it?"

"Of course. I've got to eat. I've got to pay the electric bill. I'm considering marriage. CDs. I can't survive on ideals. Cash. No checks. No charge cards. No receipt. I'll get your motorcycle. I've already packed it. Gift wrapped."

Huberman got me the package. I gave him five tens and a fifty.

"Would you have taken thirty?" I said.

"Who knows? Tell me, how's the old town? Is that little park still there, the one where they stripped me and tried to tattoo Hitler on my ass? Lord, those were gay times. But you can't go home again."

"The park is gone," I said. "It's a shopping center."

I drove to Cleveland and flew back to New York. I put the motorcycle on a shelf in my office. It looked marvelous there. I was glad to have it back. I think I would have done anything to get it.

WITH THE
ORIGINAL CAST

I n the summer of 1998 Gregory Whitten was rehearsing a seventy-fifth-year revival of George Bernard Shaw's *Saint Joan*, and Barbara Bishop abruptly called to ask me to fly back from Denver and attend a few rehearsals with her. She was playing Shaw's magnificent teenaged fanatic, a role she had not done for twenty years and never on Broadway. Still, it was an extraordinary request; she had never specifically asked for my presence before, and I wound up my business for Gorer-Redding Solar and caught the next shuttle with uncharacteristic hope. At noon I landed in New York and coptered directly to the theater. Barbara met me in the lobby.

"Austin! You came!"

"Did you doubt it?" I kissed her, and she laughed softly.

"It was so splendid of you to drop everything and rush home."

"Well—I didn't exactly drop it. Lay it down gently, perhaps."

"Could Carl spare you? Did you succeed in blocking that coalition, or can they still stop Carl from installing the new Battery?"

"They have one chance in a billion," I said lightly. Barbara always asks; she manages to sound as interested in Gorer-Redding Solar as in Shakespeare and ESIR, although I don't suppose she really is. Of late neither am I, although Carl Gorer is my brother and the speculative risks of finance, including Gorer-Redding, is my profession. It was a certain faint boredom with seriously behaved money that had driven me in the first place to take wildcat risks backing legitimate theater. In the beginning Gorer-Redding Solar was itself a wildcat risk: one chance in a hundred that solar energy could be made cheap and plentiful enough to replace the exhausted petrofields. But that was years ago. Now solar prosperity is a reality; speculations lie elsewhere.

"I do appreciate your coming, you know," Barbara said. She tilted her head to one side, and a curve of shining dark hair, still without gray, slanted across one cheek.

"All appreciation gratefully accepted. Is there something wrong with the play?"

"No, of course not. What could be wrong with Shaw? Oh, Gregory's a little edgy, but then you know Gregory."

"Then you called me back solely to marry me."

"Austin, not again," she said, without coyness. "Not now."

"Then something *is* wrong."

She pulled a little away from me, shaking her head. "Only the usual new-play nerves."

"Rue-day nerves."

"Through-the-day swerves."

"Your point," I said. "But, Barbara, you've played Joan of Arc before."

"Twenty years ago," she said, and I glimpsed the strain on her face a second before it vanished under her publicity-photo smile, luminous and cool as polished crystal. Then the smile disappeared, and she put her cheek next to mine and whispered, "I do thank you for coming. And you look so splendid," and she was yet another Barbara, the Barbara I saw only in glimpses through her self-contained poise, despite having pursued her for half a year now with my marriage proposals, all gracefully rejected. I, Austin Gorer, who until now had never ever pursued anything very fast or very far. Nor ever had to.

"Nervous, love?"

"Terrified," she said lightly, the very lightness turning the word into a denial of itself, a delicate stage mockery.

"I don't believe it."

"That's half your charm. You never believe me."

"Your Joan was a wild success."

"My God, that was even before ESIR, can you believe it?"

"I believe it."

"So do I," she said, laughing, and began to relate anecdotes about casting that play, then this one, jumping between the two with witty, effortless bridges, her famous voice rising and falling with the melodious control that was as much a part of the public's image of her as the shining helmet of dark hair and the cool grace.

She has never had good press. She is too much of a paradox to reduce easily to tabloid slogans, and the stupider journalists have called her mannered and artificial. She is neither. Eager animation and conscious taste are two qualities the press usually holds to be opposites, patronizing the first and feeling defensive in the presence of the second. But in Barbara Bishop, animation and control have melded into a grace that owes nothing to nature and everything to a civilized respect for willed illusion. When she walks across a stage or through a bedroom, when she speaks Shaw's words or her own, when she hands Macbeth a dagger or a dinner guest a glass of wine, every movement is both free of artifice and perfectly controlled. Because she will not rage at press conferences, or wail colorfully at lost roles, or wrinkle her nose in professional cuteness, the press has decided that she is cold and lacks spontaneity. But for Barbara, what is spontaneous *is* control. She was born with it. She'll always have it.

"—and so now Gregory's *still* casting for the crowd scenes. He's tested what has to be every ESIR actor in New York, and now he's scraping up fledglings straight out of the hospital. Their scalp scars are barely healed and the ink on their historian's certificates is still wet. We're two weeks behind already, and rehearsals have barely begun, would you believe it? He can't find enough actors with an ESIR in fifteenth-century France, and he's not willing to go even fifty years off on either side."

"Then *you* must have been French in Joan's time," I said, "or he wouldn't have cast you? Even you?"

"Quite right. Even me." She moved away from me toward the theater doors. Again I sensed in her some unusual strain. An actor is always reluctant to discuss his ESIR with an outsider (bad form), but this was something more.

"As it happens," Barbara continued, "I was not only French, I was even in Rouen when Joan was burned at the stake in 1431. I didn't see the burning, and I never laid eyes on her—I was only a barmaid in a country tavern—but, still, it's rather an interesting coincidence."

"Yes."

"One chance in a million," she said, smiling. "Or, no—what would be the odds, Austin? That's really your field."

I didn't know. It would depend, of course, on just how many people in the world had undergone ESIR. There were very few. Electronically

Stimulated Incarnation Recall involves painful, repeated electrochemical jolts through the cortex, through the limbic brain, directly into the R-Complex, containing racial and genetic memory. Biological shields are ripped away; defense mechanisms designed to aid survival by streamlining the vast load of memory are deliberately torn. The long-term effects are not yet known. ESIR is risky, confusing, morally disorienting, painful, and expensive. Most people want nothing to do with it. Those who do are mostly historians, scientists, freaks, mystics, poets—or actors, who must be a little of each. A stage full of players who believe totally that they *are* in Hamlet's Denmark or Sir Thomas More's England or Blanche DuBois's South because they *have* been there and feel it in every gesture, every cadence, every authentic cast of mind—such a stage is out of time entirely. It can seduce even a philistine financier. Since ESIR, the glamour of the theater has risen, the number of would-be actors has dropped, and only the history departments of the world's universities have been so in love with historically authentic style.

"Forget the odds," I said. "Who hasn't been cast yet?"

"Well, we need to see," she said, ticking off roles on her fingers. I recognized the parody instantly. Gregory Whitten himself. Her very face seemed to lengthen into the horse-faced scowl so beloved by Sunday-supplement caricaturists. "We must have two royal ladies—no, they must absolutely look royal, *royal*. And DeStogumber, I need a marvelous DeStogumber! How can anyone expect me to direct without an absolutely wonderful DeStogumber—"

The theater doors opened. "We are ready for you onstage, Miss Bishop."

"Thank you." The parody of Whitten had vanished instantly; in this public of one stagehand she was again Barbara Bishop, controlled and cool.

I settled into a seat in the first row, nodding vaguely at the other hangers-on scattered throughout the orchestra and mezzanine. No one nodded back. There was an absurd public fiction that we, who contributed nothing to the play but large sums of money, were like air: necessary but invisible. I didn't mind. I enjoyed seeing the cast ease into their roles, pulling them up from somewhere inside and mentally shaking each fold around their own gestures and voices and glances. I had not always known how to see that. It had taken me, from such a different set of signals, a long time to notice the tiny adjustments that go, rehearsal by rehearsal, to create the illusion of reality. Perhaps I was slow. But now it seemed to me that I could spot the precise moment when an actor has achieved that precarious balance between his neocortical knowledge of the script and his older, ESIR knowledge of the feel of his character's epoch, and so is neither himself nor the playwright's creation but some third, subtler force that transcends both.

Barbara, I could see, had not yet reached that moment.

Whitten, pacing the side of the stage, was directing the early scene in which the seventeen-year-old Joan, a determined peasant, comes to Captain Robert de Baudricourt to demand a horse and armor to lead the French to victory over the English. De Baudricourt was being played by Jason Kellig, a semisuccessful actor whom I had met before and not particularly liked. No one else was onstage, although I had that sensation one always has during a rehearsal of hordes of other people just out of sight in the wings, eyeing the action critically and shushing one another. Moths fluttering nervously just outside the charmed circle of light.

"No, squire!" Barbara said. "God is very merciful, and the blessed saints Catherine and Margaret, who speak to me every day, will intercede for you. You will go to paradise, and your name will be remembered forever as my first helper."

It was subtly wrong: too poised for the peasant Joan, too graceful. At the same time, an occasional gesture—an outflinging of her elbow, a sour smile—was too brash, and I guessed that these had belonged to the Rouen barmaid in Joan's ESIR. It was very rough, and I could see Whitten's famous temper, never long in check, begin to mount.

"No, no, no—Barbara, you're supposed to be an *innocent*. Shaw says that Joan answers 'with muffled sweetness.' You sound too surly. Absolutely too surly. You must do it again. Jason, cue her."

"Well, I am damned," Kellig said.

"No, squire! God is very merciful, and blessed saints Catherine and Margaret, who speak to me every day, will intercede for you. You will go to paradise—"

"Again," Whitten said.

"Well, I am damned."

"No, squire! God is very merciful, and the blessed saints Catherine and Margaret, who speak to me every—"

"No! Now you sound like you're sparring with him! This is not some damned eighteenth-century drawing-room repartee! Joan absolutely *means* it! The voices are absolutely real to her. You must do it again, Barbara. You must tap into the religious atmosphere of your ESIR. You are not trying! Do it again."

Barbara bit her lip. I saw Kellig glance from her to Whitten, and I suddenly had the impression—I don't know why—that they had all been at one another earlier, before I had arrived. Something beyond the usual rehearsal frustration was going on here. Tension, unmistakable as the smell of smoke, rose from the three of them.

"Well, I am damned."

"No, squire! God is very merciful, and the blessed saints Catherine and Margaret, who speak to me every day, will intercede for you. You will go to paradise, and your name will be remembered forever as my first helper."

"Again," Whitten said.

"Well, I am damned."

"No, squire! God is—"

"Again."

"Really, Gregory," Barbara began icily, "how you think you can judge after four words of—"

"I need to hear only *one* word when it's as bad as that! And what in absolute hell is that little flick of the wrist supposed to be? Joan is not a discus thrower. She must be—" Whitten stopped dead, staring off-stage.

At first, unsure of why he had cut himself off or turned so red, I thought he was having an attack of some kind. The color in his face was high, almost hectic. But he held himself taut and erect, and then I heard the siren coming closer, landing on the roof, trailing off. It had come from the direction of Larrimer—which was, I suddenly remembered, the only hospital in New York that would do ESIR.

A very young man in a white coat hurried across the stage.

"Mr. Whitten, Dr. Metz says could you come up to the copter right away?"

"What is it? No, don't hold back, damn it, you absolutely must tell me now! *Is* it?"

On the young technician's face professional restraint battled with self-importance. The latter won, helped perhaps by Whitten's seizing the boy by the shoulders. For a second I actually thought Whitten would shake him.

"It's her, sir. It really is. We were looking for fifteenth-century ESIR, like you said, and we tried the neos for upper class for the ladies-in-waiting, and all we were getting were peasants or non-Europeans or early childhood deaths, and then Dr. Metz asked—" He was clearly enjoying this, dragging it out as much as possible. Whitten waited with a patience that surprised me until I realized that he was holding his breath. "—this

neo to concentrate on the pictures Dr. Metz would show her of buildings
and dresses and bowls and stuff to clear her mind. She looked dazed and
in pain like they do, and then she suddenly remembered who she was,
and Dr. Metz asked her lots of questions—that's his period anyway, you
know; he's the foremost American historian on medieval France—and
then he said she was."

Whitten let out his breath, a long, explosive sigh. Kellig leaned forward
and said "Was . . ."

"Joan," the boy said simply. "Joan of Arc."

It was as if he had shouted, although of course he had not. But the
name hung in the dusty silence of the empty theater, circled and under-
lined by everything there: the heavy velvet curtains, the dust motes in
the air, the waiting strobes, the clouds of mothlike actors, or memories
of actors, in the wings. They all existed to lend weight and probability
to what had neither. One in a million, one in a billion.

"Is Dr. Metz sure?" Whitten demanded. He looked suddenly violent, capable of disassembling the technician if the historian were not
sure.

"He's sure!"

"Where is she? In the copter?"

"Yes."

"Have Dr. Metz bring her down here. No, I'll go up there. No, bring
her here. Is she still weak?"

"Yes, sir," the boy said.

"Well, go! I told Dr. Metz I wanted her here as soon as he absolutely
was sure!"

The boy went.

So Whitten had been informed of the possibility earlier. I looked at
Barbara, suddenly understanding the tension on stage. She stood smiling,
her chin raised a little, her body very straight. She looked pale. Some
trick of lighting, some motionless tautness in her shoulders, made me
think for an instant that she was going to faint, but of course she did
not. She behaved exactly as I knew she must have been willing herself
to, waiting quietly through the interminable time until Joan of Arc should
appear. Whitten fidgeted; Kellig lounged, his eyelids lowered halfway.
Neither of them looked at Barbara.

The technician and the historian walked out onto the stage, each with
a hand under either elbow of a young girl whose head was bandaged.
Even now I feel a little ashamed when I remember rising halfway in my
seat, as for an exalted presence. But the girl was not an exalted presence,

was not Joan of Arc; she was an awkward, skinny, plain-faced girl who had once *been* Joan of Arc and now wanted to be an extra in the background of a seventy-five-year-old play. No one else seemed to be remembering the distinction.

"You were Joan of Arc?" Whitten asked. He sounded curiously formal, as out of character as the girl.

"Yes, I . . . I remember Joan. Being Joan." The girl frowned, and I thought I knew why: She was wondering why she didn't *feel* like Joan. But ESIR, Barbara has told me, doesn't work like that. Other lives are like remembering someone you have known, not like experiencing the flesh and bone of this one—unless this one is psychotic. Otherwise, it usually takes time and effort to draw on the memory of a previous incarnation, and this child had been Joan of Arc only for a few days. Suddenly I felt very sorry for her.

"What's your first name?" Whitten said.

"Ann. Ann Jasmine."

Whitten winced. "A stage name?"

"Yes. Isn't it pretty?"

"You must absolutely use your real name. What acting have you done?"

The girl shifted her weight, spreading her feet slightly apart and starting to count off on her fingers. Her voice was stronger now and cockier. "Well, let's just see: In high school I played Portia in *The Merchant of Venice*, and in the Country-Time Players—that's community theater— I was Goat's Sister in *The Robber Bridegroom* and Arla in *Moondust*. And then I came to New York, and I've done—oh, small stuff, mostly. A few commercials." She smiled at Whitten, then looked past him at Kellig and winked. He stared back at her as if she were a dead fish.

"What," said Kellig slowly, "*is* your real name?"

"Does it matter?" The girl's smile vanished, and she pouted.

"Yes."

"Ann Friedland," she said sulkily, and I knew where the "few commercials, mostly" as well as the expensive ESIR audition had come from. Trevor Friedland, of Friedland Computers, was a theater backer for his own amusement, much as I was. He was not, however, a cobacker in this one. Not yet.

At the Friedland name, Kellig whistled, a low, impudent note that made Whitten glance at him in annoyance. Barbara still had not moved. She watched them intently.

"Forget your name," Whitten said. "Absolutely forget it. Now I know this play is new to you, but you must read for me. Just read cold; don't be nervous. Take my script and start there. No—there. Jason, cue her."

"You want me to read Joan? The part of *Joan?*" the girl said. All her assumed sophistication was gone; her face was as alive as a seven-year-old's at Christmas, and I looked away, not wanting to like her.

"Oh, really, Greg," Kellig said. Whitten ignored him.

"Just look over Shaw's description there, and then start. I know you're cold. Just start."

"Good morning, captain squire," she began shakily, but stopped when Barbara crossed the stage to sit on a bench near the wings. She was still smiling, a small frozen smile. Ann glanced at her nervously, then began over.

"Good morning, captain squire. Captain, you are to give me a horse. . . . " Again she stopped. A puzzled look came over her face; she skimmed a few pages and then closed her eyes. Immediately I thought of the real Joan, listening to voices. But this *was* the real Joan. For a moment the stage seemed to float in front of me, a meaningless collection of lines and angles.

"It wasn't like that," Ann Friedland said slowly.

"Like what?" Whitten said. "What wasn't like what?"

"Joan. Me. She didn't charge in like that at all to ask de Baudricourt for horse and armor. It wasn't at all . . . she was more . . . insane, I think. What he has written here, Shaw . . . " She looked at each of us in turn, frowning. No one moved. I don't know how long we stayed that way, staring at the thin girl onstage.

"Saint Catherine," she said finally. "Saint Margaret." Her slight figure jerked as if shocked, and she threw back her head and howled like a dog. "But Orléans was not even my idea! The commander, my father, the commander, my father . . . oh, my God, my dear God, he made her do it, he told me—they all *promised*—"

She stumbled, nearly falling to her knees. The historian leaped forward and caught her. I don't think any of us could have borne it if that pitiful, demented figure had knelt and begun to pray.

The next moment, however, though visibly fighting to control herself, she knew where—and who—she was.

"Doctor, don't, I'm all right now. It's not—I'm all right. Mr. Whitten, I'm sorry, let me start the scene over!"

"No, don't start the scene over. Tell me what you were going to say. Where is Shaw wrong? What happened? Try to feel it again."

Ann's eyes held Whitten's. They were beyond all of us, already negotiating with every inflection of every word.

"I don't have to feel it again. I remember what happened. That wave of... I won't do that again. It was just when it all came rushing back. But now I remember it, I have it, I can *control* it. It didn't happen like Shaw's play. She—I—was used. She did hear voices, she was mad, but the whole idea to use her to persuade the Dauphin to fight against the English didn't come from the voices. The priests insisted on what they said the voices meant, and the commander made her a sort of mascot to get the soldiers to kill. . . . I was *used*. A victim." A complicated expression passed over her face, perhaps the most extraordinary expression I have ever seen on a face so young: regret and shame and loss and an angry, wondering despair for events long beyond the possibility of change. Then the expression vanished, and she was wholly a young woman coolly engaged in the bargaining of history.

"I know it all, Mr. Whitten—all that *really* happened. And it happened to me. The real Joan of Arc."

"Cosgriff," Whitten said, and I saw Kellig start. Lawrence Cosgriff had won the Pulitizer Prize for drama the last two years in a row. He wrote powerful, despairing plays about the loss of individual morality in an institutionalized world.

"My dear Gregory," Kellig said, "one does not simply commission Lawrence Cosgriff to write one a play. He's not some hack you can—"

Whitten looked at him, and he was quiet. I understood why; Whitten was on fire, as exalted with his daring idea as the original Joan must have been with hers. But no, of course, she hadn't been exalted, that was the whole point. She had been a dupe, not a heroine. Young Miss Friedland, fighting for her name in lights, most certainly considered Joan the Heroine to be an expendable casualty. One of the expendable casualties. I stood up and began to make my way to the stage.

"I'm the real thing," Ann said. "The *real* thing. I'll play Joan, of course."

"Of course," Kellig drawled. He was already looking at her with dislike, and I could see what their rehearsals would be: the chance upstart and the bit player who had paid largely fruitless dues for twenty years. The commander and the Dauphin would still be the male leads; Kellig's part could only grow smaller under Ann's real thing.

"I'll play Joan," she said again, a little more loudly.

Whitten, flushed with his vision, stopped his ecstatic pacing and scowled. "Of course you must play Joan!"

"Oh," Ann said, "I was afraid—"

"Afraid? What is this? You *are* Joan."

"Yes," she said slowly, "yes, I am." She frowned, sincerely, and then a second later replaced the frown with a smile all calculation and relief. "Yes, of course I am!"

"Then I'll absolutely reach Cosgriff's agent today. He'll jump at it. You will need to work with him, of course. We can open in six months, with any luck. You *do* live in town? Cosgriff can tape you. No, someone else can do that before he even—Austin!"

"You're forgetting something, aren't you, Gregory, in this sudden great vision? You have a contract to do Shaw."

"Of course I'm not forgetting the contract. But you absolutely must want to continue, for this new play . . . Cosgriff . . . " He stopped, and I knew the jumble of things that must be in his mind: deadlines, backing (Friedland Computers!), contracts, schedules, the percentage of my commitment, and, belatedly, Barbara.

She still sat on the bench at stage left, half in shadow. Her back was very straight, her chin high, but in the subdued light her face with its faint smile looked older, not haggard but set, inelastic. I walked over to her and turned to face Whitten.

"I will not back this new play, even if you do get Cosgriff to write it. Which I rather doubt. Shaw's drama is an artistic masterpiece. What you are planning is a trendy exploitation of some flashy technology. Look elsewhere for your money."

Silence. Whitten began to turn red, Kellig snickered—at whom was not clear. In the silence the historian, Dr. Metz, began timidly, "I'm sure Miss Friedland's information would be welcomed warmly by any academic—"

The girl cried loudly, "But I'm the real thing!" and she started to sob.

Barbara had risen to take my arm. Now she dropped it and walked over to Ann. Her voice was steady. "I know you are. And I wish you all luck as an actress. It's a brilliant opportunity, and I'm sure you'll do splendidly with it."

They faced each other, the sniveling girl who had at least the grace to look embarrassed and the smiling, humiliated woman. It was a public performance, of course, an illusion that all Barbara felt was a selfless, graceful warmth, but it was also more than that. It was as gallant an act of style as I have ever seen.

WITH THE ORIGINAL CAST

Ann muttered, "Thank you," and flushed a mottled maroon. Barbara took my arm, and we walked down the side aisle and out of the theater. She walked carefully, choosing her steps, her head high and lips together and solemn, like a woman on her way to a public burning.

I wish I could say that my quixotic gesture had an immediate and disastrous effect on Whitten's plans, that he came to his artistic senses— and went back to Shaw's *Saint Joan.* But of course he did no such thing. Other financial backing than mine proved to be readily available. Contracts were rewritten, agents placated, lawsuits avoided. Cosgriff did indeed consent to write the script, and *Variety* became distressingly eager to report any tidbit connected with what was being billed as JOAN OF ARC: WITH THE ORIGINAL CAST! It was a dull theater season in New York. Nothing currently running gripped the public imagination like this as-yet-unwritten play. Whitten, adroitly fanning the flames, gave out very few factual details.

Barbara remained silent on the whole subject. Business was keeping me away from New York a great deal. Gorer-Redding Solar was installing a new plant in Bogotá, and I would spend whole weeks trying to untangle the lush foliage of bribes, kickbacks, nepotism, pride, religion, and mañana that is business in South America. But whenever I was in New York, I spent time with Barbara. She would not discuss Whitten's play, warning me away from the subject with the tactful withdrawal of an estate owner discouraging trespassing without hurting local feelings. I admired her tact and her refusal to whine, but at the same time I felt vaguely impatient. She was keeping me at arm's length. She was doing it beautifully, but arm's length was not where I wanted to be.

I do not assume that intimacy must be based on a mutual display of sores. I applaud the public illusion of control and well-being as a civilized achievement. However, I knew Barbara well enough to know that under her illusion of well-being she must be hurt and a little afraid. No decent scripts had been offered her, and the columnists had not been kind over the loss of *Saint Joan.* Barbara had been too aloof, too self-possessed for them to show any compassion now. Press sympathy for a humiliated celebrity is in direct proportion to the anguished copy previously supplied.

Then one hot night in August I arrived at Barbara's apartment for dinner. Lying on a hall table was a script:

A MAID OF DOMRÉMY
by
Lawrence Cosgriff

Incredulous, I picked it up and leafed through it. When I looked up, Barbara was standing in the doorway, holding two goblets of wine.

"Hello, Austin. Did you have a good flight?"

"Barbara—what is this?" I asked, stupidly.

She crossed the hall and handed me one of the goblets. "It's Lawrence's play about Joan of Arc."

"I see that. But what is it doing here?"

She didn't answer me immediately. She looked beautiful, every illusion seeming completely natural: the straight, heavy silk of her artfully cut gown, the flawless makeup, the hair cut in precise lines to curve over one cheek. Without warning, I was irritated by all of it. Illusions. Arm's length.

"Austin, why don't you reconsider backing Gregory's play?"

"Why on earth should I?"

"Because you really could make quite a lot of money on it."

"I could make quite a lot of money backing auto gladiators. I don't do that, either."

She smiled, acknowledging the thrust. I still did not know how the conversation had become a duel.

"Are you hungry? There are canapés in the living room. Dinner won't be ready for a while yet."

"I'm not hungry. Barbara, why do you want me to back Whitten's play?"

"I don't want you to, if you don't wish to. Come in and sit down. *I'm* hungry. I only thought you might want to back the play. It's splendid." She looked at me steadily over the rim of her goblet. "It's the best new script I've seen in years. It's subtle, complex, moving—much better even than his last two. It's going to replace Shaw's play as the best we have about Joan. And on the subject of victimization by a world the main character doesn't understand, it's better than *Streetcar* or *Joy Ride*. A hundred years from now this play will still be performed regularly, and well."

"It's not like you to be so extravagant with your praise."

"No, it's not."

"And you want me to finance the play for the reflected glory?"

"For the satisfaction. And," she added quietly, but firmly, "because I've accepted a bit part in it."

I stared at her. Last week a major columnist had headlined: FALLEN STAR LANDS ON HER PRIDE.

"It's a very small role. Yolande of Aragon, the Dauphin's mother-in-law. She intrigued on the Dauphin's behalf when he was struggling to be crowned. I have only one scene, but it has possibilities."

"For you? What does it have possibilities of—being smirked at by that little schemer in *your* role? Did you read how much her agent is holding Whitten up for? No wonder he could use more backers."

"You would get it back. But that's not the question, Austin, is it? Why do you object to my taking this part? It's not like you to object to my choice of roles."

"I'm upset because I don't want you to be hurt, and I think you are. I think you'll be hurt even more if you play this Yolande with Miss Ann Friedland as Joan, and I don't want to see it, because I love you."

"I know you do, Austin." She smiled warmly and touched my cheek. It was a perfect Barbara Bishop gesture: sincere, graceful, and complete in itself—so complete that it promised nothing more than what it was, led on to nothing else. It cut off communication as effectively as a blow—or, rather, more effectively, since a blow can be answered in kind. I slammed my glass on the table and stood up. Once up, however, I had nothing to say and so stood there feeling ridiculous. What *did* I want to say? What did I want from her that I did not already have?

"I wish," I said slowly, "that you were not always acting."

She looked at me steadily. I knew the look. She was waiting: for retraction or amendment or amplification. And of course she was right to expect any, or all, of those things. What I had said was inaccurate. She was not acting. What she did was something subtly different. She behaved with the gestures and attitudes and behaviors of the world as she believed it ought to be, a place of generous and rational individuals with enough sheer style to create events in their own image. That people's behavior was in fact often uncivilized, cowardly, and petty she of course knew; she was not stupid. Hers was a deliberate, controlled choice: to ignore the pettiness and to grant to all of us—actors, audience, press, Whitten, Ann Friedland, me, herself—the illusion of having the most admirable motives conceivable.

It seemed to me that this was praiseworthy, even "civilized," in the best sense of that much-abused word.

Why, then, did it make me feel so lonely?

Barbara was still waiting. "Forgive me; I misspoke. I don't mean that you are always acting. I mean—I mean that I'm concerned for you. Standing for a curtain call at the back of the stage while that girl, that chance reincarnation . . . " Suddenly a new idea occurred to me. "Or do you think that she won't be able to do the part and you will be asked to take over for her?"

"No!"

"But if Ann Friedland can't—"

"No! I will never play Joan in A Maid of Domrémy!"

"Why not?"

She finished her wine. Under the expensive gown her breasts heaved. "I had no business even taking the part in Shaw's Joan. I am forty-five years old, and Joan is seventeen. But at least there—at least Shaw's Joan was not really a victim. I will not play her as a pitiful victim."

"Come on, Barbara. You've played Blanche DuBois, and Ophelia, and Jessie Kane. They're all victims."

"I won't play Joan in A Maid of Domrémy!"

I saw that she meant it, that even while she admired the play, she was repelled by it in some fundamental way I did not understand. I sat down again on the sofa and put my arms around her. Instantly she was Barbara Bishop again, smiling with rueful mockery at both her own violence and my melodrama, drawing us together in a covenant too generous for quarreling.

"Look at us, Austin—actually discussing that tired old cliché, the understudy who goes on for the fading star. But I'm not her understudy, and she can hardly fade before she's even bloomed! Really, we're too ridiculous. I'm sorry, love, I didn't mean to snap at you like that. Shall we have dinner now?"

I stood up and pulled her next to me. She came gracefully, still smiling, the light sliding over her dark hair, and followed me to her bedroom. The sex was very good, as it always was. But afterward, lying with her head warm on my shoulder, I was still baffled by something in her I could not understand. Was it because of ESIR? I had thought that before. What was it like to have knowledge of those hundreds of other lives you had once lived? I would never know. Were the exotic types I met in the theater so different, so less easily understood, because they had "creative temperament" (whatever that was) or because of ESIR? I would probably never know that, either, nor how much of Barbara was what she was here, now, and how much was subtle reaction to all the other things she knew she had been. I wasn't sure I wanted to know.

Long after Barbara fell asleep, I lay awake in the soft darkness, listening to the night sounds of New York beyond the window and to something else beyond those, some large silence where my own ESIR memories might have been.

Whitten banned everyone but actors and tech crew from rehearsals of *A Maid of Domrémy*: press, relatives, backers, irate friends. Only because the play had seized the imagination of the public—or at least that small portion of the public that goes to the theater—could his move succeed. The financial angels went along cheerfully with their own banning, secure in the presale ticket figures that the play would make money even without their personal supervision.

Another director, casting for a production of *Hamlet*, suddenly claimed to have discovered the reincarnation of Shakespeare. For a week Broadway was a laser of rumors and speculations. Then the credentials of the two historians verifying the ESIR were discovered by a gleeful press to have been faked. The director, producer, historians, and ersatz Shakespeare were instantly unavailable for comment.

The central computer of the AMA was tapped into. For two days executives with private face-lifts and politicians with private accident records and teachers with private drug-abuse histories held their collective breaths, cursing softly under them. The AMA issued a statement that only ESIR records had been pirated, and the scandal was generally forgotten in the central part of the country and generally intensified on both coasts. Wild reports were issued, contradicted, confirmed, and disproved, all in a few hours. An actor who remembered being King Arthur had been discovered and was going to star in the true story of the Round Table. Euripides was living in Boston and would appear there in his own play *Medea*. The computer verified that ESIR actually *had* uncovered Helen of Troy, and the press stampeded out to Bowling Green, Ohio, where it was discovered that the person who remembered being Helen of Troy was a male, bald, sixty-eight-year-old professor emeritus in the history department. He was writing a massive scholarly study of the Trojan War, and he bitterly resented the "cheap publicity of the popular press."

"The whole thing is becoming a circus," Barbara grumbled. Her shirt was loose at the breasts, and her pants gaped at the waist. She had lost weight and color.

"And this, too, shall pass," I told her. "Think of when ESIR was first introduced. A few years of wild quakes all over society, and then everyone adjusted. This is just the aftershock on the theater."

"I don't especially like standing directly on the fault line."

"How are rehearsals going?"

"About the same," she said, her eyes hooded. Since she never spoke of the play at all, I didn't know what "about the same" would be the same *as*.

"Barbara, what are you waiting for?"

"Waiting for?"

"Constantly now you have that look of waiting, frowning to yourself, looking as if you're scrutinizing something. Something only you can see."

"Austin, how ridiculous! What I'm looking at is all *too* public: opening night for the play."

"And what do you see?"

She was silent for a long time. "I don't know." She laughed, an abrupt, opaque sound like the sudden drawing of a curtain. "It's silly, isn't it? Not knowing what I don't know. A tautology, almost."

"Barbara, marry me. We'll go away for a weekend and get married, like two children. This weekend."

"I thought you had to fly back to Bogotá this weekend."

"I do. But you could come with me. There *is* a world outside New York, you know. It isn't simply all one vast out-of-town tryout."

"I do thank you, Austin, you know that. But I can't leave right now; I do have to work on my part. There are still things I don't trust."

"Such as what?"

"Me," she said lightly, and would say no more.

Meanwhile the hoopla went on. A professor of history at Berkeley who had just finished a—now probably erroneous—dissertation on Joan of Arc tried various legal ploys to sue Ann Friedland on the grounds that she "undercut his means of livelihood." A group called the Catholic Coalition to Clear the Inquisition published in four major newspapers an appeal to Ann Friedland to come forward and declare the fairness of the church at Joan of Arc's heresy trial. Each of the ads cost a fantastic sum. But Ann did not reply; she was preserving to the press a silence as complete as Barbara's to me. I think this is why I didn't press Barbara more closely about her rehearsals. I wanted to appear as different from the rest of the world as possible—an analogy probably no one made except me. Men in love are ludicrous.

Interest in Ann Friedland was not dispelled by her silence. People merely claiming to be a notable figure from the past was growing stale.

For years people had been claiming to be Jesus Christ or Muhammad or Judas; all had been disproved, and the glamour evaporated. But now a famous name had not only been verified, it was going to be showcased in an enterprise that carried the risk of losing huge sums of money, several professional reputations, and months of secret work. The public was delighted. Ann Friedland quickly became a household name.

She was going to marry the widowed King Charles of England. She was going to lead a revival of Catholicism and was being considered for the position of first female pope. She was a drug addict, a Mormon, pregnant, mad, in love, clairvoyant, ten years old, extraterrestrial. She was refusing to go on opening night. Gregory Whitten was going to let her improvise the part opening night. Rehearsals were a disaster, and Barbara Bishop would play the part opening night.

Not even to this last did Barbara offer a comment. Also silent were the reputable papers, the serious theater critics, the men and women who control the money that controls Broadway. They, too, were waiting.

We all waited.

The week that A *Maid of Domrémy* was to open in New York I was still in Bogotá. I had come down with a low-grade fever, which in the press of work I chose to ignore. By Saturday I had a temperature of 104 degrees and a headache no medication could touch. I saw everything through slow, pastel-colored swirls. My arms and legs felt lit with a dry, papery fire that danced up and down from shoulder to wrist, ankle to hip, up and down, wrist to shoulder. I knew I should go to a hospital, but I did not. The opening was that night.

On the plane to New York I slept, dreaming of Barbara in the middle of a vast solar battery. I circled the outside, calling to her desperately. Unaware, she sat reading a script amid the circuits and storage cells, until the fires of the sun burst out all around her and people she had known from other lives danced maniacally in the flames.

At my apartment I took more pills and a cold shower, then tried to phone Barbara. She had already left for makeup call. I dressed and caught a copter to the theater, sleeping fitfully on the short trip, and then I was in the theater, surrounded by first-nighters who did not know I was breathing contagion on all of them, and who floated around me like pale cutouts in diamonds, furs, and nauseating perfume. I could not remember walking from the copter, producing my ticket, or being escorted to my seat. The curtain swirled sickeningly, and I closed my eyes until I realized that it was not my fever that caused the swirls: The curtain was rising. Had the house lights dimmed? I couldn't remember anything. Dry fire danced over me, shoulder to wrist, ankle to hip.

Barbara, cloaked, entered stage left. I had not realized that her scene opened the play. She carried a massive candle across the stage, bent over a wooden table, and lit two more candles from the large one, all with the taut, economical movements of great anger held fiercely in check. Before the audience heard her speak, before they clearly saw her face, they had been told that Yolande was furious, not used to being so, and fully capable of controlling her own anger.

"Mary! Where are you sulking now, Mary?" Barbara said. She straightened and drew back her hood. Her voice was low, yet every woman named Mary in the audience started guiltily. Onstage Mary of Anjou, consort of the uncrowned Dauphin of France, crept sullenly from behind a tapestry, facing her mother like a whipped dog.

"Here I am, for all the good it will do you, or anyone," she whined, looking at her own feet. Barbara's motionless silence was eloquent with contempt; Mary burst out with her first impassioned monologue against the Dauphin and Joan; the play was launched. It was a strong, smooth beginning, fueled by the conviction of Barbara's portrait of the terrifying Yolande. As the scene unfolded, the portrait became even stronger, so that I forgot both my feverish limbs and my concern for Barbara. There were no limbs, no Barbara, no theater. There was only a room in fifteenth-century France, sticky with blood shed for what to us were illusions: absolute good and absolute evil. Cosgriff was exploring the capacities in such illusions for heroism, for degradation, for nobility beyond what the audience's beliefs, saner and more temperate, could allow. Yolande and Mary and the Dauphin loved and hated and gambled and killed with every fiber of their elemental beings, and not a sound rose from the audience until Barbara delivered her final speech and exited stage right. For a moment the audience sat still, bewildered—not by what had happened onstage, but by the unwelcome remembrance that they were not a part of it, but instead were sitting on narrow hard seats in a wooden box in New York, a foreign country because it was not medieval France. Then the applause started.

The Dauphin and his consort, still onstage, did not break character. He waited until the long applause was over, then continued bullying his wife. Shortly afterward two guards entered, dragging between them the confused, weeping Joan. The audience leaned forward eagerly. They were primed by the wonderful first scene and eager for more miracles.

"Is *this* the slut?" the Dauphin asked, and Mary, seeing a woman even more abused and wretched than herself, smiled with secret, sticky joy. The guards let Joan go, and she stumbled forward, caught herself, and staggered upward, raising her eyes to the Dauphin's.

"In the name of Saint Catherine—" She choked and started to weep. It was stormy weeping, vigorous, but without the chilling pain of true hysteria. The audience shuffled a little.

"I will do whatever you want, I swear it in the name of God, if you will only tell me what it is!" On the last word her voice rose; she might have been demanding that a fractious child cease lying to her.

I leaned my head sideways against one shoulder. Waves of fever and nausea beat through me, and for the first time since I had become ill I was aware of labored breathing. My heart beat, skipped, beat twice, skipped. Each breath sounded swampy and rasping. People in the row ahead began to turn and glare. Wadding my handkerchief into a ball, I held it in front of my mouth and tried to watch the play.

Lines slipped in and out of my hearing; actors swirled in fiery paper-dry pastels. Once Joan seemed to turn into Barbara, and I gasped and half-rose in my seat, but then the figure onstage was Ann Friedland, and I sat down again to glares from those around me. It *was* Ann Friedland; I had been a fool to doubt it. It was not Joan of Arc. The girl onstage hesitated, changed tone too often, looked nervously across the footlights, moved a second too late. Once she even stammered.

Around me the audience began to murmur discreetly. Just before the first-act curtain, in a moment of clarity, Joan finally sees how she is being used and makes an inept, wrenchingly pathetic attempt to manipulate the users by manufacturing instructions she says come from her voices. It is a crucial point in the play, throwing into dramatic focus the victim who agrees to her own corruption by a misplaced attempt at control. Ann played it nervously, with an exaggerated grab at pathos that was actually embarrassing. Nothing of that brief glimpse of personal power she had shown at her audition, so many weeks ago, was present now. Between waves of fever, I tried to picture the fit Whitten must be having backstage.

"Christ," said a man in the row ahead of me, "can you believe that?"

"What an absolute travesty," said the woman next to him. Her voice hummed with satisfaction. "Poor Lawrence."

"He was ripe for it. Smug."

"Oh, yes. Still."

"Smug," the man said.

"It doesn't matter to me what you do with her," said Mary of Anjou, onstage. "Why should it? Only for a moment she seemed . . . different. Did you remark it?" Ann Friedland, who had not seemed different, grimaced weakly, and the first-act curtain fell. People were getting to their feet, excited by the magnitude of the disaster. The house lights went up. Just as I stood, the curtains onstage parted and there was some commotion, but the theater leaped in a single nauseous lurch, blinding and hot, and then nothing.

"Austin," a voice said softly. "Austin."

My head throbbed, but from a distance, as if it were not my head at all.

"Austin," the voice said far above me. "Are you there?"

I opened my eyes. Yolande of Aragon, her face framed in a wool hood, gazed down at me and turned into Barbara. She was still in costume and makeup, the heavy, high color garish under too-bright lights. I groaned and closed my eyes.

"Austin. Are you there? Do you know me?"

"Barbara?"

"You are there! Oh, that's splendid. How do you feel? No, don't talk. You've been delirious, love, you had such a fever . . . this is the hospital. Larrimer. They've given you medication; you're going to be fine."

"Barbara."

"I'm here, Austin, I'm right here."

I opened my eyes slowly, accustoming them to the light. I lay in a small private room; beyond the window the sky was dark. I was aware that my body hurt, but aware in the detached, abstract way characteristic of EL painkillers, that miracle of modern science. The dose must have been massive. My body felt as if it belonged to someone else, a friend for whom I felt comradely simulations of pain, but not the real thing.

"What do I have?"

"Some tropical bug. What did you drink in Bogotá? The doctor says it could have been dangerous, but they flushed out your whole system and pumped you full of antibiotics, and you'll be fine. Your fever's down almost to normal. But you must rest."

"I don't want to rest."

"You don't have any choice." She took my hand. The touch felt distant, as if the hand were wrapped in layers of padding.

"What time is it?"

"Five A.M."

"The play—"

"Is long since over."

"What happened?"

She bit her lip. "A lot happened. When precisely do you mean? I wasn't there for the second act, you know. When the ambulance came for you, one of the ushers recognized you and came backstage to tell me. I rode here in the ambulance with you. I didn't have another scene anyway."

I was confused. If Barbara had missed the entire last act, how could "a lot have happened"? I looked at her closely, and this time I saw what only the ELs could have made me miss before: the signs of great, repressed strain. Tendons stood out in Barbara's neck; under the cracked and sagging makeup her eyes darted around the room. I felt myself suddenly alert, and a fragment of memory poked at me, a fragment half-glimpsed in the hot swirl of the theater just before I blacked out.

"She ran out on the stage," I said slowly. "Ann Friedland. In front of the curtain. She ran out and yelled something. . . . " It was gone. I shook my head. "On the *stage*."

"Yes." Barbara let go of my hand and began to pace. Her long train dragged behind her; when she turned, it tangled around her legs and she stumbled. The action was so uncharacteristic, it was shocking.

"You saw what the first act was. A catastrophe. She was trying—"

"The whole first act wasn't bad, love. Your scene was wonderful. Wait—the reviews on your role will be very good."

"Yes," she said distractedly. I saw that she had hardly heard me. There was something she had to do, had to say. The best way to help was to let her do it. Words tore from her like a gale.

"She tried to do the whole play reaching back into her ESIR Joan. She tried to just feel it, and let Lawrence's words—her words—be animated by the remembered feeling. But without the conscious balancing . . . no, it isn't even balancing. It's more like imagining what you already know, and to do that, you have to *forget* what you know and at the same time remember every tiny nuance. . . . I can't explain it. Nobody ever really *was* a major historical figure before, in a play composed of his own words. Gregory was so excited over the concept, and then when rehearsals began . . . but by that time he was committed, and the terrible hype just bound him further. When Ann ruined the first act like that, he was just beside himself. I've never seen him like that. I've never seen anybody like that. He was raging, just completely out of control. And onstage

Ann was coming apart, and I could see that he was going to completely destroy her, and we had a whole act to *go*, damn it! A whole fucking act!"

I stared at her. She didn't notice. She lighted a cigarette; it went out; she flung the match and cigarette on the floor. I could see her hand trembling.

"I knew that if Gregory got at her, she was done. She wouldn't even go back out after intermission. Of course the play was a flop already, but not to even *finish* the damn thing . . . I wasn't thinking straight. All I could see was that he would destroy her, all of us. So I hit him."

"You what?"

"I hit him. With Yolande's candlestick. I took him behind a flat to try to calm him down, and instead I hit him. *Without knowing I was going to.* Something strange went through me, and I picked up my arm and hit him. Without knowing I was going to!"

She wrapped her arms around herself and shuddered. I saw what had driven her to this unbearable strain. *Without knowing I was going to.*

"His face became very surprised, and he fell forward. No one saw me. Gregory lay there, breathing as if he were just asleep, and I found a phone and called an ambulance. Then I told the stage manager that Mr. Whitten had had a bad fall and hit his head and was unconscious. I went around to the wings and waited for Ann. When the curtain came down and she saw me waiting for her, she turned white, and then red, and started shouting at me that she was Joan of Arc and I was an aging bitch who wanted to steal her role."

I tried to picture it—the abusive girl, the appalled, demoralized cast, the director lying hidden, bashed with a candlestick—*without knowing I was going to!*—and, out front, the polite chatter, the great gray critics from the *Times* and the *New Yorker*, the dressed-up suburbanites from Scarsdale squeezing genially down the aisles for an entr'acte drink and a smoke.

"She went on and on," Barbara said. "She told me *I* was the reason she couldn't play the role, that I deliberately undermined her by standing around like I knew everything, and she knew everybody was expecting me to go on as Joan after she failed. Then suddenly she darted away from me and went through the curtains onto the stage. The house lights were up; half the audience had left. She spread out her arms and *yelled* at them."

Barbara stopped and put her hands over her face. I reached up and pulled them away. She looked calmer now, although there was still an underlying tautness in her voice. "Oh, it's just too ridiculous, Austin. She made an absolute fool of herself, of Lawrence, of all of us, but it wasn't her fault. She's an inexperienced child without talent. Gregory should have known better, but his egomania got all tangled up in his ridiculous illusion that he was going to revitalize the theater, take the next historical step for American drama. God, what the papers will say. . . . " She laughed weakly, with pain. "And I was no better, hitting poor Gregory."

"Barbara . . . "

"Do you know what Ann yelled at them, at the audience? She stood on that stage, flung her arms wide like some martyr . . . "

"What did she say? What, love?"

"She said, 'But I'm the *real thing*!' "

We were quiet for a moment. From outside the window rose blurred traffic noises: therealthingtherealthingtherealthing.

"You're right," I said. "The whole thing was an egomaniacal ride for Whitten, and the press turned it into a carnival. Cosgriff should have known better. The real thing—that's not what you want in the theater. Illusion, magic, imagination. What should have happened, not what did. Reality doesn't make good theater."

"No, you still don't understand!" Barbara cried. "You've missed it all! How can you think that it's that easy, that Gregory's mistake was to use Ann's reality instead of Shaw's illusion!"

"I don't understand what you—"

"It's not that clear!" she cried. "Don't you think I wish it were? My God!"

I didn't know what she meant, or why under the cracked makeup her eyes glittered with feverish, exhausted panic. Even as I reached out my arm, completely confused, she was backing away from me.

"Illusion and reality," she said. "My God. Watch."

She crossed the room to the door, closed it, and pressed the dimmer on the lights. The room faded to a cool gloom. She stood with her back to me, her head bowed. Then she turned slowly and raised her eyes to a point in the air a head above her.

"In the name of Saint Catherine—" she began, choked, and started to weep. The weeping was terrifying, shot through with that threat of open hysteria that keeps a listener on the edge of panic in case the weeper should lose control entirely, and also keeps him fascinated for the same reason. "I will do whatever you want, I swear it in the name of God, if you will only tell me what it is." On the last word her voice fell, making the plea into a prayer to her captors, and so the first blasphemy. I caught my breath. Barbara looked young, terrified, pale. How could she look pale when a second ago I had been so conscious of all that garish makeup? There was no chance to wonder. She plunged on, through that scene and the next and all of Joan's scenes. She went from hysterical fear to inept manipulation to the bruised, stupid hatred of a victim to, finally, a kind of negative dignity that comes not from accomplishment but from the clear-eyed vision of the lack of it, and so she died, Cosgriff's vision of the best that institutionalized man could hope for. But she was not Cosgriff's vision; she was a seventeen-year-old girl. Her figure was slight to the point of emaciation. Her face was young—I *saw* its youth, felt its fragile boniness in the marrow of my own bones. She moved with the gaudy, unpredictable quickness of the mad, now here, now darting a room's length away, now still with a terrible catatonic stillness that excluded her trapped eyes. Her desperation made me catch my breath, try to look away and fail, feeling that cold grab at my innards: It happened. And it could happen again. It could happen to me.

Her terror gave off a smell, sickly and sour. I wanted to escape the room before that smell could spread to me. I was helpless. Neither she nor I could escape. I did not want to help her, this mad skinny victim. I wanted to destroy her so that what was being done to her would not exist any longer in the world and I would be safe from it. But I could not destroy her. I could only watch, loathing Joan for forcing me to know, until she rose to her brief, sane dignity. In the sight of that dignity, shame that I had ever wanted to smash her washed over me. I was guilty, as guilty as all those others who had wanted to smash her. Her sanity bound me with them, as earlier her terror had unwillingly drawn me to her. I was victim and victimizer, and when Joan stood at the stake and condemned me in a grotesque parody of Christ's forgiving on the cross, I wanted only for her to burn and so be quiet, so release me. I would have lighted the fire. I would have shouted with the crowd, "Burn! Burn!" already despairing that no fire could sear away what she, I, all of us had done. From the flames, Joan looked at me, stretched out her hand, came toward me. I thrust out my arm to ward her off. Almost I cried out. My heart pounded in my chest.

"Austin," she said.

In an instant Joan was gone.

Barbara came toward me. It was Barbara. She had grown three inches, put on twenty pounds and thirty years. Her face was tired and lined under gaudy, peeling makeup. Confusedly I blinked at her. I don't think she even saw the confusion; her eyes had lost their strained panic, and she was smiling, a smile that was a peaceful answer to some question of her own.

"That was the reality," she said, and stooped to lay her head on my chest. Through the fall of her hair I barely heard her when she said that she would marry me whenever I wanted.

Barbara and I have been married for nearly a year. I still don't know precisely why she decided to marry me, and she can't tell me; she doesn't know herself. But I speculate that the night A *Maid of Domrémy* failed, something broke in her, some illusion that she could control, if not the world, then at least herself. When she struck Whitten with the candlestick, she turned herself into both victim and victimizer as easily as Lawrence Cosgriff had rewritten Shaw's *Joan*. Barbara has never played the part again. (Gregory Whitten, no less flamboyantly insensitive for his bashing with a candlestick, actually asked her.) She has adamantly refused both Joans, Shaw's heroine and Cosgriff's victim. I was the last person to witness her performance.

Was her performance that night in my hospital room really as good as I remember? I was drugged; emotion had been running high; I loved her. Any or all of that could have colored my reactions. But I don't think so. I think that night Barbara Bishop *was* Joan, in some effort of will and need that went beyond both the illusions of a good actress and the reality of what ESIR could give to her, or to Ann Friedland, or to anyone. ESIR only unlocks the individual genetic memories in the brain's R-Complex. But what other identities, shared across time and space, might still be closed in there beyond our present reach?

All of this is speculation.

Next week I will be hospitalized for my own ESIR. Knowing what I have been before may yield only more speculation, more illusions, more multiple realities. It may yield nothing. But I want to know, on the chance that the yield will be understandable, will be valuable in untangling the endless skein of waking visions.

Even if the chance is one in a million.

IN THE PENAL
COLONY

I t's a remarkable piece of apparatus," said the officer to the explorer and surveyed with a certain air of admiration the apparatus which was after all quite familiar to him. The explorer seemed to have accepted merely out of politeness the Commandant's invitation to witness the execution of a soldier condemned to death for disobedience and insulting behavior to a superior. Nor did the colony itself betray much interest in this execution. At least, in the small sandy valley, a deep hollow surrounded on all sides by naked crags, there was no one present save the officer, the explorer, the condemned man, who was a stupid-looking wide-mouthed creature with bewildered hair and face, and the soldier who held the heavy chain controlling the small chains locked on the prisoner's ankles, wrists and neck, chains which were themselves attached to each other by communicating links. In any case, the condemned man looked so like a submissive dog that one might have thought he could be left to run free on the surrounding hills and would only need to be whistled for when the execution was due to begin.

The explorer did not much care about the apparatus and walked up and down behind the prisoner with almost visible indifference while the officer made the last adjustments, now creeping beneath the structure, which was bedded deep in the earth, now climbing a ladder to inspect its upper parts. These were tasks that might well have been left to a mechanic, but the officer performed them with great zeal, whether because he was a devoted admirer of the apparatus or because of other reasons the work could be entrusted to no one else. "Ready now!" he called at last and climbed down from the ladder. He looked uncommonly limp, breathed with his mouth wide open and had tucked two fine ladies' handkerchiefs under the collar of his uniform. "These uniforms are too heavy for the tropics, surely," said the explorer, instead of making some inquiry about the apparatus, as the officer had expected. "Of course," said the officer, washing his oily and greasy hands in a bucket of water that stood ready, "but they mean home to us; we don't want to forget about home. Now just have a look at this machine," he added at once, simultaneously drying his hands on a towel and indicating the apparatus. "Up till now a few things still had to be set by hand, but from this moment it works all by itself." The explorer nodded and followed him. The officer, anxious to secure himself against all contingencies, said: "Things sometimes go wrong, of course; I hope that nothing goes wrong today, but we have to allow for the possibility. The machinery should go on working continuously for twelve hours. But if anything does go wrong it will only be some small matter that can be set right at once.

"Won't you take a seat?" he asked finally, drawing a cane chair out from among a heap of them and offering it to the explorer, who could not refuse it. He was now sitting at the edge of a pit, into which he glanced for a fleeting moment. It was not very deep. On one side of the pit the excavated soil had been piled up in a rampart, on the other side of it stood the apparatus. "I don't know," said the officer, "if the Commandant has already explained this apparatus to you." The explorer waved one hand vaguely; the officer asked for nothing better, since now he could explain the apparatus himself. "This apparatus," he said, taking hold of a crank handle and leaning against it, "was invented by our former Commandant. I assisted at the very earliest experiments and had a share in all the work until its completion. But the credit of inventing it belongs to him alone. Have you ever heard of our former Commandant? No? Well, it isn't saying too much if I tell you that the organization of the whole penal colony is his work. We who were his friends knew even before he died that the organization of the colony was so perfect that his successor, even with a thousand new schemes in his head, would find it impossible to alter anything, at least for many years to come. And our prophecy has come true; the new Commandant has had to acknowledge its truth. A pity you never met the old Commandant!—But," the officer interrupted himself, "I am rambling on, and here stands his apparatus before us. It consists, as you see, of three parts. In the course of time each of these parts has acquired a kind of popular nickname. The lower one is called the 'Bed,' the upper one the 'Designer,' and this one here in the middle that moves up and down is called the 'Harrow.' " "The Harrow?" asked the explorer. He had not been listening very attentively, the glare of the sun in the shadeless valley was altogether too strong, it was difficult to collect one's thoughts. All the more did he admire the officer, who in spite of his tight-fitting full-dress uniform coat, amply befrogged and weighed down by epaulettes, was pursuing his subject with such enthusiasm and, besides talking, was still tightening a screw here and there with a spanner. As for the soldier, he seemed to be in much the same condition as the explorer. He had wound the prisoner's chain round both his wrists, propped himself on his rifle, let his head hang and was paying no attention to anything. That did not surprise the explorer, for the officer was speaking French, and certainly neither the soldier nor the prisoner understood a word of French. It was all the more remarkable, therefore, that the prisoner was none the less making an effort to follow the officer's explanations. With a kind of drowsy persistence he directed his gaze wherever the officer pointed a finger, and at the interruption of the explorer's question he, too, as well as the officer, looked round.

"Yes, the Harrow," said the officer, "a good name for it. The needles are set in like the teeth of a harrow and the whole thing works something like a harrow, although its action is limited to one place and contrived with much more artistic skill. Anyhow, you'll soon understand it. On the Bed here the condemned man is laid—I'm going to describe the apparatus first before I set it in motion. Then you'll be able to follow the proceedings better. Besides, one of the cog wheels in the Designer is badly worn; it creaks a lot when it's working; you can hardly hear yourself speak; spare parts, unfortunately, are difficult to get here.—Well, here is the Bed, as I told you. It is completely covered with a layer of cotton wool; you'll find out why later. On this cotton wool the condemned man is laid, face down, quite naked, of course; here are straps for the hands, here for the feet, and here for the neck, to bind him fast. Here at the head of the bed, where the man, as I said, first lays down his face, is this little gag of felt, which can be easily regulated to go straight into his mouth. It is meant to keep him from screaming and biting his tongue. Of course the man is forced to take the felt into his mouth, for otherwise his neck would be broken by the strap." "Is that cotton wool?" asked the explorer, bending forward. "Yes, certainly," said the officer, with a smile, "feel it for yourself." He took the explorer's hand and guided it over the bed. "It's specially prepared cotton wool, that's why it looks so different; I'll tell you presently what it's for." The explorer already felt a dawning interest in the apparatus; he sheltered his eyes from the sun with one hand and gazed up at the structure. It was a huge affair. The Bed and the Designer were of the same size and looked like two dark wooden chests. The Designer hung about two meters above the Bed; each of them was bound at the corners with four rods of brass that almost flashed out rays in the sunlight. Between the chests shuttled the Harrow on a ribbon of steel.

The officer had scarcely noticed the explorer's previous indifference, but he was now well aware of his dawning interest; so he stopped explaining in order to leave a space of time for quiet observation. The condemned man imitated the explorer; since he could not use a hand to shelter his eyes he gazed upwards without shade.

"Well, the man lies down," said the explorer, leaning back in his chair and crossing his legs.

"Yes," said the officer, pushing his cap back a little and passing one hand over his heated face, "now listen! Both the Bed and the Designer have an electric battery each; the Bed needs one for itself, the Designer for the Harrow. As soon as the man is strapped down, the Bed is set in motion. It quivers in minute, very rapid vibrations, both from side to side and up and down. You will have seen similar apparatus in hospitals; but in our Bed the movements are all precisely calculated; you see, they have to correspond very exactly to the movements of the Harrow. And the Harrow is the instrument for the actual execution of the sentence."

"And how does the sentence run?" asked the explorer.

"You don't know that either?" said the officer in amazement, and bit his lips. "Forgive me if my explanations seem rather incoherent. I do beg your pardon. You see, the Commandant always used to do the explaining; but the new Commandant shirks this duty; yet that such an important visitor"—the explorer tried to deprecate the honor with both hands, the officer, however, insisted—"that such an important visitor should not even be told about the kind of sentence we pass is a new development, which—" He was just on the point of using strong language but checked himself and said only: "I was not informed, it is not my fault. In any case, I am certainly the best person to explain our procedure, since I have here"—he patted his breast pocket—"the relevant drawings made by our former Commandant."

"The Commandant's own drawings?" asked the explorer. "Did he combine everything in himself, then? Was he soldier, judge, mechanic, chemist and draughtsman?"

"Indeed he was," said the officer, nodding assent, with a remote, glassy look. Then he inspected his hands critically; they did not seem clean enough to him for touching the drawings; so he went over to the bucket and washed them again. Then he drew out a small leather wallet and said: "Our sentence does not sound severe. Whatever commandment the prisoner has disobeyed is written upon his body by the Harrow. This prisoner, for instance"—the officer indicated the man—"will have written on his body: HONOR THY SUPERIORS!"

The explorer glanced at the man; he stood, as the officer pointed him out, with bent head, apparently listening with all his ears in an effort to catch what was being said. Yet the movement of his blubber lips, closely pressed together, showed clearly that he could not understand a word. Many questions were troubling the explorer, but at the sight of the prisoner he asked only: "Does he know his sentence?" "No," said the officer, eager to go on with his exposition, but the explorer interrupted him: "He doesn't know the sentence that has been passed on him?" "No," said the officer again, pausing a moment as if to let the explorer elaborate his question, and then said: "There would be no point in telling him. He'll learn it on his body." The explorer intended to make no answer, but he felt the prisoner's gaze turned on him; it seemed to ask if he approved such ongoings. So he bent forward again, having already leaned back in his chair, and put another question: "But surely he knows that he has been sentenced?" "Nor that either," said the officer, smiling at the explorer as if expecting him to make further surprising remarks. "No," said the explorer, wiping his forehead, "then he can't know either whether his defense was effective?" "He has had no chance of putting up a defense," said the officer, turning his eyes away as if speaking to himself and so sparing the explorer the shame of hearing self-evident matters explained. "But he must have had some chance of defending himself," said the explorer, and rose from his seat.

The officer realized that he was in danger of having his exposition of the apparatus held up for a long time; so he went up to the explorer, took him by the arm, waved a hand towards the condemned man, who was standing very straight now that he had so obviously become the center of attention—the soldier had also given the chain a jerk—and said: "This is how the matter stands. I have been appointed judge in this penal colony. Despite my youth. For I was the former Commandant's assistant in all penal matters and know more about the apparatus than anyone.

My guiding principle is this: Guilt is never to be doubted. Other courts cannot follow that principle, for they consist of several opinions and have higher courts to scrutinize them. That is not the case here, or at least, it was not the case in the former Commandant's time. The new man has certainly shown some inclination to interfere with my judgments, but so far I have succeeded in fending him off and will go on succeeding. You wanted to have the case explained; it is quite simple, like all of them. A captain reported to me this morning that this man, who had been assigned to him as a servant and sleeps before his door, had been asleep on duty. It is his duty, you see, to get up every time the hour strikes and salute the captain's door. Not an exacting duty, and very necessary, since he has to be a sentry as well as a servant, and must be alert in both functions. Last night the captain wanted to see if the man was doing his duty. He opened the door as the clock struck two and there was his man curled up asleep. He took his riding whip and lashed him across the face. Instead of getting up and begging pardon, the man caught hold of his master's legs, shook him and cried: 'Throw that whip away or I'll eat you alive.'—That's the evidence. The captain came to me an hour ago, I wrote down his statement and appended the sentence to it. Then I had the man put in chains. That was all quite simple. If I had first called the man before me and interrogated him, things would have got into a confused tangle. He would have told lies, and had I exposed these lies he would have backed them up with more lies, and so on and so forth. As it is, I've got him and I won't let him go.—Is that quite clear now? But we're wasting time, the execution should be beginning and I haven't finished explaining the apparatus yet." He pressed the explorer back into his chair, went up again to the apparatus and began: "As you see, the shape of the Harrow corresponds to the human form; here is the harrow for the torso, here are the harrows for the legs. For the head there is only this one small spike. Is that quite clear?" He bent amiably forward towards the explorer, eager to provide the most comprehensive explanations.

The explorer considered the Harrow with a frown. The explanation of the judicial procedure had not satisfied him. He had to remind himself that this was in any case a penal colony where extraordinary measures were needed and that military discipline must be enforced to the last. He also felt that some hope might be set on the new Commandant, who was apparently of a mind to bring in, although gradually, a new kind of procedure which the officer's narrow mind was incapable of understanding. This train of thought prompted his next question: "Will the Com-

mandant attend the execution?" "It is not certain," said the officer, wincing at the direct question, and his friendly expression darkened. "That
is just why we have to lose no time. Much as I dislike it, I shall have to
cut my explanations short. But of course tomorrow, when the apparatus
has been cleaned—its one drawback is that it gets so messy—I can
recapitulate all the details. For the present, then, only the essentials.—
When the man lies down on the Bed and it begins to vibrate, the Harrow
is lowered onto his body. It regulates itself automatically so that the
needles barely touch his skin; once contact is made the steel ribbon stiffens
immediately into a rigid band. And then the performance begins. An
ignorant onlooker would see no difference between one punishment and
another. The Harrow appears to do its work with uniform regularity. As
it quivers, its points pierce the skin of the body which is itself quivering
from the vibration of the Bed. So that the actual progress of the sentence
can be watched, the Harrow is made of glass. Getting the needles fixed
in the glass was a technical problem, but after many experiments we
overcame the difficulty. No trouble was too great for us to take, you see.
And now anyone can look through the glass and watch the inscription
taking form on the body. Wouldn't you care to come a little nearer and
have a look at the needles?"

The explorer got up slowly, walked across and bent over the Harrow.
"You see," said the officer, "there are two kinds of needles arranged in
multiple patterns. Each long needle has a short one beside it. The long
needle does the writing, and the short needle sprays a jet of water to wash
away the blood and keep the inscription clear. Blood and water together
are then conducted here through small runnels into this main runnel
and down a waste pipe into the pit." With his finger the officer traced
the exact course taken by the blood and water. To make the picture as
vivid as possible he held both hands below the outlet of the waste pipe
as if to catch the outflow, and when he did this the explorer drew back
his head and feeling behind him with one hand sought to return to his
chair. To his horror he found that the condemned man too had obeyed
the officer's invitation to examine the Harrow at close quarters and had
followed him. He had pulled forward the sleepy soldier with the chain
and was bending over the glass. One could see that his uncertain eyes
were trying to perceive what the two gentlemen had been looking at, but
since he had not understood the explanation he could not make head or
tail of it. He was peering this way and that way. He kept running his
eyes along the glass. The explorer wanted to drive him away, since what
he was doing was probably culpable. But the officer firmly restrained the

explorer with one hand and with the other took a clod of earth from the rampart and threw it at the soldier. He opened his eyes with a jerk, saw what the condemned man had dared to do, let his rifle fall, dug his heels into the ground, dragged his prisoner back so that he stumbled and fell immediately, and then stood looking down at him, watching him struggling and rattling in his chains. "Set him on his feet!" yelled the officer, for he noticed that the explorer's attention was being too much distracted by the prisoner. In fact he was even leaning right across the Harrow, without taking any notice of it, intent only on finding out what was happening to the prisoner. "Be careful with him!" cried the officer again. He ran round the apparatus, himself caught the condemned man under the shoulders and with the soldier's help got him up on his feet, which kept slithering from under him.

"Now I know all about it," said the explorer as the officer came back to him. "All except the most important thing," he answered, seizing the explorer's arm and pointing upwards: "In the Designer are all the cogwheels that control the movements of the Harrow, and this machinery is regulated according to the inscription demanded by the sentence. I am still using the guiding plans drawn by the former Commandant. Here they are"—he extracted some sheets from the leather wallet—"but I'm sorry I can't let you handle them, they are my most precious possessions. Just take a seat and I'll hold them in front of you like this, then you'll be able to see everything quite well." He spread out the first sheet of paper. The explorer would have liked to say something appreciative, but all he could see was a labyrinth of lines crossing and re-crossing each other, which covered the paper so thickly that it was difficult to discern the blank spaces between them. "Read it," said the officer. "I can't," said the explorer. "Yet it's clear enough," said the officer. "It's very ingenious," said the explorer evasively, "but I can't make it out." "Yes," said the officer with a laugh, putting the paper away again, "it's no calligraphy for school children. It needs to be studied closely. I'm quite sure that in the end you would understand it too. Of course the script can't be a simple one; it's not supposed to kill a man straight off, but only after an interval of, on an average, twelve hours; the turning point is reckoned to come at the sixth hour. So there have to be lots and lots of flourishes around the actual script; the script itself runs round the body only in a narrow girdle; the rest of the body is reserved for the embellishments. Can you appreciate now the work accomplished by the Harrow and the whole apparatus?—Just watch it!" He ran up the ladder, turned a wheel, called down: "Look out, keep to one side!" and everything started working.

If the wheel had not creaked, it would have been marvelous. The officer, as if surprised by the noise of the wheel, shook his fist at it, then spread out his arms in excuse to the explorer and climbed down rapidly to peer at the working of the machine from below. Something perceptible to no one save himself was still not in order; he clambered up again, did something with both hands in the interior of the Designer, then slid down one of the rods, instead of using the ladder, so as to get down quicker, and with the full force of his lungs, to make himself heard at all in the noise, yelled in the explorer's ear: "Can you follow it? The Harrow is beginning to write; when it finishes the first draft of the inscription on the man's back, the layer of cotton wool begins to roll and slowly turns the body over, to give the Harrow fresh space for writing. Meanwhile the raw part that has been written on lies on the cotton wool, which is specially prepared to staunch the bleeding and so makes all ready for a new deepening of the script. Then these teeth at the edge of the Harrow, as the body turns further round, tear the cotton wool away from the wounds, throw it into the pit, and there is more work for the Harrow. So it keeps on writing deeper and deeper for the whole twelve hours. The first six hours the condemned man stays alive almost as before, he suffers only pain. After two hours the felt gag is taken away, for he has no longer strength to scream. Here, into this electrically heated basin at the head of the Bed, some warm rice pap is poured, from which the man, if he feels like it, can take as much as his tongue can lap. Not one of them ever misses the chance. I can remember none, and my experience is extensive. Only about the sixth hour does the man lose all desire to eat. I usually kneel down here at that moment and observe what happens. The man rarely swallows his last mouthful, he only rolls it round his mouth and spits it out into the pit. I have to duck just then or he would spit it in my face. But how quiet he grows at just about the sixth hour! Enlightenment comes to the most dull-witted. It begins around the eyes. From there it radiates. A moment that might tempt one to get under the Harrow oneself. Nothing more happens than that the man begins to understand the inscription, he purses his mouth as if he were listening. You have seen how difficult it is to decipher the script with one's eyes; but our man deciphers it with his wounds. To be sure, that is a hard task; he needs six hours to accomplish it. By that time the Harrow has pierced him quite through and casts him into the pit, where he pitches down upon the blood and water and the cotton wool. Then the judgment has been fulfilled, and we, the soldier and I, bury him."

The explorer had inclined his ear to the officer and with his hands in his jacket pockets watched the machine at work. The condemned man watched it too, but uncomprehendingly. He bent forward a little and was intent on the moving needles when the soldier, at a sign from the officer, slashed through his shirt and trousers from behind with a knife, so that they fell off; he tried to catch at his falling clothes to cover his nakedness, but the soldier lifted him into the air and shook the last remnants from him. The officer stopped the machine, and in the sudden silence the condemned man was laid under the Harrow. The chains were loosened and the straps fastened on instead; in the first moment that seemed almost a relief to the prisoner. And now the Harrow was adjusted a little lower, since he was a thin man. When the needle points touched him a shudder ran over his skin; while the soldier was busy strapping his right hand, he flung out his left hand blindly; but it happened to be in the direction towards where the explorer was standing. The officer kept watching the explorer sideways, as if seeking to read from his face the impression made on him by the execution, which had been at least cursorily explained to him.

The wrist strap broke; probably the soldier had drawn it too tight. The officer had to intervene, the soldier held up the broken piece of strap to show him. So the officer went over to him and said, his face still turned towards the explorer: "This is a very complex machine, it can't be helped that things are breaking or giving way here and there; but one must not thereby allow oneself to be diverted in one's general judgment. In any case, this strap is easily made good; I shall simply use a chain; the delicacy of the vibrations for the right arm will of course be a little impaired." And while he fastened the chains, he added: "The resources for maintaining the machine are now very much reduced. Under the former Commandant I had free access to a sum of money set aside entirely for this purpose. There was a store, too, in which spare parts were kept for repairs of all kinds. I confess I have been almost prodigal with them, I mean in the past, not now as the new Commandant pretends, always looking for an excuse to attack our old way of doing things. Now he has taken charge of the machine money himself, and if I send for a new strap they ask for the broken old strap as evidence, and the new strap takes ten days to appear and then is of shoddy material and not much good. But how I am supposed to work the machine without a strap, that's something nobody bothers about."

The explorer thought to himself: It's always a ticklish matter to intervene decisively in other people's affairs. He was neither a member of the penal colony nor a citizen of the state to which it belonged. Were he to denounce this execution or actually try to stop it, they could say to him: You are a foreigner, mind your own business. He could make no answer to that, unless he were to add that he was amazed at himself in this connection, for he traveled only as an observer, with no intention at all of altering other people's methods of administering justice. Yet here he found himself strongly tempted. The injustice of the procedure and the inhumanity of the execution were undeniable. No one could suppose that he had any selfish interest in the matter, for the condemned man was a complete stranger, not a fellow countryman or even at all sympathetic to him. The explorer himself had recommendations from high quarters, had been received here with great courtesy, and the very fact that he had been invited to attend the execution seemed to suggest that his views would be welcome. And this was all the more likely since the Commandant, as he had heard only too plainly, was no upholder of the procedure and maintained an attitude almost of hostility to the officer.

At that moment the explorer heard the officer cry out in rage. He had just, with considerable difficulty, forced the felt gag into the condemned man's mouth when the man in an irresistible access of nausea shut his eyes and vomited. Hastily the officer snatched him away from the gag and tried to hold his head over the pit; but it was too late, the vomit was running all over the machine. "It's all the fault of that Commandant!" cried the officer, senselessly shaking the brass rods in front, "the machine is befouled like a pigsty." With trembling hands he indicated to the explorer what had happened. "Have I not tried for hours at a time to get the Commandant to understand that the prisoner must fast for a whole day before the execution. But our new, mild doctrine thinks otherwise. The Commandant's ladies stuff the man with sugar candy before he's led off. He has lived on stinking fish his whole life long and now he has to eat sugar candy! But it could still be possible, I should have nothing to say against it, but why won't they get me a new felt gag, which I have been begging for the last three months. How should a man not feel sick when he takes a felt gag into his mouth which more than a hundred men have already slobbered and gnawed in their dying moments?"

The condemned man had laid his head down and looked peaceful, the soldier was busy trying to clean the machine with the prisoner's shirt. The officer advanced towards the explorer, who in some vague presentiment fell back a pace, but the officer seized him by the hand, and drew him to one side. "I should like to exchange a few words with you in confidence," he said, "may I?" "Of course," said the explorer, and listened with downcast eyes.

"This procedure and method of execution, which you are now having the opportunity to admire, has at the moment no longer any open adherents in our colony. I am its sole advocate, and at the same time the sole advocate of the old Commandant's tradition. I can no longer reckon on any further extension of the method, it takes all my energy to maintain it as it is. During the old Commandant's lifetime the colony was full of his adherents; his strength of conviction I still have in some measure, but not an atom of his power; consequently the adherents have skulked out of sight, there are still many of them but none of them will admit it. If you were to go into the teahouse today, on execution day, and listen to what is being said, you would perhaps hear only ambiguous remarks. These would all be made by adherents, but under the present Commandant and his present doctrines they are of no use to me. And now I ask you: because of this Commandant and the women who influence him, is such a piece of work, the work of a lifetime"—he pointed to the machine—"to perish? Ought one to let that happen? Even if one has only come as a stranger to our island for a few days? But there's no time to lose, an attack of some kind is impending on my function as judge; conferences are already being held in the Commandant's office from which I am excluded; even your coming here today seems to me a significant move; they are cowards and use you as a screen, you, a stranger.—How different an execution was in the old days! A whole day before the ceremony the valley was packed with people; they all came only to look on; early in the morning the Commandant appeared with his ladies; fanfares roused the whole camp; I reported that everything was in readiness; the assembled company—no high official dared to absent himself—arranged itself round the machine; this pile of cane chairs is a miserable survival from that epoch. The machine was freshly cleaned and glittering, I got new spare parts for almost every execution. Before hundreds of spectators—all of them standing on tiptoe as far as the heights there—the condemned man was laid under the Harrow by the Commandant himself. What is left today for a common soldier to do was then my task, the task of the presiding judge, and was an honor for me. And then the execution began! No discordant noise spoilt the working of the machine. Many did not care to watch it but lay with closed eyes in the sand; they all knew: Now Justice is being done. In the silence one heard nothing but the condemned man's sighs, half muffled by the felt gag. Nowadays the machine can no longer wring from anyone a sigh louder than the felt gag can stifle; but in those days the writing needles let drop an acid fluid, which we're no longer permitted to use. Well, and then came the sixth hour! It was impossible to grant all the requests to be allowed to watch it from near by. The Commandant in his wisdom ordained that the children should have the preference; I, of course, because of my office had the privilege of always being at hand; often enough I would be squatting there with a small child in either arm. How we all absorbed the look of transfiguration on the face of the sufferer, how we bathed our cheeks in the radiance of that justice, achieved at last and fading so quickly! What times these were, my comrade!" The officer had obviously forgotten whom he was addressing; he had embraced the explorer and laid his head on his shoulder. The explorer was deeply embarrassed, impatiently he stared over the officer's head. The soldier had finished his cleaning job and was now pouring rice pap from a pot into the basin. As soon as the condemned man, who seemed to have recovered entirely, noticed this action he began to reach for the rice with his tongue. The soldier kept pushing him away, since the rice pap was certainly meant for a later hour, yet it was just as unfitting that the soldier himself should thrust his dirty hands into the basin and eat out of it before the other's avid face.

The officer quickly pulled himself together. "I didn't want to upset you," he said, "I know it is impossible to make those days credible now. Anyhow, the machine is still working and it is still effective in itself. It is effective in itself even though it stands alone in this valley. And the corpse still falls at the last into the pit with an incomprehensibly gentle wafting motion, even although there are no hundreds of people swarming round like flies as formerly. In those days we had to put a strong fence round the pit, it has long since been torn down."

The explorer wanted to withdraw his face from the officer and looked round him at random. The officer thought he was surveying the valley's desolation; so he seized him by the hands, turned him round to meet his eyes, and asked: "Do you realize the shame of it?"

But the explorer said nothing. The officer left him alone for a little; with legs apart, hands on hips, he stood very still, gazing at the ground. Then he smiled encouragingly at the explorer and said: "I was quite near you yesterday when the Commandant gave you the invitation. I heard him giving it. I know the Commandant. I divined at once what he was after. Although he is powerful enough to take measures against me, he doesn't dare to do it yet, but he certainly means to use your verdict against me, the verdict of an illustrious foreigner. He has calculated it carefully: this is your second day on the island, you did not know the old Commandant and his ways, you are conditioned by European ways of thought, perhaps you object on principle to capital punishment in general and to such mechanical instruments of death in particular, besides you will see that the execution has no support from the public, a shabby ceremony— carried out with a machine already somewhat old and worn—now, taking all that into consideration, would it not be likely (so thinks the Commandant) that you might disapprove of my methods? And if you disapprove, you wouldn't conceal the fact (I'm still speaking from the Commandant's point of view), for you are a man to feel confidence in your own well-tried conclusions. True, you have seen and learned to appreciate the peculiarities of many peoples, and so you would not be likely to take a strong line against our proceedings, as you might do in your own country. But the Commandant has no need of that. A casual, even an unguarded remark will be enough. It doesn't even need to represent what you really think, so long as it can be used speciously to serve his purpose. He will try to prompt you with sly questions, of that I am certain. And his ladies will sit around you and prick up their ears; you might be saying something like this: 'In our country we have a different criminal procedure,' or 'In our country the prisoner is interrogated before he is sentenced,' or 'We haven't used torture since the Middle Ages.' All these statements are as true as they seem natural to you, harmless remarks that pass no judgment on my methods. But how would the Commandant react to them? I can see him, our good Commandant, pushing his chair away immediately and rushing on to the balcony, I can see his ladies streaming out after him, I can hear his voice—the ladies call it a voice of thunder—well, and this is what he says: 'A famous Western investigator, sent out to study criminal procedure in all the countries of the world, has just said that our old tradition of administering justice is inhumane. Such a verdict from such a personality makes it impossible for me to countenance these methods any longer. Therefore from this very day I ordain . . .' and so on. You may want to interpose that you never said any such thing, that you never called my methods inhumane, on the contrary your profound experience leads you to believe they are most humane and most in consonance with human dignity, and you admire the machine greatly—but it will be too late; you won't even get onto the balcony, crowded as it will be with ladies; you may try to draw attention to yourself; you may want to scream out; but a lady's hand will close your lips—and I and the work of the old Commandant will be done for."

The explorer had to suppress a smile; so easy, then, was the task he had felt to be so difficult. He said evasively: "You overestimate my influence; the Commandant has read my letters of recommendation, he knows that I am no expert in criminal procedure. If I were to give an opinion, it would be as a private individual, an opinion no more influential than that of any ordinary person, and in any case much less influential than that of the Commandant, who, I am given to understand, has very extensive powers in this penal colony. If his attitude to your procedure is as definitely hostile as you believe, then I fear the end of your tradition is at hand, even without any humble assistance from me."

Had it dawned on the officer at last? No, he still did not understand. He shook his head emphatically, glanced briefly round at the condemned man and the soldier, who both flinched away from the rice, came close up to the explorer and without looking at his face but fixing his eye on some spot on his coat said in a lower voice than before: "You don't know the Commandant; you feel yourself—forgive the expression—a kind of outsider so far as all of us are concerned; yet, believe me, your influence cannot be rated too highly. I was simply delighted when I heard that you were to attend the execution all by yourself. The Commandant arranged it to aim a blow at me, but I shall turn it to my advantage. Without being distracted by lying whispers and contemptuous glances—which could not have been avoided had a crowd of people attended the execution—you have heard my explanations, seen the machine and are now in course of watching the execution. You have doubtless already formed your own judgment; if you still have some small uncertainties the sight of the execution will resolve them. And now I make this request to you: help me against the Commandant!"

The explorer would not let him go on. "How could I do that," he cried, "it's quite impossible. I can neither help nor hinder you."

"Yes, you can," the officer said. The explorer saw with a certain apprehension that the officer had clenched his fists. "Yes, you can," repeated the officer, still more insistently. "I have a plan that is bound to succeed. You believe your influence is insufficient. I know that it is sufficient. But even granted that you are right, is it not necessary, for the sake of preserving this tradition, to try even what might prove insufficient? Listen to my plan, then. The first thing necessary for you to carry it out is to be as reticent as possible today regarding your verdict on these proceedings. Unless you are asked a direct question you must say nothing at all; but what you do say must be brief and general; let it be remarked that you would prefer not to discuss the matter, that you are out of patience with it, that if you are to let yourself go you would use strong language. I don't ask you to tell any lies; by no means; you should only give curt answers, such as: 'Yes, I saw the execution,' or 'Yes, I had it explained to me.' Just that, nothing more. There are grounds enough for any impatience you betray, although not such as will occur to the Commandant. Of course, he will mistake your meaning and interpret it to please himself. That's what my plan depends on. Tomorrow in the Commandant's office there is to be a large conference of all the high administrative officials, the Commandant presiding. Of course the Commandant is the kind of man to have turned these conferences into public spectacles. He has had a gallery built that is always packed with spectators. I am compelled to take part in the conferences, but they make me sick with disgust. Now, whatever happens, you will certainly be invited to this conference; if you behave today as I suggest the invitation will become an urgent request. But if for some mysterious reason you're not invited, you'll have to ask for an invitation; there's no doubt of your getting it then. So tomorrow you're sitting in the Commandant's box with the ladies. He keeps looking up to make sure you're there. After various trivial and ridiculous matters, brought in merely to impress the audience— mostly harbor works, nothing but harbor works!—our judicial procedure comes up for discussion too. If the Commandant doesn't introduce it, or not soon enough, I'll see that it's mentioned. I'll stand up and report that today's execution has taken place. Quite briefly, only a statement. Such a statement is not usual, but I shall make it. The Commandant thanks me, as always, with an amiable smile, and then he can't restrain himself, he seizes the excellent opportunity. 'It has just been reported,' he will say, or words to that effect, 'that an execution has taken place. I should like merely to add that this execution was witnessed by the famous explorer who has, as you all know, honored our colony so greatly by his visit to us. His presence at today's session of our conference also contributes to the importance of this occasion. Should we not now ask the famous explorer to give us his verdict on our traditional mode of execution and the procedure that leads up to it?' Of course there is loud applause, general agreement, I am more insistent than anyone. The Commandant bows to you and says: 'Then in the name of the assembled company, I put the question to you.' And now you advance to the front of the box. Lay your hands where everyone can see them, or the ladies will catch them and press your fingers.—And then at last you can speak out. I don't know how I'm going to endure the tension of waiting for that moment. Don't put any restraint on yourself when you make your speech, publish the truth aloud, lean over the front of the box, shout, yes indeed, shout your verdict, your unshakable conviction, at the Commandant. Yet perhaps you wouldn't care to do that, it's not in keeping with your character, in your country perhaps people do these things differently, well, that's all right too, that will be quite as effective, don't even stand up, just say a few words, even in a whisper, so that only the officials beneath you will hear them, that will be quite enough, you don't even need to mention the lack of public support for the execution, the creaking wheel, the broken strap, the filthy gag of felt, no, I'll take all that upon me, and, believe me, if my indictment doesn't drive him out of the conference hall, it will force him to his knees to make the acknowledgment: Old Commandant, I humble myself before you.—That is my plan; will you help me to carry it out? But of course you are willing, what is more, you must." And the officer seized the explorer by both arms and gazed, breathing heavily, into his face. He had shouted the last sentence so loudly that even the soldier and the condemned man were startled into attending; they had not understood a word but they stopped eating and looked over at the explorer, chewing their previous mouthfuls.

From the very beginning the explorer had no doubt about what answer he must give; in his lifetime he had experienced too much to have any uncertainty here; he was fundamentally honorable and unafraid. And yet now, facing the soldier and the condemned man, he did hesitate, for as long as it took to draw one breath. At last, however, he said, as he had to: "No." The officer blinked several times but did not turn his eyes away. "Would you like me to explain?" asked the explorer. The officer nodded wordlessly. "I do not approve of your procedure," said the explorer then, "even before you took me into your confidence—of course I shall never in any circumstances betray your confidence—I was already wondering whether it would be my duty to intervene and whether my intervention would have the slightest chance of success. I realized to whom I ought to turn: to the Commandant, of course. You have made that fact even clearer, but without having strengthened my resolution, on the contrary, your sincere conviction has touched me, even though it cannot influence my judgment."

The officer remained mute, turned to the machine, caught hold of a brass rod, and then, leaning back a little, gazed at the Designer as if to assure himself that all was in order. The soldier and the condemned man seemed to have come to some understanding; the condemned man was making signs to the soldier, difficult though his movements were because of the tight straps; the soldier was bending down to him; the condemned man whispered something and the soldier nodded.

The explorer followed the officer and said: "You don't know yet what I mean to do. I shall tell the Commandant what I think of the procedure, certainly, but not at a public conference, only in private; nor shall I stay here long enough to attend any conference; I am going away early tomorrow morning, or at least embarking on my ship."

It did not look as if the officer had been listening. "So you did not find the procedure convincing," he said to himself and smiled, as an old man smiles at childish nonsense and yet pursues his own meditations behind the smile.

"Then the time has come," he said at last, and suddenly looked at the explorer with bright eyes that held some challenge, some appeal for co-operation. "The time for what?" asked the explorer uneasily, but got no answer.

"You are free," said the officer to the condemned man in the native tongue. The man did not believe it at first. "Yes, you are set free," said the officer. For the first time the condemned man's face woke to real animation. Was it true? Was it only a caprice of the officer's, that might change again? Had the foreign explorer begged him off? What was it? One could read these questions on his face. But not for long. Whatever it might be, he wanted to be really free if he might, and he began to struggle so far as the Harrow permitted him.

"You'll burst my straps," cried the officer, "lie still! We'll soon loosen them." And signing the soldier to help him, he set about doing so. The condemned man laughed wordlessly to himself, now he turned his face left towards the officer, now right towards the soldier, nor did he forget the explorer.

"Draw him out," ordered the officer. Because of the Harrow this had to be done with some care. The condemned man had already torn himself a little in the back through his impatience.

From now on, however, the officer paid hardly any attention to him. He went up to the explorer, pulled out the small leather wallet again, turned over the papers in it, found the one he wanted and showed it to the explorer. "Read it," he said. "I can't," said the explorer, "I told you before that I can't make out these scripts." "Try taking a close look at it," said the officer and came quite near to the explorer so that they might read it together. But when even that proved useless, he outlined the script with his little finger, holding it high above the paper as if the surface dared not be sullied by touch, in order to help the explorer to follow the script in that way. The explorer did make an effort, meaning to please the officer in this respect at least, but he was quite unable to follow. Now the officer began to spell it, letter by letter, and then read out the words. " 'BE JUST!' is what is written there," he said, "surely you can read it now." The explorer bent so close to the paper that the officer feared he might touch it and drew it farther away; the explorer made no remark, yet it was clear that he still could not decipher it. " 'BE JUST!' is what is written there," said the officer once more. "Maybe," said the explorer, "I am prepared to believe you." "Well, then," said the officer, at least partly satisfied, and climbed up the ladder with the paper; very carefully he laid it inside the Designer and seemed to be changing the disposition of all the cogwheels; it was a troublesome piece of work and must have involved wheels that were extremely small, for sometimes the officer's head vanished altogether from sight inside the Designer, so precisely did he have to regulate the machinery.

The explorer, down below, watched the labor uninterruptedly, his neck grew stiff and his eyes smarted from the glare of sunshine over the sky. The soldier and the condemned man were now busy together. The man's shirt and trousers, which were already lying in the pit, were fished out by the point of the soldier's bayonet. The shirt was abominably dirty and its owner washed it in the bucket of water. When he put on the shirt and trousers both he and the soldier could not help guffawing, for the garments were of course slit up behind. Perhaps the condemned man felt it incumbent on him to amuse the soldier, he turned round and round in his slashed garments before the soldier, who squatted on the ground beating his knees with mirth. All the same, they presently controlled their mirth out of respect for the gentlemen.

When the officer had at length finished his task aloft, he surveyed the machinery in all its details once more, with a smile, but this time shut the lid of the Designer, which had stayed open till now, climbed down, looked into the pit and then at the condemned man, noting with satisfaction that the clothing had been taken out, then went over to wash his hands in the water bucket, perceived too late that it was disgustingly dirty, was unhappy because he could not wash his hands, in the end thrust them into the sand—this alternative did not please him, but he had to put up with it—then stood upright and began to unbutton his uniform jacket. As he did this, the two ladies' handkerchiefs he had tucked under his collar fell into his hands. "Here are your handkerchiefs," he said, and threw them to the condemned man. And to the explorer he said in explanation: "A gift from the ladies."

In spite of the obvious haste with which he was discarding first his uniform jacket and then all his clothing, he handled each garment with loving care, he even ran his fingers caressingly over the silver lace on the jacket and shook a tassel into place. This loving care was certainly out of keeping with the fact that as soon as he had a garment off he flung it at once with a kind of unwilling jerk into the pit. The last thing left to him was his short sword with the sword belt. He drew it out of the scabbard, broke it, then gathered all together, the bits of the sword, the scabbard and the belt, and flung them so violently down that they clattered into the pit.

Now he stood naked there. The explorer bit his lips and said nothing. He knew very well what was going to happen, but he had no right to obstruct the officer in anything. If the judicial procedure which the officer cherished were really so near its end—possibly as a result of his own intervention, as to which he felt himself pledged—then the officer was doing the right thing; in his place the explorer would not have acted otherwise.

The soldier and the condemned man did not understand at first what was happening, at first they were not even looking on. The condemned man was gleeful at having got the handkerchiefs back, but he was not allowed to enjoy them for long, since the soldier snatched them with a sudden, unexpected grab. Now the condemned man in turn was trying to twitch them from under the belt where the soldier had tucked them, but the soldier was on his guard. So they were wrestling, half in jest. Only when the officer stood quite naked was their attention caught. The condemned man especially seemed struck with the notion that some great change was impending. What had happened to him was now going to happen to the officer. Perhaps even to the very end. Apparently the foreign explorer had given the order for it. So this was revenge. Although he himself had not suffered to the end, he was to be revenged to the end. A broad, silent grin now appeared on his face and stayed there all the rest of the time.

The officer, however, had turned to the machine. It had been clear enough previously that he understood the machine well, but now it was almost staggering to see how he managed it and how it obeyed him. His hand had only to approach the Harrow for it to rise and sink several times till it was adjusted to the right position for receiving him; he touched only the edge of the Bed and already it was vibrating; the felt gag came to meet his mouth, one could see that the officer was really reluctant to take it but he shrank from it only a moment, soon he submitted and received it. Everything was ready, only the straps hung down at the sides, yet they were obviously unnecessary, the officer did not need to be fastened down. Then the condemned man noticed the loose straps, in his opinion the execution was incomplete unless the straps were buckled, he gestured eagerly to the soldier and they ran together to strap the officer down. The latter had already stretched out one foot to push the lever that started the Designer; he saw the two men coming up; so he drew his foot back and let himself be buckled in. But now he could not reach the lever; neither the soldier nor the condemned man would be able to find it, and the explorer was determined not to lift a finger. It was not necessary; as soon as the straps were fastened the machine began to work; the Bed vibrated, the needles flickered above the skin, the Harrow rose and fell. The explorer had been staring at it quite a while before he remembered that a wheel in the Designer should have been creaking; but everything was quiet, not even the slightest hum could be heard.

Because it was working so silently the machine simply escaped one's attention. The explorer observed the soldier and the condemned man. The latter was the more animated of the two, everything in the machine interested him, now he was bending down and now stretching up on tiptoe, his forefinger was extended all the time pointing out details to the soldier. This annoyed the explorer. He was resolved to stay till the end, but he could not bear the sight of these two. "Go back home," he said. The soldier would have been willing enough, but the condemned man took the order as a punishment. With clasped hands he implored to be allowed to stay, and when the explorer shook his head and would not relent, he even went down on his knees. The explorer saw that it was no use merely giving orders, he was on the point of going over and driving them away. At that moment he heard a noise above him in the Designer. He looked up. Was that cogwheel going to make trouble after all? But it was something quite different. Slowly the lid of the Designer rose up and then clicked wide open. The teeth of a cogwheel showed themselves and rose higher, soon the whole wheel was visible, it was as if some enormous force were squeezing the Designer so that there was no longer room for the wheel, the wheel moved up till it came to the very edge of the Designer, fell down, rolled along the sand a little on its rim and then lay flat. But a second wheel was already rising after it, followed by many others, large and small and indistinguishably minute, the same thing happened to all of them, at every moment one imagined the Designer must now really be empty, but another complex of numerous wheels was already rising into sight, falling down, trundling along the sand and lying flat. This phenomenon made the condemned man completely forget the explorer's command, the cogwheels fascinated him, he was always trying to catch one and at the same time urging the soldier to help, but always drew back his hand in alarm, for another wheel always came hopping along which, at least on its first advance, scared him off.

The explorer, on the other hand, felt greatly troubled; the machine was obviously going to pieces; its silent working was a delusion; he had a feeling that he must now stand by the officer, since the officer was no longer able to look after himself. But while the tumbling cogwheels absorbed his whole attention he had forgotten to keep an eye on the rest of the machine; now that the last cogwheel had left the Designer, however, he bent over the Harrow and had a new and still more unpleasant surprise. The Harrow was not writing, it was only jabbing, and the bed was not turning the body over but only bringing it up quivering against the needles. The explorer wanted to do something, if possible, to bring the whole machine to a standstill, for this was no exquisite torture such as the officer desired, this was plain murder. He stretched out his hands. But at that moment the Harrow rose with the body spitted on it and moved to the side, as it usually did only when the twelfth hour had come. Blood was flowing in a hundred streams, not mingled with water, the water jets too had failed to function. And now the last action failed to fulfil itself, the body did not drop off the long needles, streaming with blood it went on hanging over the pit without falling into it. The Harrow tried to move back to its old position, but as if it had itself noticed that it had not yet got rid of its burden it stuck after all where it was, over the pit. "Come and help!" cried the explorer to the other two, and himself seized the officer's feet. He wanted to push against the feet while the others seized the head from the opposite side and so the officer might be slowly eased off the needles. But the other two could not make up their minds to come; the condemned man actually turned away; the explorer had to go over to them and force them into position at the officer's head. And here, almost against his will, he had to look at the face of the corpse. It was as it had been in life; no sign was visible of the promised redemption; what the others had found in the machine the officer had not found; the lips were firmly pressed together, the eyes were open, with the same expression as in life, the look was calm and convinced, through the forehead went the point of the great iron spike.

As the explorer, with the soldier and the condemned man behind him, reached the first houses of the colony, the soldier pointed to one of them and said: "There is the teahouse."

In the ground floor of the house was a deep, low, cavernous space,

its walls and ceiling blackened with smoke. It was open to the road all
along its length. Although this teahouse was very little different from the
other houses of the colony, which were all very dilapidated, even up to
the Commandant's palatial headquarters, it made on the explorer the
impression of a historic tradition of some kind, and he felt the power of
past days. He went near to it, followed by his companions, right up
between the empty tables which stood in the street before it, and breathed
the cool, heavy air that came from the interior. "The old man's buried
here," said the soldier, "the priest wouldn't let him lie in the churchyard.
Nobody knew where to bury him for a while, but in the end they buried
him here. The officer never told you about that, for sure, because of
course that's what he was most ashamed of. He even tried several times
to dig the old man up by night, but he was always chased away." "Where
is the grave?" asked the explorer, who found it impossible to believe the
soldier. At once both of them, the soldier and the condemned man, ran
before him pointing with outstretched hands in the direction where the
grave should be. They led the explorer right up to the back wall, where
guests were sitting at a few tables. They were apparently dock laborers,
strong men with short, glistening, full black beards. None had a jacket,
their shirts were torn, they were poor, humble creatures. As the explorer
drew near, some of them got up, pressed close to the wall, and stared at
him. "It's a foreigner," ran the whisper around him, "he wants to see
the grave." They pushed one of the tables aside, and under it there was
really a gravestone. It was a simple stone, low enough to be covered by
a table. There was an inscription on it in very small letters, the explorer
had to kneel down to read it. This was what it said: "Here rests the old
Commandant. His adherents, who now must be nameless, have dug this
grave and set up this stone. There is a prophecy that after a certain
number of years the Commandant will rise again and lead his adherents
from this house to recover the colony. Have faith and wait!" When the
explorer had read this and risen to his feet he saw all the bystanders
around him smiling, as if they too had read the inscription, had found
it ridiculous and were expecting him to agree with them. The explorer
ignored this, distributed a few coins among them, waiting till the table
was pushed over the grave again, quitted the teahouse and made for the
harbor.

The soldier and the condemned man had found some acquaintances
in the teahouse, who detained them. But they must have soon shaken
them off, for the explorer was only halfway down the long flight of steps
leading to the boats when they came rushing after him. Probably they

wanted to force him at the last minute to take them with him. While he was bargaining below with a ferryman to row him to the steamer, the two of them came headlong down the steps, in silence, for they did not dare to shout. But by the time they reached the foot of the steps the explorer was already in the boat, and the ferryman was just casting off from the shore. They could have jumped into the boat, but the explorer lifted a heavy knotted rope from the floor boards, threatened them with it and so kept them from attempting the leap.

JEFFTY IS FIVE

When I was five years old, there was a little kid I played with: Jeffty. His real name was Jeff Kinzer, and everyone who played with him called him Jeffty. We were five years old together, and we had good times playing together.

When I was five, a Clark Bar was as fat around as the gripping end of a Louisville Slugger, and pretty nearly six inches long, and they used real chocolate to coat it, and it crunched very nicely when you bit into the center, and the paper it came wrapped in smelled fresh and good when you peeled off one end to hold the bar so it wouldn't melt onto your fingers. Today, a Clark Bar is as thin as a credit card, they use something artificial and awful-tasting instead of pure chocolate, the thing is soft and soggy, it costs fifteen or twenty cents instead of a decent, correct nickel, and they wrap it so you think it's the same size it was twenty years ago, only it isn't; it's slim and ugly and nasty-tasting and not worth a penny, much less fifteen or twenty cents.

When I was that age, five years old, I was sent away to my Aunt Patricia's home in Buffalo, New York, for two years. My father was going through "bad times" and Aunt Patricia was very beautiful, and had married a stockbroker. They took care of me for two years. When I was seven, I came back home and went to find Jeffty, so we could play together.

I was seven. Jeffty was still five. I didn't notice any difference. I didn't know: I was only seven.

When I was seven years old I used to lie on my stomach in front of our Atwater-Kent radio and listen to swell stuff. I had tied the ground wire to the radiator, and I would lie there with my coloring books and my Crayolas (when there were only sixteen colors in the big box), and listen to the NBC Red network: Jack Benny on the *Jell-O Program*, *Amos 'n' Andy*, Edgar Bergen and Charlie McCarthy on the *Chase and Sanborn Program*, *One Man's Family*, *First Nighter*; the NBC Blue network: *Easy Aces*, the *Jergens Program* with Walter Winchell, *Information Please*, *Death Valley Days*; and best of all, the Mutual Network with *The Green Hornet*, *The Lone Ranger*, *The Shadow*, and *Quiet, Please*. Today, I turn on my car radio and go from one end of the dial to the other and all I get is 100 strings orchestras, banal housewives and insipid truckers discussing their kinky sex lives with arrogant talk show hosts, country and western drivel, and rock music so loud it hurts my ears.

When I was ten, my grandfather died of old age and I was "a troublesome kid," and they sent me off to military school, so I could be "taken in hand."

I came back when I was fourteen. Jeffty was still five.

When I was fourteen years old, I used to go to the movies on Saturday afternoons and a matinee was ten cents and they used real butter on the popcorn and I could always be sure of seeing a western like Lash LaRue, or Wild Bill Elliott as Red Ryder with Bobby Blake as Little Beaver, or Roy Rogers, or Johnny Mack Brown; a scary picture like *House of Horrors* with Rondo Hatton as the Strangler, or *The Cat People*, or *The Mummy*, or *I Married a Witch* with Fredric March and Veronica Lake; plus an episode of a great serial like *The Shadow* with Victor Jory, or *Dick Tracy* or *Flash Gordon*; and three cartoons; a James Fitzpatrick TravelTalk; Movietone News; a sing-along and, if I stayed on till evening, Bingo or Keno; and free dishes. Today, I go to movies and see Clint Eastwood blowing people's heads apart like ripe cantaloupes.

At eighteen, I went to college. Jeffty was still five. I came back during the summers, to work at my Uncle Joe's jewelry store. Jeffty hadn't changed. Now I knew there was something different about him, something wrong, something weird. Jeffty was still five years old, not a day older.

At twenty-two I came home for keeps. To open a Sony television franchise in town, the first one. I saw Jeffty from time to time. He was five.

Things are better in a lot of ways. People don't die from some of the old diseases any more. Cars go faster and get you there more quickly on better roads. Shirts are softer and silkier. We have paperback books even though they cost as much as a good hardcover used to. When I'm running short in the bank I can live off credit cards till things even out. But I still think we've lost a lot of good stuff. Did you know you can't buy linoleum any more, only vinyl floor covering? There's no such thing as oilcloth any more; you'll never again smell that special, sweet smell from your grandmother's kitchen. Furniture isn't made to last thirty years or longer because they took a survey and found that young homemakers like to throw their furniture out and bring in all new, color-coded borax every seven years. Records don't feel right; they're not thick and solid like the old ones, they're thin and you can bend them . . . that doesn't seem right to me. Restaurants don't serve cream in pitchers any more, just that artificial glop in little plastic tubs, and one is never enough to get coffee the right color. You can make a dent in a car fender with only a sneaker. Everywhere you go, all the towns look the same with Burger Kings and McDonald's and 7-Elevens and Taco Bells and motels and shopping centers. Things may be better, but why do I keep thinking about the past?

What I mean by five years old is not that Jeffty was retarded. I don't think that's what it was. Smart as a whip for five years old; very bright, quick, cute, a funny kid.

But he was three feet tall, small for his age, and perfectly formed: no big head, no strange jaw, none of that. A nice, normal-looking five-year-old kid. Except that he was the same age as I was: twenty-two.

When he spoke it was with the squeaking, soprano voice of a five-year-old; when he walked it was with the little hops and shuffles of a five-year-old; when he talked to you it was about the concerns of a five-year-old . . . comic books, playing soldier, using a clothes pin to attach a stiff piece of cardboard to the front fork of his bike so the sound it made when the spokes hit was like a motorboat, asking questions like *why does that thing do that like that*, how high is up, how old is old, why is grass green, what's an elephant look like? At twenty-two, he was five.

Jeffty's parents were a sad pair. Because I was still a friend of Jeffty's, still let him hang around with me in the store, sometimes took him to the county fair or to the miniature golf or the movies, I wound up spending time with *them*. Not that I much cared for them, because they were so awfully depressing. But then, I suppose one couldn't expect much more from the poor devils. They had an alien thing in their home, a child who had grown no older than five in twenty-two years, who provided the treasure of that special childlike state indefinitely, but who also denied them the joys of watching the child grow into a normal adult.

Five is a wonderful time of life for a little kid . . . or it *can* be, if the child is relatively free of the monstrous beastliness other children indulge in. It is a time when the eyes are wide open and the patterns are not yet set; a time when one has not yet been hammered into accepting everything as immutable and hopeless; a time when the hands cannot do enough, the mind cannot learn enough, the world is infinite and colorful and filled with mysteries. Five is a special time before they take the questing, unquenchable, quixotic soul of the young dreamer and thrust it into dreary schoolroom boxes. A time before they take the trembling hands that want to hold everything, touch everything, figure everything out, and make them lie still on desktops. A time before people begin saying "act your age" and "grow up" or "you're behaving like a baby." It is a time when a child who acts adolescent is still cute and responsive and everyone's pet. A time of delight, of wonder, of innocence.

Jeffty had been stuck in that time, just five, just so.

But for his parents it was an ongoing nightmare from which no one— not social workers, not priests, not child psychologists, not teachers, not friends, not medical wizards, not psychiatrists, no one—could slap or shake them awake. For seventeen years their sorrow had grown through stages of parental dotage to concern, from concern to worry, from worry to fear, from fear to confusion, from confusion to anger, from anger to dislike, from dislike to naked hatred, and finally, from deepest loathing and revulsion to a stolid, depressive acceptance.

John Kinzer was a shift foreman at the Balder Tool & Die plant. He was a thirty-year man. To everyone but the man living it, his was a spectacularly uneventful life. In no way was he remarkable . . . save that he had fathered a twenty-two-year-old five-year-old.

John Kinzer was a small man; soft, with no sharp angles; with pale eyes that never seemed to hold mine for longer than a few seconds. He continually shifted in his chair during conversations, and seemed to see things in the upper corners of the room, things no one else could see . . . or wanted to see. I suppose the word that best suited him was *haunted*. What his life had become . . . well, *haunted* suited him.

Leona Kinzer tried valiantly to compensate. No matter what hour of the day I visited, she always tried to foist food on me. And when Jeffty was in the house she was always at *him* about eating: "Honey, would you like an orange? A nice orange? Or a tangerine? I have tangerines. I could peel a tangerine for you." But there was clearly such fear in her, fear of her own child, that the offers of sustenance always had a faintly ominous tone.

Leona Kinzer had been a tall woman, but the years had bent her. She seemed always to be seeking some area of wallpapered wall or storage niche into which she could fade, adopt some chintz or rose-patterned protective coloration and hide forever in plain sight of the child's big brown eyes, pass her a hundred times a day and never realize she was there, holding her breath, invisible. She always had an apron tied around her waist, and her hands were red from cleaning. As if by maintaining the environment immaculately she could pay off her imagined sin: having given birth to this strange creature.

Neither of them watched television very much. The house was usually dead silent, not even the sibilant whispering of water in the pipes, the creaking of timbers settling, the humming of the refrigerator. Awfully silent, as if time itself had taken a detour around that house.

As for Jeffty, he was inoffensive. He lived in that atmosphere of gentle dread and dulled loathing, and if he understood it, he never remarked in any way. He played, as a child plays, and seemed happy. But he must have sensed, in the way of a five-year-old, just how alien he was in their presence.

Alien. No, that wasn't right. He was *too* human, if anything. But out of phase, out of sync with the world around him, and resonating to a different vibration than his parents, God knows. Nor would other children play with him. As they grew past him, they found him at first childish, then uninteresting, then simply frightening as their perceptions of aging became clear and they could see he was not affected by time as they were. Even the little ones, his own age, who might wander into the neighborhood, quickly came to shy away from him like a dog in the street when a car backfires.

Thus, I remained his only friend. A friend of many years. Five years. Twenty-two years. I liked him; more than I can say. And never knew exactly why. But I did, without reserve.

But because we spent time together, I found I was also—polite society—spending time with John and Leona Kinzer. Dinner, Saturday afternoons sometimes, an hour or so when I'd bring Jeffty back from a movie. They were grateful: slavishly so. It relieved them of the embarrassing chore of going out with him, of having to pretend before the world that they were loving parents with a perfectly normal, happy, attractive child.

And their gratitude extended to hosting me. Hideous, every moment of their depression, hideous.

I felt sorry for the poor devils, but I despised them for their inability to love Jeffty, who was eminently lovable.

I never let on, of course, even during the evenings in their company that were awkward beyond belief.

We would sit there in the darkening living room—*always* dark or darkening, as if kept in shadow to hold back what the light might reveal to the world outside through the bright eyes of the house—we would sit and silently stare at one another. They never knew what to say to me.

"So how are things down at the plant?" I'd say to John Kinzer.

He would shrug. Neither conversation nor life suited him with any ease or grace. "Fine, just fine," he would say, finally.

And we would sit in silence again.

"Would you like a nice piece of coffee cake?" Leona would say. "I made it fresh just this morning." Or deep-dish green apple pie. Or milk and tollhouse cookies. Or a brown betty pudding.

"No, no, thank you, Mrs. Kinzer; Jeffty and I grabbed a couple of cheeseburgers on the way home." And again, silence.

Then, when the stillness and the awkwardness became too much even for them (and who knew how long that total silence reigned when they were alone, with that thing they never talked about any more, hanging between them), Leona Kinzer would say, "I think he's asleep."

John Kinzer would say, "I don't hear the radio playing."

Just so, it would go on like that, until I could politely find excuse to bolt away on some flimsy pretext. Yes, that was the way it would go on, every time, just the same . . . except once.

"I don't know what to do any more," Leona said. She began crying. "There's no change, not one day of peace."

Her husband managed to drag himself out of the old easy chair and went to her. He bent and tried to soothe her, but it was clear from the graceless way in which he touched her graying hair that the ability to be compassionate had been stunned in him. "Shhh, Leona, it's all right. Shhh." But she continued crying. Her hands scraped gently at the antimacassars on the arms of the chair.

Then she said, "Sometimes I wish he had been stillborn."

John looked up into the corners of the room. For the nameless shadows that were always watching him? Was it God he was seeking in those spaces? "You don't mean that," he said to her, softly, pathetically, urging her with body tension and trembling in his voice to recant before God took notice of the terrible thought. But she meant it; she meant it very much.

I managed to get away quickly that evening. They didn't want witnesses to their shame. I was glad to go.

And for a week I stayed away. From them, from Jeffty, from their street, even from that end of town.

I had my own life. The store, accounts, suppliers' conferences, poker with friends, pretty women I took to well-lit restaurants, my own parents, putting anti-freeze in the car, complaining to the laundry about too much starch in the collars and cuffs, working out at the gym, taxes, catching Jan or David (whichever one it was) stealing from the cash register. I had my own life.

But not even *that* evening could keep me from Jeffty. He called me at the store and asked me to take him to the rodeo. We chummed it up as best a twenty-two-year-old with other interests *could* . . . with a five-year-old. I never dwelled on what bound us together; I always thought it was simply the years. That, and affection for a kid who could have been the little brother I never had. (Except I *remembered* when we had played together, when we had both been the same age; I *remembered* that period, and Jeffty was still the same.)

And then, one Saturday afternoon, I came to take him to a double feature, and things I should have noticed so many times before, I first began to notice only that afternoon.

I came walking up to the Kinzer house, expecting Jeffty to be sitting on the front porch steps, or in the porch glider, waiting for me. But he was nowhere in sight.

Going inside, into that darkness and silence, in the midst of May sunshine, was unthinkable. I stood on the front walk for a few moments, then cupped my hands around my mouth and yelled, "Jeffty? Hey, Jeffty, come on out, let's go. We'll be late."

His voice came faintly, as if from under the ground.

"Here I am, Donny."

I could hear him, but I couldn't see him. It was Jeffty, no question about it: as Donald H. Horton, President and Sole Owner of The Horton TV & Sound Center, no one but Jeffty called me Donny. He had never called me anything else.

(Actually, it isn't a lie. I *am*, as far as the public is concerned, Sole

Owner of the Center. The partnership with my Aunt Patricia is only to repay the loan she made me, to supplement the money I came into when I was twenty-one, left to me when I was ten by my grandfather. It wasn't a very big loan, only eighteen thousand, but I asked her to be a silent partner, because of when she had taken care of me as a child.)

"Where are you, Jeffty?"

"Under the porch in my secret place."

I walked around the side of the porch, and stooped down and pulled away the wicker grating. Back in there, on the pressed dirt, Jeffty had built himself a secret place. He had comics in orange crates, he had a little table and some pillows, it was lit by big fat candles, and we used to hide there when we were both . . . five.

"What'cha up to?" I asked, crawling in and pulling the grate closed behind me. It was cool under the porch, and the dirt smelled comfortable, the candles smelled clubby and familiar. Any kid would feel at home in such a secret place: there's never been a kid who didn't spend the happiest, most productive, most deliciously mysterious times of his life in such a secret place.

"Playin'," he said. He was holding something golden and round. It filled the palm of his little hand.

"You forget we were going to the movies?"

"Nope. I was just waitin' for you here."

"Your mom and dad home?"

"Momma."

I understood why he was waiting under the porch. I didn't push it any further. "What've you got there?"

"Captain Midnight Secret Decoder Badge," he said, showing it to me on his flattened palm.

I realized I was looking at it without comprehending what it was for a long time. Then it dawned on me what a miracle Jeffty had in his hand. A miracle that simply could *not* exist.

"Jeffty," I said softly, with wonder in my voice, "where'd you get that?"

"Came in the mail today. I sent away for it."

"It must have cost a lot of money."

"Not so much. Ten cents an' two inner wax seals from two jars of Ovaltine."

"May I see it?" My voice was trembling, and so was the hand I extended. He gave it to me and I held the miracle in the palm of my hand. It was *wonderful*.

You remember. *Captain Midnight* went on the radio nationwide in 1940. It was sponsored by Ovaltine. And every year they issued a Secret Squadron Decoder Badge. And every day at the end of the program, they would give you a clue to the next day's installment in a code that only kids with the official badge could decipher. They stopped making those wonderful Decoder Badges in 1949. I remember the one I had in 1945: it was beautiful. It had a magnifying glass in the center of the code dial. *Captain Midnight* went off the air in 1950, and though I understand it was a short-lived television series in the mid-Fifties, and though they issued Decoder Badges in 1955 and 1956, as far as the *real* badges were concerned, they never made one after 1949.

The Captain Midnight Code-O-Graph I held in my hand, the one Jeffty said he had gotten in the mail for ten cents (*ten cents*!!!) and two Ovaltine labels, was brand new, shiny gold metal, not a dent or a spot of rust on it like the old ones you can find at exorbitant prices in collectible shoppes from time to time . . . it was a *new* Decoder. And the date on it was *this* year.

But *Captain Midnight* no longer existed. Nothing like it existed on the radio. I'd listened to the one or two weak imitations of old-time radio the networks were currently airing, and the stories were dull, the sound effects bland, the whole feel of it wrong, out of date, cornball. Yet I held a *new* Code-O-Graph.

"Jeffty, tell me about this," I said.

"Tell you what, Donny? It's my new Capt'n Midnight Secret Decoder Badge. I use it to figger out what's gonna happen tomorrow."

"Tomorrow how?"

"On the program."

"*What* program?!"

He stared at me as if I was being purposely stupid. "On Capt'n *Midnight*! Boy!" I was being dumb.

I still couldn't get it straight. It was right there, right out in the open, and I still didn't know what was happening. "You mean one of those records they made of the old-time radio programs? Is that what you mean, Jeffty?"

"What records?" he asked. He didn't know what *I* meant.

We stared at each other, there under the porch. And then I said, very slowly, almost afraid of the answer, "Jeffty, how do you hear *Captain Midnight*?"

"Every day. On the radio. On my radio. Every day at five-thirty."

News. Music, dumb music, and news. That's what was on the radio every day at 5:30. Not *Captain Midnight*. The Secret Squadron hadn't been on the air in twenty years.

"Can we hear it tonight?" I asked.

"Boy!" he said. I was being dumb. I knew it from the way he said it; but I didn't know *why*. Then it dawned on me: this was Saturday. *Captain Midnight* was on Monday through Friday. Not on Saturday or Sunday.

"We goin' to the movies?"

He had to repeat himself twice. My mind was somewhere else. Nothing definite. No conclusions. No wild assumptions leapt to. Just off somewhere trying to figure it out, and concluding—as *you* would have concluded, as *any*one would have concluded rather than accepting the truth, the impossible and wonderful truth—just finally concluding there was a simple explanation I didn't yet perceive. Something mundane and dull, like the passage of time that steals all good, old things from us, pack-ratting trinkets and plastic in exchange. And all in the name of Progress.

"We goin' to the movies, Donny?"

"You bet your boots we are, kiddo," I said. And I smiled. And I handed him the Code-O-Graph. And he put it in his side pants pocket. And we crawled out from under the porch. And we went to the movies. And neither of us said anything about *Captain Midnight* all the rest of that day. And there wasn't a ten-minute stretch, all the rest of that day, that I didn't think about it.

It was inventory all that next week. I didn't see Jeffty till late Thursday. I confess I left the store in the hands of Jan and David, told them I had some errands to run, and left early. At 4:00. I got to the Kinzers' right around 4:45. Leona answered the door, looking exhausted and distant. "Is Jeffty around?" She said he was upstairs in his room . . .

. . . listening to the radio.

I climbed the stairs two at a time.

All right, I had finally made that impossible, illogical leap. Had the stretch of belief involved anyone but Jeffty, adult or child, I would have reasoned out more explicable answers. But it *was* Jeffty, clearly another kind of vessel of life, and what he might experience should not be expected to fit into the ordered scheme.

I admit it: I *wanted* to hear what I heard.

Even with the door closed, I recognized the program:

"There he goes, Tennessee! Get him!"

There was the heavy report of a squirrel-rifle shot and the keening whine of the slug ricocheting, and then the same voice yelled triumphantly, "*Got him! D-e-a-a-a-a-d center!*"

He was listening to the American Broadcasting Company, 790 kilohertz, and he was hearing *Tennessee Jed*, one of my most favorite programs from the Forties, a western adventure I had not heard in twenty years, because it had not existed for twenty years.

I sat down on the top step of the stairs, there in the upstairs hall of the Kinzer home, and I listened to the show. It wasn't a rerun of an old program; I knew every one of them by heart, had never missed an episode. Further evidence that this was a new installment: there were occasional references during the integrated commercials to current cultural and technological developments, and phrases that had not existed in common usage in the Forties: aerosol spray cans, laserasing of tattoos, Tanzania, the word "uptight."

I could not ignore the fact: Jeffty was listening to a *new* segment of *Tennessee Jed*.

I ran downstairs and out the front door to my car. Leona must have been in the kitchen. I turned the key and punched on the radio and spun the dial to 790 kilohertz. The ABC station. Rock music.

I sat there for a few moments, then ran the dial slowly from one end to the other. Music, news, talk shows. No *Tennessee Jed*. And it was a Blaupunkt, the best radio I could get. I wasn't missing some perimeter station. It simply was not there!

After a few moments I turned off the radio and the ignition and went back upstairs quietly. I sat down on the top step and listened to the entire program. It was *wonderful*.

Exciting, imaginative, filled with everything I remembered as being most innovative about radio drama. But it was modern. It wasn't an antique, re-broadcast to assuage the need of that dwindling listenership who longed for the old days. It was a new show, with all the old voices, but still young and bright. Even the commercials were for currently available products, but they weren't as loud or as insulting as the screamer ads one heard on radio these days.

And when *Tennessee Jed* went off at 5:00, I heard Jeffty spin the dial on his radio till I heard the familiar voice of the announcer Glenn Riggs proclaim, "*Presenting Hop Harrigan! America's ace of the airwaves!*" There was the sound of an airplane in flight. It was a prop plane, *not* a jet! Not the sound kids today have grown up with, but the sound *I* grew up with, the *real* sound of an airplane, the growling, revving, throaty sound of the kind of airplanes G-8 and His Battle Aces flew, the kind Captain Midnight flew, the kind Hop Harrigan flew. And then I heard Hop say, *"CX-4 calling control tower. CX-4 calling control tower. Standing by!"* A pause, then, *"Okay, this is Hop Harrigan . . . coming in!"*

And Jeffty, who had the same problem all of us kids had had in the Forties with programming that pitted equal favorites against one another on different stations, having paid his respects to Hop Harrigan and Tank Tinker, spun the dial and went back to ABC where I heard the stroke of a gong, the wild cacophony of nonsense Chinese chatter, and the announcer yelled, *"T-e-e-e-rry and the Pirates!"*

I sat there on the top step and listened to Terry and Connie and Flip Corkin and, so help me God, Agnes Moorehead as the Dragon Lady, all of them in a new adventure that took place in a Red China that had not existed in the days of Milton Caniff's 1937 version of the Orient, with river pirates and Chiang Kai-shek and warlords and the naïve imperialism of American gunboat diplomacy.

Sat, and listened to the whole show, and sat even longer to hear *Superman* and part of *Jack Armstrong, the All-American Boy* and part of *Captain Midnight*, and John Kinzer came home and neither he nor Leona came upstairs to find out what had happened to me, or where Jeffty was, and sat longer, and found I had started crying, and could not stop, just sat there with tears running down my face, into the corners of my mouth, sitting and crying until Jeffty heard me and opened his door and saw me and came out and looked at me in childish confusion as I heard the station break for the Mutual Network and they began the theme music of *Tom Mix*, "When It's Round-up Time in Texas and the Bloom Is on the Sage," and Jeffty touched my shoulder and smiled at me, with his mouth and his big brown eyes, and said, "Hi, Donny. Wanna come in an' listen to the radio with me?"

Hume denied the existence of an absolute space, in which each thing has its place; Borges denies the existence of one single time, in which all events are linked.

Jeffty received radio programs from a place that could not, in logic, in the natural scheme of the space-time universe as conceived by Einstein, exist. But that wasn't all he received. He got mail-order premiums that no one was manufacturing. He read comic books that had been defunct for three decades. He saw movies with actors who had been dead for twenty years. He was the receiving terminal for endless joys and pleasures of the past that the world had dropped along the way. On its headlong suicidal flight toward New Tomorrows, the world had razed its treasure-house of simple happinesses, had poured concrete over its play-grounds, had abandoned its elfin stragglers, and all of it was being impossibly, miraculously shunted back into the present through Jeffty. Revivified, updated, the traditions maintained but contemporaneous. Jeffty was the unbidding Aladdin whose very nature formed the magic lampness of his reality.

And he took me into his world with him.

Because he trusted me.

We had breakfast of Quaker Puffed Wheat Sparkies and warm Ovaltine we drank out of *this* year's Little Orphan Annie Shake-Up Mugs. We went to the movies and while everyone else was seeing a comedy starring Goldie Hawn and Ryan O'Neal, Jeffty and I were enjoying Humphrey Bogart as the professional thief Parker in John Huston's brilliant adap-tation of the Donald Westlake novel SLAYGROUND. The second feature was Spencer Tracy, Carole Lombard and Laird Cregar in the Val Lewton–produced film of *Leiningen Versus the Ants*.

Twice a month we went down to the newsstand and bought the current pulp issues of *The Shadow, Doc Savage*, and *Startling Stories*. Jeffty and I sat together and I read to him from the magazines. He particularly liked the new short novel by Henry Kuttner, "The Dreams of Achilles," and the new Stanley G. Weinbaum series of short stories set in the subatomic particle universe of Redurna. In September we enjoyed the first install-ment of the new Robert E. Howard Conan novel, ISLE OF THE BLACK ONES, in *Weird Tales*; and in August we were only mildly disappointed by Edgar Rice Burroughs's fourth novella in the Jupiter series featuring John Carter of Barsoom—"Corsairs of Jupiter." But the editor of *Argosy All-Story Weekly* promised there would be two more stories in the series, and it was such an unexpected revelation for Jeffty and me that it dimmed our disappointment at the lessened quality of the current story.

We read comics together, and Jeffty and I both decided—separately, before we came together to discuss it—that our favorite characters were Doll Man, Airboy, and The Heap. We also adored the George Carlson strips in *Jingle Jangle Comics*, particularly the Pie-Face Prince of Old Pretzleburg stories, which we read together and laughed over, even though I had to explain some of the esoteric puns to Jeffty, who was too young to have that kind of subtle wit.

How to explain it? I can't. I had enough physics in college to make some offhand guesses, but I'm more likely wrong than right. The laws of the conservation of energy occasionally break. These are laws that physicists call "weakly violated." Perhaps Jeffty was a catalyst for the weak violation of conservation laws we're only now beginning to realize exist. I tried doing some reading in the area—muon decay of the "forbidden" kind: gamma decay that doesn't include the muon neutrino among its products—but nothing I encountered, not even the latest readings from the Swiss Institute for Nuclear Research near Zurich, gave me an insight. I was thrown back on a vague acceptance of the philosophy that the real name for "science" is *magic*.

No explanations, but enormous good times.

The happiest time of my life.

I had the "real" world, the world of my store and my friends and my family, the world of profit&loss, of taxes and evenings with young women who talked about going shopping or the United Nations, of the rising cost of coffee and microwave ovens. And I had Jeffty's world, in which I existed only when I was with him. The things of the past he knew as fresh and new, I could experience only when in his company. And the membrane between the two worlds grew ever thinner, more luminous and transparent. I had the best of both worlds. And knew, somehow, that I could carry nothing from one to the other.

Forgetting for just a moment, betraying Jeffty by forgetting, brought an end to it all.

Enjoying myself so much, I grew careless and failed to consider how fragile the relationship between Jeffty's world and my world really was. There is a reason why the present begrudges the existence of the past. I never really understood. Nowhere in the beast books, where survival is shown in battles between claw and fang, tentacle and poison sac, is there recognition of the ferocity the present always brings to bear on the past. Nowhere is there a detailed statement of how the Present lies in wait for What-Was, waiting for it to become Now-This-Moment so it can shred it with its merciless jaws.

Who could know such a thing . . . at any age . . . and certainly not at my age . . . who could understand such a thing?

I'm trying to exculpate myself. I can't. It was my fault.

It was another Saturday afternoon.

"What's playing today?" I asked him, in the car, on the way downtown.

He looked up at me from the other side of the front seat and smiled one of his best smiles. "Ken Maynard in *Bullwhip Justice* an' *The Demolished Man*." He kept smiling, as if he'd really put one over on me. I looked at him with disbelief.

"You're *kid*ding!" I said, delighted. "Bester's THE DEMOLISHED MAN?" He nodded his head, delighted at my being delighted. He knew it was one of my favorite books. "Oh, that's super!"

"Super *duper*," he said.

"Who's in it?"

"Franchot Tone, Evelyn Keyes, Lionel Barrymore, and Elisha Cook, Jr." He was much more knowledgeable about movie actors than I'd ever been. He could name the character actors in any movie he'd ever seen. Even the crowd scenes.

"And cartoons?" I asked.

"Three of 'em: a *Little Lulu*, a *Donald Duck*, and a *Bugs Bunny*. An' a *Pete Smith Specialty* an' a Lew Lehr *Monkeys is da C-r-r-r-aziest Peoples.*"

"Oh boy!" I said. I was grinning from ear to ear. And then I looked down and saw the pad of purchase order forms on the seat. I'd forgotten to drop it off at the store.

"Gotta stop by the Center," I said. "Gotta drop off something. It'll only take a minute."

"Okay," Jeffty said. "But we won't be late, will we?"

"Not on your tintype, kiddo," I said.

When I pulled into the parking lot behind the Center, he decided to come in with me and we'd walk over to the theater. It's not a large town. There are only two movie houses, the Utopia and the Lyric. We were going to the Utopia and it was only three blocks from the Center.

I walked into the store with the pad of forms, and it was bedlam. David and Jan were handling two customers each, and there were people standing around waiting to be helped. Jan turned a look on me and her face was a horror-mask of pleading. David was running from the stockroom to the showroom and all he could murmur as he whipped past was "Help!" and then he was gone.

"Jeffty," I said, crouching down, "listen, give me a few minutes. Jan and David are in trouble with all these people. We won't be late, I promise. Just let me get rid of a couple of these customers." He looked nervous, but nodded okay.

I motioned to a chair and said, "Just sit down for a while and I'll be right with you."

He went to the chair, good as you please, though he knew what was happening, and he sat down.

I started taking care of people who wanted color television sets. This was the first really substantial batch of units we'd gotten in—color television was only now becoming reasonably priced and this was Sony's first promotion—and it was bonanza time for me. I could see paying off the loan and being out in front for the first time with the Center. It was good business.

In my world, good business comes first.

Jeffty sat there and stared at the wall. Let me tell you about the wall.

Stanchion and bracket designs had been rigged from floor to within two feet of the ceiling. Television sets had been stacked artfully on the wall. Thirty-three television sets. All playing at the same time. Black and white, color, little ones, big ones, all going at the same time.

Jeffty sat and watched thirty-three television sets, on a Saturday afternoon. We can pick up a total of thirteen channels including the UHF educational stations. Golf was on one channel; baseball was on a second; celebrity bowling was on a third; the fourth channel was a religious seminar; a teenage dance show was on the fifth; the sixth was a rerun of a situation comedy; the seventh was a rerun of a police show; eighth was a nature program showing a man fly-casting endlessly; ninth was news and conversation; tenth was a stock car race; eleventh was a man doing logarithms on a blackboard; twelfth was a woman in a leotard doing setting-up exercises; and on the thirteenth channel was a badly animated cartoon show in Spanish. All but six of the shows were repeated on three sets. Jeffty sat and watched that wall of television on a Saturday afternoon while I sold as fast and as hard as I could, to pay back my Aunt Patricia and stay in touch with my world. It was business.

I should have known better. I should have understood about the present and the way it kills the past. But I was selling with both hands. And when I finally glanced over at Jeffty, half an hour later, he looked like another child.

He was sweating. That terrible fever sweat when you have stomach flu. He was pale, as pasty and pale as a worm, and his little hands were gripping the arms of the chair so tightly I could see his knuckles in bold relief. I dashed over to him, excusing myself from the middle-aged couple looking at the new 21" Mediterranean model.

"Jeffty!"

He looked at me, but his eyes didn't track. He was in absolute terror. I pulled him out of the chair and started toward the front door with him, but the customers I'd deserted yelled at me, "Hey!" The middle-aged man said, "You wanna sell me this thing or don't you?"

I looked from him to Jeffty and back again. Jeffty was like a zombie.

He had come where I'd pulled him. His legs were rubbery and his feet dragged. The past, being eaten by the present, the sound of something in pain.

I clawed some money out of my pants pocket and jammed it into Jeffty's hand. "Kiddo . . . listen to me . . . get out of here right now!" He still couldn't focus properly. "*Jeffty,*" I said as tightly as I could, "*listen to me!*" The middle-aged customer and his wife were walking toward us. "Listen, kiddo, get out of here right this minute. Walk over to the Utopia and buy the tickets. I'll be right behind you." The middle-aged man and his wife were almost on us. I shoved Jeffty through the door and watched him stumble away in the wrong direction, then stop as if gathering his wits, turn and go back past the front of the Center and in the direction of the Utopia. "Yes, sir," I said, straightening up and facing them, "yes, ma'am, that is one terrific set with some sensational features! If you'll just step back here with me . . . "

There was a terrible sound of something hurting, but I couldn't tell from which channel, or from which set, it was coming.

Most of it I learned later, from the girl in the ticket booth, and from some people I knew who came to me to tell me what had happened. By the time I got to the Utopia, nearly twenty minutes later, Jeffty was already beaten to a pulp and had been taken to the manager's office.

"Did you see a very little boy, about five years old, with big brown eyes and straight brown hair . . . he was waiting for me?"

"Oh, I think that's the little boy those kids beat up."

"What!?! *Where is he?*"

"They took him to the manager's office. No one knew who he was or where to find his parents—"

A young girl wearing an usher's uniform was kneeling down beside the couch, placing a wet paper towel on his face.

I took the towel away from her and ordered her out of the office. She looked insulted and snorted something rude, but she left. I sat on the edge of the couch and tried to swab away the blood from the lacerations without opening the wounds where the blood had caked. Both his eyes were swollen shut. His mouth was ripped badly. His hair was matted with dried blood.

He had been standing in line behind two kids in their teens. They started selling tickets at 12:30 and the show started at 1:00. The doors weren't opened till 12:45. He had been waiting, and the kids in front of him had had a portable radio. They were listening to the ball game. Jeffty had wanted to hear some program, God knows what it might have been, *Grand Central Station, Let's Pretend, Land of the Lost,* God only knows which one it might have been.

He had asked if he could borrow their radio to hear the program for a minute, and it had been a commercial break or something, and the kids had given him the radio, probably out of some malicious kind of courtesy that would permit them to take offense and rag the little boy. He had changed the station . . . and they'd been unable to get it to go back to the ball game. It was locked into the past, on a station that was broadcasting a program that didn't exist for anyone but Jeffty.

They had beaten him badly . . . as everyone watched.

And then they had run away.

I had left him alone, left him to fight off the present without sufficient weaponry. I had betrayed him for the sale of a 21″ Mediterranean console television, and now his face was pulped meat. He moaned something inaudible and sobbed softly.

"Shhh, it's okay, kiddo, it's Donny. I'm here. I'll get you home, it'll be okay."

I should have taken him straight to the hospital. I don't know why I didn't. I should have. I should have done that.

When I carried him through the door, John and Leona Kinzer just stared at me. They didn't move to take him from my arms. One of his hands was hanging down. He was conscious, but just barely. They stared, there in the semi-darkness of a Saturday afternoon in the present. I looked at them. "A couple of kids beat him up at the theater." I raised him a few inches in my arms and extended him. They stared at me, at both of us, with nothing in their eyes, without movement. "Jesus Christ," I shouted, "he's been beaten! He's your son! Don't you even want to touch him? What the hell kind of people are you?!"

Then Leona moved toward me very slowly. She stood in front of us for a few seconds, and there was a leaden stoicism in her face that was terrible to see. It said, *I have been in this place before, many times, and I cannot bear to be in it again; but I am here now.*

So I gave him to her. God help me, I gave him over to her.

And she took him upstairs to bathe away his blood and his pain.

John Kinzer and I stood in our separate places in the dim living room of their home, and we stared at each other. He had nothing to say to me.

I shoved past him and fell into a chair. I was shaking.

HARLAN ELLISON

I heard the bath water running upstairs.

After what seemed a very long time Leona came downstairs, wiping her hands on her apron. She sat down on the sofa and after a moment John sat down beside her. I heard the sound of rock music from upstairs.

"Would you like a piece of nice pound cake?" Leona said.

I didn't answer. I was listening to the sound of the music. Rock music. On the radio. There was a table lamp on the end table beside the sofa. It cast a dim and futile light in the shadowed living room. *Rock music from the present, on a radio upstairs?* I started to say something, and then *knew* . . . Oh, God . . . *no!*

I jumped up just as the sound of hideous crackling blotted out the music, and the table lamp dimmed and flickered. I screamed something, I don't know what it was, and ran for the stairs.

Jeffty's parents did not move. They sat there with their hands folded, in that place they had been for so many years.

I fell twice rushing up the stairs.

There isn't much on television that can hold my interest. I bought an old cathedral-shaped Philco radio in a second-hand store, and I replaced all the burnt-out parts with the original tubes from old radios I could cannibalize that still worked. I don't use transistors or printed circuits. They wouldn't work. I've sat in front of that set for hours sometimes, running the dial back and forth as slowly as you can imagine, so slowly it doesn't look as if it's moving at all sometimes.

But I can't find *Captain Midnight* or *Land of the Lost* or *The Shadow* or *Quiet, Please.*

So she did love him, still, a little bit, even after all those years. I can't hate them: they only wanted to live in the present world again. That isn't such a terrible thing.

It's a good world, all things considered. It's much better than it used to be, in a lot of ways. People don't die from the old diseases any more. They die from new ones, but that's Progress, isn't it?

Isn't it?

Tell me.

Somebody please tell me.

AIR RAID

I was jerked awake by the silent alarm vibrating my skull. It won't
shut down until you sit up, so I did. All around me in the darkened
bunkroom the Snatch Team members were sleeping singly and in pairs.
I yawned, scratched my ribs, and patted Gene's hairy flank. He turned
over. So much for a romantic send-off.

Rubbing sleep from my eyes, I reached to the floor for my leg, strapped
it on, and plugged it in. Then I was running down the rows of bunks
toward Ops.

The situation board glowed in the gloom. Sun-Belt Airlines Flight
128, Miami to New York, September 15, 1979. We'd been looking for
that one for three years. I should have been happy, but who can afford
it when you wake up?

Liza Boston muttered past me on the way to Prep. I muttered back
and followed. The lights came on around the mirrors, and I groped my
way to one of them. Behind us, three more people staggered in. I sat
down, plugged in, and at last I could lean back and close my eyes.

They didn't stay closed for long. Rush! I sat up straight as the sludge
I use for blood was replaced with supercharged go-juice. I looked around
me and got a series of idiot grins. There was Liza, and Pinky, and Dave.

Against the far wall Cristabel was already turning slowly in front of the
airbrush, getting a Caucasian paint job. It looked like a good team.

I opened the drawer and started preliminary work on my face. It's a
bigger job every time. Transfusion or no, I looked like death. The right
ear was completely gone now. I could no longer close my lips; the gums
were permanently bared. A week earlier, a finger had fallen off in my
sleep. And what's it to you, bugger?

While I worked, one of the screens around the mirror glowed. A
smiling young woman, blond, high brow, round face. Close enough.
The crawl line read *Mary Katrina Sondergard, born Trenton, New Jersey,
age in 1979: 25.* Baby, this is your lucky day.

The computer melted the skin away from her face to show me the
bone structure, rotated it, gave me cross sections. I studied the similarities
with my own skull, noted the differences. Not bad, and better than some
I'd been given.

I assembled a set of dentures that included the slight gap in the upper
incisors. Putty filled out my cheeks. Contact lenses fell from the dispenser
and I popped them in. Nose plugs widened my nostrils. No need for
ears; they'd be covered by the wig. I pulled a blank plastiflesh mask over
my face and had to pause while it melted in. It took only a minute to
mold it to perfection. I smiled at myself. How nice to have lips.

The delivery slot clunked and dropped a blond wig and a pink outfit
into my lap. The wig was hot from the styler. I put it on, then the
pantyhose.

"Mandy? Did you get the profile on Sondergard?" I didn't look up; I
recognized the voice.

"Roger."

"We've located her near the airport. We can slip you in before takeoff,
so you'll be the joker."

I groaned and looked up at the face on the screen. Elfreda Baltimore-
Louisville, Director of Operational Teams: lifeless face and tiny slits for
eyes. What can you do when all the muscles are dead?

"Okay." You take what you get.

She switched off, and I spent the next two minutes trying to get dressed
while keeping my eyes on the screens. I memorized names and faces of
crew members plus the few facts known about them. Then I hurried out
and caught up with the others. Elapsed time from first alarm: twelve
minutes and seven seconds. We'd better get moving.

"Goddam Sun-Belt," Cristabel groused, hitching at her bra.

"At least they got rid of the high heels," Dave pointed out. A year

earlier we would have been teetering down the aisles on three-inch plat-
forms. We all wore short pink shifts with blue and white diagonal stripes
across the front, and carried matching shoulder bags. I fussed trying to
get the ridiculous pillbox cap pinned on.

We jogged into the dark Operations Control Room and lined up at
the gate. Things were out of our hands now. Until the gate was ready,
we could only wait.

I was first, a few feet away from the portal. I turned away from it; it
gives me vertigo. I focused instead on the gnomes sitting at their consoles,
bathed in yellow lights from their screens. None of them looked back at
me. They don't like us much. I don't like them, either. Withered, emaciated, all of them. Our fat legs and butts and breasts are a reproach to
them, a reminder that Snatchers eat five times their ration to stay presentable for the masquerade. Meantime we continue to rot. One day I'll
be sitting at a console. One day I'll be *built in* to a console, with all my
guts on the outside and nothing left of my body but stink. The hell with
them.

I buried my gun under a clutter of tissues and lipsticks in my purse.
Elfreda was looking at me.

"Where is she?" I asked.

"Motel room. She was alone from ten P.M. to noon on flight day."

Departure time was one-fifteen. She had cut it close and would be in
a hurry. Good.

"Can you catch her in the bathroom? Best of all, in the tub?"

"We're working on it." She sketched a smile with a fingertip drawn
over lifeless lips. She knew how I liked to operate, but she was telling
me I'd take what I got. It never hurts to ask. People are at their most
defenseless stretched out and up to their necks in water.

"Go!" Elfreda shouted. I stepped through, and things started to go
wrong.

I was facing the wrong way, stepping *out* of the bathroom door and
facing the bedroom. I turned and spotted Mary Katrina Sondergard
through the haze of the gate. There was no way I could reach her without
stepping back through. I couldn't even shoot without hitting someone
on the other side.

Sondergard was at the mirror, the worst possible place. Few people
recognize themselves quickly, but she'd been looking right at herself. She
saw me and her eyes widened. I stepped to the side, out of her sight.

"What the hell is . . . hey? Who the hell—" I noted the voice, which
can be the trickiest thing to get right.

I figured she'd be more curious than afraid. My guess was right. She came out of the bathroom, passing through the gate as if it wasn't there, which it wasn't, since it only has one side. She had a towel wrapped around her.

"Jesus Christ! What are you doing in my—" Words fail you at a time like that. She knew she ought to say something, but what? *Excuse me, haven't I seen you in the mirror?*

I put on my best stew smile and held out my hand.

"Pardon the intrusion. I can explain everything. You see, I'm—" I hit her on the side of the head and she staggered and went down hard. Her towel fell to the floor. "—working my way through college." She started to get up, so I caught her under the chin with my artificial knee. She stayed down.

"Standard fuggin' *Oil!*" I hissed, rubbing my injured knuckles. But there was no time. I knelt beside her, checked her pulse. She'd be okay, but I think I loosened some front teeth. I paused a moment. Lord, to look like that with no makeup, no prosthetics! She nearly broke my heart.

I grabbed her under the knees and wrestled her to the gate. She was a sack of limp noodles. Somebody reached through, grabbed her feet, and pulled. *So long, love! How would you like to go on a long voyage?*

I sat on her rented bed to get my breath. There were car keys and cigarettes in her purse, genuine tobacco, worth its weight in blood. I lit six of them, figuring I had five minutes of my very own. The room filled with sweet smoke. They don't make 'em like that anymore.

The Hertz sedan was in the motel parking lot. I got in and headed for the airport. I breathed deeply of the air, rich in hydrocarbons. I could see for hundreds of yards into the distance. The perspective nearly made me dizzy, but I live for those moments. There's no way to explain what it's like in the pre-meck world. The sun was a fierce yellow ball through the haze.

The other stews were boarding. Some of them knew Sondergard so I didn't say much, pleading a hangover. That went over well, with a lot of knowing laughs and sly remarks. Evidently it wasn't out of character. We boarded the 707 and got ready for the goats to arrive.

It looked good. The four commandos on the other side were identical twins for the women I was working with. There was nothing to do but be a stewardess until departure time. I hoped there would be no more glitches. Inverting a gate for a joker run into a motel room was one thing, but in a 707 at twenty thousand feet...

The plane was nearly full when the woman Pinky would impersonate sealed the forward door. We taxied to the end of the runway, then we were airborne. I started taking orders for drinks in first.

The goats were the usual lot, for 1979. Fat and sassy, all of them, and as unaware of living in a paradise as a fish is of the sea. *What would you think, ladies and gents, of a trip to the future? No? I can't say I'm surprised. What if I told you this plane is going to—*

My alarm beeped as we reached cruising altitude. I consulted the indicator under my Lady Bulova and glanced at one of the restroom doors. I felt a vibration pass through the plane. *Damn it, not so soon.*

The gate was in there. I came out quickly, and motioned for Diana Gleason—Dave's pigeon—to come to the front.

"Take a look at this," I said, with a disgusted look. She started to enter the restroom, stopped when she saw the green glow. I planted a boot on her fanny and shoved. Perfect. Dave would have a chance to hear her voice before popping in. Though she'd be doing little but screaming when she got a look around. . . .

Dave came through the gate, adjusting his silly little hat. Diana must have struggled.

"Be disgusted," I whispered.

"What a mess," he said as he came out of the restroom. It was a fair imitation of Diana's tone, though he'd missed the accent. It wouldn't matter much longer.

"What is it?" It was one of the stews from tourist. We stepped aside so she could get a look, and Dave shoved her through. Pinky popped out very quickly.

"We're minus on minutes," Pinky said. "We lost five on the other side."

"Five?" Dave-Diana squeaked. I felt the same way. We had a hundred and three passengers to process.

"Yeah. They lost contact after you pushed my pigeon through. It took that long to realign."

You get used to that. Time runs at different rates on each side of the gate, though it's always sequential, past to future. Once we'd started the Snatch with me entering Sondergard's room, there was no way to go back any earlier on either side. Here, in 1979, we had a rigid ninety-four minutes to get everything done. On the other side, the gate could never be maintained longer than three hours.

"When you left, how long was it since the alarm went in?"

"Twenty-eight minutes."

It didn't sound good. It would take at least two hours just customizing the wimps. Assuming there was no more slippage on 79-time, we might just make it. But there's *always* slippage. I shuddered, thinking about riding it in.

"No time for any more games, then," I said. "Pink, you go back to tourist and call both of the other girls up here. Tell 'em to come one at a time, and tell 'em we've got a problem. You know the bit."

"Biting back the tears. Got you." She hurried aft. In no time the first one showed up. Her friendly Sun-Belt Airlines smile was stamped on her face, but her stomach would be churning. *Oh God, this is it!*

I took her by the elbow and pulled her behind the curtains in front. She was breathing hard.

"Welcome to the twilight zone," I said, and put the gun to her head. She slumped, and I caught her. Pinky and Dave helped me shove her through the gate.

"Fug! The rotting thing's flickering."

Pinky was right. A very ominous sign. But the green glow stabilized as we watched, with who knows how much slippage on the other side. Cristabel ducked through.

"We're plus thirty-three," she said. There was no sense talking about what we were all thinking: things were going badly.

"Back to tourist," I said. "Be brave, smile at everyone, but make it just a little bit too good, got it?"

"Check," Cristabel said.

We processed the other quickly, with no incident. Then there was no time to talk about anything. In eighty-nine minutes Flight 128 was going to be spread all over a mountain whether we were finished or not.

Dave went into the cockpit to keep the flight crew out of our hair. Me and Pinky were supposed to take care of first class, then back up Cristabel and Liza in tourist. We used the standard "coffee, tea, or milk" gambit, relying on our speed and their inertia.

I leaned over the first two seats on the left.

"Are you enjoying your flight?" Pop, pop. Two squeezes on the trigger, close to the heads and out of sight of the rest of the goats.

"Hi, folks. I'm Mandy. Fly me." Pop, pop.

Halfway to the galley, a few people were watching us curiously. But people don't make a fuss until they have a lot more to go on. One goat in the back row stood up, and I let him have it. By now there were only eight left awake. I abandoned the smile and squeezed off four quick shots. Pinky took care of the rest. We hurried through the curtains, just in time.

There was an uproar building in the back of tourist, with about sixty percent of the goats already processed. Cristabel glanced at me, and I nodded.

"Okay, folks," she bawled. "I want you to be quiet. Calm down and listen up. *You*, fathead, *pipe down* before I cram my foot up your ass sideways."

The shock of hearing her talk like that was enough to buy us a little time, anyway. We had formed a skirmish line across the width of the plane, guns out, steadied on seat backs, aimed at the milling, befuddled group of thirty goats.

The guns are enough to awe all but the most foolhardy. In essence, a standard-issue stunner is just a plastic rod with two grids about six inches apart. There's not enough metal in it to set off a hijack alarm. And to people from the Stone Age to about 2190 it doesn't look any more like a weapon than a ball-point pen. So Equipment Section jazzes them up in a plastic shell to real Buck Rogers blasters, with a dozen knobs and lights that flash and a barrel like the snout of a hog. Hardly anyone ever walks into one.

"We are in great danger, and time is short. You must all do exactly as I tell you, and you will be safe."

You can't give them time to think, you have to rely on your status as the Voice of Authority. The situation is just *not* going to make sense to them, no matter how you explain it.

"Just a minute, I think you owe us—"

An airborne lawyer. I made a snap decision, thumbed the fireworks switch on my gun, and shot him.

The gun made a sound like a flying saucer with hemorrhoids, spit sparks and little jets of flame, and extended a green laser finger to his forehead. He dropped.

All pure kark, of course. But it sure is impressive.

And it's damn risky, too. I had to choose between a panic if the fathead got them to thinking, and a possible panic from the flash of the gun. But when a 20th gets to talking about his "rights" and what he is "owed," things can get out of hand. It's infectious.

It worked. There was a lot of shouting, people ducking behind seats, but no rush. We could have handled it, but we needed some of them conscious if we were ever going to finish the Snatch.

"Get up. Get *up*, you *slugs!*" Cristabel yelled. "He's stunned, nothing worse. But I'll *kill* the next one who gets out of line. Now *get to your feet* and do what I tell you. *Children first! Hurry*, as fast as you can, to the front of the plane. Do what the stewardess tells you. Come on, kids, *move!"*

I ran back into first class just ahead of the kids, turned at the open restroom door, and got on my knees.

They were petrified. There were five of them—crying, some of them, which always chokes me up—looking left and right at dead people in the first class seats, stumbling, near panic.

"Come on, kids," I called to them, giving my special smile. "Your parents will be along in just a minute. Everything's going to be all right, I promise you. Come on."

I got three of them through. The fourth balked. She was determined not to go through that door. She spread her legs and arms and I couldn't push her through. I will *not* hit a child, never. She raked her nails over my face. My wig came off, and she gaped at my bare head. I shoved her through.

Number five was sitting in the aisle, bawling. He was maybe seven. I ran back and picked him up, hugged him and kissed him, and tossed him through. God, I needed a rest, but I was needed in tourist.

"You, you, you, and you. Okay, you too. Help him, will you?" Pinky had a practiced eye for the ones that wouldn't be any use to anyone, even themselves. We herded them toward the front of the plane, then deployed ourselves along the left side where we could cover the workers. It didn't take long to prod them into action. We had them dragging the limp bodies forward as fast as they could go. Me and Cristabel were in tourist, with the others up front.

Adrenaline was being catabolized in my body now; the rush of action left me and I started to feel very tired. There's an unavoidable feeling of sympathy for the poor dumb goats that starts to get me about this stage of the game. Sure, they were better off; sure, they were going to die if we didn't get them off the plane. But when they saw the other side they were going to have a hard time believing it.

The first ones were returning for a second load, stunned at what they'd just seen: dozens of people being put into a cubicle that was crowded when it was empty. One college student looked like he'd been hit in the stomach. He stopped by me and his eyes pleaded.

"Look, I want to *help* you people, just . . . what's going *on?* Is this some new kind of rescue? I mean, are we going to crash—"

I switched my gun to prod and brushed it across his cheek. He gasped and fell back.

"Shut your fuggin' mouth and get moving, or I'll kill you." It would be hours before his jaw was in shape to ask any more stupid questions.

We cleared tourist and moved up. A couple of the work gang were pretty damn pooped by then. Muscles like horses, all of them, but they can hardly run up a flight of stairs. We let some of them go through, including a couple that were at least fifty years old. *Je*-zuz. Fifty! We got down to a core of four men and two women who seemed strong, and worked them until they nearly dropped. But we processed everyone in twenty-five minutes.

The portapak came through as we were stripping off our clothes. Cristabel knocked on the door to the cockpit and Dave came out, already naked. A bad sign.

"I had to cork 'em," he said. "Bleeding captain just *had* to make his grand march through the plane. I tried *every*thing."

Sometimes you have to do it. The plane was on autopilot, as it normally would be at this time. But if any of us did anything detrimental to the craft, changed the fixed course of events in any way, that would be it. All that work for nothing, and Flight 128 inaccessible to us for all Time. I don't know sludge about time theory, but I know the practical angles. We can do things in the past only at times and in places where it won't make any difference. We have to cover our tracks. There's flexibility; once a Snatcher left her gun behind and it went in with the plane. Nobody found it, or if they did, they didn't have the smoggiest idea of what it was, so we were okay.

Flight 128 was mechanical failure. That's the best kind; it means we don't have to keep the pilot unaware of the situation in the cabin right down to ground level. We can cork him and fly the plane, since there's nothing he could have done to save the flight anyway. A pilot-error smash is almost impossible to Snatch. We mostly work midairs, bombs, and structural failures. If there's even one survivor, we can't touch it. It would not fit the fabric of space-time, which is immutable (though it can stretch a little), and we'd all just fade away and appear back in the ready room.

My head was hurting. I wanted that portapak very badly.

"Who has the most hours on a 707?" Pinky did, so I sent her to the cabin, along with Dave, who could do the pilot's voice for air traffic control. You have to have a believable record in the flight recorder, too. They trailed two long tubes from the portapak, and the rest of us hooked in up close. We stood there, each of us smoking a fistful of cigarettes, wanting to finish them but hoping there wouldn't be time. The gate had vanished as soon as we tossed our clothes and the flight crew through.

But we didn't worry long. There's other nice things about Snatching, but nothing to compare with the rush of plugging into a portapak. The wake-up transfusion is nothing but fresh blood, rich in oxygen and sugars. What we were getting now was an insane brew of concentrated adrenaline, supersaturated hemoglobin, methedrine, white lightning, TNT, and Kickapoo joyjuice. It was like a firecracker in your heart; a boot in the box that rattled your sox.

"I'm growing hair on my chest," Cristabel said solemnly. Everyone giggled.

"Would someone hand me my eyeballs?"

"The blue ones, or the red ones?"

"I think my ass just fell off."

We'd heard them all before, but we howled anyway. We were strong, *strong*, and for one golden moment we had no worries. Everything was hilarious. I could have torn sheet metal with my eyelashes.

But you get hyper on that mix. When the gate didn't show, and didn't show, and *didn't sweetjeez show* we all started milling. This bird wasn't going to fly all that much longer.

Then it did show, and we turned on. The first of the wimps came through, dressed in the clothes taken from a passenger it had been picked to resemble.

"Two thirty-five elapsed upside time," Cristabel announced.

"Je-zuz."

It is a deadening routine. You grab the harness around the wimp's shoulders and drag it along the aisle, after consulting the seat number painted on its forehead. The paint would last three minutes. You seat it, strap it in, break open the harness and carry it back to toss through the gate as you grab the next one. You have to take it for granted they've done the work right on the other side: fillings in the teeth, fingerprints, the right match in height and weight and hair color. Most of those things don't matter much, especially on Flight 128 which was a crash-and-burn. There would be bits and pieces, and burned to a crisp at that. But you can't take chances. Those rescue workers are pretty thorough on the parts they *do* find; the dental work and fingerprints especially are important.

I hate wimps. I really hate 'em. Every time I grab the harness of one of them, if it's a child, I wonder if it's Alice. *Are you my kid, you vegetable, you slug, you slimy worm?* I joined the Snatchers right after the brain bugs ate the life out of my baby's head. I couldn't stand to think she was the last generation, that the last humans there would ever be would live with nothing in their heads, medically dead by standards that prevailed even in 1979, with computers working their muscles to keep them in tone. You grow up, reach puberty still fertile—one in a thousand—rush to get pregnant in your first heat. Then you find out your mom or pop passed on a chronic disease bound right into the genes, and none of your kids will be immune. I *knew* about the paraleprosy; I grew up with my toes rotting away. But this was too much. What do you do?

Only one in ten of the wimps had a customized face. It takes time and a lot of skill to build a new face that will stand up to a doctor's autopsy. The rest came premutilated. We've got millions of them; it's not hard to find a good match in the body. Most of them would stay breathing, too dumb to stop, until they went in with the plane.

The plane jerked, hard. I glanced at my watch. Five minutes to impact. We should have time. I was on my last wimp. I could hear Dave frantically calling the ground. A bomb came through the gate, and I tossed it into the cockpit. Pinky turned on the pressure sensor on the bomb and came running out, followed by Dave. Liza was already through. I grabbed the limp dolls in stewardess costume and tossed them to the floor. The engine fell off and a piece of it came through the cabin. We started to depressurize. The bomb blew away part of the cockpit (the ground crash crew would read it—we hoped—that part of the engine came through and killed the crew: no more words from the pilot on the flight recorder) and we turned, slowly, left and down. I was lifted toward the hole in the side of the plane, but I managed to hold onto a seat. Cristabel wasn't so lucky. She was blown backwards.

We started to rise slightly, losing speed. Suddenly it was uphill from where Cristabel was lying in the aisle. Blood oozed from her temple. I glanced back; everyone was gone, and three pink-suited wimps were piled on the floor. The plane began to stall, to nose down, and my feet left the floor.

"Come on, Bel!" I screamed. That gate was only three feet away from me, but I began pulling myself along to where she floated. The plane bumped, and she hit the floor. Incredibly, it seemed to wake her up. She started to swim toward me, and I grabbed her hand as the floor came up to slam us again. We crawled as the plane went through its final death agony, and we came to the door. The gate was gone.

There wasn't anything to say. We were going in. It's hard enough to keep the gate in place on a plane that's moving in a straight line. When a bird gets to corkscrewing and coming apart, the math is fearsome. So I've been told.

I embraced Cristabel and held her bloodied head. She was groggy, but managed to smile and shrug. You take what you get. I hurried into the restroom and got both of us down on the floor. Back to the forward bulkhead, Cristabel between my legs, back to front. Just like in training. We pressed our feet against the other wall. I hugged her tightly and cried on her shoulder.

And it was there. A green glow to my left. I threw myself toward it, dragging Cristabel, keeping low as two wimps were thrown headfirst through the gate above our heads. Hands grabbed and pulled us through. I clawed my way a good five yards along the floor. You can leave a leg on the other side and I didn't have one to spare.

I sat up as they were carrying Cristabel to Medical. I patted her arm as she went by on the stretcher, but she was passed out. I wouldn't have minded passing out myself.

For a while, you can't believe it all really happened. Sometimes it turns out it *didn't* happen. You come back and find out all the goats in the holding pen have softly and suddenly vanished away because the continuum won't tolerate the changes and paradoxes you've put into it. The people you've worked so hard to rescue are spread like tomato surprise all over some goddam hillside in Carolina and all you've got left is a bunch of ruined wimps and an exhausted Snatch Team. But not this time. I could see the goats milling around in the holding pen, naked and more bewildered than ever. And just starting to be *really* afraid.

Elfreda touched me as I passed her. She nodded, which meant well-done in her limited repertoire of gestures. I shrugged, wondering if I cared, but the surplus adrenaline was still in my veins and I found myself grinning at her. I nodded back.

Gene was standing by the holding pen. I went to him, hugged him. I felt the juices start to flow. *Damn it, let's squander a little ration and have us a good time.*

Someone was beating on the sterile glass wall of the pen. She shouted, mouthing angry words at us. *Why? What have you done to us?* It was Mary Sondergard. She implored her bald, one-legged twin to make her understand. She thought she had problems. God, was she pretty. I hated her guts.

Gene pulled me away from the wall. My hands hurt, and I'd broken off all my fake nails without scratching the glass. She was sitting on the floor now, sobbing. I heard the voice of the briefing officer on the outside speaker.

" . . . Centauri Three is hospitable, with an Earth-like climate. By that, I mean *your* Earth, not what it has become. You'll see more of that later. The trip will take five years, shiptime. Upon landfall, you will be entitled to one horse, a plow, three axes, two hundred kilos of seed grain . . . "

I leaned against Gene's shoulder. At their lowest ebb, this very moment, they were so much better than us. I had maybe ten years, half of that as a basket case. They are our best, our very brightest hope. Everything is up to them.

" . . . that no one will be forced to go. We wish to point out again, not for the last time, that you would all be dead without our intervention. There are things you should know, however. You cannot breathe our air. If you remain on Earth, you can never leave this building. We are not like you. We are the result of a genetic winnowing, a mutation process. We are the survivors, but our enemies have evolved along with us. They are winning. You, however, are immune to the diseases that afflict us. . . . "

I winced and turned away.

" . . . the other hand, if you emigrate you will be given a chance at a new life. It won't be easy, but as Americans you should be proud of your pioneer heritage. Your ancestors survived, and so will you. It can be a rewarding experience, and I urge you . . . "

Sure. Gene and I looked at each other and laughed. *Listen to this, folks. Five percent of you will suffer nervous breakdowns in the next few days, and never leave. About the same number will commit suicide, here and on the way. When you get there, sixty to seventy percent will die in the first three years. You will die in childbirth, be eaten by animals, bury two out of three of your babies, starve slowly when the rains don't come. If you live, it will be to break your back behind a plow, sun-up to dusk. New Earth is Heaven, folks!*

God, how I wish I could go with them.

THE DANCER FROM THE DANCE

"I'll be your dog!"
—*KIA-ORA* ADVERTISEMENT

The city has always been full of little strips and triangles of unused land. A row of buildings falls down in Chenaniaguine—the ground is cleared for further use—elder and nettle spring up—nothing is ever built. Or else the New Men set aside some park for a municipal estate, then quarrel among themselves: a few shallow trenches and low brick courses are covered in a season by couch-grass and "fat hen." Allmans Heath, bounded on two sides by empty warehouses, an abattoir, and a quarantine hospital, and on its third by a derelict reach of the canal, looks like any of them.

A few houses stare morosely at it from the city side of the canal. The people who live in them believe that insects the size of horses infest the Heath. Nobody has ever seen one, nevertheless once a year the large wax effigy of a locust, freshly varnished and with a knot of reed-grasses in its mouth, is brought out from the houses and paraded up and down the towpath. In the background of this ceremony the Heath seems to stretch away forever. It is the same if you go and look from the deserted pens of the cattle market, or one of the windows of the old hospital. To walk round it takes about an hour.

Every winter years ago, little girls would chalk the ground for "blind michael" in a courtyard off the Plaza of Realized Time. (It was on the left as you came to the Plain Moon Cafe where even in February the tables were arranged on the pavement, their planished copper tops gleaming in the weak sun. You turned down by an ornamental apple tree.) Generally they were the illegitimate children of midinettes, laundry women who worked in Minnet-Saba, or the tradesmen from the Rivelin Market. They preserved a fierce independence and wore short stiff blouses which bared the hollow of their backs to the grimmest weather. If you approached them properly one of them would always tuck her chalk down her grubby white drawers, lick the snot off her upper lip, and lead you to Orves; it was hard work to keep up with her in the steep winding streets.

Most sightseers changed their minds as soon as they saw the shadow of the observatory falling across the houses, and went back to drink hot genever in the Plain Moon. Those who kept on under the black velvet banners of the New Men, which in those days hung heavily from every second-floor window, would find themselves on the bank of the canal at Allmans Reach.

There was not much to see. The cottages were often boarded up at that time of year. A few withered dock plants lined the water's edge where the towpath had collapsed. No one was in sight. The wind from the Heath made your eyes water until you turned away and found the girl standing quite still next to you, her hands hanging at her sides. She would hardly look at you, or the Heath; she might glance at her feet. If you offered her money she would scratch her behind, screech with laughter, and run off down the hill. Later you might see her kneeling on the pavement in some other part of the Quarter, the wet chalk in her mouth, staring with a devout expression at something she had drawn.

Vera Ghillera, Vriko's immortal ballerina, had herself taken to Allmans Reach the day she arrived in the city from Sour Bridge. She was still a provincial and not more than a child herself, as thin and fierce and naïve as any of them in the courtyard off the Plaza, but determined to succeed; long in the muscle for classical dance, perhaps, but with a control already formidable and a sharp technical sense. It was the end of a winter afternoon when she got there. She stood away from her guide and looked over the canal. After a minute her eyes narrowed as if she could see something moving a great distance away. "Wait," she said. "Can you—? No. It's gone." The sun was red across the ice. Long before the city knew her lyrical port de bras, she knew the city. Long, long before she crossed the canal she had seen Allmans Heath and acknowledged it.

Everyone has read how Vera Ghillera, choreographed by Madame Chevigne, costumed by Audsley King, and dancing against sets designed by Paulinus Rack from sketches attributed to Ens Laurin Ashlyme, achieved overnight fame at the Prospekt Theater as Lucky Parminta in *The Little Hump-backed Horse*; how she was courted by Rack and Ingo Lympany amongst others, but did not marry; and how she kept her place as principal dancer for forty years despite the incurable fugues which compelled her to attend regularly and in secret the asylum at Wergs.

Less of her early life is public. In her autobiography, *The Constant Imago*, she is not frank about her illness or how it came about. And few of her contemporaries were ever aware of the helplessness of her infatuation with Egon Rhys, leader of the Blue Anemone Ontological Association.

Rhys was the son of a trader in fruit and vegetables at Rivelin—one of those big, equivocally natured women whose voice or temper dominate the Market Quarter for years on end, and whose absence leaves it muted and empty. He had been in and out of the market since her death, a man enclosed, not much used to the ordinary emotions, not interested in anything but his own life. He tended to act in good faith.

He was shorter than Vera Ghillera. As a boy, first selling crystallized flowers round the combat rings, then as the apprentice of Osgerby Practal, he had learned to walk with a shambling gait that diverted attention from his natural balance and energy. This he retained. (Later in life, though his limbs thickened, his energy seemed to increase rather than abate—at seventy, they said, he could hardly stand still to talk to you.) He had large hands and a habit of looking at them intently, with a kind of amused indulgence, as if he wanted to see what they would do next.

His heavy, pleasant face was already well-known about the rings when Vera came to the city. Under the aegis of the Blue Anemone he had killed forty men. As a result the other "mutual" associations often arranged a truce among themselves in order to bring about his death. The Feverfew Anschluss had a special interest in this, as did the Fourth of October and the Fish Head Men from Austonley. At times even his relations with the Anemone were difficult. He took it calmly, affecting an air of amusement which—as in other notorious bravos—seems to have masked not anxiety but an indifference of which he was rather ashamed, and which in itself sometimes frightened him. He let himself be seen about the Quarter unaccompanied; and walked openly about in the High City, where Vera first observed him from an upper room.

The Little Hump-backed Horse was history by then: she had carried a lamp in *Mariana Natesby*, overcome with furious concentration the debilitating danse d'école work and formalism of Lympany's *The Ginger Boy*. She had danced with de Cuevas, then past the height of his powers, and been his lover; she had had her portrait painted once a year for the oleograph trade, as "Delphine," "Manalas," and—looking over a parapet or smiling mysteriously under a hat—as the unnamed girl in *The Fire Last Wednesday at Lowth*. She had got her full growth. At work, though she was so tall, her body seemed compacted, pulled in on itself like the spring of a humane killer: but she looked exhausted when the makeup came off, and somehow underfed as she slumped awkwardly, legs apart, on a low chair in her sweat-stained practice clothes. She had forgotten how to sit. She was "all professional deformity in body and soul." Her huge eyes gave you their attention until she thought you were looking at someone else, then became blank and tired.

She never lost her determination, but an unease had come over her.

In the morning before practice she could be seen in the workmen's cafes down by the market, huddled and fragile-looking in an expensive woolen coat. She listened to the sad-sounding traders' calls in the early fog; hearing them as remote, and as urgent as the cries of lookouts in the bows of a ship. "Two fathoms and shelving!" She watched the girls playing blind michael in the courtyard off the Plaza of Realized Time; but as soon as they recognized her walked quickly away. "One fathom!"

The first time she saw Egon Rhys she ran down into the street without thinking and found him face to face with two or three members of the Yellow Paper College. It was a fraught moment; razors were still out in the weird Minnet-Saba light, which lay across the paving stones the color of mercury. Rhys had his back to some iron railings, and a line of blood ran vertically down his jaw from a nick under one eye.

"Leave that man alone!" she said. At ten years old in the depressed towns of the Midland Level she had seen unemployed boys fighting quietly under the bridges; building fires on waste ground. "Can't you find anything better to do?"

Rhys stared at her in astonishment and jumped over the railings.

"Don't ask me who she was," he said later in the Dryad's Saddle. "I legged it out of there faster than you could say, right through someone's front garden. They're hard fuckers, those Yellow Paper men." He touched the cut they had given him. "I think they've chipped my cheekbone."

He laughed.

"Don't ask me anything!"

But after that Vera seemed to be everywhere. He had quick glimpses

of a white face with heavily made-up eyes among the crowds that filled
the Market Quarter at the close of every short winter afternoon. He
thought he saw her in the audience at the ring behind the Dryad's Saddle.
(She was blinking in the fumes from the naphtha lamps.) Later she
followed him from venue to venue in the city and brought him great
bunches of sol d'or whenever he won.

With the flower-boys she sent her name, and tickets to the Prospekt
Theater. There he was irritated by the orchestra, confused by the constant
changes of scene, and embarrassed by the revealing costumes of the
dancers. The smell of dust and sweat and the thud of their feet on the
stage spoiled the illusion for him: he had always understood dancing to
be graceful. When Vera had him brought up to her dressing room afterwards he found her wearing an old silk practice top rotting away under
the arms, and a pair of loose, threadbare woolen stockings out of which
someone had cut the feet. "I have to keep my calves warm," she explained
when she caught him staring at them. He was horrified by the negligent
way she sprawled, watching him intently in the mirrors, and he thought
her face seemed as hard and tired as a man's; he left as soon as he could.

Vera went home and stood irresolutely near her bed. The geranium
on the window sill was like an artificial flower on a curved stem, its white
petals more or less transparent as the clouds covered and uncovered the
moon. She imagined saying to him,

"You smell of geraniums."

She began to buy him the latest novels. Just then, too, a new kind of
music was being played everywhere, so she took him to concerts. She
commissioned Ens Laurin Ashlyme to paint his portrait. He couldn't be
bothered to read, he said; he listened distractedly to the whine of the cor
anglais then stared over his shoulder all evening as if he had seen someone
he knew; he frightened the artist by showing him how good an edge his
palette knife would take. "Don't send so many flowers," he told her.
Nothing she could offer seemed to interest him, not even his own
notoriety.

Then he watched a cynical turn called *Insects* at the Allotrope Cabaret
in Cheminor. One of the props used in this was a large yellow locust.
When they first dragged it onto the cramped Allotrope stage it appeared
to be a clever waxwork. But soon it moved, and even waved one of its
hands, and the audience discovered among the trembling antennae and
gauze wings a naked woman, painted with wax, lying on her back with
her knees raised to simulate the bent rear legs of the insect. She wore to
represent its head a stylized, highly varnished mask. Fascinated, Rhys

leaned forward to get a better view. Vera heard his breath go in with a hiss. He said loudly, "What's that? What is that animal?" People began to laugh at his enthusiasm; they couldn't see that the double entendre of the act meant nothing to him. "Does anyone know?" he asked them.

"Hush!" said Vera. "You're spoiling it for everyone else."

Poor lighting and a smell of stale food made the Allotrope a cheerless place to perform; it was cold. The woman in the insect mask, having first adjusted it on her shoulders so that it would face the audience when she did, stood up and made the best she could of an "expressive" dance, crossing and uncrossing her thick forearms in front of her while her breath steamed into the chilly air and her feet slapped one two three, one two three on the unchalked boards. But Rhys would not leave until the bitter end, when the mask came off and under it was revealed the triumphant smile, disarranged chestnut hair and tired puffy face of some local artiste hardly sixteen years old, to whistles of delight.

Outside, their shadows fell huge and black on the wall that runs, covered with peeling political cartoons, the length of Endingall Street. "It doesn't seem much to stand in front of an audience for," said Vera, imitating the barren, oppressive little steps. "I would be frightened to go on." She shuddered sympathetically. "Did you see her poor ankles?"

Rhys made an impatient gesture.

"I thought it was very artistic," he said. Then: "That animal! *Do* things like that exist anymore?"

Vera laughed.

"Go on Allmans Heath and see for yourself. Isn't that where you're supposed to go to see them? What would you do if you were face to face with it now? A thing as big as that?"

He caught her hands to stop her from dancing. "I'd kill it," he said seriously. "I'd—" What he might do he had to think for a moment, staring into Vera's face. She stood dead still. "Perhaps it would kill me," he said wonderingly. "I never thought. I never thought things like that might really exist." He was shivering with excitement: she could feel it through his hands. She looked down at him. He was as thick-necked and excitable as a little pony. All of a sudden she was sharply aware of his life, which had somehow assembled for itself like a lot of eccentric furniture the long perspective of Endingall Street, the open doors of the Allotrope Cabaret, that helpless danseuse with her overblocked shoes and ruined ankles, to what end he couldn't see.

"Nothing could kill you," she said shyly.

Rhys shrugged and turned away.

For a week or two after that she seemed to be able to forget him. The weather turned wet and mild, the ordinary vigor of their lives kept them apart.

His relations with the Blue Anemone had never been more equivocal: factions were out for him in High City and Low. If Vera had known he was so hard put to it in the alleys and waste ground around Chenaniaguine and Lowth, who can say what she might have done. Luckily, while he ran for it with an open razor in one hand and a bunch of dirty bandages coming unraveled from the other, she was at the barre ten hours a day for her technique. Lympany had a new production, *Whole Air:* it would be a new *kind* of ballet, he believed. Everyone was excited by the idea, but it would mean technique, technique, technique. "The surface is dead!" he urged his dancers: "Surface is only the visible part of *technique!*"

Ever since she came up from the Midlands Vera had hated rest-days. At the end of them she was left sleepless and irritated in her skin, and as she lay in bed the city sent granular smoky fingers in through her skylight, unsettling her and luring her out so that late at night she had to go to the arena and, hollow-eyed, watch the clowns. There while thinking about something else she remembered Rhys again, so completely and suddenly that he went across her—snap!—like a crack in glass. Above the arena the air was purple with Roman candles bursting and by their urgent intermittent light she saw him quite clearly standing in Endingall Street shivering in the grip of his own enthusiasm, driven yet balked by it like all nervous animals. She also remembered the locust of the Allotrope Cabaret. She thought,

" 'Artistic!' "

Though on a good night you could still hear the breathy whisper of twenty-five thousand voices wash across the pantile roofs of Montrouge like a kind of invisible firework, the arena by then was really little more than a great big outdoor circus, and all the old burnings and quarterings had given place to acrobatics, horse-racing, trapeze acts, etc. The New Men liked exotic animals. They did not seem to execute their political opponents—or each other—in public, though some of the aerial acts looked like murder. Every night there was a big, stupid lizard or a megatherium brought in to blink harmlessly and even a bit sadly up at the crowd until they had convinced themselves of its rapacity. And there were more fireworks than ever: to a blast of maroons full of magnesium and a broad falling curtain of cerium rain, the clowns would erupt bounding and cartwheeling into the circular sandy space—jumping up, falling down, building unsteady pyramids, standing nine or ten high on one another's shoulders, active and erratic as grasshoppers in the sun. They fought, with rubber knives and whitewash. They wore huge shoes. Vera loved them.

The greatest clown of his day, called by the crowd "Kiss-O-Suck," was a dwarf of whose real name no one was sure. Some people knew him as "Morgante," others as "Rotgob" or "The Grand Pan." His legs were frail-looking and twisted, but he was a fierce gymnast, often able to perform four separate somersaults in the air before landing bent-kneed, feet planted wide apart, rock steady in the black sand. He would alternate cartwheels with handsprings at such a speed he seemed to be two dwarfs, while the crowd egged him on with whistles and cheers. He always ended his act by reciting verses he had made up himself:

Codpoorlie—tah
Codpoorrrlie—tah!
Codpoorlie—tah! tah! tah!
Dog pit.
   Dog pit pooley
   Dog pit pooley
   Dog pit have-a-rat
   tah tah tah
   (ta ta).

For a time his vogue was so great he became a celebrity on the Unter-Main-Kai, where he drank with the intellectuals and minor princes in the Bistro Californium, strutted up and down in a padded doublet of red velvet with long scalloped sleeves, and had himself painted as "The Lord of Misrule." He bought a large house in Montrouge.

He had come originally from the hot bone-white hinterlands of the Mingulay Littoral, where the caravans seem to float like yellow bird cages at midday across the violet lakes of the mirage "while inside them women consult feverishly their grubby packs of cards." If you are born in that desert, its inhabitants often boast, you know all deserts. Kiss-O-Suck was not born a dwarf but chose it as his career, having himself confined for many years in the black oak box, the gloottokoma, so as to stunt his growth. Now he was at the peak of his powers. When he motioned peremptorily the other clowns sprang up into the air around him. His voice echoed to Vera over the arena. "Dog pit pooley!" he chanted, and the crowd gave it him back: but Vera, still somehow on Endingall Street with Egon Rhys trembling beside her, heard, "Born in a desert, knows

all deserts!" The next day she sent him her name with a great bunch of
anemones. "I admire your act." They met in secret in Montrouge.

At the Bistro Californium, Ansel Verdigris, poet of the city, lay with
his head sideways on the table; a smell of lemon gin rose from the
tablecloth bunched up under his cheek. Some way away from him sat
the Marquis de M——, pretending to write a letter. They had quarreled
earlier, ostensibly about the signifier and the signified, and then Verdigris
had tried to eat his glass. At that time of night everyone else was at the
arena. Without them the Californium was only a few chairs and tables
someone had arranged for no good reason under the famous frescoes.
De M——would have gone to the arena himself but it was cold outside
with small flakes of snow falling through the lights on the Unter-Main-
Kai. "Discovering this about itself," he wrote, "the place seems stunned
and quiet. It has no inner resources."

Egon Rhys came in with Vera, who was saying:

"—was sure he could be here."

She pulled her coat anxiously about her. Rhys made her sit where it
was warm. "I'm tired tonight," she said. "Aren't you?" As she crossed
the threshold she had looked up and seen a child's face smile obliquely
out at her from a grimy patch in the frescoes. "I'm tired." All day long,
she complained, it had been the port de bras: Lympany wanted something
different—something that had never been done before. " 'A new *kind* of
port de bras'!" she mimicked, " 'A whole new *way* of dancing'! But I
have to be so careful in the cold. You can hurt yourself if you work too
hard in weather like this."

She would drink only tea, which at the Californium is always served
in wide china cups as thin and transparent as a baby's ear. When she
had had some she sat back with a laugh. "I feel better now!"

"He's late," said Rhys.

Vera took his arm and pressed her cheek briefly against his shoulder.

"You're so warm! When you were young did you ever touch a cat or
a dog just to feel how warm it was? I did. I used to think: 'It's alive! It's
alive!' "

When he didn't respond she added, "In two or three days' time you
could have exactly what you want. Don't be impatient."

"It's already midnight."

She let his arm go.

"He was so sure he would be here. We lose nothing if we wait."

There things rested. Fifteen minutes passed; perhaps half an hour. De
M——, certain now that Verdigris was only pretending to be asleep to

taunt him, crumpled a sheet of paper suddenly and dropped it on the floor. At this Rhys, whose affairs had made him nervous, jumped to his feet. The Marquis's mouth dropped open weakly. When nothing else happened Rhys sat down again. He thought, "After all I'm as safe here as anyone else in the city." He was still wary, though, of the poet, whom he thought he recognized. Vera glanced once or twice at the frescoes (they were old; no one could agree on what was represented), then quickly down at her cup. All this time Kiss-O-Suck the dwarf had been sitting slumped on a corner of the mantelpiece behind them like a great doll someone had put there for effect years before.

His legs dangled. He wore red tights, and yellow shoes with a bell on each toe; his doublet was made of some thick black stuff quilted like a leather shin-guard and sewn all over with tiny glass mirrors. Immobility was as acceptable to him as motion: in repose his body would remember the gloottokoma and the hours he had spent there, while his face took on the look of varnished papier-mâché, shiny but as if dust had settled in the lines down the side of his hooked nose down to his mouth, which was set in a strange but extraordinarily sweet smile.

He had been watching Vera since she came in. When she repeated eventually, "He was so sure he could be here," he whispered to himself: "I was! Oh, I was!" A moment later he jumped down off the mantelpiece and blew lightly in Egon Rhys's ear.

Rhys threw himself across the room, smashing into the tables as he tried to get at his razor, which he kept tucked up the sleeve of his coat. He fetched up against the Marquis de M——and screamed, "Get out of the fucking way!" But the Marquis could only stare and tremble, so they rocked together for a moment, breathing into one another's faces, until another table went over. Rhys, who was beginning to have no idea where he was, knocked de M——down and stood over him. "Don't kill me," said de M——. The razor, Rhys found, was tangled up with the silk lining of his sleeve: in the end he got two fingers into the seam and ripped the whole lot down from the elbow so that the weapon tumbled out already open, flickering in the light. Up went Rhys's arm, with the razor swinging at the end of it, high in the air.

"Stop!" shouted Vera. "Stop that!"

Rhys stared about him in confusion; blinked. By now he was trembling too. When he saw the dwarf laughing at him he realized what had happened. He let the Marquis go. "I'm sorry," he said absentmindedly. He went over to where Kiss-O-Suck had planted himself rock-steady on his bent legs in the middle of the floor, and caught hold of his wrist.

"What if I cut your face for that?" he asked, stroking the dwarf's cheek as if to calm him down. "Here. Or say here. What if I did that?"

The dwarf seemed to consider it. Suddenly his little wrist slipped and wriggled in Rhys's grip like a fish; however hard Rhys held on, it only twisted and wriggled harder, until he had let go of it almost without knowing. (All night after that his fingers tingled as if they had been rubbed with sand.)

"I don't think she would like that," said Kiss-O-Suck. "She wouldn't like you to cut someone as small as me."

He shrieked; slapped Rhys's face; jumped backwards from where he stood, without so much as a twitch of intent, right over the table and into the hearth. Out of his doublet he brought a small jam jar, which he put down in the center of the table. It contained half a dozen grass-hoppers, a gray color, with yellowish legs. At first they were immobile, but the firelight dancing on the glass around them seemed to invigorate them and after a moment or two they started to hop about in the jar at random.

"Look!" said the dwarf.

"Aren't they lively?" cried Vera.

She smiled with delight. The dwarf chuckled. They were so pleased with themselves that eventually Egon Rhys was forced to laugh too. He tucked his razor back up his sleeve and stuffed the lining in after it as best he could. Thereafter strips of red silk hung down round his wrist, and he sometimes held the seam together with his fingers. "You must be careful with that," said Vera. When she tapped the side of their jar, one or two of the grasshoppers seemed to stare at her seriously for a moment, their enigmatic, horsey little heads quite still, before they re-newed their efforts to get out, popping and ticking against the lid.

"I love them!" she said, which made Egon Rhys look sidelong at the dwarf and laugh even louder. "I love them! Don't you?"

The Marquis watched incredulously. He got himself to his feet and with a look at Ansel Verdigris as if to say "This is all your fault," ran out on to the Unter-Main-Kai. A little later Rhys, Vera, and the dwarf followed. They were still laughing; Vera and Rhys were arm in arm. As they went out into the night, Verdigris, who really had been asleep, woke up.

"Fuck off then," he sneered. His dreams had been confused.

The day they crossed the canal they were followed all the way up to Allmans Reach from the Plain Moon Cafe. The mutual associations were

out: it was another truce. Rhys could distinguish the whistles of the Fish
Head Men, January the Twelfth, the Yellow Paper College (now openly
calling itself a "schism" of the Anemone and publishing its own broad-
sheet from the back room of a pie shop behind Red Hart Lane). This
time, he was afraid, the Anemone was out too. He had no credit anywhere. At Orves he made the dwarf watch one side of the road while he
watched the other. "Pay most attention to doorways." Faces appeared
briefly in the cobbled mouths of alleys. Vera Ghillera shivered and pulled
the hood of her cloak round her face.

"Don't speak," warned Egon Rhys.

He had a second razor with him, one that he no longer used much.
That morning he had thought, "It's old but it will do," and taken it down
off the dusty windowsill where it lay—its handle as yellow as bone—
between a ring of his mother's and a glass of cloudy water through which
the light seemed to come suddenly when he picked it up.

Though he was careful to walk with his hands turned in to the sides
of his body in such a way as to provoke no one, he had all the way up
the hill a curious repeating image of himself as somebody who had *already*
run mad with the two razors—hurtling after his enemies across the icy
treacherous setts while they stumbled into dark corners or flung themselves over rotting fences, sprinting from one feeble refuge to another.
"I'll pen them up," he planned, "in the observatory. They won't stop
me now. Those bastards from Austonley . . . " It was almost as if he had
done it. He seemed to be watching himself from somewhere behind his
own back; he could hear himself yelling as he went for them, a winter
gleam at the end of each wildly swinging arm.

"We'll see what happens then," he said aloud, and the dwarf glanced
up at him in surprise. "We'll see what happens then." But the observatory
came and went and nothing happened at all.

By then some of the Austonley men were no longer bothering to hide,
swaggering along instead with broad grins. Other factions soon fell in
with them, until they formed a loose, companionable half-circle ten or
fifteen yards back along the steep street. Their breath mingled in the cold
air, and after a few minutes there was even some laughter and conversation
between the different parties. As soon as they saw he was listening to
them they came right up to Rhys's heels, watching his hands warily and
nudging each other. The Yellow Paper kept itself apart from this: there
was no sign of the Anemone at all. Otherwise it was like a holiday.

Someone touched his shoulder and, stepping deftly away in the same movement, asked him in a soft voice hardly older than a boy's, "Still got that old ivory bugger of Osgerby's up your sleeve, Egon? That old slasher of Osgerby Practal's?"

"Still got her there, have you?" repeated someone else.

"Let's have a look at her, Egon."

Rhys shrugged with fear and contempt.

It was bitterly cold on the canal bank. Vera stood listening to the rush of the broken weir a hundred yards up the reach. Sprays of scarlet rose hips hung over the water like necklaces tossed into the frozen air; a wren was bobbing and dipping among the dry reeds and withered dock plants beneath them.

"I can't see what such a little thing would find to eat," she said. "Can you?" No one answered.

The sound of the weir echoed off the boarded-up house-fronts. Men from a dozen splinter groups and minor factions now filled the end of the lane to Orves, sealing it off. More were arriving all the time. They scraped heavily to and fro on the cinder path, avoiding the icy puddles, blowing into their cupped hands for warmth, giving Rhys quick shy looks as if to say, "We're going to have you this time." Some were sent to block the towpath. Presently the representatives of the Blue Anemone Ontological Association came out of one of the houses, where they had spent the morning playing black-and-red in a single flat ray of light that slanted between the boards and fell on a wooden chair. They had some trouble with the door.

Rhys brandished his razors at them.

"Where's the sense in this? Orcer Pust's a month dead; I put Ingarden down there with him not four nights ago—where was the sense in that?"

Sense was not at issue, they said.

"How many of you will I get before you get me?"

The representatives of the Anemone shrugged. It was all one to them.

"Come on then! Come on!" Rhys shouted to the bravos in the lane. "I can see some bastards I know over there. How would they like it? In the eyes? In the neck? Facedown in the bath-house tank with Orcer Pust?"

Kiss-O-Suck the dwarf sat down suddenly and unlaced his boots. When he had rolled his voluminous black trousers up as far as they would go he made a comical face and stepped into the canal, which submerged him to the thighs. He then waded out a few yards, turned round, and said quietly to Rhys, "As far as they're concerned you're as good as dead already." Further out, where it was deeper, probing gingerly in the mud

with his toes, he added, "You're as good as dead on Allmans Heath."
He slipped: swayed for a moment: waved his arms. "Oops." Shivering
and blowing he climbed out onto the other side and began to rub his
legs vigorously. "Foo. That's cold. Foo. Tah." He called, "Why should
they fight when they've only to make sure you go across?"

Rhys stared at him; then at the men from the Anemone. "You were
none of you anything until I pulled you out of the gutter," he told them.
He ran his hands through his hair.

When it was Vera's turn, the water was so cold she thought it would
stop her heart.

Elder grew in thickets on the edge of the Heath as if some attempt at
habitation had been made a long time ago. Immediately you got in among
it, Vriko began to seem quiet and distant; the rush of the weir died away.
There were low mounds overgrown with nettle and matted couch-grass;
great brittle white-brown stems of cow parsley followed the line of a
foundation or a wall; here and there a hole had been scraped by the dogs
that swam over in the night from the city—bits of broken porcelain lay
revealed in the soft black soil. Where brambles had colonized the open
ground water could be heard beneath them, trickling away from the canal
down narrow, aimless runnels and trenches.

It was hard for the dwarf to force his way through this stuff, and after
about half an hour he fell on his back in a short rectangular pit like an
empty cistern, from which he stared up sightlessly for a moment with
arms and legs rigid in some sort of paralytic fit. "Get me out," he said
in a low, urgent voice. "Pull me out."

Later he admitted to Vera:

"When I was a boy in the gloottokoma I would sometimes wake in
the dark not knowing if it was night or day; or where I was; or what period
of my life I was in. I could have been a baby in an unlit caravan. Or
had I already become Kiss-O-Suck, Morgante, 'the Grand Little Man
with the crowd in the palm of his hand'? It was impossible to tell: my
ambitions were so clear to me, my disorientation so complete."

"I could never get enough to eat," said Vera. "Until I was ten years
old I ate and ate."

The dwarf looked at her whitely for a moment.

"Anyway, that was how it felt," he said, "to live in a box. What a
blaze of light when you were able to open the lid!"

Elder soon gave way to stands of emaciated birch, in a region of shallow
valleys and long spurs between which the streams ran in beds of honey-
colored stone as even as formal paving; a few oaks grew in sheltered

positions among boulders the size of houses on an old alluvial bench. "It seems so empty!" said Vera. The dwarf laughed. "In the south they would call this the 'plaza,' " he boasted. "If they knew about it they'd come here for their holidays." But after a mile or so of rising ground they reached the edge of a plateau, heavily dissected into a fringe of peaty gullies each with steep black sides above a trickle of orange water. Stones like bits of tile littered the watershed, sorted into curious polygonal arrays by the frost. There was no respite from the wind that blew across it. And though when you looked back you could still see Vriko, it seemed to be fifteen or twenty miles away, a handful of spires tiny and indistinct under a setting sun.

"This is more like it," said Kiss-O-Suck.

Egon Rhys blundered across the entangled grain of the watershed, one peat hag to the next, until it brought him to a standstill. The very inconclusiveness of his encounter with his rivals, perhaps, had exhausted him. He showed no interest in his surroundings, but whenever she would let him he leaned on Vera's arm, describing to her as if she had never been there the Allotrope Cabaret—how pretty its little danseuse had been, how artistically she had danced, how well she had counterfeited an animal he had never imagined could exist. "I was amazed!" he kept saying. Every so often he stood still and looked down at his clothes as though he wondered how they had got dirty. "At least try and help yourself," said Vera, who thought he was ill.

The moment it got dark he was asleep; but he must have heard Kiss-O-Suck talking in the night because he woke up and said,

"In the market when my mother was alive it was always, 'Run and fetch a box of sugared anemones. Run, Egon, and fetch it now.' " Just when he seemed to have gone back to sleep again, his mouth hanging open and his head on one side, he began repeating with a kind of infantile resentment and melancholy, " 'Run and fetch it now! Run and fetch it now! Run and fetch it now!' "

He laughed.

In the morning, when he opened his eyes and saw he was on Allmans Heath, he remembered none of this. "Look!" he said, pulling Vera to her feet. "Just look at it!" He was already quivering with excitement.

"Did you ever feel the wind so cold?"

A cindery plain stretched level and uninterrupted to the horizon, smelling faintly of the rubbish pit on a wet day. The light that came and went across it was like the light falling through rainwater in empty tins; and the city could no longer be seen, even in the distance. To start with it was loose uncompacted stuff, ploughed up at every step to reveal just beneath the surface millions of bits of small rusty machinery like the insides of clocks; but soon it became as hard and gray as the sky, so that Vera could hardly tell where cinders left off and air began.

Rhys strode along energetically. He made the dwarf tell him about the other deserts he had visited. How big were they? What animals had he seen there? He would listen for a minute or two to the dwarf's answers, then say with satisfaction, "None of those places were as cold as this, I expect," or: "You get an albino sloth in the south, I've heard." Then, stopping to pick up what looked like a very long thin spring, coiled on itself with such brittle delicacy it must have been the remains of some terrific but fragile dragonfly: "What do you think of this, as a sign? I mean, from your experience?" The dwarf, who had not slept well, was silent.

"I could go on walking forever!" Rhys exclaimed, throwing the spring into the air. But later he seemed to tire again, and he complained that they had walked all day for nothing. He looked intently at the dwarf.

"How do you explain that?"

"What I care about," the dwarf said, "is having a piss." He walked off a little way and gasping with satisfaction sent a thick yellow stream into the ground. "Foo!" Afterwards he poked the cinders with his foot and said, "It takes it up, this stuff. Look at that. You could water it all day and never tell. Hallo, I think I can see something growing there already! Dwarfs are more fertile than ordinary people." (That night he sat awake again, slumped sideways, his arms wrapped round his tucked-up knees, watching Vera Ghillera with an unidentifiable expression on his face. When he happened to look beyond her, or feel the wind on his back, he shuddered and closed his eyes.)

"When I first saw you," Vera told Egon Rhys, "you had cut your cheek. Do you remember? A line of blood ran down, and at the end of it I could see one perfect drop ready to fall."

"That excited you, did it?"

She stared at him.

He turned away in annoyance and studied the Heath. They had been on it now for perhaps three, perhaps four days. He had welcomed the effort, and gone to sleep worn out; he had woken up optimistic and been disappointed. Nothing was moving. The dwarf did not seem to be able to give him a clear idea of what to look for. He had thought sometimes that he could see something out of the corner of his eye; but this was only a kind of rapid, persistent fibrillating movement, never so much an insect as its ghost or preliminary illusion. Though at first it had aggravated him, now that it was wearing off he wished it would come back.

"My knee was damaged practicing to dance Fyokla in *The Battenberg Cake*. That was chain after chain of the hardest steps Lympany could devise, they left your calves like blocks of wood. It hurt to run down all those stairs to help you."

"Help me!" jeered Rhys.

"I'm the locust that brought you here," she said suddenly.

She stood back on the hard cinders. One two three, one two three, she mimicked the poverty-stricken skips and hops that pass for dance at the Allotrope Cabaret; the pain and lassitude of the dancer who performs them. Her feet made a faint dry scraping sound.

"I'm the locust you came to see. After all, it's as much as *she* could do."

Rhys looked alertly from Vera to the dwarf. Ribbons of frayed red silk fluttered from his sleeve in the wind.

"I meant a real insect," he said. "You knew that before we started."

"We haven't been lucky," Kiss-O-Suck agreed.

When Rhys took hold of his wrist he stood as still and compliant as a small animal and added, "Perhaps we came at the wrong time of year."

Something had gone out of him: Rhys gazed down into his lined face as if he was trying to recognize what. Then he pushed the dwarf tenderly onto the cinders and knelt over him. He touched each polished cheek, then ran his fingertips in bemusement down the sides of the jaw. He seemed to be about to say something: instead he flicked the razor into his hand with a quick snaky motion so that light shot off the hollow curve of the blade. The dwarf watched it; he nodded. "I've never been in a desert in my life," he admitted. "I made that up for Vera. It sounded more exotic."

He considered this. "Yet how could I refuse her anything? She's the greatest dancer in the world."

"You were the greatest clown," Rhys said.

He laid the flat of the razor delicately against the dwarf's cheekbone, just under the eye, where there were faint veins in a net beneath the skin.

"I believed all that."

Kiss-O-Suck's eyes were china-blue. "Wait," he said. "Look!"

Vera, who had given up trying to imitate locust or danseuse or indeed anything, was en pointe and running chains of steps out across the ash, complicating and recomplicating them in a daze of technique until she felt exactly like one of the ribbons flying from Rhys's sleeve. It was a release for her, they were always saying at the Prospekt Theater, to do the most difficult things, all kinds of allegro and batterie bewilderingly entangled, then suddenly the great turning jump forbidden to female dancers for more than a hundred years. As she danced she reduced the distinction between Heath and sky. The horizon, never convinced of itself, melted. Vera was left crossing and recrossing a space steadily less definable. A smile came to Kiss-O-Suck's lips; he pushed the razor away with one fat little hand and cried:

"She's floating!"

"That won't help you, you bastard," Egon Rhys warned him.

He made the great sweeping cut which a week before had driven the razor through the bone and gristle at the base of Toni Ingarden's throat.

It was a good cut. He liked it so much he let it pass over the dwarf's head; stopped the weapon dead; and, tossing it from one hand to the other, laughed. The dwarf looked surprised. "Ha!" shouted Rhys. Suddenly he spun round on one bent leg as if he had heard another enemy behind him. He threw himself sideways, cutting out right and left faster than you could see. "And this is how I do it," he panted, "when it comes down to the really funny business." The second razor appeared magically in his other hand and between them they parceled up the emptiness, slashing wildly about with a life of their own while Rhys wobbled and ducked across the surface of the desert with a curious, shuffling, buckle-kneed, bent-elbowed gait. "Now I'll show you how I can kick!" he called.

But Kiss-O-Suck, who had watched this performance with an interested air, murmuring judicially at some difficult stroke, only smiled and moved away. He had the idea—it had never been done before—to link in sequence a medley of cartwheels, "flying Dementos," and handsprings, which would bounce him so far into the smoky air of the arena, spinning over and over himself with his knees tucked into his stomach, that eventually he would be able to look *down* on the crowd, like a firework before it burst. "Tah!" he whispered, as he nerved himself up. "Codpoorlie, tah!"

Soon he and Rhys were floating too, leaping and twirling and wriggling higher and higher, attaining by their efforts a space that had no sense of limit or closure. But Vera Ghillera was always ahead of them, and seemed to generate their rhythm as she went.

Deserts spread to the northeast of the city, and in a wide swathe to its south.

They are of all kinds, from peneplains of disintegrating metallic dust—out of which rise at intervals lines of bony incandescent hills—to localized chemical sumps, deep, tarry and corrosive, over whose surfaces glitter small flies with papery wings and perhaps a pair of legs too many. These regions are full of old cities that differ from Vriko only in the completeness of their deterioration. The traveler in them may be baked to death; or, discovered with his eyelids frozen together, leave behind only a journal which ends in the middle of a sentence.

The Metal Salt Marches, Fenlen Island, the Great Brown Waste: the borders of regions as exotic as this are drawn differently on the maps of competing authorities: but they are at least bounded in the conventional sense. Allmans Heath, whose borders can be agreed on by everyone, does not seem to be. Neither does it seem satisfactory now to say that while those deserts lie outside the city, Allmans Heath lies within it.

The night was quiet.

Five to eleven, and except where the weir agitated its surface, the canal at Allmans Reach was covered with the lightest and most fragile web of ice. A strong moon cast its blue and gamboge light across the boarded-up fronts of the houses by the towpath. "They don't look as if much life ever goes on in them," thought the watchman, an unimaginative man at the beginning of his night's work, which was to walk from there up to the back of the Atteline Quarter (where he could get a cup of tea if he wanted one) and down again. He banged his hands together in the cold. As he stood there he saw three figures wade into the water on the other side of the canal.

They were only ten yards upstream, between him and the weir, and the moonlight fell on them clearly. They were wrapped up in cloaks and hoods, "like brown paper parcels, or statues tied up in sacks," he insisted later; and under these garments their bodies seemed to be jerking and writhing in a continual rhythmic motion, though for him it was too disconnected to be called a dance. The new ice parted for them like damp sugar floating on the water. They paid no attention to the watchman, but forded the canal, tallest first, shortest last, and disappeared down the cinder lane that goes via Orves and the observatory to the courtyard near the Plain Moon Cafe.

The watchman rubbed his hands and looked round for a minute or two, as if he expected something else to happen. "Eleven o'clock," he called at last; and though he couldn't commit himself to a description which seemed so subject to qualification as to be in bad faith, added: "And all's all."

Introduction by Stephen R. Donaldson—Copyright © 1993 by Stephen R. Donaldson. Used by permission of the author. • "The Aleph" by Jorge Luis Borges—From *The Aleph and Other Stories* by Jorge Luis Borges, translated by Norman Thomas di Giovanni. Translation copyright © 1968, 1969, 1970 by Emece Editores, S.A. and Norman Thomas di Giovanni. Used by permission of the publisher, Dutton, an imprint of New American Library, a division of Penguin Books USA Inc. • "Lady of the Skulls" by Patricia A. McKillip—Copyright © 1993 by Patricia A. McKillip. Used by permission of the Howard Morhaim Literary Agency, Inc. • "As Above, So Below" by John M. Ford—Copyright © 1980 by John M. Ford. Reprinted by permission of the author and his agent, Valerie Smith. • "Eumenides in the Fourth-Floor Lavatory" by Orson Scott Card—Copyright © 1979 by Orson Scott Card. Reprinted by permission of the author. • "Narrow Valley" by R. A. Lafferty—Copyright © 1966 by R. A. Lafferty; first appeared in *The Magazine of Fantasy & Science Fiction*; reprinted by permission of the author and the author's agent, Virginia Kidd. • "The Dreamstone" by C. J. Cherryh—Copyright © 1979 by Jessica Amanda Salmonson. First appeared in *Amazons!* Reprinted by permission of the author. • "The Storming of Annie Kinsale" by Lucius Shepard—Copyright © 1984 by Lucius Shepard. First appeared in *Isaac Asimov's Science Fiction Magazine*. Reprinted by permission of the author. • "Green Magic" by Jack Vance—Copyright © 1963 by Mercury Press, Inc. First appeared in *The Magazine of Fantasy & Science Fiction*. Reprinted by permission of Ralph M. Vicinanza, Ltd. • "The Big Dream" by John Kessel—Copyright © 1984 by Davis Publications, Inc. First appeared in *Isaac Asimov's Science Fiction Magazine*. Reprinted by permission of the author. • "The House of Compassionate Sharers" by Michael Bishop—Copyright © 1977 by Baronet Publishing for *Cosmos*. Reprinted by permission of the Howard Morhaim Literary Agency, Inc. • "The Fallen Country" by Somtow Sucharitkul—Copyright © 1982 by Somtow Sucharitkul. First appeared in *Elsewhere*, *Vol. II*. Reprinted by permission of the author. • "Strata" by Edward Bryant—Copyright © 1980 by Mercury Press, Inc. First appeared in *The Magazine of Fantasy & Science Fiction*. Reprinted by permission of the author. • "And Now the News . . . " by Theodore Sturgeon—Copyright © 1956 by Mercury Press, Inc. Reprinted by permission of The Pimlico Agency, Inc. • "The White Horse Child" by Greg Bear—Copyright © 1979 by Greg Bear. First appeared in *The Magazine of Fantasy & Science Fiction*. Reprinted by permission of the author. • "Prince Shadowbow" by Sheri S. Tepper—Copyright © 1985 by Sheri S. Tepper. Reprinted by permission of the Howard Morhaim Literary Agency, Inc. • "The Girl Who Went to the Rich Neighborhood" by Rachel Pollack—Copyright © 1984 by Rachel Pollack. Reprinted by permission of the author. • "Consequences" by Walter Jon Williams—Copyright © 1990 by Walter Jon Williams and the Liavek Co-op. Reprinted by permission of the author and his agent, Ralph Vicinanza. • "The Stone Fey" by Robin McKinley—Copyright © 1985 by Robin McKinley. First published in *Imaginary Lands*. Reprinted by permission of the author and Writers' House Inc. • "Close of Night" by Daphne Castell—Copyright © 1984 by The Estate of Daphne Castell. First appeared in *The Magazine of Fantasy & Science Fiction*. Reprinted by permission of the Estate and Estate's agent, Virginia Kidd. • "Hogfoot Right and Bird-Hands" by Garry Kilworth—Copyright © 1987 by Garry Kilworth. First published in *Other Edens*. Reprinted by permission of the author. • "Longtooth" by Edgar Pangborn—Copyright © 1970 by Mercury Press, Inc. First appeared in *The Magazine of Fantasy & Science Fiction*. Reprinted by permission of Richard Curtis Associates, Inc. • "My Rose and My Glove" by Harvey Jacobs—Copyright © 1984 by Harvey Jacobs. First appeared in *OMNI*. Reprinted by permission of the author. • "With the Original Cast" by Nancy Kress—Copyright © 1982 by Omni Publications International, Ltd. First appeared in *OMNI*. Reprinted by permission of the author. • "In the Penal Colony" by Franz Kafka—From *Franz Kafka: The Complete Stories* by Franz Kafka, edited by Nahum N. Glatzer. Copyright 1946, 1947, 1948, 1949, 1954 © 1958, 1971 by Schocken Books, Inc. Reprinted by permission of Schocken Books, published by Pantheon Books, a division of Random House, Inc., and Martin Secker & Warburg, London. • "Jeffty Is Five" by Harlan Ellison —Copyright © 1977 by Harlan Ellison. Reprinted by arrangement with, and permission of, the author and the author's agent, Richard Curtis Associates, Inc., New York. All rights reserved. • "Air Raid" by John Varley—Copyright © 1977 by John Varley. Reprinted by permission of The Pimlico Agency, Inc. • "The Dancer from the Dance" by M. John Harrison—Copyright © 1985 by M. John Harrison. Reprinted by permission of the author.